OTHER BOOKS BY GEOFF MICKS

Inca

Copyright

Copyright © 2012 Geoff Micks

ISBN-13: 978-1481871143 · ISBN-10: 1481871145

Version 1.2 - Last Edited December 29, 2012

All rights reserved. No part of this publication may be reproduced by any means without written permission except for brief quotations for review purposes.

http://faceintheblue.wordpress.com

Cover and map composed by Geoff Micks with art from the public domain.

The following is a work of fiction. All characters including those based on recorded historical figures are the product of the author's imagination and are used fictitiously

Acknowledgments

This book is for Valda Schaller, my high school Latin teacher.

She doesn't know it exists, but I began writing it as her student. That woman glowed with her passion for the written word. What I know about the mechanics of the English language I learned under her firm tutelage. I've written half a dozen drafts of this paragraph, but I can't properly express the debt my prose and worldview owe to her influence. I admire and respect that woman as an educator and an intellectual of the highest order, and for all her quirks and foibles I wouldn't trade my four years in her class for the world. Valda, I forgive you for the curse you put upon a 17-year-old boy in Sorrento, Italy. "You are going to the school of fools, and that's not a school you graduate from. The universe is out to get you." I've lived a life full of adventure with my chin up because of your warning, and I'm a better person for having had you shape me. Thank you.

As with my first published novel, this book is built upon the encouragement, patience, and generosity of so many people. My parents, Paulette and Terry, are my foundation and my champions. I'm also indebted to Kathy Hibbert and Colleen Sadler for their support in my earliest fumbling attempts at a first draft. Special mention should also go to Seana Dawson, Chris Bourque, Jillian Warring-Bird, Jeremy Desat, and Matt Cimone, people who have put up with my enthusiasm for this subject matter for most of their adult lives. I must also commend Leigh Beadon, an editor and a friend of incredible talents. Finally, I'd like to mention Meghan Kelly and Heather Zak, women whose opinions of this story mean a great deal to me.

There are hundreds of others, of course. From teachers and authors to friends and total strangers, those of you who have helped me in thought or word or deed, I am grateful to you all.

Any errors you find in these pages are mine and mine alone. Many of them are deliberate after a great deal of thought, and the rest are not for want of trying.

Cheers!

Quotations

"Whatever happens, we have got

The Maxim gun, and they have not."

--Hilaire Belloc

"Dulce et decorum est pro patria mori."

It is a sweet and fitting thing to die for one's country.

--Horace

Map

KwaZulu and Surrounding Territories

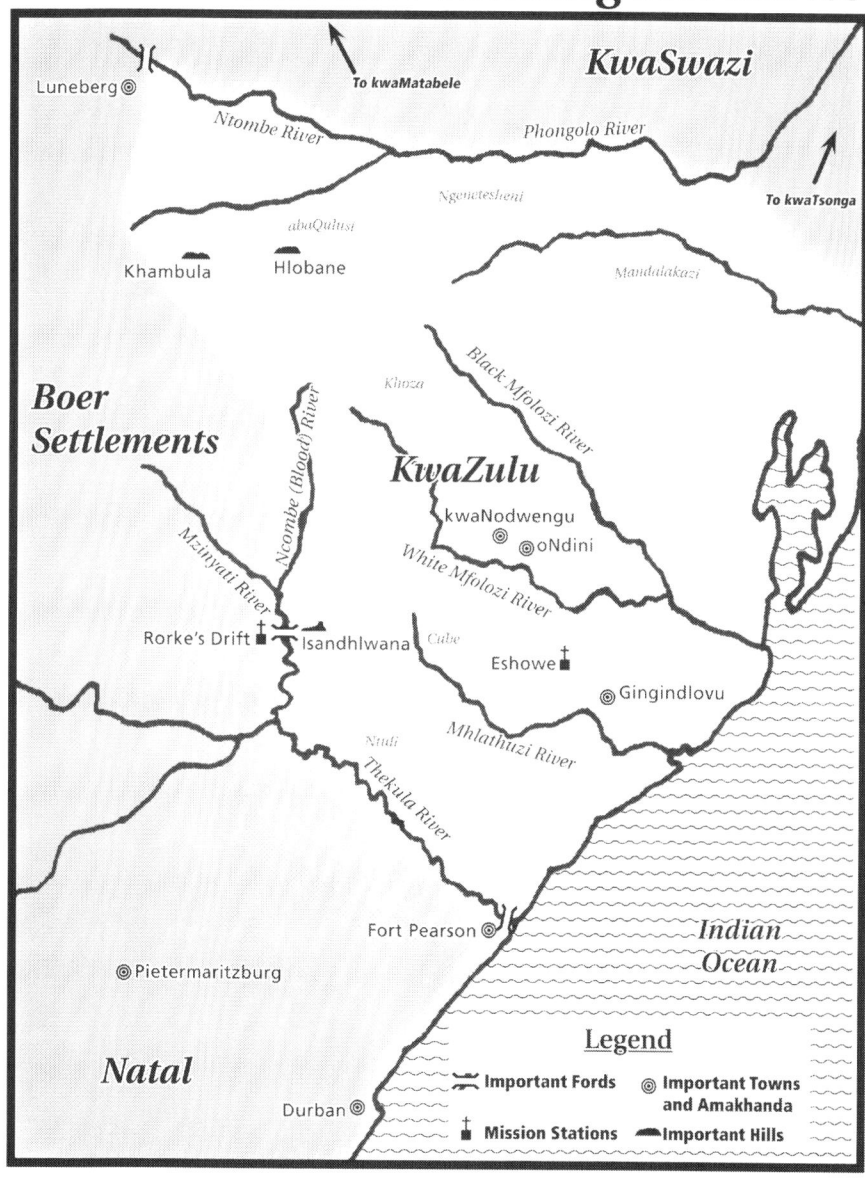

Please note there are glossaries of characters and terms at the end of the novel.

Chapter 1

It began with a creak, then the clinking of metal on metal, sounds strange and unfamiliar to the sourveld grasses that hemmed in the Valley of the Three Homesteads. The herd boys looked at one another with wide eyes; none of them could identify the intrusion into their world, and that frightened them.

It was Ingonyama --not the oldest of the assembled cousins but the strongest-- who took action. He reached out and tapped his brother Mbeki on the side of the head, gesturing to the crest of the ridge above them. The sounds came from that direction, and they could not go unchallenged before the cattle were allowed to disperse among the shade trees to chew their cud and wait out the worst of the afternoon's heat.

"Stay here," Ingonyama told the others.

One by one his cousins muttered, "It is heard," the traditional response to a command. Each of them would have liked to have gone with the two kaJama brothers, but Ingonyama was their induna, and his word was law out in the fields.

Mbeki and Ingonyama worked their way up the side of the hill. The younger son of Jama betrayed his apprehension by swinging his sticks in sharp strikes at any blade of grass that grew above its fellows.

He thinks too much, Ingonyama thought. That's his problem. There's no sense worrying until there's something to worry about. He flashed his brother a lopsided smile to reassure him.

"What do you think it is?" Mbeki asked.

"We'll find out soon enough."

Mbeki frowned at his older brother's nonchalance. Mbeki did not like mysteries, and the weight in his stomach told him there was something to fear in the next valley over.

They climbed higher still, and Ingonyama did his best to portray an unflappable confidence for both Mbeki and their cousins watching below. No one could tell how tense he was, for he squared his shoulders and walked with his chin held high. The sun beat down upon him, and he stretched out his arms to relish its warmth. It was not until his eyes crested the ridge that he betrayed his own fear: He dropped down onto his belly, dragging his brother with him.

"What is it?" Mbeki hissed. He was a head shorter than Ingonyama, and he had not seen what had driven the easy smile from his brother's face.

"Just crawl. You'll see for yourself."

"Why?"

"Just crawl!" Ingonyama hissed. To stand would silhouette them against the sky to the strangers working their way down the face of the opposite hill; even as a child Ingonyama had sense enough not to give up the element of surprise to his enemies.

When they had slithered through the grass far enough to see without being seen, both boys lay still and pondered the monsters in the distance. Mbeki was first struck by their clothes: As herd boys, the two of them both went about naked except for a small gourd that protected their privates from the cruel barbs of the tall grass; even their father and uncles did not wear much more than a loincloth outside of winter, when they might throw a blanket around their shoulders. That was the way of the Zulu, but the men marching slowly towards them were dressed in thick wool from the nape of their necks all the way down to their ankles.

Mbeki was at a loss. He had never seen anything like the distant figures before. They had cloth on their arms, although Mbeki did not have a word for sleeves. A man on a horse wore knee-high boots: In kwaZulu footwear had been outlawed since the days of King Shaka, so that all boys would grow into men who could run across any terrain on tough, calloused feet.

"Who are they?" Mbeki asked. Never in his young life had he seen a white man, but his sharp eyes could pick out dozens of pink faces shining with sweat as they trudged forward at the speed of their slowest wagon. It was the pace of a funeral march, and Mbeki felt the presence of death lurching towards him.

"They must be Boers!" Ingonyama grunted.

Mbeki winced. Their Uncle Punga was the valley's storyteller, and few of his tall tales were laced with more horror than those of what the pale marauders had done to the people of the Kingdom of Heaven. Thirty years ago the boys' grandfather had died at Blood River along with three thousand other warriors who charged the invaders' laagered wagons. Boers stole cattle and overthrew kings. Out in the fields the herd boys ruled their world with songs and sticks, but neither would be of use against the guns of white men. They needed an adult.

"Where's Baba?" Mbeki asked. Their father was the man to deal with this. Jama could handle anything.

"I don't know. He's smithing today. He could be anywhere." Their father worked his iron in the woods, far from the eyes of the herd boys. "Uncle Punga might know where he is…" Ingonyama suggested without much enthusiasm. His eyes never left the shouldered muskets.

Mbeki grimaced, thinking over the possibilities: Uncle Punga was not the man to deal with a crisis, but their Uncle Khandla was out of the valley on regimental business. There was not another warrior in the Valley of the Three Homesteads, and trying to keep Uncle Punga out of it would see them get a whipping at the end of the day. "Yebho," he gave his reluctant agreement.

The decision made, the two wormed their way backwards. When they were well below the ridge-line they turned and ran down the hill to the waiting herd boys below. Mbeki's mouth got the better of him, and from a hundred paces out he began to shout, "Boers! Boers are coming!"

Ingonyama shot his brother a stern look, worried now that their cousins would panic. Before the murmurs could grow too loud he took charge, ordering each of the boys to take some of the herd off into different dongas throughout the valley, hiding their families' wealth from the intruders in the shadowed depths of dried stream beds.

"And what will you do?" Hlubi asked. He was Punga's eldest son, and he often challenged Ingonyama's authority.

"Mbeki and I will go get your father," Ingonyama said.

"I should go too," Hlubi said. "He's my Baba." Hlubi's younger brothers also wanted to find their father, but Ingonyama had no patience for their demands.

"It doesn't take all of us. We have to divide the cattle. Hlubi? You're in charge while I'm away." That was enough to win his elder cousin's agreement, and the rest of the herd boys soon fell into line, taking their cows and heading off in different directions. The sounds were growing clearer now, and the rumble of wagon wheels and the lowing of oxen under snapping trek whips drove the two kaJama brothers into a jog trot towards their uncle's homestead, the grass flying beneath them.

Punga was outside the thorn palisade of his kraal, singing to keep a rhythm while he chopped his firewood into manageable pieces. One of his daughters was stacking the finished wood, and he smiled at her. The smile froze on his face when he saw two of his nephews making their way towards him. It was just after noon --far too soon to drive the herd home for the night. Something was wrong.

Mbeki and Ingonyama ran up to their uncle, pointing behind them and telling their story through their gasps. Punga's sweat went cold on his body despite the day's heat, but he did his best to hide his fear from the children.

"What do we do?" Mbeki asked as he finished his report.

"We find your father," Punga said. "Jama will know what to do."

Ingonyama and Mbeki traded a knowing look. "Do you know where he's smithing today?" Ingonyama asked.

"He'll be taking a snuff break by now. It's too hot to be working over a fire." Punga's eyes swept the hillsides towards Jama's homestead, looking at the copses and spinneys where his brother-in-law worked. "Let's go."

The three ran through fields of sweetveld, the sweat running down their chests. Punga's paunch --a sign of too much soft living and too little recent campaigning-- bounced in rhythm to the practiced swing of his legs. He carried his axe in one hand, and the boys had their sticks. It was a pitiful arsenal compared to the Boers' guns, but that would be Jama's problem. Jama would know what to do.

The boys' father squatted over the embers of a dying fire. Though the trees and brambles were thick enough to screen him from the fields, through their branches he could see his sons and Punga from a long way off. He frowned as he took a pinch of snuff from his horn and sneezed. "What's all this about?" He wondered. He had not seen Punga run like that since his brother-in-law sewed on the head ring of a married man. He stood up stiffly, rubbing his hip with one hand and waving with the other. "I see you, Punga!"

"Jama!" Punga huffed as he saw his brother-in-law through the brambles. "The boys saw Boers!"

Jama's reached down and snatched up his assegai from the pile of equipment scattered around his hearth. Whatever was happening, he wanted his spear with him. "Where?"

The three pointed south, back over their shoulders to where he knew the herd was grazing. He sprinted out towards them, the scar tissue on his hip turning an angry red. "How far away are they?" Jama asked. The three turned and ran with him towards the coming white men.

"They're in the next valley over," Punga said.

"How many of them are there?" Jama asked. If there were two or three riders, they might be able to scare them off. If a dozen of them had banded together for a cattle raid Jama would send Ingonyama to the kaMajeke brothers and their cousins who lived two valleys further to the north.

"Almost a hundred," Punga replied. Jama's lurched to a halt so suddenly that Punga and his sons continued on for a dozen long strides before realizing he had stopped.

"How many?" There had only been a hundred Boers at Blood River, and twelve thousand Zulus had been unable to defeat them. It had almost been the end of the kingdom.

"Almost a hundred," Punga said again, looking to his nephews for confirmation. The boys nodded in unison.

"How many horses? I mean obviously one for each man, but how many extra per man?" Jama's eyes swept the horizon looking for the dust cloud of such an invasion. If the Boers had a number of extra horses they could move fast, getting deep into kwaZulu before King Mpande could muster an impi to oppose them. *What have we done to provoke them this time?* He wondered.

"There's only one horse," Mbeki said, confused.

Jama rounded on his youngest son, his expression stormy. "One horse? What sort of story is this? The Boers ride those damned ponies everywhere. That's how they do anything! What are these Boers doing? Walking?" It struck Jama as ridiculous that a Boer would separate from his horse for anything other than food and sleep.

"Yebho, Baba," Ingonyama said, hurt that Jama did not believe them. "They are all walking together in a rectangle, neat as warriors about to parade before the king. They have one Boer on a horse out in front and wagons behind. They're even all dressed alike in red jackets with funny black leggings and white headdresses, and--"

"Those are British, not Boers! You three give me chest pains!" Jama laughed, a smile of relief spreading across his face before it flickered and died. "What are redcoats doing on our side of the Thekula River?"

He did not wait for Punga to reply; instead, he began to run again, this time at the more controlled pace of the jog trot.

From the top of the southern-most ridge Jama could see the company of British regulars advancing slowly in the terrible heat, made worse by their woolen uniforms. They marched in step with their heavy Enfield muskets resting on their shoulders. He could pick out the Africa veterans among them, because they had known to dye their white helmets a dun colour with old tea leaves. On the brown veldt their red jackets were not nearly as eye-catching as those impossibly white helmets.

Jama crawled over the crest of the ridge with Punga and the boys following his example. Moving like a snake through the tall grass, Jama worked his way down the opposite slope without disturbing the tops of the slowly waving sourveld. With hand signals he ordered Punga and the boys to break off to either side. When they were in position in front of the column's path all he could do was crouch as the cadence of the British boots drew closer.

He waited, hidden by the tall grass and confident in his plans. There was no war with the British. If he was firm from the very beginning he would have control of the situation. He listened to the squeak of wagon wheels and the lowing of the oxen, hearing the assorted clinking and clattering of the soldiers' canteens, belt buckles, and other paraphernalia. It all seemed so awkward, noisy, and slow to Jama. When they were not singing, Zulu warriors moved across the land like ghosts. How did these white men ever conquer forty lands, each greater than kwaZulu? Jama wondered. He had great respect for the redcoats' ability to kill, but that did not mean he understood it.

When the horse was only a few spear-lengths ahead of him he rose up as if he had sprung from the earth itself. "Why do you come to the Valley of the Three Homesteads?" The officer's horse reared and then backed up a step as Punga and the boys also stood, forming a semicircle in the path of the intruders.

The officer spoke something in his barbaric tongue. Jama did not move. He stood calm, staring down the man as he would a misbehaving cow. The officer would flinch first. Jama was a master at holding eye contact.

Mbeki watched his father stand before the horseman without fear. The officer was pale, and he held his head as if he had a smell under his sharp and narrow nose. Just for a moment Mbeki wondered if the man's thin mustache was actually filth, but he decided the officer's uniform was too clean for his face to be dirty.

Jama may not have had a small army at his back like the officer, but he did not feel at a disadvantage. Jama had the black head ring of a married man circling his crown, and the necklace of interlocking willow wood that wrapped twice around his neck was his nation's highest mark of bravery. If these decorations were not impressive enough, Jama also wore the brass armbands of a royal favourite, announcing to anyone who understood them that this man was special.

The officer did not understand their significance, and he sniffed again. He spoke the same words, loudly and slowly, this time waving his arm as if to brush Jama away. Jama smiled the lopsided grin Ingonyama had inherited and continued to bar the horse's way. The officer could not lock eyes with Jama any longer. He turned and called something back to his soldiers. A black man was pulled out of one of the wagons and brought forward.

"I see you, Nkosi," The man began tentatively, calling Jama a lord. "I am Phalo." He wore a red calico cloth around his head, marking him so that the British could tell which black men were in their service.

"Are you a Zulu, Phalo?" Jama asked. He did not return the polite, 'I see you.'

"Cha." The negative answer was what Jama had expected.

"Then you are a monkey." The word monkey was the same as the word for stranger, but when a Zulu called a black man from outside the kingdom a stranger it was not a polite thing. Phalo opened his mouth to argue, but Jama just smiled and ordered, "Say it with me now. You are a--"

"Monkey," The man gulped, subdued. Jama knew that Phalo or his parents had left kwaZulu to seek an easier living among the white men of British-controlled Natal. Phalo's kind had abandoned their pride to find cheap brides, plentiful cattle, and the other scraps they could gather from the table of the British and the Boers.

"Now tell your officer that I am Jama kaZuya of the Hunters Regiment, and that my land is not crossed without my permission." Just as he had stared down the officer Jama now locked eyes with Phalo, but the interpreter looked at the ground in shame immediately.

"My master says--"

"He's your master, is he? Sold yourself for a piece of red cloth?"

Phalo tugged at the headband as he continued. "My master says he comes here on the order of the Great White Queen, ruler of all Africa. He says that King Mpande makes trouble in the West, and that the Great White Queen does not like it. He is going to the kraal of kwaNodwengu to give King Mpande the message..."

Phalo asked the officer to repeat part of his gibberish. "That this is the Year of our Lord Eighteen Sixty-Six, not the days of King Shaka, and that today Africa belongs to the Great White Queen..." His voice trailed off as he saw Jama set his jaw. The officer shifted in his saddle, and Phalo remembered the rest of the message without further prompting. "My master demands--"

"Demands?" Jama interrupted again, and watched Phalo tremble. Am I so intimidating? He suppressed a laugh, knowing he must appear hard as stone. Personally, he found it all very amusing that the British thought they ruled the whole world.

Phalo gulped again, but continued as if he had not been interrupted. "He demands two cows to feed his men, a place to make camp near your homestead for the night, and a guide to kwaNodwengu. He will pay you in golden sovereigns for these things." Jama forgot his earlier levity and stood there, smoldering.

The British must have brought food with them, so the demand for livestock was a well-studied insult, and staying in his valley over night would subject Jama to still more pompous behaviour. Then the officer wanted Jama's family to do without one of its men for however long it took the slow-moving column to reach the Royal Court? In exchange for these outrages he was offered bits of metal whose only use to him would be as baubles to string onto a necklace for one of his wives, but which one?

No, the whole thing was unacceptable, and Phalo's shudders of ill-concealed terror at Jama's expression began to upset the officer's horse. At last Jama said, "Cha." He set his jaw again. He would say nothing other than this blunt refusal. Anything else might be interpreted as weakness.

"What?" Phalo asked with such a tremor in his voice that Jama looked up to make sure the sky was not falling.

Jama kept his voice gentle, worried now that poor Phalo's heart might burst at the sound of a raised voice. "Translate what I said, Monkey."

Phalo gave his master Jama's reply.

The British officer looked down on the two Zulu warriors and the herd boys with contempt. The whole continent irritated him. His career up to this point had been spent in India, a land that knew the power of the British Empire. Here he was negotiating with barefooted herdsmen? He had been ordered out on this embassy in force to intimidate King Mpande into making concessions in the West, and the officer decided he might as well begin by showing his strength to this upstart.

Jama watched the officer ride his horse back towards his men, who wheeled from column of march into line abreast with a precision born from long practice. It was Jama's turn to be afraid now, for the British infantry began to load their muskets.

"My Master says he will deliver his message to the king, and you will give him all that he has asked for."

Jama's eyes never left the soldiers hands as their ramrods went down the muzzles of their heavy Enfields. "Tell your master this: The far side of the hill behind me is my family's land. He will not cross my fields without my permission, or my king will hear of it. If he heads further west he can find a free place to make camp for the night. There are many thorn bushes and deep dongas to slow his wagons, but if he starts now he can be around my pastures before nightfall. If he's hungry, he has an entire company of soldiers to go shoot his dinner, or wagons full of black men to open up the tins and mealie bags he has brought with him. If he wants a guide, he should have hired one on the border, just as the rest of the king's petitioners and supplicants do.

"This is kwaZulu, and I am a friend of my king, Nkosi Nkulu Mpande kaSenzangakhona. I am a smith. I make assegais. I am going back to my homestead now, where I will teach my sons the differences between a hunting spear and a war spear. That's something they will need to know the next time they see redcoats in kwaZulu uninvited. Go well, Phalo." With that Jama turned his back on the loading muskets and began to walk up the hill.

Phalo stammered the polite, "Stay well, Jama," before turning and speaking urgently to his master.

A bead of sweat rolled down Jama's face that had nothing to do with the heat, and he put one foot in front of the next with great concentration. Behind him he heard a hundred flinted dogheads pull back to full cock. The British officer gave a curt command.

It had gotten away from him somehow, and now the officer was about to do something beyond stupidity. Wars started this way, but that would mean nothing to Jama if he was a corpse. He worked it out in his head: A hundred muskets, each throwing a bullet as heavy as my thumb at a speed covering three hundred paces in the time it takes to draw a breath... This could be my last moment. This could be my last moment. This could be my last moment. The mental mantra was repeated with each footfall, but still the officer did not give the command to fire.

Mbeki watched as the officer's face went crimson with impotent fury. He decided that if he ever owned a white man he would make him angry all the time just so he would turn that colour. Realizing Jama was leaving, Punga gathered up the two boys with his arms and hurried to join Jama's dignified withdrawal.

"Don't run," Jama hissed under his breath. "If that officer thinks we're afraid, he might shoot us down despite the good advice Phalo is giving him against killing a man wearing brass armbands."

"But Baba, we're not afraid," Ingonyama said.

"Yes we are." Jama looked down at his eldest and realized his son did not understand. "Do you know the size of the hole one of those bullets can put through you?" Ingonyama shook his head, and Jama held up a clenched fist by way of demonstration. "That's how my father met his end, boy. It's a terrible way to die. We aren't always going to be able to stare down the giant, Ingonyama. One day he is going to crush us." Ingonyama blinked, unable to imagine his father afraid of anything.

It was only when they were all over the crest of the ridge and out of sight of the terrible guns that Jama at last collapsed into the grass, weak and trembling.

Chapter 2

"Your brother is dead," the guardsman huffed, his chest heaving from the long run through the darkness.

Prince Inyati nodded, numb for reasons besides the predawn chill. His older brother the heir, Matshobana, had fallen to Lobengula's supporters. Inyati was not quite a man yet, but even he had known this news was coming: No one had liked his brother except his father, and King Mzilikazi of the Matabele was dead almost a moon now.

Somewhere out there his half-brother's executioners hunted for him, but that thought did not bother him as much as it should. The new king, Lobengula, was not a cruel man: He just wanted Inyati gone, and whether that meant death or exile, he would get his wish.

"What are your orders, Lord Prince?"

Inyati turned to face the head of his guard, tipping his head back and trying to make his false smile look confident. "We go south. I am not the first man with Zanzi blood to carve out a kingdom for himself!"

His eight warriors all joined him in his smile, drawing comfort and inspiration from their shared history: Inyati's father had been Mzilikazi of the House of Kumalo, a noble who fled from King Shaka of the Zulu in the time of their grandfathers. With three hundred warriors Mzilikazi had built the Matabele, the People of the Long Shields, a nation of raiders feared by all who knew of them. Their young prince had his father's Zanzi blood, and a dream all his own. They would go south.

"How do we begin?" One of them asked.

Inyati felt his heart might burst at the faith they placed in him. He was only on the cusp of adulthood, but these veterans trusted him with their lives and the lives of their families who waited with a few cattle in the donga behind him. Their trust would not be misplaced.

"We fire our kraals and head for the Swazi. Should anyone try to bar our path, we shall say a Prince of the House of Kumalo is on his way to offer his spear to the Swazi king. Who knows? We might even find people want to join us: The Swazi are a prosperous people, and they do not fear the Zulu."

"They will take us in?" The question sought reassurance: These men did not know the workings of other tribes.

"Of course!" Inyati laughed, even though doubt gnawed his heart until his chest felt hollow. "In a few years I will be grown enough to challenge Lobengula for the kingship. You know who I am! I speak the Boer language, and I can run and fight all day, thanks to your training. I can be a king one day, with luck, and when the Swazi take me in they will always have the option of supporting me, gaining a friendly neighbour to their north." Inyati hoped that was true. If he was wrong, they would flee death at home to be murdered in foreign lands.

"I shall miss this place," one of his guards admitted.

"I will too," Inyati reached out to touch the warrior's elbow. "But we will make a new home among the Swazi. They don't have fighters like the Matabele. You will all be treated as princes there, just for the way you handle a spear and an axe."

The men perked up at this, looking to one another with hope where before they had seen only despair. "Will there be cattle?"

"The Swazi are famous for their herds!" Inyati promised.

"And women?"

"Broad backsides, impeccable tits," He assured his guards, echoing one of his late father's favourite praises for his many wives.

Now his followers were talking among themselves, sharing the few things they knew about the Swazi. One called out to his wife in the darkness, and when the women and children came up to join their prince they felt a wave of enthusiasm and merriment among their menfolk. They all agreed they would go south, where the future would be brighter than the coming dawn.

Inyati smiled and laughed and joked along with the rest, but inside he knew his life was now out of his control. He would go south, and no one knew what would happen to him. He was among people who depended upon him, but he had known since the moment of his father's death that he was all alone in the world.

Chapter 3

Nandhi composed her features, a difficult thing for a little girl to do. It was going to be a hard day out in the fields, and that had nothing to do with the work.

"Your father is a beast, Nandhi!" Mnkabayi hissed with her usual venom. "Look what he's done to my son!"

Nandhi looked at her half-brother as he bent low to pull another weed out of the sorghum field. He seemed no worse than usual when their father's temper got the better of him: Jobe's nostrils were black with clotted blood, and his cheeks were thick with the rough scabs of friction burns where the back of Prince Hamu's hands had crashed again and again. Their father could be a hard man. Nandhi chose to say nothing, bending over to pull a weed of her own.

"He's working with the women!" Mnkabayi spat, waving her hands over her head at the cruelty of her husband. The rest of the royal harem --wives and daughters and servant women-- worked their crops without looking up. This was not Mnkabayi's first tantrum. In a way, she and her husband were a matched set: They both vented their fury for all the world to see. "Is my son six? No! Jobe has been a herd boy for more than half his life. His place is with the cattle!"

"I deserve this, Mother," Jobe honked around his stuffed up nose.

"What did you do?" Nandhi asked. If she was to spend the day listening to Mnkabayi rail against her fate at being sent to marry a northern baron again, she might as well get a good story out of it first.

"I spat at the mention of Prince Cetshwayo," Jobe hung his head even lower in shame.

"I don't understand," Nandhi admitted. "Baba hates Cetshwayo."

Mnkabayi grabbed her son's shoulder and shook him like a straw doll. "Not in front of a royal messenger, he doesn't! Jobe, you know better than that! Your father sided with Cetshwayo at the Battle of Ndondakusuka. Cetshwayo will one day become our next king because of Hamu's support! How much favour can we expect to receive when that messenger returns to the King's Great Place and tells the Crown Prince of the Zulu that Hamu raises his sons to spit when they hear his name?"

Nandhi closed her eyes and held her peace that Mnkabayi could swing so quickly from hating her husband to berating her son.

"I did not mean to embarrass Baba, Mother," Jobe cringed. The women within earshot murmured their agreement at that: Prince Hamu had no more loyal dog than Jobe. When he grew up, command of Hamu's secret regiment would fall to him. The hopes of a proud and independent Ngenetsheni Clan would one day rest on this youth's shoulders.

"Well you shouldn't be out here with us! Go tend to the cattle!" Mnkabayi shoved her son away, pointing to the pasture closest to Prince Hamu's kraal.

"But Baba—-"

"Your father sent you to the fields to work with the women. You've done that. Now I have sent you to the herd where your brothers and cousins will spend the day mocking you for doing women's work. Your father will like that too. Now go!"

Tears welled up in Jobe's eyes, tears that had not appeared even as his father beat him. He ran from the sorghum field so that the women would not see how his mother's words cut him.

Nandhi watched him leave and was careful not to sigh. That was the way of Hamu's children: They were raised to obey his whims. *And what does he want for me?* The little girl asked herself. *I'm to work his fields until I'm old enough to marry, and then I'm to be sold off for cattle and an alliance. I am one small step towards my father's independence from the Zulu Royal Court. Is that all my life is for?*

Nandhi bent over and pulled another weed, ignoring Mnkabayi's often repeated tirade about her lot in life. If Nandhi was back in Hamu's royal quarters she could have prepared one of her special dishes to soothe everyone's nerves, but here in the field she could do nothing to lighten the mood. Nandhi smiled down at the weed as she pulled it: Perhaps it would not be so bad to be married away from this place. Her father had the reputation for being the cruelest clan chief in kwaZulu. Did that not mean anyone else's kraal would be an improvement?

Chapter 4

"You shouldn't have made the bet, Mbeki," Langa said, using one of his sticks to wipe a crushed cowpat from his calloused foot.

"You two shouldn't have backed me up," Mbeki kaJama laughed at his cousins, smacking one of his father's cows forward.

Mbeki, Langa and Bikswayo were working the rear of their families' herd as a punishment for daring to defy the leader of the herd boys. Where the rest of their brothers and cousins held station to the sides and front of the drive, clear of the worst of the dust and flies and dung, they brought up the rear, doing the dirty work.

Mbeki laughed again, shaking his head a little at the hubris he had shown in daring to doubt his older brother's supremacy over their little corner of kwaZulu, the Place of the People of Heaven. He should have known that lopsided grin could not be beaten. Ingonyama always won.

The day had begun like any other, with the herd boys rising before dawn to lead the cattle out to pasture. It was late summer, and the pumpkins were ripe enough for a game of skill to pass the idle hours out in the fields. Under Ingonyama's whispered orders, Mbeki and his cousin Hlubi had each stolen one of the gourds from the pumpkin patch as they passed by, concealing themselves among the cows afterwards so no adult would see their ill-gotten burdens.

Once the herd was watered and let loose to graze in a lush meadow, the boys had formed a line half way up the side of a nearby hill. Ingonyama posted the youngest cousins out as sentries to keep an eye out for any parents before producing the hunting spears he had hidden in a faggot of brush. Someone struck up a praise song for his courage in borrowing his father's weapons without permission, but Ingonyama waved them to silence. "Are we ready to play?" Their cheer was his answer.

One by one, the boys took it in turn to roll a pumpkin down the slope, throwing the spears at its bouncing, receding form. Whenever a pumpkin was hit the thrower took ten steps up the slope, and the first person to the top would be declared the winner, mightier than all his brothers and cousins until the next day, the next game.

No one had doubted Ingonyama would win. He always won. At twelve Ingonyama was already almost as tall as a man. He had his father's broad shoulders and narrow waist, and where Mbeki's ten-year-old chest still had some puppy fat, Ingonyama was lean and muscled.

No one could outrun or outwrestle him. No one could beat him at stick fighting. No three herd boys together could pull Ingonyama off his feet at a game of tug of war. Ingonyama was unbeatable. That was the rule, but that morning Mbeki had felt the rule was about to be broken.

Mbeki's gifts were a sharp mind and keen eyes. He noticed things, the little things that sometimes he could not describe in the torrent of words that spilled from his mouth at the slightest provocation. That morning Mbeki sensed that Ingonyama did not seem satisfied when he stretched out his arms; nor did the clumsy follow through when his brother took his turn with the spears escape Mbeki's notice. The younger son of Jama knew that the drawback to growing so big so young would be growing pains, and whether it was an awkward night's sleep or a muscle twinge after carrying the brushwood, something was bothering Ingonyama that morning.

Mbeki, on the other hand, felt wonderful, and each of his casts was a fluid movement, bringing his spear's long thin blade into the pumpkin's hard body again and again. Mbeki had almost reached the top before any of the other boys had scored a hit, and his success went to his head and out his overactive mouth in a fit of enthusiasm.

"I'm going to beat you, Ingonyama!" Mbeki crowed, doing a little dance and waving his fighting sticks.

"You couldn't beat the dust out of a blanket," Ingonyama called from down the slope. He sounded bored.

"Big talk from a big man!" Mbeki yelled back.

"I play to win, and I always win," Ingonyama assured him. Ingonyama's credo was backed by a lifetime of victories, but Mbeki had tasted his coming triumph, and it was sweet.

"I'll bet you lose today!" Mbeki cried before he knew what he was saying. He heard his cousins Langa and Bikwayo teasing Ingonyama, who smiled his lopsided grin at all three of them as he would at a barking puppy.

"What do you want to bet?" The eldest son of Jama asked.

"When I win, I want to lead the herd into Punga's homestead tonight!" Mbeki demanded. He was smart enough to make his prize more one of pride than of possession.

"You'll be at the back with these two, dodging steaming piles of it," Ingonyama had predicted, swinging his arm forward and backward, working the kinks out.

Now the three of them drove the slow forward with practiced flicks of their sticks, reminding the faster cows what would happen if they stopped to forage. "I still can't believe he hit that pumpkin fifteen times in a row. You only had to hit it twice!" Bikwayo protested, bringing his stick down with a thwack against the rump of a pregnant heifer.

"Not so hard. We're almost there," Mbeki murmured.

The three homesteads of the valley each took turns sheltering the cattle, and tonight the honour was Punga's. As the herd began entering the cattle kraal, Ingonyama and Punga's son Hlubi stood to either side of the gate, shouting out the praise song for each cow.

"Black Flanks, impregnator of the chaste!" Ingonyama called out as the stud bull went into the kraal.

"Twisted Horn, whose milk is like honey!" Hlubi cried with disappointment that his turn was a second rate cow.

"Patched Hide, of nimble feet and worn teeth!" Ingonyama sang, and on it went until the last cow went inside. "Split Hoof, soon to be beef!" The steer twisted its head around, as if in understanding.

"Brown Queen, she of the violent temp--" Hlubi broke off in mid-praise as he realized that Brown Queen had not entered, nor was she outside. "Where's Brown Queen?"

"I thought she was up with Black Flanks," Mbeki's tone was defensive: As one of the three watching the rear of the herd he might be responsible for the missing cow. Black Flanks was always at the front and thus out of Mbeki's responsibility.

"She was caught lame on a thorn this morning. She should have been in the back with Split Hoof," Ingonyama said in a tone that was not to be overruled.

"Well she wasn't back here, and she certainly didn't get past us," Langa said with more confidence than he felt.

"Could we have left her down by the pond?" Bikwayo asked.

"Not unless she's shrunk to ankle height." Hlubi's voice dripped sarcasm.

"What about when we were playing with the pumpkins? I remember she was by the dead acacia when we started. Where was she when we finished?" Mbeki asked. None of the herd boys had an answer.

"Hlubi, tell your father that Brown Queen is missing. Bikwayo, Langa, you check the east side on your way home. Mbeki and I'll sweep the west." One by one Ingonyama assigned the herd boys a task. "It'll be dark soon, and there's no moon tonight," He said as he finished. A small shudder went through the group of boys. A moonless night was when the evil spirits were at their most powerful. "If no one finds her before dark, we'll have to wait until morning to do a proper search."

Mbeki and Ingonyama saw no sign of their missing cow on the long walk home, and their shame grew with each footfall: Every Zulu man spent his childhood tending to the herds. From a hundred paces a herd boy could tell which of his precious bovines has stepped on a painful rock, needed milking, or had found a warm spot in the swaying grass. Losing a cow from sheer negligence was the worst thing either boy could imagine doing, and their hearts sank at the thought of having to admit their failure to their father.

Chapter 5

Jama kaZuya leaned the largest pieces of wood together to meet at his shoulder height. The sun was setting to welcome a moonless night, and his cattle kraal was empty: When these two things coincided, it was his preference to build a great bonfire in the centre of his homestead to burn throughout the night and allow no darkness to linger within his thornbush palisade. It was an extravagance, but within his own home such a whim had the force of law, and so his three wives were taking it in turn to bring him armloads of wood from the pile by the perimeter fence. It was his eldest wife, Manase, who decided it was time to reign in her husband's monument to flame.

"That should be high enough, Jama. Besides, the boys will be home soon: If you don't have it lit by then, they'll fight over who gets to do it for you."

Jama gave her his best lopsided grin. He rarely showed it in the presence of his boys, but around Manase he fell into the carefree ways of his youth, especially when he was making a fool of himself. "You're right, of course. Would someone get me my flint and steel? I left them with my smithing tools."

It was his youngest wife, Namgoqu, who left to fetch the tools to start the fire. Namgoqu had done as little of the fetch and carry of wood and tinder as possible, so now she went to get the steel in an effort to do her part. She had done so little because of Bhibhi, the newborn daughter who slept in the crook of one of Namgoqu's slender arms.

Jama watched the play of emotion across his two elder wives faces once Namgoqu had her back turned. Manase was older than Jama, and her two sons were all she would give her husband. Mpikasi, Jama's second wife, was barren. Now Namgoqu had a beautiful baby girl, and the hearts of the other two women squeezed that the child was not theirs.

Jama saw the small gestures his wives made to mark their place in the family: Manase wore a kirtle of her own design, decorated with hundreds of beads that spoke in the hidden language of such designs that she was the senior wife of the love of her life; Mpikasi chose to go around bare-chested like a maiden. Without a baby to swell her breasts, her bosoms stood higher and firmer than any other woman of her age, and so she flaunted them in the privacy of their homestead walls, saying to her husband and his wives that there were some small advantages to bearing no children.

When Namgoqu returned, her behavior was the clearest of all: She handed Jama the fire equipment with a slight bow and a muttered, 'Nkosi,' which was a title that he was entitled to as the head of his household, but one he never asked for from his family. She then bowed again to Manase and Mpikasi before taking her place to their far left with the baby in her left arm. All these spoke of her shame. She would always be his most junior wife.

Namgoqu was ten years younger than Mpikasi and twenty years younger than Manase. Jama had paid a huge bride price in cattle to bring her into his home in the hopes of having new sons. Instead he had Bhibhi, a colicky daughter, mercifully silent now only because she slept. Worse still, Namgoqu had suffered so in her delivery that Jama would not lie with her again. He meant it as a kindness, but she took it as something just short of being abandoned.

Ah, well, Jama thought. There's no understanding how to please women. "I praise you, Namgoqu," he said, giving the closest the Zulu tongue had to a thank you. He crouched down to reach the soft, tinder dry heart of the pyre, and a shot of pain from his hip made him grimace.

Manase made a little mew of sympathy, but it was more one of habit than of concern. The ugly scar that sat high on Jama's hip and dragged down his thigh was only an inconvenience. He might never again dance like a young man, but he could run across the kingdom if ordered. Besides, that scar had earned him the willow-wood necklace of bravery that was looped around his neck; it had also graced his forearms with the brass armbands of a royal favourite. A little pain was a small price to pay for the elevation in station it had given to a simple blacksmith.

It was at this moment, before the first spark was struck, that Ingonyama and Mbeki entered through the gates of the kraal with long faces. They did not rush into Manase's arms, as she expected. They did not each demand the privilege of starting the fire, as Jama expected. They did not rough house with such volume as to risk waking little Bhibhi, as Mpikasi and Namgoqu expected. The two brothers marched in lockstep to their father's side and sank down onto one knee, like warriors reporting a defeat to their king.

"What is it?" Jama asked, his eyes moving from one son to the other.

Ingonyama began to tell his father about Brown Queen's disappearance in clipped military sentences, but Mbeki kept cutting in with a storyteller's flourish. Neither was happy with how the story ended in being told, but Jama just nodded. His smile was nowhere to be seen now. He turned back to the pyre and threw several long sparks off the flint scraper with a scrap bit of steel. The fire began in a small nest of dry sourveld grass, and he fed it twigs like a mother bird bringing worms home to her chicks, all the while his mind was working.

When he was sure his fire would burn without further care he turned back to his sons. The sun was now so low on the horizon that the fire did more to light them than the sky. Ingonyama looked so much like Jama's father that it made the blacksmith's chest hurt at times. He started with his eldest.

"So how do we know if any of Kandhla's or Punga's boys found our missing cow?"

"They'll tell us in the morning," Ingonyama replied.

"And if they haven't found her yet, are we to wait for all the boys to do their chores and drive the herd out before we start looking for her?" Ingonyama went to open his mouth, but Jama was trying to teach his son something, and his vocal participation was not part of the lesson. "That cow is worth a third of a wife, boy! Brown Queen makes enough milk to keep you in amasi throughout the summer. She calves as easily as she defecates. She never catches a chill. She's a complainer, but at least that means you always know what's wrong with her. She is a wonderful heifer, and you lost her."

He waited for that to sink in. "When you have different groups looking for something, you should always have a signal to sound the all clear. That's just good tactics, Ingonyama. You should have thought of that!"

Manase watched her eldest son stiffen, and she hid her smile. Ingonyama's dream was to be a famous warrior one day, and he had the heart for it. Even as a toothless infant he had bit her finger so hard as to leave it tender. That was why her husband had named him Ingonyama, He is a Lion. But heart was not enough in Jama's opinion: Jama's father had been as brave as any man alive, but he had died rushing the Boers' wagon laager at Blood River. Charging a fortified position defended by muskets was bad tactics, and Jama wanted better for Ingonyama.

Manase saw her youngest son drinking in what Jama was saying, and she reached out to pat Mbeki's head. Mbeki always paid attention, even when it did not matter. Mbeki would do the military service required of every Zulu, but his life would be spent following Jama into the blacksmithing trade. His future was secure, and as safe as he cared to make it.

"What can we do about it now, Jama?" Mpikasi asked. She feared the night would be spent reprimanding the sons who were not hers, and so she hoped to cut to the end of the lecture.

"There's nothing we can do, now that it's dark. We'll have to spend the night hoping she's been found. Tomorrow Mbeki will go to Punga's at dawn and Ingonyama will go to Khandla's. If no one saw her in the night, all the other herd boys will go about their normal chores, and I'll take these two out to find Brown Queen."

Mbeki looked over at Ingonyama, blinking in surprise. That did not sound like a punishment. A warmth began in the pit of his stomach, and Mbeki felt the corners of his mouth pull up into the beginnings of a grin. "Baba?" He asked.

"Yebho?"

"Aren't you mad?"

"Nothing's happened to my cow yet that I know about. Tomorrow we will see if I'm mad."

Mbeki looked into the fire, his smile dazzling. "That's fair, Baba. Tomorrow will be a great day." He felt it in his stomach and all the way down to his toes: Searching for Brown Queen would be something he would remember until the day he died.

"Not if we don't find her, boy. You two won't be able to sit down for days if you lost my cow."

Ingonyama grimaced at that, for Jama almost never hit his sons. Mbeki kept on smiling. "Baba, we'll find Brown Queen. I know we will. Tomorrow will be a great day!"

Chapter 6

Mbeki made his way along the crest of the hills hemming in the western side of the Valley of the Three Homesteads. The false dawn was giving way to the true beginning of the day, and as the first edge of the sun's blood red orb cleared the horizon Mbeki increase speed to the comfortable and familiar jog trot. This pace was learned when a boy first left his mother's side in the fields at the age of six, and it became so ingrained in a Zulu's life that even a man gone to seed like Punga could run all day across rough terrain with no aches or pains the next morning.

As the sun rose higher still, its light spilled over the eastern ridges hemming in his family's holdings, illuminating some of the best cattle country in the world. The Valley of the Three Homesteads was a trench of rich green sweetveld, surrounded on all sides by corrugated ridges swathed in brown sourveld and dotted with spindly acacias, dark thickets, and rocky outcroppings. The dongas were so deep that the diagonal light of the new sun did not reach their bottoms, producing thick black lines across the pastures and meadows below.

Mbeki was oblivious to the beauty of it, his mind racing faster than his legs. All through the night before he had sensed an inexplicable anticipation for today, and now that it was here he knew he would not be disappointed. Their father had sent Mbeki and his brother out to notify the other kraals that he would find Brown Queen with his sons, and now Mbeki hurried to Punga's homestead, taking the highest ground in the hopes of spotting their lost heifer on his way.

What am I so excited about? Mbeki asked himself as he ran. Is it that Baba is taking his spears? Mbeki shrugged away the thought, for it was not unusual for Jama to walk his lands with weapons in his hand. Whatever it was Mbeki was looking forward to, he knew he would have to be careful to be the first to tell their story when he got back to the other herd boys: Ingonyama could make strangling a mamba sound like digging a hole.

The shadows cast by the young sun would have hidden the faint impression from the untrained eye, but Mbeki's time in the fields had long ago taught him how to read spoor over broken ground. He dropped down into a crouch over the patch of grass that had caught his attention, his hands hovering over the dimpled earth.

Even as he watched, the early morning breeze began to worry at the soil at the lip of what could only be a hoof print. The herd was still in Punga's kraal, so this must have been left by Brown Queen. Mbeki frowned as he examined further. The print was much deeper at the front of the hoof, implying she was moving fast, but Ingonyama had said she was lame. Brown Queen was famous for her tantrums, but she had a low pain threshold. She would not have run injured unless it was away from something.

Mbeki stood and looked around. Brown Queen was nowhere in sight. She must have left the valley, he thought. Committing this intuition and the location of the spoor to memory, Mbeki ran even faster to complete his task.

When Mbeki returned to his homestead and told his father and brother what he had seen, the three of them set off at a trot towards the site of the hoof print. A strong breeze had come up out of the east as Africa burned under the morning sun. By the time Mbeki brought them to the hoof print it was only the faintest windblown impression.

Jama worked his way back and forth along Brown Queen's trail, only speaking when he was sure of what he said. "She favors her rear right leg and takes the easiest route. She moves faster than she wants to. Here and here she pauses as if hesitating or listening. Mbeki, when did Uncle Punga say the last lion had been in our valley?"

Thrown off by the unexpected question, Mbeki stumbled for a moment before recalling from rote one of Uncle Punga's fables. "In the time of King Dingaan, when blood was on the earth and the Boer stole many cattle, a lion stalked our herds and ate his fill. The lion was--"

"I praise you, Mbeki." Jama interrupted. Mbeki could recount almost anything, but at times he spoke far too much. "Tell Punga he needs to think up a new story. That one needs replacing: Brown Queen smelled a lion."

"Baba, there's no lion spoor, and if lions ran down a lame cow last night there would be vultures in the sky." Mbeki kept his tone neutral. Beside him Ingonyama trembled with excitement.

"With lions that would be true, but ours is a single lion, a male long past his prime who's been forced from his pride."

"Baba, how can you know that? Where are the signs?" Mbeki asked.

"You ask too many questions!" Ingonyama blurted, afraid his father would dismiss the idea.

"There's a kudu in one of the thickets where I smith. The kudu's been mauled by a lion recently. The lion's spoor is marked with a painful limp. Only the luckiest ambushes can make up for his lack of speed. Also, I have smelled the lion's musk in those woods; he is marking his territory trying to attract a new female, the randy old goat." His father chuckled, and Mbeki was fascinated at the thought that one could smell a lion.

"Where is the lion now, Baba?" Ingonyama asked, twisting his head around as if the violent motion of his skull would bring the predator into view.

"Yesterday the lion stalked Brown Queen here but couldn't catch her because he is as lame as she is. If he came up here from my forest, he won't go all the way back there. He'll find another thicket, full of thorns and high up, away from any boys. He'll sleep during the day and try his luck again this evening."

Ingonyama looked like his heart had shattered. Mbeki decided to voice his brother's thoughts. "This evening? We must deal with the lion before it kills a calf."

"We?" Jama asked, arching an eyebrow.

"Uncle Punga is out collecting honey," Mbeki said.

"And Uncle Kandhla has gone to the ikhanda of the Hunters Regiment!" Ingonyama said it with joy, for it invited him to hunt a lion.

"Baba, you know where the lion is right now." Putting action to word, Mbeki gestured with an open hand towards a spinney of thorn bushes and acacias three hundred paces away. To point with a single finger was the height of rudeness, but his open-handed gesture was not just a social consideration: It was an invitation, and a challenge.

"Uncle Punga says you killed fifteen lions before you were twenty, Baba," Ingonyama said, allowing a little bit of a challenge to creep into his voice too.

"Uncle Punga also says he once had a white bull that only mated black cows and produced only brown calves. What have we learned about Uncle Punga?"

"Uncle Punga speaks of swamp water as honey," The two sang their uncle's praise song.

"Still, you're right. I would prefer to wait for Kandhla, but you two will have to do. That said, you boys will never see the lion until it is dead, is it heard?" He waited for them to nod. He set down the spears in his hands. "Each of you take a spear--"

"Yebho, Baba!" Ingonyama cried with glee, snatching up the massive broad-bladed war assegai that could burst a man's heart with the effort in took to pull a cow's udder.

"Each of you take a hunting spear." Jama put heavy emphasis on the word hunting and took the assegai from Ingonyama's reluctant fingers. "I want you to circle up around the thicket so that you're behind and upwind of him. Then I want you to come through the trees making as much noise as you can. Scream, chant, sing songs, move your spears through the brush. The lion will move downhill to get away from you, and I shall be here with this." He hefted the assegai with grim purpose. Killing a lion with a spear was not something to be taken lightly, but he knew the old tom was ailing. It could be done with equal parts of care, courage, and experience.

Ingonyama and Mbeki nodded their understanding at their father's plan before making their way over the crest of the ridge and loping along the side of the steep hill to circle around in behind the spinney. As they passed to windward Mbeki thought he smelled a heavy scent that made his eyes water; his mind raced at the thought that it might be the musk of a lion.

"Mbeki... What if we went into the thicket quietly? Wouldn't Baba be pleased if his boys killed a lion and saved the herd?" Ingonyama kept his tone neutral, as if it was a passing thought. The twitching spear in his hand betrayed his heart's desire.

"Wouldn't Baba be pleased if the lion killed his boys and saved him the trouble of feeding us anymore? Baba said to make noise, and I am going to make that lion think the regiments of Shaka are coming for him." The war-like reference took the sting out of Mbeki's refusal, and soon the two brothers were advancing towards the woods at a trot, screaming back and forth the war cries and marching songs of their grandfather's father's youth.

Before they had time to grow nervous the boys were under the trees' canopy. The pleasant shade and the gray thorn bushes seemed too peaceful to hide a monster. Mbeki noticed the smell was much stronger here. The woods darkened still further. They had not seemed this deep from the outside. Mbeki wanted to call out to his father, but Jama could not respond; if the lion suspected the boys were merely beaters for a trap he would escape another way, or even double back on them.

One moment they were singing, and the next they both fell silent. Mbeki felt a lump of anticipatory dread clench in the pit of his stomach, and when he froze Ingonyama's voice trailed off. In the time it took for Ingonyama to turn his head to inquire what was wrong their whole world changed: A lion with a mane stiff with mud materialized out of the brush in front of them and leapt towards Mbeki.

In Mbeki's mind the world slowed down, and he saw every detail with an infinite patience. The old tom reeked of musk and the smell of stale blood. He saw the angry scab on the lion's front paw that oozed a sickly yellow puss as the great cat extended his claws. The beast's eyes swam with pain and age and anger, and Mbeki squinted as the cat roared its fury from between urine-coloured fangs spiderwebbed with saliva. Somewhere he heard a little boy's scream, but it was far away. It did not seem possible that the sound came from his own strained throat.

To Ingonyama the world was fast, and he was faster. Without thought he twisted his body perpendicular to the path of the lion and raised his spear over his head with both hands gripping the base of the blade. Like a long-practiced dance, the lion passed in front of him with the top of his filthy mane level with Ingonyama's armpit. Ingonyama drove his weapon down with all his young strength at the point where the beast's head met its neck. The lion could only take the blow, dying without a sound as the point of the blade found the meeting place between the spine and the base of the skull.

Mbeki saw his brother move and watched as the lion's eyes went dead, but that changed nothing. The body still came towards him, driven by inertia and the hatred of the lion's cheated spirit. Mbeki felt as if a mountain was falling upon him, and the terrified scream he had heard was cut short by a muffling thump. After that there was a crushing weight and all went dark.

Jama took an eternity to abandon his ambuscade and move into the thicket to find out why Ingonyama kept shouting, "Ngadla!" The traditional Zulu war cry 'I have eaten' that is called by the vanquisher over the still warm body of the vanquished.

"What's all this about?" Jama asked, only changing his tone after he came up through the brush.

"Ingonyama, Baba." He is a lion, Father. The flush of pride warmed Jama's heart, but a shiver ran up his spine at the risk his son must have taken: The hunting spear stuck straight up from the cat's neck like a flag pole.

"Ngwenyama," Jama replied, trying to hide his smile. He was a lion. "Now he's dead. Where's Mbeki?" Ingonyama looked blank for a moment before sucking air through his teeth and pointing at the dead cat. Jama lifted his chin for a moment, not understanding, and then he saw the small foot projecting out from under the monster's ribcage. He rushed as fast as his old wound would allow him, heaving with every muscle and sinew to roll the beast off his second born.

He stood there for a long while, frozen in a position of exertion; only his face moved, twitching as if the convulsion of his cheeks was the last force necessary to shift the great weight. Jama felt the lowest parts of the lion begin to lift off the ground; the cool soil beneath his feet pulled the body back like iron to a magnet. Slowly he felt the carcass's center of gravity edging further and further over. He grunted with effort.

At last the lion rolled over onto its side, and Jama dropped to the ground in exhaustion beside his freed son. Mbeki and Jama lay next to each other, their chests heaving in unison. At last, Mbeki took Jama's limp hand and patted himself on the head with it. They lay sprawled together like that until Mbeki choked out, "I see you, Baba."

Jama replied after much effort, "I see you, son." That was all they ever said about it.

When the enormity of what had happened moved from the present to the past, Jama rose to his feet and set to work skinning the lion with the razor-sharp edge of his war assegai. His sons watched, missing nothing, until he felt the need to speak. "Fifteen?" Jama asked, pulling out the claws and teeth of the animal with a practiced flick of the wrist upon the base of the war assegai's blade.

"Baba?"

"Did Uncle Punga say fifteen before I was twenty?"

"Yebho, Baba."

"Tell Uncle Punga he's wrong... It was thirty-four." The boys opened their mouths to shout and scream for details. "But before I married your mother I lived in the north where lions are more common. Besides, I didn't hunt them alone. Only a fool would hunt a lion alone." He locked eyes with his eldest, a warning in his voice. Ingonyama tried to hold his father's gaze but could not. His point made, Jama returned to his work.

When he was finished, the two boys followed their father back down the hill. The fresh lion skin was rolled up and carried over Jama's shoulder, a few trickles of cat blood rolling down his chest and flat belly. The claws and teeth swung inside a bag made of the lion's stomach, tied with sinew to the string of Jama's loincloth.

"What will you do with the skin, Baba?" Ingonyama asked.

"It's the biggest lion I've ever seen!" Mbeki cried.

"You've never seen a lion before." Jama tried to keep a toothy grin off of his face. He had two fine sons. He could not think of a person who would deny it.

"Well that makes it the biggest then," Mbeki said with such enthusiasm that Jama could not help but give a single bark of quickly strangled laughter. Both boys stopped for a second at the sound before tagging along again.

"The skin needs to be properly cleaned, stretched, and dried, then we must give it to the king's representative."

Ingonyama stopped again. "You're going to give it up? Baba, the skin is--"

"The property of the king. That is the law, and it is a good one." Jama continued to walk, but when Ingonyama did not follow he stopped and said without turning, "The king isn't as wealthy as you think. He is just one man, just like me and you." Ingonyama puffed up at being called a man, but he still did not move.

"Everything the king has the people gave him. Everything the king has, in the end, belongs to the people. Your skin will be a royal gift to someone some day. King Mpande will give it to someone as a token of his respect. Now don't be selfish and come along." He put enough steel in his voice that Ingonyama fell into step behind his father without another word of complaint.

When they reached the valley floor they saw Langa and Bikwayo's father Kandhla standing with the rest of the herd boys some distance away from the grazing cattle. He stood in the full military regalia of the Hunters ibutho: A headdress with bunches of sakahuli feathers attached to either side, a white shield with black speckles in his hand, and a loincloth of genet skins around his waist. Mbeki noticed Kandhla did not have nearly as many oxtails of courage bound to his knees and biceps as his father wore when Jama put on his formal uniform.

"Shi! Shi! Shi! Shi-shi-shi!" Kandhla called the regimental war cry, an imitation of hunting dogs running through long grass, smashing his assegai against his shield for added effect.

"I see you, Kandhla. Is there any news of Brown Queen?"

"She came back this morning to my kraal. Her eyes are glassy with fear, but her hide is unmarked. She'll make a good cow to give to the ikhanda."

"They want a cow?" Jama frowned.

"Yebho." Kandhla's tone did not hide the disgust he and Jama both felt over that matter. The Hunters Regiment had been married and sent to their homesteads for twelve years now; feeding the ikhanda garrison was a burden the valley should not have to carry.

"What else did you hear at eSangweni?" Jama asked, naming the royal homestead from which Kandhla had just returned.

"The date for the umKhosi Festival has been set for the next full moon. The king wants all his royal favourites to go to kwaNodwengu as soon as possible."

King Mpande's Great Place in the heart of kwaZulu was one of the few amakhanda large enough to host the umKhosi Festival, the Festival of First Fruits that would cleanse the nation spiritually and ensure a good harvest. It was also the time each year when the king would interview each of his favourites to insure there were no problems in his land that he was not aware of.

Jama straightened his shoulders and lifted his chin. Although he was only a little higher up the slope than Kandhla he seemed to tower over the other man, even in his simple loincloth with a bloody skin slung over one shoulder. "I'll leave in three days. I can tell the king how the British tried to treat us, although I doubt mine will be the only complaint he'll have heard about them. I'll also mention the cow."

Mbeki looked again at the brass armbands and willow wood necklace. In Mbeki's daydreams of the future, filled with smithing and hunting and herding, he also fantasized about having brass enclosing his forearms to mark him as special. One did not need to be a great warrior to win the status of royal favourite. The fleet, the smart, and the brave had just as much claim to them as the warrior without peer. A quick glance at Ingonyama pricked his heart with jealousy; Ingonyama would have the armbands and willow wood necklace at twenty. That was just who Ingonyama was and what he did. He always succeeded.

"You will talk to the king?" Ingonyama asked.

"What did you think the brass armbands meant, Ingonyama?" Mbeki asked.

"I knew he earned them doing great things; I didn't know he had access to the king," Ingonyama replied. "Why would the Nkosi Nkulu listen to a blacksmith?"

"Didn't Uncle Punga tell you how I got my scar?" Jama asked, surprised that his brother-in-law had somehow neglected to tell his sons about his moment of glory.

"Cha, Baba," Mbeki answered.

"Don't go out to the herds tomorrow. Come with me to do some smithing. I'll give you a lesson, and we can talk about things." Jama reached out and patted Mbeki on the head before walking away towards his home, still carrying the bloody skin of the dead lion.

Chapter 7

Mbeki felt warm and safe under his blanket of monkey skins. His head was elevated off the floor by a wooden headrest his Uncle Kandhla had carved for him. The inside of the hut was gently lit by light filtering around the door cover. The distant lowing of cattle was an unnecessary lullaby. It was morning, and Mbeki drifted aimlessly in semiconscious thought. All was peaceful and serene.

Should I get up? Mbeki asked himself. His eyes snapped open. "Of course I should get up! Today is the day. It's tomorrow already, and yesterday Baba said that tomorrow he would take us smithing!" Iron working fascinated Mbeki, and Jama had also promised a good story to pass the time. He yawned once, comfortable beneath his fur kaross, but chided himself for the unmanly indulgence of sloth.

Before he could succumb to idleness and close his eyes again Mbeki was out from under the covers and rolling up his sleeping kaross. He set the blanket and headrest at the back of the boys' hut before stretched his sleep-indulged muscles up to the domed roof of the beehive structure. As he lowered his arms he gave an appreciative squeeze to one of his stringy biceps. He was nowhere near as strong as Ingonyama, but each month Mbeki wondered if he should ask his cousin Bikwayo for a rematch at wrestling. "I might be able to take him this time," He lied to himself.

From a tin biscuit box at the side of the hut Mbeki brought out his penis cover. The metal container had been discarded by one of the passing white soldiers, but Mbeki could not see anything wrong with it: With its lid on it was almost water tight; it was certainly sturdy, and it kept valuables out of the mouths of vermin or insects.

With a practiced motion Mbeki thrust his big toe into his brother's blanket. One good kick each morning would remind Ingonyama that Mbeki was always up first. Mbeki's foot moved through the blanket without meeting resistance, and Mbeki --braced for a jarring contact-- was thrown off balance and nearly fell.

Mbeki blinked twice, staring at the empty blanket in confusion. On the rare mornings when Ingonyama awoke first he avenged his pride by waking Mbeki with his feet. Mbeki ran his hands down his ribs and flanks, looking for any tender spot which could be a newly formed bruise. He found one that was several days old and a scab that was healing nicely, but there was no sign of a recent kicking that he might have slept through. "Where's Ingonyama?" He muttered.

Mbeki ducked out through the low door and looked around. Jama's kraal was the typical Zulu homestead: A circle of huts around a courtyard that served duty as a cattle pen during the night, with an outer wall of thorn brush to keep out scavengers.

The herd had already left in the hour before dawn, driven through the single gate in the outer palisade by Mbeki's cousins. The fresh churned earth and damp leavings told Mbeki that the herd had not been gone long. Usually he would have been up earlier to help work the cattle, but only half of the rapidly rising sun had breached the horizon. He had not overslept by much.

He did not like it when his brother disappeared. It often meant Mbeki was an unwitting mouse to Ingonyama's cat. Perhaps Ingonyama would stalk him silently until he went to relieve himself. Often when Mbeki was at his most vulnerable Ingonyama would rush up behind him with a shove and a war cry. Mbeki remembered the last time his brother had played that game: Even after a month some of the boys still used the praise song,

Steps in his own Urine, Shrieks to the Stars,

With Ingonyama on the prowl

Mbeki should cross his legs.

It was humiliating, and neither son of Jama bore disgrace well. Mbeki resolved not to empty his bladder until after he knew where his brother had gone. "Ingonyama?" He called. There was no reply. "Where are you?" As if hearing his question, Jama and Ingonyama emerged from the Manase's hut carrying a number of pieces of partially worked iron.

"Were you planning to sleep all day? Get the bellows and powdered shell out of the spare hut!" The second son jumped at once to obey his father's order.

The extra hut stood opposite the boys' hut, to the right of the gate. It was for guests and storage, but Mbeki found it amusing that the blacksmith tools were given a hut of higher authority within the homestead than the two boys. As Mbeki ducked into the beehive structure to fetch out the equipment the junior wife's baby began to wail.

"Namgoqu, what's wrong with Bhibhi?" Jama boomed, almost causing Ingonyama to drop his load as he teetered under the day's provisions of amasi and boiled millet. Jama's daughter had been born last fall, and already she had earned a praise song among the three families of the valley: 'Bhibhi, who squeals like an elephant.' Punga swore he could hear her tantrums in his kraal on the far side of the valley, but Mbeki doubted even a determined little girl like Bhibhi could be that loud. It only felt like it.

"She's fine, Nkosi. She'll be asleep once she's done feeding." Namgoqu walked out from behind her hut as Mbeki came back into the cattle pen. She cradled her child, who sucked hungrily on a bare teat between shrieks of discontent.

"Good," Jama said. Bhibhi's wails could set anyone's teeth on edge, and the promise of relief was warming. "Manase! Mpikasi! Work on the lion skin while we're away. I know it won't be finished in time, but do the best you can." His other two wives sang their understanding. "Mbeki! Oh, there you are. Help Ingonyama with the water pots. We'll do some quenching today."

"We aren't doing hoes, then?" Mbeki asked, running down to the opposite end of the kraal to grab the empty pots from Ingonyama's overburdened arms. Quenching was a difficult and time-consuming thing. Jama could hammer out three or four hoes of softer iron in the time it would take to quench something into true hardness.

"You don't give King Mpande gardening tools. We need a gift for the umKhosi Festival." Mbeki felt stupid for not having thought of that himself. Hoes were women's tools. A king would want spearheads to distribute to his royal favourites. Mbeki began to tie the tools into bundles for easier carrying.

"What were you doing up so early?" Mbeki asked Ingonyama as they gathered the smithing paraphernalia.

"The sooner I was up, the sooner Baba's up, then out to the forest, hear the story, and finish the smithing as soon as possible," Ingonyama grunted, lifting stacks of iron ingots. Ingonyama endured smithing, but he found no pleasure in it. The promise of a good story was what was driving his eagerness today.

"You didn't kick me this morning."

"Didn't I? Oh, well, I'll make it up to you by kicking you a few times tonight." Ingonyama flashed his lopsided grin and began piling provisions into a basket that he then heaved onto Mbeki's crown.

When the two boys had their heavy loads balanced upon their heads, shoulders, backs, and arms, Jama led his two sons out of the gates and up-valley towards one of his forests. Jama carried only a sheepskin to sit upon, but to Mbeki and Ingonyama this showed their father's generous nature. As a father Jama did not need to carry anything at all; taking even the light sheepskin by himself was one less item to be added to the colossal weight in Mbeki's trembling arms.

They stopped to fill the water vessels at the brook halfway along their trip, and from that point the boys' journey was unbearable. They groaned with pain and exertion, young bodies shrieking for release as they carried ingots of iron, leather bellows, stone and iron tools, and containers of food, water, and clay uphill.

The sun made its way through an eighth of the sky before they reached Jama's smithy, and every step was torture. Their muscles ached and sweat streamed down their faces. Once it was clear of the horizon the sun's rays lost their cool dawn pretense to blaze with unremitting heat and light on the world below.

"So really, why didn't you kick me?" Mbeki wheezed.

"Foresight," Ingonyama panted, hiding his smile: He liked it when he thought of a way to seem intelligent to his younger brother.

"Foresight?" Mbeki wheezed again, oblivious of Ingonyama's concealed admiration.

"If I crippled you, I'd have to carry your load as well as mine." Mbeki laughed, and Ingonyama joined him.

The two climbed higher and higher, always careful of their footing: A single thorn or sharp rock could cause them enough pain to lose their balance and drop their load, and that was unthinkable. If either spilled so much as a basket of the curdled milk called amasi they would be told to fetch another one, and the torture would begin again.

They wove their way along the rocky footpath and into the forest without losing any of the precious liquid in the heavy gourds. Quenching took a lot of water, and the boys would already have to make at least one trip back to the stream before their job was done. Any water wasted in transit would be replaced later with sweat and toil.

If it was not for blind obedience and long experience, Mbeki might have asked why they went so far from the stream to do the smithing. Jama would not have had an answer, for the truth was lost in history: Smiths had been making the tools of war since before oral tradition.

No king in the remembered history of all the Bantu peoples, of whom the Zulu are just one branch, had ever gone to war without fine iron or steel weapons in his warriors' hands. Smiths had long ago turned their skill into a cult. Only by bringing religion into the trade and conducting their work in the deepest recesses of a forest could the smiths preserve their power from successful imitators.

Jama was an aberration, a strange duck in the smithing community's pond. Jama and his sons were of the Cube clan, an ancient sect of smiths. Jama had learned blacksmithing from his father in the dark recesses of the Nkhandla Forest to the north. When Jama's father had died in the service of King Dingaan he had left Jama in the hands of Uncle Punga's father, who was of the non-smithing Ntuli clan in the kingdom's south. Moving here meant Jama had to acquire workable iron ore from traveling smiths and royal couriers, but his skills were sufficient to make that cost effective. Mbeki knew Jama was one of the greatest smiths in kwaZulu. Ingonyama's pride would have made him say the very best, but Mbeki knew if Jama was the best he would live in the king's ikhanda working exclusively for royalty.

"This should do," Jama announced at last, spreading the sheepskin next to an old hearth. A clay furnace in the shape of a pregnant woman's torso squatted at one end of a pile of ashes. The area was surrounded by thick woodland, forbidden to every other occupant of the valley.

Jama mumbled a few prayers. When working by himself or with his sons he was not a scrupulous observant of the smith cult; if a client had come to visit he would have been obliged to put on a shaggy horned costume to assume the form of a monstrous smith spirit, but he was glad to do without it. Working iron was hot enough without being bundled up in a thick cloak. The spears worked with or without the incantations, so he did not see the point unless a visitor was paying extra for the show.

Ingonyama and Mbeki set down their burdens with muffled noises of relief. Working quickly to keep their muscles from stiffening, the two dug up the old smithy with a hoe blade, carefully banking the sides to reflect the heat inwards instead of letting it spill out; a small effective forge was more comfortable and efficient to use, and it was less work to feed.

Jama watched them critically while taking a little snuff from his container and sneezing deliciously. When the hearth was deep enough he gestured for them to stop, and they sank to the ground to best enjoy the momentary break.

"Firewood," Jama ordered. Mbeki was up and back within moments. One of his chores was to collect firewood and stack it near all of Jama's hearths for quick use. The wood was dry and hard, perfect for their purpose.

"You can start the fire, Ingonyama." Mbeki bit his lower lip in envy as his brother arranged the tinder at the bottom of the trench and struck steel against flint. Both boys fed the quickly growing fire with larger and still larger pieces of wood, until it burned high and bright. There were no pops or snaps of steam escaping and sap exploding, just the roar of tormented air.

"Charcoal?" Jama rarely took the boys to help him in his task, but now that he had helpers he took deep contentment in watching them. He knew that Mbeki showed a real aptitude for smithing, and Ingonyama was at least too stubborn to ever quit a task that needed doing.

Repeating his order with feigned impatience he watched as Ingonyama finally produced three pieces of charred wood from the bottom of a leather satchel. Nervous at the heat and flame Ingonyama set them upon the fire with an inexpert hand, leaving too much room between the pieces. As they lay, the fire would receive too much air and would continue to produce flames.

With a small grunt of pain Mbeki reached into the hearth and moved the charcoal logs to their proper positions. "I praise you, Mbeki," Jama gave some recognition for his son's attention. For just a moment Ingonyama's eyes clouded over with something approaching jealousy before they returned to the stare of dutiful, uninterested attention.

The charcoal worked its magic, turning the flames from a fast, high-burning inferno into a slow-burning furnace with white hot coals almost unmarred by visible flame. This fire would go through its fuel slowly and transfer the maximum amount of heat to the iron ingots. A bead of sweat rolled down Jama's forehead; between the fire and the sun it would be an uncomfortably hot day.

"Bellows." At Jama's word both boys began to pump the goatskin bellows, turning the coals whiter and still whiter. "More wood. It needs to be hot!" Mbeki carefully placed more wood on the fire, watching with satisfaction as it incinerated into white coals with almost no smoke or flame. "That's good," Jama again lauded his younger son. Mbeki was careful not to show his pleasure; doing so was the easiest way to lose more praise in the future.

"Baba--" Ingonyama began, speaking between blows of the bellows. "Yesterday you said you would tell us the story of how you--" Another pump of the bellows paused the eldest son. "Got your scar."

"Did I?" Jama asked, as if searching his memory. His sons voiced their indignation at his serious tone. "Ah, I remember now. Keep the fire hot, Mbeki. Those bellows need to go a little harder, Ingonyama. If this fire gets cold we'll waste the day." The boys complied as best they could while straining to hear over the roar of the coals and whoosh of the bellows.

Jama let his sons wait in suspense. There was work to be done; he set five iron ingots onto the coals. His task was made much easier by one of his most prized tools: A set of European blacksmith's tongs. Zulu smithing could not dependably bend or punch metal, as would be necessary to forge tongs, so Jama had bought the tool for two goats as a young man. The hinge fascinated him, and he had tried a number of times to duplicate it without success.

His task done, he leaned back on his sheepskin. He debated taking some more snuff, but his sons seemed ready to riot. Boys are not known for their patience, he thought with a chuckle. He began, "Our King Mpande is different from all the other kings of the Zulu. Do you know why?"

Ingonyama was careful not to make a face. When Uncle Punga told a story it began with the hero's moment of triumph and then went back to fill in the details; Jama, on the other hand, always began with a question, and Ingonyama never guessed the right answer. Mbeki could think of any number of reasons why King Mpande was different but wisely kept his silence. When neither boy rose to the challenge Jama answered his own riddle. "Unlike Shaka and Dingaan, Mpande had children."

Ingonyama looked blank. Mbeki smiled in understanding. Jama now took a pinch of snuff before continuing. "Shaka killed his opponents, but was then murdered by his brothers. Of those brothers Dingaan became king, but he was deposed and died because of his brother Mpande. Mpande doesn't have any more brothers, but he has had many sons, and that was a problem."

The air was sticky with humidity, and the heat of the fire was oppressive. The two boys were coated in the itchy salt of dried perspiration and were impatient for the story to begin in earnest. "What was the problem, Baba? Prince Cetshwayo will be the king one day. The Zulu will always have an Nkosi Nkulu," Ingonyama asked, still working the bellows.

"Every Zulu king since Shaka has become Nkosi Nkulu by killing his predecessor. Mpande knew that if he chose one of his sons to be his heir there was nothing to stop that son from murdering him and becoming the Great Elephant." Mbeki nodded. However unsavoury, that was the way of kings. "So Mpande did not choose an heir, but his sons were not content to stay little boys forever. All too soon they had narrowed themselves down to two possible successors: Cetshwayo and Mbuyazi. Mbeki, keep the fire hot!

"Here Mpande thought he had his solution: If he never chose between those two sons, neither could kill him. No murderer could become king without being challenged by his brother. The two princes demanded an answer, and the more Mpande refused, the more the princes went to the clan chiefs for support. Here Cetshwayo gained the upper hand, and he called his supporters the 'uSuthu' after the great black bulls of the west. Mbuyazi decided if he stayed in kwaZulu he would one day be stabbed to death out in the fields, or drowned while bathing, strangled while he slept, or poisoned while he drank."

"Is Cetshwayo a bad man, Baba?" Mbeki asked.

"Cha, and keep that fire fed! Cetshwayo is a fine man and a strong leader, but ambition can make a prince do terrible things. I doubt Cetshwayo would have killed Mbuyazi until he became king. On the other hand, Mbuyazi would have killed Cetshwayo without hesitation. Wicked men expect wicked deeds-- Oh, wait a bit, boys!"

Jama took the hot irons from the fire and placed them on a flat stone. He hammered the edges out into a spear point, and only stopped when the metal became too cool to warp. He then generously coated each piece of hot iron with powdered sea shells; this, combined with a healthy amount of ash from the fire, would turn the iron into a low-grade steel. When Jama had replaced each ingot on the fire, Mbeki felt he needed a gentle prompt to keep the story going.

"So is Mbuyazi a bad man?" Mbeki asked, adding still more wood to the fire. He had never heard of Mbuyazi before, but there were so many princes. Senzangakhona, Shaka's father, had sired almost fifty sons. Mpande was well on his way to duplicating the feat.

"He was, and he would have been a bad king." Mbeki nodded, glad to know the man was dead. "He knew that when Mpande wanted to be king instead of his brother Dingaan, Mpande went south to the white men for support. So Mbuyazi gathered all of his followers and headed to the southern border of kwaZulu, the Thekula River. Cetshwayo knew that with the help of the Whites, Mbuyazi might one day become king, and so he gathered all of his uSuthu and followed his brother."

"What does all this have to do with your scar, Baba?" Ingonyama asked, pausing at the bellows.

"You have enough breath to ask questions, but not enough to keep pumping?" Ingonyama returned to the bellows with more effort but less enthusiasm. "When Cetshwayo called his uSuthu to march, I joined the rest of the Hunters Regiment and followed him after Prince Mbuyazi."

"Wo! Do not go. Cetshwayo will kill you!" Mbeki quoted the famous advice given by a clan chief to a man who had wanted to flee with Mbuyazi. Uncle Punga's version of history was more colourful than Jama's, and Mbeki now remembered hearing some of this story before.

"Yebho. There is a song about Cetshwayo:

"The restless black one moved on,

"leaning on his barbed spear,

"and striking terror into the hearts of his opponents.

"We sang that all the way to the Thekula. Mbuyazi had judged his moment badly. The river was in flood. It was so swollen --and he had so many followers-- that it would take great care and time to ford. We were upon them almost before they had asked the British on the opposite shore for permission to cross."

Jama looked into the fire, watching the wood burn and the metal glow. "It was a battle from out of song, boys. Twenty thousand uSuthu in full war dress faced off against seven thousand of Mbuyazi's warriors and tens of thousands of his followers. We had them trapped against the flooding river. They had no place to go." Jama's voice began to monotone, remembering the events without giving them the proper flourish and flair that Punga would have used.

"Our right was beaten back by some Englishmen and Boers with guns. Our left crushed his right with assegais covered with blood up to the butt of the handle. Then the ostrich feather in Mbuyazi's headband blew off, and our center charged forward under that good omen."

"Were the Hunters in the center?" Ingonyama asked. Mbeki's mouth twitched just a little in amusement; battles were part of his brother's soul.

Jama snapped from his reverie, remembering he had an audience. "Yebho, we were the young battle veterans of the Swazi campaigns. The Hunters regiment was the most dependable ibutho Cetshwayo brought onto the field that day. We moved forward at a full out charge, screaming our war cries. That's when I twisted my ankle on a rock."

"What?" Both boys chorused in surprise. They had to wait with visible impatience as their father pulled the spearheads from the fire and dipped them into a hollowed gourd filled with water. The container hissed with steam as the metal was quenched, and he muttered a few incantations whose real purpose was to measure the time necessary to keep the iron in the water long enough to cool down.

When he had finished praising the iron god, the earth mother, the wood nymph, and all his smith ancestors, Jama began coating the cooled metal with clay. This was one of the great secrets that set Jama apart from other smiths. It was the technique given to Jama by a traveling foreign smith named Mbeki, who was honoured to this day by Jama's second born. Jama was careful to keep the clay thickest in the center and thinner towards the edges. Only when each spearhead was well-coated and placed onto the coals did Jama sit back and resume his story.

"I was running down the slope like a stud bull to a cow when a stone under my foot shifted, and I twisted my ankle. I was a hundred paces or more behind the fighting, and I couldn't move. My friends ran into action, and I couldn't even hobble."

"So you missed the battle?" Ingonyama's face fell, shamed at his father's misfortune.

"I watched as Prince Cetshwayo and some of his advisors came up after the impi. He sent his personal guard into the battle when it became obvious we would win. He was thirty paces behind me, and when I turned to him his eyes were filled with scorn. Then I heard, 'Laba! Laba! Laba! Laba!' I looked back towards the battle and saw eight of Mbuyazi's men had broken through our lines and were running towards Cetshwayo as fast as their legs would take them. His guards had all left to join the slaughter. He was defenseless."

Jama began speaking in an offhand way, as if the next part was of no real importance and should not be mentioned among the other great deeds of that day. Jama was not a braggart. "Well they were running right towards me, and so I stabbed the first through the chest. The next tried to run past me, so I jumped sideways to reach him. I landed on my bad foot, which hurt," He sounded apologetic. "So I killed him in anger. I just cursed and stabbed. He fell."

Jama realized he was giving too much detail, and he shook his head. "I couldn't tell you what I did with the other six, except that I stabbed one in the throat and another found his guts in the grass. By the time I had stopped panting and cursing and stabbing, I was surrounded by eight bodies. I had been stabbed in the hip, and gashed down the leg, and my twisted ankle was now broken. Cetshwayo had watched the whole thing and asked me my name. When he returned to his father, I was made a royal favourite, for without me King Mpande would have lost two heirs instead of only one."

"What happened in the rest of the battle?" Ingonyama asked, looking at his father's scar with new interest.

"It turned from a retreat to a rout. Even cattle stampeding will head in one direction, but that mob just flew apart. Everyone was running, but no one was working together. Some ran for the river. Others thought they could hide in their camp. Some tried to surrender, while others tried to fight their way past us. We drove them into the flooded river. Not just the men, but the women and the children... And the cattle."

"Not the cattle!" Mbeki cried, aghast: Women and children were supposed to be butchered. That was war. Cattle were treasure to be taken by the victors.

"Even the cattle. The Thekula River turned red. Women upstream all the way to the ocean couldn't do their washing or fetch water for cooking. Sharks, which are like lions of the sea, prowled the mouth of the river like a regiment dancing for their king. It is said that bodies washed up on beaches all up and down the coast for days afterwards.

"No one knows how many people Prince Mbuyazi had with him, tens of thousands certainly. Not one hundred of them survived. The Battle of Ndondakusuka was the bloodiest battle in Zulu history, and it was neither a victory nor a defeat. It was just something that had to be done."

"Now one day Prince Cetshwayo will be king." Ingonyama wiped the sweat from his brow, still pumping the billows rhythmically up and down.

"Yebho."

"So we have to visit him and bring him gifts," Mbeki huffed, adding more fuel to the fire.

"Well, the gifts are for Mpande, but Cetshwayo will be there at his side. Now go get some more water."

Mbeki carried the emptied gourds back down the hill, thinking about what his father had said. Tens of thousands of people killed in a single day. Mbeki had trouble imagining that. Math was not an exact science to the Zulu, and it took Mbeki a long time to work out that if he took a hundred cows from the valley's herd and each of those cows was a hundred people he would still only be approaching the numbers his father had talked about.

He reached a shallow pool beside the brook and set the gourds down. Mbeki picked up a pebble from the bank, holding it in his hand and watching his reflection in the still water. He went to toss the stone into the stream, but the pebble slipped from his finger and rolled back down his hand into his cupped palm.

"How did I do that?" Mbeki had been watched his reflection, and it had seemed as if he had thrown the stone only for it to vanish into thin air. Mbeki tried to repeat the trick. "It looked like the rock disappeared!" Over and over he tried to duplicate the sleight of hand but failed each time. He focused all his attention upon the act, his mind working the problem, trying to master the trick of reflex and misdirection. Only when he heard Ingonyama working his way down the hill did he realize he should have been back to the smithy long ago.

"Baba is furious! The spearheads can't stay on the fire this long! Where's the water?" Ingonyama did not pause to hit his brother. He knew Jama would do that. Instead he grabbed the pots, scooped them into the stream heedless of the extra sediment this method produced, and took off at a run uphill. He could no longer bother about spilling the odd drop.

Mbeki swallowed hard and tucked the pebble into the waistband of his loincloth. If the spearheads were spoiled, at least the rock might cheer him up after his bottom became unsittable. Mbeki snorted with amusement and took off after his brother up the hill.

"Are they ruined, Baba?" Mbeki asked as his father pulled the spearheads, now wrapped in terra cotta cocoons, from the recently fetched water.

"We will have to see." His voice was hard, but Mbeki knew he was being fair. If they were ruined Mbeki deserved his punishment. If they were all right then no harm had been done. Jama placed the first of the pottery-encased spearheads on his stone anvil and smashed it with his hammer. The clay shattered, and with much labour he chipped and pulled the wrapping from the metal face of the blade. The steel had crystallized inside its baked clay sheath. There were large, tough crystals in the center where the clay had been thickest, and the spear's edge now held smaller, softer crystals that could be easily sharpened.

The rest of the day was spent grinding the spears with whet stones and polishing them with animal fat. Many smiths used human fat from dead criminals, but the nearest place of execution was at the uSixepi ikhanda several days away, and the idea of carrying human fat that would go rancid in the heat all that way turned Jama's stomach.

Jama waited until the spears were done before he finally relieved Mbeki's worry, "The blades are harder than they should be, but once we sharpen them they will almost never dull. From now on we will wait longer for the water."

As the day ended Jama led them back to their homestead. His only rebuke of Mbeki was that he made his youngest son add the sheepskin mat to his load. Mbeki did not mind the extra burden now. The food, water, and clay containers were all empty, and their journey was downhill. Both Mbeki and Ingonyama crawled into their fur karosses exhausted, but Mbeki did not sleep. He spent the night trying to repeat his magic trick in the dark.

Chapter 8

It was two days later when Jama and the boys set out for kwaNodwengu, the great ikhanda of King Mpande. Jama wore his full-dress uniform, and he was adorned in so many cow tails of bravery that almost no skin on his torso or legs could be seen from under the white mass.

"Aren't those hot Baba?" Mbeki asked, shifting his heavy burden from the back of his head to balance more evenly on his crown.

"They are hot, but they aren't heavy. Besides, they keep the flies away." Jama tried to keep the irritation out of his voice. He would have preferred flies: The fluffy tails irritated his skin. At least he knew from experience that after the rash broke he would have no more itching problems until the next time he put on the tails.

When Mbeki was confident he could balance the load on his head with a single hand, he took the pebble out of his loincloth and began playing with it. He had repeated the trick several times now, and was confident he could make the stone not only disappear but reappear at will.

The three walked far from their valley, farther than the boys had ever gone before, and Mbeki saw just how big the world was. They passed by the great Nkhandla Forest where the rest of the Cube clan worked their steel in secret. They journeyed across the Mhlathuze River two days after they left home and forded the White Mfolozi two days after that. There could be no mistaking that they were now in the heart of the kingdom. Here, between the White and Black Mfolozi Rivers, a traveler was never out of sight of dozens of homesteads, and as they went closer to the king's Great Place they could see two or three amakhanda perched on different plains no matter where they were.

An ikhanda was like a larger version of a homestead. It still had a single gate leading through the circular outer wall into a great cattle enclosure with huts lining the inner perimeter, but instead of the four or five huts you would find at a homestead, even the smallest ikhanda had almost a hundred. An ikhanda was not so much a home as a center of power. When an ibutho, a regiment, was unmarried they lived in an ikhanda. When the king traveled through his lands, which he did less and less as he aged, the different amakhanda became his country residences.

To the ikhanda taxes were paid. To the ikhanda the local people would go to arbitrate disputes or request royal support. Each and every ikhanda had some relative of the king within, so that no one was ever more than a couple of days' travel from the judgment and power of the Zulu Royal Family. "How many amakhanda are there?" Mbeki asked as they passed the thirteenth they had seen since on their journey.

"Over thirty. Most of them are around the White and Black Mfolozi Rivers, but there are perhaps ten to the south and four or five to the north. Those are the ones that belong to the king, anyway."

"There are others?" His father's talkative mood encouraged him to ask as many questions as he wanted. Mbeki liked to imagine his memory was like Uncle Kandhla's sea sponge, and that anything said around him was sucked up like water.

"There aren't supposed to be, but the kingdom isn't as strong as it once was." Jama's tone was irritated. "The Great Men of the Nation are more powerful now than they have been since Shaka conquered and subjugated their grandfathers. Many of them have set up mini-kingdoms, paying only lip service to King Mpande." Jama spat to emphasize his feeling.

"It's especially bad in the North, where Mpande has never been popular. They build their own kraals, create small amabutho for themselves, and pass judgments of life and death over their subjects. That's a power which only the King should have."

Mbeki nodded. "Why doesn't Mpande have them killed?"

"Why don't they have Mpande killed?" Jama replied, then changed the subject. "Look boys: There's kwaNodwengu!" He gestured an open hand to an ikhanda off in the distance.

Mbeki could tell at once that this was Mpande's capital. It was a massive complex that must have stripped a good-sized forest to construct. Almost a thousand huts in four rows ringed the massive parade square, with an immaculate palisade around the outside and another within separating the cattle pen from the first row of huts. The country around the Great Place was ablaze in yellow and pink-petalled mimosa trees and wild flowers in bloom. Jama watched as a mass of white the size of a mealie field stood up from beyond the gate and moved like a cloud upon the earth, streaming into the kraal.

"What is that, Baba?" Ingonyama asked. Mbeki's eyes were sharper; he thought he knew what was going on.

"I don't recognize the uniform. It must be Mpande's new ibutho, the Skirmishers. They were only mustered earlier this year. They look like they are in good shape." Mbeki's eyes could just make out some of the individual warriors. The young men wore leopard skin headbands decorated with feathers, and they carried their black and white shields easily as they ran. Their cow tails, though far less thick and numerous than his father's, still made them seem large and fluffy, so that in a mass at a distance they were like a rolling fog.

Within the great circular parade square of kwaNodwengu the ibutho formed into a single file and began to dance and sing as they marched pass the seated figure on the opposite side of the kraal from the great gate. "Mbeki, your eyes are better than mine: Is there a big man standing off to the king's right?"

Mbeki did not need to squint. "Yebho, Baba."

"Then Cetshwayo has come in from oNdini. Good, he's the reason I'm an advisor to the king. Now I won't have to remind Mpande why I'm here." The three made their way to the ikhanda at a steady pace. All around them the grass had been beaten down by thousands of feet and devoured by the vast herds that the amabutho had driven before them.

"Will all those men be staying in kwaNodwengu, Baba?" Mbeki asked, seeing another regiment of warriors heading towards the gate. These men wore headbands decorated with black ostrich plumes with longer white feathers piled above those. They carried red and white shields.

"Cha, only the king's favourite ibutho, the Chieftains, will be staying in kwaNodwengu. The rest will stay in the other amakhanda, and once those are all full, the most junior amabutho will sleep out here in the pastures," Jama said it with the offhand manner of one whose regiment guaranteed him a hut to sleep in. "Here comes the Frost. Punga has a cousin in there somewhere."

Mbeki looked at the red and white-shielded ibutho with interest. "Why are they called the Frost, Baba?"

"Why do you ask so many questions?" Jama's rebuke hid his ignorance. He did not know why any of the regiments received the names they did.

Jama and the boys waited at the gate as the Frost filed in, jumping and shouting out their war songs, smashing their shields with their sticks. Mbeki knew that no one would have their spears with them. To brandish a spear in the King's Great Place was punishable by death.

Only the royal bodyguard --the Invincibles-- were armed with assegais around the Nkosi Nkulu. Each of them was a man beyond suspicion of treachery.

At last the final warrior was through the entrance, and Jama led the two boys through the outer gate into the great kraal. "Jama kaZuya! Is that you?" The deep voice that boomed out from a narrow opening in the inner fence belied the short man who stepped out to greet them. He had the frost of age at his temples, but his arms and chest still spoke of great strength. His pugnacious face made it clear that he was not one to back down from a fight.

"Ntsingwayo!" Jama called, the lopsided grin that Ingonyama had inherited parting his features. "You must be dead by now old man. You were a hero from Dingaan's days!" This seemed to please Ntsingwayo a great deal. His stern continence broke into a rare smile.

"Who are these boys? They can't be yours. They're too good looking!"

"These are my two sons, Ingonyama and Mbeki. Boys, this is Nkosi Ntsingwayo kaMahole, chief of the Khoza Clan. This man is one of the most powerful advisors of King Mpande, and King Dingaan before him."

Ntsingwayo had first seen potential in Jama during the Swazi campaigns, and Ndondakusuka had only reinforced his approval. The two met infrequently, usually at umKhosi festivals, but when they did it was always memorable. Ntsingwayo's favour had brought Jama's family many head of cattle over the years.

"I see you, Nkosi Ntsingwayo," Ingonyama said boldly; he attempted a bow, but thought better of it when the load on his head began to shift. Mbeki held his tongue. He did not understand why his father was so friendly with a man of such power. Jama would have been Ingonyama's age when Dingaan was king, and here before him was a hero of his grandfather's generation.

"Ha! He's a bold one, Jama." If Ntsingwayo had been a woman Ingonyama would be having his cheek pinched; instead, the chief heaped praise upon the father. "I remember you told me you had a son right after Ndondakusuka, but has it really been that long now? What is he? Fifteen?"

Ingonyama's chest puffed up with pride. "I am almost thirteen, Nkosi Ntsingwayo."

Mbeki seethed that he had not been as forward as Ingonyama. Here was a Great Man of the Nation, and Mbeki had not said a single word. "What did you do for King Dingaan, Nkosi?"

"Oh! The little one speaks too?" Ntsingwayo's eyes never left Jama, marveling that the passing years hardly touched the blacksmith. "We'll, I led one or two minor skirmishes--"

"Minor skirmishes!" Jama snorted. "Boys, this is the greatest fighting general since Shaka and Ndlela."

"I didn't want to upset your youngest. He'd cry if I told him some of the things you and I used to do."

The two laughed and swapped old remembrances. Mbeki shut his mouth and resolved not to open it again. Whereas Ingonyama had received praise, Mbeki had been clearly snubbed. He comforted himself with the knowledge that he had the answer to how his father knew this man and he did not really need to know anything else.

"I suppose you are here to answer the King's summons for the royal favourites?" Ntsingwayo asked.

"Yebho, Nkosi."

"None of that Nkosi stuff from you. After you're settled in and paid your respects to the Nkulu Nkosi, find me up on the left, three rows in, four huts from the wall of the royal quarters. Two of my sons are ready for good spears, and I don't want to give them the usual rubbish." Jama nodded in understanding. With the influx of European metalwork, many Zulu blacksmiths were growing shoddy in their craftsmanship. It was not unheard of for new assegais to bend when they made contact with an enemy's ribs. Jama's spears had no such defects.

"Yebho, but why aren't you in the royal quarters? Surely Mpande isn't making a chief sleep out with the men?" Ntsingwayo gave a wave of his hand, dismissing the allegation as unimportant. "How is the King's mood?" Jama turned his head to look through the gate at the distant figure seated on his little stool. He looked fat and bored.

"Good! He's just interviewed Prince Hamu--"

"That's put him in a good mood? I thought Prince Hamu was hated at court."

"The Great Elephant said something that scared Hamu so much the 'Great Man of the North' almost had his penis cover fall off. Cetshwayo's raising a levy of fresh taxes from the northern lands, and

Mpande is sending an entire ibutho to help." Mbeki looked to his father for further explanation, but Ntsingwayo was not done. "Everyone knows Hamu runs the Ngenetsheni Clan like they were his own private kingdom. Now he has to torch his amakhanda and disband his ibutho before any of the King's men arrive to find them."

Ntsingwayo sighed, feeling his age. "I wish Mpande would put that fool in his place more often. Hamu gets so full of himself when he comes to the capital: He looks around and dreams what it would be like to be king."

Jama nodded again. Ntsingwayo and Jama were both members of the uSuthu faction, and they had not killed Mbuyazi to let Hamu become the Great Elephant. "He doesn't seem to understand his corpse lies between him and the throne," Jama murmured. "Oh, Ntsingwayo, you must see this: Mbeki, where shall I find the Nkosi?" Jama asked playfully.

"Up on the left, three rows in, four from the wall of the royal quarters." Mbeki dutifully recalled the old man's directions. "Baba, left of what?"

Ntsingwayo was impressed. He clapped his hands together once, as a child does when presented with a new toy. "I wasn't even talking to him... Can he do that all the time?"

"He has quite a memory." Jama patted Mbeki's shoulder, careful not to disturb the load balanced on his son's head.

"Hmm..." Ntsingwayo murmured. Just as a herdsman could judge a heifer at a glance, Ntsingwayo understood men. He collected them, helped them, used them to build a power base for his clan and his king and the uSuthu faction. Jama was one of his early finds, and the smith had shown his worth many times over the years. Now his sons were growing up, and Ntsingwayo liked the look of them too. He came back to the present, where Jama and his sons were watched him curiously. "Well, I'll see you afterwards." He turned on his heel, his mind elsewhere.

The three continued through the main gate; the entrance way fifty paces deep to account for the distance between the inner and outer palisade. Once into the great parade ground Jama led the boys left and through a much humbler gate in the inner palisade. Surrounded on all sides now by huts and strangers, Jama led them up a row and then down a lane then up another row, all the while his head swiveled from side to side examining the identical beehive structures. "This one!" Jama announced, pointing at a hut which seemed identical to all the others around it.

Ingonyama threw his load inside the door, and Mbeki followed suit after a moment's hesitation. Jama grabbed a stick from the ground and stuck it into the thatch wall of the hut. "Mbeki, remember that we are half way up on the left, outer row, with the stick above the door. Do you have all that?"

"Yebho Baba, but--"

"Just remember it, take this, and come with me." He said, forcing a bundle into Mbeki's hands. Again they worked their way through the maze of yellow and brown, Mbeki noticed now how all the huts had some subtle marker to distinguish them from their fellows: This one had a bowl outside the door; that one had a blanket over the entrance; another one had a round stone over the threshold. Apparently, if there was no marker and there were no items inside, the hut was unoccupied.

By now the Frost Regiment was finished their dance and stood in formation along a section of the inner palisade. Another ibutho, Mbeki thought it might be the Weepers judging from their song, had formed up outside the gates. This break between performances was the perfect time for a royal interview, and Jama marched up to the King's low throne with all the confidence expected of a war hero. When he was five paces away he dropped to the ground, prostrating himself.

"Bayete, Nkosi Nkulu." Jama gave the royal salute, his genuflection made more sincere with the knowledge that Mpande did not like him much, and that a wave of a bored hand could have him killed.

"I see you, Jama," Mpande sighed. Jama waited a heartbeat before he rose from the ground. He seated himself on his calves, careful to keep his head below the level of his king's. The two boys sat cross legged behind him.

His father and the king made polite conversation. Jama was careful not to commit himself too strongly to anything he said, lest Mpande disagree. Each royal favourite had the right to bring problems and concerns to the attention of the royals, but aside from the British officer's rudeness and eSangweni demanding a cow, there was little for Jama to complain about. The British had been sent back without meeting Mpande, which was all the King could offer Jama by way of action. As for eSanweni, Mpande ruled that the cow must go to them. It was his ikhanda, after all.

King Mpande's whole body conveyed his utter lack of interest in the visit; he had done several hundred already this umKhosi season, and could only look forward to a hundred or so more. Mbeki tried to pay attention to what was said, but it was the mind-numbing chatter of people who could not wait for the interview to end.

Mpande was fat, but it was not the healthy kind of fat to which successful Zulu men aspired. It was not the fat of prosperity, but the fat of sloth and uneasiness. It was the result of gorging while he worried, and idleness when he should have been out walking or traveling the country. His beady eyes were glazed over with a look Mbeki had seen in a thousand cows: The stupid blank stare of an animal repeating what it had done its entire existence. It was that look that had kept Mpande alive where all his brothers had been murdered.

Mpande kaSenzangakhona was a brother of Shaka and Dingaan, both kings before him. As dozens of his other brothers were murdered for being a threat to first one's throne, and then the other's, Mpande had survived the fratricide by playing the family idiot. Both kings had felt Mpande was too harmless to kill, too stupid to ever try for power. Behind those stupid eyes Mpande was a genius at political survival; when Dingaan was at his weakest after the disaster at Blood River, Mpande had launched a Boer-supported civil war and won. King Mpande had continued to play his political games with his children until that had ended with the slaughter at Ndondakusuka.

Mbeki suspected that the king, for all his power, felt like he was a puppet now. A glance over the King's shoulder made it clear who was the puppet's master. Prince Cetshwayo, the dutiful son, listened to everything his father said to his favourite. Mbeki felt much better knowing that this man would one day replace the current Nkosi Nkulu.

Cetshwayo sat behind and to one side of his father on a carved ebony stool, and another man sat at the king's other shoulder. The two were obviously related, for the royal family had a strong tendency towards chubby thighs and generous paunches. It was also clear that this second prince was not happy. He scowled at everything through his thin beard, and whenever Mpande turned to Cetshwayo with a question or opinion the frown creased deeper into his soft, plump face. Mbeki felt the anticipation again as a weight in his stomach: This man would bring him much grief.

A servant brought a mug of beer to the prince. Mbeki watched as he took one sip and backhanded the servant, hissing something about more honey. The servant slunk away like a beaten dog. The droning conversation did not cease. That no one took any notice told Mbeki that it happened quite often. The man with the plump face radiated tension like brooding dark clouds on the horizon.

Jama reached his hand back to take a parcel from Mbeki's lap. "My King, may I present you with some gifts? I'm sure your wisdom can find some use for these humble items." Avarice momentarily flashed across Mpande's eyes before they glazed over again.

"First, I have five spearheads of the new kind I told you about on my last visit. These are even better than usual: I've been experimenting with different lengths of time in the final heating, and--"

"I am sure they are magnificent, Jama, but do not tell me how you do it. That is what smiths are for." The King gave a slight nod of his head, and an Invincible came forward and took the spearheads. "What is your other gift?" The larger parcel still sat in a pile next to Ingonyama.

"My son Ingonyama killed a lion with great skill, Great Elephant. Here is its skin." Jama unrolled the hide, and there were some mutters from the Royal Court as they saw the single hole at the base of the head.

"Your son must be a fine young man, Jama. Has he mustered into the Skirmishers? Why haven't you brought him with you?" Prince Cetshwayo asked.

Jama smiled. "Cha, Nkosi! This is my son, Ingonyama. He made his kill with a single stab at the age of twelve!"

"Wo! Truly, you breed fine sons, Jama. He won't join an ibutho for years yet, but he hunts lions better than most warriors who wear the head ring," Mpande smiled, pleased to have his boredom broken.

"More praise than he deserves, Nkosi." Both Ingonyama and Jama wore broad grins. Their modesty was transparent, but no one expected anything else. Mbeki found himself playing with his pebble again, making it appear and disappear at will. He hoped the interview would end soon. He was bored.

"Do that again!" Cetshwayo demanded. Mbeki's head snapped up to realize that all eyes had focused on him. Mbeki made as if to throw the stone away, palmed it into his hand, made an elaborate effort to find it where it should have landed, then made it appear out of his ear. He looked up expecting applause, but instead the three royal figures glowering at him with rage. "I see you, Wizard of kwaZulu!"

The smile on Jama's face turned sickly, but he could not quite remove it. In his youth the cry 'kill the wizards!' had gone from homestead to homestead. Thousands of witch doctors had been pulled from their huts and impaled upon sharpened stakes. Their corpses had decorated the gates of every ikhanda in the kingdom for the crime of frightening the populace more than King Dingaan could.

"Nkosi, he's just a boy! He doesn't--"

"Silence!" The brooding man behind Mpande slashed the air with his hand. "He used magic near the King before the umKhosi Festival! For anyone other than a royal isangoma, that is punishable by death. The harvest is at stake!" Mpande nodded in agreement. The spirit of the Nkosi Nkulu had to be kept clean before a ceremony of this magnitude.

"Are you Prince Hamu?" Mbeki asked, his mind racing.

"Yebho." Hamu's eyes were needles that he used to impale whatever he looked upon. Mbeki felt their sting and could not hold eye contact.

When an argument rose up among the herd boys out in the field Mbeki always tried to divide the issue so Ingonyama was on his side. At the Royal Court it was Mpande and Cetshwayo who would prevail no matter what, and so it was Hamu who must lose so Mbeki could live. "I'm told your penis cover almost fell off earlier. Maybe if you were given a smaller one it would fit better." Both Cetshwayo and Mpande roared with laughter. Hamu clenched his teeth and snarled. He was always careful to wear a thick loincloth, but it was his secret shame that Mbeki's delaying tactic was true. Through his teeth he cried, "Send for my isangoma!"

Mbeki leaned back in terror as a wild-haired man ran out of the royal quarters' gate: The isangoma's body was painted in whirl patterns; his necklace was of human knucklebones, and his kilt was studded with tiny bundles of leather. He got down on his hands and knees, sniffing the earth like a dog and shrieking, "I smell evil!"

Mbeki turned from the isangoma to Mpande, trying hard not to tremble and keep his voice steady. "He does smell evil, Nkosi Nkulu. Please ask this man not to eat rotting mutton anymore."

Mpande chuckled again, but now that his boredom was broken he was not about to end his entertainment so quickly. Jama's eyes darted between Mbeki and the isangoma, trying to think of something. Ingonyama sat silent and helpless beside his brother.

"There! There is your evil Great Elephant!" The isangoma pointed at Mbeki, who flinched. Mpande's eyes, alive with interest only moments before, fogged over again with boredom. Executions were not a novelty to the King of the People of Heaven.

Mbeki took a deep breath. Time, he thought. I need time, and I will think of something to save me. "My King, I don't think this man is an isangoma at all. Any fool can coat himself in mud, never clean his hair, and shriek like a baboon in labour. He doesn't know any real magic!"

The isangoma blinked once behind his makeup, surprised that the child had not been dragged away in tears yet. "I don't need to prove myself to you!"

"Go ahead, Zungu Nkulu! It's been too long since we had a good display." Prince Hamu never took his eyes off the blacksmith's son, boring a hole into the boy who should have been beneath his notice. The child had mocked his manhood; he would wash the outrage away with the boy's blood. When Hamu had found Zungu Nkulu years ago in a mangrove swamp the locals had been worshipping him as a god. He was the finest wizard in the land, and some said even Shaka's chief isangoma could not have performed the miracles of Zungu Nkulu, Zungu the Great.

Mbeki watched the wizard's every movement as he jumped and twitched, wailing his incantations. His heart sank as he realized the skill of the sorcerer: Zungu spoke a dozen tongues of gibberish. He was fleet of foot, and his arms and legs were painted to add a blurring effect to his erratic motions. Mbeki lived a great distance from the capital, but even he had heard of Hamu's prized wizard.

As Mbeki saw it, there were two possibilities: If magic was real and Zungu was a true magician, then he was dead. On the other hand, Punga had used a magical explanation to end too many unbelievable stories for Mbeki's taste. Just as Mbeki's sleight of hand was not magic, so too might the isangoma's show be a trick. His life depended upon that chance.

Mbeki felt his concentration slip as the crushing weight of the danger he was in distracted him, but he remembered himself just in time to see the wizard's hands slide into two of the leather pouches on his kilt. Though it was over in a moment and the hand came out without cupping or clenching into a fist, Mbeki knew that Zungu was holding something.

Mbeki wiped the sweat out of his eyebrows, not paying any further attention to the sporadic choreography of the unwashed man. All his attention was focused on the bags that jangled and danced upon his kilt; he knew his salvation was in those two little pouches.

Zungu Nkulu got down on all fours again, jumping over a tiny fire which was kept going a few paces from their little group and cackling until flecks of froth gathered in the corner of his mouth. Across the parade square warriors of the Frost ibutho watched with interest. Mbeki blinked and missed the isangoma emptying the contents of his hands into the fire in one of his jumps, but he could watch nothing else as Zungu howled, and the fire burst into searing white light and terrible yellow smoke. It was brighter than the sun and stank of rotten eggs and homemade gunpowder. When Zungu flashed his palms towards the sky Mbeki could see his hands were empty, and he sagged with relief that the fire was no act of the ancestors.

Shaking his whole body, the wizard rolled his eyes and addressed the boy. "There is nothing wrong with my magic!"

Mbeki sighed. His bowels stopped churning, and his hands stopped trembling in his lap. If he could keep Mpande entertained while he dealt with the isangoma, he would be all right. "There was nothing magical about what I did, and there was nothing magical about what you did. Anyone can open and close his hands at the right time with practice. Even a little boy can show his King how you did that."

Mpande gasped with pleasure. A fraud recognizes a fraud, and the king had played the family idiot long enough to know Zungu was nothing better than a talented performer. Still, Hamu's star wizard was too good for Mpande to do away with. If the blacksmith's son could reveal Zungu Nkulu as a charlatan, Mpande would gladly spare his life. "Jama, What is your boy's name?" the King leaned his ponderous bulk forward. Hamu scowled and leaned back. Cetshwayo sat rock still, his mind considering things from every angle.

"M-Mbeki, Nkosi." Jama was stunned that his son's carcass was not already impaled by the main gate.

"Mbeki? What a shame. I think the 'Wizard of kwaZulu' would suit him better." Mpande ran his fingers through his hair. The whole court waited for him to speak. "Mbeki? If you can do what he just did without using magic, you will live and he will die in your place."

Mbeki frowned, for he did not want anyone to die, but he rose and walked over to the isangoma, who bared his teeth and hissed but did not move. He was surrounded by the King's Invincibles, and were Zungu to do anything to stop the child it would be his body decorating the gates of kwaNodwengu.

Mbeki reached into the two pockets that the isangoma had used, walked over to the fire, and dropped first a silver rock and then a yellow one into the fire. The small lump of magnesium --brought all the way from the Portuguese trading post at Delogoa Bay-- burned as bright as the sun on the earth, and the stink of rotting eggs clogged his nostrils as the sulfur oxidized. Mbeki did not understand the chemistry of it, but the stones saved his life.

"Wo, Mbeki kaJama, the Wizard of kwaZulu!" Cetshwayo laughed, clapping his hands with relief that all had ended well. The fate of Hamu's wizard did not bother him at all. "You can bring your boys back anytime, Jama." He shot a quick grin at Hamu, who glowered at Zungu Nkulu.

King Mpande nodded his fat head in agreement. "I praise you, Jama, for bringing your sons to kwaNodwengu. I thought this was going to be a dull day." With a flick of his wrist Mpande dismissed them.

Mbeki did not see the other signal Mpande gave that ordered the two Invincibles forward. They grabbed Zungu by the arms and dragged him away kicking and biting, but otherwise totally silent.

"We must remember the kaJama boys," Mpande murmured to Cetshwayo as a weak-kneed Jama disappeared through a gate in the inner perimeter and a new royal favourite made his slow approach towards the throne. "They'll grow up to be fine men some day, and the kingdom could use fine men."

"I still think we should call him the Wizard of kwaZulu. The ancestors know Hamu doesn't seem to be able to provide us with one." Cetshwayo smiled broadly.

Prince Hamu snorted and excused himself. There was murder in his heart as he left the Royal Court.

Chapter 9

The umKhosi Festival, the unifying ceremony of the Zulu Kingdom, began the next day. A sea of young warriors smashed their sticks against their shields, roaring their martial pride so that from a distance the noises blended into the sound of an ocean storm breaking against a rocky shore. For a day's walk in all directions wild animals fled from the might and fury of the Zulu impi. Every kopje and donga echoed to the steady pulsing thunder coming from kwaNodwengu.

A mammoth black bull, dark as a midnight sky reflected in a muddy pool, was driven into the parade square by two nervous boys. The bull's name was Trampler of Children, for he had killed a herd boy on his way to Mpande's Great Place. He had been selected from all the herds of the Zulu for his glossy black coat, his sharp horns, and his violent temper. The bull swung his head to the right, and the boy captured by his baleful glare quailed in terror.

Trampler of Children's shoulders were the height of a man, and were that man to stretch out his arms his hands could not encompass the breadth of the bull's horns. The assembled multitude smiled at one another, knowing the monster in the center of the kraal promised a year of prosperity. The better the bull the better the harvest, and Trampler of Children was the greatest bull in all of kwaZulu. Upon the completion of the proper magic rituals the next year would be one of plenty.

King Mpande walked out of the gate of his royal quarters wearing his best leopard skin cloak and a necklace made from the cat's claws. "Bayete!" The crowd roared the royal salute with such force that the king was pushed back a step. After that first titanic cry a deathlike silence fell over kraal, broken only by the snorting of the bull.

Mbeki shifted his weight from one foot to the other. He had to pee like a milch cow just back from the stream, but he knew that this part of the ceremony might take all morning. He hopped up and down for a moment, hoping to bounce his bladder into submission. He could not move from his spot, and he could not urinate in the great parade ground of kwaNodwengu during the single most important religious event of the year. The situation was hopeless.

The two kaJama brothers were among a number of boys who had come to the umKhosi Festival as porters for their fathers. The group was formed up in the same manner as a regiment, and now they stood in the place of least status and honour on the left side of the ikhanda's main gate. Ingonyama and Mbeki had managed to push their way into the front row before the induna put in charge of them had ordered everyone to stand still.

The most important part of the festival, the Great umKhosi, was still some days away, so only the young unmarried amabutho were here in their full strength. Despite the absence of many of the older regiments, the great kraal was still completely ringed by warriors, standing five or six rows deep in their colour coded costumes and shields; behind them stood women and children from the surrounding homesteads, ready to add their high voices to the songs and chants to the festival when needed.

Mbeki wondered how many more people would arrive when all the warriors of the Zulu assembled. The Great Place seemed full now, but regiments like the two-thousand-strong Hunters, his father's ibutho, had only a hundred or so warriors representing them for this part of the umKhosi.

"Who shall it be, Nkosi Nkulu? Who shall kill the bull?" A voice called from Mbeki's end of the kraal where the younger amabutho stood stripped of their formal attire. One of these regiments would have to rush forward, unarmed, and slay the great beast in the center of the cattle pen.

"I do not know which ibutho should go. None look strong enough for Trampler of Children." The King's voice carried across the entire parade square. There was a rustling from the thousands of shields as the distressed youths heard his words.

One young man ran forward from the Skirmishers ibutho. "Bayete, Great Elephant! Choose the Skirmishers! We shall kill all our enemies, thus! And thus!" The man began to jump and spin in a shadow fight. He slashed with his stick at an invisible enemy before him and blocked an imaginary assegai thrust from his phantom foe. This was the giya, the fighting dance of warrior prowess.

The eyes of the assembled regiments turned to the youth with approval. Under Mpande's predecessor, King Dingaan, the man might have been killed for dancing so well: Dingaan had once boasted he was the nimblest dancer in kwaZulu, and he had refused to let age and corpulence rob him of his title. The People of Heaven were happy they lived in a less-oppressive age. They could still be killed at a whim, but Mpande suffered from such urges less often than his two brothers before him.

Another young man from the Weepers ran from his ranks and cried, "Bayete! Do not choose the Skirmishers, Nkosi Nkulu! Choose the Weepers! I've seen wet nurses braver than the Skirmishers!" He too began to dance. Soon men from all five of the full-strength young amabutho stepped forward to giya for their regiments' chance to rush upon Trampler of Children's horns.

"Enough!" The King's word froze every dancer in whatever gesture or contortion he was currently assuming. The king pointed with an open palm to the Skirmishers, and a wild cheer went up from the chosen warriors. Resuming discipline at once, their izinduna ordered them to set their shields and sticks onto the ground. They would run against the bull with only their hands and teeth as weapons.

"uSuthu!" The chief induna of the Skirmishers cried.

"uSuthu!" The ibutho replied, stomping their feet for effect, working up the courage to charge. The smile on Mpande's face did falter, but Mbeki knew his King would be angry to have his crown prince's war cry used so openly against him. uSuthu was the name of a breed of large black cattle from the west: Trampler of Children was an uSuthu bull, and the double meaning of the war cry would protect the Skirmishers from punishment.

The warriors moved forward at a trot, surrounding Trampler of Children in a circle a hundred paces across with the beast at its center. "Bayete!" Their induna prompted.

"Bayete!" The multitude roared. Before they lost their nerve the induna ran towards the bull, his men following his example. The bull hesitated for only a moment before he charged forward, swinging his massive horns from side to side. Two, three, four men were tossed into the air. Their bellies torn open or their lungs punctured or their hearts burst; then the bull was engulfed. Two thousand men swarmed upon him like ants onto a caterpillar, but still Trampler of Children's mighty strength shone through, so that the ground beneath the heap of bodies was soon slick with the blood of brave men.

In ones and twos, youths with mangled limbs and bleeding bodies fell out of the pile. Truly, this bull was a marvel. At this point the king could allow an isangoma to run up with a spear to end the slaughter, but his anger at the uSuthu war cry held his tongue.

With a thump the bull finally collapsed to the earth. Now the struggle entered a new stage as each man reached in with his hands to finish the bull. If Trampler of Children somehow freed himself they would have to begin again.

Shouting encouragement to one another, twenty men who had already braved the horns of the monster to reach his head moved in for the kill. While the sheer weight of warriors pinned the enraged creature to the ground, the twenty took hold of anything they could find. They pulled the bull's tattered ears, his gore-drenched horns, his raw bleeding lips, and every struggling thing in between. Chanting to coordinate their efforts, they twisting in unison until sweat streamed down their bloody bodies, and the bull's bellows of anger turned to desperation, then terror.

They twisted and pulled and pushed and cursed and wrenched with all their strength as the head turned further and impossibly further. They looked at each other in awe at the titan they had borne to the ground. It was only after an unbearable time that Trampler of Children's neck broke with an explosive crack. Even then the beast twitched in his death throws with such force that two more men flew through the air, and one more had his head cracked like an egg by a stray hoof.

Shakily, the regiment pulled itself away from the bull and the broken bodies surrounding it. "Bayete!" They cried once more. Hundreds of hands lifted the bull up onto their shoulders and carried his limp form like a bit of flotsam in a mighty river. The body was taken up the kraal and into the cattle pen in front of the royal quarters.

A team of izangoma received it there with reverence while another arrived at the place of the kill. These wizards and witches set about gathering every bit of the bull left behind, from the tufts of hair, to the blood-soaked earth, to a single massive eyeball that one of the warriors had gouged out with his fingers during the desperate struggle. Nothing could be left behind.

The Skirmishers returned to the far end of the Great Place and another aching silence fell over the assembled men as they waited for word from their King. "I praise you, Skirmishers. The greatest beast of the Zulu lies dead by your hands. The beast fed from our soil, which will soon bring forth a harvest as great as the beast. I praise you!" Mpande smiled, his anger forgotten.

"Bayete!" The izinduna of the Skirmishers prompted.

"Bayete!" They echoed the royal salute with joy and pride. The men missing from their ranks had been sacrificed for the good of the people. There were no regrets.

"Now the bull's magic must be given to the young. None may be wasted!"

"Cha, Sire!" Fifteen thousand throats roared.

Mpande nodded seriously. "Magic earned with brave men's blood is the most expensive. It must be given to the children."

The warrior in charge of the herd boys turned to face them. "Go to the King now. Do not speak or laugh. This is a great honour for you all. Don't ruin it." Mbeki and the other boys trotted forward, crossing the parade ground to stand before Mpande.

"Children of the Zulu! You shall go into the royal cattle enclosure and eat the great bull. Its strength will become your strength, and you shall not come out of the pen until this time tomorrow. Eat your fill, and then eat more!" Mbeki licked his lips in anticipation. That was a lot of beef, and if he was going into the cattle pen there would be a place where he could empty his throbbing bladder: The place was ankle-deep in cow pats anyway.

"The flesh of the Bull is magical! None must go to waste! You shall not relieve yourselves until you are out of the pen, or the harvest is cursed. Is it heard?"

Mbeki's mind panicked, and he almost blurted a startled request for Mpande to repeat the last part of his command. Instead he heard his voice echo with all the other boys, "It is heard, Nkosi Nkulu. Bayete!" Meek as a calf to the slaughter, he followed the other boys into the pen. The izangoma had already removed the bull's skin and innards, and a great fire was ready for cooking. The cattle pen smelled of fodder and blood, dung and urine. Mbeki felt as if he was going to burst.

A massive piece of seared flesh was forced into Mbeki's hands by a smiling isangoma. He mechanically began to eat it. Blood and other juices ran down his chin and chest. It was delicious, but all he could think of was how many times he normally peed in a day. The mental tally was disturbing: Once before dawn and again after the cattle went to pasture; at least once before supper, and again before sleeping. With the excitement and distraction of the umKhosi Festival he had not relieved all day, and he would not be allowed to do so until mid-afternoon tomorrow.

Groaning around a mouthful of beef, Mbeki walked over to the fence of the cattle pen to watch more of the ceremony. Another isangoma rushed out of the royal quarters carrying a bowl filled with a black liquid. The witch doctor reached the King and offered him the dish with a deep bow. Mpande took the shallow container of goo in his left hand and used the index and middle fingers of his right to scoop out some of the black sludge and put it in his mouth.

"The King puts magic in his mouth!" The wizard cried.

"Bayete!" The crowd roared.

Mpande puffed out his cheeks and pulled his lips back to squirt the black goo through his teeth in a high arc. "The King spits magic!"

"Bayete!"

The King repeated the process, forcing more and more of the black liquid out through his teeth, filling his mouth from the dish as needed.

"I have to pee! Pee, pee, pee!" Mbeki muttered under his breath. The pulsing stream of liquid from between Mpande's teeth inflamed Mbeki's keen ears. His active imagination could not stop thinking about his need.

Another boy came up beside him, watching the long black jets fly through the air. "I wonder if the King practices that before the ceremony." He handed Mbeki another piece of steaming meat. "Here. Your brother asked me to give this to you: Roast kidney. It's so tender you'd think you were eating a piece of fruit."

Miserably, Mbeki began to eat. It was so juicy that he imagined he could feel his bladder swell with the extra fluid. "I have to piss like you wouldn't believe."

The other boy's eyes widened. "You can't do that!"

"What does peeing have to do with the harvest?"

"Do you see those Invincibles? Any boy who takes off his penis cover dies. Now keep your jokes to yourself. You're making me have to go too." The boy wandered away, squeezing his legs together and cursing under his breath.

When Mpande finished he led the warriors out of the ikhanda to sing and sacrifice to his ancestors; only with their blessing would the coming year be good. The day wasted away, and the boys ate and ate. No sooner would they sit down, convinced that they were about to burst, when a wizard or a royal bodyguard would come along and encourage them back to the fire for more meat. First they cajoled, then they ordered, then they began to threaten.

"There is still so much meat. All you boys can't handle that beef? You can't be Zulu! Get up and eat!"

"Don't hold your belly and groan at me. You're not fooling anybody. Go and eat!"

"I tell you this beef is delicious. When was the last time you got your choice of the cut of meat? Eat it now!"

"You there! Where do you think you're going? Do you want to ruin our harvest and see us all die of famine? You pee everyday of your life, you can miss a day now!"

So it went until at dusk the King and the crowd returned. Again the warriors lined the inner wall and listened as their king spoke. He talked until after the sun set about the nation, the harvest, the past and the future. Just before he dismissed them he said what all the unmarried men had been straining to hear all day. "I suppose you want to know which ibutho shall sow on the head ring this year and be allowed to marry?"

"Yebho, Nkosi Nkulu!" More than one young man cried out. The head ring was the mark of a full adult, a man who could own his own cattle, trade them for wives, and run his own homestead. A head-ringed man only served in his regiment at the umKhosi Festival and during times of war. Every unmarried warrior waited for the day his King allowed him to sew on the head ring and go in search of his first bride.

"I shall give you a hint, but no more. You'll have to wait for the end of the umKhosi to find out. Is it heard?"

"It is heard, Baba!" One of the boys from the Frost yelled. There was more laughter this time, because calling the King father, while acceptable, was still a transparent attempt to curry favour.

"The ibutho that shall sew in the head ring this year is famous for its war cry." Mpande smiled at his cleverness as he walked into his royal quarters. The ikhanda buzzed liked a hive of bees as each man turned to his neighbour to puzzle out the clue. Every regiment had famous war cries, but each thought their own was special.

"Perhaps it is the Skirmishers? Didn't we get his attention with uSuthu?" A youth cried hopefully. The Frost warriors further up laughed with contempt.

"Don't bet on it, puppy! You're hardly off your mother's teat! Your regiment only formed this year! Why would he marry you off?"

"It won't be the Frost either. Whoever remembers your songs?" A warrior of the Mongrel Regiment taunted.

"Famous war song? What is more famous than Du Du Du?" An induna of the Du Du Du ibutho called out. His warriors began beating the shields, stomping their feet, and singing, "Du! Du! Du! The sound of men running forward! Du! Du! Du! The sound of the men who will kill you!"

Soon the whole kraal was filled with the sound of competing songs, and as the izinduna led the young men out of the ikhanda to sleep a few stick fights broke out between the amabutho.

Throughout the long night the boys were driven back again and again to the cooking fires. For them, sleep was out of the question. Their bodies were coated head to toe in beef grease. Their bellies were rigid to the touch. The izangoma no longer prepared the meat for them; now each boy had to cut off what he wanted, cook it as he preferred, and stuff it into his reluctant mouth.

Many of the boys burned their meat so they would have more time between feedings. Even Ingonyama, whose praise song since he was weaned onto solid food was 'The voracious devourer of beef' tottered and groaned, clutching his stomach and swearing to anyone who would listen that his skin was stretching tighter than a drumhead.

Dawn found the boys almost unable to stand, so they were ordered to crawl back to the bull. Now they did little more than burn the beef until it was black as a cinder and then suck on it without swallowing. Although this slowed down their intake even further it did nothing to relieve the terrible pressure on their bladders. Every boy was convinced he was carrying an Mfolozi River's worth of urine half way between his navel and his groin.

By the afternoon the boys were so far gone that a number needed help to totter out of the cattle pen. The bull carcass was picked clean down to the bones, and izangoma burned the remaining scraps down to ashes. Mbeki and the other boys tried hard to stand in neat lines before the King, but the constant shifting from one foot to the other, the clutching of stomachs and the muffled curses, reduced any semblance of order to a mockery of discipline.

"Now you know why the boys who have been here before always hide when the first bull is being killed," Mpande smiled. The boys could not bring themselves to reply. The watching ranks of warriors grinned too, fondly remembering their own youths: Many among them had once eaten the bull.

"This parade square is looking very dry. Nothing will grow here anymore. It has been so long since we had a good rain," Mpande said. The boys stared at him blankly, for there had been several showers over the last few days. Mbeki needed no further prompting. He pulled aside his loincloth, took off the gourd covering his manhood and peed in a high arc for a very, very long time.

Others wasted no time in following his example, and soon all the boys was relieving themselves and trying not to step in the growing puddles. The adults laughed so hard that many fell to the ground with the strength of their guffaws. By the time the boys had finished they too were laughing, and the Great Place of the Great Chief of the People of Heaven was a very happy place.

"I would have to say we are going to get a lot of rain this year." The King choked out through his mirth. It rained for the next three days, and when the weather cleared the Great umKhosi Festival began.

Chapter 10

The ranks of the amabutho at kwaNodwengu swelled as new warriors arrived. Every man save the old, the sick and the rebellious made the journey to the center of the kingdom. The Zulu did not fear an enemy taking advantage of their undefended borders; indeed, their neighbours knew this was the worst time to challenge the izimpi of the Zulu: Almost forty thousand warriors were gathered in the Great Place of the King of KwaZulu.

Each warrior was there in all his finery; every regiment in its own distinct uniform. There were the youngest amabutho: the Skirmishers, the Weepers, the Mongrels, the Frost and the Du Du Du, each with their dark shields and elaborate headpieces hiding their lack of head rings. These warriors were in the prime of their lives, and their formal attire did not bear the marks of age. They sought to impress the older amabutho of their fathers and older brothers.

Next were the middle-aged regiments: The Young Mambas, the Adult Mambas, the Chieftains, the Hunters, the Wild Pigs and the Worriers. Some were head ringed, others not, and their shields mixed dark and light colours. Most of these regiments were hardened fighters from Ndondakusuka, the Swazi Campaigns, and any number of border skirmishes. They moved through the amakhanda between the Mfolozis with all the confidence their position demanded. They were crack veterans, the backbone of the Zulu impi.

The older amabutho certainly did not feel unwelcome. The Ambush Battle, Sharp Youth, and the Snake Regiments stood proud with their white shields, crane feathers, and head rings. They were the elders, and whatever their juniors thought in private, everyone showed them the respect they deserved. There were even a few hundred old men from the truly ancient Stabbers and the Stumbling Blocks regiments. These grandfathers had seen Shaka when they were boys, rushed the Boer muskets at Blood River, fought in Mpande's civil war, and were the fathers and grandfathers of the men who today made up all but the eldest of the other regiments. Their fighting days were long over, but the young crowded around their campfires to hear their stories.

The last arrivals were the semiautonomous abaQulusi, a tribe that guarded the Zulu's northwestern border with fanaticism. Because of their distant base and their crucial strategic importance they alone, of all the clans of kwaZulu, were allowed to keep their warriors for a local independent regiment made up from warriors of all ages.

Led by the exiled Swazi Prince Mbilini waMswati, the abaQulusi left their homes before the date of the umKhosi Festival was set: If they had waited for a royal messenger, they would not have had enough time left to cross the Kingdom to participate.

The amabutho lined up in strict order of age and paraded outside the Great Place before King Mpande. Thousands of the warriors had brought their families, and so women and children watched the parade with a carnival atmosphere.

Mbeki cheered and stomped his feet as the Hunters marched past. As a royal favourite Jama marched in the file closest to the king and crowd, and he could see him clearly. As each row got close to Mpande, the warriors bowed from the waist until their heads were at the level of their knees as they passed in front of him. The ranks began straightening up again as they passed, but they were not fully upright again until they had passed the next nearest ikhanda over a thousand paces away.

Mbeki regarded the King's guests with a mix of curiosity and trepidation. Dozens of white men stood to one side of Mpande, surrounded by his bodyguard of Invincibles. There were Boers with their hair and beards the colour of straw, wearing wide brimmed hats and tall leather riding boots. They were here to trade, or petitioning to hunt, or just to say they had visited the court of King Mpande kaSenzangakhona, ruler of the mighty Zulu.

Apart from the Boers stood the Englishmen in their heavy coats and wool pants, their clean shaven or mustachioed faces sweating. Their heads were covered in all manner of queerly shaped hats. They came for much the same reason as the Boers, but a number had also come on yet another diplomatic mission to make unreasonable demands upon the King. Mpande allowed them to visit provided they remembered their manners, and their place.

Finally there was John Dunn, an Englishman dressed like a Boer, who had sat as a member of the Zulu Royal Court for almost his entire adult life. Mbeki had heard it said that the English called Dunn the White Chief of the Zulu. John Dunn was so important to the Zulu as both a gun runner and as an insight into the white mind that he had been granted his own royal fief in the extreme south-east of kwaZulu, along with many wives.

"See, Jonani?" An older boy nearby gestured at the object of Mbeki's attention to his friend. The Zulu had trouble with words that did not end in vowels, so John Dunn had answered to Jonani since he was a teenager.

"Yebho," replied the other boy.

"My Baba is going to buy a gun off of him before we leave," The first said proudly.

"Cha," The second laughed with mock disbelief.

"Yebho, he's going to spend four cows on a double barreled shotgun. The shells are as big as your thumb, and they can drop a buffalo at five hundred yards."

Mbeki thought of the old tower musket Jama kept in Mpikasi's hut. It was a muzzle loader with no sights, a thinning barrel, and poor flint. His father had received it from the king as a gift; it was worth a goat. "Your father must be a very rich man to waste four cows on a noisemaker," Mbeki murmured to himself.

"What did you just say?"

Mbeki winced, but saw no advantage in lying now that he had been heard. "Your father seems to have cows to waste: Once the ammunition that comes with it is gone, your homemade powder and shot will ruin the barrel. After that it won't kill a crane at ten yards, let alone a buffalo at five hundred." Mbeki knew a little about guns.

"I know you. You're that kaJama boy!" The second boy pointed at Mbeki's face with a single finger.

"My Baba isn't very happy with you," The first menaced. Mbeki made eye contact with the older boy for the first time, and he took a step back in shock. Sometimes two bulls are put into the same kraal, and when they lock eyes everyone present knows only one will prevail. It was inexplicable, unreasonable, but Mbeki knew that this boy had just become his enemy.

"Who's your Baba?" Before the older boy could answer Mbeki continued, "Does your mother even know?" Mbeki began to edge away from the two of them. If he could find Ingonyama he would be all right.

"My father is Prince Hamu kaNzibe, and I know something a little smaller than a buffalo he might like to shoot with his new gun." Jobe remembered the beating he had suffered last night for a minor infraction of house rules; far from blaming his father, Jobe knew it was Mbeki's fault for making his father so angry in the first place. The welts on his buttocks were hidden by the back flap of his loincloth, but nothing could hide his shame at being beaten like a servant.

Hamu's son lunged towards Mbeki, who turned and ran as fast as he could. Mbeki began to pull ahead of them, but when he turned his head to see how much of a lead he was gaining he crashed headlong into a fat woman. She started berating him for his clumsiness, but she was interrupted when two other boys fell upon him.

Mbeki cursed as the two boys tried to roll him over to hit his front. Twisting an arm loose, Mbeki smacked one of the boys in the throat. He was up and running again before the other boy could react. "Where's Ingonyama?" He huffed to himself. He remembered his brother taking his leave after the parade, but he could not remember which way he had gone. Mbeki's thigh hurt where one of the boys' blows had landed, and he knew he could not outpace them much longer.

"Ingonyama!" He shouted; he could hear the heavy breathing of the two boys behind him.

"Yebho?" He heard a reply, ahead and to his left.

"Come here--" A flying tackle from Hamu's son sent Mbeki to the ground again. This time he twisted around onto his back and kicked out with his leg. With a sickening crunch he felt something give, and a gurgle of pain escaped from the kaHamu boy's lips as his nose broke in a welter of blood. He fell backwards, cupping his hands over his face. Mbeki lay toe to toe with him, panting. Ingonyama and the other boy arrived to see the two lying there.

"You'll pay for this, kaJama," The Jobe whimpered. Blood seeped between his fingers and ran down his forearms. "When my Baba finds out what you did--"

"What did you do, Mbeki?" Ingonyama asked, only now realizing he had missed a fight. The boy with the broken nose shot a look of pure venom at Mbeki.

Mbeki sat mute, staring at his opponent's face and wondering just what sort of cow pat he had stepped in. Ingonyama and the injured boy's friend squared off against each other, not sure what to do.

"My name is Jobe kaHamu, and you're going to wish you never met me." With as much dignity as he could manage with blood smeared all over his face, Jobe allowed the other boy to help him to his feet and walked away, muttering threats until he was out of earshot.

"Hamu's son? You know how to pick them Mbeki." Ingonyama hoisted his brother up, and the two went into kwaNodwengu.

With the parade over, the amabutho were back on the parade ground of the Great Place again. This time the kraal was ringed in rows twenty deep, and even then the youngest regiments and most of the crowd had to remain outside the gate. Ingonyama and Mbeki scrambled up onto the roof of one of the huts just in time to see the King appear from the royal quarters.

Mpande wore a hooded cloak of woven corns stalks, decorated with beads and bells and strips of white cloth rubbed with broken berries to produce splotchy stains. The air, heavy with the rains of the last few days, was absolutely still as he walked from the royal quarters into the cattle kraal. Flies buzzed; a baby wailed; the little bells of his costume jingled, then all was again silent.

"Stand!" He cried. No one answered.

"Stand!" He tried again, still no response.

"Stand!" He roared the word for a third time, commanding the nation to hail him as its king for another year.

This time the whole Zulu nation cried out, "Bayete!" It echoed off the walls of the ikhanda like thunder.

"Stand!"

"Bayete!" It shook the thatch upon which the boys sat.

"Stand!"

"Bayete!" The third thunder-crack scared birds out of the surrounding mimosa trees. Hailing their chief, the amabutho began to sway and sing songs in praise of their king, then they lifted their voices to pray for a good harvest. The multitude ended with the Zulu national anthem that was only ever sung during the umKhosi Festival.

An isangoma ran from the royal quarters carrying a dozen calabashes in a net. The crowd shifted and muttered. Here was deep magic: Each gourd was filled with the water of a different lake, river, or sea from the Land of the People of Heaven. Into it was mixed magic herbs, black medicines, ashes from the bull killed during the opening of the umKhosi Festival, and other mystical ingredients.

Mpande took the first calabash and held it over his head as he ran towards the crowd. He hurled it against the shields of his warriors, and the nation cheered. He threw again and again, shattering the gourds and showering his warriors with magic. The ubiquitous izangoma were on their hands and knees among the crowd, picking up the pieces of the calabashes. Only by salvaging every scrap could they be sure the magic could not be taken by an enemy and used against the Zulu in times of war.

When the last gourd was smashed, Mpande waited for the crowd to still, then cried, "Bring out the Bull!" Without waiting to be obeyed he turned and returned to the royal quarters. Another bull was brought out, this time stolen from the herds of an enemy nation. Long before the Du Du Du ibutho fell upon it, Mbeki and Ingonyama had climbed off the hut in unseemly haste. They fled through the gates and tore off across the fields, followed by many other veterans of the first bull killed in the umKhosi ceremony. The adults smiled and shook their heads before turning their attention back to the bull. Children were funny sometimes.

Chapter 11

"What is this?" Hamu glared at his son's face. Jobe stood before the northern prince, his head hung with shame. He had avoided his father's huts all day, but at last the pain in his nose became unbearable, and he had snuck into Hamu's section of the royal quarters in search of his mother. His sister Nandhi had directed him towards the right hut, but the moment he passed the first of Hamu's guards with dried blood all down his chin, neck, and chest, he was dragged before the prince. One of his father's retainers had fetched his mother as well.

"It is nothing," Jobe said.

Hamu smacked his son across the face, jarring Jobe's nose and sending a fresh coppery tang of blood up into his sinuses. "Do not lie to me! Ever!" Jobe realized is father was in one of his rages, but the anger was not at anything Jobe had done. He needed only to endure until the storm passed.

Jobe's mother, however, was not prepared to humour her ill-tempered husband. "Don't you yell at him! He's done nothing wrong! You're mad because of your public embarrassments, not because of his nose!"

Hamu turned to face her. "Stay out of it, Mnkabayi!" His blood was boiling: Zungu Nkulu had killed Mpande's executioners, strangling them with his bare hands before escaping out into the plains. Hamu had been delighted, sending four of his best men to collect Zungu.

Even away from the Royal Court a wizard of Zungu's reputation was worth a thousand warriors to Hamu, but Zungu had killed three of Hamu's men too, leaving the fourth with two broken arms and a message: "Tell Hamu that I am done with him. I'm going North, and I will have no master there except myself."

Hamu had spent years and hundreds of cows cultivating that wizard's loyalty, and it had all been ruined by one little boy. Zungu's disappearance had shaken the North's web of alliances, and one by one Hamu was watching his flies drop into other spiders' outstretched arms; already, four minor chieftains had switched loyalties to the Mandlakazi clan led by Zibhebhu, his northern rival. Another two were making advances to the abaQulusi under Cetshwayo's pet Swazi, Mbilini. Oh, to have that kaJama boy alone for just a short while, Hamu thought.

"I will not stay out of it! Jobe has nothing to do with Zungu! This is all Mbeki kaJama's fault!" Mnkabayi saw her husband clench his fists in impotent fury, and she began to screech: "Mbeki kaJama! Mbeki kaJama! You were beaten by a child!" The fire in the hut's hearth did not light all the way to the walls, but Hamu could still see his attendants, normally stony faced, begin to smile as he was berated by his wife. He felt hot bile rise up his throat at the humiliation. "Why not blame Mbeki kaJama for Jobe's nose while you're at it?"

Hamu opened his mouth to shout her down again, but Jobe interrupted him. "It was him! Mbeki broke my nose!" Jobe's anger made him speak. It was a mistake that would haunt him for the rest of his life.

Mnkabayi shrieked with laughter harsh enough to curdle milk. At last she contained herself, clutching her sides and swaying. "That little boy is a wonder, Hamu! Maybe he's why you're going bald?" She cackled again, watching as Hamu stood there, his mouth slack in disbelief. "Maybe he's why you're so fat?" She loathed him, hated his clammy embraces and sloppy kisses. She laughed at a sudden thought. "Maybe he's why you have such a small penis!" There was a collected gasp from everyone else in the hut.

"Zokufa!" Hamu barked. His head steward knew what had to be done. The tall man stepped out of the shadows and stabbed Mnkabayi in the back with a broad-bladed war assegai. Her face froze in surprise, and Zokufa helped her sink to her knees. Mnkabayi looked up at Hamu. "I didn't think you had the balls," she murmured, the light going out of her eyes.

Jobe ran to his mother, shaking her and crying. Everyone in the hut watched him until he was all cried out.

"I did not kill your mother, Jobe," Hamu said softly. "Nor did Zokufa." The steward melted back into the shadows. "Your mother killed herself when she mocked me. You killed your mother when you said Mbeki broke your nose. Ultimately, Mbeki killed your mother. She would still be alive were it not for that blacksmith's son."

Zokufa murmured from the darkness, "What do we do now, Nkosi? If we take her outside for the jackals someone might see the hole in her back."

Hamu breathed in through his nose and out through his mouth, savouring the smell of her blood. He felt goosebumps rising up all over his skin at the thought of Mnkabayi's angry shade still hanging in the room. Her last words had been immensely gratifying. I have the balls to do anything, he thought. Tomorrow that kaJama boy will learn to leave me and mine alone!

"We'll bury her under the floor." He watched a few of his men shiver with superstitious dread and noted them as being unsuitable for bloody business. "I will move my quarters to another hut. Three or four of my wives and daughters can sleep in this one once we have the grave covered over."

That satisfied everyone, and soon five men had hoes out, scraping up the packed clay floor and pulling up the dry earth underneath. They put Mnkabayi's body into the hole and began to scrape the dirt back over her. "Wait," Hamu ordered. He knew his son had been coddled by this woman. "Jobe, you finish it." The boy looked at his father, his once-handsome face ruined by his broken nose. In a daze, he took one of the hoes and began to drag the soil onto his mother. "You're burying your mother because of Mbeki, boy. We'll bury him tomorrow too."

Jobe could not see his mother's body through his tears, but he nodded his head at his father's words. Mbeki kaJama would die for what he had done. Jobe swore it with every pull of his hoe.

Chapter 12

Mbeki danced around the fire all night, enjoying the songs of the Hunters ibutho. Ingonyama was learning to giya, and all of Jama's friends were impressed at how high he could jump. All around them were happy, laughing people. The nation had come together in one place, and there were as many campfires on the earth as there were stars in the heavens.

Hlubi and Punga were nearby at another campfire telling the story of Ingonyama hunting a ferocious man eater, all by himself, with only a wet loincloth as a weapon. Elsewhere people played tag in the dark, or drank sorghum beer, or swam in the river. Whatever they did, every Zulu settled in for an evening of festivities, everyone except the King.

Mpande's fat thighs ached as he spent the night squatting over the inkatha of the Zulu people. It was the most magical charm in the arsenal of the Zulu: A grass rope wrapped in a python's skin, stuffed with over seventy years', four kings' and thirty clans' worth of talismans. Tradition demanded the king to squat over the inkatha to bring good fortune. It was a long, torturous affair, and he grunted his prayers to his ancestors, desperate for the next day's sun to release him from the ordeal.

At dawn the next morning the parade ground of kwaNodwengu was filled with people ready for the last part of the Great umKhosi Festival. Mpande emerged from the royal quarters, weary from his night's vigil over the inkatha. He shuffled forward on stiff legs, and his ponderous gut seemed to sag.

Beneath his cloak of corn stalks he was painted from head to foot with white swirls, chevrons, squares, stars, squiggles and splotches; it was the dark medicine that leached all the malignant spirits out of the land and onto the King's skin. He walked as a man lost, staggering a little this way and that, slowly making his way across the parade ground through the gates and out into the fields beyond. The nation followed in silence.

Mpande meandered, never walking far in any one direction. Though he was supposed to be heading for the river, he never went straight for it; there were times he even headed back towards kwaNodwengu. Slowly, ever so slowly, he came closer and closer to the river until finally, standing on its bank, he removed his corn stalk cloak. The amabutho ran downstream and into the water. Without looking to see whether his people were ready, Mpande stepped into the river and began to wash off all the evil spirits painted onto his skin.

Mbeki and Ingonyama watched as izangoma burned the corn stalk cloak, and the ashes were thrown into the water around the king. The current pulled the dark magic downstream, and when the king was at last clean the nation gave a mighty roar of approval. Mpande emerged from the water smiling and happy again. The nation gave the royal salute, and he signaled for beer to be distributed among his people.

The kaJama brothers returned to their father's hut in kwaNodwengu, unaware of the eyes that followed them. They packed up their belongings without any premonitions of danger. "We'll probably leave as soon Baba's back. Maybe we'll wait until after the head ring announcement is made," Ingonyama said. Mbeki nodded his agreement. As the boys ducked to enter the low doorway, strong arms seized them and shoved them up against the side of the hut.

"Look what you've done to my son!" Prince Hamu barked. Eight tall men flanked him, and two more held the boys firmly against the thatch. Jobe stood next to his father, the center of his face was a violent, swollen purple; his eyes spoke of murder.

"Take your hands off of me!" Ingonyama shouted into the face of the man before him. Mbeki could not speak.

"You embarrass me in front of the King. You disgrace my wizard. You break my son's nose. There is justice in the land, and it is on my side." Hamu's needle eyes seemed to pierce Mbeki's heart, and Mbeki writhed under their attention. Hamu gave a decisive gesture with his head and two of his men produced short stabbing spears from under their cow tails.

Mbeki could not think, could not focus on anything except the sun glinting off the naked steel. Like a mouse mesmerized by a mamba, he stood there pinned against the wall, watching the two men draw closer. They held their spears with ease, preparing an underhanded stabbing stroke that they had practiced since infancy. Mbeki opened his mouth and closed it again. He could smell the stale sweat of the man holding him down.

"You didn't bathe with the King!" He burst. The man flinched. "That's not allowed! Every Zulu warrior has to go to the stream and bathe when the Nkosi Nkulu bathes. You didn't! You stink!" Mbeki's words were playing on the supernatural fears of the man; the sins of the warrior had not been ritually washed away. They would cling to him like a shroud, dooming him. Just as Mbeki realized he had hit the right note he lost it again. His accusation turned to babbling. "You're dry! You didn't bathe! You still have evil spirits on you! You've--"

"Shut up!" The man shook him like a straw doll. The ones with spears had also paused. Inside Mbeki was screaming, I have to keep talking. What else can I say? He could not breathe. He felt like a python was wrapping around his chest.

"Kill him!" Hamu ordered again. The men with spears shook their heads a moment, clearing their ears of the little boy's damning words.

"What is going on here?" A new voice boomed. Ntsingwayo kaMahole stood down the row, still dripping from the river.

"You haven't seen anything old man, turn around and walk away." Hamu had iron in his voice, but his heart skipped a beat: Ntsingwayo was the chief of a clan as powerful as his own, and he was a loyal supporter of both Mpande and Cetshwayo.

"What are you doing to my sons?" Jama also appeared up the aisle, along with several other wet men.

"And what are you doing with those spears, Nkosi?" Ntsingwayo rumbled. "The King will hear about this, Hamu. Men more powerful than you have died for less."

Hamu flinched. "Your boys are pests. See that they don't bother me or my sons again." Hamu turned on his heel and walked away, followed by his men. A group of warriors from the Hunters Regiment followed him, mocking him and grabbing at his followers' shoulders; Ingonyama joined them, heaping abuse upon Hamu's name.

Mbeki stood quaking beside the hut. Jama took his son by the shoulder, but Mbeki did not notice. "I couldn't think of anything... I couldn't think of anything..." His whisper was lost in his father's soothing shushing.

Ntsingwayo walked up and whispered in Mbeki's ear, "Prince Hamu is a mamba: If he finds you while you're sleeping you're a dead man, but if you stomp your feet and threaten him the snake will flinch first. You're safe now. I promise." Ntsingwayo said with a smile that transformed his stern face into that of a jolly old man. "Now come on, let's see which ibutho will sew in the head ring this year. I have a daughter I'd like to marry off to someone close to my kraal, and there's a good man from the Du Du Du whose family lives only a day away."

They walked out to the parade ground where the king, freshly toweled with the fleece of a lamb, stood before his young regiments. "This year the Kingdom is in good hands. All the omens have been promising: Our cattle grow fat, our crops grow tall, and our children grow old. It has been three years since an ibutho has sewn on the head ring; three years since I have ordered a regiment of young men to become full adults. I can tell you now that next year I shall not say it has been four years!" There was a murmur of approval at that.

"The ibutho I pick will sew on the head ring and may marry their appropriate female age group." This brought on still more pleasant mutterings, for there had been years when female age groups had been wed into warriors of older regiments; many a young warrior had watched through gritted teeth as some old man walked off with his sweetheart. "This year I have chosen..." Mpande waited until all the young men were leaning forward to hear his words. "The Adult Mambas ibutho to sew in the head ring."

"Mina! Mina! Mina! Hhahe!" The regiment gave their war cry. Other regiments gave some polite insults to the lucky new future husbands, and the regiments melted away.

"I guess I'll have to marry my daughter a little further from home than I would have liked," Ntsingwayo sighed.

Ingonyama and Mbeki returned to the hut for Jama's possessions without mishap, and soon they were on their way back to the Valley of the Three Homesteads. All around them others also returned to their kraals: New bachelors dressed in their colourful courting gear wandered the country looking for brides; the royals returned to the royal amakhanda, and the herd boys were allowed to play reed flutes until the harvest. Mbeki was very good with the instrument, but Ingonyama was all thumbs.

Hamu returned to his clan holdings in the north with a much-reduced retinue: His wizard was gone, a wife was dead, two of his personal guards had been executed for having their spears out in the Great Place, and three more had been killed by Zungu Nkulu. This year's umKhosi festival had been a disaster for the Ngenetsheni Clan.

Hamu swung around to make sure his retinue was in order and his daughter Nandhi caught his eye. Which one is she? He wondered. My seventh, so that would make her fourteen. She was a late bloomer with only the first bud of breasts now appearing on her naked chest and the merest beginnings of womanly curves at her sides. I'll have to start considering who to marry her off to. If I leave it too long she might find some young man she would prefer to the randy old goat I'll want her to wed. He warmed just a little at the thought. If Nandhi became as attractive as her mother, Hamu would be able to build an alliance with any chief in the land.

Jobe wandered into his field of view, and even that tiny good mood left him. His eldest son's flattened nose ruined an otherwise handsome face. His future heir had been disfigured by a child whose very presence seemed to throw a black cloud of bad luck over every one of Hamu's plans. "I will remember the name Mbeki kaJama." His voice was cold, which was how Hamu worked best. He allowed himself to imagine the little boy's blood spilling into the dust and felt some of his anger and tension relax.

His temper had clouded his reasoning; there had been better ways to kill the kaJama boy, but he had not thought the matter through. He would do better next time. He was not a fool: It took someone very clever to rise over the handicap of poor lineage to become a serious contender for the throne, but he had done that. Eventually he would be king, and then anyone who had ever bothered him would pay.

"I will remember the name kaJama. I'll be saying it to a royal executioner someday." Mbeki kaJama had made an enemy, and Hamu intended for him to regret it. With one more turn of his head to look back at Mpande's Great Place, Hamu pulled his cloak a little tighter against the drizzle and walked north.

Chapter 13

Prince Inyati kaMzilikazi ran south through the tall grass with his Matabele guards at his back. The years as an exile had been kind to the Prince of the House of Kumalo: He had grown tall, with long limbs well formed. He wore a black kilt of monkey pelts, and his hair pulled out into high spikes, decorated with red feathers. Today would be his day, and the sun would not set before he had shown his keepers his true worth.

Around him birds exploded up out of the undergrowth as the Swazi ran through the tall grass. They wore black and white ostrich feathers piled up high on their heads to make them seem taller. They moved without discipline, drunk on their own heady success and hubris.

Inyati felt a gnawing doubt at the corner of his mind: Zulu do not run. We don't know how many of them there are, but there could be even more of them than there are of us. Plus, we've crossed the Phongolo into kwaZulu. This is their land now, and the Swazi have never chased a Zulu impi back onto their home soil before.

Another part of Inyati was elated. After years of waiting and training, finally he ran out to war, and it was only through war that he would impress the Swazi lords who controlled his fate. Only through war would he one day return to his lost home, far to the north. Inyati had worked every day under his guardsmen's instructions to hone his strength and skill. Now, at last, he could begin to build his name and reputation in the eyes of these foreigners. Even if they lacked the prowess of his Matabele, it was only with their help that he could build his future.

The Zulu had been enemies of the Swazi since their two borders first met, but the Swazi's stoic resistance and their distance from the two Mfolozi Rivers had saved them the full wraith of King Shaka. King Dingaan had been too occupied with the Boers to bother with the Swazi, and King Mpande had tried feebly several times to conquer them without success.

This latest attack was little more than a cattle raid in force: Something to blood the young regiments. The Zulu had looted Swazi homesteads and rustled vast herds of Swazi cattle. As the impi withdrew back towards kwaZulu, the Swazi king had gathered his forces, Inyati among them, and set off in pursuit. Unburdened by the booty of a successful raid, the Swazi impi was catching up.

Since the beginning of the pursuit, Inyati had waited for the Zulu to turn and fight. The classic Zulu battle tactic was the Bull Buffalo formation: Their army would be divided into two horns made up of the youngest and fastest regiments on either side of the head, made up of slower and more powerful regiments. Behind the head and horns would be the loins, a reserve force set to one side for the crucial moment. When battle was joined, the head would engage the enemy straight on while the horns wrapped around the flanks. The head would hold the enemy's attention until this had been accomplished, and then when the enemy was surrounded on all sides the loins would be committed and their weight would carry all before them.

The Bull Buffalo formation had been developed by King Shaka, and it always brought victory to an assegai-wielding army. What it lacked was subtlety, and the further Inyati chased the Zulu into their Kingdom without seeing the head and horns form up in front of him, the more he worried.

"We've caught them!" The cry came from the Swazi vanguard, and Inyati gave his Matabele a hand signal to increase their pace. He would have to be in the front to choose his place on the battlefield: Only where the fighting was thickest would his reputation be made.

There was a thin screen of brush to be passed through, and on its far side Inyati and his men came to a sudden, jarring halt. Around them their Swazi allies whooped their delight at having overtaken the Zulu, but the Matabeles' trained eye for terrain told them they had come upon a place of death. Inyati shook his head, but he could say nothing. He would not be invited to the Swazi war council, if indeed they bothered to hold one. There was no one he could tell, 'We didn't catch the Zulu. They led us here to be slaughtered.'

The kloof cut across the plains from east to west as far as the eye could see. The bottom and steep sides of the ravine were rutted by the thousands of feet and hooves that had crossed this obstacle only a short time ago. The dust churned up by their passing still hung suspended in the air, so that the ground was veiled under a golden brown fog. One the heights on the far side of the kloof Inyati could see the horns of kwaSwazi's stolen cattle.

"This is going to be bad," Inyati muttered over his shoulder. One of his men grunted an agreement. "Are you still with me?"

"Yebho, Nkosi!"

"We will not stay long. The Swazi don't have the stomach to stay down there and fight for long. We will go no further than the stream that runs through the middle of the valley floor: We'll kill any Zulu that crosses that stream until our generals order a retreat, then we will retire in good order. We will be remembered for our skill today, where everyone else tries to forget their shame. Is it heard?"

"It is heard, Nkosi!" The eight cheered him. He was their prince, and they knew he would not be careless with their lives.

"Let's see what these Swazi are going to do, then."

The Swazi lined up on the lip of the kloof in three or four ranks and began to shout and jeer across the valley at their foes. "All gods spit on the Zulu impi!"

"The little girls ran all the way home!"

"That's all the Zulu are good for: Running!"

Zulu of the Frost and Hunters amabutho stepped up to their own edge of the kloof, less than half the number of the Swazi ibutho. They too began to taunt and mock.

"Hey Swazi? Where were you when I fired your kraal?"

"Give my regards to your king! I think I saw him hiding under his sleeping kaross!"

"We have all your miserable excuses for cattle. They're pretty thin looking, but I suppose if it's the best you had they'll have to do."

More than one Swazi youth began to run down into the kloof at the mention of their cattle. Their izinduna tried to call them back, but the ravine was so deep that many just stopped rather than bother to climb back up.

"What will a retreat out of this place look like?" Inyati asked his guardsmen.

"It will be hard, Nkosi: We should walk down when the Swazi run, so that we will still have our lungs to get back up here after we lose."

After we lose, Inyati agreed. The Swazi do not know what war is about, but the Zulu do. Not one of these Swazi have wondered where the younger Zulus are. The Frost and Hunters are already veterans. King Mpande blooded them against the Swazi when I was a babe in arms. Where are the warriors who are getting their first taste of war?

Chapter 14

Mbeki threw down the pot of beer with relief and had the sack of millet eased from his back by another porter. Their long march was over, for the time being. It was time for the Zulu impi to brush off their Swazi pursuers. He exhaled his relief and sank into the grass for some much needed rest. He nodded a silent thanks to the boy who had helped him.

Ahead of him the stolen Swazi cattle lowed with concern, twisting their heads from side to side to see where their stick-wielding tormentors had gone. Mbeki handed the beer pot over to the other porter, gesturing for him to take a drink. "Go ahead. If I'm old enough to keep track of the takings, I'm old enough to give you a drink." The boy looked around for a moment before taking a nervous swallow from the jug. They were both too young to drink beer, but the army was behind them, facing the other way.

The youth nodded his gratitude. "Will there be a battle?" He asked, wiping the suds from his upper lip.

"It's good ground for us to fight on, but the Swazi will have to be pretty stupid to let us choose the field." Both boys turned from the herd to look behind them. The kloof dropped away before them, giving them a perfect view of what they could only hope would be a place of slaughter for their enemies.

"Well I'm glad for the break, battle or not. Three days of hard marching..." The boy squatted down in the grass, rubbing his aching feet. A rock embedded in the kloof wall had cut him just above the thick callus on his sole, and the wound was plugged with dust kicked up by the herd. "That's all well and good for the impi, but the cattle have lost all condition." The boy smacked his lips and picked up the beer pot again.

"Three days where they can only forage when they should be sleeping, and only get watered as they're driven through a stream. By the time we get them home their meat will be so tough even children won't eat it." The boy tipped his head back again, the lump in his throat bobbing up and down as he drank long and deep.

Mbeki nodded: The cattle were being driven so fast that even the milch cows were having their udders pulled as they ran. He understood the need to retreat at speed --this had been a raid, not an invasion-- but the cattle were suffering for it.

Mbeki had come on the raid to help his father and brother: Ingonyama was eighteen now, and a member of the new Humbler of Kings regiment. Jama was here in a small contingent of the Hunters ibutho. Warriors had other concerns besides the day to day chores of camp, so Mbeki started their fires, cooked their food, carried their supplies, and all the other tasks necessary to keep them comfortable in the field.

General Ntsingwayo kaMahole of the Khoza Clan was the leader of this expedition, and when the first loot had come in he remembered Mbeki's gift for memory: At fifteen, Mbeki was put in charge of keeping a running tally of everything the raid captured in the name of King Mpande. Even now Mbeki's mind clicked back and forth like an abacus, adding the last Swazi homestead burned and subtracting the ox whose heart had burst climbing the side of the kloof. He would not disappoint Ntsingwayo.

Mbeki's thoughts turned from arithmetic back to his family: The day had come almost a year ago when Ingonyama had decided it was time to leave his home and muster at the local ikhanda to join a newly forming regiment. The time to go was always the choice of the youth, but Ingonyama had been in no danger of dragging his feet.

"Baba, I want to join the new ibutho," He had said, his voice unsteady. At seventeen he was younger than the norm, but he had grown into a big man. Jama had smiled his lopsided smile and told his son to go pack. The two of them had gone to the local ikhanda, and Ingonyama had joined the other boys in his area who had reached the mustering age. When all the local companies of that age group were put together they had become the King's new regiment, the Humbler of Kings.

Every Zulu man spent his childhood preparing to join an ibutho. Every boy could dance and sing and fight with sticks. They could already run all day and tend the king's herds and fields. While they lived in the ikhanda their new izinduna would take these skills and improve on them: Ingonyama learned to run in formation, to fight with throwing spears and stabbing assegais. He learned to smash an opponent off balance with his shield and stab for the exposed belly with an underhanded stroke.

"What?" Mbeki said, for the other boy had spoken.

"I said, why do you suppose the Humbler of Kings have gone to ground?" The boy repeated. He had suspected Mbeki had not been paying attention.

Mbeki looked around at the warriors of the Humbler of Kings regiment. Almost four thousand youths squatted down in the grass. Not one of them would be visible from the far side of the kloof.

"The Swazi will only have the Frost and Hunters to count now. Ntsingwayo's planned this very well. He was right to retreat so far into kwaZulu." The other boy snorted, angry at himself for asking the question, angrier still for not having come up with the answer himself. "Here they come." Mbeki kept his voice calm.

The Swazi formed up along the top of the kloof, working up their courage by shouting challenges across to the Zulu. Mbeki sensed their reckless enthusiasm: They were in kwaZulu, and they could only see a few hundred Zulu warriors on the opposite side of the kloof. The Swazi must number two thousand at least.

As the two sides traded insults, small groups of the Swazi began to work their way down the nearly vertical face of the kloof. Unable to restrain them, the Swazi general waved the rest of his men forward with a great war cry, and his warriors fell like stones in an avalanche from the top of the kloof.

"uSuthu!" The Zulu cried back, holding their ground. Mbeki watched the Swazi come, picking their way down the hill, across the flat bottom, over the little trickle of a stream, reaching the base of the Zulu slope. A golden fog of dust obscured their legs, so that they seemed to float towards him, screaming their obscenities.

Ntsingwayo gave a wave of his assegai, and the Humbler of Kings rose from the long grass, crying their war chant: "Hohho! Hohho! Hohho!" As one, they turned their mottled shields edge on to the enemy, and then full towards: The sight of four thousand shields moving in perfect discipline unnerved the Swazi, and Mbeki watched as the warriors below him counted the spears above them shining in the late afternoon light. It was with little surprise that he heard the Swazi induna call out, "Fall back and regroup!"

The Swazi began to retreat, but with another roar of "uSuthu!" the Zulu poured down into the kloof in pursuit. Mbeki rose up and cheered them on: His brother was out there somewhere, running into his first battle.

Ingonyama had waited all day for the Swazi to come. Moments before his regiment was ordered to go to ground the war doctors had made their rounds, and he could feel the magical powder they had sprinkled on him giving him super-human strength. He could hear his blood roaring in his ears, and his vision was clouded with red.

A tiny voice deep inside him spoke of terrible things, of pain and death, fear and failure. Ingonyama imagined a great weight, a mountain of crushing stone, and he put his doubt beneath that mental burden. Only later, much later, would he take that voice out from under his mountain and tell it how wrong it had been.

A deep breath, and another, and another, the magical powder was in his mind, and he felt a thousand feet tall. He was powerful and deadly. Ingonyama knew he was ready to kill. "Hohho! Hohho! Hohho!" He barked as he dove down into the gorge. The Swazi were in full retreat before him, but running down the kloof face gave him such momentum that he soon found himself at the heels of his enemy.

"Ngadla!" He shouted, reaching forward and putting his spear into a man's kidney. The Swazi clutched his side, stumbled, and fell in a heap; Ingonyama did not stop to finish him off: That was for the slow to do. Like a lion in among a herd he ran up behind another man, lengthening his stride and controlling his breathing, getting the most speed for the least effort. "Ngadla!" He cried again, stabbing this one between the shoulder blades. He heard the snick as the vertebrae separated, and he felt hot blood spray over his hand and arm as the Swazi heart burst.

At the stream running down the center of the valley floor a Swazi turned to fight, but Ingonyama put his shield into the man's face, knocking him over backwards into the water. Another swung the edge of his assegai at Ingonyama's head like an axe, but Ingonyama jumped back and smiled, showing his strong teeth. "I'm Ingonyama kaJama of the Humbler of Kings ibutho. Who are you?"

The Swazi gaped at this blood smeared youth, lost his nerve and ran. Ingonyama gave a good-natured laugh and charged at the next group that looked like it was rallying. He worked his way up and down the valley floor, well out ahead of the rest of his regiment. In many cases there were whole companies of Swazi between him and the next Zulu, but he moved through the enemy ranks like a spirit, killing and maiming, and each time crying, "Ngadla! I have eaten!"

As Ingonyama pulled his assegai out of the sucking flesh of another foe, someone new caught his eye. This man was only a little older than the first son of Jama, but he was neither a Zulu nor a Swazi. He was as tall as Ingonyama, and his hair was pulled out into high spikes and decorated with red feathers so that he seemed taller still. Eight similar but less impressive men flanked him. Their eyes locked, and both nodded to the other.

The man threw his shoulders back and dropped his shield. One of his subordinates tossed him a vicious looking axe that he caught neatly in his left hand. Now with spear in one hand and axe in the other he did a courtly bow and smiled, waited for Ingonyama to do something.

Ingonyama blinked, recognizing the danger in front of him. This was no fleeing Swazi. "I am Ingonyama kaJama of the Cube Clan. I serve in the Humbler of Kings ibutho."

The other man's smile grew wider. "I am Prince Inyati kaMzilikazi of the House of Kumalo. I have pure Zanzi blood, and I serve myself."

Ingonyama blinked again. He had been right in thinking the man was not Swazi. The House of Kumalo had been one of the most noble clans of Shaka's kingdom, but they had gone rogue and fled far to the North to form a new nation, the Matabele, the People of the Long Shields. There was no other tribe who had won the Zulu's respect and fear at the point of a spear. Mzilikazi was the Matabele King, and here before Ingonyama stood his son. Inyati would have been trained since he was weaned to kill with as little hesitation as a man crushes a fly.

"I see you, Inyati," he said, eyeing the prince's spear and axe.

"Shall we?" Inyati laughed, enjoying the nervous look on his opponent. The prince crossed the ten paces separating them in three long strides, bringing his axe crashing down Ingonyama's shield; Ingonyama lurched back at the force of the blow, and Inyati brought his assegai around, searching for Ingonyama's exposed side.

Ingonyama jumped backwards again and smashed his shield into Inyati's face with all his strength while the prince's arm was still stretched out. Both stepped back and circled each other for a moment, dancing up on the balls of their feet. They smiled at each other as they moved, working themselves up for the next lunge.

In a flash of blurring steel, Inyati parried a thrust with the haft of his axe and Ingonyama took his opponent's spear on his shield. Gasping and straining, they both leaned in to bring their full strength to bear on the other. Ingonyama butted his forehead into the Matabele's exposed face, and then had the same done to him. They broke apart again, each having taken the measure of the other.

"You're a long way from home, Kumalo," Ingonyama said, trying to ignore the pain in his nose, sniffing at the coppery smell of blood.

"Oh, I don't know: The House of Kumalo started a few days' march that way, didn't it?" Inyati replied, gesturing with his spear over Ingonyama's shoulder. The first son of Jama did not remember all of Punga's stories, as Mbeki did, but he knew enough about the Matabele to feel an icy barb of fear reach up from the ground and through his stomach.

In the days of Shaka, Mzilikazi of the House of Kumalo had been a great general. One day Mzilikazi kept more than his share of looted cattle, and Shaka ordered him to explain his actions at the kwaBulawayo ikhanda. Mzilikazi knew that to go to the Place of Killing would end with his body lying below the Executioner's Rock to be devoured by the vultures that had come to be called Shaka's chickens, so he took three hundred of his clan and fled north.

Mzilikazi had become a Shaka in his own right, killing hundreds of thousands on his march. The survivors of each shattered tribe were incorporated into his new nation, the Matabele. Legions of warriors, trained in Shaka's fighting disciplines, served the House of Kumalo with unblinking obedience. Within five years there had been five thousand of them. Today, they were almost as numerous as the Zulu themselves.

"I don't know where you started, but I know where you're going to finish." Ingonyama raced forward again, using his shield to knock aside Inyati's guard and stabbing for the torso. Inyati stepped to one side with the easy grace of a boy taunting a bull. They blinked at each other for a moment: It was a new experience for both of them to have an opponent of equal mettle.

Ingonyama did not mean to move, but the dust caking his sweat-stained legs irritated him, and the first twitch saw his reflexes to take over, driving him towards the Matabele with his shield still badly positioned. Inyati saw the weakness and hooked his spear around behind Ingonyama's shield, pulling hard. Ingonyama lost his balance and only luck saw him fall forward below the arc of Inyati's swinging axe.

He landed face first in the dust, making no effort to cushion the fall with his hands. He rolled in the dirt desperately and lashed out with his assegai to keep the Matabele back; Inyati had already stepped forward to finish his prone opponent, and the tip of Ingonyama's assegai scored the flesh across the son of Mzilikazi's thigh.

Inyati retreated from Ingonyama's flailing spear. His men saw their leader's shallow wound and moved forward with murder in their hearts.

"Cha!" Was Inyati's word of command, and they halted, frozen in their positions but ready at any moment to kill for their prince.

Ingonyama rose from the ground and nodded his thanks to the prince. He was impressed with the Matabeles' discipline, but not surprised. The Matabele had taken the finest traditions of Shaka but had never settled down to defend what they had conquered. They were a raider nation; every year the entire male population would be sent against a foe and would not return to plant their crops until their enemy was destroyed, his cattle stolen, and his women brought home to become the mothers of future Matabele.

Twice the Zulu had sent armies to defeat the People of the Long Shields, and both times the izimpi had been smashed. Even the Boers had only been able to drive the Matabele further north, and they had used guns and horses that the Matabele had never seen before to do so.

"Pick up your shield," Inyati offered.

Ingonyama began to obey but stopped himself. "Cha."

Inyati smiled, expecting nothing less. He dropped his axe in response and lunged towards Ingonyama, as if just the momentum of his charge would force the spearhead into his enemy's heart. The two collided with enough force to knock the air out of their lungs, and they leaned into each other, trying to throw off the other's balance. Both had their spears hovering over his opponent's heart, the thrust resisted by his opposite's left hand on his wrist.

They grunted with effort, shuffling their feet around to gain some advantage. The eight Matabele watching could only tell their leader from his foe by the red feathers in his hair, and the violent spinning and twisting was shaking even these telltales out of place and down into the waist-high dust cloud surrounding them.

Inyati shoved his knee into Ingonyama's groin. Ingonyama bit into Inyati's taut right biceps. Inyati brought his chin down onto Ingonyama's crown, but then regretted it as Ingonyama's head snapped up. His opponent disoriented, Ingonyama brought his foot up against the Matabele chest and pushed off, sending both tumbling backwards. Inyati spat, shaking his head. His smile was grim now. He gave a curt order to his men in a language Ingonyama did not understand.

A calabash left one of the Matabele's belts and sailed through the air. The son of Mzilikazi caught the gourd in his empty hand, removed the stopper with his teeth, and drank deeply from the cool, sweet water.

Ingonyama watched, his mouth gummy from the dust and exertion. When Inyati was done he smiled again and tossed the container to Ingonyama. Ingonyama ached to drink, but his eyes were on Inyati's spear.

"My oath on my Zanzi blood I won't kill you until you're done." Ingonyama nodded and tipped the gourd skyward over his open mouth.

While he waited, Inyati looked around: Everywhere the golden dust of the kloof floor hung in clouds that danced in the sunlight, allowing only the silhouettes of dying men to filter through the haze. He shook his head. "These Swazi don't know what war is all about. Do they?"

"Cha," Ingonyama agreed with a laugh. The Swazi were forming a skirmish line a hundred yards behind him, but only half of them had rallied to fight. Now outnumbered almost five to one the ground shook with the beat of running feet, drumming war shields, and the other sounds of battle. The Zulu's victory was a given.

"Are you done drinking?"

"Yebho."

Both sides burst into sudden motion, and before the falling calabash hit the ground they met: This time Ingonyama brought his free arm between Inyati's legs and lifted up, sending Inyati flying through the air. He bit back a curse as he felt Inyati's assegai drag along his back, sending hot blood running down onto his loincloth. Inyati landed well, rolling like an acrobat, but Ingonyama took his assegai in two hands and swung it against the Matabele head.

There was no conscious decision, but the moment before impact Ingonyama twisted his weapon so it landed with the flat of the blade instead of with the cutting edge. The thunderclap of impact was the same sound as an axe being brought against dead wood, and the thick wood along the tang cracked at the force of it. Inyati's eyes rolled into the back of his head, and he collapsed at Ingonyama's feet.

This time there was no Prince of the Matabele to stop them, and the eight, shocked at their induna's defeat, moved forward as one. Ingonyama's stomach dropped, knowing each of these men would be the equal of the Invincibles of the Zulu royal guard.

"Kill me!" Ingonyama roared. The eight stopped for a moment. "Kill me, if you can." Ingonyama snatched up a discarded throwing spear and took a deep breath to steady his arm. "You! You, at the back! Step forward!"

The Matabele blinked at being picked out, and he was even more surprised when Ingonyama launched his spear in the smooth flowing motion practiced every pumpkin season for twelve years. The spear hit the warrior in the forehead, and he fell backwards, dead before he hit the ground. The spearhead was set so deep into his skull that the long haft stuck into the air like a gate post.

The seven remaining Matabele stood stunned for a moment; one turned to run, but a curt order from the senior man called him back. The Matabele formed a phalanx seven-wide, their shields forming a solid wall.

In vain Ingonyama looked for some gap in their defenses, knowing he could put a spear into anything the size of a fist at this range, but only the Matabeles' toes appeared at the bottom of their shields, and only their blood hazed eyes peeked over the top. They were the People of the Long Shields, and they softly tapped the sides of the spears against their shields' edges: Instead of the smashing thunder of the Zulu, it was the gentle death rattle of the Matabele, and Ingonyama heard his doom in the gentle sound.

A stream of profanity that would have left the saltiest campaigner impressed poured from Ingonyama's dust-choked throat. Every invective, curse, or jibe that he had ever heard spewed forth without slowing the seven warriors in the slightest. Ingonyama picked up Inyati's axe and sent it tumbling end over end to smash into the cliff face of shields. Ever so slowly the phalanx moved towards him, shuffling their feet so that no shield moved ahead or behind the others. It was a perfect barricade that rebuffed Ingonyama's weapons as easily as his insults. Now ten paces away, now five, then it stopped.

"uSuthu!" The Zulu war cry tore from hundreds of throats as the last Swazi resistance collapsed and their warriors fled for the imagined safety of the kloof wall. The senior Matabele lowered his shield just enough to be sure of the situation, then issued a curt command. As one they turned their shields edge on to Ingonyama, placed their hands over their hearts and bowed to their fallen prince. Then, still in perfect discipline, they turned and retreated in good order.

Ingonyama watched them go; sure that he had just seen the finest warriors on Earth. It was only when the men of the Frost began to pass him that he allowed his knees to give out, and he collapsed on top of the Kumalo prince, weeping tears of pent-up emotion.

He knelt there for a long time, feeling the burning of the flesh wound on his back, the aching in his crotch, and the throbbing of his nose. Every muscle was tight; his chest hurt; his bones felt like they were turning to powder. His skull felt as if it was shrinking. He was so caught up in his discomfort that for a moment he was not sure if his ears were playing tricks on him.

"Ten."

He paused, his face still turned to the earth, wet with tears.

"Ten."

He lifted his face to the sky and saw Ntsingwayo smiling down at him.

"Ten," The old man repeated again.

"What, Nkosi?" Ingonyama murmured, surprised he still had a voice.

"You killed ten men. I watched you. You are your father's son, boy. Jama could not have done it better himself when he was your age."

"I-- He--"

"Yes, he was a difficult one. But now he's-- He's still alive!" Ntsingwayo barked, his smile disappearing. "Finish him!"

"Cha... Cha! He's a prince of the Matabele."

"Matabele? What are those bastards doing here?" Ntsingwayo's gruff voice hid his fear: In his youth he had gone on one of the expeditions to punish the Matabele; he had lost many friends on that campaign.

"I don't know, but I don't think we should kill him. That's for the King to decide." Ingonyama rose shakily to his feet, dark wet tracks cutting through the dust and grime on his face.

"Alright: Nine, and a captured prince," The general replied. "Now go wash your face in the stream or they'll never sing songs of how brave you were today."

Ingonyama staggered away, and with a signal Ntsingwayo brought over some men who trussed up the prince of the House of Kumalo. Warriors ran past their general, chasing the Swazi up the side of the kloof. Ntsingwayo allowed himself a broad grin. It was another great victory for the Zulu Kingdom, and he knew people would remember that it had been his plan that had created such a decisive triumph.

The Matabele rolled his head and moaned. Ntsingwayo frowned down at the prisoner, prodding him with a calloused foot. "What are we going to do about you?" He asked himself. "Ah, well. Mpande doesn't like your kind any more than I do. You'll be dead soon enough."

Chapter 15

Throughout the night Zulu warriors trickled back to the impi's camp. They had chased the Swazi all the way to the Phongolo, and though no one had counted the dead, Ntsingwayo was sure the Swazi would never cross the river again. The next day he ordered his army to begin a leisurely march back to kwaNodwengu.

For ten days the impi moved south, slowed by the weight of their booty. Across field and stream, windblown kopje and the tropical vegetation of the ravines, they marched, greeted everywhere by the cheering local Mandlakazi clan, pleased that the Swazi to their north had been humbled. Here was some of the richest cattle country on earth, and every morning Mbeki woke up to the smell of the rich dark earth freshly churned by the hooves of the herds.

Inyati's bound wrists were tethered to the horns of a bull. If he failed to keep pace or fell the bull would drag him along until he recovered unassisted. Despite old Ntsingwayo's easy pace, by the time the procession reached the Great Place the son of Mzilikazi was almost dead.

kwaNodwengu had aged and matured in the years since Mbeki's first umKhosi Festival. The tall mimosa trees had grown statelier; the earth had been trampled and packed to a clean brown surface all in and around the ikhanda; the ever-present fields of mealie had spread even further, carefully tended for the Great Elephant by the unmarried amabutho. The Humbler of Kings and the companies of the Frost and the Hunters filed through the gate in their full regalia. The King and the great men of the nation watched them dance and boast with suitably regal airs.

At length the warriors grew subdued, and the izinduna trotted forward to give their reports to the King. Ntsingwayo ran up, then the induna of the new Humbler of Kings, followed by Jama who represented the contingents from the Hunters and the Frost. At each report King Mpande gave a weak nod and gestured for the man join the ranks of the great men of the nation and royal favourites who stood behind him.

When the izinduna were dealt with an Invincible roared out, "Mbeki and Ingonyama kaJama, the King summons you!" Both boys gave a startled 'Bayete!' and trotted forward.

Mbeki reached Mpande first and prostrated himself, repeating the royal salute. His brother joined him in a moment, but Mbeki strained to hear the faint, "I see you, sons of Jama."

King Mpande did not look well. Sweat hung heavy across his brow and chest, despite the modest heat. The warrior who held a shield over Mpande's head waved it slowly up and down but could do little to shoo away the flies that buzzed around the king. Death isn't really a smell, Mbeki thought, but Mpande smells of death. All around Mpande his council tried to ignore their King's state.

Mbeki rose up to kneel on his legs, and Ingonyama followed. From over the King's shoulder Cetshwayo asked, "What was our total take from the raid, Mbeki?"

The second son of Jama froze for a moment before replying, "Nine hundred and ten cows, four of them stud bulls so black they don't even shine when they sweat. Seventeen men's worth of beads--" There were some impressed intakes of breath at that. Glass beads, imported from Arabia via the Portuguese or from England via Natal, were an extremely valuable trade item. Four pounds of beads could buy a heifer just entering into her calf-bearing years. Even four or five beads could purchase a chicken if the buyer was a good haggler. A man could carry over sixty pounds of beads, so the beads alone would be worth over two hundred and fifty cows.

"We also took three hundred-odd other livestock, and enough grain and beer to bring the impi home without foraging from any Zulu lands. We burned over forty homesteads in Swazi territory, and any foodstuffs we could not carry we otherwise destroyed. Of the impi they sent against us they lost several hundred at least, including a prince of the House of Kumalo--"

"Matabele princes don't wander around kwaSwazi," Prince Dabulamanzi interrupted. Mbeki smiled at the man, who was a great general and widely respected despite his affinity for gin.

"A sheep has killed an elephant, Nkosi," Ingonyama gave the popular phrase for the impossible happening. The prince grunted, accepting the truth without liking it.

"You were the one who captured this... man?" Sihayo, another great man of the nation, asked. His hands held woodworking tools, and a half-finished headrest lay at his feet. Sihayo often worked wood at official functions, much to the quiet amusement of court.

"Yebho, Nkosi." Ingonyama said.

"What was that like?" Prince Ndabuko, one of Cetshwayo's youngest brothers, asked. He had been a child when the Zulu had gone to fight the renegade induna Mzilikazi and his raider nation. Unlike many of the grey heads on the council, he did not have a host of fears and memories to suppress.

"Hard, Nkosi. If he had fought as he was taught, instead of dropping his axe to make it a fair fight, I would be dead now." Many of those who had the frost of age at their temples shuddered in sympathy.

"Of course he's a monster: He's Matabele!" The rancour in Godide's voice spoke volumes. His father had led one of the assaults against Mzilikazi, and all of his sons had inherited his anger and resentment at having been bested.

"The Matabele prove that our way can overcome anyone else on earth," Sihayo said, chiseling a chevron pattern around the base of his piece.

"I don't want proof when it is used against us," Ntsingwayo rebutted. There was no sign of his smile now. His stern face seemed set in stone.

"The Matabele are a people to be watched, but they are far away. Except for one: Where is this spawn of Mzilikazi?" The King's voice was a whisper, but it silenced all of his advisors. Mbeki was fascinated by the rattle in Mpande's throat, likening it to two dead reeds scraping against each other in the winter winds.

"Bring forward the prisoner!" An Invincible bellowed. A new figure emerged from the gate at the opposite end of the kraal. He squared his shoulders for only a moment before a stick crashed into the small of his back, knocking him forward. Inyati was bound at the wrists with a length of leather rope and another piece, only the length of an arm, joined his ankles. Even as the guard hurried him along he was unable to make much progress.

Twice he crashed to the ground and was kicked brutally until he regained his feet unassisted. When he reached a point ten paces from the King and his entourage he again tried to stand tall, but this time a stick was brought against the back of his knees, toppling him into a kneeling position. A firm hand on the back of his neck shoved his forehead into the dirt.

"Leave him," The King ordered, trying to speak up. He coughed once, miserably, and a fleck of blood-tinged phlegm appeared on his lips. Reverently an isangoma wiped the red mucus away with his index finger and deposited it on a pillow of dry grass wrapped in python skin.

None of the King's body dirt must ever be left unattended to, lest an enemy use it to reap black magic.

Reluctantly the guard stepped back, and Inyati tottered again to his feet. His back and arms were worn raw where the bull had dragged him when his strength had failed. Even this last show of bravado was beyond him, and he swayed for a moment before lowering himself back into a kneeling position.

"Who are you?" Mpande wheezed.

Inyati's eyes were fogged with pain, but he spoke with the pride of the doomed. "I am Inyati kaMzilikazi, son of the killer of thousands. My blood is pure Zanzi, and once the House of Kumalo was as noble here as the Mandlakazi, the Buthelezi, or the Zulu. I demand--"

"You will demand nothing! You will ask nothing! You will not even beg! I have to decide what to do with you now, because someone refused to kill when he had the chance!" The rasp of the King's voice made Ingonyama flush, but he remained silent. "Why were you in kwaSwazi? What is your father planning with them?" Inyati said nothing.

"You will answer the King," Zibhebhu, another of the northern princes, ordered. There was steel in his voice.

"Bayete, Great Dying King! I piss on you and all your generations!" Angry growls rose from each man's throat, and Mbeki decided on another reason why no spears were permitted near the King: It would be too easy for subordinates to butcher someone being interviewed.

"So help me, if Mzilikazi thinks he can come back here--" Mpande wheezed, his chest clearly hurting him.

"My King," Prince Hamu murmured, for one does not interrupt the King lightly. "There are rumours that Mzilikazi is... Dead."

"Eh?"

"Yebho, they are only rumours, but it's said the ague and gout finally took him. I have some... small connections with the Matabele, and this is what I've heard."

Prince Cetshwayo snorted. If Hamu said small connections, it meant he had close ties to the renegades, perhaps even representatives at their court.

"Why was I not informed? A blood enemy of our people dies, and you don't think it fit to tell me?" Mpande rasped.

Hamu quailed. "It's all rumour Nkosi Nkulu, but it is said he's been dead for a few years--"

"Years?" The king spluttered.

"Years," Hamu began again. "And there was a brief civil war. Two sons went for the throne: one succeeded, and one failed. It is whispered to me that a new King, Lobengula, has come to power."

Before anyone's mind could turn to the similarities between the Matabele succession and Ndondakusuka, Inyati burst, "Lobengula! So long as I'm relieving myself, some of it can go his way too!"

"You're against Lobengula?" Zibhebhu asked.

Inyati knew the interview would end with his death, so he let his anger pour out. "He was not eldest or smartest or even Baba's favourite. In fact, when Mzilikazi was dying Lobengula was hiding in the hills from Baba's executioners! My brother was the eldest son, but now he's dead."

"So what are you doing out here?" Godide hissed.

"I was a boy. I backed the wrong brother."

"Why aren't you in a shallow grave somewhere?" Ntsingwayo asked, his tone making it clear that's where he wanted the man.

Inyati began to speak fast, his accented Zulu dropping back into his native Sindebele. Flecks of foam appeared at the corner of his mouth. "Lobengula killed the rightful heir, but he didn't kill all of his supporters. I wanted to wait in exile for my chance, and—-"

"My King, I have an idea," Hamu purred.

"I never doubted it," Mpande replied, struggling to breathe.

"We have a son of Mzilikazi who is a wanted outlaw of the King of the Matabele. Think what you would pay to have someone who was a threat to your succession completely in your power." Hamu did not linger on the point; Hamu was himself a threat to the Zulu throne. "I don't think a thousand cows would be too much to ask of Lobengula to have a visit from his dear brother."

"A thousand cows?" Mpande asked. A thousand cows would generously reward a hundred favourites, or set up ten of his regimental izinduna as wealthy men. An infusion of a thousand cows into the royal herd would stabilize the Kingdom while he recovered from whatever his ancestors were inflicting upon him.

"Easily," Hamu replied, knowing he would ask his Matabele contacts for three, settle for fifteen hundred, and keep the difference. "It would take eight months, perhaps a year to negotiate. I can send a messenger."

"See to it. Yebho, a thousand cows... The Matabele have those big white ones, don't they? With the upturned horns?"

"Yebho, my King."

"Very well, his execution is postponed for one year... Either this Lobengula pays for the privilege, or we'll do it for free..." Mpande sucked in a breath, then drew in another without exhaling. When he spoke again it was at normal volume. "Ingonyama kaJama of the Humbler of Kings Regiment, every commander has said you were like a lion at the battle of the ravine. I make you a royal favourite."

Before Ingonyama could begin the obligatory denials the King continued, worried that he should not be able to start again. "I grant you five cows from the captured herd and ten pounds of beads. I grant you twenty cow tails of bravery. I grant you the willow wood necklace of courage." With each new honour Ingonyama's chest swelled a little more and his head bowed closer to the earth so that no one would see his inappropriate joy. "I also grant you membership to the Invincibles. Mbejane?" The leader of the King's Bodyguard stepped forward. "See to it."

Before Ingonyama could again try to speak, Mpande's eyes turned to Mbeki. "Youngest son of Jama, my little wizard, you shall be this prince's keeper. Keep him safe for one year, then deliver him back here to me. Do this and you shall be rewarded. Is it heard?"

"Yebho, Sire, it is heard."

"Good, because I... I don't think I could say it again..." Shaken at this public admission of the king's failing health, the great men and royal favourites watched as four Invincibles stepped forward and lifted up the King's throne, carrying him inside the royal quarters. "Bring me Magema the Healer," He whispered to his servants. Only behind the high walls of the Black Royal Quarters could Mpande lie down, struggling to breathe, without shame.

Mbeki watched the king leave, before turning his head to see the dull, pain-clouded eyes of Inyati kaMzilikazi boring into him. "It will be a long year..."

The Matabele Prince coughed once before muttering an obscenity by way of in agreement.

Chapter 16

Summer gave way to the cool chill of autumn, and each dawn saw the grasses of the valley coated in thicker and thicker layers of hoar frost. As remorseless as a stone rolling down the side of a ravine, the sky went from a deep blue to a grey overcast that seemed to suck the warmth out of the land a little bit more each day. The Valley of the Three Homesteads prepared for the coming winter as best it could.

Jama, Kandhla and Punga organized their families to work together in the long and arduous task of reaping the harvest, working each field in turn. First, the millet and the maize were scythed down by the older women and put into large wicker baskets by the younger wives and children. Once the staple foods were in, the lesser crops of squash, other gourds, beans, fruits, and greens were collected with equal efficiency, if less enthusiasm.

After the easily ruined crops were gathered, the tubers were hauled up, cleaned, and then dried. Being careful to do as little of the work as possible, as was their right, the men supervised as their families carried the winter's provisions into the deep storage pits within the palisades of the homesteads. Well satisfied with their efforts, the men slaughtered a young steer and all three families ate their fill.

The harvest done for another year, each homestead readied itself for the coming cold in its own way: Jama traded hoe blades for extra fur sleeping karosses for each of his wives; Kandhla gave his sons woolen sweaters brought all the way from the mission station at Eshowe in the east; Punga sent his children out into the glens around the valley, stacking mountains of firewood within his walls.

Of course, no Zulu man could think of the welfare of his kith and kin without worrying about his cattle, and soon they too were pampered and protected against the cold. Many the thin-skinned milch cow and expectant heifer sported a blanket draped over her soft hide. Each herd boy walked through the field with a soft leather towel over one shoulder to dry their bovines' mud caked hooves to prevent infection and arthritis. Fires were kept lit in the cattle pen all night to hold off the chill, and the boys would wake even earlier in the mornings to agitate the older cows into motion, keeping them warm with the movement of their stiff bodies and the beating of their mighty hearts. Still all these nurturing treatments would be for naught if the herd died of starvation, and so Mbeki and his charge were sent out to survey the winter grazing.

Inyati and Mbeki wandered the ridges of the valley seemingly at random. As happened every year with the coming of fall, the sweetveld of the valley floor had begun to whither and die. The combination of morning frost, scant precipitation and poor sunlight had combined to starve the tender early-ripening grass. Now the sourveld which coated the walls of the valley in thick brown swaths became critical. If it was not for the sourveld's late season and resistance to the extremes of fall and winter the Zulu would have needed to migrate far to the north every year in search of grazing for their cattle. As it was, the two young men were judging the quality of the sourveld with the expert eye of long experience. Sourveld was never as good as sweetveld, and so it was very important to decide where and when to allow the herd to graze.

"This far, higher in perhaps four or five days. The sourveld here is almost sweet." Inyati spoke with authority, but Mbeki shook his head.

"We don't need to come up this high yet. The base of the slope hasn't been grazed over, and it's as ripe as the sweetveld was last summer." Inyati grunted an acknowledgement and flexed his hand open and closed, a gesture Mbeki had noticed he repeated whenever he was annoyed or impatient.

"Is there a problem?" Mbeki asked. He knew what the answer would be.

The prince was thinking the five hundred miles north and a few years ago it would have been unthinkable for a commoner like Mbeki to contradict him. Instead Inyati said, "I am a prince of the House of Kumalo, and I've already done my time as a herd boy. This work is beneath me."

Mbeki looked at his ward for a long moment. Inyati still had a regal air about him despite his lack of royal paraphernalia. "What do you suggest?" Perhaps in kwaMatabele being a Prince to the monster Mzilikazi meant something, but in kwaZulu Mbeki had seen many watch the prince pass with murder in their eyes. "What manlier pursuits would you prefer? You don't smith; you don't carve; you don't gather honey. What is it that you want to do, oh Prince?"

"Why do you still herd? There are five other boys here in this valley. Why don't you do something else?" Inyati's change of subject paused Mbeki for a moment. It was true, the older boys, Hlubi, Ingonyama, Bikwayo, and Langa had all mustered into the Humbler of Kings, but both Punga and Kandhla had produced fine strapping boys to take their place. The eldest of these herd boys was twelve, far too young to be anything but a bother to his older cousin.

"The herd is my task for now," Mbeki replied, but Inyati thought he saw a flicker of interest. Mbeki was bored with the herd boy's life and had been ever since he had returned from the raid against the Swazi.

"Why don't we go hunting?"

Mbeki exploded, "I see! Alright! Wonderful! What an idea! I'll just run off and get you a spear!" Each of Mbeki's replies drove the scowl deeper and deeper into Prince Inyati's chiseled features.

"There's no need to be so sarcastic. If I wanted to escape, I could do it as easily now as I could with a spear. Where is your father? Or Punga? Or Kandhla? Even your cousins can't see us from up here. I could snap your neck, hide you in that thicket over there, and I would have a day's head start on any pursuit."

Mbeki laughed without humour, accepting that the prince had regained his strength. It had taken almost a month of eating well and working hard, but Inyati was once again as strong as Ingonyama. Mbeki had stared down too many cows in his life to blink before this bluster. "Alright, do it and see how far you get." Despite his brave words Mbeki took a step back and brought his sticks up to guard himself.

Inyati eyed the sticks, appreciating Mbeki's skill with them. He gave a melancholy smile. "What good would it do me, Mbeki? Where would I go? Where can I run? Home is almost two months' trek north, and all that waits for me there is a quick and messy execution. Run south to the Whites? Do you know how the Boers feel about Matabele?" Mbeki could imagine, but Inyati did not wait for a reply.

"The English don't know us, but they'll ask the Boers for an opinion; after that it's either a bullet in the back of my head or chains on my wrists. Besides, Mpande can send thirty thousand warriors to any corner of the kingdom to find me. No, I'm going to stay right here and hope it all works out."

"You're a dead man no matter what happens."

"I'm damned if I do, and I'm damned if I don't," Inyati replied in Cape Dutch. Mbeki looked at him blankly. "I think your Uncle Punga is a loud mouth baboon." Inyati tried again, but still Mbeki did not understand. "You have a face that makes women cry. I think you can't understand a word I'm saying and it's driving you mad. Am I right?" He said the last in Zulu.

"What was that?" Mbeki had concentrated, but it was so different from the lilting music of Zulu. It was harsh and cruel, guttural and sharp. It ended in hard sounds and much of it was from the back of the throat. It fascinated him.

"That's Boer Dutch, which they call Afrikaans. You Zulus have had more dealings with them than the Matabele: Don't you speak Afrikaans?" Mbeki shook his head; Inyati sensed he had bait. "What about Sindebele?" Inyati asked in that language, a bastardized form of Zulu.

Mbeki furrowed his brows. "I followed that, but it's hard."

"Your cows are thin and puny, not one of them is fit to be bred into our herds. I look at your amabutho and laugh: I've seen better warriors doing bead work and massaging women's feet. I think the Zulu language is the most pompous overblown piece of dog's filth I've ever had to learn. Sindebele is far better. It says what it means, fast and easy." He switched back to Zulu. "How much of that did you understand?"

He listened with a slack jaw as Mbeki repeated it back to him in exactly the same tone then said, "I remember the words, but a lot of the meaning is missing."

Inyati involuntary grunt of appreciation was high praise. "I'll tell you what: If we go hunting, I'll teach you Afrikaans and Sindebele. I'm sure I can teach you those languages in a year." Inyati had not actually decided his opinion of the youngest son of Jama yet. To be sure his father was respectable, and his older brother was a worthy, but this young one...

Mbeki still looked hesitant, so Inyati decided to make the big push, "I give you my word on my Zanzi blood I won't try to escape while hunting." Mbeki did not need too much persuading after that, and it was not long before they had returned to Jama's kraal for equipment.

"What did you want to hunt?" Mbeki came out of his hut with four long-shafted hunting spears.

"Lion? Elephant? Gnu?" Inyati joked. Mbeki frowned, envying the prince's upbringing. North of the Phongolo the land was still thick with game, but the Zulu Kingdom was largely hunted out: Here the elephant were gone, shot down by white men in exchange for trade goods; the Gnu had been butchered for meat and to keep them from competing for grazing land with the cattle; as for the lions, they were a pestilence destroyed on sight before they could harm the herds.

"How about something for the pot?" Mbeki prompted. The valleys nearby were still rich in all manner of buck, bird, boar and fowl. He knew if he came home with some meat for the family he would be warmly received.

"Kudu?" Inyati asked, arching an eyebrow.

Mbeki frown deepened at the implication that his home did not even offer kudu. "Of course kudu... There's good ground for them a quarter day's run from here. I'll just tell Bhibhi where we're going. Bhibhi!" Mbeki called to his little sister, who shot her head out of one of the huts with a load of beads in her hands.

"Yebho?" She said it with all the respect a little girl should show an older brother, but her eyes were on Inyati's handsome face, and a small note of alarm sounded in Mbeki's head. Bhibhi was nine, and that was old enough for crushes. Mbeki would have to make sure any attraction Bhibhi might be feeling was nipped in the bud by one of Jama's wives. The prince was destined to die.

"We're going to hunt kudu to the west. Tell Baba when he gets back." She bobbed her head in agreement, but lingered in the doorway of the hut, trying to think of something to say to extend the conversation. "What?" Mbeki asked at last.

"I don't know," Bhibhi never took her eyes off Inyati, who was beginning to shift uncomfortably under the little girl's gaze.

"Get back to your beadwork, Bhibhi. Inyati will still be handsome when we get back, I promise," Mbeki said. Bhibhi looked horrified for a moment, then ducked back into the hut and out of sight of the Kumalo prince. "I think you're in there." Mbeki deadpanned. Inyati grunted an acknowledgement then hefted one of the hunting spears to check its balance.

The two young men ran from the circle of huts at the jog trot that came as easily to them as breathing. The sun rose higher into the sky, and the frost melted back to dew before evaporating altogether. Mbeki detoured just far enough to shout to his younger cousins where the cattle should graze that afternoon, then they were off in earnest.

To the west of the valley there was an escarpment, then a narrow strip of sourveld and elephant grass. Beyond that the terrain dissolved into a chaos of woods and kopjes, meadows and donga, perfect terrain for kudu. Mbeki lengthened his stride, stretching every muscle with pleasure. Inyati took the extended pace as a challenge, and soon they were racing towards the edge of an escarpment with reckless abandon, each pouring on his reserves in a battle of wills and bodies.

"I'm... Going... To... Win.... You... Know," Inyati puffed, speaking only in place of exhaling. Mbeki did not even have enough air left over to speak; he swallowed the bitter phlegm in his throat and lowered his head into the buffeting wind.

They flew through the grass swift as springbok. It was only as they reached the top of the cliffs that Mbeki came to a sudden jarring stop; there was that old familiar weight in his stomach. Something bad was about to happen. He caught just the telltale flicker of movement below him before Inyati crashed into him, sending both men end over end towards the yawning drop at the edge of the precipice.

"Why don't you look where you're--" The anger flared.

"If you hadn't stopped--"

The reply was hot and vicious, "Shut up!"

"Stick it in your ear!"

"You Zulu--"

"Matabele monkey!" Mbeki knew he had gone too far the moment he had said it.

The prince's face darkened and his eyes went from white to the smoky yellow of rage, "Monkey?" His voice almost broke with his anger. It was the most racist of terms which the Zulu used upon any other black man in Africa. "Look how far the mighty Zulu have come, from being the latrine of the world to the world's rulers. Too bad no one bothered to rinse the shit out of your mouth."

Mbeki's eyes fell with shame. The man before him was no monkey. In another time and place he would have been entitled to the leopard skins and heron feathers of Zulu royalty. It was only a cruel trick of their mutual ancestors that Inyati was sentenced to death instead of sentencing men to death. "There was a column of men; that's why I stopped," Mbeki murmured by way of apology.

"You stopped because you were tired. I won." Inyati was too angry to accept the peace offering.

"You're tired too," Mbeki replied.

"I am not!"

"Your chest is going like a bellows," Mbeki said.

"Well look at you: I've seen puff adders less enthusiastic!"

"You're like a little girl, spluttering after trying to swim!" They argued for a while, neither used to having someone else with a sharp enough tongue to keep up.

"Well where is this column of men?" Inyati finally asked, hoping it had been a quick and clumsy lie.

"Right there!" Mbeki gestured with open hand; the decisive move was an announcement of victory. Inyati strained his eyes searching the woods for signs of men. At length he agreed, but only after ten warriors emerged from the treeline heading towards the base of the escarpment, with dozens of moving forms behind them.

"How many do you suppose there are?" He asked, watching as warrior after warrior emerged from the thicket.

"Over fifty from the Humbler of Kings, but I can't imagine what they're doing out here." The two watched as the company trotted forward in single file. They were stripped for fighting; their ceremonial garb either left at their ikhanda or worn only in an abbreviated version.

At their head was a face Mbeki recognized from half a mile out. "Cha... It can't be!" The breath hissed out of his lungs, and Inyati looked at him with some interest.

"You're not going to have a heart attack, are you?"

Mbeki ignored the jibe and strained his senses, hoping he had been wrong, but there was no mistaking the flattened nose, the callous scowl, and the look of pure venom coming from the induna of the company; it was Jobe kaHamu.

"I see you, Jobe!" Mbeki called once they were within hailing distance of one another. The distant induna paused in his stride before ordering his men to form up in a line abreast with a hand signal.

Jobe waited until he was much closer before he replied, "I see you, Mbeki kaJama." The six years had been kind to the young noble: Jobe had thickened across his waist and chest, but had not yet put on the fat common to the Zulu royal family. He wore a short cloak of leopard skin to mark his distant regal blood. Across Jobe's chest there was a bandoleer filled with crudely made shotgun shells; a man to his right carried a heavy double barreled weapon, its muzzle scared from the imperfect projectiles and overgenerous charges of gunpowder.

Jobe followed the path of Mbeki's eyes and scowled. "Yebho, it's the same one. My father has bought two more since. They're better guns anyway. What are you doing way out here?"

"I'm not far from my home. We live just over that way." He gestured to the east.

Jobe was surprised. "But you're Cube: your clan smiths in the Nkhandla forest."

"I am Cube, but my father lives with the Ntuli. He's related to Punga and Kandhla of the Ntuli on his mother's side." Mbeki could smell the smoked biltong in the leather pouch hanging from Jobe's loincloth; he wondered absently if the hunger from his exertions was making him too friendly with the son of Hamu.

The next words from Jobe's mouth dispelled any relaxing of the tensions between them. "My men are hungry, and I am on the king's business. I'll take four cows from your father's herd as provisions." While it was true an impi on the march could gather food from the passing homesteads, a company on its way to border patrol was more than capable of foraging for game. To further add to the unmistakable insult, fifty men could not possibly eat four cows; most of the meat would be left for the jackals.

"Cha."

"What?" Jobe smiled, unsurprised but prepared to feign confusion: With fifty men at his back, he could do whatever he wanted.

"Cha! You're not on the king's business. You are on your way to sit on your rump on top of a hill and look down into a valley. Giving you four cows will certainly give you more to sit on, but it won't help you in the King's work."

"You have no right to deny me anything!"

"True, but it's also true that they're not my cows, and I don't have them with me. If you want to get the haft of a spear shoved through your front teeth, you can take it up with my Baba. They're his cows."

Jobe fumed but saw the truth in it. As the induna of a company of warriors he would have been able to make this simple herd boy hand over four cows. As an unmarried youth he could hardly demand the same from a battle-hardened head-ringed counselor to the crown prince, who was also a company induna in his own right, and of a more senior regiment too.

Jobe was infuriated to have been caught so easily. "What about you?" Jobe turned on Inyati. "Why are you here instead of with your regiment? You'll be Humbler of Kings, by the age of you. Come with me. I'm calling you up for border patrol."

Inyati's stared at Jobe until the induna looked away. Mbeki made the introductions. "This is Prince Inyati kaMzilikazi of the House of Kumalo. Prince, this is Jobe kaHamu of the Zulu royal family."

"Oh! Yebho!" Inyati seemed pleased; Jobe almost smiled at this royal knowing his family. "Your father is the one who Mzilikazi bribed when he fled north. Our family is still stunned that it cost us eight hundred cows to go a single day through Hamu's territory."

"That's not true! It can't be true! My father would only have been a boy when Mzilikazi went north!" Jobe pulled himself together, remembering where he was and who he was talking to. "I'll have your lying tongue cut out for that!" He nodded once to one of his men, who stepped forward uncertainly.

Mbeki leaned forward, grabbing the man's ankle and tipping him over backwards. He jumped over the falling man, with Inyati joining him in a mad downhill dash.

The warriors turned to chase Mbeki and Inyati down the escarpment they had just climbed, but Jobe realized his men stood little chance of catching the two. These were not Ngenetsheni, and they did not share his family's motivations to run Mbeki to ground and punish him. They did not understand that the boy had embarrassed his father, weakened his clan's position at court, and his actions had resulted in his mother's death. In Jobe's mind Mbeki was a weed to be pulled, a beetle to be crushed, garbage to be burned. With the thin cruel smile of his father, Jobe ordered his men to huddle around him for new orders.

Inyati and Mbeki ran until they were deep into the forest. Both had heard Jobe call off his men, and so they knew that they were safe when they collapsed against each other shrieking with laughter.

"Did you see his face?" Mbeki hooted.

"The man is a pig!" Inyati laughed.

"How do I say that in Afrikaans?" Mbeki asked.

"Die man is aan vark," Inyati laughed.

Repeating it a couple of times to himself to fix it in his memory, Mbeki untied the bundle of hunting spears he had been carrying and handed two to the son of the monster Mzilikazi with a smile.

Both Inyati and Mbeki were natural hunters, using skills they had practiced throughout their childhood. They began with slow lazy spirals from their starting position until Mbeki caught sight of the most obvious spoor there was, droppings. He caught Inyati's attention with a wave of his hand then crouched above the sign. The smell was pungent, the leavings still damp, and the shape was distinctively kudu.

From the size of the scat and the poorly chewed greens inside of it he knew that an old bull had left this behind. Mbeki touched it once to gauge the temperature, and found it was only beginning to cool; the big bull had defecated no later than when Mbeki had first seen Jobe's column of men. They were close.

Up and moving again, they no longer stopped when they caught spoor, just waving of the hand to signal it as they passed: a bent twig, a plucked shoot of grass, even a hoof mark in some scummy soil loosened by melted frost. The bull was careless and confident, moving deeper into his woods. They followed as he meandered across a shady glen, down into a donga, then began scaling the side of a rocky kopje. Once they had begun climbing they actually heard the distant scuffing and scraping of the kudu's feet against the rocky outcropping.

"Wind?" Inyati whispered, concerned that the direction of the breeze might change.

"Cha," Mbeki replied. They were upwind, and they would stay that way. He knew from a lifetime's experience that the wind would blow west all day, then switch suddenly in the evening to the east. It was only midday, and the kudu bull could not be more than fifty paces from them. The wind would not alert him to their presence.

With a wave Mbeki ordered Inyati off to one side and forward again. Every footfall was a slow and cautious one now, for a kudu's vision was as good as a man's. With the bull uphill only a careful approach would get them within spear-throwing range.

They found the creature eating the grass growing out of the cracks of the kopje, and Mbeki's mouth twitched into a smile: The old bull had a sweet tooth. The greens up here would get the most sunlight and the least frost. The shoots would be delicious, and soft enough for the bull's old teeth to handle.

Inyati raised his first spear to the ready, and a squeal erupted from the rock face. A troop of hyraxes had dug their burrows near the kudu's meal, and one of the rodents had spotted the prince's motion, sounding the alert. The kudu leapt forwards, leaving Inyati and Mbeki cursing behind him. "Rock rats!" The prince shook a fist at the tiny sentinel.

"Wait!" Mbeki urged. Both watched as the kudu jumped higher and higher up the kopje before curiosity overcame him, and he turned back to see what had been after him. This was the fatal flaw of the kudu that all hungry hunters had learned to be grateful for. In unison the two threw their spears, but Mbeki saw the animal was no longer paying attention to them: his head snapped up in alarm at the last moment, and the kudu never saw the spear that killed it.

"Jee!" Inyati gave the Matabele victory cry, and both men went up the slope to the carcass. Inyati pulled his spear out of its heart and smiled hugely. "It must be fifteen years old if it's a day! I hope your father likes them gamey, because this one here is going to need some tenderizing. Still, did you see him jump when that hyrax barked? He had some life in him yet! Help me gut him here; no sense carrying the extra weight home-- What's the matter with you?" He asked, looking up from the kill for the first time to see Mbeki's horrified face.

Mbeki had climbed up to the kopje's top wondering what the old bull had found so interesting: Up this high he could see over the trees below all the way to the top of the escarpment where the two of them had left Jobe fuming. Now it was the cliff top that was smoldering as fire licked its top, fed by the strong westerly breeze. "Veldt fire," He whispered.

Inyati's jaw hung slack: Veldt fire, the words made any herdsman quake. At best a prairie blaze destroyed the crucial grazing pastures the cattle would need for an entire season; at worst the fire could destroy homes, roast herds alive, and kill every man, woman, and child in the inferno's path. This was the worst season for a veldt fire: the vegetation was so dry that there would be little smoke to warn people a fire was coming.

If the wind was blowing into Inyati's face it would not have been so bad, for the forest was unpopulated; instead it was blowing on the back of his head, and he was looking towards the Valley of the Three Homesteads.

Mbeki ran downhill with reckless abandon, spears, water gourds, and leather riem cord all dropping behind him. "Hey!" Inyati called, "What about the kudu? Do we just leave him here?" His keeper's receding form was answer enough, and he too stripped himself of any extra weight, and with a little sigh to the lost bull he began to descend the rocky path.

Faster, faster, faster... Faster. Mbeki repeated the word over and over in his head, putting on more and more speed. All thought of pacing himself was forgotten. This was a sprint, a twice over the horizon sprint. Mbeki leapt over a donga in a single bound, running through the forest without bothering to weave around the thickets and brambles. It was only when he began working his way up the escarpment face that Inyati caught up to him, both sucking in lungfuls of cold air while they could, both knowing how hot it would be at the top of the cliff.

"What's the plan?" Inyati gasped at Mbeki's climbing back.

"Don't burn to death... Go home... Make sure no one else burns to death." Mbeki pulled himself up the cliff face as fast as a baboon, dragging himself arm over arm straight up with a newfound strength born of fear. He was at the top of the cliff and running again before Inyati was even half way up the easier grade.

The grey air at the top was filled with suspended ash, and Mbeki could not help but take it into his lungs. The ground was hot under his feet, and cinders found every vulnerable spot between his toes, under his nails, along his cuticles. His mouth tasted like soot and felt like it was filled with sand. Tears streamed down his face, leaving it sticky and black where the filth clung to it.

His chest grew tight and his heart beat like a deep drum reaching crescendo. The fire had already burned itself out here; there was too little fuel on the veldt to keep it going in any one place, but he despaired with the thought that if this was the burned out grassland, what would running through the fire be like?

As he got closer to the flaming ground his feet began to blister; then the blisters broke and his bleeding feet began to burn. He could smell burning hair as his eyelashes disintegrated and his hair smoked. His lungs seemed to fill with rocks; his chest was alive with their grinding and tearing. By the time he was within a few paces of the highest flames he sank to his knees. Mbeki struggled to rise, but in vain. The heat was too much and the air too little.

Before Mbeki could collapse into the ashes he was scooped up by the strong arms of the Prince of the House of Kumalo. Inyati had paced himself better and wrapped his loincloth over his mouth to filter out the worst of the ash. Now with the weight of Mbeki across his shoulders he staggered through the fire, wishing desperately he could have used his loincloth to protect his genitals from the brief kiss of the flames.

The air was much colder and fresher when he was out the other side to the west of the fire, but the damning wind continued to blow towards the valley, and Inyati knew he could not stop to rest for fear the fire would overtake him. "Wake up!" He wheezed at his burden through a heat-tortured throat. He was racked by piercing coughs, and Mbeki weakly coughed with him. Inyati grinned with relief, his big white teeth appearing out of his grey soot stained face. In Afrikaans he said, "That's a good boy! Now get off me and do your own damned running!"

Mbeki opened one eye slowly, "That's Boer isn't it?"

"Oh, I get it!" Inyati laughed, dropping Mbeki onto the ground.

Mbeki got up and spat out a black gobbet of ash-filled spit. "The man is a pig!" He barked in Afrikaans. The two laughed through their coughs, slightly unhinged by their experience. The crackle of the advancing fire brought them back to their senses, and they ran together at the jog trot all the way back to Jama's kraal.

Jama thought he was looking at two demons when the young men ran through to the gates of his homestead: They were grey, brown, black, and white, where they were not red with blood. They shrieked with laughter and anger and fear, babbling over each other, their eyelashless eyes wide with emotion. If they had not been the same height as his youngest son and his eldest son's prisoner he would have stabbed them both on sight.

"Quiet! Say it again!" The two began speaking over one another. He waited only a moment before he ordered, "Stop! You: Say it again! You: Shut up!"

He had pointed at the taller one to speak, and this time the youths were more composed, "Nkosi, there is a veldt fire coming from the east. It's burning strong and is being pushed forward by the wind!"

"Wo!" It was not of disbelief or despair, merely acknowledgement. Jama's mind was already working. "We'll take axes and hoes and start a fire break at the top of the eastern ridge! Bhibhi!" He did not wait for her to speak, "Run to Punga and Kandhla! Get their sons to drive the cattle up the western side of the valley! Tell them the boys, my wives and I are making a firebreak on the eastern side, and they are to bring everyone they can to help. Do you have that?" The little girl bit her lip as she nodded her head. "Go!"

Both demon boys and the little girl ran off on their errands while Jama called out his three wives to help. Soon every person who was not driving cattle was at the eastern ridge building a fire break.

"For such a catastrophe I was hoping there'd be more smoke. There's hardly any smoke!" Punga complained, working the turf loose with a hoe.

"By this time next year your campfire stories will say the sky was black," Jama assured him.

The work was fast and furious: Every tree, log, branch, or bush had to be cut and thrown down the side of the ridge; then the topsoil needed to be turned over to bury the dry, flammable sourveld and leave nothing to burn. It was the work of days, and they had mere hours.

Their hope was that by the time the fire reached the valley the firebreak would have stripped the blaze of any fuel, containing the flames and stopping them from spreading down into the valley. It was a weak hope; the wind was strong, the firebreak narrow, the grass on both sides of the break was dry, and a single spark carried by the wind over the bare patch of earth would burn on the other side, rendering all of their work for naught.

Inyati and Mbeki lay under the shade of an acacia halfway down the slope. Their feet were raw; their breath came in wheezy gasps, and their bodies were coated in a patina of white ash stained dark grey under the arms by sweat. They had tried to help with the firebreak, but Inyati had passed out while cutting down a young Mopane tree, and Mbeki had been left with barely enough time to gloat before he had stepped on a thorn with his scorched feet; his shriek would have stopped a charging impi.

"Do you think they'll finish in time?" Inyati asked, repeating the question in Afrikaans at Mbeki insistence.

"Cha, I think the fire will come too fast," Mbeki replied, then listened as Inyati repeated Mbeki's response in Boer. His mind was detached from the crisis, turning over the new sounds as a way of distracting himself from the tragedy bearing down on his family.

"We didn't start any fires. Do you think the not-so-handsome prince is responsible?" Inyati asked.

Mbeki waited for the Boer version before replying, "Which not-so-handsome prince? You made me break my promise to Bhibhi about bringing you home presentable. It'll be a while before any girls will chat with you: It's not often the cremated walk around making polite dinner conversation you know."

"You're not--"

"Ah, ah, ah! In Boer!"

"Afrikaans! Boer is the people, Afrikaans is the language. Sometimes they call it Cape Dutch."

"Fine, say it to me in Afrikaans."

"I can't, I forgot what you said." The prince chuckled and rolled onto his side. "Seriously, that kaHamu lit the fire, didn't he?"

Mbeki sighed, "Yebho."

"What are we going to do about it?"

"Nothing, what is there to do?" Silence fell between them. The fire reached the valley as dusk fell. The people of the three homesteads watched as the fire licked closer and closer to the break. Every popping log or disintegrating blade of grass was scrutinized for sparks might carry across their meager protection. When the sun had set over the horizon there was still light in the east. The fire was burning high and strong.

"Come on! Burn out!" Punga muttered.

"All ancestors, bear witness! I'll slaughter a calf in your memory if you put that fire out," Kandhla added. An eerie wail came from the fire.

"What is that?" Bhibhi shrunk against her mother's side in terror. From out of the flames shot a fiery comet, wailing and screeching. The people of the valley gasped as it flew across their fire break and fell off the top of the ridge, tumbling end over end to land in one of the piles of brush.

The burning carcass of the antelope was the spark the tinder had been waiting for, and even before the buck's fat burned off, the fire had spread throughout the woodpile. The veldt fire was now on both side of the firebreak. They watched as the flames licked higher and higher, leaning over towards them greedily. "Do we run?" Punga asked, wringing his hands. Jama gathered his wives together in his arms, unsure what to do.

Mbeki watched the fire light up the clouds overhead. Through the thin smoke he could see he the reflection of a group of campfires to the south. That'll be Jobe's patrol, he thought. They didn't bother to move too far, did they? "Do you suppose you get to decide what sort of spirit you get to be? When you're an ancestor, I mean."

Punga looked at him as if he was deranged, but Jama answered evenly. "I don't see why not. It's your death. I take it you have an opinion?"

"I think I'd like to be the spirit that punishes arsonists." Heads nodded. Mbeki felt something cool on the back of his ears, and for a moment thought he was sinking backwards into a pool of water, but he was standing on the side of a hill. He turned around, and now the cool feeling was all over his face. It was the evening breeze, and his back was to the fire. As steady as the rise and fall of the sun, the wind had shifted for the day.

The valley's inhabitants watched in silence; their eyes glowed with hope. The breeze was as strong easterly as it had been westerly, and the fire was being blown back over its own ashes. It struggled for hours, smoking and flaming, but by the middle of the night all that was left was smoking ground. The sky above had cleared and the moon had risen and begun to fall again before Jama spoke for the first time. "Do you still want to punish arsonists?" The moon was full, and all eyes went to his face, hard as granite.

"Yebho Baba, but not as a spirit," Mbeki replied. Inyati and Mbeki each took a pair of sandals from Jama's wives. The law forbade men to wear sandals so that they would grow thick, calloused feet for faster mobility in war, but they would move faster without their blistered feet holding them off rocky ground, so this once they indulged themselves. Without any further discussion Jama started handing out the brush clearing axes. Keeping one for himself, Jama led them in single file in the direction they had seen the distant campfires.

As they moved through the night Mbeki ran his hand over the blade of his axe: It was nicked and weathered, with the first hints of rust were appearing on its finish. He could feel the sticky sap of the day's cleared brush, and he knew he wanted blood. The night was cold, and none of them had brought a cloak, but there was no shivering. When they finally reached the company's campsite, all five of them were hot with their anger.

The men of the valley disdained stealth. The warriors of Jobe's company were all curled up in their karosses. This deep in kwaZulu, and with such an inexperienced induna in command, they had posted no sentries. It was with relish that Mbeki unrolled Jobe from his monkey-skin blanket and stood on his left arm, and Inyati stood on his right. The son of Hamu awoke trapped beneath the ash-white bodies of his enemies; Jobe's scream was high-pitched and heartfelt.

The warriors of the company exploded out of their beds in confusion while their induna screamed for their help. The ghosts of two dead men hung over him, and he was trapped beneath them. His warriors froze in shock, for none of them could mistake the spirits in their midst; if that was not enough to give them pause, three middle-aged men surrounded their induna wielding woodcutters' axes.

"I think the King would be very interested to know what you've done here, you piece of shit!" Jobe's shriek was less shrill, as it was Jama who had spoken to him. Mbeki's head snapped towards his father. The penalty for arson was death, and Mbeki saw no reason to get the King involved.

"Jobe kaHamu, I charge you with setting fire to the veldt near the Valley of the Three Homesteads. I arrest you for arson, and I leave it to the king to decide your fate, as is his royal duty!" Jama turned back to the men of the company. "Who is second in command here?" One raised his arm, hesitantly. "You're the new induna. Break camp and leave us, now!" With barely a 'Yebho, Nkosi.' the man and the others left, none looking at their former commander.

"This, this is assault on a member of the royal family, and I command you to stop." Jobe's eyes were huge; he still was not sure if the shades of Mbeki and Inyati standing above him.

To allay his fears, Inyati kicked him in the mouth. "Shut your ugly face!" He ordered, he then repeated it in Boer for Mbeki's benefit.

Chapter 17

Cetshwayo sat on the throne naturally, hiding his uncertainty from the eyes of his councilors. Mpande was not yet dead, but the king could hardly attend to his royal duties while vomiting blood and losing control of his bowels. As the heir, Cetshwayo was regent, and he was slowly pulling the threads of power towards him, but he must not overreach himself, not yet.

"Jobe kaHamu," He spoke softly, as a wise man would. He saw Ntsingwayo give a nod of support, Godide a scowl of rejection, and Prince Hamu a look of absolute loathing. I should burn your son alive; that's the way to treat an arsonist, Cetshwayo thought. "Kneel while I pass judgment."

Hamu raged at fate: Mpande was dying, his best moment to contest the succession lay before him, and this was the moment his son decided to embarrass him before the whole court. "Kneel, boy," Hamu grunted. Jobe trembled as he sank to his knees.

Cetshwayo said, "Of arson I find you guilty. After the testimony we have heard, no one doubts you lit a series of fires and ordered your men to build them up and then leave them untended. You did this knowing whose home was downwind of the blaze you created. That's arson, a crime punishable by death." Cetshwayo looked to his left and right. Most of the great men were in support, but those few who looked prepared to argue could not be ignored. "However--" With this word Jobe's head snapped up. "I am not the Nkosi Nkulu, and despite what many chiefs think, only the king may pass sentence of death."

"I therefore sentence you to a fate worse than death: No longer are you a member of the Humbler of Kings ibutho! You shall never don the head ring and become a man. You shall never own property or cattle. You may never speak for the Ngenetsheni or run a household. To disobey this decree is also punishable by death, and I assure you there will be a king on the throne if I ever see you again. Is it heard?"

"It is heard," Jobe replied, misery in his voice. "Very well, the Regent has spoken! His voice is the voice of King Mpande kaSenzangakhona."

"Yebho," Chorused the assembled men.

Jobe rose from the ground with effort, the full implications of his sentence feeling like a weight across his shoulders. His legs shook as he saw his father excuse himself from the royal presence and walk briskly towards him. Hamu took his son by the arm and pulled him over to the inner palisade wall. "If you weren't my son I would be digging another hole under my hut for what you have done to me today! I could have made my case to challenge the succession were it not for you! You want that kaJama boy dead? So do I, but I could have ordered him killed on a whim as the Nkosi Nkulu! Your way just cost me kwaZulu, and in sparing you Cetshwayo is already building his reputation as a just king! Get yourself up into our family's holdings and serve me well enough that I forget about this, or so help me you will become one of my ancestors." Jobe nodded, but Hamu was still not satisfied.

Hamu spat on the packed earth of kwaNodwengu's parade ground. The foul taste in his mouth did not go away. Somewhere in this kraal Jama kaZuya, Mbeki kaJama and Inyati Mzilikazi would be raging that Jobe had been spared the death sentence he deserved, but they would never know how Cetshwayo's mercy had spared them. I can't kill them after today, Hamu knew. If anything happens to them, all will know it was me, and the wrath that should have taken my son will find me instead.

Hamu tugged at his thin beard, adjusting his plans in light of the regent's sentence. Above him, unnoticed, a vulture circled; it smelled death on the wind.

Chapter 18

King Mpande died twisting in pain, each cough forcing more of his bleeding insides out through his mouth. Even Magema the Healer, the most famed isangoma in kwaZulu, could do nothing further for him. The Great Survivor, the last of Shaka's brothers, was finally gone.

He died in the late winter, but Prince Cetshwayo made excuses whenever his father's duties should have brought him to court. He needed time to climb onto the shaky throne, and so Mpande was dead and buried for an entire season before kwaZulu was told to grieve. A somber umKhosi Festival followed, during which Cetshwayo performed all the rituals without flaw, and making great tribute at his father's grave.

The sun was setting as women moved through the ikhanda, lighting rush torches and lamps of animal tallow. A carnival atmosphere filled the people with boisterous good humour. The umKhosi Festival's prophecies foretold nothing but good harvests and good fortunes to come under their new Nkosi Nkulu; Ingonyama, however, was not happy.

The eldest kaJama carried his spear loose in one hand and his shield firmly in the other; an Invincible was never unarmed, for he was always on the king's business. He moved the spearhead slowly through the air as he worried: When Prince Hamu made up the guest list for his post-umKhosi dinner party, only the greatest men in the nation were invited. Ingonyama was making a name for himself in King Cetshwayo's service, but that was hardly a singular distinction in the Land of the People of Heaven. He did not know how he had earned an invitation, and that made him nervous.

The evening air was warm and humid, and Ingonyama drew it into his lungs as if he was about to dive under water. *Why should I have to go? The man has hated my family since I was twelve.* He watched the torch-lighters at work and shuddered with a sudden thought: *Hamu likes a late meal. What if he expects me to stay the night?* The Invincible mentally kissed the Humbler of Kings' umKhosi beer bash goodbye and forced the lopsided grin onto his face.

He could hear hearty laughter from beyond the high wall of the royal quarters, and his smile lost some of its falseness. The umKhosi Festival was done for another year, and Ingonyama could feel the nation relax around him to know that the death of their King had not cursed them to a year of misery, as had the deaths of Dingaan and Shaka.

He looked at the fresh-cut mopane palisade: It was a beautiful new ikhanda. After Cetshwayo made Mpande's death known to the kingdom, kwaNodwengu had been abandoned as a mark of respect to the late king. Cetshwayo had set up his own Great Place in the nearby ikhanda of oNdini, but he had spared no expense in building this new kwaNodwengu. The new king had ordered it made large enough to continue hosting umKhosi festivals, and so over a thousand huts ringed the parade square in orderly rows of yellow beehives.

It had been seen as quite a coup when Prince Hamu beat off Zibhebhu and Ntsingwayo to occupy the new ikhanda's royal quarters during the festival. His dinner parties were famous, and the giant huts of the new royal homestead would make a fine place for him to hold his feast. Of course, now that the umKhosi was over, he would return to his own ikhanda in the north as soon as this last party was over.

The guard at the door to the royal quarters pulled himself to an approximation of attention. "Halt. Are you expected?" The question was followed by a lazy yawn. There were only a hundred Invincibles, and Ingonyama was far from the least of them; still, if he failed to challenge a single guest Hamu would punish him.

"Yebho, I am invited to dinner." The guard let him pass.

The royal quarters were where the master of the ikhanda lived with his harem, court functionaries, treasuries, and magical charms. The royal quarters were better lit and less cramped than the rest of the ikhanda, and many of the huts were massively proportioned. Each of these huts would house some of the royal wives or concubines, and beneath their hearths would be buried the treasures of the nation. Ingonyama followed the path to one of the largest huts.

He took another deep breath as he bent over to enter the low door. The inside was filled with posts holding up the high roof. He was enveloped in sweet-smelling smoke and the laughter of middle-aged men well into their cups. He stood there for a long moment, uncertainty written all over his face. A pretty young woman rose from her place along the hut's wall to greet him. "I see you, Nkosi. May I help you?"

"I am Ingonyama kaJama of the Invincibles." He bowed lower than politeness required, for she was beautiful. The silence between them stretched; finally he looked up and smiled in embarrassment. He had been so eager to introduce himself he had forgotten to answer her question. "I've never been to a royal dinner before. Where should I sit?"

It was a serious matter, for men always sat on the right side of the hut with the most senior and important people furthest from the entrance. With another rush of embarrassment he saw where she had gestured: He was to sit closest to the door. Dozens of men sat in the hut, and he was the most junior guest. He lay his shield down to mark his spot and looked around the hut.

She laughed at his expression. "It's not as bad as all that. Of course you're going to have a junior seat. Almost all of the guests are princes or chiefs. I think my brother Jobe is the only other unmarried man here." Ingonyama's smile froze on his face: This beauty must be one of Hamu's daughters. He was glad she had said something before he began to flirt in earnest. He had mistaken her for a common serving girl.

Laughter from the farthest end of the hut distracted him. Prince Zibhebhu smiled hugely under his tilted head ring as Hamu, Godide, Mbilini, and Ntsingwayo slapped their thighs with enjoyment. "So I told him, 'You can't milk a bull,' and it took him quite a while to realize what he'd done." Fresh guffaws came from the great men, and Godide roared so hard he knocked his head on one of the wooden posts behind him; this did nothing to relieve the others' mirth.

Prince Dabulamanzi waited for the laughter to subside before snapping his fingers. "I think that calls for another drink!" There were roars of approval, and a servant appeared at his elbow with a bottle of gin. The prince watched the clear liquor tumble into his mug and on an impulse passed it to Hamu. "Go on, cousin! Puts beer to shame, and you don't gain any weight from it!"

Hamu took the cup firmly, threw it back, and felt the warmth spread through him. It is too dangerous to have so much alcohol in a single mug, he thought to himself idly, deciding not to indulge in Dabulamanzi's habit again. "Not bad," He declared, smacking his lips. "But I prefer my daughters' beer!"

At the mention of the dozen maidens arrayed around the room the men cheered again, each tipping his mug to the ceiling, downing the contents as only men well into an evening's drinking can do. Prince Mbilini hiccupped once, gave a passing servant girl an affectionate pat on the bottom and called for more beer. "Exactly how much have they had so far?" Ingonyama asked the princess.

The maiden's laughter was like tiny bells. "They've been here since the umKhosi finished, and of course no one can refuse a host's beer."

"Perish the thought," He said gallantly. She smiled at him, a smile that did more to light the dim hut than any of the low burning torches. Ingonyama decided he did not care if she was Hamu's daughter.

"Would you like a drink?" So graceful were her movements that the mug seemed to materialize in her hands.

"Of course," He laughed, taking the cup of frothy brewed sorghum.

"I'm Nandhi. You said you were in the Invincibles?"

"Yebho."

"So were you at the skirmish of the Phongolo marshes?"

The two young people talking by the door had drawn more than a few eyes to them, and before Ingonyama could reply Prince Mbilini answered for him. "Was he there? He was in command! Thirty Invincibles crossed the river and spent all night stealing cattle. By dawn two hundred Swazi caught him driving the herd through the marsh. Sixty dead men later, thirty Invincibles and a hundred cows arrived at oNdini."

Mbilini waMswati was known as the Hyena of the Phongolo. A renegade Swazi prince, ejected from his kingship by the convolutions of royal politics, Mpande had set him up as a leader to the abaQulusi tribe which guarded the northwestern frontier. Mbilini smiled with crooked teeth, showing there were no hard feelings for killing his fellow countrymen.

"Then there was the skirmish at Three Gorges," Zibhebhu added, taking a long pull on his beer mug.

"And Shaka's Rock," Godide piped in, rubbing the back of his head.

"And the Qwabe uprising," Ntsingwayo's grin was dazzling, for Ingonyama was his protégé.

"And he's only been in the Invincibles a year," Hamu finished dryly. He did not like the way his daughter was looking at Mbeki's brother. She was here to turn the head of one of the princes, not associate with nobodies.

Normally, Ingonyama would never have received an invitation to the most prestigious party of the year. The kaJama boys were constant reminders of the loss of his wizard and the blow that had struck to his prestige at court. The new royal isangoma was one of Dabulamanzi's local wizards, and the royal prince was basking in the influence and power that should have belonged to Hamu.

Ingonyama's invitation to dinner was for a specific purpose. Everyone was here for one reason or another, and Hamu planned to amuse himself by steering conversation from one objective to another until each of the men in his hut would render him some service in the coming year. No part of Hamu's plans involved Nandhi and this young man. He would have to do something about that.

"Were you in the Invincibles for the coronation of Cetshwayo?" Prince Ndabuko asked.

"Oh, don't get me started on that," Godide muttered. "Damn silly if you ask me, getting some white man to put a metal circle on Cetshwayo's head." Hamu was please Godide was so openly opposed to the whole ridiculous idea.

It was a bone of contention among many of the great men. Cetshwayo had become Nkosi Nkulu of kwaZulu with all the proper ceremonies, and then he had crowned himself again by European custom. Their new king had invited hundreds of white men into the heart of the kingdom to participate in the coronation; then, before his people, Cetshwayo had dressed up in a silly costume and become a monarch in the eyes of the Great White Queen of England. In exchange, more than one man in the hut felt he had prostituted his honour for closer ties to the British.

"I was in the Invincibles when he was crowned, and the entire royal guard was present," Ingonyama replied. He had not understood why Cetshwayo would debase himself like that either until Mbeki had given him a thorough explanation.

"It's all very simple," Mbeki had said. "Cetshwayo isn't steady on the throne. There are too many princes, too much ambition, and too many promises made and favours owed for him to just succeed. He needs allies from outside the court, powerful backers to recognize his power."

His brother's body language implied this was all obvious, but Ingonyama still did not understand. "So why did he have to involve the British?" Ingonyama had tried to take in what his brother was saying, but his mind refused to put it together.

"Because Prince Hamu and Prince Zibhebhu and half a dozen others all would like to be king, or at the very least they'd like to establish their own kingdoms; with the recognition of the Whites, Cetshwayo can use the fear of those white guns to keep the other royals in line until he's established. After that the English can go sit on a bull's horn."

"If he fears for his throne he should send Mbejane and the Invincibles out. We could kill a few royals, burn a few amakhanda, and be back before the flies had settled on the corpses." That was Ingonyama's view of politics.

"Cetshwayo doesn't want to claim the throne by murdering his opponents. That's what has been wrong with our system from the beginning." Ingonyama could agree with that: Shaka had killed his brother; then he was assassinated by a brother who also killed most of his brothers, who was then betrayed by another brother who forced him into exile and death. Cetshwayo's was the first peaceful succession in three generations. "Cetshwayo wants a return to the old ways. Senzangakhona was the last Zulu Nkosi Nkulu who didn't kill his predecessor for the throne, and that was back when the Zulu tribe was only a few hundred warriors' strong."

"I understand Cetshwayo needs the English now, but when he's done with them what favours will he grant them for their support?" Mbeki had not had an answer to that.

"And what are you're opinions on the matter, Ingonyama?" Ntsingwayo asked, snapping Ingonyama from his recollections.

"What our King does with foreigners is his business. What does that metal head ring mean? Did we pay good cows for it? Did we marry off our daughters to the English? All our King did was bring white men into kwaZulu and show them our strength. He had forty thousand warriors there when he was crowned. The English will think twice before bothering us," Ingonyama said the words reasonably, though they were not his own. Mbeki and Ntsingwayo had talked late into the night yesterday, and he had listened with half an ear.

"It just better not come back and bite me in the ass," Mbilini said.

Ntsingwayo looked over at the Swazi prince in surprise, for Mbilini was one of Cetshwayo's staunchest supporters: As leader of the abaQulusi, the renegade already had the autonomy so desired by Hamu and Zibhebhu. Closer ties to the British should not have threatened any of his ambitions. "What do you mean?" The Khoza chief asked.

"I mean the damned Boers, what else would I mean? Always putting down claim markers in my territory and evicting my men from 'their' property. If the British back the Boer grazing rights, Cetshwayo might give it to them as a way of paying back his debt for their coronation ceremony. In an afternoon that golden head ring of his might cost my abaQulusi what they've been fighting to keep since Shaka's days."

"Cetshwayo is never going to give away a third of the North just to please the Whites," Zibhebhu said.

"Why not? All of Natal used to be Zulu territory. Shaka and Dingaan and Mpande each gave away huge swaths of good cattle land to please the Boers and the British. Now the Whites are asking for more. Is anyone surprised? They won't be satisfied until they have all of it, and anyone who doubts that a war is coming is a damned fool," Mbilini spat back. War was something the Swazi prince understood, but he knew many of the men in the hut did not have the stomach to face British rifles and cannon.

"If Cetshwayo wants to give away your lands that is his right as King. If Cetshwayo decides to go to war to protect you lands that is also his right as King," Ntsingwayo barked, unhappy at the whole discussion.

Hamu could feel the shifting allegiances in the room and reveled in the power of being able to judge their currents. "Why should Cetshwayo make that decision? Why should he have that power?"

"Because he is our King, Prince Hamu," Ingonyama said. Hamu almost smiled as his plans began to unfold. "Tell me why Cetshwayo must be king at all?" He gestured for the young man to sit with an open hand.

"Because he was Mpande's heir," The Invincible said.

"Oh, to be sure he was, but why was he the crown prince?" Hamu tried to keep from smirking, but failed.

"Because he was the eldest son, and the strongest, and he beat off all the pretenders." Ingonyama meant for the pretender remark to irk the prince, but Hamu let it go.

"Really?" The Prince's expression was one of rapt fascination. Ntsingwayo glowered but did not interrupt. "The eldest son is the heir?"

"That is the law, and it is a good one." Ingonyama lifted his stubborn head to lock eyes with Hamu.

"Then I should be king," Hamu purred.

Godide swallowed the wrong way, and Zibhebhu slapped him on the back with undue force. Both stared at Hamu, trying to figure out why he was bringing that old story up again.

Ingonyama knew he was being toyed with, but could not help himself. "Everything I've just said--"

"Proclaims me as the king of our people," Hamu's laugh was bitter. "I am Mpande's eldest son. I am strong, and I have spent my life beating off pretenders. I should be your Nkosi Nkulu."

"You're not Mpande's son. Your name is Hamu kaNzibe."

"That is my name, but Nzibe was not my father. When a prince dies without an heir, the extended family must provide him with one; that way, the royal family never shrinks. Nzibe died several years before I was born, and it was Mpande who sired me. Mpande wasn't king at the time: He was the family idiot, and no one ever thought his eldest boy would one day be heir to the Kingdom. I was disposable.

"They gave me to Nzibe's widows, and Mpande's second eldest, Cetshwayo, became the heir when my father became king." Ingonyama looked at Ntsingwayo for some denial but saw none.

"I was adopted by the family of dead Nzibe, and like a seed pod in a strong breeze everything drifted away. I lost my royal birthright, my claim to the throne, my authority, my standing," Hamu was working himself into a rage. "My fate, my glory, and my destiny, it was all stripped of me because some rotting corpse had been sterile in life.

"I am the eldest kaMpande! Me! Cetshwayo is second. Second eldest, second smartest, second strongest, and he has never been denied anything. He doesn't know how to fight for what he wants."

"Ndondakusuka," Ntsingwayo murmured.

"What?" Hamu snapped. His performance was for Ingonyama's benefit, and Ntsingwayo's interruption was not a welcome one.

"He fought Prince Mbuyazi for what he wanted." Ntsingwayo did not understand this display of temper. In the old chief's experience Hamu was a snake: He should not be hissing and spitting unless he was ready to strike. Ntsingwayo's mind flew to the latest reports from his spies, wondering if he had missed something.

"And who helped him? Whose factions favoured Cetshwayo and carried the day? My Ngenetsheni, and Zibhebhu's Mandlakazi!"

"You put him on the throne that day, so live with it. Or say something else so I can order this Invincible to arrest you." Hamu and Ntsingwayo pulled their lips off their teeth like snarling dogs, and they were only moments away from coming to blows before Zibhebhu let the pressure off.

"Cousin Hamu, let's not worry about things we can't change tonight. Cetshwayo is the Great Elephant; the umKhosi is over; the harvest looks good, and we have a score of your prettiest daughters here to pretend they're fascinated by anything we have to say." A few of the young women bobbed their heads in appreciation of the honourable mention.

Godide burped once, then chuckled. Soon the beer and the company were thawing Hamu's cold stare, and Ntsingwayo leaned back, if not happy, at least no longer furious. "So let's discuss something else, alright?" Zibhebhu was smooth and charming, all smiles, while inside his mind was working: Hamu was inclined to throw fits of temper, especially when he was suffering a setback, but such rages were almost never verbal. Hamu vented his anger physically. He smashed things, kicked dogs, beat wives, a hundred other things. Words were for solving problems. What is the boy doing here? Zibhebhu wondered.

"You're right of course, old friend. Let's eat and talk about something else," Hamu said, satisfied that he had made a beginning with the Invincible. There was still time. A wave of his hand brought young serving girls forward with shallow bowls of water; each of the guests carefully washed their hands and toweled them on a clean piece of cotton the girls carried.

With another wave Hamu beckoned still more women to bring in the food platters: There was crumbly maize porridge, stamped maize, the same with beans, coconuts and dried fish brought by fast runners from the coast, tomato slices, chopped or whole fruit, duck glazed with honey, spiced snake meat, grilled gazelle liver, and savory lamb stew.

The guests ate with delight, for it was a well laid banquet. Each spooned what they wanted from a platter onto their wooden plate, and ate with enthusiasm. Cup after cup of beer washed down the mouthfuls, and more than one of the men noticed the beer was laced with fruit nectar to sweeten it.

Ingonyama rubbed his belly to show his appreciation of the brewer's skill, and Nandhi lowered her eyes demurely. Hamu saw the boy was engaging his daughter again, and decided to interrupt. "Pass the fish, Ingonyama." The eldest son of Jama looked down the hut to Hamu then at the fish next to his knee. He picked up the platter with his right hand, supporting his elbow it with his left hand as manners demanded, and passed it down the line to Hamu.

Ingonyama felt the need to reconcile the mood of the hut from the previous argument. "The dried fish in sea salt are good Nkosi, but have you ever thought of bringing fresh fish inland?"

"It can't be done," Hamu said dismissively, though he wished it could. He hated salted fish, which was why his daughters had put it on the farthest platter from him in the first place. Now it was the only thing near Ingonyama and he would have to choke some of it down.

"Couldn't you keep the fish alive in pots of water?" Ingonyama maneuvered his question between two bites of the duck.

"The water gets too warm for the fish, and they go belly up." Hamu saw the blank look on the youth's face. "That's what fish do when they're dead." Ingonyama nodded in understanding. He had never seen the ocean, and the brooks around the Valley of the Three Homesteads were too swift for dead fish to linger.

"I'm surprised there isn't a pot that would stay cool. I bet my brother could think of something; he's quite clever, you know." Ingonyama's attention was already drifting back towards Hamu's daughter. Like iron to a magnet, he could not turn away. Ntsingwayo beamed around his mouthful of porridge as Hamu made the obligatory noncommittal noise.

Godide burst out in drunken enthusiasm; "Tidal pools! You could catch them in tidal pools. The fish there like the warmer water anyway. Or crayfish!" The ideas scattered and shifted from the mouth of the prince; he was well and truly soused. "Crayfish could go around in the pots! Oh, you must come to the coast for crayfish! Flesh as soft as amasi and creamy as fresh milk." Godide ruled the coastal lowlands and was famous for his broad palette. Ingonyama felt a little queasy at eating an armored fish with legs like a spider and pinchers like a scorpion, but he remained quiet.

"Our young friend is heading to the coast," Hamu replied, honeying his voice. He was glad the conversation had stumbled in the direction he wanted. One of his seeds was already sown in Ingonyama's mind, but it was for the future, planted for a contingency that would be allowed time to take root and might never need to be harvested. His next seed for Ingonyama was about to be planted, and its purpose was much more immediate.

"Oh?" Ntsingwayo arched an eyebrow.

"I've been put in charge of the party to collect tribute from the Tsonga." The eyes around the table went wide, and with good cause. In the days of Shaka the izimpi had roamed the land, subjugating thousands, and there was one land that had been particularly ripe for the taking: The Tsonga were a peaceful people who lived on the coast far to the north in a land of plenty. They had rare and beautiful animal pelts, feathers, copper, cowrie shells, and a fine harbour in which Europeans would come to trade all manner of useful things.

Shaka had wanted the riches of the Tsonga, but any conquest so far from kwaZulu would need to be followed by a heavy-handed occupation and a permanent garrison. To spare their lives and save Shaka the trouble, the Tsonga had agreed to an annual tribute of their riches.

Over the years this tribute had grown to staggering proportions and was now vital to the Zulu economy. There was not a single regiment that did not wear the skins and feathers of kwaTsonga; almost all the beads, pots, guns, mirrors, knives, and quality gunpowder came from those lands. Without the Tsonga tribute life in the Zulu kingdom would be little different than it was two hundred years ago. The King would be a pauper, and his warriors would go into battle with nothing more inspiring than grass headdresses and leather kilts.

The collection of tribute from the richest and most important vassal nation was an incredible command for one so young. No one but Mbejane had commanded that procession since he first became head of the Invincibles ten years before.

"Why you?" Nandhi's estimation of Ingonyama had gone up. Nandhi knew her father had ordered her here to catch the eye of one of the princes, but she wondered if her father may have misjudged this young man's worth. Besides, he had a nice smile.

"Mbejane doesn't wish to travel this year," Ingonyama said, omitting his own pride at being picked as Mbejane's replacement over scores of warriors with more seniority.

"Too much chance of revolt. The King's Champion and commander of the Royal Bodyguard should be with Cetshwayo at a time like this." Everyone ignored Ntsingwayo, even Ingonyama, who should have known better.

"You should be careful on your return leg; there are many bandits in the land." Hamu lowered his chin and spoke seriously. He could not be too blunt or blatant. Ingonyama was not the brightest torch in the ikhanda, but he was not stupid; besides, Ntsingwayo's suspicions about

Hamu's conversations with the young Invincible could not be ignored.

"I am taking twenty-five Invincibles and fifty warriors from the Humbler of Kings regiment. Who would be stupid enough to attack me?" It was a serious question on a serious matter, and Ingonyama's tone made it clear whoever replied had better be sober. Godide held his peace.

"I would say the northern lands have grown wild. The thieves are banding together under robber barons. It is most distressing," Hamu said, casting his eyes about with feigned worry.

Hamu was setting something up, and Ntsingwayo did not like it. "Those are your lands, aren't they?" He asked pointedly.

"Mine and Zibhebhu's," Hamu agreed, trying to brush off the Khoza chief.

"Then perhaps I should tell our King. I'm sure he'd be more than happy to build a new ikhanda up there. Perhaps the Red Needle ibutho could garrison it, or part of the Humbler of Kings." Ntsingwayo's tone was of mock concern; his eyes were simply mocking.

"The problem is nothing we cannot settle by ourselves with time, but at the moment there are many who would try for our young friend's procession on the return leg of his journey. One man springs to mind..."

"Who?" Ingonyama leaned forward, his hand tightened on the haft of his spear.

"A warlock who dwells near the mangrove swamps of the Phongolo delta," Hamu began. Zibhebhu was careful to remain silent and still. He now knew why Ingonyama had been invited to this feast. "He has the local men banded into his own private ibutho, and I could see him daring to attack your command."

Zibhebhu was glad Hamu had not mentioned that the man had been successfully raiding commerce in their territory for three years with impunity. The two northern barons had needed to dig deep into their coffers to make up Mpande's share of the stolen goods. If the late king had lost a single cowry shell, one glass bead, or a single ratty blanket he would have sent an impi to pacify the trade routes and built the ikhanda that would rob the two princes of any pretense of autonomy. They had almost bankrupted themselves to keep their secret, for a garrison in the north would ruin them.

Prince Zibhebhu marveled at Hamu's ingenuity: Cetshwayo can't spare Mbejane, so he sends a youth with the king's authority and a war band of elite men to the north. Both of the northern princes had their private regiments, but to use them would be a declaration of independence neither was ready for.

Zibhebhu's mind saw Hamu's goal with admiration. *This boy will remove the thorn from our sides without a thought, and he lacks the authority to put a garrison in the north. Very clever, I must congratulate Hamu. I also must remember to find better spies: I didn't know Mbejane would not be going on his annual trip.* Zibhebhu settled in, content with the evening.

Ingonyama had taken Hamu's statement at face value, never wondering about Hamu and Zibhebhu's cunning expressions. "Well I'd be a fool to wait for my return leg! There's no sense risking the porters and their load; I'll wipe out this man on my way to kwaTsonga then carry on as planned. A two-day detour at the most. You will of course provide a guide?"

"Of course," Hamu and Zibhebhu chorused. *The youth is no fool,* Zibhebhu mused. *He is a Lion very much lives up to his name. I should reinforce his command before the battle. He is doing me a favour, after all.*

"While you're up there, Ingonyama, see if you can't renegotiate the trade agreements. It seems to me we should be able to get about twenty percent more tribute from those Tsonga monkeys, eh?" Ntsingwayo chuckled. Hamu and Zibhebhu looked at him with eyes of obsidian; they had always kept the extra as a levy for moving the tribute through their territory.

"Nonsense! The Tsonga are stretched to the breaking point. There isn't an extra civet skin to spare in the entire country!" Hamu protested.

"Oh, I don't know about that. It seems to me there must be around twenty percent more beads, blankets, guns, feathers, precious woods, skins, and bangles up in that country." Ntsingwayo smiled sweetly. His spies had finally been able to give him the outrageous rates Hamu and Zibhebhu were skimming off the top, and he would make sure they felt the pinch.

Ingonyama watched as the men argued over numbers of this, and ratios of that, and was very glad he was not a great man of the nation. He had no idea how many shells equaled how many feathers, and could not have cared less about the exchange rates between gunpowder casks and copper ingots. It all went over his head, and it was not long before his attention shifted from the princes to Nandhi.

"What would you say if I said you were the most beautiful woman I've ever seen?" It was not something he would have tried without the help of six or seven mugs of beer, and even after he said it he was glad the senior end of the table was busy arguing. He would hate to have a wrathful Hamu eject him from the hut before he got an answer.

"I'd say you have good taste," She began, smiling coyly. "But I don't think there's much you can do about it." Her tone invited him to try. The combination of alcohol and mutual youth in the company of elders fanned the flames of attraction. Sparks flew. Pulses quickened. Ingonyama looked to the end of the table to confirm no one was paying attention to them.

"I know a party going on down by the laundry pool."

"There's a party going on right here." Nandhi looked over at her brother Jobe, but he was asking Mbilini about Swazi ambush tactics. Convinced no one would notice her, she lowered her chin and gave Ingonyama a seductive look.

"That's true..." Ingonyama paused momentarily, mesmerized by her expression. "But here they're talking about how many cowry shells to the cow, and whether or not garrisons should be placed in Mandlakazi lands." He paused to make sure she found that as boring as he did. "My party down by the laundry pool is going to have three or four hundred people dancing and singing until dawn."

"Is that right?" She stuck the pink of her tongue out, whetting her upper lip.

"That's right." He winked.

"Well what kind of fool would want to stay here then?" She teased. He looked down the table as Godide took another swallow of beer and leered at one of Hamu's daughters. Her eyes followed his, and Ingonyama's took the opportunity to study her form.

Her figure was perfect: She was short and ever so slightly plump, with generous hips and thighs; her face was blessed with full lips and a high forehead. She turned back from looking at Godide to see his appraising look, and she laughed her ringing bell laugh again.

With unspoken consent she signaled to two of the servant girls who had set the table. They stepped forward with due reverence and offered a shallow bowl of water to each of them. Ingonyama rinsed his mouth carefully before spitting the water back into another bowl, then he and Hamu's daughter slipped out of the hut into the night.

Chapter 19

Nandhi's head swam with introductions and jokes and the newly learned slang of good common people. This was a different world from her upbringing in the tightly chaperoned community of Hamu's royal quarters in the North. But I am not mixing with commoners, she thought with a laugh. There's nothing common about Ingonyama.

Her Invincible escort led her to a new clutch of people. "Boys, may I introduce my princess, Nandhi?" Half a dozen fit young men raised their mugs and voices in greeting, and she laughed, waving them off with one hand. She was not sure if they were cheering her, or the fact that Ingonyama was escorting royalty to a party, but it was a welcome change from her father's court, where no one was supposed to notice her unless Hamu made a point of bringing her to their attention; even then it was always a silent scrutiny, judging, weighing her value as a cook or a future wife.

Oh, what have I missed? She realized Ingonyama had just introduced her to the warriors. "How do you do?" She asked politely, not having caught a single name. Without knowing it, she had asked exactly the right question.

"We feel so good! Oh! We feel so good! Oh!" They chanted in unison, each 'Oh!' followed by a pelvic thrust whose enthusiasm was explained when they tipped their mugs skyward with a practiced movement. Their throats bobbed up and down, and when each was done they wiped the suds from their lips with their forearms in perfect synch. It was a game, a male ritual of camaraderie that they had practiced all night. She clapped in applause, and they took their bows before heading off to refill at the beer pots.

"You have interesting friends," She said.

"What?" He said, not having heard her for the drums playing in the background.

"I said you have interesting friends!" She shouted.

Ingonyama worried that his comrades' boorish display might have offended her, so he snatched up two full mugs from a passing youth, gave one to her, and led her away from the party and out onto a grassy hill.

Nandhi walked beside him with complete trust, knowing she was safe with an Invincible. They walked through the thigh-high grass, dew drops running down their calves feeling cool and comfortable. The two climbed higher and higher up the slope until the sound of the drums was only a faint suggestion, like a heartbeat. At last Ingonyama dropped his shield onto the grass to form a flat dry spot and offered it to her with an open hand.

She sat, and the view took her breath away. Below them lay oNdini and kwaNodwengu, all lit up with lamps and torches to form two glowing rings of yellow set in the darkness. The moonlight had transformed the green-brown of the White Mfolozi River into a silver ribbon. The grass around them was blue in the dimness, but the dew drops on the undisturbed blades caught the moon too, glowing like stars descending from heaven to float around the two of them. "Beautiful," She murmured.

Ingonyama sank down into the grass beside her, propping himself on one elbow, "Yebho, you are."

Nandhi smirked, remembering his earlier tactless advances, amused and surprised that her decision to encourage them had led them up here rather than to some drinking competition during which she would find herself disgusted with him and leave. "Why are we here?"

After a silence he said, "I wanted to see what kind of person you are."

She laughed again. "And?"

"I like what I see," He said, smiling again. "From your father and your brother I expected you to be a brooder, or at least have a temper."

There's that honesty again, and the bluntness, she thought. "That's fair, but we are not our brothers, or our fathers. After all, you're not a liar or a cunning little cheat." She had meant it as a joke, a light-hearted poke at his family to negate his own truths about hers, but instead of the anticipated chuckle he recoiled from her as if he had been lying beside a snake.

"What?" He asked. His voice was rough.

"Your father is Jama, the one who brought trumped up charges of arson against my brother? And your brother is Mbeki, the one who is coordinating with Cetshwayo to humiliate and isolate my Baba at Court, yebho?" She asked, mystified.

"Cha!" He said, his brows knitting. He dropped his elbow to lie on his back, staring skyward. Clearly, he was trying to think.

"Oh! Oh, my mistake! When I heard kaJama I assumed you were a son of Jama kaZuya, the Cube smith who lives with the Ntuli." She laughed in relief, trying to soothe him.

"I am." Her laughter died, and a long silence stretched between them. "You seem to have some funny ideas about my family," Ingonyama said at last.

"Well, everyone's family has its troublemakers. My father might make some hard decisions, but at least he never tried to have one of Jama's sons killed, like your father did with that ridiculous arson story—-"

"All the high pasture between my home and the escarpment was burned to ash, and I personally took the statement of a company of Humbler of Kings that said your brother ordered that fire." She gaped at him, knowing from the stillness of his face that he was not lying, and yet his story was completely at odds with what her family had told her. "As for your father trying to kill one son, that's never happened." She opened her mouth to speak, but he continued, "He's tried to kill both of us."

"Say that again." She was focusing all of her attention on him.

"When I was twelve, and my brother was, oh, nine or ten, we came to our first umKhosi Festival as my Baba's mat carriers. That was when Mbeki broke Jobe's nose, remember?" She felt a pang, remembering that was when Jobe's mother had disappeared. "We were almost stabbed to death among the huts by Hamu's guards."

"That can't be true," She said. "If my Baba wanted you dead, you would be, and you certainly wouldn't be coming to dinner with us."

"I'm sure I was invited to serve a purpose," He said, only realizing it as he spoke. "That's how your father works." She was on her feet before she knew it, kicking him in the ribs.

"That's not true!" She was not sure why she was so angry. He was on his feet in a blur, easily catching her wrists to keep her from clawing him.

"And what about you?" He asked her while she twisted and turned, trying to get a hand free to scratch him. "Why does he have you out here with me? What can he get out of me through you that he couldn't get out of a prince like Ndabuko, or Dabulamanzi, or a great chief like Ntsingwayo?"

"Stop it!" She shouted.

"Answer my question."

"Cha!"

"Answer my question!" He let go of her and took a step back, the two of them squaring off. Uphill of them a cricket began to chirp.

"My Baba is a good man who resorts to bad things to achieve his goals," She said, not believing it.

"My brother is a good person, and so is my father, and so am I." He locked eyes with her, but she broke the unequal contest. "Is it heard?"

"It is heard." She sank back down onto her shield. At length he lay down in the grass, but further from her. There was a rift now. The silence stretched. She felt the ox hairs of the shield tickle her, smelled the wet grass, and slowly, gently, she calmed herself. "You've met my family. I've never met yours. All I know about them is what I hear from Jobe and Baba. You're telling me something different, and I'm wrong to think you're lying. If you have something good to say about your brother, say it. I'll listen."

"Mbeki is..." Ingonyama trailed off. He was not a teller of stories, but he needed a good one, one to dispel her beliefs about those closest to him. Without knowing where it came from, he told the first thing that came to mind. "When I was growing up with Mbeki I had almost three years on him, but he always wanted to compete against me. Of course he couldn't win, but he wanted the feeling of triumph." She listened, trying to imagine the young man, so demonized by her family, as a little boy playing in the fields. "So I took to making bets with him. Instead of trying to outrun me, outswim me, outfight me, I would say he couldn't do something, and then he would do it."

"Like what?" She said, glad that his voice was losing its ice.

"Small things when he was young: 'I bet you can't climb to the top of that rock face, Mbeki.' 'I bet you can't catch that lizard with your bare hands, Mbeki.' When he had done it, I would heap him with praise and spend the next few days listening to him taunt me."

He smiled, and her heart warmed. She had feared she would not see that smile again. "Then one day he was almost grown up. He was as tall as our Baba; he could throw a spear into the eye socket of a bull's skull at twenty-five paces, and he could jog trot all day and all night, just like a grown man. All of a sudden I didn't want to make him feel good. I wanted to humble him. I wanted to feel good about myself at his expense."

She heard a trace of anger and of loathing in his voice, and she tensed for a moment before relaxing again. Since she was old enough to stand those tones were the signal to get out of her father's presence. She did not feel the violence from the Invincible though, even though in one short year in the Royal Guard he had killed more men than her father probably had in all his years of political intriguing. "What happened?"

"I was teasing him. After our visit to court he had taken the praise name 'the Wizard of kwaZulu,' and I told him his magic was nothing compared to my strength. That's true, of course, because my brother isn't an isangoma, but I said it in front of our cousins, and he couldn't back down. He demanded a test, and where before I would have given him something he could do, now I dared him to do the impossible: I bet him he couldn't lift a stone, weighing more than he did, and move it up to the top of this marula tree that stood in our southern-most meadow.

"I couldn't have done it. The stone was a hundred paces from the tree, and the tree was fifteen paces high. You know what those trees are like: They have lots of branches leading off the trunk, but the branches are too far apart to move from one to the other while carrying something. I expected him to get angry, perhaps to hit me and start a wrestling match where I could leave him in the dust. I would have stood over him, and at the time I thought that would have made me happy. Instead he accepted, asking only that I give him some time to do it."

"What did you say to that?"

"I laughed at him. I made all my cousins laugh at him. I said he could wait until we were old and grey: The tree could fall down, and he still wouldn't be able to move that stone to the top of it. I sounded like a big man, but I felt very small inside. He just looked at me, laughing at him, and he gave me his stakes."

"Stakes?"

"His wager. He named his price for moving the stone to the top of the tree."

"So what did you bet him?" She asked, wondering where the story was going. Already her ideas about Jama's family were fading away, but she did not know what would replace them.

"He asked for my respect, and it was like a slap in the face for him to say that he did not have that already. He is my brother." Ingonyama said simply. For a long time he stared down into the plain below, watching the fires dance. Nandhi grew impatient, and eventually cleared her throat. Ingonyama came out of his reverie and continued as if he had not stopped. "He sat on the rock for the entire afternoon looking at the tree, and then when he came back the next day he had three of my Baba's wood axes with him."

"He was going to chop down the tree?"

"I told him that wasn't allowed, and he just said, 'I know.'" Ingonyama smiled, still remembering the scorn his brother had put into that phrase, taking Ingonyama's statement as an insult. "Do you know what he did? He chopped off all the branches on one side of the tree, even the ones that made the climb easy. It took him three days, and when he was done Baba had to rework all three axes. Their cutting edges were flat."

"Then what happened?"

"He spent two days clearing away the fallen branches, and any rocks at the base of that side of the tree. Then he took every fingerlength of leather riem cord he could lay his hands on; not just our homestead's supply, either. He borrowed from my Uncle Punga, my Uncle Khandla, even went to the kaMajeke brothers homestead, which, in itself, was half a day's trip. He had a pile of riem higher than I am tall, a thousand times more than would be required to tether the stone to his back. All told, it probably weighed half as much as the rock."

"Why?" She asked, not understanding the spreading smile on Ingonyama's face. It's lopsided, she realized, finding the unusual cocky smile very attractive.

"I asked him that, and he just kept saying, 'you'll see.' He used a very small portion of the riem and four days of back-breaking labour to move that stone to the base of the tree. Every day I'd lead my cousins to the marula tree, and we'd laugh at his progress, assuring him that there was just no way when it took him four days to move the boulder to the base of the tree that he was ever going to get it to the top, especially when he had it at the base of the tree on the side with no branches above. He just kept saying, 'You'll see.'"

"Did he move the rock?"

"He didn't even come near it for five days. He took the riem and braided it, like you braid an oxtail, except in five strands so the rope was as thick as three of my fingers when he was done, and it stretched maybe three hundred paces. Then do you know what he did?"

"Cha," She said.

"He soaked the whole thing in a stream so that the leather shrank and the rope braid became one piece. He borrowed half a dozen hides worth of premium leather and he ruined it all. My father raged at him. My uncles raged at him. The kaMajeke brothers sent word that if they caught him in their valley they'd whip him. Everyone was asking, 'Why? Why?' And do you know what he said?"

"'You'll see,'" She said, clapping her hands and laughing.

"'You'll see.' He tied that stone in thirty, forty paces of line, using knots I've never seen before. He dug under it, holding it up with some of the discarded branches so that he could attach it underneath. That stone was perfectly secured."

"But it would still be impossible for him to lift it up the tree, no matter how tightly the rope held the rock," She protested.

"Are you kidding? He could barely lift the rope up the tree."

"The rope?"

"He tied the free end around his waist and climbed the tree with the line snaking out behind him, dragging him backwards. Twice he fell and caught himself. At this point I went to him to call off the bet. I didn't want him breaking his neck. But he just told me, 'You'll see.'" Ingonyama shook his head. "Once he had the end at the top, we all waited for him to try and lift the stone, but instead he tossed the rope through the highest crotch of the tree and climbed down the other side with the rope still in his loincloth."

She watched Ingonyama try to describe it with his hands, Mbeki going up and coming back down so that the line formed a triangle with the rock and his brother at the two bottom corners and the highest part of the tree at the top. "Then he spent two days hauling pots of water up the tree, leaving them in every fork and crotch. When we asked him what he thought he was doing he just said--"

"'You'll see,'" they said in unison.

"Finally the big day came, and he announced we could watch him move the stone into place as long as we never came within a hundred paces of the tree, no matter what. We all promised, and when we arrived we saw him moving three steers to the side of the tree with branches and attaching the rope to wooden bars across their chests, as if they were the oxen we had seen pulling white men's wagons.

"Mbeki took a handful of pebbles, put them in a pouch, and climbed the marula. Then from the highest point of the tree he made the herd boy's distress call, the one that meant danger was near, and the cows began to move away from him. Their harnesses jerked them up short, for they were attached by the rope to the rock via the top of the tree, so they stopped. Of course cows would prefer to stand rather than to pull.

"Then Mbeki started throwing the pebbles at them. He continued his distress call, and the painful stings of the stones hitting their hindquarters sent them away from him. The rock began to lift, but even from where we sat we could see the rope catching on every scrap of bark, especially at the top crotch itself. Mbeki kept shouting and throwing, all the while dumping pot after pot of water onto the rope to keep it from snapping at the friction."

"And?" She asked, anxiously.

"The stone made it up the tree and came to rest on the highest crotch, and he cut the rope with an axe before the cows could drag it over the top. The stone was up there, and he put his foot up on it and shouted, 'Behold, the Wizard of kwaZulu! I told you all that you would see!' Then he began to laugh, and he laughed so hard he fell, hitting four branches before catching the fifth.

"When he made it to the ground he had dislocated his shoulder, but that stone is still on top of that marula tree, and he has my respect. To this day when a stranger comes to our valley and asks after the stone we tell him the wizard of kwaZulu put it there with his magic." He smiled again, but became serious. "Now you understand that just because my brother humiliated your father to save his life, I can't excuse you for speaking ill of him."

"I was wrong to say it," She apologized.

"Don't worry about it. You understand now; how could you have known before?" There was another silence between them, but it was a comfortable silence. Somewhere between the argument and the story they had moved from acquaintances to friends. "Shit," Ingonyama muttered then remembered the company he was keeping, "I mean, oh dear."

"What?" She asked, suddenly concerned.

"Look who's coming up the hill." At the base of the slope an unmistakable giant was climbing towards them; it was Mbejane, the King's Champion.

"My Baba must have sent him," Nandhi sighed, knowing that if Mbejane was checking an empty hillside, he had already ransacked half a dozen kraals and parties, which meant Hamu had sent him searching almost as soon as she had disappeared and would now be furious.

"You aren't going to tell your father I deflowered you, are you?" He asked.

She laughed hard, reminding him again of the sound of bells tinkling. "You're terrible."

"All right, all right, fair enough. All I ask, then, is when you do tell him, tell him I was good."

"Oh, you're good all right." The two watched as Mbejane came within hailing distance, standing awkwardly with his spear loose in his hand, unsure of how to summon her. "Princess?" He said at last, stiffly. "Prince Hamu requests you return to the banquet." Nandhi rose and Ingonyama began to get up too. "Not you, Ingonyama. Your presence has been appreciated enough for today." There was an undertone of humour in the champion's usual deep, deadpan voice; Hamu had stopped inviting Mbejane to his umKhosi feasts for much the same reason Ingonyama would never again be welcomed. *That prince is a danger to my king*, the giant thought, *but he has some beautiful daughters.*

Nandhi stood there for a long moment before making up her mind. She turned from Mbejane and gave Ingonyama a quick kiss. "Until next time," She whispered in his ear as she pulled away. She squared her shoulders, mentally preparing herself for her father's verbal barrage. *It was worth it*, she thought to himself. *You only live once, and Ingonyama promises to make life interesting.* Head high and heart pounding, she followed the King's Champion down the hill.

Chapter 20

"Well?" Inyati asked in the language of the Boers, their secret tongue.

"He's been there since midmorning," Mbeki replied.

Inyati put on his most chipper and mischievous expression. "Let's play chaperone, shall we?"

"What's the harm?" Mbeki spread his arms wide, as if he could not think of a reason against the idea.

"Well, he could wring both of our necks and leave us for dead." The two grinned at each other, egging themselves to do the deed. "Come on Chomper!" Inyati settled the matter and called for the dog. He had been just a puppy at the time of the fire; now he was almost fully grown. Chomper rose to his feet with a bone in his mouth, and came to heel at Inyati's side. "Find Ingonyama!" The dog relinquished the bone to Inyati's waiting hand and took off, hard on the scent.

Both boys knew where Mbeki's brother was, but they followed the dog anyway. They took great pride in having trained a hunting dog to obey commands in Afrikaans, and even more in having a pet that could find any of a dozen friends by smell alone.

The dog worked his way through the Great Place of King Cetshwayo, pausing near the royal quarters to draw in Ingonyama's scent. Mbeki's elder brother spent most of his day here, and his smell was strong but old. With a wag of his tail Chomper picked up the fresh trail and took the boys off in another direction. They went across the great parade square and down the inner palisade before slipping into a row of huts.

Warriors of the Chieftain ibutho smiled as the boys passed their quarters. "Heading home soon?" Inyati asked.

"Yebho," They replied one after the other. Their eyes shone with the expectation of the overdue reunion with their wives, children and cattle. The Chieftain ibutho was the regiment immediately younger than Jama's Hunters, and they should have returned home the umKhosi Festival. Married men were not on active duty, and more than one of the warriors resented their orders; still, Cetshwayo had been a warrior of their regiment and Hamu was their induna: The two royals found reason after reason to keep their favourite regiment at the capital.

"That's good. You're starting to stink up the place." A few laughed, most scowled; foreign prince or no, Inyati wore no head ring and should not count himself the equal of married men.

"We're just off to break up a love nest, want to come?" Mbeki's eyes laughed as the men dissolved without a word into every available hut and out every available gate. "I'll take that as a refusal," He said to the empty air.

At last Chomper sat at the threshold of a hut with a jackal-skin cloak over the entrance and looked back at Inyati. Before the dog could give their presence away, Inyati set the bone in his jaws and patted him on the head.

Mbeki leaned in to the door. "He is a Lion! See how he whelps those cubs?" There was no answer from the other side of the cloak. Ingonyama, He is a Lion, was not surprised to hear from them.

Inyati nodded his head, liking the pun. He too yelled through the door, "If you're not careful she might catch a Shaka!" Shaka had been the first great king of the Zulu, but his name meant stomach beetle. The future king had been conceived out of wedlock, and to hide his embarrassment the virile father has said his latest lover had merely been infected by a Shaka, which often mimicked the signs of pregnancy. When the bastard child was born he had been dutifully named stomach beetle.

Mbeki muffled his laugh with the back of his hand: Inyati's joke worked on two levels, for Shaka's mother had been named Nandhi, just like Ingonyama's girlfriend. Before the next jeer, Mbeki's older brother pulled aside the jackal skin and stuck his head out of the door.

"Can I help you boys?" He tried to look stern, but his lopsided grin was irrepressible.

"Oh, I don't know. It seems to me you have your hands full at the moment." Mbeki guffawed just a little too hard, and fast as lightning Ingonyama was out of the hut with one leg behind Mbeki and a practiced hand pushing into his brother's sternum. Mbeki fell into a tangled heap of long legs and developing arms.

"You two have had your fun. Just let me say go well." Ingonyama leaned in through the door to give the traditional Zulu farewell.

Mbeki and Inyati chorused in singsong voices, "Go well, Nandhi!"

"Ingonyama, if those two disturb us one more time I'll get my Baba to cut a couple of things off, and I'm not talking about their heads!" The boys winced in mock pain, but her threat did not keep them from dragging Ingonyama back from the door. They knew Nandhi was not really mad.

"Come on Chomper!" The dog rose to follow Inyati.

"Can't you speak to that mutt in Zulu?" Ingonyama's pride was hurt at having been the source of their levity.

"You want me to speak Zulu? Absolutely! So, how was she?" Inyati's expression was lewd.

"Get yourself a girl, and then we'll talk."

"Are you kidding? I'm older than you, and a prince to boot! I--"

"Shut up!"

"You're not planning on marrying her are you? There are plenty of cows in the field," Mbeki teased.

"Is it such a ridiculous idea?" Ingonyama snarled.

Both of the other boys stopped for a heart beat. "Are you serious?" Inyati burst.

"Why not?"

"You don't have a head ring for one thing! You won't get one for another ten years at least!" Inyati's tone was reasonable and Mbeki nodded his support, but Ingonyama had a reply ready.

"The Invincibles can request a head ring as a royal boon. You don't think I have enough clout with the King to ask for the right to marry?"

"Favour with the king is one problem. What about the other problem?"

"What other problem?"

"Hamu," Inyati and Mbeki said together.

"Wouldn't he want his daughter to be happy?" They both laughed at the very idea. "If I asked the King for Hamu's daughter as a wife, she'd be mine!"

"Well what about the bride price?" Mbeki asked, his concern rising. This isn't just an idea, he realized. He's got this into his head, and he's too stubborn to get it out again.

"Bride price?"

"Yebho! You know, the time-honoured tradition whereby the groom gives the bride's family compensation for the loss of their beautiful daughter?" Mbeki's patronizing tone did not play well with his brother.

"I know what a bride price is! I'll manage! The going rate is two or three cows. Baba still has my five cows from capturing your Matabele friend here. He'll let me use them."

"That would get you a common girl."

"She's not a common girl!"

"That's my point! You want to marry someone who'll give your children a royal bloodline? That's a hundred calf-bearing cows, minimum!" Ingonyama took a step back, shaken. Jama, Punga, and Kandhla's combined herd was a hundred and thirty cows, bulls, steers and calves, and that was after a lifetime of good business acumen, drought free pastures, and generous gifts from the king. A hundred cows was an impossible sum to spend on a wife, beyond the reach of any but the richest great men of the nation.

"A hundred cows..." Ingonyama's voice trailed off, lost in the vastness of the concept.

"Minimum. That's if Hamu likes you, which he doesn't."

"He'll probably ask for two hundred," Inyati piped in. Ingonyama's hand rush towards his face. The Matabele winced, but the blow stopped a finger's breadth from his eye.

"I hear what you're saying, but that's just a delay: Not an impossibility. I'll figure it out." That was all the compromise he was willing to make.

They walked on for a long while in silence before Inyati said, "So be honest: You're impotent, aren't you?" It was such a ridiculous statement that they all started laughing, and it was a happier mood that brought them to their daily mid-afternoon spectacle.

"We almost missed the show!" Mbeki crowed. Inyati and the younger kaJama settled down in the grass on the side of the hill while Ingonyama set down his shield and sat upon it. Below them spread the White Mfolozi and their way of passing the hottest part of the day.

Whenever he was at oNdini, Mbejane, the commander of the Invincibles, came to the spot below them to exercise. He was the biggest man any of them had ever seen, and more than one Englishman waiting at the King's Great Place for permission to hunt had remarked that the Royal Champion looked like a circus strong man.

Mbejane may well have been at one point: No one knew where he came from. He had no acknowledged clan, no patronym; his skin was as dark as the hide of an uSuthu bull, and he spoke Zulu with an unplaceable accent. On the other hand, Mbejane had the strength of ten oxen and had sworn allegiance to the King of the Zulu. That made him a very important man.

"Hey, Jojo! Come on up!" A young Invincible rose from the grass below them and made his way uphill, teetering under the weight of a pot of beer, the awkwardness of four giant mugs, and the steep pitch of the slope. He was as young as Ingonyama, which made him unusual for one of the King's bodyguard. He was a man of few words and fewer bright ideas, but he was loyal to a fault and followed Ingonyama around like a puppy.

They sat in the grass together, drinking and playing with Chomper as they watched Mbejane conduct his daily ritual. First the giant swam into the cool waters of the river without a care for the crocodiles or currents. He would emerge carrying a large round boulder that weighed more than Mbeki did.

With the sound of a grunting hippo exploding from deep in his chest, the King's Champion lifted the rock to the full outstretch of his arms, straight up over his head. Every muscle in his chest and arms pulled taut at the effort. There was no fat on the hulking man: It was all curving, pulsing, bulging muscle.

"One!" The boys cheered, and counted over and over until Mbejane had done five reps of five, all before the four boys had emptied their beer pot. If the stone had ever fallen on a lesser man that poor unfortunate's head would have crushed down between his shoulders. Ingonyama and Inyati both maintained the rock would crack in two if it ever bounced off Mbejane's ugly skull.

The induna of the Invincibles repeated his exercise with smaller stones, stretching them out in front of him or off to either side. Mbejane was soon lathered with sweat like a zebra after a stampede, but his exercise did not end there: Throwing the rocks back into the river for safe keeping, he made his way to the obstacle course.

Some time ago Mbejane had found a thick bed of thorn bushes amid a smattering of Mopane saplings. Cutting the trees to leave posts, he had tied leather cord into a spider's web of trip wires, snares, obstacles, and barriers. Throughout the field, leather bags full of sand waited like so many sullen sentinels.

Mbejane snatched up his assegai and tore through the course, lifting his knees up so high they almost touched his heaving chest. As he passed each leather bag he stabbed it within the blink of an eye, leaving sand streaming out of a yawning hole. The obstacle course was twice the length of Jama's homestead, and the trip wires were viciously high and terribly low. If Mbejane stumbled even once he would bleed from a hundred holes, for he allowed the thorns to grow thick everywhere but on the few small foot holes.

Mbejane covered the distance in the time with such speed and grace that the boys never tired of watching him, and in his wake he left thirty leaking sandbags and thirty cries of 'Ngadla' to die in the wind. By tomorrow his wives would have patched the holes and woven a new web from the leather cords. Every day Mbejane ran a new course, so he could not memorize a path and dull the thrill of his peculiar sport.

"Glad he's on our side," Jojo murmured, pleased he had thought of something to say.

"We could've used a few more like him up in kwaMatabele," Inyati agreed.

"He's the one who's going to kill you, isn't he?" Ingonyama's lack of tact was typical, if not pleasant.

"At least he'll do a competent job of it." Inyati looked at the sandbags. "One fluid motion... Mbeki, remind me to ask for it in the chest, would you? I'd hate to die of a belly wound." The festival atmosphere died, for Inyati's day of reckoning was near at hand. The four of them were left to their thoughts.

"Look!" Jojo pointed above them, where a messenger was running down the hillside to reach them.

"You are Inyati kaMzilikazi, Prince of the Matabele?" The messenger puffed.

"I have more titles, but those are some of them." Inyati attempted to be nonchalant, but there was only one reason a messenger would come for him, and he felt his knees go weak.

"King Cetshwayo requests your presence."

"What was King Lobengula's decision?"

"You will come with me now."

Jojo reached for his spear to enforce the messenger's order, but Ingonyama shook his head. "He'll come, but first tell him whether he'll die here, or whether his brother wants the execution to happen in kwaMatabele."

"Here."

Inyati's sphincter clenched. "Fine." He squared his shoulders, wanting to look strong for his friends and show no sign of his burbling bladder or his palpitating heart.

"I have an idea," Mbeki said. All eyes turned to him.

"He can't run away, if that's the Great Wizard of kwaZulu's plan. Whether I like him or not, I won't let him go." Ingonyama used Mbeki's nickname to aggravate him, but his brother would not be deterred.

"Just listen." The four huddled together as Mbeki gave his plan. The messenger shifted from one foot to the other, but he was not prepared to chide two Invincibles. At last they finished.

"I like it," Ingonyama said, and Jojo nodded as well. He did not really understand what had been said, but it had Ingonyama's approval, and that was good enough for him.

"It's worth a try," Inyati agreed.

"Well, it makes sense if you think about it." Mbeki said, trying to convince himself as much as anyone. Inyati's life depended on it.

Chapter 21

Cetshwayo sat upon his stool of a throne in regal dignity, flanked on either side by imposing shafts of ivory and a dozen Invincibles. His cloak was a leopard skin neatly draped over one shoulder and reaching to below his loincloth at the front and back. His head ring was level and true. Mbeki was proud to have such a king over him, but he worried that the smile and laugh were missing from his sovereign's features.

"Bayete, Great Elephant." Ingonyama genuflected. The other youths repeated his words.

"I see you, Invincibles. I see you, young wizard. I see you, dead man." Cetshwayo let the last greeting hang. A Matabele hyena had been let into his sheep pen during the lambing season. He felt no regret at his late father's decision to destroy it.

"My King," Prince Inyati began carefully, "What was my brother's reply to Prince Hamu's messenger?"

"Lobengula said, 'Why should I strip my nation of cows until the grass grows too high to see over? A Zulu spear will kill as well as a Matabele one.'"

"But what if there was no spear, Great King?" Mbeki asked, his tone light.

"What?"

"Do you remember Mbilini waMswati of the Swazi?"

"Yebho," The King said. He could order Inyati killed at once and no one would question his command, but he considered himself a patient and thoughtful man.

"Prince Mbilini is sentenced to death in his own land, but if just a few of his relatives were to die--"

Mbeki was cut off as the King finished his sentence. "He becomes the King. That is why my father gave him asylum in kwaZulu."

"Inyati is also an heir to a throne. Besides his brother Lobengula, all of the Matabele princes are either dead or too timid to rule. Why should you kill a man who can be of use to you in the future?" Mbeki waited for the King's response. Cetshwayo tilted his head to the side at the idea, as if examining it from a new angle; it took only a moment for him to find a flaw and snort at the idea.

"Mbilini is loyal to the Zulu by oath and blood and politics. I wouldn't trust your young pup here to guard my privy for fear I'd find a spear up my bottom while stooping over my piss pot." A few of his councilors chuckled, and Cetshwayo smiled at Mbeki, hoping there was more to the suggestion than that.

As if on cue, Inyati dropped to one knee. "By blood I am a Zulu who has simply lost his way. By oath I now swear allegiance to King Cetshwayo kaMpande of kwaZulu and pledge my country to his service should I claim my throne."

"An oath under a death sentence is no oath." Cetshwayo was amused, but would take no action until he had considered all possibilities.

"The law says it is."

"Laws are made by kings, puppy. When you are the King, you can decide this oath of yours means nothing at all."

"By blood and oath and politics Mbilini is bound to you. You have my blood. You have my oath. As for politics, if I claim the throne of kwaMatabele I will only be doing so with the help of the Zulu. Killing me gets you nothing, Great Elephant. Letting me live costs you nothing."

Cetshwayo tilted his head the other way. He smiled, but there was no warmth behind it. "And would you need to be a chief like Mbilini? Would I have to keep you in feathers and beads, cattle and girls, as I do for the fair Swazi Prince who guards my border with the Boers?"

Inyati gave his most charming grin. "I wouldn't kick and scream if you offered me such things, but I would be content with a pardon from my death sentence."

"Ah yes! The death sentence my father gave you." The King looked to his advisors and gauged their expressions. His birthright, political savvy, European support, and Invincibles had put him on the throne, but he was under no illusions as to whose good graces kept him there. Ntsingwayo was open and receptive, but the rest frowned and scowled at the notion of letting the Matabele live. He judged their mood with a practiced eye before he made his decision. As with so many of Cetshwayo's rulings, it would be a compromise.

"My father, King Mpande, was a wise man," Cetshwayo began. "But he was under a great deal of stress from his illness when he ordered your death. At noon tomorrow Mbejane shall execute Inyati as my father ordered, but Inyati shall be armed in the manner of his choosing and may fight for his pardon.

"If he defeats my champion, then clearly my father's spirit has helped him in an impossible task. If my father regrets his words, he shall help Prince Inyati tomorrow." The wave of murmuring swept up and down the great men and for a moment Cetshwayo thought he had miscalculated.

At length one of the great men rose from his squatting position. "Bayete!"

"Bayete!" The rest echoed.

Cetshwayo bowed his head at their approval. To refuse out of hand would have made him seem stubborn. To grant the pardon would have made him appear soft. This compromise would still see the Matabele dead, as his council wanted, but it would be seen as a token of generosity by those who did not like to see a proud man butchered like cattle. As a bonus, Cetshwayo would finally see Mbejane in action, something he had not witnessed since becoming King.

Inyati stood with slack lips, remembering the towering black mountain of muscle that was the King's Champion. It was worse than a death sentence: An execution was at least a comforting certainty. This was a mockery, a hopeless hope, an impossible possibility of life.

Mbeki's plan had been based on the belief that the King would exert his independence and make this small move to prove his authority; instead, Cetshwayo had decided the matter was too small to risk angering the great men, and now Inyati was going to die within sight of his pardon.

Inyati barely remembered to mumble the royal salute before leaving the royal presence. In his mind the King's words echoed like the insides of a deep drum, "At noon tomorrow, Mbejane shall execute Inyati as my father ordered."

Mbeki spent the rest of the afternoon looking for the Matabele prince and only found him as the sun was setting. Inyati had returned to Mbejane's training ground. Mbeki watched from the hillside as Inyati tortured himself.

First the prince of the House of Kumalo swam far out into the stream, but he could not lift even the smaller stones Mbejane used for his lesser exercises, let alone the great boulder. Before Inyati could give up the treacherous current swept him under, and he dragged himself soaking and miserable to the riverbank almost a hundred paces downstream.

Next he shooed Mbejane's wives from the obstacle course with the necessary amount of male arrogance before beginning his run. Inyati's progress was rapid and sure, and it was a moment of guilt for Mbeki as he thought, maybe it's not so hard after all. Before even that small praise could fully register, Inyati tripped and fell into the thorns with a yelp of pain and hurt pride.

The second son of Jama took his time walking down the hill, but Inyati did not rise from the thicket. It took a long while for Mbeki to reach him, but the Matabele never shifted or tried to protect himself from the cruel thorns. Their eyes met, and an understanding passed between the two of them. "I'm a dead man."

"Yebho."

"But even in an execution, at least there's the comfort of a hopeless situation."

"Yebho."

"Not like this."

"Cha."

"What am I going to do?"

Mbeki watched as the tiny pinpricks of the thorns wept tears of blood down Inyati's side and flanks. Finally he shrugged. "A hero dies in heroism."

"A hero dies in heroism?" It was the warrior's credo taught by every father to his son as he cradled the boy in his arms. It was the war cry of the herd boys in their games, and the urging of a young wife to her husband as he went off to war. It was the last utterance of a man who would have songs sung of him, and it was the perfect summary of the spirit of a warrior nation.

"Yebho, At least you'll die with a weapon in your hands. You won't have to kneel down and ask him as a personal favour to stab you in the chest. There is no submission, no surrender. You will die a hero's death." Mbeki hauled Inyati to his feet.

"A hero's death?" The old familiar grin reappeared, and Mbeki felt his heart warm. "You really are full of big steaming chunks of it, aren't you?" Mbeki laughed, but Inyati was not done. "I'm being serious here! A hero's death? Who needs that? How about a coward's life? As for that stabbing in the chest thing, that's the best way to go! One fluid motion to the heart, and boom, that's the sound of your corpse hitting the ground. No cry of pain, no shrieking from a belly wound. Chest wound all the way."

Their gallows humour saw them all the way back to oNdini, but Inyati did not sleep that night. It was a haggard and drawn prince of the House of Kumalo who appeared before the king at noon. "There shall be no witnesses?" He asked.

Cetshwayo shook his head. "This is not something I want made into a public spectacle."

"Yebho, Nkosi. My death's just the business of me," Inyati pointed to his chest with an open hand, "my killers," he pointed with a single finger to the king and his champion, "and the people who'll bury me." A final jerk of the thumb to Ingonyama and Mbeki finished his sentence.

Cetshwayo let the man's comments stand. "Don't forget my personal healer, Magema. He shall attend to you."

The reed-thin old man next to Cetshwayo gave a little bow but lost none of his stature. It was a bow of arrogance and pride, not respect and subservience. In his hand he carried a leather satchel filled with instruments he had boiled to devoid of evil spirits. He was the oddest medicine man anyone had ever seen. He wore no magic charms or protective layers of filth, in fact he bathed with hot water and soap twice a day and shaved all the hair from his body. Despite these obviously unsanitary, unholy practices, the royal physician had the highest success rate for saving lives of any healer in kwaZulu.

Inyati was less than pleased. He knew why Magema the Healer was present. "You're too kind, Nkosi. You mean even if I somehow manage to scratch your big ox, he'll be bandaged up before I'm cold?"

"Quiet, puppy!" Mbejane barked. He did not like this situation at all. His king knew his knee was still healing from a bad fall. Every day his leg groaned in torment after his exercises. Magema the Healer had promised it would regain its former strength soon, but if he was not fit to lead the kwaTsonga tribute this year, why should he have to duel with this prince? Had he somehow lost Cetshwayo's favour? If any of his subordinates saw him stumble today, they might challenge him for his position as King's Champion.

"You may find this puppy has teeth, monster." Inyati gave a dazzling smile. He turned to Ingonyama to collect his war axe and a spear.

"Remember, you play to win, and you always win." Ingonyama murmured his motto, and Inyati shook his head.

"Right now, I'm hoping the game will just be called off. Maybe Mbejane could forfeit?"

"You would have beat me, if you had fought as you had been trained." Ingonyama said.

"You were easy. Mbejane will be hard," Inyati said. He turned back to the leader of the Invincibles. "Hey monster, a request?"

"Of course, young prince."

"Give it to me in the chest?"

"What?" The giant rumbled.

"One fluid motion," Mbeki elaborated.

"Of course, young prince," The great bull of a man repeated in the same tone, as if he had been asked to pass a platter at a dinner party. Mbejane lifted his great shield and assegai high. "uSuthu!"

"Jee!" The deep call of the Matabele ripped from Inyati's throat. He felt the warm pool of fear begin to boil in his belly and opened and closed his hand around the handle of his axe.

Inyati needed the battle over as soon as possible, knowing his strength could never match the vast reserves of his opponent. Mbejane also wanted a quick fight. With a sudden rush they were at each other.

To the onlookers the blades moved with dizzying speed as each fighter sought some weakness to exploit and found none. Although both men cut distinctive figures, they fought with such energy, working on instinct and intuition, that it was difficult to follow who was doing what. They broke apart so abruptly that Mbeki could not see the cause, except that Inyati had dropped his axe and Mbejane his shield: Both still held their assegais.

Inyati and Mbejane launched themselves back towards each other, locking into a twisting, turning, spinning ball of loose arms and legs, like two leopards fighting over a carcass. Inyati despaired at the force of those massive arms closing around him, and the bite of Mbejane's spear as it climbed from the small of his back to between his shoulder blades. He dropped to the ground and rolled away before the King's Champion could make good his killing stroke.

No sooner was he free then Inyati dove back at the King's Champion, smashing into him with the thump of a steak slamming onto a wooden platter. Mbejane began throttling Inyati with his free hand. Inyati was holding off Mbejane's killing stroke with a combination of his spear arm's shoulder and his own empty hand, but the muscles bunched hard as steel in Mbejane's arm, and the spear was inexorable.

In desperation Inyati kicked at Mbejane's knee, and to his surprise he felt something give. Unbalanced, Mbejane could not prevent Inyati's blow from reaching his chest, but Inyati had given up his hold on Mbejane's own spear to make the killing blow. With a hot rush of blood over their hands, both knew they had scored deep and hard.

"Jee!"

"Ngadla!"

Mbejane and Inyati looked one another in the eye, startled by what the other's victory cry meant. Only then did they feel their own pain: Each of them had a piece of burnished steel embedded deep into their bodies. Inyati began laughing the shrieking cackle of the doomed.

"Shut your ugly face!" Mbejane roared his grief.

"Go curl up and die!" Inyati spat back. Both sank to their knees then fell onto their backs, their prostrate forms oddly comical, each with a spear handle the length of their arm sticking up from their body. Inyati's spear was buried high up into Mbejane's right breast, and already the red foam of a lung wound was welling up around the steel. Mbejane's spear had caught the Matabele just to the left of the navel.

Ingonyama, Mbeki, and Magema the Healer rushed to Inyati's side. Mbejane was doomed: A lung wound was a death sentence, but for Inyati there was hope. If only the blade was not as deep as it looked. If only by some miracle the assegai had missed the thousand crucial pieces in the young prince's abdomen.

"Belly wound? Belly wound!" Inyati spun himself around in the dirt and lashed a kick into Mbejane's unprotected groin. "You've killed hundreds of people, and with all that practice the best you could give me is a belly wound? You big stupid ox!"

Mbejane grunted in pain, air hissed and burbled through the red bubbles of his holed lung. He tried to smile, but could manage nothing more than a grimace. "What would you have preferred, puppy?"

The pain was setting in, deep and aching. The adrenaline of combat was seeping out of him, and Inyati found only his anger allowed him to speak. Sweat beaded the Matabele's brow, and the working of his lungs aggravated his belly. "A chest wound! I asked for a chest wound!" He paused as the pain washed over him.

"Next time perhaps you should paint a target for me," Mbejane said, feeling his wound too.

"I don't think there'll be a next time for either of you." Ingonyama was too blunt to hide the truth; he had not been a warrior long, but he knew a lung wound and a belly wound were two of the worst injuries a spear could inflict upon a man.

Inyati blinked back tears and looked at the spear sticking into the air. He swallowed nervously and looked over at Magema. "Hey, old man, take this thing out of me."

"It's plugging the wound. If we remove it you may bleed to death."

"I'm not going to live long with this thing sticking out of me, am I?" Inyati gestured at the spear handle, wincing at the pain of the motion. His voice was getting thin and raspy.

Magema the Healer shrugged. "This isn't going to be pleasant." As the spear was removed bit by agonizing bit, Inyati gasped like a fish out of water. A whistle from deep in his throat turned into a thunder, then a roar.

"Did that hurt?" Mbejane's sarcasm was heavy, offensive.

"Hurt? Did it hurt?" Before anyone could stop him Inyati reached over and pulled the spear out of the great chest of the King's Champion. The gaping hole between his ribs quickly filled with the frothy crimson foam of hot lung blood.

"Puppy..." Mbejane could not manage a snarl, his eyes going dim.

"Monster," Inyati whispered, touching his fist to his heart in mock salute as the life drained out of Mbejane.

"Stop moving!" Magema ordered.

"Stop? Does that mean you can save him?" Mbeki's question was enough to make Inyati looked down at himself, but he knew the answer: Blood was shooting out of him like water from the trunk of an elephant.

"What can I do to help?" Mbeki asked. Without a word the old man took Mbeki's hand and drove it impossibly deep into the warm sticky red void of his friend's belly. With wonder and horror Mbeki felt a pulsing, twitching worm between his fingers; it was the source of the gushing blood that had already engulfed his hand to the wrist.

"Pinch that, or he's a dead man. He's already lost a lot of blood, and if I don't stop the artery from bleeding he'll pump himself dry." Mbeki pinched the writhing tube between his thumb and forefinger until the flow of blood stopped. "You!" Magema looked at Ingonyama. "Hold him down for me. He should be too weak to struggle, but I don't want to risk it."

Magema the Healer was swift and competent, taking boiled cat gut and a long thin needle from his bag and putting both hands deep inside Inyati's abdomen. Mbeki could not tell where his friend's crimson insides stopped and the old man's blood-caked hands began. He felt the artery slip from between his fingers, but Magema only grunted and shifted position.

After a moment the old man ordered, "Get you hand out of there now. It's in my way." Mbeki obeyed. "Hand me the lamb's fleece from my bag." Magema began sponging the blood out of the wound. "Another." He worked again. "Another." Finally Mbeki could see all the way down inside the Matabele and recognized what he saw from a hundred slaughtered cows and sheep.

There the stomach lay, exposed and brown, delicately laced with blood vessels. Next to it the large intestine loomed pink-gray and foreboding. Between them a network of veins and arteries worked their way back and forth in a tangle of blue and red; three of them had ugly cat gut knots holding them together. Mbeki shook his head in amazement: With his hands submersed in blood, the old man had found and repaired three tiny blood vessels. It was magic far more real than any of the gibberish and tricks izangoma could perform.

The old man looked down upon the stomach and intestines, seeing all the nooks and crannies where the evil black blood and yellow pus could grow. If there was true magic in the world, he thought, I would put it in there, and no harm would come to this man.

With a belly wound there was no possibility of second chance through amputation. Magema would either do it right the first time or Inyati would die slowly and horribly, racked by fever and delusions until there was not enough of his body working to keep his spirit trapped within. With a few mumbled incantations Magema sewed the lips of the wound together again.

"That's amazing," Ingonyama murmured.

"I am the best," Magema the Healer agreed; he had never been one for false modesty.

"So is he all right?" Mbeki asked. Inyati lay in a pool of his own drying blood. His face was slack, and his breathing shallow.

The old man took his time in replying. He bandaged the whole abdomen with absorbent lambs fleece gauze and brilliantly clean wool wrapping. It was with satisfaction he saw the deep injury fail to bleed through his dressing.

"Well, he'll have a scar to rival your father's." Magema the Healer waited for a chuckle and was relieved when it failed to come. He understood humour to the same extent he understood modesty. "The first three days will decide his fate. It's a belly wound, and in this heat he should begin to rot by then. If he survives the first three days he has a chance. If he lives for twenty days he'll live until the next damn stupid thing he does." Mbeki nodded his understanding.

"Give him plenty of weak beer, at least six mugs a day, and he'll need lots of fresh beef every day as well."

"And as for you," The old man turned from Mbeki to his patient. Inyati's eyes were glassy with pain, but he was awake. "You'll never put spices in your food again without regretting it. You'll have an ulcer by thirty, and if you ever stuff yourself to bursting, you'll feel the spear stick into you again. You won't get off your back for at least a month, and don't bother trying to walk for a very long time. You've shaved ten years off your life today, and if you break my stitching before you mend, you'll lose the rest." Inyati's only response was to close his eyes.

"Not a bad trade, seeing as how he wasn't supposed to see tomorrow." Ingonyama's comment was ignored.

"Now about my fee..." The old man looked to Mbeki, who felt his stomach flip over at the prospect of having to pay the king's personal healer the price he so obviously deserved.

Ten cows from the royal herd," Cetshwayo spoke from his throne.

Mbeki stood slack jawed. "The King is generous!"

"I did not think he would live. Now that he's going to, I might as well be generous about it."

Four Invincibles brought out a frame with animal skins pulled taut over it. Gently lifting Inyati's limp form onto this stretcher, they carried him away to the royal quarters. Another Invincible stood over the corpse of his former commander; he would keep the vultures off Mbejane's corpse until someone came to dispose of it.

Chapter 22

The three days passed in an agony of nerves as Mbeki waited for Inyati's insides to reek of mortification. The first dark clouds of the coming rainy season moved across the edge of the horizon; the flowers were off the mimosa trees, and the freshly cut mopane poles wept sap onto the ground; everywhere one looked one saw signs that the ancestors were not in a good mood.

For three days Inyati could drink only sparingly from a mug of beef broth, and he did not pass water at all into the waiting chamber pot. Magema the Healer was too professional to wring his hands, but on every visit he put his face over the bandages and breathed in deeply, trying to smell the ill humours.

"Well?" Mbeki was anxious; the old man had given no sign as to how the wound was mending. Inyati had said nothing, nor had he seemed to show any signs of recovery.

Magema the Healer held off answering. "What has he had to eat and drink?"

"A little more than a mug full of broth." Mbeki held up the fired clay cup; it was not large.

"Has he peed?"

"Cha."

The old man leaned over the wound again, gently pressing against the bandaged abdomen with his clean fingers. Inyati groaned a little but kept his eyes closed. The old man threw his mind back to his days as an orderly at a hospital in Natal. The long years since had seen his knowledge of medicine expand and grow as he combined white medicine with black medicine, but what needed to be done now was something both schools of thought agreed upon. "Bathe him." It was neither a question nor a suggestion.

"What?" Mbeki looked blank.

"He's not bleeding inside, and I don't smell mortification, but the bandages are damp from stale sweat. You should have been bathing him everyday, but as that hasn't happened we might as well start now. We'll take him outside for some fresh air, bathe him, and change his dressings."

"Why isn't he using the chamber pot?"

"Maybe his body needs the fluids." Mbeki did not like the sound of Magema saying maybe, but he decided not to press the point. The old man called for boiling water.

"We can't put him in boiling water!"

"First we cool it to warm water, then I wash him a little at a time with a cloth and you dry him gently with a towel." It happened just as Magema the Healer ordered, and Inyati seemed to settle in to the comfort of his sponge bath without complaint.

"Why boil the water first?" Mbeki asked, dabbing Inyati's head with a clean cloth.

"The same reason you should always drink boiled water or beer. River water, especially slow moving river water, causes dysentery and diarrhea; water that's been heated or turned into beer doesn't."

"I'm going to cut the bandages free, but the ones that are caked into the blood will stay with him. I'll just put fresh bandages over them." He waited for the inevitable question. Magema always explained what he was about to do first: It was too distracting trying to answer while working on the patient.

"Why?" Asking questions seemed to be the only thing Mbeki did anymore.

"It's part of the scab. If I cut the bloody dressing out the scab will go with it, and we'll have a new open belly wound. Then we have to wait another three days for signs of gangrene." The answer seemed to satisfy Mbeki and he watched as the old man cut loose the bandages that were free, then examine those that had been encased in the coagulated blood. "Good," Magema the Healer murmured. "Good!"

Mbeki helped Magema rebind the wound then took some herbs to mix into the beef broth. At the sight of Mbeki's long face the old man broke character and gave some kind words. "He's through the hardest part, which is more than I thought would happen. It's very important he lie still and have plenty of broth until he can eat beef. Bathe him every day, and I'll visit after his bath to change the dressings. He looks good. He looks very good."

The next day he did not look good at all. Inyati lay on the stretcher and tried with all his feeble strength to toss and turn. His skin was hot to the touch, and his occasional murmurings were incoherent. Death stalked him, and Mbeki felt its presence in the room. The old man came as soon as Mbeki's message found him.

"How long?"

"It started at dawn."

"And you are only calling me now?" Any warm feeling towards the boys was masked now at his frustration at Inyati's inability to heal and Mbeki's inability to know what was worth mentioning to him. "Cold compresses. Go get them now."

"What?"

"Get your fingers out of your ears and listen! Go get cold compresses." Mbeki looked at him blankly and Magema reigned in his impatience. "Put a clean piece of cotton in cold water that has been boiled and put it on Inyati's skin to cool him down." Mbeki and an Invincible left and came back with the damp cloths. By noon Inyati's fever had dried them as a hot rock dries laundry.

"Do it again." The Healer was busy over a burbling pot into which he threw dozens of herbs to strengthen the blood, cool a fever, kill the ill humours, and force Inyati to urinate. He did not believe magic chants did anything, but they did not hurt and it was expected of him, so he sang off key and boiled and sang some more. When he was finished the old man sieved the water to leave a heavily steeped, bitter tea. "He must drink this."

His tone was decisive, but Mbeki looked to Inyati's comatose form. "How?"

"Tip his head back and hold his nose." Mbeki obeyed, and Magema the Healer poured his concoction into Inyati's mouth. His patient began to gag, but the old man held Inyati's mouth firmly shut and massaged his throat until he swallowed three lip-curlingly bitter swallows. Inyati lurched, and Mbeki brought the chamber pot up to his mouth, but the old man knocked it away. "If he throws it up we have to do it again!" Inyati must have heard through his delirium, for he choked down the rising bile with great effort.

For a long while the old man looked down on Inyati's naked form. He pulled each eyelid back to look at his pupils, rested a hand on his laboring chest, pinched his wrist to feel his pulse, all the while watching Mbeki through the corner of his eye. None of these actions would have been done by an isangoma; a witch doctor would have pranced and jingled bells, lit incense and chanted hymns. If the isangoma ever did deign to touch the patient it would be with hands caked with dirt and filth, and his magic would be made of lizard dung and baboon heart.

The Healer knew if Mbeki tried to stop him, he would lack the strength to resist and Inyati would die, but Mbeki did nothing. He is a smart lad, the old man decided. New things do not frighten him, and that is a rare.

After careful observation he noted the first signs that the medicine was working. "Good. Now it's for his ancestors to decide." That seemed to satisfy Mbeki, and the healer went to fetch a pot of beer.

They waited long into the night, calling for new lamps as the old ones sputtered and died. It was in the evening guard's second watch when Inyati's skin cooled and his thrashing subsided from harried to uncomfortable. By dawn the next day Inyati peed down his thigh before Mbeki could reach him with the chamber pot. His urine was a deep amber colour, like the honey at the heart of a bee hive, almost brown. Magema the Healer's smile was infectious, and he even allowed a chuckle as Inyati murmured, "I've been waiting for that." With that, the Matabele prince fell back into a soothing dreamless sleep.

The strength flowed back into him in the days that followed, and it was not long before his restless nature turned him into the worst kind of bedridden patient. "I'm fine, let me up."

"Lie back down or I'll brain you with a war club," Mbeki threatened, wishing the old man was with him.

"Can't I even sit up? I'm lying on a rock." Mbeki gently lifted Inyati into a sitting position but found no stone beneath him.

"Liar."

"I'm not dead. It couldn't have hurt me." The Matabele was careful not to wince at the sharp pain as his abdomen contracted.

"Well I'm putting you back down."

"What? Why?"

"Too much excitement for one day."

"Excitement? I got to see what the inside of this hut looks like when my head is off the ground. My heart's going like a wedding drum."

"Back." A gentle but firm hand pushed the Matabele back to the floor.

"Can I at least have some visitors?"

"Like who?"

"Well your brother the ox for starters."

"He's organizing the party to collect the Tsonga tribute."

"Oh... Is your father around?"

"Not since Jobe's trial. You know that..."

"Ah ha! Nandhi! I want to talk to Nandhi. You go get her, and I'll just lie here quietly." It did not happen exactly that way; Mbeki had the good sense to send a guard to fetch Hamu's daughter, but it was not long before Inyati had his guest.

"What? No witty remark?" She smiled and squatted down next to him.

"I'm working on it. I'm working on it."

"I don't have all day."

"Okay, I'll skip the pleasantries then. How's the outside looking? Is the sky still blue? Are women still pretty? I'm starved for news in here."

Nandhi did not seem to notice the prince's petulant mood. "I'm sure Mbeki could answer questions like that."

"Well, how's Ingonyama then?"

"Busy," She sighed. Since Mbejane's death Ingonyama had gone about his duties with the kind of bull-headed tenacity that could only earmark him for greatness later in life. In the meantime he was not spending nearly enough time with her.

Behind her Mbeki sat bolt upright with alarm, muttered something about leaving something on a cooking fire, and left the hut with alacrity. Inyati looked after him for a moment, mystified, before returning his attention to his guest. "Busy? I take it that doesn't sit too well with you?"

She was laying out the contents of a basket of food, but stopped to reply. "He spends too much time with his men."

"Well Invincibles are like that." Inyati was getting bored, but he tried to fight it. All he could think about was how good it would feel to run through the tall grass, the seed-heavy tops tickling his thighs, and the gentle swish swish as his legs kept up a steady cadence. It would be a long time before he would have that simple pleasure again.

"Not like this," She said. "Mbejane's dead, and of course the Invincibles are all too noble to want command." Her tone made it clear she did not think them all that noble at all.

Knowing it was expected of him, Inyati murmured his support, "Of course," before reaching for one of the honey cakes she had brought.

"Ingonyama wants the job," She said seriously. "He could do it. The King's Champion --He'd be good at it, don't you think?"

"Oh, yebho!" He said around a mouthful of cake. He wondered if he had been agreeing with Ingonyama's suitability, or if he had just been overwhelmed at how good the cake was. What did she put in these things?

"Still, he works from dawn until dusk readying his men for the Tsonga tribute, then he takes the dusk to midnight shift guarding the royal quarters, and then do you know what he does?"

"Goes and sees you?" Inyati wanted her to keep talking so he could stuff another one of the cakes into his mouth. If the ancestors had known there was food this good, they would have reconsidered dying.

"Cha! He sleeps!" She said it with such outrage that for a moment he thought that he was the only one who really needed sleep and everyone else had just been humouring him all these years.

"Well--" He never finished, which was just as well; talking around two honey cakes was quite a challenge.

"Here I am at my most radiant, and he sleeps!" He could tell from her tone she was not really angry; it was more of a playful sense of frustration. Ingonyama, He thought, You get a beauty, a cook, and a sense of humour, and I get a spear in the guts. Where's the justice?

"The nerve. The guy works three quarters of his life and sleeps the other quarter." He reached for a sliver of glazed duck breast and almost cursed as the tart flavor exploded in his mouth. The saliva rushed into his mouth with such enthusiasm he spluttered as if drowning.

"I know." Of their own accord her shoulders shuddered, and she chuckled quietly.

"What?" He asked, putting half a duck breast into his mouth at once.

"Nothing, nothing, just a wicked thought."

He swallowed with interest. There was nothing like a wicked thought to liven up the bedridden. "You have to share those around you know. You can't keep those to yourself."

"Well," she leaned forward, naturally her breasts were exposed but leaning forward made the view superb, and Inyati almost swallowed the wrong way in surprise. "What I'd really like to do is teach him a lesson."

"I like what I'm hearing so far." And what I'm seeing, but he did not speak the thought. Where else am I supposed to look, the wall?

"I thought of a good prank, but I could never do it."

"I'm sure you could. What is it?"

"Well, just imagine we waited until he was sound asleep one night, then tied his feet to the horns of a bull, and--"

"That's a good one!" Look at her face, he ordered himself. Reluctantly his eyes obeyed. "I can see him now, sound asleep, then all of a sudden he's pulled right out of his hut and out of the gates of the ikhanda. He'd be as far as the river before he'd think to cut the rope." Inyati exaggerated, of course. Ingonyama would have himself loose before he was out of his hut, but it would be a funny prank none the less.

"What do you think he'd do to us?" Her whisper was conspiratorial; her eyes twinkled with merriment.

"To me? Nothing, I'm a poor helpless cripple. To you? Well, I imagine there'd be a stern talking to, and he'd probably watch you like a hawk." His eyes drifted back down to her breasts, and he had to make the conscious effort to look up when she spoke.

"That sounds perfect," She purred, and Inyati was hard put not to see what the sound would do to the area below her neck. Outside, a pebble shifted as Mbeki returned. They shushed each other with such enthusiasm that they were giggling by the time Mbeki came in.

"What's so funny?" Nandhi and Inyati's looked at each other; a silent consent passing between them.

"Nothing," Inyati tried to dead pan it, but a snicker broke through his self control. He watched with a detached interest as the muscles in Mbeki's neck bunched.

"Well if that's how you feel she can play your nursemaid! It's not my fault! Everybody gets loose bowels once in a while! I'm stuck in here with you all day, and I'm not eating properly. I—- Oh, damn!" As quickly as his fragile dignity would allow Mbeki flew out of the hut and his footfalls receded into the distance.

Nandhi and Inyati looked at one another again and tried hard not to break into new fits of laughter. When they finally had themselves under control Nandhi said, "Well that's different."

"Yebho."

"Poor Mbeki."

"Poor... Liquid-stooled Mbeki." They laughed.

"Stop it," she finally gasped. "That's so cruel!"

"It's only cruel if he takes offense, and he did that before I said anything. It can't get crueler." He propped himself up on an elbow and took a little amasi. *There is no way this can taste any different from anyone else's amasi.* He reasoned. *It's just curdled sour milk. How can she make that any different than anyone else?* It was only as he put it into his mouth that he wondered what the green flecks were. He let it sit on his tongue and inhaled; even breathing tasted wonderful.

"Speaking of crueler, when do you think you'll be up to our little surprise?"

"Me?" He gulped, regretting losing the lump of amasi, but consoled by the sizeable basket in front of him.

"A princess can hardly sneak into an Invincible's hut in the dead of night, drive a bull into position, go outside, tie the knots, then convince the bull to move."

"She can't? She managed to come up with the idea."

"So we know where her gifts lie, don't we?" Nandhi received no reply, so she poked Inyati in the ribs. "Don't we?"

"I can't walk," He said.

"We'll do it when you can."

"I'm not supposed to get up for--"

"But you want to, so get better faster."

He tried again. "Healing is like boiling a pot of water; it only takes forever when you want it over quickly."

"Are you saying I should light a fire under you?"

"The hole in my belly was enough."

"You can't be that sick. You've been wolfing down my food and staring at my chest since I got here. If you had your spear next to you, and if you didn't have so many witty things to say, you could be Ingonyama." He could not think of a reply to that, and a gentle scuffling outside signaled Mbeki's return. "I'll visit you tomorrow," She announced, then left the hut.

Inyati lay still for a long time after her departure, and Mbeki was still uncomfortable enough not to break the silence. There was a tug of war going on in Inyati's mind between his fidelity to his friends and his sudden desire to spend more time in Nandhi's company. It was a disturbing realization that he knew the right choice to make, but he refused to make it. "Bad things are going to come of this," He whispered to himself. He closed his eyes and slept.

Chapter 23

Darkness was her cloak, and under its protection she crept through the inner fence gate and into the row of huts. The lamps and torches had all burned out, so by the feeble light of the stars alone she worked her way to Ingonyama's hut.

"The door with the wild dog skin..." She strained her eyes for the telltale piece of splotchy hide. At last she saw it and tugged twice on the coarse grass rope in her hand. The waiting tug was not long in coming, and with a quick intake of breath she steeled herself to commit the deed.

She pushed aside the skin and waited for her eyes to adjust to the darker interior. Ingonyama never slept deep and dreamless, and she could not enter until she was sure she could do it quietly. Only after she put her first foot across the threshold did she remember the glass beads on the floor. The delicate clicking as they were disturbed would be more than enough to wake her negligent boyfriend, and she might have some explaining to do, encumbered as she was with a sturdy noose and near-total darkness.

Wobbling for balance she retracted her foot and leaned forward. With her hands to smother any noise the glass might make, she silently began to move them aside. Without slowing from her task she remembered the day Mbeki had given Ingonyama the idea.

"For a handful of beads you can sleep in the Great Place with peace of mind." Nandhi thought Mbeki's enthusiasm always seemed to carry the argument; Ingonyama was less than convinced.

"I sleep with peace of mind now," He had muttered, sharpening his spear in Inyati's hut.

"You sleep like a baby, and you're just as innocent. The Royal Court can be a dangerous place." Mbeki was careful to sheath as much of the rebuke as possible in the guise of concern, but Ingonyama was not prepared to take it that way.

"My brother wants to give me advice about court security," He had said it to her, but Mbeki had grit his teeth at the slight and carried on.

"You're not a minor court guard anymore, Ingonyama. You're a possible successor to Mbejane."

"Possible? Who else might become King's Champion?"

"Anyone a man like Hamu wants if your throat is slit while you sleep." Inyati had propped himself up on one elbow to look the Invincible square in the eye. "What does it hurt to take Mbeki's advice? It's the matter of a few moments work each morning to gather the beads, meanwhile you never receive unexpected guests in the night. Mbeki's no courtier, but he knows how the world works."

Ingonyama had grumped and harrumphed, but he knew he was outmatched. His brother and the Matabele could take any side of an argument and debate it until their cause seemed the only right one. Ingonyama could never find the words; they were fleeting and elusive. He did not mind, though. One day he would be the King's Champion, and that was worth much more than pretty turns of phrase.

Nandhi wished Inyati and Mbeki had been a little less persuasive as she painstakingly collected the beads.

"Another night," Inyati had beseeched her earlier. Beyond all prediction he could walk with the help of two well-formed sticks after only a month.

"He leaves the day after tomorrow," She had said.

"I can do the bull; I can just barely do the bull, but there's no way I can sneak up on that ox. He has the ears of a bat, and he sleeps with an assegai." Despite his joking tone, she saw real fear in his eyes at the mention of the spear.

"I can't do it!" She hissed.

"I'll do the knots. You just loop it over his feet and pull it snug." So here she was, and with the last bead out of her way she crossed the threshold. Ingonyama had thrown off his kaross in the warm evening air, and his naked form lay sprawled across half the floor, bathed in cool moonlight that seeped through the doorway. She took a cautious step forward and then another. His legs were spread apart, but she knew she had to get the noose over both ankles if she did not want him to break something; within a moment she had a plan.

Walking around him until she was up near his head, she began to gently blow on his ear; nothing forceful, nothing annoying, just a delicate movement of air. He sniffed once in his sleep and she stopped. She waited for her heartbeat to slow before she began again, blowing softly, fading in and out so that no part of Ingonyama's senses might have mistaken it for breathing.

"Mbeki close the flap," He muttered in his sleep; she suppressed an inappropriate giggle. She continued exhaling slowly, moving her attention from his ear to the side of his neck, watching in the dim light as the hairs rearranged themselves to deal with the direction of this unexpected breeze.

"I'm cold," He murmured, moving an arm. "Jojo, throw more wood on the fire..." She almost screamed as the rope jerked in her hand. Inyati was getting impatient. She gave one slow silent tug and hoped he would take the hint. She blew again, this time letting the air breeze across his bare chest. His breathing remained slow and steady, but she watched as each nipple went hard at the cold.

Encouraged, she moved her gentle ministrations lower, blowing across his belly and the rippling muscle just under the skin. She heard him curse gently in his sleep, using language he would never have dared to use in her presence if he had been awake. She could imagine him working her name into the sentence and nearly slapped him at his illusionary impertinence.

With a smile that could only be followed by a vengeful act she began her blowing even further down, and watched in rapt interest as his manhood reacted to the unpleasant cool sensation. Like a frightened turtle, she decided without embarrassment. With a shudder, the sleeping form turned over onto his side, shielding his groin from the cold. She looked down at his ankles, and, sure enough, his rolling had brought them together.

As quiet as a snake in a maize field she crept down to his feet. It has to be one fluid motion, she knew. I have to grab his feet, lift them up, put the noose around them, and tug the line, all before he realizes what happens. She tensed herself then stopped. Did Ingonyama just move? She waited in the darkness but he did not do it again.

She spread her hands out in the darkness, visualizing the movements. It had to be perfect; this was something she would remember as long as she lived, and it had to be just right. Without conscious decision she lifted his feet, moved the noose over them, and--

"What are you doing, Nandhi?" He had been wide awake the whole time. She opened her mouth in shock, but she had already thought her actions through so thoroughly that she gave a savage jerk on the line.

Outside on the parade ground, Inyati opened and closed his hand around the head of one of his canes. *Too long, it's been too long.* His impatience and nervousness were taking equal parts in his anxiety. He should never have come, never actually acted on her idea, but he found he could not say no to her. He knew it was wrong, but he looked for flirtation in everything she said to him, and she was always so kind when he agreed to help her. It was a weakness, but he comforted himself with the knowledge that nothing would come of it.

With a startled rush of relief he felt the line jerk and brought one of his sticks against the broad backside of a red bull. With a bellow of outrage it took off, and his whoops and war cries spurred it on to an ambitious charge for the far end of the kraal. All around the ikhanda, fresh torches were lit from the smoldering fires, and lamps were rekindled with burning twigs; hundreds of men and women appeared from their huts to watch the commotion as Ingonyama shot out the gate of the inner palisade.

He was dragged across the beaten earth of the parade square, clawing frantically for purchase in the packed soil. His spear was still in his hut and he had no means of cutting the tether tying him to the enraged bull. Ingonyama felt the skin peel from his backside and was grateful he was not sliding on his belly. The growl of a cornered lion escaped from his lips, and as he passed through the main entrance gate of the kraal he reached out and grabbed the mopane pole with a bone-jarring effort.

The cow strained against this unexpected impediment, and the rope groaned under the tension. Ingonyama felt every sinew pop and strain as he held on to the gate for dear life. His teeth grinding with effort, he pulled himself forward the width of a finger at a time, slowly inching his way towards the inner wall. The bull felt this pull backwards and rebelled with new fury, pawing and stamping and bucking the rope, tossing Ingonyama's lower body through every combination of up and down, left and right.

Inyati watched in horror as Ingonyama began slipping, losing the battle as the stamina of the bull overcame even Ingonyama's great strength. *Where is his assegai?* He thought. *He always carries that damn thing loose in his hand!*

"Someone cut him loose!" He yelled, but the watching crowd was slow to move. This was totally unexpected: It was like watching a falling star, but even a falling star might be repeated, and they all knew they would never see this again in their lives. "Someone cut him loose!" He cried again, and only a few snapped out of their awed daze and began to move drunkenly to help.

Ingonyama felt his little finger slip off the smooth wood and knew he would not be able to put it back. His fingernails had broken and bled digging for purchase, and he clenched his jaw so hard his ears popped. There was no breath left to cry out; no air to spare on a grunt or a moan. He was clinging on for dear life, and with a shudder he felt another finger go.

"Someone cut him loose!" He heard Inyati say it again, but the responding footfalls were impossibly far away. I'm going to die, He admitted to himself. He heard that little voice of fear deep within him again and he knew he did not want to die. He wanted to live. He wanted to marry Nandhi and be the King's Champion and hear songs sung of him and have sons to carry his spears and shields for him.

You're going to die, said the little voice, but with a surge he decided the little voice was wrong. He imagined a great mountain, a towering mass of granite reaching up to the sky, and he imagined it falling on his fear.

"I'm going to live," He woofed, and felt the last of his fingers go. With a rush of pain he was dragged backwards through the gate. Outside the kraal, the freshly packed earth gave way to the tall dry grass of last season's sweetveld, and it tore and caught against him until all the skin on his lower body was cut and sliced open, raw and bleeding. He felt a rock connect with the side of his head, and stars exploded before his eyes that had never graced the cattle kraal of heaven. He felt a tree stump's jagged top zip along his leg, and felt the sticky warmth of blood.

"I'm going to live," He announced again, but even to his own ears the words were drowned out by the rushing of the grass. Ahead of him the bull slowed to gather its strength, and Ingonyama knew this was his moment.

With a pull of his abdominal muscles he jack knifed over until his head touched his knees. He was slowly sliding forward on his buttocks now, and he felt the last scraps of skin catch on every ant hill and grass blade. He bent his knees, forcing his shins to bear the sharp edges of the grass and further slowing his progress.

The rope was not especially good; if it had been leather riem cord, he knew he would have died. Instead he brought his big teeth against the grass that had already endured the same lacerations upon him. He worried it as a rat worries the tough oxhide of a shield, and he felt a strand part. "I'm going to live," He said around a mouthful of blood-covered grass.

The bull ahead of him was getting tired, and Ingonyama heard its low of distress. You'd better moan. He thought, grinding his teeth against the cord. When I get done here, I'm going to drink your blood from a beer pot, swallow your heart raw, grind your hooves for stew, and then-- He felt another strand part. And only then am I'm going to kill you! With only two strands left and the bull beginning to veer and shift in his course, the rope parted, and with a sudden jolt Ingonyama was tumbling end of end until his head smashed into the bole of a mimosa tree, and all went dark.

"Ingonyama," The voice was distant. He did not want to wake up.

"Ingonyama," His mind rebelled, and he refused to answer.

"Ingonyama," It was only with the third repetition that he realized it had been said by three different people, and the sun behind his closed eyelids had been in three different places in the sky.

"What?" His tone was surly, and he felt he had a right to such an attitude.

"Ingonyama!" A number of voices spoke one on top of the other, and rather than pick one he waited for them all to be quiet.

"Open your eyes," It was the voice of Ntsingwayo, and grudgingly Ingonyama cracked one eye. He was on a stretcher to one side of the royal court. They had been conducting the business of the day while waiting for him to wake up. "There, that's better."

"It will never happen again!" Nandhi burst from over Ntsingwayo's shoulder.

"We thought you would cut yourself lose!" Inyati said.

"Who thought the bull could pull you that far?" Nandhi begged him to understand.

Ingonyama murmured the most terrible soldier's curses he could imagine, all the while probing each tooth with his tongue to make sure they were all still there. He felt as if his entire body was covered by bee stings rubbed with salt, and only after he realized everyone was watching in awe at the stream of profanity coming from his mouth did he stop and say, "My wife will never do anything like that ever again." Her head snapped up; her smile was blinding.

"What?" The new voice was flat, and he opened his other eye to bring Nandhi's father into view.

"I said no wife of mine will ever pull that sort of thing again." I'm alive, and I just proposed and she smiled at me. If Hamu has a problem with that he can stick it in his ear.

"You do not have my consent," The northern prince replied with reptile coldness.

"He doesn't need it; he has mine," Cetshwayo's friendly boom overpowered his cousin.

"My daughter--"

"You have a hundred daughters, maybe two hundred. You won't miss one."

"I want two hundred cows for the bride price." No one spoke. It was an awesome sum beyond even the king's ability to dispose of casually.

"You'll get it," Ingonyama announced through cracked lips. He did not know how, but he would get it. He looked down at himself and realized he was covered in scabs and friction burns. He moved an arm and did not feel as much discomfort as he had expected. "How long have I been asleep?"

"All day," Cetshwayo said.

"Have I missed the Tsonga tribute?"

"I delayed it for you," said.

"He can't possibly go now!" Nandhi objected, but Ingonyama was already heaving his scarred body out of the cot.

"Of course I can." Ingonyama was already hobbling on aching, unsteady legs towards the gate. Jojo tossed him his spear which he caught in one hand without turning his head.

"Of course he can," Inyati muttered. Ingonyama stiffened and turned to the Matabele. He advanced on him slowly, still getting used to the complaints from his joints and the tightness of his scarred back.

"You!" He pointed with a single finger, but Inyati was too worried to be insulted. The spear in Ingonyama's hand was polished to a high shine, but Inyati could already picture it painted red with Zanzi blood. "The next time you want to get a laugh out of me... Piss in my beer cup." Before the lopsided grin could appear on Ingonyama's features he turned back towards the gate. "Invincibles!" He let his voice echo off the palisade. "Let's go!" Seventy-five men fell in behind their battered leader, and with only a little hesitation he broke into the jog trot of a Zulu warrior.

Chapter 24

They marched north and east, taking the easiest path not for their own benefit but to find a trail kind enough for the heavily burdened procession they would be returning with. Ingonyama's men went out as fast as a hungry mamba, but they knew they would be returning from kwaTsonga bloated like a well fed python, swollen by the weight of the annual tribute. For the first several days they spent each night in an ikhanda, then as they went further and further from the heart of the kingdom they settled into homesteads and finally the open rolling veldt.

Ingonyama had noticed a steady cooling to the welcome his men received as they traveled. At first they were greeted as heroes, then welcomed as the King's men, then treated as tolerable strangers, now even that reception was becoming elusive. They were in Prince Zibhebhu's fief, and no warriors on the King's business was welcome here.

For two decades Zibhebhu's clan, the warlike Mandlakazi, had considered themselves to be a de facto independent kingdom. Zibhebhu had his own ikhanda, his own ibutho of Mandlakazi warriors, and had the right of life and death over his subjects. In those same twenty years the only non-Mandlakazi warriors in this land had been here for reprisals, or the collection of Zibhebhu's annual tribute, or to pillage supplies from the countryside as they passed through on their way to foreign conquest.

Ingonyama saw harsh accusation in every pair of baleful eyes, and each night he had to sheepishly ask for supplies from the locals.

"The rainy season comes, Invincible. I need everything I have for the planting." The man was short and fat, with a graying pate and a scowl deep enough to swallow a spear.

Ingonyama was careful not to mention the man had already planted his fields, his children did not seem emaciated by hunger, nor was the King's man so tired he could not smell the sweet scent of mealie cakes baking behind the palisade of the Mandlakazi's homestead. "I suppose you don't have any goats to spare either?" It was a weak question, and he regretted asking it immediately.

"That's right. The nannies are all with kid or already have a young one who hasn't been weaned yet. As for billies, I only have the one stud. If you take him I'm ruined." The man stuck out his unimposing chest, put both hands on his hips, and attempted to look menacing. The effect was lost, however, when he had to tilt his head back to look Ingonyama in the eye.

Ingonyama steered clear of pointing out that there was obviously a great number of goats in the flock and that even a couple of kids would feed his men. "Chicken? Beer?" It was a firmer tone this time, but he knew the answer.

"My chickens are all laying eggs, and it must have slipped my mind to brew enough beer for an entire company of thirsty men."

Ingonyama held his temper with great effort. The man was a fool if he thought he could send hungry young warriors away emptied handed. In fact, Ingonyama was within his rights to confiscate everything this man owned if that was his desire. "Very well, you leave me little choice." The man's hard eyes softened with fear for just a moment before they filled with venom again. "I'm taking a cow. That one there: The piebald heifer long past her calving years." It was a merciful choice that deprived the man of little more than four hooves and a mouth, but the Mandlakazi was in no mood to be thankful.

"You've beggared me! I have four sons to marry off! Not my cow! I'll give you a dozen chickens! Four kids! Come back with my cow!" His wail was long and drawn out as two of Ingonyama's men drove the cow from the rest of the herd. They left the homestead with the man still shrieking abuse. Ingonyama wondered how much of the pillaging of this area had been caused by the stubborn nature of the Mandlakazi.

As dusk fell Ingonyama and Jojo discussed the situation over the last of the cow. "It's like we're invading them," Jojo muttered.

"We are," Ingonyama rumbled, picking the last meat off of a rib.

"I don't feel safe sleeping in the open." They were on a gentle slope only a short march away from the Mandlakazi's kraal. Only the odd acacia tree and a cluster of boulders near the top of the ridge broke the monotony of the landscape.

"We'll camp among the rocks over there. I want eight shifts of four sentries each during the night. Every man sleeps with his weapon, and we are up before dawn. Is it heard?"

"It is heard, Nkosi."

Ingonyama awoke in a cold sweat, cursing. It had happened again. Ever since he had left the King's Great Place he had spent the day straining his battered body and spent the night suppressing his fears. He knew he would never be bodily pulled from sleep and across the plains to his death, but his dreams told him differently.

Each night was the same: He heard the glass beads over his threshold being carefully moved, and without opening his eyes his hand tightened on his spear. There was a gentle footfall, then another, and there was a sound in the background as well; the sound was amplified by the night, and after much thought he placed it as the sound of beads on a woman's loincloth gently bouncing against the leather cloth itself.

"Nandhi," he almost said each night, but the dream would not let him. He had let go of his spear. Defenseless he lay there with his eyes closed and legs sprawled as Nandhi began skillfully to disturb the air around him. He always took it for a game, some bizarre form of foreplay. When the cool breeze reached his loins each time, he suppressed a shudder and finally rolled away, inadvertently bringing his feet together.

"What are you doing Nandhi?" But from there his dream changed from memory to a new and harsh fantasy. The bull was being driven by his ancestors, translucent men of shadow and smoke. Beyond the gates of the kraal lurked their land where the ancestors went when they were not bothering the course of their descendants' lives. He knew without being told that no man could go to that place and return; if he crossed the threshold, if he passed the gate, all his earthly delights would be gone forever.

"You're going to die!" The voice was no longer little: It was a grown man who stood beside him as the bull pulled him towards death. His back was on fire with pain, but he turned his head towards the voice and saw Hamu's plump face split to reveal a toothy grin. "You're going to die!"

"Cha!" He said in every dream, but the word seemed strained and without real conviction. The gate drew near, and the bull turned its head impossibly far over its shoulder to look back at him; its eyes were two orbs of blood red, and its cavernous nostrils each puffed out a thin tendril of smoke.

"There's the pole. Grab it, son!" Jama appeared beside Hamu, arms raised to cheer on his first born.

"Yebho, Baba," He would say, but now he was not being dragged across the ground by a bull: He was hanging from the pole with both hands with the bull and all its weight hung suspended from his feet, and below that was the Land of Death.

"You're going to die!" Hamu whispered, and Ingonyama looked up into the prince's joyful face. Hamu and Jama floated above him, watching as each one of his fingers slowly slipped, and the incredible pressure of the bull's dead weight dragged him backwards into the abyss.

He fell for a long time into a world of mist and fog. The gate to the land of life receded into a tiny dot of light above him, impossibly far away. "You're going to die!" The voice was beside him, and he turned his head to see the sun-bleached bones of a man with an assegai blade and handle stuck out from between his ribs. His arms and legs were missing. His skull watched him through its empty orbits.

"You're dead," The skeleton announced in the little voice he knew so well. Ingonyama reached out to the body, but there was no flesh on his hand or arms. With that he awoke. He breathed deep, knowing he would not be going back to sleep. Each night the dream came earlier, more realistic than before. Ingonyama got up from his kaross and went to relieve one of the pickets; he might as well let someone else rest. He would not fall asleep again.

The following morning before dawn, when only the cattle's horns are silhouetted against the lightening sky, his warriors were awake and alert. Their marching finery had been set aside, and they crouched among the rocks and the tall grass stripped for fighting.

Dawn was the perfect time for an attack. The Mandlakazi were a militant people, and that man and his four sons would have little trouble finding enough friends to avenge his cow. Ingonyama strained his ears to the dying night but heard nothing. There was no sign of smoke over the Mandlakazi's homestead and no sign that the herd was being driven out today. That did not bode well.

A pebble shifted down the slope, and seventy-five hands tightened on their spears. Another pebble followed, then a distant whisper; none of Ingonyama's men were down there. He pulled in a lung full of air, and then let it out. He pulled in another, and released that too in a huff. He sucked up a heaping chest full and roared, "Who are we?" The silence was shattered, just as the first boom of thunder breaks the calm before the storm.

"The Invincibles!" Was the reply, and even the fifty men from the Humbler of Kings Regiment shouted the words, volume having greater importance than heraldry.

"Who are we?" It was like a musket shot in the early dawn, and a startled kite flew out of a nearby acacia in alarm.

"The Invincibles!" They cried.

"Who are we?" His tone had not changed, but there was menace in his words now. Three was the magic number, and the Mandlakazi could not be sure the Invincibles would not come down the hill in all their fury after the third repetition.

"The Invincibles!" His men strained their voices, drawing out the words in deep sonorous chorus. Their tone begged him to release them against their assailants.

"Who is he?" Jojo bellowed, and there was a heartbeat's pause, for this was a new chant.

"Ingonyama!" They replied.

"Who is he?"

"He is a Lion!"

"Who is he?"

"He is a Lion!"

The light grew stronger to reveal over a dozen men running away, the young warriors' laughter nipping at their heels all the way across the valley.

The Tsonga Tribute set out that day in high spirits, and moved at a blistering pace across the terrain. Not one of them was over thirty and most were not even twenty, so there were no older men to slow their pace or dampen their enthusiasm. By the late afternoon it was understandably something of a shock then for the rearguard to find the main body had halted.

"What's the problem?" One asked of the main body.

"Vanguard's made contact with an armed party," Someone answered.

"Then why aren't we killing them?"

"Give it time."

Ingonyama and Jojo stood with the vanguard and watched a company of armed men deploy into line abreast, as if preparing to skirmish. There was no sign of his lopsided smile. The strangers were mostly in their thirties, each carrying a black shield and a spear with streamers tied to their tops. The strong wind fluttered these pennants and ruffled the warriors' feathered headdresses. This was not one of Cetshwayo's units, nor was it Swazi or Tsonga. Jojo noticed Ingonyama's frown and adopted a similar one.

"What regiment are you?" He asked, his voice carrying across the forty paces separating his force from theirs.

"We serve Zibhebhu. We are his men."

"Mandlakazi?"

"Yebho."

"There is no Mandlakazi ibutho." His tone left no room for argument.

"Not officially."

"So you haven't answered my question." He let the silence hang until finally they acknowledged his superiority.

"I am of the Mongrel ibutho."

"Young Mambas."

"Du Du Du," A smattering of other middle-aged regiments were named. Serving in the Mandlakazi ibutho or not, every man among them was a warrior in an official ibutho, every man but one.

"I serve in the Hamu ibutho. I also command it." A man with the flattened nose stepped forward and the other men stepped back, as if to distance themselves from him.

"There is no Hamu ibutho." Ingonyama's tone had not changed, but inside he was rocked back on his heels. Did this man openly admit he was the induna of the Hamu ibutho? By the King's decree he was not allowed to belong to any regiment at all.

Jobe kaHamu was not prepared to be cowed by Ingonyama. "There are five hundred men in Hamu's ibutho, and I am their induna."

Ingonyama decided not to press the matter; of course there was a Ngenetsheni ibutho that was privately loyal to Hamu. At the same time it was just as obvious that an Invincible would never admit the existence of a body of Zulu warriors serving someone other than King Cetshwayo. "Are you going to guide me to this Bandit King? Or did you just run out here to burn the fat off your thighs?" There were chuckles, and not all of them were from Ingonyama's side of the field.

"I am your guide and your guard. From here on my men will escort you through Mandlakazi territory." Jobe looked good, Ingonyama admitted. Hamu's son wore a necklace of leopard claws and a length of black wool over one shoulder and across his chest. The bandoleer of shotgun shells was draped over the other shoulder, and he held the gun behind his shield with a practiced arrogance. Ingonyama was not willing to let this man get too full of himself.

"This is Zulu territory. Shaka proved it at the tip of a spear; Dingaan proved it with a wave of his hand; Mpande proved it with reprisals, and if Cetshwayo has to prove it, I will help him."

"But not this trip," Jobe said.

"Cha."

"Then I can live with that." So Jobe's hundred joined Ingonyama's seventy-five, and they began their jog trot again. For the rest of the day they moved towards the eastern horizon, then they swung north and continued on through the darkness. They finally stopped at a small ikhanda that did not officially exist. It had been built and garrisoned by the Mandlakazi ibutho, and Ingonyama could tell from the soot stains in the thatch roofs it had been here a long time.

"If there are reprisals, you'll wish you hadn't shown me this place. Unauthorized amakhanda are put to the torch." Ingonyama was not really threatening, merely getting ready to excuse himself for the evening. Sleep would probably elude him; he almost hoped it would, but he had to try.

"Within a fortnight this ikhanda will be abandoned, and the ibutho will have built a new one somewhere else." Jobe watched Ingonyama begin to rise to the statement and decided with regret that the Invincible was too stubborn to let him get the last word. "Let's not argue, shall we? Tomorrow we'll be at the warlock's lair."

"He is a warlock, then?"

"Oh yes. He's a fully trained isangoma, master of the black arts, and a god if the locals are to be believed."

Ingonyama knew no man gained such a reputation without good cause. "What can he do?"

"He can make trees speak, talk to the ancestors, raise the dead, breathe fire and spit honey, if you believe what his people say." Jobe rolled his eyes and downed a mug of beer in one long swallow.

"How many followers does he have?"

"Two hundred, maybe."

"Two hundred?" Ingonyama was not worried about the numbers: His seventy-five were some of the best in kwaZulu, and Jobe had brought a hundred of Zibhebhu's men to help. Ingonyama just could not understand how a simple wizard had raised a private ibutho in kwaZulu.

Jobe read his temporary ally's expression. "I know, I know: It's outrageous. He's got Mandlakazi, Tsonga, Swazi, and people from a dozen other clans and tribes thinking he's a god. He even trades with the Portuguese. It's amazing." He stopped, realizing he had gone too far.

"How long has this warlock been out here?" Trading with the Portuguese was not the work of a couple of months.

"All his life, I suppose."

"I mean, how long has he been a Bandit King?"

"Three years?" Jobe had not paid much attention at Hamu's party, but with a sinking feeling he knew the conversation was getting away from him. Did Baba and Zibhebhu say something different? He wondered.

"Really?" With the germ of an idea forming, Ingonyama got up and found an empty hut to try to sleep in.

Chapter 25

The Strangler Fig lives only by murdering the forest, and the cold breeze that blows through its small sharp leaves is heavy with the pungent reek of malice and evil. As a sapling the fig grows at the base of a mighty tree and sends a frail shoot upwards, ever upwards, climbing and twisting around the great trunk like the tentative slither of a newly hatched mamba. To the grandfather of the forest such a shoot carries the promise of a slow, inexorable death.

Once that first delicate tendril reaches the light, another and another soon follow, wrapping themselves lightly around the body of the tree. At first these tiny climbing tentacles seem laughable compared to the powerful column of ancient wood, but it is not long before each shoot is as thick as an arm, then a leg, then sometimes a waist. Within a few short years a hundred twisting, turning fig trunks hide the great tree from view, covering it in a sickly gray sheath, smothering as a blanket and tight as a noose.

Unable to expand and grow, the tree strangles until it stands dead in the tight embrace of its killers. Over decades the tree within rots and disappears, leaving just a hollow space within the heart of a knotted stand of strangler figs. Meanwhile, the figs strangle other trees and each other. They breed and strangle, to breed again, spreading like a plague throughout ancient stands of timber. Within the life of a single gargantuan tree the forest it grew in can disappear behind the murderous grey veil of the Strangler Fig. It was such a forest Ingonyama now saw.

It was a dark and loathsome place, a crazy knot of slim gray limbs and tangled gray trunks. The figs had grown together, overlapping and strangling one another to form a labyrinth in three dimensions that had taken a thousand stately trees' deaths to form. He hated the brooding warren the moment he saw it. "You're sure this is the place?"

"Wouldn't you say it's the perfect place for a dark god to hold court?"

"I'd say it's begging to be chopped down, turned into a raft, and pushed out into the ocean."

"Not on Mandlakazi land."

"Anywhere I want, if that's my mission." Anger hung in the air between them. "Send your men around to the nearest homesteads. We'll need pots of animal fat, mutton drippings, and tallow." Jobe looked ready to argue Ingonyama's authority. "Do it! I want twenty pots; if they have to kill an entire flock to fill the order, so be it." Jobe turned to one of his men and gave the order.

"Why do you need that?"

"You'll see later."

"You're as bad as your brother." The statement had less hatred in it than either Jobe or Ingonyama expected.

"We'll see. Sompisi?"

"Nkosi!" A young Invincible broke from the milling mass of men.

"Take twenty men and follow the party going to the local homesteads. Remember the skirmish at Ncidi's homestead last year?"

"Yebho, Nkosi."

"You will do what my detachment did there; once you're ready, take your men around to the far side of this forest and await my signal."

"What signal, Nkosi?"

Ingonyama thought for a moment. "Mbejane." Sompisi nodded his understanding and ran back to the group of warriors, calling out names.

"What detachment did you lead at Ncidi's homestead?"

"The Right Horn, ordered out to the extreme flank. We carried the day."

"With pots of animal fat?"

"You'll see. Bambatha? Doctor the men!" Another warrior cried 'Nkosi!' before setting to work preparing the men spiritually for battle. Bambatha cried magic hymns, threw herbs and dagga weed into a low fire, and then began to giya and jump around. Every invisible stab of his giya flicked white powder off of a tassel and onto the young men crowded around; it was bravery powder, and the men grew excited and angry. They began to bellow their war songs and stab the air, working up their courage for the fight ahead.

"How do you want to pry him out?" Jobe asked.

Ingonyama shifted his weight from one foot to the other, surveying the swath of veldt between his warriors and the edge of the forest. "Why don't we ask our friend here? Stand up, boy! It's not polite to sneak up on your elders, and if you are going to try, you should be better at it. I saw you when you left the trees." A little boy rose from the grass ten feet away from them. Jobe threw a nasty look to the pickets, but he could assign no real blame: The child was laced from head to toe with riem, and tufts of sourveld were wedged between the leather cords and his skin. Even standing, the boy was difficult to discern from the meadow around him.

"I am my Nkosi's emissary."

"I notice your Nkosi was careful to send someone he wouldn't miss if we gutted you like a boar."

The boy glowered at Jobe's interruption. "He will see you now." It was imperious enough to be a summons to a royal court, and Ingonyama supposed that was how the urchin thought of it. Jobe was hard put not to guffaw. The boy wants us to go in there? Jobe did not think he looked so stupid as to walk into a pride of sleeping lions with a wedding drum under one arm.

"Very well, Jojo, Jobe, come with me." Ingonyama strode forward. The child's invitation played perfectly into his plans. Jojo followed behind him dutifully.

Jobe's jaw dropped, but he was quick to find a more useful reply. "I think I should stay out here. Someone should direct our men when you need help."

Ingonyama paused for a moment before he saw the sense in it. Aside from the fact that Jobe did not want to come, someone did have to stay outside. Within the fig stand he could be a liability; outside he might become an asset. "You're right. The signal to attack will be 'uSuthu.' Follow a groove in the forest floor and you'll find us." He looked at Jojo, who nodded in understanding. "Give me one of your Tsonga speakers and we'll go."

"Foreign Nkosi," the child said. "The forest is thick. Your shields and throwing spears will snag on every twist of the path."

"Boy, if you mean to disarm us, it will take more than some undergrowth to do it."

"A stabbing spear, ax, or war club will fit on the trail much better, foreign Nkosi." So Ingonyama, Jojo, and the Mandlakazi man discarded their large shields and throwing spears. With a spear in one hand, an ax in the other and a war club tucked into their loincloths, they prepared to advance.

Jobe stopped them with a word. "Here." A weather beaten revolver was put out handle first towards Ingonyama. "Only six shots, and don't loose the brass cartridges. They're all I have."

"I praise you, Jobe."

Hamu's son almost smiled.

The three men followed the little boy across the meadow and into the fig trees. The forest smelled musty, felt dank, and the winding footpath ahead of them was as dark as an uSuthu bull's hide. Like a heavy cloak this place seemed to hold them close, suffocating them under an invisible weight. After a hundred paces the canopy above them was unbroken, and the three grown warriors trembled at the sounds around them; high in the branches wind chimes, wooden whistles, and jugs of water sang eerie tuneless songs, like ten thousand lost souls trying to find their way out of the darkness.

Ingonyama found himself checking over and over to make sure Jojo was dragging his spearhead in the dirt. The path twisted and turned like a strand of twine in a violent spring thunderstorm; only the impressions in the trampled clay path would bring reinforcements to them, or let them find their way out again.

Jojo's jaw tightened with anxiety at this place they found themselves in. The grating sound of the spearhead against the rocks and roots on the trail set Jojo's teeth on edge; his eyes never strayed too far from the burnished blade.

The boy looked at the spear as well and cursed his ignorance; if he knew the secret hand language of the sentinels he could tell them to erase the trail. That furrow of earth would allow anyone to follow the most convoluted path to and from the heart of the forest. He shuddered at the thought of what would happen if the warlock learned he had failed even this simple task.

Every one of Ingonyama's senses scanned for danger, but the gray trunks formed impenetrable walls in every direction. All around him he heard unearthly sounds, smelled rotting vegetation, and felt the clay grow colder and colder under his bare horny feet.

The two Invincibles could feel the armed men around them, but they could not see a single human form; they never thought to look above them. On fighting platforms high in the trees the warlock's men watched the tiny party on the forest floor. They had bound fig leaves to them with leather cord to break up their outline, and many had painted themselves green to mask their skin colour. The men spoke with gestures and were careful not to shift their weight on the creaky floors. They must remain quiet; surprise and their wizard weapons would win the day; their god had foreseen it.

Without warning Ingonyama stepped into a clearing in the forest and recoiled from the harsh light as if physically struck backwards. Before his eyes could adjust he felt his heart jump as the air whooshed out of Jojo in a single hoarse word, "Tokoloshe!"

A tokoloshe lay on the ground before them, buzzing with carrion flies; it was evil given flesh, and Ingonyama felt his insides lurch as if he was falling. The corpse was only starting to rot under the flies gentle ministrations. It was the most dangerous monster in Zulu magic, and Ingonyama knew from its missing tongue and gouged out eyes that the zombie was ready to serve its master.

"Tokoloshe! Plague this man's family through all their final days!" A voice demanded. The beast did not move, but Ingonyama was not relieved. Tokoloshe only came to life at night, but there was no escape from one once its dark master had commanded it. A tokoloshe did not need food or water or air. No weapon could harm it, and no one could escape its putrid grasp. The dead man's soul was trapped in his decaying body, and the only hope of escape was to obey the wizard who had enslaved him. A tokoloshe would be unspeakably cruel in its attempt to carry out its mission.

"Who said that?" Ingonyama's voice carried more authority than he felt, but he remembered now that this was just a bandit's lair, not a place haunted by the ancestors. Surely the tokoloshe was a stage prop dug out of a fresh grave and brought here for his benefit. Only a master of black magic could raise the dead.

"I did," The most horrific man Ingonyama had ever seen stepped out of the darkness and into the light. He was completely naked, without even the simple penis cover that was the minimum of acceptable dress. Skinny and small, his body was crisscrossed with ornamental scars and tattoos highlighted with body paint and animal fat. A single copper bangle ringed his neck, and his hair was knotted and tangled like the forest in which he lived.

"You?" Ingonyama asked in disbelief.

"Do I know you?" Zungu Nkulu's horror-inducing face tightened in concentration.

"Cha," Ingonyama lied, a rare thing. Zungu Nkulu was the wizard

Mbeki had revealed as a fraud at Mpande's court over seven years ago.

"Boy!" Zungu barked at the urchin who had led them here. "How are his warriors dispositioned?"

"A few pickets, most of them well back. They are doctored for battle. Hamu's son has been left in charge. The signal to attack is 'uSuthu'."

"How many men?"

"Many men, Nkosi."

Ingonyama hid a smile; the boy could not count, which was common in rustic areas. The twenty warriors under Sompisi had not been missed, and his surprise would remain a secret. The urge to smile left him when the warlock's attention returned to this uninvited guest.

"I may not know who you are, but I know what you are. You command the Tsonga tribute, and you've come to kill me." From the darkness all around, invisible people began to hiss and spit at the very thought. Ingonyama was unfazed.

"Kill you, skin you, and make myself a throw rug." His confidence was returning as he remembered how Mbeki had discovered Zungu's methods. The man was a charlatan; his magic was all tricks and deception. The spear in Ingonyama's hand was real. Zungu's arsenal was an illusion.

The warlock grinned with broken, rotting teeth, but his smile could never be friendly or reassuring. It was the death grimace of a hyena. "Why?"

It was a question that caught the Invincible off guard. "Why?" Ingonyama repeated the question.

"Why do you want to kill me?" The skinny little man clasped both hands atop his walking stick, and became the naked mangled image of innocence.

"Because... Because you're a bandit." He looked over Zungu's shoulder at the shaded huts of a miniature royal quarters.

"True."

"A murderer." How many huts are there? Eight, ten?

"Yebho."

"A wizard." There were ten huts, and Ingonyama knew he had found the way to collect Nandhi's bride price.

"Right."

"And a self-proclaimed god."

"Self-proclaimed?" Zungu's raised his right hand above his head and made a series of signs. From the darkness around the clearing men and women appeared, singing flowery hymns and carrying riches beyond dreams of avarice: Cheetah pelts, heron feathers, baubles of ivory and ebony, trade beads, bolts of cloth, glass bottles, and all manner of steel tools and weapons. "I am a god because the people believe it. I am their god."

Ingonyama watched in confusion as the little man's followers clothed him in bright cloaks of wool and cotton, ringed his head with a crown of beaten copper, and hung an ornate golden crucifix from his belt. Zungu fingered the last with pride and looked Ingonyama square in the eyes.

"Once I was the finest wizard in the land." His eyes were obsidian, black and sharp, cold and brittle like the thin layer of ice over a watering hole in the winter. "I cured the sick, found the wicked, warded off evil, and drove out the dark forces." That was not how Ingonyama remembered it, but he kept his silence. "In truth I was nothing: A prancing jester for the amusement of a fat king and his fat princes." The Invincible let that, too, pass. "One day a boy came and showed me I was wrong to be there. I had lost touch with the spirit realm, loosened my hold on the ancestors, and allowed my well of magic to dry up." Wails went up from the crowd, and a drum beat gentle consolation.

It's all a ritual, Ingonyama realized. He does this often. Ingonyama refused to be drawn into the elaborate atmosphere of mysticism. Jojo shifted uneasily, but Ingonyama stilled him with a look. Jobe's Mandlakazi did nothing to hide his terror, but Ingonyama could not sense any danger yet.

Zungu went on. "I was ejected from the court and sentenced to death. I murdered two Invincibles with nothing but my hands and teeth." The drum beat faster. "I fled to my home in the wilderness, knowing I should never see the royal courts again. I raged and raged at fate, but all things are with a purpose!"

"One day I came upon this very forest, and I found peace with a wandering Portuguese man named Father Juan." A sigh of contentment rose up from the crowd. "He was a gentle man, quiet and pure. Juan was a shepherd seeking a flock, and I was like a lost lamb." Another sigh. "He taught me things, wondrous things about the one true God, and all the things he had done to help mankind. Then it occurred to me who I am, and what I must do." The crowd became silent.

"I listened to his words and found salvation. I read his books and learned knowledge. I knew who I was and what my destiny was."

"Who were you?" Many murmured, without any cohesion or unity. He held up a hand and the crowd fell quiet.

"I am the son of the one true God. I am Jesus Christ."

"Who is Jesus Christ?" It seemed a ridiculous name, and Ingonyama found he could not pronounce it correctly. The Zulu tongue just did not easily form words that did not end in vowels.

Zungu tilted his head to one side, birdlike, and spoke with the innocence of a child. "Long ago the son of God came to the white men; he was called Jesus Christ. He told them that the ancestors go to a wonderful place after they die if they follow simple rules." Despite himself, Ingonyama was intrigued. He leaned against a tree with arms crossed, trying to look indifferent as the warlock went on. "But there is a problem, my young Invincible. Can you guess what that problem is? The problem is that no one in the Land of the People of Heaven has ever heard of this son of God, unless it's from the thin lips of a balding white man who tells us we cannot marry more than one woman, and we cannot kill a man without first letting him speak his case. We cannot, cannot, cannot. What kind of a teaching is a list of cannots?"

"I do not understand what you mean by the son of God. Every man is a descendant of Nkulukulu," Jojo said. His father had been an isangoma. In the time it took to blink in surprise, Zungu had crossed the five paces separating him from Jojo and slapped the Invincible hard across the face. Jojo set his jaw and swung his head back to face the wizened little man, but he remained still.

"Nkulukulu is a type of devil!" Zungu eyed the young man as if he himself might be a demon as well.

"He made the world. Did the devil make the world?" Ingonyama tried to sound reasonable. Who does this little wizard think he is? Nkulukulu, the Great Great One in the sky, the god with one thousand eyes who sees everything, had made the world, and then his chosen people, the People of Heaven, the Zulu, had come down to claim this world and everything on it. Everyone knew that.

"Cha!" Zungu cried, and the crowd echoed him. "Cha!" Cried Zungu's voice from behind Ingonyama, but the old man still stood before him.

"Cha!" Said Zungu's voice above his head. "Cha!" Proclaimed Zungu's voice from between his knees. Only at this point could Ingonyama see that Zungu's mouth was slightly open, though his lips did not move. He did not know how it was being done, but Ingonyama knew that this was all a trick.

"Old man," He said firmly. "I am not here to pray to you. I am not here to seek your council. I am here to kill you." He pulled in a lung full of air to cry uSuthu, but Zungu began speaking rapidly, twitching his face and turning his head from side to side.

"Kill me? Kill me he says? Do you know that is what the Romans did to Jesus Christ?" He pronounced Romans and Jesus Christ very carefully, and both words would have been gibberish if Ingonyama had tried to repeat them. "That is the problem! That is why the Whites are stronger: They heard Jesus' words, and we did not," He was ranting now, a trickle of froth appeared from the corner of his mouth.

"Do you know why he died? Because his was a message of love!" He said the Portuguese word, amor. "Love, what is that? The Zulu do not even have a word that means love, so how could we follow the Son of God's teachings?" Zungu was doing a clumsy giya now, jumping up and down, spinning and slapping at imaginary demons all around him. The crowd was forming a wordless background chorus, accompanying each spin with a rise or fall in pitch.

"That is why I'm here. That is why I am Jesus Christ! God got it wrong the last time, because who understands what love means?" Ingonyama admitted he did not. "So my father, God, sent me to teach the Zulu with a word we all understand." He locked his eyes on Ingonyama and the Invincible saw madness swimming in their pain-filled depths. He saw the shock and loss of his discharge from the royal courts; he saw the pain of his fall from grace, his crushed self-esteem.

Within those eyes, tinged yellow with malarial influence and beginning to go milky white with cataracts or tropical opthamalia, Ingonyama saw a madness that would consume the world, and a sanity that could bring the madness to fruition. Ingonyama had stepped into a nest of serpents, and he was glad that it was his duty to kill all the young and crush the unhatched eggs.

"Death!" He had forgotten Zungu Nkulu was still speaking, and the word sent a shiver down his spine. "You see!" He cried with joy. "Even you understand death. Love is a word, and it means nothing. Death is real and now and personal. God, my father, built it into each of us to know what death is, and it will all start with you."

Ingonyama wet his lips and said, "How's that?"

"If I kill the Tsonga tribute, the Mandlakazi will flock to my victory and leave Zibhebhu to pull at his crooked head ring! If the Mandlakazi revolt, Cetshwayo will send every spear he can muster to oppose us, but with the Mandlakazi bloodlust and my father by my side we shall smite the heathen." There was another nonsense word, and Ingonyama wondered how much of it was from the Portuguese priest whose cross Zungu fingered so reverently, and how much of it was the product of Zungu's broken imagination.

"With the Zulu at my command I shall take the Swazi, and then the Pedi, the Basuto, the Matabele and the Boer. With those beneath me I shall take the British from Africa and drive them back to their old white queen. With Africa I shall take the world, and then with the world I shall march into Heaven." As if a great prophet had spoken, the people began repeating his words to themselves in hushed awe.

"So it all starts with me?" Ingonyama felt a laugh coming up but forced it down. The occasion was too solemn.

"You shall be a martyr to a cause greater than you ever imagined!" More gibberish words.

"You know what I think?" Ingonyama did not wait for an answer. "I think you're a crazy old man who lives in a swamp. I think you want to go back to the royal court, and this is how your broken head thinks it will happen. You are no wizard, old man. You know it, and I know it. My name is Ingonyama kaJama. I'm Mbeki kaJama's brother, the boy who proved you're a fake."

The three of them watched as the madness worked its way in little waves up from Zungu's heart, through his neck, to his face. Zungu swallowed twice, trying to keep the froth from appearing in his mouth again and failing. He took one step towards them, and Jobe's Tsonga speaker finally broke. "uSuthu!" he cried, then a spear flew out of the crowd and took him in the belly, toppling him forward with a mewling gurgle. The crowd that only a moment before had been a reverent chorus turned ugly. From nowhere spears and clubs appeared, and many of the women and children were filtering to the edge of the glen.

"Back!" Ingonyama hissed, Jojo guarding his back as they retreated towards the forest path. The wind in the trees had stopped, and everything had a dreamlike silence to it.

"Kill them!" Zungu's voice broke the silence, and his worshippers leapt to obey. Jojo and Ingonyama found themselves an island in a sea of armed men. Ingonyama brained one with his war club, and then reversed his stroke to catch another under the chin; blood rushing over the man's lips as he bit through his tongue. Still using the war club --The packed mass was too tight for his spear-- Ingonyama put it into the throat of one man and then broke its head off against another's shoulder.

"Jojo!" He called as he pulled Jobe's revolver out of his loincloth.

"Yebho!" His friend called, still fighting against the tightly packed fanatics on his side.

'Follow me!" Without any further warning Ingonyama put the pistol into the face of the man between him and Zungu and pulled the trigger. In the tree-lined clearing the gunshot sounded like an explosion, and a path cleared between him and the warlock. Trusting Jojo to follow him and keep his back clear, he ran towards the self-proclaimed son of God with pistol raised.

Zungu began singing something in Portuguese, and just as Ingonyama pulled the trigger a man threw himself into the line of fire and went down like a child's straw doll. Seeing the threat to their god, the crowd drew close again, and Ingonyama shot three more men to try and open a space. He felt a sharp piece of steel graze the small of his back, and he spun towards the spear wielder and put the last bullet into his face.

With a push and a shove he worked his way through the crowd to where Zungu stood stock still, singing his hymn. There were no more bullets in the gun, but Ingonyama grabbed it by the barrel and swung it like a club into Zungu's knee. Without a sound, the little man toppled over. Clumsy with haste, Ingonyama snatched up that great golden cross from Zungu's belt and threw it inside the largest of the nearby huts.

Pain shot through his ankle and he looked down to see Zungu biting deep into his flesh. The press was still too great to use his spear to good effect, so he shot his other foot out into Zungu's groin and the wizard released the ankle from his bloodstained teeth.

"Time to go, Jojo!"

"Yebho!" Leaving Zungu's prostrate form behind a wall of his followers, the two fell back with much opposition. The crowd's more enthusiastic members lay dead or dying, and most of the rest had gone to fetch their wizard weapons.

"uSuthu!" Ingonyama and Jojo took turns shouting it as they ran down the trail, following the groove. Soon they heard the answering calls and knew help was on the way.

Above him on the fighting platforms, Zungu's forest sentinels readied a calabash stuffed with gunpowder. Respectful of the temperamental fuse, they lit it with care and a muttered prayer before throwing it down at the intruders below.

The explosion was a muffled thump of black smoke, but long splinters were driven off the trunk of a tree and filled the air around the Invincibles, throwing them to the ground. Ingonyama shook his head at the ringing in his ears, feeling the sting of a dozen small cuts. "Are you hurt?" Ingonyama coughed.

"Yebho." Jojo was slick with blood, but he struggled to his feet, and they took cover behind a tree.

Outside the forest Jobe stood with the waiting warriors. He missed the comforting weight of his revolver, and regretted giving it to Ingonyama. Jobe knew his father would have spies among the Mandlakazi, and that his act of generosity would be reported and punished.

"uSuthu!" He heard it faint and muffled through the trees. Jobe did not stir, wondering if he could somehow keep the reinforcements from going to Ingonyama and Jojo's aid. The Tsonga speaker was no great loss, and the death of the two Invincibles would please his father, but he knew it would be impossible: The Invincibles would not stand by, and the Mandlakazi were as spoiling to rid the trade route of the bandits as the Tsonga tribute was. Besides, in his heart of hearts Jobe did not think he had enough iron to be the son his father wanted.

Again he heard 'uSuthu,' followed this time by a thunderclap of noise and a flicker of light. The men behind him stirred, no holding them back now. Jobe turned to them and raised his assegai. "Follow the groove in the ground. Take no prisoners!"

The Zulu moved forward at the jog trot, and Jojo joined their song:

"He is a Lion! He is a Lion!

He is even better than that:

He is a Hippopotamus!

Master of his world, killer of the careless,

whose gut is huge, and penis pendulous!"

Inside the forest Ingonyama smiled as the song filtered through the trees, muffled from time to time by the thump of exploding calabashes: It was Jama's favourite song, and the inspiration for his name. He called out for his men to watch for danger from above, and waited for them to filter up to his position.

"Well?" Jobe threw himself behind a nearby tree.

"Jojo and I took some of them at the warlock's kraal. Since we've gotten on this trail we haven't killed one, but they're using a lot of gunpowder." As if to emphasize his point another calabash bomb went off somewhere in the forest. The wails of a wounded man cut through even the deadening walls of strangler figs. "I'm afraid we lost your man."

"That's not what I was asking." Jobe set his jaw. "Do you still have my pistol?" Ingonyama tossed it over to the petty prince. Above him he heard a musket go off, then another, then another and another.

"How many muskets do they have?" Jobe asked. Ingonyama pulled up his assegai, making sure the shiny surface had not been marred by anything, and then stuck it out to reflect what was happening on the far side of the tree. He watched as teams of men worked up on the platform, firing and loading.

"Twelve muskets, but only four marksmen on that platform. How many platforms are there?" The sound of bombs and musket shots throughout the forest told him little, except that he did not have control of this battlefield. With a guilty rush he wished he had brought Mbeki.

"Sompisi?" Jojo murmured again, trying to be quiet enough that Jobe would not hear the wounded man offer Ingonyama suggestions.

"Not yet. It's our one surprise--"

"Zungu!" Someone shouted, and the firing above stopped. Boiling up from every trail in the forest, men ran forward with spears and clubs and axes.

"uSuthu!" Ingonyama called, and the Tsonga tribute and its Mandlakazi escort rose to meet the charge. The fighting was heavy, as all of Zungu's followers not in the trees had been committed to this human wave: Old men, young boys, even a few girls had come forward with kitchen utensils or farm implements. An old paunchy man appeared in Ingonyama's path and the Invincible thrust his spear into his neck.

Hot blood rushed over Ingonyama's arm and the cloying stickiness of it excited him. Ingonyama's other hand held an ax, and before he could draw his assegai out of the old man he had used the axe haft to parry a strike. He reversed his stroke and broke another man's arm. His enemies used hoes and throwing spears crudely shortened to work in the confines of the forest; his axe ruled them all.

"Jojo!" He called, and the sounds of carnage shifted as Jojo worked his way from the wall of fanatics to reach his induna's side. "See how the rest of the men are doing!" Jojo gave a quick, 'Yebho, Nkosi' and ran off down the line, clutching his bleeding side whenever a muscle rebelled at his activity.

Zungu commanded more than the two hundred bandits Jobe had predicted, but they were poorly armed, poorly trained, and their faith in a victory could only last so long against the workman-like butchery the Invincibles were performing. By the time Jojo made his way back, the first fanatics at the back of the melee were drifting away from the action and back into the warren of passages and trails through the fig stand.

"We've lost twenty or thirty of ours and Jobe's. They've lost two or three times that. I think it's time for Sompisi." Having made his report, Jojo did not wait for a reply but rushed into the fighting again, disappearing behind a wall of fanatics that he soon reduced to a floor.

"Zungu!" Came the cry from above, and the men on the ground melted back into the foliage. High-pitched screams flew through the air, followed by cries of pain and protest. Arrows, a weapon unused in Southern Africa since the bushman and their primitive bows had been driven from the plains by the advancing blacks, rained down from the fighting platforms with a ferocity which was not belied by the whistle attached to the shaft of each. The shrill scream was terrifying and did nothing to reduce the arrow's impact as it flew into a man or into the ground and trees around him.

"Take cover!" Ingonyama called, throwing himself behind the nearest tree between him and the platforms. Of course he had heard of arrows, distantly, but they had long been rejected as a tool of war. A warrior with a big ox hide shield could have stood all day behind his portable wall, impervious to such flimsy missiles. Against a warrior with a shield only a steel-tipped throwing spear stood any chance of doing damage, but here in the dense brush throwing spears were as awkward as shields, and the unexpected archer reigned supreme. Ingonyama longed for the shields his men had left in the plain behind him.

"Ingonyama?" The voice was soft, and he turned to see Jojo lying out in the open; one of the arrows was through his shoulder, and the barbed head had burrowed into the earth. He was pinned there.

"Stay still!" He ordered. If the archers above learned they had a target out in the open, Jojo would find himself riddled with arrows. "Time for Sompisi." Ingonyama had not meant to say it aloud, but from another tree over to his right he heard Jobe's reply.

"Yebho! Sompisi would definitely be a good idea right now!"

"Mbejane!" He called the signal. Jobe took it up, and soon all of the Invincibles, Humbler of Kings and Mandlakazi who could still breathe were shouting out the dead Invincible's name. "Mbejane! Mbejane! Mbejane!"

Deep in the woods behind Zungu Nkulu's royal quarters Sompisi cocked his ear to the new sound. "Is that Mbejane?" He asked one of the Invincibles. The man made a gesture of indecision; it was the fifth time Sompisi had asked that question. He was like a cattle dog tied to the gate post of a homestead. He wanted to be free to run, but he was confined until someone took his leash off. Sompisi opened his mouth and tilted his head for better hearing; 'Mbejane!' rewarded his effort.

"This is it! Light them!" Twenty men took their dry bundles of grass, dipped them into the jars of fat and animal tallow, and then lit them from a series of small fires prepared for the purpose.

"uSuthu?" He suggested.

"uSuthu!" They replied. Carrying the pots and torches with them, they advanced along the serpentine trails at the jog trot. Within five hundred paces they were passing through the deserted royal quarters, and one of the pots was emptied onto the huts. Sompisi touched his brightly burning torch to each of the beehive structures, and soon they were running through a forest much more cheerful by the firelight. After a while they came across the deserters of the fanatic impi and cut them down without mercy, sparing no one. Over each warm corpse they cried, 'Ngadla!' before running forward again.

Through the undergrowth they moved, still carrying the pots and torches. Within another hundred paces they came across the rest of the fanatics hiding behind trees and foliage, opposite Ingonyama's position. Sompisi gave sharp barking orders, and his men mowed down the exhausted and wounded men who turned to face them. By the time they reached Ingonyama they were so flushed with success that Sompisi and his men were rocked back at the carnage they discovered.

The battlefield between the gray trunks had never been more than a dozen paces wide, and the bodies were scattered in heaps and depressions. Powder smoke hung a foot above ground level in a putrid fog, and arrows were stuck into trees, the ground, the corpses, and the living. Everywhere there was silence, but Sompisi wisely ordered his men into cover. "Nkosi?" Sompisi let his voice drift across the open spaces.

"Yebho!" Ingonyama replied.

"We have cleared everything in front of you; why are you hiding?" The Invincible braced himself for the worst, his dread palpable. This forest was haunted; Sompisi was sure of it.

"Look above you." Ingonyama was watching the men on the fighting platforms as they broke out their reserves of arrows, gathered more calabash bombs, loaded their muskets, and started carrying heavy baskets from the crotches of trees to rest nearer the edge of the platforms. They were rallying, and from up there they could pick off his men one by one. The sulfur of the crudely made gunpowder burned his nostrils, and he spluttered for a moment.

"Fire..." He whispered. "Sompisi! How much of the fats and oils have you used?" Ingonyama looked at the trees around him; the figs were green and would not burn well, but the dead wood within the heart of each tangled knot would be dry as kindling.

"Almost none of it, Nkosi!"

"Burn the trees that are holding up the platforms! Go!" Hearing his words, the defenders of the platforms stopped their preparations and resumed a murderous level of fire. The forest trembled at the banshee shriek of arrows, the roar of musketry, and a new sound of heavy weights falling to the ground. Zungu's blacksmiths had fashioned heavy iron darts with a round, spiked head and heavy fins; they were as long as a man's forearm and dropped from above they landed with twice the force of a hard-swung war club. Most dropped uselessly to the ground, but the groans of newly wounded and the crunch of bones meant that some fell true.

Sompisi and his men rushed against the boles of the trees, emptying their pots onto anything combustible before touching the wood with their torches. Above the Invincibles Zungu's men let loose with a set of rockets, but their whooshing and hissing did little to dissuade Sompisi, and wherever the rockets touched down, new fires started up from the splattered paraffin fuel. A man next to Sompisi took a musket ball through the kidney and dropped to his knees. Another to his right took a dart directly on the crown of his head, and the heavy metal projectile did not stop falling until it was resting on the inside of his jaw bone, the top of his skull had crushed his brain into jelly.

Ingonyama watched this terrible courage and decided he could not hide safe behind his tree while his men died. Giving an encouraging call to any who wanted to follow his example, he rushed from behind his cover and snatched up a half-full pot from the fingers of a dying friend. He threw it against a nearby tree and someone put a torch to it. Behind him he heard a fig tree begin to pop as the water in its green wood turned to steam from the heat all around it. The forest was on fire, and the men on the fighting platforms were trapped on top of a funeral pyre. Their only way down was grass ladders, climbing down burning ropes into a burning world.

"Sompisi! Jobe! Time to go! Take all of our wounded!" Ingonyama snapped the protruding shaft from Jojo's shoulder and lifted him up until he was balanced on his induna's broad shoulders.

"What about their wounded?" Sompisi asked, throwing the last pot onto an already blazing fire.

"Let them cook."

Ingonyama watched as Zungu stumbled into view, seeing his shattered dreams burn. He was leaning on a stick, and Ingonyama felt a cool rush of hatred for the crippled little man. Zungu watched him with eyes glazed, the copper band on his head cast eerie reflections of the fires around him. His mouth opened and he said his final words, "Your family shall find no happiness in this day! I have sent a sickness on the world, and it is your fault!" Ingonyama shook his head at the feeble curse and turned away. Zungu Nkulu was a madman, and no Zulu could help feeling sorry for one in the grip of insanity. Ingonyama wished him a speedy death, but he was too busy to deliver it himself.

His men streamed out of the woods carrying their wounded with them. Before they could collapse into the soft grass, Ingonyama ordered them into a loose perimeter around the forest. No one would be allowed to escape, and anyone who left the quickly growing inferno would be put to the spear. It was not long before the first trickle of survivors began to filter out, and his men killed them from a distance with throwing spears.

The fire grew, spreading from thicket to thicket, jumping any natural openings or breaks in the forest. The rainy season was still only just beginning, and the forest was parched. In a month it would have been impossible to light a campfire under that canopy, but today the entire forest burned hot and fierce. Ingonyama watched as a blackened and charred man began pulling himself with his hands from the edge of the forest. His feet had burned off and his legs were clearly broken and cooked into uselessness. The fingers on his hands had melted together, and an inhuman caw escaped from his ruined throat. He was the crawling dead; it was only a matter of time. Two of Jobe's men looked to Ingonyama and he nodded his order.

The two men should have finished the man at once, but Ingonyama had only ordered them to kill him, he had given no instructions as to the method. One of them had snatched up a fallen bow and the other had gathered some arrows, and together they gamely tried shooting the poor burned wretch from a distance of fifty paces. After a dozen shots one arrow finally thumped through what had been the man's thigh, but there were no nerves in the cooked haunch to let the man know he was pinned to the earth, and he continued to try and pull himself along.

Sickened by the man's suffering, Ingonyama snatched up a throwing spear and put it right between the sightless dried up eyes. There was a spasm in what little of the poor wretch's body still was able to respond to the dead brain's commands. With relief, Ingonyama heard the cawing stop and saw the head hang forward to bury the dead man's face in the dirt. His hair had burned away and the white skull peeked through the redness in places, but even from a distance Ingonyama could clearly see the copper band that had been Zungu's crown.

Chapter 26

Ingonyama watched long into the night as the fire raged. Bambatha had taken the flat of his ax to the little part of the shaft sticking out of Jojo's chest, and the moans of protest as Bambatha tapped the shaft from one side and pulled the arrowhead from the other split the night.

There were more wounded than there were healthy, and Ingonyama knew the entire rainy season and all of its ill humors would come and go before he could return here to collect them. Many more of his friends were going to die. He reached back and massaged the shallow spear wound in the small of his back, ignoring the more serious bite mark on his ankle. They were both minor compared to the damage he had endured only half a moon ago.

"Ingonyama," Bambatha's arms were red up to the elbows in other men's blood.

"Yebho."

"He's going to live." Bambatha's tone implied nothing, neither happiness, nor pride, nor even relief.

"Yebho," was Ingonyama's only reply. He was too numbed to show his gratitude, and he would not have shown any if he could. A commander must never play favourites with the men under his command. He was glad Jojo would live to see the next dawn, but he wanted all of his men to have the same fate. His eyes returned to the forest, and he wondered if he had been selfish.

He had gone in there to seek his fortune, and he had found it, though it would be many moons before today's work came to fruition. By going in alone he had set a plan in motion that would end with Nandhi marrying him, but at what cost? Seventy-five of his men and a hundred Mandlakazi had gone into that forest; only a hundred men in total had come out again, and thirty of those might well die before tomorrow. Of the rest of the surviving wounded, how many would survive the malaria, the fevers, the gangrene, the dysentery, the pneumonia, and the dozen other diseases that the rainy season and the wounds would bring? Ingonyama mulled all this over, working it out in his head, trying to pretend that the numbers were not men with families.

He had nothing to be pleased about, but he felt himself fighting his lopsided grin and he hated himself for it. I'm going to marry Nandhi, and I've won that today. He would not sleep that night, and only part of the problem was his nightmares. He would wait for the dawn and spend the time between then and now deciding if he was as monstrously selfish as he felt at that moment.

The smile finally appeared on his face, and he sternly removed it. He pinched his thigh until he winced at the punishment. He ordered himself to feel bad for the hundred who were dead or were going to die, but a part of him acknowledged that even if he had not gained anything from today's butchery, he would be proud of what he and his command had done. The firelight was poor illumination for soul searching, but as the night wore on Ingonyama found his peace.

The next day they buried the Zulu warriors as their custom dictated. A man killed on the battlefield did not need the elaborate burial of a man who died at home: The dead man's face was covered with his shield, or, if there was one nearby, his body was thrown into an ant bear hole. The bodies of the enemy dead, those that had not been burned in the fire, had their bellies cut open to allow their souls to escape and were then left for the buzzards. By noon all the wounded had been left at nearby homesteads and a much reduced Tsonga tribute party set out again.

Ingonyama spent the rainy season at the Great Place of the King of kwaTsonga, but his mind was always on the stand of strangler figs. As soon as the last thunderheads had disappeared and the rich black soil of Africa put out its first tender green shoots Ingonyama was off again. He politely ignored the King's entreaties to stay as long as he wanted. He did not want to marry one of the Tsonga Nkosi Nkulu's daughters; he wanted to marry Nandhi, and he had a date with destiny.

For all his rush, Ingonyama could not speed his progress much. Hundreds of Tsonga porters carried boxes and bales, pots and baskets, crates, cases, casks and barrels, bolts and bundles of all description over rough terrain. No man could be expected to run day in and day out with half of his body weight balanced on his head, shoulders, and back. Added to this, some of the porters' sons drove cattle behind the procession, and the herd needed time each day to water and graze. To further slow Ingonyama down, once he was back in Mandlakazi territory Jobe and the men of Zibhebhu's personal ibutho finally left Ingonyama's company, and he could no longer convince the porters to set even a brisk walking pace without a number of warriors to provide an example.

Gradually they made it to the ashes of the fig stand and a joyous reunion ensued. Jojo and a dozen others had survived their bouts with malaria and dysentery, and Ingonyama gratefully thanked the heads of the homesteads that had taken them in. Ingonyama called for a day of rest, and the porters gratefully set down their burdens. No sooner had he said it then he set off with Jojo in tow for the burned out ruins of the forest.

"What?" Jojo finally asked as they walked between the charred stumps, often calf deep in ash and mud.

"You'll see." Ingonyama did not want to explain himself until he was sure he had not dreamed of his actions in the clearing. He had gone into the forest on that fateful day three moons ago with only one objective, and though he was sure he had accomplished it, he needed the proof.

"Can I have a hint?" Jojo looked around at the remnants of the forest. When he had been here the last time it had been difficult to see more than a spear length in any direction. Today he could see all the way to the horizon. The fire had reduced all the trees to stumps and had even burned the grassy clearing around the forest for a hundred paces in all directions. From his adopted homestead Jojo had watched the still smoking ashes receive the torrent of rain that had finally put out the smoldering fires.

"You want a hint? How old are you?" Ingonyama felt something hard under foot and he stooped down to wipe away the ashes. It was a crude and patchy area of terra cotta.

"Now who's acting like a child?" Jojo chuckled as Ingonyama dropped to his hands and knees, pushing the ashes out of the way with gentle caresses. "What is that?"

"This is what's left of the packed clay floor of one of the huts." The heat had baked the clay floor, and he cleared it away reverently but did not find what he was looking for.

"Very interesting." Jojo was not a good liar, but Ingonyama did not care. He was up and moving through the ashes again, pacing about in gradually increasing spirals from the first hut. His foot struck brittle clay again, and he lowered himself down to clear away the ashes. They were wet and cloying, and they caked his legs and chest and arms. He heard the teeth-jarring scrape of a heavy metal weight against the fired floor, and with excitement he redoubled his efforts.

"If you want to play in the dirt, there's a pile of cow manure behind the homestead I stayed at. The herder has an idea of using it for fertilizer." Jojo was not usually so talkative, but he felt like an idiot standing there as Ingonyama dug through the ruins of Zungu's royal quarters.

"There!" Ingonyama had cleared away the entire circular floor; prominently in the center lay Zungu's great Catholic crucifix. The heat had ruined the fine workmanship, leaving a crude lumpy cross-shaped gold stain on the floor. The term 'X marks the spot' would have been foreign to Ingonyama, but he knew that this cross marked the future he had fantasized about.

"What?" Jojo heard Ingonyama's excitement, and his hand tightened instinctively on his spear.

"Do you know what this is?"

"The floor of a hut?"

"Not just any hut; Zungu's hut." Ingonyama waited for enlightenment to dawn in Jojo's eyes but decided he did not have the patience. "I threw that gold cross into Zungu's hut." There was still no understanding in his friend's trusting brown eyes. "Zungu thought of himself as the chief of his own country, right?"

"Yebho," Jojo was confused. What is Ingonyama so happy about? We've found a dead madman's hut.

"What do chiefs bury under the floors of their huts?"

"Their wealth-- Their wealth!" Jojo had not put it all together, but at least Ingonyama could see he was excited now.   "And how long was Zungu out here?"

"Three years?" Jojo was not sure of that, but it was something like that.

"So do you think there might be, oh, I don't know... Two hundred cows worth of trade goods under our feet?" Ingonyama's lopsided smile could have turned night into day.

"You're going to marry Nandhi," Jojo laughed.

"I'm going to marry Nandhi." Ingonyama grabbed Jojo by the arm, and they spun around doing a mad, merry dance. There was joy in their hearts, and in that moment it seemed all was right with the world. It never occurred to Ingonyama that Zungu's final curse might come true, or that the future under his feet would be one of misery and pain.

Chapter 27

Ingonyama could not put his finger on it but something was wrong. It was a creeping sensation down the back of his neck, a heaviness in his stomach that he could not explain. All around him the laughter and rough-housing of children was subdued; women failed to sing in the freshly planted mealie fields; even the cows seemed scattered and depressed on the slopes of ripening sweetveld. The drizzle did not help. The rainy season was lasting longer than usual, and the sky above was a leaden sheet providing a steady shower of icy water all day.

His calloused feet squished in the sodden earth, and his thighs were soaked from the tall wet grass. The battered shield over his head deflected the worst of the downpour, but he was drenched and cold, and his scars ached at the chill. The occasional curse behind him heralded his men's mood: They slipped and skittered through the mud without the boisterous good humour he had come to expect from them.

Despite it all Ingonyama was happy. He had done it. He had the bride price. He had the glory. All he needed was the easily acquired head ring and he could marry Nandhi. "What a wife she'll be..."

"What Nkosi?" One of his men asked.

"Nothing." He imagined himself building his homestead in his father's valley with Nandhi at his side. He would not marry any other women. Nandhi was all he would ever need. She could sing, make him laugh, she was not afraid to work, and the ancestors knew she could cook. He could be fat and prosperous with her. First marriage, then secure the kingdom for his king, and then a happy life herding cows and making babies.

Ingonyama heard a clumsy man fall behind him. His warriors were clad in their fur karosses to hold off the worst of the damp, but their heavy loads had a precarious balance, and the soft slippery ground underfoot caused their stoic attitude towards hardship to slip. Muttered curses against the ancestors and spirits who would put such a quagmire between them and their home grew steadily more impassioned and imaginative as they shuffled through the uncomfortable world.

Between the vanguard and the rearguard the Tsonga tribute was even more miserable than its warrior escort: At the beginning of the day's trek their foreman had suggested it would be too much bother to get out their blankets to hold out a quick shower, and now they could not stop on the march to unpack them. Hundreds of eyes glowered at the back of the foreman's head. If this had not been the last day of their journey his bed roll would have been viciously kicked in the night.

"Tsonga tribute!" Ingonyama let his voice carry, waiting until he had the attention of the soaked and bedraggled men. "Let's go home!" He had been saving the command until the palisade of oNdini appeared on the horizon, and now he pointed it out with his spear. The rain was still damping down their enthusiasm, and only a ragged cheer managed to come up from the group. Ingonyama decided that would not do. "Jojo?"

"Yebho, Nkosi?" His friend appeared at his elbow.

"I think they need a song to keep them warm."

"Yebho, Nkosi." Jojo grinned with big square teeth. He had not liked the subdued nature of the normally rowdy company either. With the deep base notes of the trained chorus leader Jojo soon had the men singing in two rounds with harmonies, detailing their fight with Zungu Nkulu. By the time the warriors were on the seventh verse they were passing through oNdini's gates, and their song led people to abandon the shelter of their huts to welcome the Tsonga tribute home.

Inyati's procession entered the parade square with some of their expected dash; the rearguard closing up with the vanguard to strut for the benefit of the growing crowd. The Invincibles who had stayed with the King during the rainy season fell in to either side of the new arrivals as an honour guard. Ingonyama nodded at friends and grinned triumphantly at rivals.

"Ingonyama!" One of them called.

"Yebho."

"Your men are still armed!" Only sticks were allowed within Cetshwayo's Great Place of oNdini.

"My men are all Invincibles." He left the man spluttering from reasons beyond the rain and marched serenely towards the royal quarters. Until moments ago half of his command had been from the Humbler of Kings ibutho, but when Ingonyama said they were Invincibles it became a fact. The young men visibly puffed up at their new importance and followed their induna proudly onto the packed earth of the main parade square, still carrying their spears as was an Invincible's duty.

The rain stopped as Cetshwayo appeared from the royal quarters. The sweet smell of damp earth blanketed the stronger odours of cow manure and human habitation. "I see you, Ingonyama kaJama." It was hard to look anywhere else: Ingonyama pulled all eyes towards him. Within sight of the gates the Tsonga escort had taken off their karosses and they stood proud and wet, wearing only their civet skin kilts. Ingonyama was most impressive of all, for his scars crisscrossing much of his lower body. He looked like a colossal tree that an inexperienced woodcutter had tried a hundred times to fell while only scratched the surface.

"Bayete, Nkosi Nkulu." Ingonyama knelt before his king. Cetshwayo's advisors, favourites and courtiers all gathered behind their king, but Ingonyama did not understand their postures. They should have been straining forward to hear his report; instead, they hung their heads and did not smile. A depression had gripped the nation, and Ingonyama could not fathom its cause.

In the onlooking crowd Mbeki swallowed the lump in his throat and tried to be happy: His brother was home; Inyati had almost recovered from his injuries; Jama had not suffered too terribly in the disaster, and within the year he would join the king's new regiment, the Flycatcher Birds. It should be a joyous day. The first in a long time.

He watched from the crowd as his brother approached the throne, marveling at how five moons had hardened the Invincible; no one would have guessed Ingonyama's real age. His spear handle was worn so smooth from constant handling that he had carved notches into it to keep it from slipping out of his hand. His shield was solid black, but the edges were chipped and frayed, the bindings had loosened, and the water pouring down from the sodden genet skin at the top showed every dent and scratch on its faded and worn surface.

"What is he doing?" Inyati hissed from behind him. He still needed a stick for support, and he could not push through the crowd or stand on tiptoe for a better view.

"He's talking to the king... He's presenting his shield!" Mbeki doubted he could have continued narrating through so broad a grin, but fortunately Ingonyama and Cetshwayo were speaking loud enough for their voices to carry.

"I see your shield, Ingonyama." Cetshwayo was keeping his voice neutral.

"My King, the Invincibles need new shields." He steeled himself. "Their new commander asks for new shields." There were some intakes of breath from the otherwise solemn advisors. Ntsingwayo flashed a quick smile before regaining his composure. Ingonyama had declared himself for the vacant position of King's Champion.

"Hamu?" Cetshwayo turned to his cousin; according to the tradition of granting shields, a great man of the nation must step forward and accuse Ingonyama of cowardice; then argue the point to the crowd until the prospective commander either won over the crowd or withdrew his claim. Mbeki winced at Cetshwayo's choice: Hamu would not make things easy for Ingonyama.

The plump-faced man stepped out from the advisers to stand between the King and the induna of the Tsonga tribute. "Why should we grant new shields to the Invincibles?" Hamu began, his voice carrying to every ear in the ikhanda. "What has he done with the old ones? Did he fight Boers? Did he fight Swazi? What did he do, except go and come back? He is young and foolish and thinks that shields aren't earned! I ask you," He did not ask anyone, "Why in the name of the ancestors should we give new shields to cowards!" The crowd, already sullen, grumbled among themselves.

"I haven't finished!" Ingonyama stood, letting his voice carry across oNdini's parade ground. "My shields shall not only be new. They shall be white!" White shields were the symbols of married men. Ingonyama had just promised the Invincibles that under his leadership they would be allowed to wed. Each of the royal guardsmen tensed, their minds flying to the daughters of neighbours and friends. Mbeki laughed aloud, knowing Hamu would be spitting blood.

"I ask what you've done, and all you can reply is to beg for more?" Spittle flew from Hamu's lips in apoplectic rage. He was trapped into arguing against allowing the Invincibles' to marry, making enemies of the armed men at court. His temple pulsed and his little beard shook at his impotent fury. Had he been fifteen years younger and a good deal fitter he would have strangled Ingonyama. To make matters worse, the eldest son of Jama wanted the head ring so he could marry Hamu's daughter. If Ingonyama got his way, it would be another huge step back for Hamu's position at court.

"Old man," Ingonyama began, and Hamu turned his head as if slapped, for he was not yet fifty. "I have fought a dozen battles for my King, and this one from which I return was the greatest of all." With that he launched into an oration of the events before the rainy season. Behind him his men cried an occasional 'It is true' or 'Yebho, Nkosi!' When he mentioned the Mandlakazi man's aborted raid, the crowd laughed, and Zibhebhu glowered. When he spoke of Jobe commanding the illegal ibutho, Hamu cringed. When his narration reached the strangler fig forest, he began to giya as he spoke.

Ingonyama leapt high off the ground; his lean body snapped his knees up to his chin in mid-air before landing cat-like on the wet packed earth. Remembering some of Uncle Punga's oratorical gestures, he emphasized each event with a thrust of his spear, and threw aside every obstacle in his story with a shove of his shield.

The crowd sucked in their breath with vicarious fear when he mentioned the tokoloshe, then trembled at his parody of Zungu's madness. When he reached the battle Jojo and Sompisi ran forward, leaving their spears behind and taking up their sticks, raising welts and drawing blood from one another, grinning all the time to show it was nothing personal.

"Their weapons were terrible! Fire from the sky!" Mbeki listened with amazement as Ingonyama's men made the whoosh noises of the rockets. "Sticks that screamed!" The shriek of the arrow whistles filled the damp air. "Metal that would kill any man it touched!" Several of the Invincibles looked above them at the imaginary darts and then dropped prone in a pantomime of agony. The crowd groaned as he described the wizard weapons, but Mbeki was too busy trying to imagine how they were made.

"Sompisi, brave Sompisi with the pots of fat, answered my call and fell upon the foe from behind." Sompisi turned to the audience to raise an arm in salute, and Jojo promptly smacked him across the forehead with his stick. The two flew at each other again, and Ingonyama continued to dance as he told the rest of the tale, leaving out only the wealth beneath Zungu's hut. That would be for the king's ears alone.

When at last he was done he stood there panting. "Zungu Nkulu cursed us with his last words, and I laughed in his face. The man walks with the ancestors now, his hair on fire and his crazy eyes unseeing." A roar of approval ripped from every throat. The women ululated and the little boys and girls jumped up and down with excitement.

Hamu shifted his weight from one foot to the other, embarrassed at what ritual now forced him to say. "Is that all?" A hundred years of tradition forced the words out of his mouth.

"It is enough." Cetshwayo's smile was as bright as the sun, and Ingonyama knelt once more to hear his king speak. "Your shields shall be white as the lamb's wool, as white as a cumulus cloud. White as only married men should have." The Invincibles were careful not to break discipline. "Now get up, Ingonyama. The King's Champion kneels to no man, not even me."

As the crowd dispersed Mbeki raced up to his brother and spun him around. "You did it!" He laughed. "We finally have something worth celebrating!"

"What are you talking about?" Ingonyama watched in dismay as his brother's face fell.

"You don't know?"

"Cha, what happened? Is something wrong with Baba?" It was the worst thing he could think of, but his mind had no imagination for bad tidings.

"Ingonyama, since you left half of the cattle in kwaZulu have fallen dead!"

Chapter 28

Inyati could feel the cold shaft of despair rise up through his testicles and gritted his teeth at the taste of bile in his mouth; Ingonyama had come home. He was back, and now Nandhi was beyond him forever. He opened and closed the hand that was not holding his cane, remembering.

The lung disease had swept through the nation's herds, and every Zulu had gone to them. Through war and pestilence, through drought and famine, never had the kingdom felt such despair as when the cattle began to die. Nandhi and Inyati, princess and invalid though they were, could not be prevented from helping.

They had driven the first sick into quarantined paddocks, and then when it was obvious that the infection had reached all of the cows they fed fires throughout the night to keep their bovine charges warm, rubbed ointments onto their hides to aide their breathing, and eventually smoked the meat and prepared the hides of those that died.

Nandhi had been a light in the darkness. The situation was too bleak for her bell-like laughter, but she had done little things to make people's burden easier: She never stopped cooking, running meals out to the men and women in the pastures so they did not need to abandon their work to eat. She threw her voice and spoke on behalf of the sick cows, amusing the children to no end. She never shirked her work because of her royal status, and carried portions of carcass as gracefully as if the fly buzzing meat had been a bouquet of flowers. When all of her other tasks permitted her, she would visit Inyati with a kind word, a joke, or friendly concern for his nicely healing wound.

The Matabele had not rested for weeks. During the day he cared for the cattle, the faithful Chomper always at his heel, and in the night he snuck out of his hut to be with Nandhi. They played silly word games and talked about their families and watched the fires burn down to ashes. They never spoke of Ingonyama, and neither ever mentioned their midnight meetings to Mbeki. It would have been a beautiful courtship, if she had not already been betrothed.

One night they had snuck into the royal quarters, no great trespass for Nandhi but a crime for Inyati, and they had entered the hut which contained the holy inkatha. It had sat there, sheathed in python skin, the very soul of kingdom. Within that coil of twisted grass lay the life essence of every king, along with ashes from every umKhosi bull for seventy years. The thing breathed a holy awe; they had looked down on it and seen immortality.

He had whispered sweet nothings in her ear, and she had laughed her laugh. They had left as quietly as they came, but things were different after that. She was more withdrawn, more reserved. Careful now not to give him a signal, an opening he could use to make her decide between Ingonyama and himself.

What drove him mad, beyond the impossibility of having her, was her obvious desire. She wanted to be with him just as much as he wanted to be with her; he could tell. It was the little things: The looks when she thought he could not see, the special attention heaped upon him, the smile that came to her lips when she was thinking her private thoughts. He could see things from her perspective: She had two eminently suitable suitors.

How cruel was life that he had met her second? That he was recovering from a belly wound while Ingonyama rose to become King's Champion? He was a prince and she was a princess, and if their lives had taken different courses it would have been natural and right for him to claim her. He had dreamed her fiancé would never return to claim her, but now Ingonyama was back, and he would have to accept that.

The Prince of the House of Kumalo leaned on his cane, and saw Ingonyama not as his best friend's brother, but as the enemy of his happiness. Where Inyati stood awkwardly, ever conscious of the pain in his abdomen and the weakness in his limbs, Ingonyama was as tall and strong as ever, boasting scars that made him look powerful without touching his fine looks.

Inyati knew that meeting Ingonyama was the worst thing that ever happened to him. It was Ingonyama who had captured him instead of killing him in the hardest fought duel of that, tired dusty day. By taking him alive Ingonyama had subjected him to Mbejane and all the horror of that geyser of blood welling up from within him, spraying Magema the Healer's face with the hot and sticky matter of his innards. Now it was Ingonyama who was going to marry Nandhi, and there was nothing he could do about it. Inyati ached to hate him, but could not find it in him to do so. That only made it worse.

He could tell just by the change in the air that Nandhi was behind him. The sound of her running feet on the wet-packed earth was torture to his ears. A little giggle escaped her throat as she passed him, and Ingonyama's wide white grin burned his eyes. They almost embraced in public before decorum returned.

"I see you, Ingonyama." She had her back to Inyati quite unintentionally, but he still felt shut out and alone. He almost fell at the pain her words inflicted.

"I see you, Nandhi." Ingonyama's smile was still there, and Inyati watched as she bathed in his affection. In a rush they began gabbling at each other, saying all that had happened to them since last they had seen each other. Inyati stood and brooded, wanting to catch Nandhi's eyes, looking for reassurance that he was not forgotten. He never had the chance. His free hand opened and closed, opened and closed.

The four of them were too occupied with one another to notice, but there was another set of eyes watching closer than any in the circle of friends would have liked.

Hamu leaned against the inner palisade, picking his teeth with a blade of grass. The kaJama brothers and his daughter were talking back and forth; their faces animated as they all tried to speak at once. The Matabele prince leaned on a stick not far off, obviously unhappy. What I would not do to drive a wedge between those four, he thought. It was long past a simple annoyance: As leader of the Invincibles, Ingonyama had catapulted himself into the very heart of royal politics. The incorruptible are always so difficult to manage, Hamu thought. I need a way to deal with that boy.

A man ran up wearing the blue beads of a Hamu messenger. He genuflected halfheartedly, tired from the hard pace and poor weather. Hamu frowned, consciously turning his painful needle stare onto the man. "What?"

"Nkosi, your son is approaching. He shall be here shortly." The messenger bowed again and looked up at the prince expectantly: Hamu's messengers were the best paid of all the private couriers in kwaZulu. Hamu's temper snapped.

"Don't look at me! What sort of reward do you want? My messengers are supposed to be faster than swallows in flight, and yet that monstrosity--" He pointed to the Tsonga tribute unpacking on the far side of the ikhanda. "Beat you here." He cuffed the messenger across the side of the head, but decided that was not enough. "Zokufa?" One of his attendants tossed him a stick, and he smashed the messenger in the face. "Go back to your farm. I am rewarding you by not driving off your cattle! You are dismissed from my service."

The messenger blinked for a moment. The welt from the stick cut across his cheek, over his nose, and up into one eyebrow. He pulled the blue beads from around his neck and dropped them to the ground. "Yebho, Nkosi," He said, then he spat viciously onto the necklace. Hamu only stopped trembling with anger after the man had left the gates of the ikhanda.

Jobe strode through those same gates with all the confidence of a strutting ostrich. Hamu's smoldering gaze did not faze him, nor did the tense stances of his father's retainers. "Baba," He smiled.

"Don't Baba me, Jobe." Hamu was trying to rein in his temper, but he knew he did not have the willpower. No matter, he decided. All the great kings of kwaZulu had possessed explosive tempers. Shaka himself had thousands of people put to death when they did not mourn his mother's death to his satisfaction. Hamu had always liked that story; in fact, he had named Nandhi after Shaka's mother.

"Nkosi?" Jobe arched an eyebrow. He only had to call his father lord when Hamu was especially angry.

"Ingonyama has just received permission for all the Invincibles to marry." Jobe grinned ever so slightly. "Wipe that stupid smile off your face! Do you want to be heir to the king one day, or do you want to find yourself as a minor northern prince?"

Jobe stiffened. He's really mad today, he thought. He never talks about my succeeding him. "What do you want, Nkosi?"

"Look out there. What do you see?" Jobe turned his head and saw Mbeki speaking softly to Ingonyama. Nandhi never took her eyes from Ingonyama's face. Inyati was slightly apart from them, behind Nandhi, opening and closing one of his hands and trying not to scowl.

"I don't know, Ba-- Nkosi."

"That's because you're a fool. I'm surrounded by fools." His father sighed heavily, and Jobe knew Hamu was beginning to calm down. "Let me tell you what you see, Jobe, and let this be yet another example of why you should learn to read lips." Jobe frowned; his father was very proud of his ability to overhear what people were saying at great distances, but when Jobe had once eavesdropped on his father as a little boy he had been beaten until his bottom went purple.

"Mbeki has told his brother that the cattle plague has decimated the herds. Ingonyama asks how that could be. The younger kaJama explains that lung sickness must have spread from cow to cow when Cetshwayo brought all the herds together for the royal coronation, but many in the land blame it on a dark sorcerer. Now Ingonyama is thinking--"

"How do you know what he's thinking, Nkosi?"

"Look at how he stands, idiot. He has one heel back, as if bracing himself. He is thinking, 'Cattle prices will be the highest they have ever been; how can I afford the ridiculously reasonable bride price my future father-in-law demands?'" Hamu's tone was venomous.

"Baba, he can afford the two hundred cattle." Hamu snapped his head around. His needle eyes bored into his son, and Jobe quailed for a moment. "In--Ingonyama recovered the loot Zungu hid in the forest. There must be enough to buy two hundred cows."

Hamu snarled at this news: If he was tied by marriage to Ingonyama, then he would no more be able to kill Ingonyama than kill Jobe. Who would trust a man who killed his own kin? Only a king could murder his own family with impunity, and even then it was the work of tyrants. Hamu knew tyrants died tyrants' deaths. He wanted to be remembered for his wisdom, not his murders. Hamu did not want to spend his old age waiting for the spear in the night. "What do you suggest?" He snapped. He ran his fingers once through his thin beard, then through his thinning hair. This wedding was a disaster.

"What is Inyati so upset about?" Jobe asked, watching the Matabele abruptly give up standing on the outside of the circle. With a great breech of protocol he pushed Mbeki to one side with his cane and stepped into the younger kaJama's place. The circle grew wider to readmit the wizard of kwaZulu; the conversation never faltered.

"Hmm?" Hamu's eyes turned to the Prince of the House of Kumalo, and he knew he saw the solution to his problem. "Jobe, my boy, you have done well!" His son smiled at the rare compliment, but his father's attention was focused on the injured Matabele.

I know that look, Hamu thought. That's desire. What do you want, Inyati? Take care of Ingonyama for me, and you can name your price. "Who do I have following Inyati?" Before anyone could reply he remembered. "Zokufa! Send for Gumpega and get us some beer --Better yet, gin." Hamu had reconsidered his previous decision, recognizing gin now as a great source of patience when he was surrounded by incompetents. "Tell him we have business to conduct. Jobe, stay here with me. I'm going to need you."

Chapter 29

The skins were plentiful; the decimated cattle herds had contained more than enough dead white heifers to supply a hundred white shields. Ingonyama and Mbeki sat carefully on the top of a fence and supervised the shield making process. A black rubber-like ring of fungus and gum had been woven into Ingonyama's hair; it was the head ring, the mark of a man given the king's permission to wed.

Ingonyama touched the head ring unconsciously; he was wearing it ten years earlier than was usual. "Don't hack, cut," He ordered the men below. He had been back at the King's Great Place for days now, but Mbeki still had questions for him.

"So in the middle of a battle you thought to mark the site of Zungu's hut?"

"Hmm? Oh, Yebho. You there! That one has a black spot on it. Are there any black spots on a cloud? Then find a different skin."

"That was clever. So have you bought the cows yet?"

"Yebho, from old Ntsingwayo. Gave me a good deal on them too, probably just wanted to snub Hamu." Ingonyama smiled his lopsided grin but never took his eyes off the shield makers. He had told Cetshwayo of his recovery of Zungu's treasury and the king's eyes had lit up.

Cetshwayo had been struggling throughout the rainy season to find a way to loan Ingonyama the cattle to infuriate Hamu, but the lung sickness had robbed him of any surplus. When his champion offered him twenty percent of the treasure horde, he had almost embraced the man as a brother. Instead he had sent for Ntsingwayo, who had been farsighted enough to bring a few hundred head of cattle to oNdini just in case a wedding would take place. Cetshwayo and Ntsingwayo had long since realized Hamu was at his least dangerous when he was distracted and angry. This wedding would set him off like a barrel of gunpowder.

"Where are you going to build your homestead?"

"You ask a lot of questions. Look! That's the one!" He dropped down from the wall and rushed forward to help drive the brilliantly white cow into the shield yard. Where the rest of the shields were being made from the skins of the lung sickness victims, Ingonyama and Jojo would receive the special magical powers of a shield cut from a live cow.

The King's personal shield maker advanced with a razor sharp blade and bade ten men to hold the animal steady. Fast and efficient, he carved two shields out of the side of the bellowing animal, and everyone stood back as the skinned beast wailed and moaned.

"The longer it goes on like that, the stronger the shield will be," The shield maker assured them. Mbeki felt queasy at the thought of the suffering the animal was undergoing for the sake of magic, but Ingonyama did not seem to have any qualms. The cow eventually succumbed to blood loss, and the men advanced to examine the two perfect ovals of white-haired hide.

"Now I can marry Nandhi," Ingonyama sighed.

Chapter 30

"He can't marry Nandhi." Inyati turned guiltily, startled to hear his inner thoughts spoken aloud by someone emerging from the shadows. "She's beautiful, isn't she?" Jobe pointed with an open hand to the door of his father's hut. Nandhi had been summoned to an audience with her father, and Hamu's son had not needed to wait long before Inyati appeared, loitering always within sight of Hamu's temporary homestead just outside oNdini.

He had been carefully coached by his father in what to do and say, but he was still nervous. If this went off any way but the one his father had planned, Jobe might be in front of Cetshwayo receiving judgment again, and, as Cetshwayo had promised, this time there was a king on the throne.

"Is it that obvious?" Inyati had never forgiven Jobe for the veldt fire, but he was eager to share his feelings, and he had wisely avoided telling Mbeki.

"Wise men say, 'Hope does not kill; I shall live in hope of getting what I seek another day.'" Inyati knew Hamu was offering his support through Jobe, and he had to grit his teeth to resist the temptation to accept.

"You want to speak in proverbs? How about, 'Behold the lizard puffing itself out to make a man.'" It was what was said of criminals who led lives of depravity but tried to go before the executioners with honour.

Jobe ignored the insult. "Another one would be, 'The needy man laughs.' You need something. I am offering it to you, yet you spurn me. Does that lessen your need?" Inyati felt his knees wobble, and he lowered himself down to the ground, setting his cane to one side.

"'Cunning people do not deal with another.'" He regretted that one as soon as he said it, for it allowed Jobe to make some kind of offer. Before Hamu's son could say anything, Inyati added, "'You are expecting what you will never get; looking for what you will never see.'"

Jobe sighed. "Do they have the expression, 'Behold the Zulu and Ndwandwe nations at it again.' in kwaMatabele? The Zulu and the Ndwandwe were always fighting, fighting, fighting. I ask myself why? And why do you and I fight?" Inyati did no reply. "I fight with Mbeki because my father hates him, and you fight me because Mbeki is your friend. We're fighting other people's battles instead of our own." Still Inyati did not speak. Jobe began again, sympathetically, "Do they have, 'The mole that has its abode underground is fortunate, because it does not see the world.' in kwaMatabele?"

"Yebho, we also have, 'Stay-at-home enjoys his staying: Travel enjoys his traveling.'" Inyati winced, knowing he had used a weak argument intentionally.

Jobe jumped on the opening, using the traditional rebuttal, "'Stay-at-home finds nothing: Travel earns nothing.'"

Inyati knew he wanted to be convinced, and he loathed himself for it. He heard the gentle echo of feminine laughter from within the hut and his hand began to play over the scar across his belly. Ingonyama would kill me if I married Nandhi, he thought.

Hamu's son leaned in close and whispered in Inyati's ear, "We have another saying in these parts, 'No one is killed twice in kwaZulu.'" Inyati closed his eyes. "If you do this one thing for us, you can marry Nandhi and live in the North under my father's protection. From there he can agitate Lobengula in kwaMatabele, and one day you can take the throne for yourself."

Inyati imagined his homeland, where elephants roamed across high veldt prairies and impi after impi would parade before him in their glorious array. He pictured himself leading his raider nation against the dirty Shona and patrolling the border zones that no man could cross and live. To make the picture complete he imagined Nandhi at his side as his queen. As if Jobe could read his thoughts he heard a whisper, "You will see your home again. You have my father's word."

Inyati felt his resolve waiver. Since King Mzilikazi's death everything had gone wrong: The flight from his brother's executioners, falling in with the Swazi, the duel with Ingonyama, the death sentence, Mbejane, Nandhi. What would it hurt to again be in control of my destiny? Is it worth one black deed? Inyati knew the answer, but before he could stop himself he whispered, "Defeated men say to one another, 'I am old.' What must I do to go home?"

Chapter 31

The first of the cattle crested the ridge followed by its fellows. The grassy meadows near oNdini were decorated with garlands and bouquets to complement the wild flowers. Two whole cows and a number of lesser animals were spitted over bonfires, slowly rotating under the supervision of Jama's wives and Ingonyama's aunts. The party was ready to begin.

Ingonyama's lopsided grin could not be suppressed; the entire family had come up from the Valley of the Three Homesteads for the wedding. His young herd boy cousins drove the cattle with practiced taps on the hindquarters of the slowest cows. As they walked they sang wedding songs of peace and prosperity. Ingonyama knew it was the sun's early rays which opened the wild flowers on the hill, but perhaps the singing helped too.

The Zulu love to sing, and soon every guest had joined the rising harmony of bass tones, highlighted by falling contraltos from the women. The earth beneath them seemed to sigh at the sound. Ingonyama gave a nod to the body of men behind him, and they too joined the song. Deep and slow, with lips pulled back off of their big white teeth, a hundred men sang the chorus.

Ingonyama walked over to his future father-in-law and gestured with an open hand at the oncoming herd. "Well, Nkosi, here is the bride price. Two hundred cows: Nandhi is worth every heifer." Ingonyama's words had all the proper tones of respect, but to Hamu's ears it sounded like the Invincible was laughing at him. He gave a noncommittal grunt. The cows looked very good, especially considering they had just survived a cattle plague. When the herd boys brought the livestock to a stop, Hamu waved his kin forward to examine the bride price.

Jobe led his brothers and personal attendants forward, all dressed in their finest military gear. Each cow's hooves were examined for fungus or injury; then the mouth was opened to check that the molars were not worn or rotting. An ear was pressed to the cow's side to insure all the appropriate burblings and churnings were taking place in her abdomen, and then finally the tail was lifted up.

This was the most important inspection; each of these cows had birthed a calf, proving her fertility, but the stretch marks could tell the discriminating herdsman how successful future offspring would be. When each cow was inspected, one of Punga or Khandla's children would drive it to the far side of the meadow. Hamu watched impassively as all two hundred cows were scrutinized.

At last Jobe returned to his father's side. "They're magnificent, Baba. Get our best stud bull in this herd, and we'll double it in a year. No foot rot or asthma at all. No signs of arthritis. No missing teeth. I can't find a single cow that can be rejected on any grounds." Hamu nodded his head stiffly. He had expected nothing less. Ingonyama and his royal patrons would not allow the wedding to be called off over something as petty as a poor bride price.

"Nkosi," A man approached from Ingonyama's party. Hamu furrowed his brow before remembering this was his future brother-in-law, Jama. "My son has offered you the bride price, but I would like to offer you a gift as well." Hamu saw the glint of steel inside the man's leather satchel and braced himself to dodge an attack. The smith pulled back the flap to reveal a dozen exquisite spear points, each polished to a blinding finish.

"Mbeki and I have worked for almost a moon to make these. Each of them is worth a dozen lesser spears." Hamu knew there was no lie in that estimation. In a land where a spear could be purchased for a single sheep, these points would be worth an entire flock. It was almost a quarter of the value of Ingonyama's bride price.

"I praise you Jama, and your gift." Hamu did not praise Mbeki, but Jama was willing to let that minor point go. "These are very impressive." Jama was surprised to hear real emotion in Hamu's voice. The northern prince was not just being polite; he was pleasantly surprised on a day he thought would be torture.

Good, Jama thought. If they mean that much to him, I'm glad Mbeki suggested it. "Go well, Prince Hamu."

"Stay well, Jama," Hamu replied. Despite his troublesome sons, Hamu resolved to allow the smith to live when he became the Nkosi Nkulu of kwaZulu.

The hours after sunrise were not easy on Hamu. Formation singing and dancing between the different genders and families dragged on. He should have been participating, but everyone understood he was not in favour of the marriage. The women's bright coloured wraps and flamboyant headdresses did nothing to lighten his mood, and when a few dozen of his daughters ran by, their beaded necklaces and hip bands bouncing against their soft leather aprons, it occurred to him that a good portion of the bride price would be needed just to reimburse the expense of dressing his family in the manner expected of royals attending a wedding. Hamu breached his first bottle of gin and drank straight from the neck.

By noon warriors from both families arrived with their sticks and shields. A column of young women formed up next to the warriors, and Hamu and Jobe's wives began leading a spontaneous parade around the meadow with green branches cut from a nearby thicket. Their laughing and cheering grated on Hamu's nerves so that even his third bottle of gin was no comfort, and at times he physically shuddered as his concentration slipped.

At last the friendly banter of insults between the two families began, and Hamu abandoned his lonely vigil on the ridge to join his clansmen. It was a tradition for the two families to say that the other was not worth being related to, and Hamu had a few choice remarks he wanted to make. He staggered into the forefront of his sons, facing Ingonyama's infuriating lopsided grin across the field.

"You are marrying my daughter out of spite!" He shouted. The smile began to slip, and Hamu felt better. "I hate your family the way leopards hate baboons." He gestured at his leopard skin cloak, letting everyone know who the baboons were in his metaphor. There was a sickly silence from both families. Smiles stayed on faces as if there presence could keep things from worsening.

"That reminds me," A new voice said. Heads turned to see Cetshwayo working his way down the hill. A warrior held a shield over his head to ward off the worst of the sun's heat. "I forgot to give you your wedding present, Ingonyama." He snapped his fingers, and a retainer placed a bundle wrapped in calfskin into his hands. He walked between the two families. Everyone remained frozen, stopped at the moment where it had all gone terribly wrong.

"Ingonyama, you are the best of what makes a Zulu," King Cetshwayo began. "You are strong, determined, and capable. Your name does you justice: He is a Lion." With a flourish Cetshwayo pulled back the calfskin to reveal a lion skin cape. Its front legs had been left on to drape down the chest, and the skin was trimmed so it hung only a few inches below the waist at the back. The mane was still attached, stiff and proud. There was only a single puncture mark, right were the lion's head met its spine.

"Is that?" Mbeki asked from Ingonyama's side of the crowd. He remembered being trapped under the giant cat, and his father rolling it off of him, letting the sunlight pour down upon his upturned face. He remembered the skin had been present when Zungu the Great had been banished from the court, and when he had first earned Hamu's ire. The skin was part of his family's history, and he was awed at the thought that it would be returned to them on his brother's wedding day.

"It is." The King's smile was like the sun. "I remember my Baba saying, 'We must remember the kaJama boys. They'll grow up to be fine men some day, and the Kingdom could use fine men.' So I've kept that lion skin in my hut all these years. I'm glad to give it back to you." There was a sigh from the crowd. Anything that had been in the king's presence for so long was imbued with his spirit. Cetshwayo's gift was a talisman of near-invincibility.

Ingonyama donned the cape with reverence; his fingers touching the hole he had punched through the lion's neck when he was just twelve years old. The leather was oiled and well broken in. This had not been sitting in a corner. Leather in this condition had seen special attention. The cloak fit perfectly, and the mane framed his head just as it had done to the old tom cat.

"Perfect!" The king turned to Hamu. "I would say you don't hate him as a leopard hates a baboon: You hate him as a leopard hates the lion." There was laughter from the very young boys in both families. Where leopards kills baboons, lions always steal kills from leopards. Hamu's choice of animal was now the loser. Hamu stood as still as a stone at this new humiliation. Cetshwayo could see how close Hamu was to the edge. "Easy, cousin, I think the sun and the beer have you a little confused."

Seeing the king had excused Hamu's behaviour and knowing the northern prince might deny it at any moment, Mbeki cried, "Bayete!" And the crowd echoed him. "Bayete!" Cetshwayo gave a little wave of acknowledgement; then Mbeki launched into the fast staccato wedding chant. A unified response rose up from the men on both sides. Hamu, realizing the tension had eased, joined in. Mbeki gave the next lone call, and soon hands were clapping to the beat of a wedding drum. Fast and furious, the beat drove on and on until it took tremendous effort to keep a unified rhythm.

Ingonyama burst into a giya, his shield and stick in constant, blurring motion. A primal cry ripped from his throat as he struggled to keep pace with the drum. He blocked high and stabbed under his shield, killing one of his imaginary foes. Twisting around he thrust his stick-spear into an imaginary throat, and the dropping his shield he did a back flip to put his stick into a third phantom behind him. Sweat poured down him as the young girls in the audience cheered his athletic feats. Eventually he exhausted himself, and the giya ended with him struggling to stand. Both families burst into applause.

Silence fell as Nandhi appeared over the top of the ridge. She walked with measured steps down the hill, seeming to float along the ground. She stopped to touch the king's offered hand, a blessing on the marriage, before entering the space between the two families. She wore a veil of the finest silk, imported at stunning expense from the Portuguese settlements on Delagoa Bay. Her bright wrap held all the colours of the rainbow, and her beadwork said in the secret code of lovers that she had the man of her dreams.

Hamu moved to join her between the two families. Ingonyama also joined them. A butcher's knife appeared in Hamu's hand. All eyes followed the blade, waiting to see what would happen. Hamu leaned over and cut the cord holding Nandhi's veil in place. The silk floated to the ground, discarded. By showing the bride's face he had blessed the marriage and severed his family's responsibility to the girl. It was traditional for the father to say, 'You have stabbed me' to signify the pain of his lost daughter, but for Hamu this lacked enough emotion. He choked out, "You have skewered me." His breath was heavy with gin. Ingonyama smiled his thanks for performing the only mandatory function required of him without making a scene. Hamu grunted an acknowledgement.

A new song broke out, and Hamu drifted back into his family's crowd. "Jobe?" He hissed. The press of bodies was so thick he could not find the son he was looking for. "Jobe?" He did not want to attract attention to himself, but he needed to speak to his heir. He caught sight of his majordomo. "Zokufa, find Jobe." The grey-haired man nodded and began working his way through Hamu's family in a different direction.

At last Jobe's squashed nose hove into view, and Hamu pulled him out of the press. "Is our friend ready?" Jobe looked blank for a moment, and Hamu saw the fogginess of alcohol in his stare. He slapped him across the side of the head, refreshing Jobe's memory.

"About that, Baba, I was wondering if we had to do that now... It's been such a great party. Would one more day matter?"

"Idiot!" Hamu slapped his son again, harder, and then realized he must do nothing to call his actions to an onlooker's attention. He pulled Jobe even further from the party and whispered, "After tomorrow morning the wedding is done. I can't kill my daughter's husband. Do you understand?" He thumped his son between the eyes with a finger. "If it ever came out that I killed my son-in-law, I would be abandoned by my supporters! He has to die today, or not at all." He went to tap his son's head again but Jobe dodged. Enraged, Hamu slapped his son full across the face. "Do it now."

For a moment there was defiance in Jobe's eyes, and Hamu felt an alarm cry go off in his head. *My son is becoming a man, and men have their own ideas sometimes.* He filed the knowledge away for future consideration and waved the boy off on his errand. Jobe went dejectedly, having failed once again to confront his father.

Chapter 32

Dusk was falling as Chomper moved from shadow to shadow, stalking something in the grass. Inyati did not have the patience to see what kind of rodent the dog had found this time. "Heel," he ordered in Afrikaans. Chomper dutifully fell in step behind his master. Inyati felt like throwing up. It was not because of the eight mugs of beer he had consumed to work up his nerve. It was because of the mug he had in his hand: This one had come from Jobe, and it was for Ingonyama. That was all he knew. "No one said anything about poison," he whispered to himself. "But what else could it be?" He would have to dump it. He could not go through with it. It was impossible.

The beer was from Nandhi's own brew, spiced with fruit nectar and nutmeg. It did not have a foul odour, but that proved nothing. He had to get out of sight of Jobe and dump it. There was no other option. The mug felt red hot in Inyati's hand. His other palm was slick with perspiration, and it almost slipped off the head of his cane.

"Wo, are you alright?" Mbeki grabbed Inyati's elbow, steadying him. His friendly smile was a dagger in Inyati's heart. He wondered if the beer had mamba venom in it. That would be odourless and tasteless. He imagined Ingonyama drinking the potion in complete trust before dropping to the ground in agony, his insides knitting themselves into bloody knots. He could hear women screaming and someone calling his name. He shook his head.

"I said, are you okay?" Mbeki looked concerned. Inyati realized Mbeki had been saying his name for some time.

"I've just got a lot on my mind." He tried to brush the younger kaJama off, but Mbeki kept a hand on his elbow.

"Look, don't worry. Ingonyama may set up a homestead here by the Mfolozi, but you and I'll be going back to the valley. We can hunt kudu again. Remember that day?"

Inyati could feel the wizard of kwaZulu's eyes play over him, and he knew Mbeki had kept the nickname through an eerie ability to figure things out. Inyati's sense of shame was like a black blanket covering him, suffocating him, and he feared within moments Mbeki would see through him. He needed to dump the mug and forget the whole thing, and he needed to do it right now. He managed to choke out, "Yebho. Look, I'll be all right. Go enjoy the wedding; I'm just going to walk around for a while."

Mbeki nodded. Inyati was feeling ill, but he did not want to keep Mbeki from the festivities. He gave the Matabele a reassuring pat on the back and turned to go.

Inyati caught sight of Ingonyama in a circle of Invincibles ahead of him and felt the hot rush of bile rise up through his throat. He had never agreed to kill Ingonyama; He had just agreed to talk to Jobe at the wedding, and he had done that. His obligations were discharged. He tipped the mug over, spilling its contents onto the ground--

"Whoops! Hey, hey, careful! I think you've had a few too many." Mbeki turned around to see Inyati pouring the beer out. He snatched the mug out of his friend's slack fingers. "That's Nandhi's special brew there! If you want to waste beer, spill the rat piss her father brought to the party." Inyati's face was slack with horror, but Mbeki could not see any problem. "Hey, how about a toast to the happy couple, eh?" There was a mouthful of Nandhi's magic elixir left in the bottom, and he lifted the mug in salute.

Inyati's free hand came crashing down against the mug, slapping it out of Mbeki's hand and shattering it on the ground below. "What is the matter with you today?" Mbeki shouted. "Have you gone--"

A howl from below interrupted him, and the two looked down to see Chomper squealing like a gutted cat in the grass, vomiting blood and kicking his legs into the air. He was lying in the puddle of Inyati's beer. "What--Poison?" He looked at Inyati incredulously. "Who would you want to poison?" Inyati's eyes flicked towards the laughing Ingonyama. Mbeki followed his gaze, and by the time Inyati turned back to his friend it was to see a stick flashing towards his face.

Inyati tumbled over backwards. Mbeki's stick had caught him right between the eyes. Mbeki began slashing up and down the Matabele's prostrate form with his stick, all the while hissing in Afrikaans, "You and I aren't friends. Do you hear me? If I see you near my brother again I will kill you! Do you hear me?" Inyati was shielding his head with one arm and waved his cane back and forth in the air to break some of the wicked impact. Mbeki kicked him in the stomach. "Do you?" Mbeki lifted his stick again, but Ingonyama grabbed his arm. He had seen the fight start and had run to intercede.

"Mbeki, I never took you for such a mean drunk!" Mbeki looked into his brother's eyes without comprehension. "Come on over here; I have some people I want you to meet." With that Ingonyama steered his brother away from Inyati's prostrate weeping form.

Chapter 33

The evening stick fight began on schedule. Hamu's sons and Ingonyama's male relatives squared off on top of a hill, while women and non-combatants watched from the campfires at the bottom of the slope. Nandhi was a little uncomfortable as the centre of attention, so whenever someone came to congratulate her and shower her with still more womanly advice, she directed their focus to the skirmish above.

The fight was not real. It was a form of giya where the imaginary foes were the other family. Ingonyama and Jobe, as captains of their respective warriors, would keep their men under rigid control. The moment a man fell to the grass the fight would stop. When everyone stopped bleeding they would return to the bottom of the hill for more beer and beef.

"Nandhi, how are you going to grow your hair?" Nandhi sighed. Married women could grow their hair out, and it seemed as if each of Jama's wives had an opinion as to what was fashionable. She turned to see a barely pubescent girl looking up at her. "I think you should wear it long, like this." The girl giggled and threw both of her hands to her head, using her fingers to show the contours of her imagined hair style. Nandhi suppressed a shudder at its awfulness.

"Now which one are you? Punga's, Khandla's or Jama's?" Nandhi tried to remember the wave of introductions when Ingonyama's family had arrived, but she could not place the girl.

"Oh! I'm Bhibhi! Jama's my Baba, and Ingonyama's my brother." The little girl laughed again. "He sleeps in late, and he's a bit of a grouch in the morning, so be careful."

Nandhi was touched by the girl's advice. "I can't speak for when he lived with you, but now that he's an Invincible he gets up before dawn each day, and he's never a grouch." Bhibhi giggled again. She was a bubbly girl, and she realized how Nandhi must have acquired this knowledge of her brother's early morning habits.

Nandhi turned her head away in embarrassment. She had been seeing Ingonyama for over a year, but she had never done what Bhibhi's lascivious mind imagined. In fact, she had spent more evenings with Inyati than she ever had with Ingonyama. The thought --as so many that involved Inyati-- gave her pause.

Ingonyama was more than she had ever hoped for, but there was something about Inyati, so brave about his injury, that tugged at her heart. Inyati was the sort of man her father had raised her to marry: A prince with the potential to become a powerful man one day. She realized how uncomfortable she was with the whole idea, and decided to turn the girl's attention away from the bride. "Have you been to a wedding before?" She waited for the girl to shake her head. "Well both families are going to fight now, to represent how they used to be two separate groups. Then afterwards they'll bind each other's wounds to show how they've become one. Look."

Bhibhi turned her head to the oncoming show, disappointed already that Inyati was not well enough to stick fight. Even with his scar he's so handsome and funny, she thought with a sigh. And I was the first to see it. Even before Mbeki and Inyati were friends, I knew he was a good man. She already had dropped suggestions among her father's wives to begin pressuring for Inyati as a groom for his daughter when the time came.

She was so happy to be here at Nandhi's wedding. Inyati had come to the Valley of the Three Homesteads not too long ago to visit Jama, and he had made a passing mention of Nandhi that had made Bhibhi burn with jealousy. Now she's married, wonderfully married to a wonderful man, and she can leave Inyati to me. Bhibhi smiled with secret pleasure, thinking of this wedding as almost more of her day than Nandhi's. The shouting from the top of the hill broke her happy daydream.

"Ingonyama!" The war cry went up from one side.

"Hamu!" was the reply. With a rolling thunder of sticks striking shields, the two sides engaged. Mbeki was near the edge closest to the girls, and they could see he did not seem to be having a good time. His face was mottled with rage, and every slash of his stick was calculated with long practice to evade his opponent's guard without knocking him to the ground and ending the match. One after another, Hamu's kin fell back from the front of the fight, bleeding from their heads, chests, and thighs. A hole appeared in the Hamu wing, and Jobe himself moved to fill it.

"You!" Mbeki pointed a single finger at Jobe the way a man would point at the black magician who commanded a tokoloshe. With a blur of stick and shield the two engaged, Jobe reeling under Mbeki's sticks.

"Why is Mbeki so angry?" Nandhi asked her new sister-in-law. A shrug was Bhibhi's only answer. "He seems awfully serious about the fight."

On top of the hill the rest of the stick fight had veered off to one side, giving Mbeki and Jobe plenty of room. In a way this followed tradition for there was always one match that stood out from the others, bringing prestige to the participants. Usually it was between the captains, but Ingonyama did not begrudge Mbeki his fun. Clearly he had a demon or two to work out of his system.

"You gave Inyati the poison," Mbeki murmured into Jobe's ear while their sticks were locked against one another. Jobe kept his face neutral, but he slipped into a more defensive pose. "Baba's had enough of his new son-in-law already, has he?" There was the staccato click, click, clicking as their two sticks crashed against one another. Mbeki brought his shield against Jobe's shoulder, and then sliced down with his stick across his opponent's forehead. The skin parted and blood poured down into Jobe's eyes and over his crooked nose. He barely had time to grunt in pain before Mbeki landed another blow in the small of his back, causing Hamu's son to drop his stick and shield from slack hands.

Nandhi was on her feet, watching as her brother was taken apart a piece at a time. Mbeki was carefully placing his blows so that Jobe could not fall over or sink to his knees in submission. The beating was brutal and thorough, and Nandhi winced as another thunder crack caught Jobe under the jaw, lifting him off his feet. Realizing his opponent must fall to the ground, ending the match, Mbeki hit him twice more before he landed unconscious into the grass.

He slowly came out of his blood rage to see that all eyes were upon him. The fight had stopped as soon as everyone realized Jobe was in trouble. Ingonyama opened and closed his mouth, not understanding how his brother could have done what he had just seen. A cricket started chirping somewhere in the grass, further exaggerating the cone of silence around Mbeki and the fallen kaHamu.

Mbeki looked down at Jobe, then back into the awestruck crowd. Ingonyama's mouth was closed now, his jaw clenched. In a moment he would have to come across the grassy space between them and end the silence with a stick across his brother's face. "Would someone get me some water and bandages? I've... I've got to clean him up a little." A few sickly smiles appeared in the crowd, and soon there were murmurs and whispers as people discussed what a surprise the whole incident had been. The silence was broken, and things returned to normal.

The evening burned on into the wee hours of the morning, and the families slowly drifted back to oNdini, just over the hill. A bridal hut had been built near a stream leading into the White Mfolozi, and there were some lewd cheers from the men who had stayed around to witness the bride and groom enter their hut. They had only a few hours to consummate their marriage; dawn would see Nandhi's sisters banging on the walls of the hut. They would then take her to the stream for a bath and make sure she was no longer a virgin. If this last deed was accomplished, Ingonyama and Nandhi would be married.

The eastern horizon was just starting to glow when Mbeki returned from oNdini with another pot of beer. Some Invincibles had set up camp out of earshot of the bridal hut, but sitting up all night eating the feast's leftovers was thirsty work, and the partygoers had taken the beer back with them. Mbeki set down the pot with a grunt. Sompisi and Jojo cheered.

"I always figured you for a thinker, not a doer," Sompisi said, filling his mug from the pot. "But you proved me wrong today. What did Jobe ever do to you to deserve all that?" From the fire the group could just see the jackals circling the spot at the top of the hill where Jobe had fallen. They were attracted by the smell of his dried blood in the grass.

"We've never gotten along. He set a veldt fire to wipe out my family's holdings once..." Mbeki could not bring himself to tell anyone of Inyati's treachery. "I think I just had a few too many." He tipped his beer mug skyward by way of demonstration. There were murmurs of approval from the circle of men around him.

"Still, I imagine he'll walk carefully around you from now on," Bambatha said around mouthfuls of leftover beef. Jama and Punga had each brought a steer to the party, now the group of men had pulled the remaining beef close to the fire to keep scavengers from stealing it.

"Cha," Mbeki shook his head. His mind was still clear, despite the clumsy coordination of his hands. "Other men maybe, but Jobe is Ngenetsheni. He'll just hate me a little more. Theirs is not a family that gives up." Mbeki shrugged it off. Jobe had always hated him. Now he had a good reason.

"Speaking of a family that doesn't give up, they're here awfully early." Sompisi saw a long file of Hamu's daughters working their way over the hill, staying well clear of the jackals. "I guess Hamu is hoping they haven't done it yet."

Jojo snorted. "Fat chance!" It had been a quarter of the night since Ingonyama and Nandhi had retired to their bridal hut. The idea that they had not consummated the marriage yet was ridiculous.

"I think once Nandhi's away we should give Ingonyama a visit," Mbeki suggested. Each man threw his mug back by way of agreement. Everything sounded like a good idea after a long night of feasting and drinking. The men watched as Nandhi emerged from the hut, now wearing the chest covering wrap of a married woman. One of them muttered something about, 'A pity.' As she was led off to a secluded spot along the stream the men moved across the field at a clumsy jog trot, reeling and swerving from the alcohol. Long practice and a few theatrical hand gestures saw them encircle the temporary shelter.

"He is a Lion!" Sompisi shouted, swaying. "You have until the count of five to come out here and drink with us, or we're coming in!" A cheer went up from the men, and they started to count. "One! Two! Three--" One of them said four instead of three, and then half said five instead of four. Bambatha threw up his hands in disgust and started back at one, but that only confused them further.

Mbeki fell into the tall grass, laughing. Jojo walked over and shook Sompisi, who kept saying "Four... Four..." Waiting for someone else to join him. They need not have bothered with the counting. Ingonyama came out, but he was not smiling.

"What's the matter, Nkosi?" One of the Invincibles hiccupped. Ingonyama walked seemingly at random past the group and towards a spot well upstream of Nandhi. The men let him go. He would come back, and they were not entirely confident they could follow him.

Ingonyama enjoyed the cool sensation of the grass on his thighs, rubbing his jaw with one hand. "I need to shave," He murmured. The stubble under his hand prickled, but he was too preoccupied to feel the discomfort. He found a boulder by the side of the stream and sat on it, his legs dangling over the edge towards the river below.

He saw his reflection in the water; saw the bags under his eyes. He pulled his lips off his teeth in a parody of his lopsided grin but gave up. "Why?" He whispered to himself. He had a new nightmare to add to his collection. The dying dream had come less and less, and for a time he hoped he would never suffer from insomnia again. Now he was not so sure.

He remembered the night: For a little while they had talked about the future and the past; then when both felt comfortable with their new circumstances they had begun.

The inside of the hut was cozily lit by a low fire, and their naked bodies had been cushioned from the hard clay floor by a dozen soft karosses, so that they seemed to be frolicking on a cloud. He had mounted her with joy, at long last released from the social conventions that prevented him from entering her. She had arched under him, her hands running up and down his back, and he had thrust into her again and again while she moaned and writhed beneath him.

Ingonyama stared down into the water, her aching cry echoing in his brain. She had only said it once in the throws of passion, but he could not dismiss it. It echoed in his ears like a bird taught to mimic human speech. "Inyati," He repeated it to himself, unable to reason out the full implications of that simple orgasm-induced name. "Inyati..."

Chapter 34

The pair of them worked around to windward, stepping carefully as the tall grass gave way to rock and thorn. The kopje towered above them, shrouded in vegetation. The bigger man was flushed, and he pushed a sweat dampened lock of blond hair out of his eyes and back up under his wide-brimmed hat. The wind was a gentle stirring of air in his face, reassuring him that they could proceed. He turned to Mbeki and nodded, and the two spent the next several moments quietly loading their elephant guns.

They were primitive things: muzzle loaded and percussion capped with no rifling whatsoever. The only concession to comfort was a stock of walnut fitted with a leather cushion to ease the terrible recoil. Still, when hunting elephants it was best to leave the usual guns at home. The two small cannons the men loaded with familiarity would each throw a quarter of a pound of lead through bones, blood, and sinew. Nothing else on Earth could stop an elephant as quickly.

When the last snick of ramrod and click of half-cocked hammer was finished Mbeki nodded. The blond man put his face into the wind again and made his way into the thicket. The thorns pulled and worried at his clothing, their red tips looked as if they had already drawn blood. At their insistence he slowed still further, taking care to unhook each barb from his lucky blue shirt.

They felt it vibrating up from the ground before they heard it: A rumbling from up ahead. The scat Mbeki had found that morning was the size of the blond man's thigh. A quick probe with an index finger told Mbeki their prey could not be far. His leavings were still warm and moist.

The behemoth had been raiding Zulu farms in these parts for decades. His praise name was Ivory Hoes, for a long life had made the bull's tusks so heavy that one tip or the other would often drag along the ground, leaving an impression in the dirt.

As a young bull in the days of Shaka men had hunted him for his ivory, but Ivory Hoes had long since learned to deal with the miners of white gold. Any man foolish enough to simply follow the groove in the soil would find the animal doubled back into the wind constantly. At one sniff of pursuit Ivory Hoes would take off at the tumbling pace that an elephant can keep up for days and that only a man with a string of horses can hope to maintain.

Mbeki and the blond man had been out here for six months and killed many good tusks, but the blond man wanted to go home with one last trophy: The ivory on either side of Ivory Hoe's face must be a hundred and twenty pounds each. One could make a lot of billiard balls and piano keys out of two hundred and forty pounds, but the blond man had an eye for putting them over the mantle; he rarely disappointed himself.

With one last branch pushed out of the way, they entered the clearing where Ivory Hoes had decided to rest. The elephant's long experience had served him well: Ivory Hoes was surrounded on all sides by thorn thickets, and the high vaulting canopy of mopane and fever trees shielded him from the harsh rays of the sun. At first the blond man could not understand the bull's lack of activity, but another rumble explained it. Ivory Hoes was an old man now, and the idea of a nap in the hottest part of the day was difficult to resist. Ivory Hoes had not caught a whiff of Mbeki and the blond man for weeks and felt safe enough to snore peacefully, unaware that Death was stalking him.

Ivory Hoes' pebbled hide smelled of vegetation and dung. It was crisscrossed with slashes and punctures from dozens of unsuccessful blows from hunters. The blond man saw these scars and knew he could not delay taking his shot. The giant before him was the grizzled veteran of a lifetime spent as prey; he would not be so careless as to slumber too long or too deep. Even asleep, every nerve in that dust-stained body would be tensed and ready to burst into flight. The blond man would have to make his move now, in this rare window of opportunity, or go home empty handed.

The problem was the hunters' angle relative to the elephant: Ivory Hoes' rump was in front of them, and the pachyderm was turned ever so slightly to reveal the great sides of his massive ribcage. From this angle just a small portion of the back of his skull showed. There was no head shot here, and the best heart shot came when the hunter was perpendicular to the elephant. The blond man spat quietly to drive the bitter taste of disappointment from his mouth. It was no angle for a killing shot, but to move around this close to Ivory Hoes would probably alert him.

Mbeki knew the blond man's mind, could sense his impatience. The blond man would try to take the heart shot now rather than move and risk losing the kill. Mbeki knew only a bullet in the brain would stop this bull. He leaned in and whispered, "Go for the head shot. You won't get his heart." He gestured with his hand to show the shortest way to a better firing position.

The blond man grunted and crouched down, sweating through his shirt. At this angle the odds of a clean heart shot were slim. The beast could be mortally struck but might take twenty minutes to die, and Ivory Hoes could kill them both in two minutes if he knew they were there; on the other hand, to move would make noise, and those tattered ears would hear a mouse burp at a hundred paces.

His decision made, the blond man brought up the elephant gun and peered over the sights. They were really just a suggestion as the bullet could drift as much as ten degrees in any direction once it left the barrel. Muffling the sound with a callused palm, the blond man drew the hammer back to full cock. The click sounded as loud as a gunshot to him, but the giant did not stir.

He breathed in and out, in and out, slowly moving the barrel to point at that massive rib cage. The angle was wrong, he realized. If he aimed for the ribs from so far behind the bull, the slug would follow a shallow path only a foot or so under the skin. It would make a mess of one lung, but the heart would pump fast and furious. The blond man drew a bead behind the ribcage: At this angle the bullet would come in through the diaphragm and spall inside the chest cavity, mincing the heart and lungs like a fork stirring an egg.

He drew in a breath, let half out, and pulled the trigger. The blast was deafening, but the elephant's trumpet of fury was much worse. The bullet had drifted, but not forward, up, or down as the blond man had hoped. With a meaty thwack the quarter pound of lead had smashed into the beast's abdomen, moving through its entrails in a backwash of black blood. It was a mortal wound but not an instant one. The blond man thrust his hand behind him for the other loaded gun, but Mbeki was not there.

"Shit!" His gun boy had deserted him.

Mbeki was tearing through the underbrush, his sides raw and bleeding from the thorns. The thicket around him muffled the bull's squeals and the blond man's curse, but he knew it was all going horribly wrong behind him. Judging his position from a hazy notion of the size of the clearing and the distance he had covered, he burst through a stand of saplings and reappeared in the direction the bull had been facing when the shot went off.

"uSuthu!" It was the only thing Mbeki could think to shout, and it worked. The beast was swinging towards the blond man, but now the familiar war cry Zulus made when they were working up the courage to drive him from their maize fields caught his attention. Ivory Hoes had come to associate the sound with the pain of throwing spears and the illness of their infections.

Ivory Hoes moved like an avalanche, unstoppable. Mbeki stood only thirty paces in front of him, and his mouth hung open at the fury he had pulled down upon himself. The ground shook with the thunder of the charge. Mbeki's blood curdled at the elephant's shriek of anger. The world slowed down to the point where he could see each little mote of dust dance in the sunlight that filtered down through the trees. This was just like the time the lion had charged him as a boy, but now there was no Ingonyama to save him.

"Run, Mbeki!" The blond man cried, frozen to the spot at the sight before him. Dream-like, Mbeki drew the hammer back, threw his gun up to his shoulder, aimed for a point between the elephant's eyes, and pulled the trigger. Ivory Hoes was almost on top of him, rage and despair in his rheumy eyes. A long trumpet squeal tore from his throat.

The bullet went high, missing the spot that would have dropped Ivory Hoes like a mealie sack; instead, the slug sank deep into the beast's high, spongy forehead. Inside the skull a honeycomb lattice of soft bone slowed the bullet, forcing it to take the path of least resistance. By the time it touched the brain there was almost no force behind the shot.

Mbeki knew he was finished. He turned to run, dropping the elephant gun and pumping both arms to get as much power out of his legs as he could. The world was still slow, and his frantic sprinting seemed slower still. Mbeki dodged around one tree and heard a crunch as the beast's shoulder smashed against the bole, knocking the tree out of the ground. The sac of fluid and gel lining the inside of Ivory Hoes' skull was ruptured and blood was pouring into his brain. He veered left, dashing against another tree, and then right, destroying another. His broken shoulders, ruined abdomen, and the inexplicable numbness and disorientation in his head would have stopped Ivory Hoes, but another swerve brought Mbeki's running form into view.

Ivory Hoes never felt the bullet shatter his pelvis as the blond man fired his reloaded gun. Ivory Hoes never felt the ground rush up against his chest with enough force to crush his ribs. What he did feel before the light went out of his eyes was Mbeki's torso in his trunk, and his last conscious movement was to throw that fleeting contact into the air with all his terrible might.

For a long time the thicket was quiet, then a blue monkey chattered and another shrieked, and then the whole troop was howling. It drowned out the blond man's calls, and he found his gun boy only after a broad sweep of the area in front of the bull. Mbeki had landed wrong, wrenching his shoulder and spraining his wrist. A lump the size of a heron's egg was raising on his forehead, but there was a smile on his face.

"I told you to go for the head shot," Mbeki said in English.

"That you did."

"You know, I never did like you."

Holland Keech tipped his head back and laughed with relief.

Chapter 35

It had been a beautiful blue-skied day when they first met: Cetshwayo was happily accepting Zibhebhu's apology for a matter of little importance; Hamu had gone north to sulk after Ingonyama's marriage; Ntsingwayo was celebrating that he was a grandfather for the eighty-first time, and the court was unusually free from serious worries.

Mbeki stood behind his king, trying to ignore the itching. He wore the full regalia of the Flycatcher Bird regiment, and the few oxtails of bravery bestowed upon him were driving him mad. "You speak the language of the Boers, don't you Mbeki?" The question was unexpected, and Mbeki had to repeat Cetshwayo's words under his breath to make sure he had heard right.

"Yebho, Nkosi Nkulu." He tried to forget that Inyati had taught him. Inyati was dead to him.

"I want you to translate for me."

"Yebho, Great Elephant."

"Here comes the man with whom I wish to speak. Treat him kindly. I'm rather fond of him." That statement alone was a surprise. Cetshwayo was friendly with the English, but Boers were not so favoured: When Mpande had gone south to seek Boer support for his civil war he had taken his son Cetshwayo with him. The Boers had worried that if Mpande died they would not know which black boy in the King's entourage was his heir, so they had cut a chunk out of Cetshwayo's ear just as they would a promising calf sired by a famous bull. Cetshwayo often touched the missing portion of his ear when dealing with Boers to remind himself that they thought Zulu no better than cattle.

Mbeki expected the Boer to be someone special to be able to overcome Cetshwayo's childhood trauma, but even from the far side of the parade ground Holland Keech had stood out: A white man with a clean light blue shirt and clean dark blue pants, walking around in high cavalry boots; he wore no hat, spat no tobacco, sniffed no snuff, and failed to look around in disdain at the sea of black humanity into which he was engulfing himself. Mbeki liked him at once.

The man approached Cetshwayo and his royal entourage with due reverence, genuflecting. "I see you, Nkosi Nkulu," He said in Zulu. His accent was terrible, and it was clear he was using one of the few phrases he knew.

"I see you, man with the unpronounceable name," Cetshwayo replied. Mbeki translated.

The blond man smiled. "Holland Keech, your Majesty." Holland was not speaking Afrikaans, but it was similar. The king nodded that that was indeed the moniker he could not pronounce.

"May I introduce Mbeki kaJama of the Cube clan, Flycatcher Bird regiment, and Wizard of kwaZulu?" Mbeki repeated this to the man, including his nickname: False translation could lead to trouble. "Now, I have considered your request to hunt in kwaZulu..." The blond man leaned forward, but Cetshwayo would not give an answer so easily. Mbeki knew that this would not be the first such interview the man had gone through at Court.

In the days of King Dingaan white men often waited months for permission to hunt. Cetshwayo was not much better than his uncle. Any hunter who left without his permission would find himself surrounded on all sides by an impi before he was over the horizon, and it was rare for those hunters ever to receive the royal pass after such a breach. "First, I would like your opinion as a warrior on a matter of some concern to me."

Mbeki could tell the man was impatient. He tilted his head to one side, lowered his blond eyebrows in frustration, and exhaled slowly to hold his temper. "Tell your King I'd be happy to answer any questions he would like, but if he could please let me know when I might have his permission to hunt--"

It was not Afrikaans, but it was so close Mbeki's curiosity overcame his caution. "What language is that? You aren't a Boer."

The man flashed a dazzling white smile. "Nope, I'm an American." He waited expectantly, as if just the word would enlighten Mbeki. "That's, uh, a place over the sea."

"Like England?"

"Um... No. It's across the sea from England too."

"Why is American like Afrikaans?" Mbeki asked. Cetshwayo cleared his throat, irritated at this private conversation. Mbeki explained what was being said, and the King leaned back with new found patience. It was a warm day and sitting was not uncomfortable.

"It's not. I'm speaking Dutch." Again the white man acted like the word should impart an immediate understanding. "That's a language they speak in Holland--"

"Like your name!" Mbeki clapped his hands and translated for the King.

There were some chuckles from the courtiers, but the white man interrupted them with anxious words. "No, no. I speak Dutch and German because I grew up in Pennsylvania Dutch Country."

"I thought the Dutch country was Holland. Where is Pennsylvania?" Mbeki translated this, and Cetshwayo began to laugh as he saw Holland's face go red.

"Look at the colour he's turning! That's a wonderful trick, Mbeki. Now stop teasing him. Say this:" Mbeki began translating word for word. "You have seen our impi on maneuvers. How do you think the Zulu would do against the white armies who carry so many guns?" Cetshwayo tried to make the question seem airy, but behind him the chuckling councilors fell silent to hear the answer.

After the translation Holland shook his head. "I'm not sure, Your Majesty. I think thirty or forty thousand Zulu could probably take ten or fifteen thousand men with muskets out in the open." Smiles appeared on the faces of the King's advisors. The battles with the Boers had convinced many of them that war against white guns was impossible, but the British demands on Cetshwayo were becoming more and more outrageous.

"You're not asking about fighting Americans ten or twenty years ago. You want to know whether or not you could beat the English if they ever work up the nerve to hit you, is that right?" Mbeki translated it into Zulu, and Cetshwayo answered with a dignified nod.

"The problem is that guns are a lot better than they used to be." Cetshwayo furrowed his brow at that and asked for an explanation.

"May I show him?" It took a few minutes for a demonstration to be set up, but when all was ready five pumpkins stood on stools in the middle of the cattle kraal. One of the attending Invincibles had fetched two rifles from Holland's wagons, and another twenty formed a wall between the now armed white man and their King.

"Well, Your Highness, the guns you people are probably familiar with are muzzle loaders." He took the first rifle from the gun-carrying Invincible. "This is what the British army uses: Standard issue Enfield musket that a good rifleman can discharge twice a minute." Everyone in the crowd was familiar with the loading of a musket. Many Zulus owned the cheap trade muskets sold through Zibhebhu and Hamu's northern gun runners or Sihayo and John Dunn's southern contacts.

Holland laboriously loaded the weapon and discharged it. Without stopping to see how well he had done, he loaded it again and fired. When the reek of sulfur and the cloud of smoke dispersed, two pumpkins lay shattered behind their stools. There were murmurs from the crowd. Zulu marksmanship was poor, and hitting something the size of a pumpkin at thirty paces was excellent in their opinion. Holland held up one hand to silence them.

"The trouble, gentlemen, is that we are living in the year of our Lord eighteen-hundred and seventy-five, and this--" He held up the Enfield. "Is obsolete. This isn't all that different from the muskets Wellington used to beat Napoleon when my grandfather was still in diapers." Mbeki did not know how to translate half of what Holland was saying, but the American was not finished. Caught up in the moment he took the other rifle with a showman's flourish.

"This here is the future! The British army is already switching over, so this is what you can expect to see if the redcoats bother you: The breech-loading Martini-Henry. You can fire this thing fifteen times a minute until you are out of ammunition." He threw the rifle up to his shoulder and the gun spoke with a horrifying mechanical sound: Bang! Click, click, snick. Bang! Click, click, snick. Bang! Click, click, snick. The remaining pumpkins flew off their stools, disintegrating in the air at the impact of the heavy bullets. Three shots in less time than it had taken to load the Enfield that lay in the dust at Holland's feet.

Mbeki along with every other warrior in the crowd felt a cold shiver run down his spine. An army armed with such weapons would be unbeatable. The British had them. The Zulu did not. Cetshwayo cleared his throat as if unsure of his voice. "Ask him how many of those... Martini-Henrys he would be willing to offer in exchange for a hunting expedition?"

There was some muttering from his councilors. Many wanted the new rifles, but the King traditionally bought through John Dunn. While it was not a monopoly, John Dunn was very generous to his lobbyists at Cetshwayo's Court, and they did not like their Nkosi Nkulu acquiring weapons from a man who was not paying them.

"Tell your King I happened to pack ten of them and a thousand rounds of ammunition, just on the off chance he'd be interested." Holland's grin was infectious, and soon the whole court was smiling ear to ear.

After the big blond man had returned to his wagons, Cetshwayo turned to Mbeki. "You're going with him, Wizard."

"Great Elephant," Mbeki began. "I'm in the Flycatcher Bird ibutho. We're on active duty--"

"You're too good to hoe my fields and herd my cattle. That man with the unpronounceable name needs special attention; after all, he is spying on us for the British." "Nkosi Nkulu?"

"He is going to hunt between the Phongolo and Ncombe rivers. The British do not know what the land is like, and Prince Mbilini and the abaQulusi keep them from scouting out an invasion route, so they have come up with this 'hunter' idea." Cetshwayo waved his hand as if to say his intelligence network had not even been challenged to discover this fact. It had only taken five bottles of Cape Smoke brandy distributed among Holland Keech's servants as well as some pressuring on John Dunn to learn the plan.

"Sire, if this is true, why give him permission? Why even let him live?"

"Wo, you do ask a lot of questions." Just for a moment Mbeki was irritated with Cetshwayo before he remembered his place. "Very well, I shall tell you: Whether this man gives them their invasion route or not, the English seem determined to attack us." Cetshwayo's tone implied their motivation was as much a mystery to him as to Mbeki. "How do you make a herd of cows move in the direction you want them to go, Mbeki?"

Cetshwayo questions often seemed to come from nowhere, but this time Mbeki had heard him properly. "You coax the cows closest and strike the cows farthest from where you want to go."

"Yebho," He said it as if it explained everything. Mbeki made fleeting eye contact with Zibhebhu, who shrugged his shoulders. Cetshwayo realized he was not being clear. "I want peace. I do not want war. So, I will coax those Whites who want peace to support my side, and I will have this hunter tell the British who want war that the abaQulusi are vicious; the country is vast; the rivers are unfordable, and Mbilini is a monster. I will make war look like more trouble than it's worth, and thus I will have my peace."

"How are you going to do all this?" Zibhebhu asked.

"Mbeki is going to make sure the hunter is impressed with the defenses on our northern borders. While he's at it, he's also going to take Inyati with him. I don't know what has come between them, but it will be settled by the time they get back. Won't it, Mbeki?" Cetshwayo's smile did nothing to ease the sudden pain in Mbeki's head.

Chapter 36

Holland's wagons set out the next day with Mbeki rushing everything along. It was his slim hope that they could be gone before the Matabele heard of the assignment, but he knew he would be disappointed in that effort. Inyati's presence would be a constant irritant, bothering and worrying him, rubbing salt into the wound that was his shattered trust.

"Is everything ready?" Holland brought his horse alongside Mbeki with a practiced ease. Mbeki was to be his guide through kwaZulu and induna of his Zulu escort.

"Yebho, Nkosi." Mbeki's eyes were on the gate of oNdini. If they could get over the horizon before the Matabele left the gates he could tell Cetshwayo Inyati had not come.

"Funny, I don't recall ever becoming a lord." Mbeki's head snapped up at the American in surprise: All white hunters were called lord. This white man did not have that assumed superiority, and Mbeki liked that. "Call me Holland, and I'll call you Mbeki. Is that a deal?" Holland stuck out his hand.

Mbeki looked at the outstretched hand in confusion. To him the gesture was one of polite pointing, so Holland seemed to be drawing attention to Mbeki's breastbone, but he was clearly waiting for a response. Deciding mimicry would be the best response, Mbeki stuck out his open hand as well. Holland grabbed it and shook the hand twice. "Deal," He repeated. Mbeki assumed it was a way of sealing bargains among Americans.

Mbeki thought he heard his name on the wind, and his eyes returned to the gates of oNdini. He was careful not to wince as Inyati emerged, moving towards them as fast as his cane would allow, his free arm waving above his head. The oxen were already inspanned to the wagons, camp was broken, and Holland had needed only Mbeki's status to order his drivers to use their trek whips. Mbeki had been so close to making good his escape.

"Who's this?" Holland asked.

"This..." Mbeki's mind churned, trying to conceive a position high enough for an exiled prince and low enough that he would not be in constant contact with the man who had tried to kill his brother. "Is one of Cetshwayo's distant relatives. It is complicated, but he is a prince of a people called the Matabele. His place is very minor at Zulu Court, so my King and I would like him to come to supervise your camp staff."

Holland arched an eyebrow. He did not like Cetshwayo messing around with his comfortable setup; he had broken in his subordinates on the long road from Pietermartizburg to oNdini. The idea of some minor Zulu official coming in and disturbing everything was not a pleasant one. Mbeki sensed he may have picked a bad title, so he continued, "He speaks Afrikaans as well as I do. He was my teacher."

Holland was surprised to hear his warrior escort's voice tremble. He looked at the cripple, moving at a staggering jog across the veldt in obvious pain but unwilling to let the wagons leave without him. He still did not like it, but it had taken him months to earn his trip. He grunted his acceptance, and the two waited for Inyati to catch up.

The wagons rolled north and west for two weeks before Mbeki would let them set up a hunting camp. "We are too close to the Mfolozis. This area is hunted out of the game you white hunters want." That suited Holland's needs too. A decent map of the northern borders was worth five thousand golden sovereigns to him. Even just a suggested route of march would be worth a hundred pounds.

When the wagons finally stopped, Mbeki watched as the cantankerous boxes on wheels became a homestead. They were pulled into a loose circle with thorn brush surrounding to keep scavengers out. One end of the circle contained a mimosa tree for shade, and most of the other was shaded by a massive red-stripped canvas tarpaulin attached to the tops of several wagons. There was a screened off latrine, and on the opposite side of the compound a full bathtub sat inside its own collapsible canvas house.

The servants kicked into high gear with little instruction from Inyati or Mbeki. Each knew their role when establishing a camp. There was one man whose whole job was to keep a massive cauldron of water boiling all day, enough to fill the bathtub, plus laundry, cooking, tea, or any medicinal needs. Another was responsible for trickling water in the courtyard to lay the dust. Still another spent his day chopping wood in the nearest copse of trees, then carrying the sizable portions inside the stockade of thorn brush to fuel the cauldron fire, cooking fires, smoking fires, and campfires all day and all night.

There was even one who cared for Keech's chicken coop, feeding the noisy poultry, cleaning and mending their roosts, and collecting their eggs for an endless array of poached, fried, scrambled, hard and soft boiled, deviled, or omletted eggs with mushrooms and choice cuts of antelope.

In total, including Mbeki and his eight Zulu warriors, Holland was responsible for forty-seven men, and the day before the base camp was set up was the last of his sheep had been butchered. "No problem," The blond man had smiled. Mbeki had felt the rumble in his stomach, but going without meat was acceptable when other food was available. The blond man had enough cornmeal to feed an army, and his coffee, served black out of U.S. Cavalry mess cups, was exotic if bitter.

Mbeki should have known Holland had no intention of letting his men go without meat. As soon as the camp was set up to his satisfaction, he took Mbeki and the eight Zulu out onto the veldt, riding his best brown mare. The land was mountainous, and the hills were emphasized further with deep kloofs and dongas. The swaying golden grass of the veldt became the green of forest if one descended, and the dull brown and gray rock scrub of the kopje if one went up. Every kind of game imaginable thrived in this land.

"Have you ever hunted with a rifle before, Mbeki?" The Zulu shook his head; Jama's tower musket was not as accurate as his hunting spears. "I've shot men in the South, buffalo on the Prairies, and now I'm finally shooting in Africa." His rifle came out of its bucket in one smooth motion, the hammer came back, and he fired. His trained horse did not even twitch. "Go get that, will ya?"

Mbeki turned his head in the direction of the shot, only now realizing that Holland had actually shot something. A herd of antelope was running away from the shot, flying across the ground barely touching the earth, but one animal was not moving; an impala buck was on his back, legs akimbo.

"Could you repeat that in English?" It had taken almost a week for Mbeki to confirm that Americans spoke English, but that there was a region of America which spoke Dutch which was the father language of Afrikaans. He heard the request in English, and decided it was not that different from Afrikaans. He waved his men forward and they advanced at the jog trot.

The kill had been merciful. The heavy bullet went right through the young impala's heart. Several of the Zulu muttered, 'Wo' and sucked air through their teeth in appreciation of their white man's killing prowess. Before they had cleaned the impala, two more shots rang out. "That should be enough for everyone, right?"

Mbeki stood up from his task and ordered him to repeat it in English before replying, "Yebho." They left all three of the gazelles' heads and viscera out on the veldt for the hyenas. They kept only the choice meats, livers, hearts, kidneys for grilling, and a few yards of intestines to make sausages. The men returned as the sun set, the clucking of the chicken coop letting them know they were almost home despite the waning light.

The fireside that night was perfect for quiet conversation, and Mbeki decided it was time to begin following his King's orders. "You should never leave camp without my direct supervision, Holland."

"Why?" The big man gulped his coffee. He repeated it in English without prompting.

"This is the land of Mbilini waMswati, the Hyena of the Phongolo," Mbeki repeated himself in Zulu at Holland's request. The blond man originally asked out of sheer bloody mindedness, forcing Mbeki to repeat everything in a different language as he had to, but soon he found himself trying to put the words he knew together with the new ones to translate Mbeki's sentences in his head. It was interesting when he paid attention.

"Who's that? He sounds like a bandit." Holland's eyes strayed to his personal wagon. He kept his rifles there when he was not hunting, and there was a revolver under the bed he could just as easily wear on his hip if this was hostile country.

"He is not a bandit." Mbeki's mind flashed to Zungu the Great, dead more than a year now. "He is Cetshwayo's most feared general: He guards this land as a lioness guards her cubs. As a child he was wrapped in the skin of a freshly killed dog. It gives him dark powers."

Holland leaned back, interested but not impressed. This would sound wonderful in his report. "Why is he waMswati? Shouldn't that be kaMswati?" He lifted his mug to indicate it was empty and needed refilling. His steward had the cup out of his hand before his arm had fully extended. He made the drinky motion with his hand, indicating he would like some whiskey in it this time. The man nodded. Holland smiled in satisfaction. Why beat them into service, he thought, when you can give them a small bonus at the end of the year that will set them up like kings when they get back to their families? You get better service with coins than with whips.

"He is a renegade Swazi prince, and the Swazi's word for 'son of' is wa, not the ka of a civilized person. He is one of the Swazi's few great killers." Mbeki wanted to build Mbilini up, but he did not want to imply that the Swazi were good fighters. "The Swazi throne is his, but he had to flee into kwaZulu. He leads the abaQulusi regiment along the border, and he is brutal in his treatment of trespassers."

"How so?" Holland was not sure how much of this was hyperbole. A friend in Natal had warned him to watch out for some prince or another who guarded this area against all newcomers, but the Zulu had so many princes that he had not remembered the name.

"A Zulu warrior disembowels his dead opponent to set his spirit free. Mbilini disembowels his live opponent so any future enemies will be haunted by the screams." There was a crash of plates, and Holland turned to see the Matabele prince had dropped a tray of dishes. He eyed the vicious scar across the man's belly again, as he had done ever since this prince had entered his service.

"Ignore him," Mbeki advised. "He may speak Boer, and he may come from a line of proud warriors, but monkeys are not worth the attention of good people." Holland watched as the man's slack fingers opened and closed. That's something to watch, he decided. These two don't get along, and I need the smart one a lot more than the scarred one.

Months passed, and Holland and the Zulu formed an efficient hunting team. Keeping Mbeki with him as a gun boy, Holland would send the other eight around to the far side of his prey to drive them towards him. His trophy wagons slowly filled with elephant tusks, lion and leopard skins, and buffalo heads that were clumsily stuffed to survive the trip to a proper taxidermist in Natal. Every night the men ate fresh meat, and each day they headed out to hunt with haversacks stuffed with smoked sausage and venison jerky.

One day Holland emerged from his tent to the sound of men cheering. He knew that sound: It was the noise an audience made at a prize fight. He pulled the revolver out from under his mattress and ran towards the center of the crowd, pushing his otherwise docile servants out of the way. Breaking through to the open space in the middle he stopped in surprise.

He had expected it to be a fight over whose turn it was to do laundry, or one of the other menial chores that the men pawned off on each other in exchange for favours. Instead he saw Mbeki and Inyati circling each other, a stick in each hand, hissing at each other in a language too different from Zulu for him to understand.

"Don't lie to me. I was there," Mbeki said in Sindebele. He did not want their conversation to be understood by the servants or Holland. This was between them.

"I didn't do it," Inyati replied, holding his sticks on the defensive. He had at last abandoned his cane, but he was in no shape to win a stick fight against Mbeki. The precision blows directed against him were coming much too fast, skinning the bark off his saplings to reveal the green wood underneath.

"Zulu don't lie. It must be a trick the Matabele monkeys picked up in the North." Inyati's Zanzi blood pulsed through the veins in his temples, whispering for blood to avenge the insult. He took another step back; he knew he was outclassed even if his pride did not.

"I did not poison him, and if you'd just use your head you'd remember I was pouring out the beer!" His appeal to Mbeki's memory had no effect, and a fresh set of slashes rained down upon his unsteady guard. He felt himself driven back again, but this time the crowd did not open up to let him retreat. A blow connected with his right knee, and he felt himself sag. Another one caught him high on the shoulder, and he dropped his left stick numbly. He cringed back, waiting for the decisive blow.

Mbeki had spent most of his life practicing his stick fighting, and an opponent with only one stick was easily overcome. He moved his right shoulder to begin the downward swing, but found he could not move his arm. He looked over to see Holland was holding him at the wrist, shaking his head in anger. "You will not fight my staff in my camp."

"Be careful what you eat in your camp. This monkey tried to poison my brother," Mbeki said it in Zulu so that everyone could understand. There were gasps of horror, and many of the servants recoiled in disgust.

"I didn't do it!" Inyati felt his shame burst out, like puss from a weeping sore. He had come achingly close, but he had not committed the uncommittable. He lunged forward with his one stick, trying to drive his agony away by smashing Mbeki right in his lying face. He never got that far.

Holland saw the Matabele shift his weight onto the balls of his feet, and he released Mbeki's wrist. In a fluid motion he turned his body and brought his fists up. Black men had no tradition of boxing, and Inyati had no idea what was coming. Holland lashed out with a left jab, stopping Inyati's charge cold. The Matabele swayed, unsure of what had happened. Holland swung with his right in a cross, bringing his clenched fist against Inyati's temple with the force of a knobkerrie. Stars exploded in the Matabele's head, but he remained conscious.

Holland watched the Prince of the House of Kumalo stagger on his feet. He knew his point had not been made, so he uppercut Inyati's abdomen twice with his right, driving all the air out of the Matabele's lungs. Another left jab and then a right hook to the head dropped Inyati like a sack of millet.

Holland examined his knuckles, kissing each one that had broken skin. His servants stood around him, mouths agape. No one was sure what had just happened. Mbeki broke from his reverie first and advanced towards the prostrate form of Inyati. As smoothly as he had fallen into a boxing stance, Holland brought his revolver out of its holster and leveled it at Mbeki. "Turn around and go back to your wagon." Mbeki blinked once to assure himself it was not an illusion before turning, dreamlike, and walking away.

"You, you, and you," Holland said in Zulu, pointing at random into the stunned crowd. "Get him cleaned up and in bed. If Mbeki gets within ten paces of him before sundown call me, and I'll shoot him." The men nodded, and the crowd broke up. Holland examined his fist again and smiled.

Chapter 37

Most of the summer went by quietly, interrupted only by the gunshots. One day Mbeki was roused in the hour before dawn by the gentle pressure of a booted foot. "What is it?" He asked in English.

"There's movement down by the creek," Holland replied in Zulu. Neither was fluent in the other's language, but they made a game of seeing how far they could go before lapsing into their mutual Afrikaans.

"Probably wild dogs or hyenas smelling the gnu we had for dinner last night." Mbeki tried to roll over under his kaross, but the next words stopped him.

"Wild dogs don't have spears and shields. The Hyena of the Phongolo and his cronies do." Mbeki's hand reached under the cot Holland had given him and grabbed his spear.

The two slipped out of the thorn fence on the opposite side of the camp from the stream. Mbeki carried his war assegai and shield. Holland had his revolver and a rifle Mbeki had never seen before that was clearly not a muzzle loader. Using the hand signals they had devised while hunting, the two dropped down into the streambed some distance from where Holland had spotted movement.

At times this creek would have been a donga, but the rains had been good last year and the bottom was thick with reeds, slowing their stealthy movements but completely hiding them from observation from the banks.

They moved with care, pushing aside the bottom of the reeds to disturb the tops as little as possible. It took a long time to work their way forward, but at last they saw a form in the darkness. The man was well fed and head ringed, a veteran who must have grown complacent in his middle age. The man had carelessly left his spear leaning against the bank so that the spearhead stuck out the top of the creek bed. Reflected moonlight from that polished steel had caught Holland's eye. It was all going according to plan.

The two waited for the thin wisps of cirrus clouds to clear the moon. There were three of them, including the head ringed veteran. All three were abaQulusi judging by their shields and headbands. They were free of the ceremonial uniforms, the expensive items that could be damaged in action. That meant they were dressed for fighting. One of them looked to the eastern horizon, clearly waiting for the dawn. Dawn was the time for Zulu to attack.

Mbeki smiled, sure the darkness would conceal his pleasure from Holland. Mbilini was no Zulu; if he wanted them dead, he would have attacked in the wee hours when resting men were in their deepest sleep and a sentry was at his lowest ebb. That was how the abaQulusi fought, ruthlessly in the dark. Holland would not know that, and meanwhile would probably feel a gratifying sense of satisfaction to think he knew his enemy's mind.

Holland brought up his rifle, aiming for the spot between the closest man's shoulder blades. "Turn around," He whispered in Zulu. The click of a hammer coming back froze the three for a moment, but they turned to see the big blond man had all three of them covered. "This rifle can put two or three bullets into each of you before you can reach me. Is it heard?"

"It is heard, Nkosi," The three whispered.

"Who sent you?" His rifle moved from one warrior's face to another.

The three exchanged glances, consensus in their eyes. Each sucked in a great lung full of air and cried, "Mbilini!" loud enough to rouse the sleeping vulture from a nearby tree. Holland did not watch the black bird beat its great wings. He was more interested in the hundreds of warriors who materialized out of the darkness to line both steep banks of the streambed above him. "Drop your weapons," his fat prisoner ordered. Holland looked at Mbeki for advice, but his gun boy had already let go of his assegai and shield, dropping them into the ankle-deep water at his feet.

Holland looked at the packed ranks of men to either side of him. He had eight rounds in his rifle and another six in the revolver. He carried forty extra cartridges, but he knew he would never get the chance to reload. They carried stabbing assegais, but there was no need for them to bother. Behind their shields each man also carried two throwing spears, accurate to thirty yards. The closest of the warriors above him were only five yards away. He exhaled through his nose and set his rifle down on the steep sandy bank, out of the water.

"And the little gun," One of the men from the bank ordered. These men repulsed a dozen Boer raids a year; they knew what a revolver looked like. Holland took it out of its holster slowly, watching as the warriors tensed like steel springs until he had placed it beside the rifle. He set it down it so that he could snatch it up at a moment's notice: The rifle was too cumbersome, but he could take six of them to hell with him if it came to that.

From out of the crowd a short, dark man emerged. Beside some of his more impressive comrades he was physically nothing special, but the air around him was electric. With a bark he gave an order Holland did not understand, but before he could reach for his revolver he saw lit torches filter from the back ranks to the front. The abaQulusi had kept small smokeless fires going all night, screened from all directions so that no one save the owls could have known their true numbers.

The new lights revealed the little man's features and Holland nodded, thinking, He looks like a pugnacious bastard. The man's heavy brow made him seem to be perpetually frowning; his neatly trimmed goatee was earned at great expense from dull Zulu razors, judging from the scars around his mouth. The head ring placed high on his head was polished to a blinding finish with beeswax, but he looked too young to be married. Mbeki had told him that Mbilini had donned the head ring as a youth to show his royal status. The man standing on top of the bank could be no other.

"I see you, Prince Mbilini waMswati." He gave the greeting as if the meeting was taking place at the man's Hlobane homestead in the afternoon instead of standing in a stream of shallow water hours before dawn, about to die.

"I see you, Man with the Unpronounceable Name," The little man beamed. His smile did not warm the heart; it was the flash of canines that a wild dog might give to a cornered klipspringer. "Did he hurt you, Mbambo?" The old warrior whose glinting spear had been the bait in the trap shook his head. Mbilini nodded. "I have a problem you might resolve for me, White Man. You are in the land of the abaQulusi, hunting abaQulusi animals and grazing your wagons' oxen on abaQulusi grass. You do all these things to the abaQulusi, but you do not give the abaQulusi--" The next word was unintelligible. Holland whispered it over his shoulder to Mbeki who supplied, "Tribute" in Afrikaans.

"Ah," Holland tried to collect his thoughts in Zulu. "I gave your Nkosi Nkulu Cetshwayo a tribute," he rolled the new word around on his tongue, "When I began this hunt."

"I am not satisfied." Mbilini's tone made it clear he would leave satisfied. "You are using abaQulusi land without reimbursing the abaQulusi. The king has given you his permission, but you did not seek mine. That is impolite. Come with me." It was not a suggestion. Mbilini turned and walked towards Holland's camp. Behind him his men followed with their spears held ready for the underarm stabbing stroke. The empty space in the sea of warriors was moving after Mbilini, and it was clear that if Holland and Mbeki did not move with that empty space they would be cut down where they stood.

Holland left his rifle and revolver on the bank. he had no choice. Behind him one of the abaQulusi picked them up and held them high, proud of his new trophies. Mbilini's sudden appearance with hundreds of men and torches on the edge of camp did not go unremarked by Holland's camp servants, and their wails of distress clearly irritated the Hyena of the Phongolo. "Be silent!" He ordered. The servants obeyed.

The abaQulusi formed a ring shoulder to shoulder around the thorn fence of the camp. Only five including Mbambo went with Mbilini inside the camp perimeter. Back among his own people Holland felt a little better, but his good mood quickly died as Mbilini made a bee line straight to his wagon. Clearly the camp had been under observation for some time. There were sounds of tearing cloth and the clatter of glass and steel objects falling to the floor. At length Mbilini emerged with an armful of books, among them Holland's journal with his detailed maps of the land between the Phongolo, Ntombe, and Ncombe rivers. It had taken Holland three months of detailed study and constant surveying while hunting to make those charts.

"The first tribute the abaQulusi demand is one to our outraged ancestors." Mbilini's voice rang through the still night air, carrying to his men who encircled the camp. "Shaka put us here to forever protect his border. We have stood guard here for three generations, watching. When lookouts see danger, they light a pyre to attract attention. Let us honour our ancestors and send them a signal fire." He dumped his armload of books onto one of the campfires. Holland gritted his teeth. Mbeki was careful not to smile.

Again Mbilini walked to a wagon, Holland's armoury. The Swazi Prince returned with five guns of various makes and a number of brass instruments. "The next tribute the abaQulusi demand is for our women." He held aloft the rifles and there were admiring murmurs from the ring of warriors.

"You see, White Man, the abaQulusi have farmed these lands since Shaka's day. The Boers, though," There was hissing noises from the abaQulusi, "Seem to think they own all this." He gestured in every direction with a single finger. "They come across the border on their horses, put down claim markers, and then burn our huts for trespassing on their land." His voice dripped contempt.

"What does that have to do with my five very expensive hunting rifles?" Holland knew exactly what was happening. Mbeki was a little chagrined. The surveying equipment had to go, but the rifles had not been part of the plan he had worked out with his abaQulusi contacts. Mbilini was committing extortion.

"These five rifles, which make up only one third of your collection, will defend our wives and children. As for these," He held aloft the bronze surveyor instruments, crucial to replace the burned maps, "They will ease their suffering. Women have a fascination for pretty baubles, but then, so do men." He handed the whole collection over to one of his retainers.

"There is one last tribute the abaQulusi demand. This time it is for the warriors who have invested an entire night to benefit their people." Mbilini looked around the perimeter at the faces lit by firelight. "I have it on good authority that you can use your hands as clubs. Mbambo hear does not believe it. Knock him down, if you can."

"With pleasure," Holland needed to vent his frustration. Five thousand pounds sterling would have been a down payment on a good farm in Natal to settle on. A hundred pounds would not even fund another hunting expedition.

Mbambo put up his arms in front of him, as Mbeki had shown him at their clandestine meeting. Holland stepped up, wondering who the spy in his camp might be. Probably that crippled Matabele. Imagining Inyati's face on Mbambo's plump form he smashed him four times in the face, left, right, left, right. The last blow put the big man down. Holland put one foot on the man's belly, turned to the crowd, and said in a mocking voice, "Ngadla."

There were big grins and a few chuckles. Mbilini clapped his hands, the snarling dog smile was still not comforting. "Very good, White Man! To have our continued permission to hunt here every day you will give that one," He pointed with an open hand to Mbeki. "A lesson in this hand fighting. Should we ever find these lessons have ceased, we shall take another five guns as compensation. Now it remains for me to say, go well, White Man." Mbilini was positively affable. It had been a profitable night.

Holland looked over at Mbeki, the worm of suspicion burrowing into his mind. "Stay well, Mbilini waMswati."

Chapter 38

"Come on Mbeki. Turn at the hip; put your shoulder into it." Holland spoke in English. These lessons were not for the staff. "Boxing isn't about how many times you make contact. It's about how hard you hit when you get there." Holland had suspended a punching bag from a bough of the mimosa tree. It was kudu leather stuffed with grass and weight down at the bottom by mealie bags. His gun boy struck again, better this time.

"Okay, okay. Good hook. You're a natural two-fisted fighter Mbeki, but if you can get some real power in your left, that will surprise the hell out of your opponent."

"Who would I be fighting who knew anything about boxing?" Mbeki asked. He had instructed Mbilini to demand lessons because the fighting ability intrigued him. As an additional bonus it would be something he could do that Ingonyama could not. At the same time, he wished Mbilini had thought of a more subtle way than actually pointing out Mbeki in front of Holland.

"When you put up your fists and start hitting someone, anyone who is thinking on their feet will assume a right handed person is going to have more power in his right." While that was true and satisfied Mbeki, it was not what Holland was thinking. *Mbeki, you cost me five thousand pounds and change. When we get back to civilization I'll find you an opponent. Count on it.*

The two of them worked for another hour, as they had every day for the last month and a half. They would return from hunting in the late afternoon, hand the camp cook the game for the pot, and box until dinner was ready, sometimes by lantern light.

Sitting down to dinner, the two's discussion turned to the hunt. "I still think old Ivory Hoes will raid the kaSomopho brothers' mealie field tonight," Holland asserted. They had been in on-again off-again contact with the great bull elephant for weeks, and the brief glimpse of those massive tusks had set Holland's hunter heart beating faster. The bull was sixty if he was a day, maybe seventy. This was not the Limpopo River; bulls like that should all be dead. The idea that such a bull had outwitted all the hunters before Holland captivated him.

"So what? You want to sleep in the mealie field tonight and hope he doesn't come from downwind?" Although Mbeki spoke around a mouthful of kidney, his sarcasm still came through clearly. "A bull like that doesn't make those kinds of mistakes. If you want Ivory Hoes, and I'm almost sure you do given that you never shut up about him, you'll have to do it in daylight."

"Ah, what do you know? There isn't an elephant within a weeks' walk of where you grew up." Holland scooped a mouthful of boiled millet into his mouth, swallowing the mush without enthusiasm.

"What do you know? There isn't an elephant within ten thousand miles of where you grew up." Mbeki smiled. He was not sure exactly how far a mile was, but ten thousand was an awful lot of them, so he had made a point of remembering when Holland told him how far away America was.

"You want to talk about something else? What about Inyati? What happened there?"

"He was my best friend. Now he's not."

"Now I'm your best friend." Holland grinned, knowing what was coming.

"You're not my best friend," Mbeki laughed at the very idea.

"Why not?"

"Because you're White. I'm a Zulu. I'm too good for you." Mbeki's toothy smile had bits of kidney in it.

Holland laughed. "You racist bastard." The two waited for their mirth to subside, comfortable in each other's presence. "So what did he do? Something about poisoning your brother? I thought your brother was the Royal Champion."

"He is." Mbeki bobbed his head. "Inyati was poisoning him for Hamu." Mbeki still felt betrayed, but four months had eased the shock. He could talk about the incident now.

"Now which one's Hamu?" Keeping the royals straight was not one of Holland's strengths.

"Oh, he's a northern baron. His homestead is about five days' march that way." Mbeki pointed to the east with a single finger; the gesture was not lost on the American. "He seems to think he can be king. He forgets that Mpande had dozens of sons, all with better claim than him."

"So what does he have against Ingonyama?" Holland had not heard any of this before.

"Nothing, really. His problem is with me: I implied he had a small penis in front of the other royals; I disgraced his wizard; I broke his son's nose; then I almost had the same son executed for arson. Oh, and I beat his son to a pulp at his daughter's wedding." Holland whistled, impressed. Mbeki was a little surprised at how the list tallied himself; his memory recalled each insult to Hamu's honour, but it had not occurred to him that the man might have good reason to hate him. "All Ingonyama did was ask to marry Hamu's daughter, a union he condemned, and then actually came up with the impossible bride price Hamu demanded. Then he became leader of the Invincibles, and it was Hamu who had to try and deny the royal guards the right to marry--"

"Your family really likes to piss on Hamu's parade, don't they?" Holland moved his tongue around the inside of his mouth, disliking the starchy residue the boiled millet had left.

"To my knowledge my sister Bhibhi hasn't done anything to him. Mind you, she's only fourteen." They laughed again. Holland called for a bottle of whiskey.

"So what exactly did Inyati do?" Mbeki did not answer. He stared into space, remembering the cup pouring out onto the grass. He stood up from the camp stool and walked away from the fire. Holland had some idea what was about to happen. He poured himself a glass from the bottle, toasting himself.

Inyati did not socialize with the other servants, considering it beneath his station; for their part they did not want to accept an assassin into their group. Mbeki found him by the creek where he had arranged for Holland to be ambushed and robbed of all his charts and map making equipment. "I want to know why you did it," He said simply.

"I didn't--"

"Why you almost did it." He dropped down beside Inyati, their legs dangling over the edge of the bank into the space below.

"Jobe said-- Hamu offered-- Mbeki, I wanted to go home." Mbeki nodded. "Jobe said I could live in the North on his father's land. He said his father would get his contacts in kwaMatabele to agitate Lobengula. He said I could become the king one day, and I thought he meant it. I mean, if I was King I would owe Hamu a great deal. By helping me he would be helping himself."

Mbeki nodded. It was a terrible reason, but he could not think of a good one. "There's something else." Inyati was eyeing him nervously. He moved himself along the edge of the bank so that he was further from Mbeki. "Hamu said when I was king, Nandhi would be my queen."

The pieces fell together in Mbeki's mind. The pranks the two of them had done together. The time spent in each other's company. Inyati had been courting Ingonyama's fiancée. He felt his right fist clench, his shoulder and hip swivel, and the hook caught Inyati on the back of the head, sending him flying down into the shallow water of the creek. The Matabele broke the surface, his eyes wild with fear, but Mbeki was laughing. The second son of Jama was beating the earth with his hands, his great belly laughs echoing off the nearby kopjes. In the distance a lion coughed his challenge to the unusual sound.

Mbeki pulled himself up, wiping tears from his face, unsure why he found it all so funny. At length he stopped laughing, looking down at his sopping wet friend. "Have you ever slept with Nandhi?"

It was brutally blunt, the sort of thing Ingonyama would say without thinking but Mbeki would only utter after careful consideration. Every one of Mbeki's senses was focused on the Prince of the House of Kumalo. Inyati shook his head, and Mbeki relaxed, knowing it was the truth. They stayed there for a moment, Inyati looking pathetic down in the water. Another chuckle escaped Mbeki's vice-like mouth. Only when he was absolutely sure he could keep a straight face did he say, "Okay, then. You're okay."

Chapter 39

Dawn burned off the mist the way a lantern evaporates the darkness. Holland and Mbeki walked side by side through the tall sweetveld of the valley floor. The spoor was unmistakable; the mealie field behind them was in tatters. The groove marks in the earth were as wide as Mbeki's palm; the pile of scat was fresh.

Mbeki probed its depths with his index finger. The dung was still warm on the inside; it had not dried out at all, and the elephant's last set of molars were too smooth to break down the coarser fibers, a sign of old age. Mbeki turned to Holland, whispering, "Ivory Hoes was here when we were having breakfast. Unless he has picked us up, he's within an hour's walk."

"Good thing we brought the elephant guns." Holland patted the walnut stock of the crude weapon.

"We've been out here for half a year. If we take this last bull can we go home?"

"The wagon won't hold anymore," Holland promised. Mbeki nodded his relief; he needed to report back to his Cetshwayo on the Mbilini incident. "Where do you think he is?"

Mbeki swept the horizon. If the locals were right in their suspicions Ivory Hoes retreated into the mountains between raiding the farms. It made sense: Old bulls do not run with herds, and if he stayed down in the valleys he would have be seen much more often than was the case. To the west lay the Mountains of the Upturned Spears that the Boers called the Drakensbergs. The foothills of those mountains were perfect elephant country, and only a mile in that direction a forested kopje with thick thorn brush at its base stood proud and defiant against the winds and rains of erosion. "There," He decided.

"Great." Holland gave his gun boy a slap on the back. "One last set of tusks for my mantle, and then back to civilization. We can take the wagons to Luneburg then follow the road to Newcastle, Dundee, and eventually Pietermaritzburg." Mbeki looked at him in surprise. He had heard of those places, but did Holland mean he was not going back to oNdini? He voiced his question.

"Hell, no! That's sixty miles in the wrong direction. Besides, I know you've got orders to make the Zulu seem daunting to the British. Let's go to Natal, and I'll show you off."

Mbeki blinked in surprise. How long has Holland known his orders? "Show me off?"

"Young, trained Zulu warriors don't turn up in Natal very often, and when they do, they're fugitives from their own people, which tends to sap their pride. You're the brother of the King's Champion. You stand behind the King when he talks to foreigners. You're also tough as a piece of ox hide and look like you know what you're doing with a spear. Come to Natal with me, and maybe the next demand the British send to Cetshwayo will be politely worded." Holland did not mention his own designs on Mbeki. His gun boy shrugged an acceptance. "Good! Let's get us a pair of Ivory Hoes." The two set off towards the forest at the base of the kopje.

Chapter 40

Holland made clucking noises as he examined the bump above Mbeki's eyebrows. The shoulder had already been put back in place, and a sling kept the wrist from moving, but Holland could do nothing for the injury to his friend's head. "Nothing comes of bellowing over the contents of a cow's stomach," Mbeki said simply, trying to deflect Holland's ministrations.

The blond man smiled. "Maybe that lost something in the translation..." He returned to a campfire and turned over the fillets of elephant heart. After returning to camp, Holland had led the camp followers out to butcher the carcass. Ivory Hoes' namesakes leaned against the dieselboom of one of the wagons, and the most savory parts of his anatomy hung suspended over dozens of fires.

"It makes perfect sense!" Mbeki pretended to be hurt that Holland had not immediately grasped the expression he had chosen to confuse him. "When you kill a cow you spill its stomach where you've butchered it, but no matter how much the other cows bellow over the contents of their comrade's stomach, he's still dead. Complaining changes nothing."

"So, there's no sense crying over spilt milk?"

"Exactly, if a child spills milk, you beat him. You don't cry about it. That way he won't spill it in the future, and he doesn't think less of his father for weeping." Mbeki sat up and touched his injuries. They hurt, but they would heal long before Holland would be showing him off in Pietermaritzburg. He smiled a little at the thought; the Boers and British south of kwaZulu were waited on hand and foot by former Zulu who had immigrated south for a life of supposed luxury among the Whites. Mbeki and his eight warriors, trained from boyhood in the martial arts of the Zulu amabutho, would make the Whites think twice before attacking kwaZulu.

"That's not quite the point..."

"How would you two like your steaks?" Inyati laboured under a wooden platter heavy with grilled elephant steaks running the gauntlet from blue seared to extra well done.

"Medium rare," Holland replied immediately. Mbeki gestured for the same. Moving two of the steaks from his platter onto separate plates, Inyati handed the rest off to a passing servant.

"There you go." He gave them their plates. "How's he doing?"

"Just fine," Mbeki answered for Holland. He ached all over, but in a real sense he was in the best shape of his life. His twentieth birthday had come and gone, and the daily workouts, long hunting expeditions, and steady intake of meat had built up his muscles. He was no Ingonyama, but Holland assured him that he would be a dynamite light-heavy weight boxer if he ever decided to leave kwaZulu. Mbeki had laughed in his face.

"When do we break camp?" Inyati looked around at the familiar circle of huts, feeling the slightest twinge of regret that it was coming to an end. Since Mbeki had forgiven him, things had returned to the way they once were. The only unspoken rule between them was that Inyati was never to mention Nandhi. He had done so twice, and each time Mbeki's newly trained fists had necessitated the use of a gazelle stake to soothe the bruised flesh around Inyati's eye.

"I'll shoot a couple of antelope and trade them from sheep at the kaSomopho brothers' homesteads. Between that and the sausages and jerky we'll be okay for provisions. We can leave any day once the food's in order." The two ate their steaks with gusto, not worried at the juices that ran down their chins. "Do you think the weather'll hold?"

The three of them had set out from oNdini a little less than two moons after the rainy season, and their six month stay had brought them dangerously close to it again. "Hard to say." Mbeki did not want to commit himself to an uncertainty. "If it does rain, that will slow the wagons and make fording the river difficult."

"Ah, it won't rain. It'll cloud over for a week or two, but we'll be in Luneberg before the clouds burst." Holland leaned back in his camp chair and put his foot up on a stack of firewood left there for that purpose.

Two days later they broke camp in the pouring rain. The oxen were inspanned by men who slipped in the mud every other step. The servants gave up on the sopping canvas tarpaulin and threw it across the top of one of the wagons. They started at dawn, but the day seemed to get darker and darker as the cumulonimbus clouds piled inky blackness into the sky.

The trek whips cracked and popped, and the oxen whimpered at their wet discomfort. Mbeki and Holland crouched on the bench of the lead wagon under a canvas overhang they had rigged up. From behind them there was a rolling thunder. The whole world went white for a moment as a bolt struck nearby. The boom was immediate and deafening.

"Lightning!" The servants wailed. Mbeki blinked his eyes to remove the spots: Lightning was the most feared supernatural phenomenon in kwaZulu: Lightning struck the tallest and proudest trees, the most fearless bulls, and the men who were blackened with misdeeds. Lightning was the ancestors' assegais touching the Earth to punish those they felt to be wicked. "Do something, wizard!"

He looked back, startled. His title was a nickname given to him in jest for a childhood trick. He was no isangoma. When the spectacular summer storms came to the Valley of the Three Homesteads it was Jama who beseeched the ancestors to spare his family and his herd.

"What are they gibbering about?" Holland did not understand the problem. They were not out in the open; there were mountains and thick forests to either side.

"They want me to save them." Before Holland could argue, Mbeki jumped down and ran back to the next wagon, demanding a fire and certain herbs.

"How are you going to start a fire? Everything's wet!" Holland climbed down into the downpour in frustration. All of his drivers had abandoned their benches: His wagons were going nowhere.

"Shields, get your shields!" Mbeki's eight Zulu and Inyati ran for their ox hide shields to protect a quickly growing pile of tinder. Holland scowled: in search of dry wood and tinder his men were stripping the wagons of loose floor boards, discarded clothing, sawdust from the carpentry tools, even kerosene for the lanterns were all being added to a carefully prepared teepee. Mbeki leaned in with flint and steel.

"Mbeki, this is stupid! Get these boys back to work. It's just a thunderstorm." Holland looked at the black men all around them, water running down their hard faces.

Mbeki was trying to remember what his father had done to placate the spirit world. A storm like this one was a serious matter: A man struck by lightning could not be buried or mourned. A cow struck by lightning could not be eaten, but must be buried in a hole deeper than a man was tall. A tree struck by lightning could not be used in any way, and the ground at its base became cursed.

"Tshitsilikazi," Mbeki murmured, bent over the fire. It was a word Holland had never heard before. The malevolent clouds hung oppressively above him, ready to fall. "Tshitsilikazi," Mbeki murmured again. Above him the shield-bearing men began smashing their fists against their shields, screaming obscenities at the sky in defiance. Their voices bounced off the surrounding granite kopjes, coming back in odd snatches through the thick air and pouring rain. Mbeki threw the herbs he had requested onto the fire. "Tshitsilikazi!"

As Mbeki breathed in the smoke he felt his heart race and his head began to feel heavier. He waved his hands over the fire, and light danced on his finger tips. "Do you see this, anyone?" He whispered, afraid they would say no. There was another blinding flash of lightning, and a tall tree a thousand paces away exploded. The thunderclap was spectacular, and even Holland cupped his hand to his ears. Mbeki did not react, except to say, "Tshitsilikazi!"

He looked up and saw the same light on his fingertips dancing in the clouds above like giant fireflies. "Go away!" He ordered, thrusting his hands away from the camp. There was another flash, and a bolt of lightning touched the top of a kopje in the direction Mbeki had pointed. It wavered there for several moments, writhing in electric fury. Mbeki could see the light on his finger tips growing dimmer. The people around him took a step back. The Wizard of kwaZulu had just performed a miracle.

"Go away!" He ordered again, throwing his hands out in another direction. A new thunderbolt obediently stabbed down from the heavens, vapourizing a tree perched half way up the side of a barren kopje. Around him the black men's mouths hung open. Mbeki could control the storm.

Mbeki knew that the light on his finger tips, which grew dimmer and dimmer with each bolt, was the strength of the clouds above him. He had to bleed the beast to death with lightning blood. "There!" Boom. "There!" Crash. "There! There! There!" Only when his finger tips were naked of the dancing light did he stand up on aching legs. The fire had gone out, and the servants were cowering under the wagons from both the storm and the wizard. Only his trusty Zulu were still in the tall grass around him. They caught him as he collapsed.

Mbeki was hauled up onto the lead wagon, weak but pleased to hear the sound of falling rain, free from thunder. Only after the wagons were moving again did Holland lean over and ask, "Were any of those herbs you threw into the fire dried mushrooms?"

"Yebho. Why do you ask?" Mbeki answered as one does when he is trying to sleep.

"No reason." Holland flicked his whip again, driving the oxen towards Luneberg.

Chapter 41

It rained at least once a day for the entire trip to Pietermaritzburg, but there were no more great thunderstorms, and the trip passed without major incident. Mbeki did not care for the idea of roads once the wagons were on them. He kept asking, "What if we want to go over there?" Driving where a thousand others had gone before in the exact manner they had done so irritated his sense of freedom. People in kwaZulu did not need to all find a path on the veldt and follow that straight line all the way to their destination. Holland was unable to reconcile Mbeki to the idea.

When they reached the small city of Pietermaritzburg with its elegant government buildings and open gardens, Holland set up camp on the outskirts of town. "Why should I pay for a hotel when I've brought accommodations with me?" Still, he went into town to buy fresh provisions, a new suit, and to have his lucky blue shirt mended. After a few days to rest and recuperate from their long trip Holland finally called Mbeki to put on his best military regalia and follow him.

Mbeki wore a civet tail kilt, a leopard skin headband with red feathers, and a red-beaded necklace with a lion claw pendant. He then covered much of the skin on his upper arms and lower legs with cow tails of bravery. His shield was red and white, and his knobkerrie was of the finest red ivorywood. He asked if assegais would be appropriate, but Holland told him that spears were as inappropriate in the presence of white leaders as black ones.

The two walked through town, attracting a number of stares: The American because he was a stranger, and Mbeki because he walked tall and proud, uncowed by the colour of his skin or the presence of the Whites. Holland led them to a garden party in progress at the Carnarvon estate. The steward asked Holland to leave his servant at the door, but he walked right past him with Mbeki in tow. Only when he reached the carefully tended green lawn did it occur to him that he needed to have a word with Mbeki.

"Always stand a pace behind me. It is expected of you. Don't speak any English, and don't act like you understand it. Is it heard?" He said it in Zulu.

"It is heard. What about Cape Dutch?"

"I'll warn them you speak it, and that will impress them." The two walked on, passing women covered up from under the chin to the very tip of their toes in clothing, and then sporting hats and bonnets to hide what little remained beneath an ugly array of ribbons and flowers. Mbeki forced himself not to stare, but the women indulged in long looks at his iron-hard boxer's build.

The men were not much better in their dress: Each of them was also clad from under the chin down to the toe, and if they were outside they wore a plethora of hats in all shapes and sizes. They also hid their face behind every combination of mutton chops, mustaches, goatees, and beards. It staggered Mbeki that the Whites had any time to harp on the Zulu Court after worrying about fashion.

"Ah, gentlemen, may I present Mr. Holland Keech, one of the hunters we were just discussing." A tall man, handsome in the Whites' way, gestured in Holland's direction. Holland walked towards the circle, shaking hands with first the tall man then the four others already present.

Holland was all grace and charm. "Lord Carnarvon, gentlemen, this is my good friend Mbeki kaJama of the Zulu Kingdom. I must warn you that he speaks Afrikaans."

"I was just telling these fellows of the extra assignment we've been offering to hunters in Zululand." Lord Carnarvon bobbed his head, as if Holland was speaking, and he was merely agreeing. "How did you fare?"

Mbeki was careful not to tense. This was where he found out how impressive Mbilini had been. "Well," Holland began, making a casual glance around to make sure only the men in the circle were paying attention. "I'm afraid my detailed maps and surveying equipment were destroyed. I have crude drawings that may be of some use to you." There were mutters of 'What a shame' and 'Pity' from the circle.

"As for any hypothetical invasion, I'd say cavalry would be your only option." Mbeki almost winced. He did not know what hypothetical meant, but advising the use of soldiers on horseback sounded like an endorsement to him. Holland was not finished. "I worry about their chances for success: The land is rough, filled with mountain strongholds and cave networks. The locals are as warlike as the Sioux, if any of you understand that analogy, and the Zulu general Mbilini is a ruthless little dictator in his corner of the Kingdom."

Mbeki breathed out. This was better, but he wondered if Holland was using unusual words to deceive him. Lord Carnarvon spoke. "Yes, the whole country is suffering under that black blood thirsty despot Cetywayo--"

"Cetshwayo, my lord," Holland corrected.

"Yes, yes, quite. He is a godless man, and he keeps his army from marrying so their sexual frustration turns them into perfect killing machines. I've told my successor all of this, and he was quite appalled." Mbeki did not understand where the British had arrived at their conclusions: Cetshwayo was the kindest king in seventy years, and the country had never been so prosperous. As for the King's power to grant the head ring to deserving regiments, why would that concern the Whites? What did sexual frustration mean?

"Your successor, my Lord?" Holland looked at the partygoers with an inquisitive eye, worrying he was talking to a man rendered superfluous.

"Yes, Sir Bartle Frere. Excellent man, from India, you know. That's what we need here, another India. Put the whole country under a confederation so that the blacks learn Christian mores, can reach White communities in search of work, and switch their currency from cattle to sovereigns. Frere will be arriving late summer of next year, and he can pick up where I left off. Of course you're on board with my solution to the Native Question?"

"Of course, my Lord," Holland nodded.

"Yes, the Zulu Kingdom is the last great impediment to our road to peace in South Africa." Carnarvon eyed Mbeki. "Look at this one here: This man is in the full bloom of his youth, perfect for getting a good job in the gold mines or the sugarcane fields, but he can't come because his King won't let him. What's worse, all the tribes to the north of Zululand can't come because they would have to trespass across Cetywayo's territory to reach us. We are bringing in thousands of Indians when we have a labour pool right here." The circle all voiced their agreement. When the Colonial Secretary spoke, everyone fell into line.

"What we need, gentlemen, is an excuse for a quick little war. March the regiments into Zululand, break a few heads, and clean house. It worked against the Xhosa, and it would solve all our problems in a stroke." The surrounding men harrumphed their encouragement.

A liveried black man walked by carrying a tray of exquisite crystal wine flutes filled with a deep red substance. Several of the men in the circle lightened the waiter's load with a practiced hand. As the man left the circle Mbeki reached for one, but the servant gave him an imperceptible shake of the head. Mbeki put his hand down, embarrassed. On the veldt any one of these men would have needed him. Here at their garden party he attracted looks because he was not carrying a tray.

The conversation drifted from politics to economics, a discussion Mbeki found incomprehensible. From there it went to gossip, and Mbeki liked that even less. None of it was scandalous, and it was all about people he had never heard of. When it drifted to sports, though, Holland surprised him. "How's the prize fight progressing?"

"Hmm?" One of the men in the circle lifted a hairy eyebrow. "Oh, yes. Poorly, man, poorly. We have the ring and stands all set up. The tickets are sold. Gentleman Jim's boat has already arrived at Durban, and he'll be here in a few days."

"Then what's the problem?" Holland tried to look perplexed. They had asked Holland to organize the prize fight a year ago, but the money had not been worth his time; besides which, he had told them before he had left on his hunting expedition exactly what their problem would be.

Gentleman Jim was a professional heavyweight boxer who made his living touring the British Empire, beating the natives in the boxing ring to prove to the Anglo-Saxon colonials that Britannia produced the best men on Earth.

The trouble was that there were no true natives in Natal: Shaka had wiped out every man, woman, and child seventy years ago. Every black man here was a refugee from kwaZulu, and the Colonials were not afraid of refugees: They were afraid of the Zulu.

"The dirty kaffirs, of course! We offered fifty cows just to get one in the ring and another hundred if he wins, but all we could get were some hotheads from the cane fields; three or four flyweights who are willing to have their head staved in for a herd." The man looked disgusted. "They may speak Zulu, but every ticket holder will be able to tell that none of them is a warrior. Even the best of them wouldn't make it to the second round."

"Gentlemen, what if I could get you a bona fide Zulu warrior, brother to the King's Champion and a trained light heavy weight boxer?" The circle eyed Mbeki with interest. Mbeki struggled to keep from shouting an expletive at the back of Holland's blond head.

Holland held up his hands. "Gentlemen, gentlemen, I haven't asked him yet." He turned and made the offer in Zulu.

"Cha," Mbeki replied stiffly.

"Mbeki, they're over a barrel. Colonials love Gentleman Jim. Before he switched to Queensbury Rules, he once went fifty-eight rounds with an Eskimo in Canada, and forty-one rounds with an American who was shooting his mouth off in London." Holland scratched his eyebrow, telling Mbeki who the American had been.

"I will not fight your rematch, Holland."

"Not for fifty head, with another hundred if you win?" Holland was trying to appeal to Mbeki's greed, but the youngest son of Jama did not have a sweetheart with a ridiculous bride price. Such a herd would consume all of Mbeki's neighbours with jealousy, and when he was allowed to marry his homestead would soon be consumed in the bickering and squabbling of the dozens of women he could buy. "Okay, what about your King's orders? Beating Jim is going to impress every man in the audience, including officers, governors, civil servants--"

"Get them to pay me in rifles." Mbeki could see the idea made Holland uncomfortable. "Oh, I see: Willing to give the stupid kaffir a few old heifers to have his brain rearranged, but not willing to give him something he wants? A hundred rifles, at least fifty of which must be breach loaders, and all the rest must be percussion capped. Get me that, and I'll do your prize fight."

Holland turned, but he did not ask for guns. Mbeki opened his mouth to protest before he realized Holland had asked for enough money to purchase the rifles. When Holland offered half as an advance and half as the winner's purse, the man arranging the prize fight looked Mbeki up and down. He circled the warrior, tapping him once on the shoulder to assure himself that he was seeing muscle and not fat. As if he was buying a cow, he opened Mbeki's mouth to ascertain his teeth were in good order. Mbeki had no idea what this had to do with anything, but at length the man said, "Yebho." Then smiled, immensely proud that he knew a single word of kaffir talk.

Holland's camp had already unpacked the boxing equipment by the time they returned, but Mbeki took the setup with good graces. He would be beaten senseless, but returning from Natal with fifty good rifles after impressing the Whites with Zulu martial spirit would earn him a pair of brass armbands. "What are the rules of boxing?" He asked, stepping into a roped off square. He had learned to fight with his fists, but the sport itself had never been explained to him.

"As I said, Gentleman Jim fights with Queensbury Rules now, which kind of takes the fun out of things, but at least you won't die." Mbeki blinked, realizing he may have agreed to more than he bargained for. "You fight for three minutes at a time with a one-minute break between rounds. You fight with new gloves--"

"Gloves?" Mbeki looked at his hands. He had thought boxing was a bare-fisted sport.

"No, no. It's good. It makes it harder to hurt your hands, and it distributes the weight of your blow more evenly. Don't hit him below the belt, and don't hit him when he's down. If you go down or if you lean on the ropes, you've got a ten count to get up or you lose." Mbeki nodded his understanding.

"Now I fought Gentleman Jim with the old rules, and they really hurt. On the plus side, just competing got me enough money to come to Africa." He smiled, but it was pained. "Here's what I learned: Don't hit him anywhere but in the head. If you hit him anywhere else, he's not even going to slow down." Mbeki nodded. "Next, don't hit him in the nose. It makes him crazy." Mbeki nodded again, remembering Jobe. "Last, when he's bleeding, hit him where he leaks."

"That's all?"

"That's all," Holland assured him.

"Has he ever gone down?" Mbeki asked.

"Not in his professional career, no."

Inyati stepped into the ring wearing a ridiculous padded helmet. "He sounds like another Mbejane. Just be glad he doesn't have a spear."

"What are you wearing?" Mbeki looked at the padding as if it was some sort of trick or trap.

"You're going to be sparring with him." Mbeki looked down to see Holland had taken his hand and was running white adhesive tape between and around his fingers. The blond man looked up, smiling, "This'll keep you from breaking your fingers." He barked an order to one of his camp servants, and a pair of thick leather mittens flew through the air. He caught them by the lace connecting them, getting hit in the face by one of the gloves.

He slipped a glove over Mbeki's hand, who opened and closed his fist, testing the new material. "Go ahead, try it out." Mbeki took a step towards Inyati. "Oh, I almost forgot." Mbeki felt a piece of molded rubber being shoved into his mouth, sheathing his teeth like the terra cotta cocoons of his father's spears. "Go get him."

Mbeki walked up to his friend, the camp servants cheering him on. He took up the boxer's stance and put a quick left-right combo into Inyati's padded skull. The gloves felt great.

Chapter 42

The gloves itched like crazy. The tape between his fingers was driving him mad as it pulled on every invisible hair on the back of his hands. The canvas sides of his tent flapped in the breeze, disconcerting him. Outside he could hear the roar of the crowd, cheering for the match to begin.

"I'm not ready," Mbeki said. He had been allowed to keep the stripped down version of his native dress, and he was even allowed to forgo shoes, which he found uncomfortable in the extreme. They wanted a Zulu warrior in the ring, and Mbeki would oblige them. An official lifted up his mitt to examine it for any violation of the rules. There were no nails or razors or bits of glass. Holland wanted his revenge on both Gentleman Jim and Mbeki to be fair and honest.

"You're ready," Holland assured him. "Now remember, dance around him. Better to giya than just stand there letting him slug you, right? Use your left a lot. He's right-handed. Oh, and Mbeki?"

"Yebho?"

"Don't die." The blond man flashed his easy smile. Mbeki was coaxed to his feet by strong arms all around him. He was led down a path between two sets of towering bleachers. On the opposite side of the ring, a similar path between seats stood empty. Mbeki had asked that the servants be allowed to watch, but Holland had blanched at the thought of finding seats for so many black men at an event that was already sold out. He had allowed Inyati and Mbeki's eight Zulu to help him in Mbeki's corner. It was the best he could do.

"My Lords, Ladies, and Gentlemen!" A short, round man said from the center of the ring. "It is my pleasure to introduce to you, in this corner, weighing in at one hundred and seventy-five pounds, The Wizard of Zululand, Mbeki kaJama!" There were boos from the stands, but they had been set far enough back that no one dared throw anything for fear of hitting the aristocracy ringside.

The booing turned to cheers, and for a moment Mbeki thought there had been a change of heart; instead, he saw Gentleman Jim climb into the opposite corner of the four-sided ring. "And in this corner, weighing in at two hundred and twenty pounds --all of it Kent muscle-- Gentleman Jim!" The cheering grew louder, until Mbeki could hear the hoarse croak of men who had strained their voices. He shook his head in private amusement: In kwaZulu it was the cursed man indeed who could not shout and sing all day. The best parts of life were loud.

Gentleman Jim slipped off his robe, and there were some muttered exclamations from the audience. The boxer was shorter than Mbeki by the width of a palm, but he was completely encased in rippling muscles. The muscles in his arms and legs stood up under the skin like knots in a leather cord. Mbeki's keen eye suspected the beginnings of a paunch in the man's front, but the high waist of his trunks hid it from view.

The man was completely bald, but Mbeki judged only part of it was from age; the rest was helped with one of the fine steel razors the British produced. Gentleman Jim's mustache was pulled out into little spikes fixed with beeswax. His nose had been broken many times and set with something less than precision. His eyes were clever and merry.

The two walked to the center of the ring and had the rules explained to them so there could be no confusion. Gentleman Jim eyed Mbeki curiously, for he looked stronger and more capable than the usual fighters the colonies found for him. He remembered the aborigine in Australia who had been in secret training for two years. That Aussie black man had cracked four of Gentleman Jim's ribs and dislocated his right shoulder before he had finally gone down. He hoped this would not be a repeat of that unpleasantness.

"Does he speak English?" He asked the referee. The man shook his head. Mbeki did not enlighten him. "Have a good fight, Kaffir. I will make it as painless as possible." They touched gloves and returned to their corners.

With the ding of a bell the first round began, and the two came out to circle one another. Mbeki's Zulu cheered for him, singing regimental war songs and swishing the air with their sticks. Mbeki never took his eyes off of Gentleman Jim's shoulders, for Holland had told him they always predicted the blow. The right shoulder twitched, and Mbeki stepped to the left, jabbing Gentleman Jim above the eye while his opponent's blow found empty air. Another shoulder moved, and this time Mbeki stepped back, dancing away from the punch.

What's wrong with his right shoulder? Mbeki wondered. The first time Gentleman Jim had punched, his shoulder had twitched before his arm moved. Now the twitch seemed to be a spasm, a weakness. Mbeki dodged again then feinted twice with his right before bringing his left cross against Gentleman Jim's head. The crowd moaned, realizing the blow had possessed surprising force.

Gentleman Jim shook his head at the impact, sure now that this was no lamb led to the slaughter. The fight promoter had promised a good match, and they had found an opponent who knew how to box. He had better turn on the talent. He used the old one-two: Left jab, right cross. The black man dodged and danced and blocked, but some of the force leaked through. He could see the man reeling under his blows and threw every ounce of his extra forty-five pounds into his fists. Mbeki was backed up into a corner, unable to move, and Gentleman Jim managed to get a powerful hook behind Mbeki's guard, connecting with the Zulu's jaw.

The bell mercifully rang, and the two returned to their corners. Mbeki spat out the mouth piece and took a sip of water from Inyati's hands. "He only hit me once, but it hurt," he said.

The Matabele arched an eyebrow. "Have you said anything to him? Play with his mind!"

Mbeki nodded. Holland gave him a few pointers. The bell rang again, and Mbeki's world returned to the man opposite him.

The two advanced, but this time there was no preliminaries. Mbeki tried a cross to Gentleman Jim's head, and when the blow did not land he threw himself into a clinch with him. "I shall eat your heart. I shall slit open your belly. Never have you known a Zulu wizard. Never shall you meet another!" He said it in Zulu into the mustachioed fighter's ear, but the menace was there in any language. The two flew apart, and as Gentleman Jim again brought up his fists the right shoulder spasmed again.

Mbeki knew the fight was young, so he decided to experiment. Instead of punching for the well protected head, he would hit that right shoulder a few times. Gentleman Jim was right handed, and if his main stopping power could be disabled he might be taken apart a piece at a time. Two jabs to the right shoulder quickly had Gentleman Jim protecting it, and when he made a clumsy try for a left cross to Mbeki's face the Zulu stepped out from under it and hit the shoulder three times in quick succession. He felt something move under the muscle and gristle, and from the anguished groan he knew the man had an old injury there that still bothered him.

The round ended, and Holland asked Mbeki what he thought he was doing. "I said go for the head shot! He doesn't feel those body blows. I've broken two of his ribs myself. It doesn't stop him." Mbeki did not tell him his intuition. The sweat was streaming down him, and these short breaks between rounds were already blessed respites. He saw Gentleman Jim sitting in his own corner; one of his managers was massaging his right shoulder. Mbeki smiled around his mouth guard.

Rounds came and went, and Mbeki continued to smash Gentleman Jim's right shoulder and whisper curses in his ears. The crowd knew something was wrong with their champion, and soon they booed every glove that touched his shoulder, and any blow that was landed with his right fist, however feeble, was cheered as a major coup. Round nine saw Mbeki back in his corner, a cold compress shoved against the open wound above his eye. His left ear was cauliflowered, and his lips were swollen. Gentleman Jim's head and face were intact, but Mbeki could see that his right arm was nearly useless. It was time to step up the pressure.

"Make a cut and then hit him where he's bleeding?" Holland had told him these things, but all the blows to the head had clouded Mbeki's vaunted memory. Holland nodded, understanding the significance of Mbeki's lapse. He thumped Mbeki on the back and shoved him off the stool at the bell.

Mbeki no longer danced. He staggered. It took a great effort to keep up the footwork necessary to sidestep Gentleman Jim's blows. Fortunately, without his right Gentleman Jim had lost two-thirds of his fighting power and half of his ability to block head shots. Mbeki was careful to only make his strikes from Jim's right side, even if it did leave himself open to his opponent's left hooks. He hit Gentleman Jim once, twice, thrice in the head, all above the right eye. The boxer's head snapped back each time, but his skin refused to break.

The crowd had settled down to watch the two pugilists struggle, but this new tactic on the Zulu's part had them on their feet demanding Gentleman Jim to put the kaffir away. They had sat for nine and a half rounds as the black man had taken away Jim's arm and the white man had taken away Mbeki's dodge, but now their champion did not have the ability to hit the black man while he stood still, and the repeated jabs to the head looked bad.

"I'll put a dog on the roof of your hut," Mbeki hissed, punching into Gentleman Jim's block. "I'll set a tokoloshe upon you." He smashed his opponent's right shoulder again, forcing Gentleman Jim to lower his left arm from his head. "I shall drive your herd away and burn your kraal to the ground!" Mbeki used the left cross Gentleman Jim had come to fear, and he felt the glove come back sticky with the white man's blood. The bell rang, but the crowd roared: They wanted the two to fight through the break. Their champion was blooded.

With another ding the two were thrust back out of their corners. Mbeki's Zulu screamed their bloodlust, but he could barely hear them over the din of the crowd. He advanced jerkily towards Gentleman Jim, looking at the stupid spiked mustache. It struck him as ridiculous that they had been fighting this long and that waxed mustache had not been disturbed. His opening blow bristled the neat spike into a bottle brush, but the top of his fist caught the tip of Gentleman Jim's nose and pushed it back against the rest of his face until the cartilage snapped. Gentleman Jim's eyes, previously glazed over, snapped open, awakened by this new and outrageous pain. Mbeki was caught by a surprise right uppercut, a blow that must have hurt the champion almost as much as it hurt his opponent.

Mbeki reeled back as left jabs and crosses mixed with a few powerful right hooks and uppercuts. Everywhere that Gentleman Jim's blows landed --and the white man's rage did not lend itself to selective targeting-- clouds of sweat burst up like throwing a stone into a puddle. When the bell rang both fighters returned to their corners. Mbeki was battered and bruised all up and down his torso and head. Gentleman Jim was exhausted from his sudden burst of energy.

Two rounds later the two could barely stand. Gentleman Jim was a wreck, his right arm was not just useless: It was rigid, and the slightest motion inflicted upon it was unbearable. Mbeki dealt with aches and pains all over his body, and one of his eyes was swelled shut. The crowd was on their feet again, for their champion had done well in the previous round, but he was all used up.

Mbeki did something new, uppercutting Gentleman Jim in the abdomen, driving the air from his lungs. Then he smashed both fists, one after the other, into the cut above Gentleman Jim's eye. The crowd booed and hissed, but the Englishman could do nothing to defend himself. He landed a left jab under Mbeki's guard, but it lacked the strength to crack a rib. Mbeki hit him again and again, the way he pummeled his punching bag.

Gentleman Jim may have spent his career fighting poorly trained opponents, but he could take a beating. It was with surprise, then, that he felt himself falling backwards to the ground. Mbeki kept swinging at the air where Gentleman Jim had been standing, but Holland called him over to his corner to see if the champion would rise. Mbeki went to his sanctuary gratefully, but Holland would not allow him to sit, and Mbeki could not figure out why.

The official was counting, one, two, three, and Gentleman Jim was struggling to rise. The crowd was howling, and his manager was ordering him, pleading with him, to get up. The show had sold out to prove that an Anglo-Saxon was the physical superior of any Kaffir, even the Zulu, but Gentleman Jim lay on his back like an overturned turtle, desperate to suck air into his lungs.

Four, five, six. Gentleman Jim rolled over onto his belly and crawled to the edge of the ring. He hooked one blood-smeared glove over the ropes, then the other. There was a trail of blood on the white floor, some of it from his head and some of it from his mitts. He heaved up, but the muscles in his right shoulder refused to clench.

Seven, eight. Gentleman Jim had his legs under him, and he extended them painfully, as if he was carrying a rucksack loaded with bricks. He stood on his feet, swaying, and he let go of the ropes. The official stopped counting. The crowd roared their encouragement. The bell rang, and Gentleman Jim needed two of his assistants to lower him onto his stool.

"He's finished, Mbeki! Just plant one or two between his eyes and it's over." Holland was pouring water down Mbeki's front and shoulders, trying to rinse off the worst of the blood and spit and sweat. "Cetshwayo will give you a set of brass armbands for this!"

Mbeki looked down at his arms in a daze. What brass armbands? His head hurt, and he was thirsty. Holland would not give him anything to drink, too worried that someone would throw it up. Does he mean me? Mbeki wondered. He heard the evil ding again and hauled himself to his feet. His good eye would only half open now, and he had to scan the ring to see his opponent lurch to his feet and stagger to the center of the ring with knees locked, lest they buckle beneath him.

Mbeki went out to meet him, and he felt a fist connect with the blind side of his head. The crowd roared, but something was wrong: The room tipped up on its side, and the floor rushed up to meet his face. He heard a man counting in English, 'One, two, three.'

"Wo, I'm down." He laughed with relief.

'Four, five, six.' The counting annoyed him. It was comfortable on the ground.

"Get up Mbeki! Get up!" He heard Holland calling him, and he brought himself up on his hands and knees. There was a reason why he was supposed to stand up, but he could not remember what it might be. 'Seven, eight, nine.' He was on his feet and swaying. His half open eye caught sight of Gentleman Jim leaning against the ropes in his corner, waiting for the ten count. "Go get him, Mbeki! Go!" Holland and the Zulu were the only ones cheering for him; everyone else booed and hissed. A gin bottle flew through the crowd, smashing on the entry pathway he had walked down an eternity ago.

Gentleman Jim and Mbeki hobbled towards each other, every step an agony. Mbeki's bad eye was showing him things that were not there, and halfway to his opponent he threw up his block at an imaginary hail of blows. The crowd fell silent as Mbeki rocked under an invisible assault. Gentleman Jim stopped too, unsure of himself. Inyati clenched his teeth. "Mbeki, uSuthu!" The Zulu echoed his war cry. "Ingonyama!" They repeated that one too.

Mbeki lowered his guard, hearing his brother's name. The white man stood before him, battered and bruised. He took a step towards him, and another. "I'm going to make your balls into a necklace, you cattle stealing, baby eating, mother raping white bastard." He said in English. Gentleman Jim's eyes flew open in surprise, and he watched as Mbeki's right jab caught him right between the eyebrows. He fell backwards, and he did not get back up.

Mbeki staggered back to his corner, ignoring the crowd's booing and his friends' cheering. A bottle of whiskey was thrust into his mouth, and he took two hard swallows, ignoring the alcohol burning his crushed lips. Behind him a man was saying something about a winner, and Mbeki felt someone grab his right hand, lifting it skyward. He did not have the strength to protect himself from the coming blows. It did not seem to matter, though. No one was hitting him.

Gentleman Jim walked up to shake the hand that beat him so mercilessly. He looked Mbeki in the eyes, the blood craze leaving them both. "I've got to ask you, do you speak English?" The man shook his head as if to drive out an echo trapped inside the cave of his skull.

"What?" Mbeki asked in Zulu. Only when Gentleman Jim had left did he finally smile, knowing the champion would remember his English words forever as a delusion.

Chapter 43

Ingonyama greeted them at the gates of oNdini with a stranger's face. There were bags under his eyes, unshaven stubble on his jaw, and a desperate look in his eyes. The smile he had been forming at the sight of his long-absent brother froze into a grimace as soon as he saw Inyati walking at Mbeki's side.

The life of the King's Champion had been far from rosy while Mbeki was away. He found no peace in his wife's company. Inyati's name echoed in his head whenever he saw her, so he spent very little time with Nandhi for fear he would come out and ask what he dared not know for sure. Instead he made every excuse to be in the field with his men, seeking escape in company he trusted implicitly.

Ingonyama looked at Jojo and Sompisi, who were smiling and slapping Mbeki on the shoulder in welcome. The two of them were his rocks, the unmovable foundations upon which he depended. With Nandhi he was always worrying, always wondering, but these two never let him brood. You can trust a man more than a woman, he thought, then chided himself. He did not know if Nandhi was faithless, and it was the not knowing that ate at his heart.

Maybe we should have a child, he thought to himself for the hundredth time. He had spent months casting about for a way to heal the rift between them without asking his wife about Inyati. A boy --a son-- as trustworthy as these two. That will fix everything, he lied to himself.

In his worst moments, lying alone beside her in their hut, he threw the darkest possible light onto the possibilities: Nandhi had seemed a virgin when they had been wed, but even the most cursory interrogation of the local medicine women had told him virginity could be faked with enough notice to prepare. So Inyati and Nandhi might have become lovers when he was dealing with Zungu Nkulu and the Tsonga Tribute; if Mbeki had found out about the affair during the wedding that would explain why he had beaten Inyati so mercilessly. It all fit together so well.

Yet here his brother stood with the man who had made a cuckold of him. Ingonyama knew Mbeki too well to think his brother could have discovered Inyati and Nandhi's secret and then forgiven the Matabele. Something was not right. Ingonyama mulled it over even while Mbeki spoke to him.

"Ingonyama, can you hear me?"

"What?"

"What would you like me to do with all these rifles?" Mbeki casually gestured to the two wagons he had bought to haul his winnings to oNdini, as if he always brought home a hundred precious firearms.

In that moment the insomnia, the paranoia, the self-doubts and worries were all put away. Ingonyama was working again, and his work always came before his personal problems. "We'll move them into the armouries in the royal quarters." Ingonyama supervised the transfer of the rifles from Mbeki's wagons, talking all the time about Mbeki's adventures with the white hunter. He was careful not to mention or look at Inyati.

Only when the transfer was well underway, with dozens of porters streaming from the wagons to the royal quarters and back, did Ingonyama focus on one aspect of the small talk. He was not satisfied with Mbeki's explanation as to how he had come by the guns. It seemed incredible to him that the British would give away so many good rifles just to see two men fight. "So what is this boxing, exactly?" He asked, toying with his brother.

"You clench your hands into fists, like this, and then beat the other man unconscious." Mbeki demonstrated, feeling marvelous that all his bruises and aches had finally left him.

"Like this?" Ingonyama clenched his right hand as Mbeki had demonstrated.

"Yebho," Mbeki laughed, his pride getting the best of him. He had stood toe to toe with a world champion and won. "Go on, take your best shot." Mbeki was still smiling when Ingonyama brought his fist against the side of his skull. He was still smiling when his eyes rolled back into his head. Somewhere between standing and lying in the dust the smile left him.

"Like that?" Ingonyama asked, wishing the blow had struck Inyati.

"Something like that," Mbeki agreed, his face in the dirt of the parade ground.

Inyati was careful neither to laugh nor move. He had read Ingonyama's body language from a hundred paces. The King's Champion was tight across the shoulders; his brows were knit with unpleasant thoughts. He knows, thought Inyati. He knows about Nandhi, maybe even suspects the poisoning. It will only take the smallest of confirmations from me, and I am a dead man. Ingonyama was laughing now, but Inyati heard no joy in those deep booms. Ingonyama was like a gutshot elephant: All he needed was someone to gore.

Chapter 44

"Life is good," Mbeki sighed, rolling the stalk of grass from one side of his mouth to the other. Jama made a noise of agreement. The two sat by the hearth, sweating and content, watching the clay encasing the spears harden in the heat. The two had spent the day smithing in Jama's forest, and now they could relax.

"Bhibhi's preparing supper tonight," Jama said. "She's turned into quite the little woman, let me tell you. Cooks, cleans, and she has a gift with the garden."

Mbeki nodded. He had not spent much time at home while Bhibhi was growing up, and when he had been here he had been out in the pastures while she had always been within a few paces of her mother, but there was no denying she was the most eligible single woman in the valley; Punga's daughters had all inherited his ugly face and irritating personal habits.

In a few more years Bhibhi's female age group would be allowed to marry. Mbeki wondered if she had any admirers; he remembered her girl's crush on Inyati, but she had hardly seen him in years, and he doubted that infatuation would have survived the intervening time.

"So how many were killed?" Jama finally asked. He had avoided discussing the matter for Mbeki's entire visit, but it was why his son had come in the first place; when Cetshwayo had granted Mbeki the brass armbands of a royal favourite he had also made him a royal messenger. Ever since that day, over a year ago now, Mbeki had been running the length and breadth of kwaZulu giving the King's instructions or spreading important news.

"Seventy-five," Mbeki said slowly. The heat was not the only thing making him uncomfortable. Last year Cetshwayo had given the Chieftain ibutho, made up of men only a few years younger than Jama, the right to marry any girl in the land between nineteen and twenty-one years of age. The Chieftains were Cetshwayo's favourite regiment, he had even been a member before becoming King, but the girls in question had been expecting to marry men their own age from the Humbler of King's regiment. The young men had been forced with gritted teeth to stand by while their sweethearts were married off to men twice their age.

The girls had not been happy either. There had been a number of refusals, and many girls had declared they would not marry anyone outside the Humbler of Kings ibutho. Cetshwayo had been furious; the right to declare who married whom was one of the few royal powers that had never been usurped by the great men of the nation. He had sent Ingonyama and his Invincibles out with orders to kill any woman who refused to marry. They returned with seventy-five dead maidens' blood on their spears.

"How could Ingonyama be a part of that?" Jama was proud of his sons, but they no longer lived with him. Bhibhi had become the center of his world, and he could not imagine his little girl being cut down in her youth for refusing to marry a man old enough to be her father.

"He was only following orders, Baba."

"That's no excuse, and you know it."

"That is the law, and it is a good one," Mbeki said. Jama nodded his reluctant acceptance. The two sat in silence until the clay coating the spearheads had hardened to the consistency of a brittle stone, then they hauled them out of the ashes and smashed off the terra cotta cocoons. They sharpened and polished, careful not to mar the surface of the blades. The umKhosi Festival was coming again and, as every year since Jama had been made a royal favourite, he would take spearheads to his king as a gift.

"So how is Ingonyama?" Jama asked as they descended the slope, both of them heavily laden with equipment. Jama had only seen his eldest son once since his marriage two and a half years ago, and his son had seemed disturbed. Physically he was as fit as ever, but there was something haunting in his expression; he did not seem to get much sleep, and he was throwing himself into his work with a dedication that bordered on madness.

"About the same. He has days where he is his happy old self, but those are usually days where the king orders him out into the field, taking tribute or skirmishing on the borders. When he killed a Boer who was driving off some cattle he smiled all the way back to oNdini, but as soon as he saw the gates on the horizon his smile disappeared."

"He only has the one wife, doesn't he?" The question was rhetorical. If there had been any other marriages Jama would have known about it. Mbeki did not bother to answer in the negative; he was still hot. "It sounds like he has trouble at home, but with only one wife what could the problem be?"

Jama and Mbeki shook their heads in unison; whenever there was trouble at Jama's homestead it was when one of the wives was having it out with another one, and all three demanded Jama be present to mediate. Mbeki was just as puzzled by Ingonyama's behaviour as Jama; Inyati's infatuation with Nandhi and contemplation of poison were unknown to his brother, and much better left that way.

"Well, what about my grandson?" Jama's solemn face broke into his lopsided grin. The fact that he was a grandfather ten years earlier than he had expected did not bother him at all. It just meant he would be around to spoil the boy that much longer.

"Galazi is well, if a one-year-old is ever well. His mother dotes on him, but that's to be expected." Jama nodded his head. Ingonyama was a father, but that did not seem to have brought him peace from whatever his demons were. Still, Jama delighted in his grandson. When he went to oNdini for the umKhosi Festival he would drop in on the boy with a toy wooden spear Kandhla had carved for him. That would make Galazi's eyes light up.

The two returned home, each lost in their own thoughts. Bhibhi's meal was not comparable to Nandhi's banquets, but it was filling and country flavoured. Mbeki slept in the guest hut with the blacksmith tools, and the next day Mbeki and Jama, borrowing two of Punga's youngest sons as bearers, started off towards oNdini.

The actual umKhosi Festival would be held at kwaNodwengu, the rebuilt homestead of dead Mpande, but Cetshwayo's court was at oNdini, so when they arrived on the ikhanda-filled plain beside the White Mfolozi they headed straight for the King's Great Place. Mbeki pointed out Ingonyama's homestead perched atop a nearby ridge, and Jama nodded in appreciation. There were five huts, which was a lot for a single wife and one child, but perhaps Ingonyama was of a mind to have more children, maybe even more wives. It did not occur to Jama that Ingonyama slept in a separate hut from his wife most nights, or had huts for his Invincible friends to sleep in whenever they were too drunk to stagger home.

The two approached Cetshwayo's throne with care, as there was a loud argument going on between Hamu, Cetshwayo, and the induna of the Humbler of Kings.

"It is unreasonable, Cousin. Unreasonable!" Hamu's thin beard trembled with fury. He had neglected to call Cetshwayo by any title but that of a relation, and the insult was not lost on anyone. "The Chieftains are the greatest regiment, and oNdini does not have room to house them and four thousand puppies!" Hamu was the induna of the Chieftains ibutho, but that gave him no right to launch such a tirade at the king.

"The Chieftains, even with the additional men I have put into them to keep their numbers up, have only twenty-five hundred warriors; the Humbler of Kings number four thousand. There are fourteen hundred huts here at oNdini. I assure you, everyone will fit." Cetshwayo's voice was heavy with authority, but he refused to raise his voice to an issue he considered minor enough to be beneath his notice, and so some of the effect was lost. He was twice the king his father was; everyone acknowledged it, but where Mpande's umKhosi festivals had been spent greeting old friends and settling old scores, Cetshwayo had to deal with Hamu every single year.

"It's not a question of fitting!" Hamu threw his hands up into the air in exasperation. "My men have brought their wives with them, and they can't spend a moment in their company without some boy telling them to clear out of the hut because he wants to sleep." No one was foolish enough to mention that many of the Chieftains' wives had been the Humbler of Kings' girlfriends. Those events were still too raw, and Cetshwayo could easily explode at anyone who questioned his decision yet again. Even faithful Ntsingwayo had disagreed with his King on that fiasco; Cetshwayo admitted to himself that the matter had gotten away from him, but publicly he could not waiver.

"Hamu, this is an order to the induna of my best ibutho," Cetshwayo gestured to his cousin. "And to the induna of my strongest ibutho," He gestured to the other man. "Deal with it between yourselves. The Humbler of Kings shall one day take the Chieftains' place as my best and most-favoured men. That day is not here yet, but it is coming. I will not allow my two favourite regiments to quarrel on the happiest holiday of the year. You are dismissed." Hamu stood there trembling for a moment before he joined the Humbler of Kings' induna in genuflection. They departed in different directions.

When Mbeki and Jama finally moved from the inner palisade wall to kneel before the king, Cetshwayo was in no mood for their visit. "Jama I will speak with. Mbeki, follow Hamu. Make sure he doesn't do anything foolish."

"Yebho, Nkosi Nkulu," Mbeki jumped up, glad to be excused. As a royal messenger he had dozens of royal interviews in a year, and the novelty had worn off. He slipped between the palisade fences and worked his way up the right side of the ikhanda. Everywhere there was discontent and shouting. Young men disrespected their elders and refused to take the beatings that the old men felt would put their inferiors in their place. Mbeki even saw three Humbler of Kings dragging a Chieftain out of his hut by his ankles as his wife screamed from within. This chaos could not go on.

Eventually he worked his way to within sight of the hut Hamu had set aside as the headquarters of the Chieftains ibutho. Every hut in the file and for ten huts in either direction along the four rows was filled with Chieftains, and a constant guard of Chieftains prevented any Humbler of Kings from entering this one oasis of sanity. Mbeki was of the Flycatcher Bird ibutho, which was so closely associated with the Humbler of Kings that he too was denied entry.

Mbeki watched from as near as the Chieftains would allow him as induna after induna entered Hamu's hut. Hamu was the regimental induna of the Chieftains, but it seemed that each company induna or member of the Chieftains who had royal lineage had been invited to this meeting. Mbeki hoped Hamu was merely venting his rage on his subordinates, but he did not think so. Mbeki watched with mounting suspicion as Jobe exited the hut. No one else left, and the meeting was clearly not over, but Hamu's disgraced son was leaving the Chieftain's secure zone as fast as he could without drawing attention to himself.

Mbeki was torn, knowing he had been ordered to watch Hamu but suspecting that Jobe was up to something. The squash-nosed man was trying to act nonchalant, and that made him all the more conspicuous. Mbeki made his decision and followed Hamu's son.

Just as there was a Chieftains safe zone in the right wing, the left wing of Cetshwayo's Great Place held a safe zone four huts wide by twenty huts long guarded by the toughest and least respectful members of the Humbler of Kings. Jobe had no regiment, but his age group put him in the Red Needle ibutho, just a couple of years older than the Humbler of Kings; he entered freely. Mbeki's Flycatcher Bird uniform and brass armbands got him passed the pickets as well.

Mbeki watched as Jobe entered the headquarters of the Humbler of Kings, but knew he had no excuse to get close enough to eavesdrop. To hear a normal conversation inside a hut from outside one might need to go so far as to press an ear against the thatch. He was bound to be noticed doing such a rude thing, and at the very least he would be dragged before Cetshwayo for punishment, losing track of Hamu's son.

Mbeki watched as a man ran out of the hut and returned with four friends, each of them staggering under the weight of beer pots. The noise within the hut gradually grew loud enough to be heard from where he stood, but it was not an argument; it was the sound of a party. More beer went in, empty pots went out, and anyone who left to throw up quickly had his place inside taken by someone eager to join the drunken carousal. When Jobe stumbled out around midnight, falling down drunk, Mbeki had long since gone to bed; he had dismissed Jobe's presence there as nothing more than a young royal looking for a good time. He could not have been more wrong.

Chapter 45

The next day was the start of the Great umKhosi Festival, and the two amabutho inside oNdini reluctantly formed up on the great parade ground. They would have to march out to kwaNodwengu one at a time, for the gate was not wide enough for both to file out together, but neither wanted to be the first to go. Cetshwayo had already gone to nearby kwaNodwengu, which was just far enough away to be inconvenient for him to be summoned to settle the dispute.

"You can go first: Yours is the junior regiment, and this isn't really your ikhanda. Besides, my men would not trust you to be around our huts unsupervised. I have already had complaints of theft, and my men all swear they are not to blame." Hamu's needle eyes played over his opponent, secretly delighting in his discomfort.

"Oh, don't go on and on, Hamu. It's too early in the day." The chief induna of the Humbler of Kings held his head with one hand, his hangover raging. He did not know what had started the party at his headquarters last night, but almost every one of his izinduna was recovering from its effects. "My men are still eating..." His mouth tasted like it was full of cotton. "You can go first; we will follow you as soon as we are done." Both knew no one was eating out of hunger. His izinduna were desperately trying to sober up, chewing dry mealie cakes, drinking boiled water, sticking their heads over fires burning scented woods or precious used coffee grounds.

"Very well," Hamu gave a hand signal to the Chieftain induna closest to the main gate, and soon the whole ibutho was up and streaming towards the kraal's gate. Any second now... Hamu thought. This will be the cheapest victory I have ever earned. It had cost him one good ox to buy enough beer to inebriate the Humbler of Kings commanders and two more oxen to buy the actions of a single boy. If only I had thought of this years ago.

Near the main gate the youth was sweating despite the cool dawn light. His oxen were safe at his father's homestead up in Hamu's country, and now he had to earn them. His swished his stick through the air, assuring himself once more than he still had the vital piece of lumber. The Chieftain commander was coming closer and closer to the main gate, closer and closer to the young man. "Boys!" The youth shouted.

"Would you have these Chieftains go first, while better men have to wait?" The young men around him looked startled, but the commander who should have defused the situation was huddled over a fire by the royal quarters waiting for the wedding drum in his head to stop beating.

"They marry our girls; they order us around, and now they will be the first to see the king. I've had enough of this!" The youth jumped forward, slashing his stick against the side of a passing Chieftain's face. The nearest Chieftain induna had been expecting the blow for some time, and he ordered his company to engage the youths with sticks. The battle grew and grew, and Hamu's smile spread wider as each new company from both sides rushed into the fight.

"Now, now, boys, don't fight," Hamu said loud enough for the drunken izinduna of the Humbler of Kings to hear him, but not loud enough to persuade any of the fighting men to stop. Slowly his smile dimmed. His Chieftains were being beaten; the youths outnumbered his men two to one, but somehow he had not expected the puppies to beat the dogs. "These young ones are spilling blood on our best dancing gear. Take your assegais to them! It's the King's fault for shoving them into our place!" He had planned to order this when the stick fighting became vicious, but now that the possibility of defeat was looming, he moved his schedule forward. The izinduna of the Humbler of Kings looked at him in horror.

Jobe and the Chieftain izinduna ordered their warriors furthest from the fight to rush to their spears. The ones closest to the fracas ordered their men to push the Humbler of Kings out of the gates, preventing them from reaching their own weapons. One of the Humbler of Kings izinduna rushed up to Jobe, trying to reason with him, but Hamu's son pulled out his revolver and shot him through the forehead.

Mbeki awoke at the sound of the shot and tore out from under his kaross as if on fire. A gun had been fired inside the Great Place of the Great Chief of the People of Heaven: there was no possibility that something good was about to happen. He entered the parade ground with a stunned expression on his face. The Humbler of Kings regiment had been driven out of the ikhanda, leaving half a dozen bodies behind. He scampered on top of the nearest hut to get a good view of what was happening outside.

The Humbler of Kings had reformed by Ingonyama's homestead, but they were only armed with sticks while the Chieftains had spears. The two regiments stood facing each other in battle formations, their full dancing regalia soaked in blood so that the white ox tails had turned to a nauseating pink. Most men had bleeding welts from the stick fight, but those would heal; the Chieftains' assegais would not be as forgiving as their sticks.

Ingonyama emerged from his kraal along with Jojo and Sompisi. They strode between the two regiments, trying to calm them down. They were heavily armed, as Invincibles always are, and the Chieftains were reluctant to face the three giants.

"Return to your huts!" Ingonyama boomed. It was the wrong order, for both sides started buzzing like angry bees. They lived in the same huts, and neither would ever share quarters again; the blood on their clothes was proof of that. "Put down your spears! This is the umKhosi Festival, not the Swazi campaigns." That was another mistake: The Chieftains had fought valiantly in the failed Swazi campaigns, and they were enraged that yet another young man mocked the memory of their hard fighting youth.

"Chieftains!" The war cry went up.

"uSuthu!" The Humbler of Kings replied. The two regiments charged against one another, and Ingonyama was engulfed in mayhem as uncles killed nephews and cousins killed cousins.

Standing on the hut Mbeki could not see what had happened to his brother. He strained for the snow white shields of the Invincibles, but three men in the blizzard of black and white and red shields did not stand out.

"You!" His head snapped down to look at three middle-aged men on the ground below him. "Get down from there! You aren't welcome in oNdini anymore!"

"I'm not in the Humbler of Kings!" Mbeki protested. "I'm a royal messenger!"

"I don't care if you're royalty, pup! When you boys learn to respect your elders, we'll treat you like adults. Until then, get your ass out to pasture like a good herd boy." One of them lunged up the side of the hut, trying to grab Mbeki's ankle.

"I haven't done anything to you!" Mbeki said.

"We don't care!" The three began to scale the side of the hut, grabbing the bindings that held thatch and pole together. Their combined weight pulled it one way, and the pressure of Mbeki's retreating feet across the top of the dome pulled another. A rift appeared under Mbeki, and he was falling into the hut before he had time to cry out.

He lay there for a long time in a semiconscious daze, while flashes of light danced in the murkiness of his mind. When he awoke he got to his feet shakily and exited the ruined hut. His tormentors must have left him once the fight had gone out of him. Mbeki staggered out into the parade ground. Lit only by torches, Cetshwayo was passing judgment. Ingonyama stood behind him with his assegai coated in dried blood. The King's Champion was unhurt, but Mbeki knew he would be one of the only ones who had escaped unscathed.

Cetshwayo could not hide his scorn for all involved. "I fine every man of the Humbler of Kings one beast. They shall sleep in the fields tonight and every night until the umKhosi Festival is done." The old familiar weight appeared again in Mbeki's stomach, the one that intuited the future for him, and Mbeki knew that this would be the last umKhosi Festival the Zulu Kingdom would ever hold. The realization made him sad. "I blame Hamu for this fight. If he had not called for spears, I would still have two hundred of my finest warriors by my side." There were rumblings from the crowd. Clearly they thought Hamu was the one in the right and the king was wrong.

Hamu smiled as he listened to the Great Elephant's proclamations. Earlier that day Zokufa and Jobe had dragged a body to him for his inspection; it had once been the stupid boy who had taken two of his oxen. He had already sent word by fast messenger to reclaim them. He would accept whatever fine Cetshwayo imposed with humility. The people knew he had done what was in their best interest. Hamu would retire to his mini-kingdom in the North. The King would never dare to interfere with his fief now that the Chieftains considered Hamu to be the wiser ruler. For one ox's worth of beer, Hamu had advanced his career ten years. Only a war could interfere with his plans, and he had ideas about that too. The sun had set in the sky, but it shone brightly on Hamu.

Chapter 46

Nandhi moved from pot to kettle to pan with an effortless grace. She had decided on an outdoor lunch in the center of the homestead's courtyard. From here the cool autumn breeze would erase the smell of cow dung without detracting from the aroma of the food, and the view of the oNdini kraal below Ingonyama's hillock was as beautiful as when they had first climbed it the night they had met. She sighed, enjoying her own company and the bubble and burble of her cooking. Behind her, Mbeki stood at the kraal's gate, watching her. "I see you, Nandhi."

She spun around, surprised that he was early. "I see you, Mbeki." She gave him one of her most dazzling smiles; inside she sensed danger, knowing Mbeki was too good at seeing hidden things.

"Where's Galazi?" He asked, crossing the threshold into the courtyard.

"I gave him to a neighbour to watch for me. He's old enough to make a pest of himself at meals, and I wanted to talk with you without interruption."

"I can't be long." He touched his brass armbands. "I'm off on another trip." Ntsingwayo had lobbied the king for years to make Mbeki a royal messenger when he was old enough, but now that he had the job that he realized it was no favour: Being a royal messenger was hard work, and time passed by too quickly when you were never in one place for long.

"Where are you going this time?" Nandhi asked, positioning exactly the right sized piece of wood under the pot to speed up the stew without burning it.

"I'm heading south with new policies for the clan chiefs concerning the British."

"War measures?" She asked. A new barrage of demands had reached the Court, demanding the abaQulusi territories be handed over to the Boer land claimants. Ntsingwayo was forming a political faction to lobby the King to let a war come and settle things once and for all. Cetshwayo, for his part, could not understand the Whites' insistence: He had done nothing to provoke them except lead his people in a more fair and just way than his predecessors.

The kettle began to sing, so she took it off the fire and put it onto a circle of smooth river rocks. "Trade restrictions and court gossip," Mbeki replied, walking towards her little picnic in the making, gratefully taking the bowl of warm water she offered him to rinse his hands, face, and mouth; in the back of his head he felt a tingling, knowing something was not right. "But you didn't invite me up here when your husband and son were gone to talk about my trip."

She sighed again, taking the fillets from the pan and put them onto two wooden platters before replying. "I wanted to speak to you about your brother."

Mbeki dropped his shield to the ground and sat on it. He took the platter from her, taking a bite of the meat and swallowing before he replied. He let the taste linger, admitting to himself that the woman worked miracles. Finally he answered, "You really mean you want to talk about Inyati."

She sucked air in through her mouth as if the fillet was too hot, as opposed to the perfect temperature. "You know?" She was not sure if that would make things easier or harder.

"That Ingonyama is running around like a bull about to be turned into a steer? That Inyati has been living with my father and avoiding this place like the plague? That you and he were only flirting, but that somehow Ingonyama suspects there's more to it than that, but he's too proud to bring it out into the open?"

"What should I do?" She stood up, unable to sit still with her pent up frustration. *One slip, one clumsy little slip, and I have ruined my marriage!* She had raged against herself ever since her wedding night, but at the same time she was furious with Ingonyama for even suspect her of impropriety. *What low opinion could he have of me that he would think I would do such a thing?*

Almost three years had passed without seeing Inyati, but still Ingonyama had neither unbent nor just come out and brought matters to a head. There was a wall between them, invisible but sturdy, and only rarely did they see glimpses of their former comfort.

For a while Galazi had brought them together, but soon enough Ingonyama had accused her of coddling the boy. She had replied that he was never around, so of course she was raising their son, and before she knew it the old wall was back, higher and thicker than before, and with still fewer cracks. Quietly she asked, "What can I do?"

"What do you think of Inyati?" Mbeki remained sitting, taking another bite of his fillet. His eyes never left her face.

"What do you mean, what do I think of him?" She replied defensively. Inside she was trembling. Ingonyama was so unstable, always suspicious, always worrying. He never got a whole night's sleep in her hut, and he would yell at Galazi whenever their boy disturbed their uncomfortable silences. When he was gone she wished he was home, but when he was home she counted the days until he had to leave again.

Inyati was settled. He did not spend all his time with warriors, as if he was deliberately avoiding her. The first night had been a slip of the tongue, but every day since she had thought of the Matabele prince and wondered what her life would have been like if she had made a different choice.

"You know exactly what I mean: I am your husband's brother, and as I am the only one in this entire family who knows what everyone else knows, as well as what everyone else thinks. Tell me what you want."

"I would not betray Ingonyama," She said.

A sudden thought occurred to him. "What set Ingonyama off in the first place? He doesn't know anything for sure, or he would have done something about it. He suspects, and my brother's imagination doesn't work from nothing." As he spoke he realized this could only be something Nandhi had done. "What have you said to him, woman?" His question was cutting, and he saw his brother's wife flinch.

"I called out Inyati's name on our wedding night."

Now it was Mbeki's turn to suck in a breath of air. He felt as if he had swum down to the bottom of a lake and only now was he emerging to the light. Poor Ingonyama! Inyati is lucky my brother has not mentioned this to me. The look on my face would have had another assegai in the Matabele's belly before I could ever have calmed him down. "That was stupid of you."

She stood there in silence, glad that something would be done. "It was a mistake." Mbeki said nothing; she could see his mind working behind his eyes, weighing options and discarding plans. "What can I do?" She asked, desperate for him to speak again.

"You can do nothing. You will say nothing about any of this to him. If you two were going to sort this out on your own, you would have done it by now. I'll have to tell him in my own way at the right time. Do you understand me?" She nodded. Mbeki decided that was not enough. "This will take time; I don't see him that often. Not a word from you, is it heard?"

"It is heard," She murmured.

"Fine," He stood, realizing the food had been a trap; she had lured him in and lowered his defenses to trick him into dealing with his brother. "This has been going on for three years? In three years you two couldn't talk to each other? Now I'm supposed to fix everything in exchange for lunch, am I?" He threw his platter to the ground, tipped her stew into the ashes, and knocking her kettle over. He walked out of the kraal without looking back, not caring how hard she wept.

Chapter 47

Mbeki took a pinch of snuff. The mixture of noxious powders made him sneeze, driving out any evil influences he might have inhaled during his long run south. He rubbed his chin, feeling the rasp of stubble beneath his fingers. Maybe I should grow a goatee, he thought absently.

He stood at the top of the kraal, ignoring the ache in his legs. At least the running kept him warm. The winter winds could chill an idle man to the bone, but Mbeki had been far from idle: Sihayo's kraal was as far south as the Valley of the Three Homesteads and further to the west, but Mbeki had made it here from north of the Black Mfolozi in just seven days. The Mzinyathi River was just out of sight beyond the hills to the west, and beyond that lay Natal.

"I see you, Mbeki," Sihayo said, not rising from his woodworking. He was carving a decorative detail onto a milk pale with wood chisels; he clearly did not want to set aside such worthy work to speak to a royal messenger who would be bringing bad news.

"I see you, Nkosi." Sihayo was the chief of Qungebe, the clan that held this stretch of the river in the name of Cetshwayo and Sihayo, not necessarily in that order. "I bring tidings from oNdini. Negotiations do not go well."

Sihayo set aside his carvings with a sigh. If war with the British came his people would be the first to suffer; kwaJim, or Rorke's Drift as the Whites called it, was almost opposite his kraal. It was one of the few places anywhere on the Mzinyathi and Thekula Rivers where a large force could cross quickly in numbers sufficient to make resistance impossible. "Tell me."

It had been more than a year since the Lord Carnarvon Mbeki had met at the party had been replaced with Sir Bartle Frere, and the new man had even less tact and diplomacy than his predecessor. As one trader had told Cetshwayo, "He wants to treat the kaffirs like wogs!" Mbeki assumed that wogs must have inhabited the land of India that Carnarvon said Frere previously governed. Whatever Frere's plans were, his demands were insane.

"The white men are saying all sorts of things were promised during Cetshwayo's coronation ceremony. They demand the abaQulusi territory for Boer settlers. They demand that no one may be killed according to our laws unless they have first had the trial prescribed by their laws. They demand that every warrior in Cetshwayo's army be allowed to marry and return to civilian life. Their demands are impossible. They know they are being impossible!

"Already a white impi is being gathered at Natal. Our spies say there is a transportation shortage; the white settlers won't give the army enough wagons and oxen to move all of their equipment, but it is only a matter of time. All Frere needs is an excuse, and he will start a war."

Sihayo shook his head. Just as Zibhebhu and Hamu traded with the Portuguese for luxuries, rarities, firearms and other goods, Sihayo and his sons traded with the Boers and British. War would change all that, probably forever. He looked at his kraal around him, knowing it would be the first target on the British general's list; every white man who knew anything about kwaZulu knew of Sihayo's kraal. "What else?" While this news was bad enough, Sihayo's own contacts across the river had already told him of it. Mbeki had come for another reason.

"Two things: First, there was an evil omen seen at oNdini. The Royal Court watched above it as an eagle circled above us. From nowhere four hawks appeared; they broke the eagle's wings, and when it fell to the ground they devoured it while it was still alive." Sihayo's eyes went wide. "The izangoma were sent for, and their prediction was that the Zulu Kingdom is about to be set upon from all sides by our enemies. Without great luck we shall not prevail." Sihayo took some snuff from his own container, agreeing that what Mbeki said was true.

"Second, my King knows that you have many dealings with the men south of the Mzinyathi River." Sihayo's jaw set. "He asks only that you do not send any warriors into Natal for the next few months. Tell your business partners to come here. There is too much danger of an incident if Zulu warriors cross the river."

A gunshot echoed off the hills, and the two sat still for a long time. "What was that?" Mbeki asked.

"My son and some of my followers have retrieved a wife of mine; the second time they have fetched one back for me, as a matter of fact. The whores' fathers married them to me for the bride price, and then my wives both fled west to be with their lovers." Mbeki's heart sank. There were no homesteads west of Sihayo's kraal and east of the Mzinyathi.

"They went into Natal and brought your wives back?" He imagined Zulu warriors bursting into a Natal homestead and dragging the women out by their hair. "What was the gunshot? A signal to let you know they had returned?" Mbeki did not think it was a signal.

"Cha, my son killed both of them. That is the punishment for adultery."

"It is the punishment a king can order, no one else!" Mbeki shook with fury.

"Why take them all the way up to oNdini, when killing her here sets an example for my other wives?" Sihayo asked, picking up his milk pail again. Mbeki was already up and running for the gate of the kraal. "Go well, Mbeki!" He received no reply. Mbeki would have to tell Cetshwayo as soon as possible: Frere had his excuse.

Chapter 48

The squeak of hemp rope running through block and tackle was painful to the ears, and Mbeki looked at the whole apparatus in sickly fascination. He stood upon a floor of planks lashed to pontoons that was being dragged across the surface of the water by a rope and pulley system attached to both banks of the Thekula River. The barge had been designed to carry an entire company of British regulars, and it seemed ricketier with only the few dozen aged and withered Zulu men and Mbeki upon its heaving deck. This was the largest party of councilors Cetshwayo had yet sent to negotiate with the British; Mbeki had been brought along to confirm the White interpreter's translations.

He pulled at his goatee, glad that the morning's shower had reduced the air's mugginess. Early summer was hot and damp, and the negotiators must not be seen sweating. "That's far enough!" A redcoat on the bank ordered in English. The barge stopped five paces short of the Natal shore. Mbeki wondered if the Zulu emissaries would even be allowed to set foot upon British soil. "Know this, wise men of kwaZulu!" The translator's Zulu was excellent. "You come onto our soil to take back a message to your King, nothing more. Is it heard?"

"It is heard," The men replied. The traditional military phrase raised their spirits slightly. Mbeki knew it would not last.

The squealing began again as the rope resumed its movement, and soon the barge hit the bank with a force that threw the men forward against one another and into the rails. They got off the contraption haughtily, many saying they would have preferred to swim the river than be carried across on the back of a wooden turtle.

An awning had been erected under a large Natal fig tree. In the distance the new earthworks of Fort Pearson loomed, threatening to vomit forth its garrison if the elderly Zulu did not behave. Sixty-five unarmed redcoats already surrounded the negotiations. Mbeki suppressed a smirk. What did the British think is going to happen? Are these elders the vanguard of an impi?

The meeting started off well. The British had ruled in favour of the Zulu on the matter of the abaQulusi land claims. The old men were careful not to smile, nor did they break their facade when they ate a roast ox and drank large tumblers of sugar-water. These councilors had haggled for their king many times, and they knew when they were being softened up. At last the British laid down their latest demands.

"In thirty days you shall surrender Sihayo's sons to stand trial for murder and kidnapping. You shall also pay a fine of five hundred head of cattle for invading our lands. As well, Cetshwayo shall disband his regiments and abolish the ibutho system. Any man may marry when he wishes and need not serve their King as warriors or as servants." The old men remained stone-faced until a man from Durban photographed them. The flash startled them, and for a moment their faces showed their confusion and fear.

At length they conferred with one another and bade Mbeki to ask a simple, "Why?"

"Your king is a tyrant," The Whites' Zulu speaker said. "He can order any one of you killed without trial. He forbids men to marry until they are old, so their sexual frustration makes them into killing machines. Your people groan under his rule, yearning to be free."

The old men rocked back as if bitten. They could not have been more stunned if the man had burst into flames. "Have the Zulu complained?" One asked. Mbeki did not bother to translate, but the white interpreter did and waited for an answer, which he gave them.

"That is not important. Our cause is just, and our demands will rectify the situation."

The old men spoke in whispers. Mbeki spoke in English for them while the Whites eyed him suspiciously. "Lords of the British, deputies of the Great White Queen, our king did not order Sihayo's wives to be killed. It was an act of rash boys. In your land, is the queen held responsible when one of her soldiers commits murder while on leave from the army? Our king's laws oppress no one, while your laws would have a man cruelly imprisoned if he is found guilty.

"As for the ibutho system, surely you know what you ask of us is impossible? The amabutho are not part of the Zulu State; they are the Zulu State. The regiments guard our borders, tend the king's cattle and fields, build the king's kraals and enforce the king's laws. The Zulu Kingdom can no sooner abolish the ibutho system than a man can rip out his heart and lungs.

"Finally and most importantly, thirty days is not enough time for our king to do any one of the things you ask. Do you not realize that this will lead to war?"

Mbeki thought it was well said, but the British did nothing to change their ultimatum. The negotiators were hustled back onto the barge and ferried across the Thekula twice as fast as they had been crossed it the first time.

As soon as the river mud was under his feet Mbeki began to run. It still took him five whole days out of the thirty to reach oNdini.

Chapter 49

"It is like warding off a falling tree: I stand in the forest; the tree beside me comes crashing down, and all I can do is throw up my hands and wait." Cetshwayo rubbed the knock in his ear absently. "Very well, Sihayo's son shall be handed over, and Sihayo shall be stripped of every cow. The remainder of the fine will be paid equally by all the great chiefs. Is that agreed?" It had taken the King and his advisors three days to hammer out these terms.

The King and the Great Men of the Nation sat in front of the royal quarters of kwaNodwengu, sweating under the summer sun and the strain of their unpleasant choices. All eyes focused on Cetshwayo, who kept rubbing his ear. The silence stretched.

"What of the ibutho system, cousin?" Hamu asked. This was the first time Hamu had returned to oNdini since the stick fight almost a year before. Neither the king nor the northern baron had made any moves towards reconciliation.

"You and I both know that is impossible: Without the Zulu izimpi there is no law, no peace and no umKhosi. We would become a collection of tribes as we were before Shaka. I want peace as much as you, but I want peace without surrender. I have already sent word by fast messenger to the Whites asking for more time, requesting alterations to their ultimatum..." Cetshwayo's trailed off.

"My King," Mbeki began slowly. He was a royal favourite and entitled to speak his mind, but he did not want to anger the two highly charged sides of the Court. Hamu's followers were demanding peace at any price, and Ntsingwayo's side wanted freedom even if it meant war. "You have conceded all you can. Your reasonable offer is on its way and will arrive before the thirty days has expired. We must be ready for the worst. Call up the amabutho. Mobilize the izimpi."

Cetshwayo sighed, adding Mbeki's name to the war faction. "How would you deploy our warriors, oh Wizard?" The disposition of the izimpi had been discussed in fits and starts since the very beginning, but only now was Cetshwayo ready to make the decision.

"Great Elephant, our sources tell us that the British have divided their forces into five izimpi, three of which shall attack us: One on the coast, one from kwaJim, and one through the land of the abaQulusi." Heads nodded. The Zulu spy network was highly organized, and it was easy to follow the thousands of slow moving men, horses, oxen, and wagons that constituted the British armies. "Our best envoys to the Swazi court have promised us their neutrality; we must take them at their word." The Zulu were spread too thin to guard against every possible foe.

"So where would you put the actual men?" Hamu's needle eyes bored in, hoping that by forcing Mbeki as the war faction's least influential member to speak on their behalf the King would not feel compelled to take his advice.

"I would leave the abaQulusi and their allies to guard the West. They are the furthest away, and their mountains are perfect for the harassing attacks Mbilini prefers. In the East I would keep nine or ten thousand warriors: The men who live on the coast and therefore have the most to lose if the White impi gets through." The war council made noises of agreement. The peace party murmured their continued objection. Cetshwayo silenced both with a wave of his hand.

Mbeki continued. "Here at oNdini I would keep any man over sixty who answers the call to muster. It isn't much of a reserve, Nkosi Nkulu, but we will need every fighting man on the front." A few of the leaders over sixty harrumphed their disapproval of the suggestion, but as Great Men of the Nation they would not be held in reserve. "Finally, our main Impi, which should have between twenty-five and thirty thousand warriors, should fall on the British column crossing at Rorke's Drift."

"Why attack their center? Why not the coast? Forty thousand warriors could smash the white's coastal Impi into dust." Hamu did not like how Mbeki had presented his case: It was simple and persuasive; Hamu sensed the weaker members of his peace party slipping over into the war camp.

"The Whites' center impi is their strongest. It is also the closest to oNdini, which must be where the Whites are heading; also, their overall commander marches in the centre. Tell me, if we faced five amabutho of Swazi and their king led one of them, would we attack the weaker amabutho first or would we throw as much as possible against their leader?" Mbeki never raised his voice, but the war faction knew he had put Hamu in his place.

Cetshwayo knew it too. "Well said, Mbeki. It shall be so. Mbilini shall lead the forces of the West. Godide shall lead the forces in the East. I shall lead the old men here at oNdini if the situation calls for it. As for the Great Impi, it shall be commanded by Ntsingwayo kaMahole." The old Khoza chief nodded his head in gratitude, accepting the heavy burden. "Send the mobilization orders out. Tell the men to leave their dancing gear at home and come stripped for fighting."

Cetshwayo turned to his councilors and they could see the heartache their King suffered. "These are your orders, and you shall follow them if you wish to prevail: Never attack a fortified position, never cross into Natal, and set a pace that will not tire the men before battle. Catch the British in the open. Is it heard?"

"It is heard," They answered. Mbeki saw several men in both the peace and the war parties move their lips without speaking the words.

As the meeting broke up Prince Zibhebhu took Mbeki by the arm. Despite being a separatist, Zibhebhu was a member of the war party, so Mbeki felt compelled to speak to the man, whatever his personal loyalties to Cetshwayo. "Is Inyati still hiding out down in your valley?" The prince asked from under his tilted head ring.

"Last I heard. I think it is better he avoid any contact with Ingonyama until I've gotten some things straightened out."

"So he won't be mustering to fight?"

"How can he? Oh, I suppose he's strong enough now, but as an Invincible, Ingonyama might go to any front, so what army could Inyati join where he can avoid Ingonyama?"

"My army," Zibhebhu said.

"That's not funny." Mbeki pulled his arm loose from Zibhebhu's grip.

"Not that army. I'm a loyalist for the duration of the war. There's no sense in my siding with the Whites: That's trading a king I see every day for a queen I will never see in my life. Cha, I was talking about Cetshwayo's spy network; he's put me in charge of it. Doesn't Inyati speak English and Afrikaans?"

"Yebho, Nkosi."

"I'll send a runner down to your valley. The position I have in mind will get him out of kwaZulu for the duration of the war. I'd like to be able to say you suggested it." Zibhebhu flashed his smile, and Mbeki saw how seductive the dashing northern prince could be. Hamu was ice and fire, but Zibhebhu had warmth and charm.

Damn me if I don't like him, Mbeki thought. "If you're a loyalist for the rest of the war, then you're on my side. Tell him whatever you like to get him to do it, but also tell him I still haven't dealt with Ingonyama."

The northern prince patted Mbeki on the arm twice and left, still smiling.

Chapter 50

The greatest impi since Shaka's day, more than twice the size of the one Dingaan had sent against the Boers, ringed the king's kraal in ranks thirty deep; even this level of crowding forced the youngest regiments to stand outside the gate. No one was sure of the exact count, but somewhere between twenty-five and thirty thousand warriors had answered their king's summons to the Great Place. To the west another three thousand guarded the mountains from the strongholds of the abaQulusi. In the east eight thousand men were ready to fight a holding action. To the north many more men stayed home, unwilling to fight for the king unless ordered to do so by their separatist barons, like Hamu.

Mbeki felt strange standing at the most senior position in the kraal, directly in front of the royal quarters; the rest of his regiment was outside the kraal. The white shield was also something of a shock, but Ingonyama had insisted. "You're too good for the Flycatcher Birds, Mbeki. How many men your age do you know who have been royal favourites for over two years? You have more seniority than the izinduna in your regiment, and they're twice your age. Cha, it's the Invincibles for you. After the war you can go back to your messenger position or your smithing, but right now I need you." The last words had convinced him.

Joining the Flycatcher Birds outside the kraal were the Humbler of Kings, kept outside as the next most junior ibutho, because of their size, and most importantly because no one was sure if the Chieftains and the Humbler of Kings could be trusted in the same ikhanda again. Just inside the kraal was the Red Needles, and opposite them in the next most junior position was the Red Leopards ibutho.

Although the regiments had been ordered to form up without the ceremonial dancing gear that would only be dirtied or damaged in the coming campaign, it was still easy to distinguish the amabutho by their shields; there were clear colour divisions allowing Mbeki to see where the Skirmishers stopped and the Weepers began, and again with the Mongrels, the Frost, and the Du Du Du. Their dark shields filled the lower half of the kraal with an impressive show of military might.

Further up were the middle-aged regiments, married and out of active service except in times of war, but all the more valuable to the King because they were blooded veterans of proven bravery: The Young Mambas, the Adult Mambas, the Chieftains, the Hunters, the Wild Pigs, and the Worriers all stood tall and proud, the odd paunch or bald spot not detracting from their impressive martial display.

At the very top of the kraal to the immediate left and right of the Invincibles stood the truly ancient regiments made up of men too old to fight but too young to be sent away. The Ambush Battle, Sharp Youth, and the Snake Regiments stood in their finest attire, submerged in a sea of feathers and beads and cow tails, determined to be present at the greatest moment in their kingdom's history, even if their orders held them in reserve garrison duty.

At a word, Ingonyama had the Invincibles part and swing aside like a double door to allow their king to walk out onto the parade square. "Bayete!" The thousands roared. "Bayete!" They repeated. "Bayete!" Again the royal salute echoed out, and this time every man raised his right foot chest high and drove it into the ground so that the earth itself shook and the rumbling murmur of a wide and shallow drum could be heard.

"My children," Cetshwayo began, throwing his voice so that all could hear him. "War has come."

"Bayete!" The warriors called.

Cetshwayo held up a hand. "Cha, my children, this is not a matter for celebration. These Whites will be a difficult foe, and the road to victory will be long and hard. The Whites do not want peace, and we will have to convince them of its benefit through killing and dying." He put his arms out from his chest in a gesture of innocence. "I have never gone over the ocean and said to the Great White Queen, 'Your laws, which were good enough for all your ancestors since the time Nkulunkulu made you, are not good enough now. Disband your army for it threatens us. Give us the son who revenged his cuckolded father so we can shoot him.'" Beside Mbeki, Ingonyama tensed. "And yet that is what the Great White Queen's emissaries have told me to do. What can be done?"

"Leave it with us, Great Elephant! We shall teach the Whites their view is wrong!" A youth called from the Red Needles. The crowd roared its approval, and Cetshwayo had to hold up his hand again for silence.

"That is my thought too, my children. Your cause is just. You fight to defend you kingdom, your king, your homes and your families. These Whites want to take that all away. We must show them they are wrong, and war is the only thing they seem to understand."

"Bayete!" The Great Impi roared, drumming on their shields and stamping their feet. Again, Cetshwayo gestured for silence.

"You shall march south against their most powerful impi, and you shall crush it. Move slowly so that you are not tired when the attack comes. Do not cross into Natal, for this shall drive them crazy, and they will make no peace until every last Zulu is dead. Finally, do not attack the Whites when they are behind their fortifications; many of you were at Blood River," He gestured to the eldest regiments, "and the rest of you have heard of the death at that place. Take your time, attack them in the open, and do not enter their lands. Do this, and after a battle or two they will make peace. Is it heard?"

"It is heard!" The Impi roared. "uSuthu! uSuthu! uSuthu!" Cetshwayo lowered his head, overcome at the loyalty of these men who would brave the gunfire for him and his cause.

"Go well, my children," He called.

Chapter 51

An impi on the move overloads the senses. The ground trembles to the pounding of feet, so that a man standing still will feel his ankles ache at the vibrations. The air shimmers with the sparkling reflections from polished steel and glistening black bodies, the thousands drifting in and out of focus as they run through the waving grass, disappearing and reappearing from the clouds of dust. One can taste the sweat the impi exhales. The musk is irrepressible and unmistakable, and no one who smells it can doubt its power.

But it is the sounds, the sounds of an impi that are most impressive. The noise of an impi echoes from every cliff face. Animals flee, fish sink to the bottom of ponds, birds throw themselves aloft, all to avoid the overwhelming force of the sounds. Every man in every regiment sings his war cries, smashes his shield with his spear, and pounds the grass into the dirt with his callused feet. Behind them young boys drive cattle, adding to the ruckus with the pounding of hooves, lowing of distress, the sound of sticks meeting rumps, and the songs of the herd.

In the middle of the rainy season it could almost be mistaken for thunder, but it was too rhythmic, too unceasing. The noise went on and on and on, and anyone who knew its source trembled at the power it implied. Thirty thousand men were on the move, and anything that stood before them would be blown away like dust in the wind.

The Zulu Kingdom had peaked, and all its strength and glory now ran out to meet the future.

Chapter 52

The air was electric, charged and muggy like before a thunderstorm. The sky was overcast. The grass was wet. The men were well-rested but uncomfortable with their impatience. Off to the right they could hear the distant sound of gunfire as a diversionary skirmishing force pulled a British detachment further and further away from the Whites' camp, which was only just over the horizon. Soon they would charge the guns of the weakened camp, and each man felt the rush of excitement and the weight of dread resting equally upon him.

The Great Impi was bivouacked in the Ngwebeni Valley, a deep and grassy kloof with a trickling stream running down the bottom. Everywhere men huddled around smokeless fires, cooking their mealies in three-legged iron pots. No one had an appetite, but all would take what they could get. It would pass the time while the izinduna decided.

The Invincibles sat in silence, feigning indifference to the crucial war council taking place across the valley. When the orders came they would follow them; that was all there was too it. They could not help but be anxious, though, wanting it to begin so that it could end. Ingonyama's good example made each man more aware of his own impatience.

Ingonyama lay on the ground with his ankles crossed and his hands folded behind his head. He looked as if he was ready for a nap, and it was driving his men crazy. His shield was propped up above him so that its shadow hid his face from the young sun's light. He was convincing in his calm and comfortable posture, but if any one had put their head to Ingonyama's chest they would have heard his heart going far too fast for his carefree facade.

Normally Mbeki and Ingonyama would have gone themselves to the war council, especially as the impi was being led by their family's old friend Ntsingwayo kaMahole. Direct orders had kept them with their men to restrain the impetuousness of the young regiments billeted all around them. With so many of the senior izinduna away at the meeting Ntsingwayo wanted good examples present to keep the younger warriors from acting without orders. Besides, he knew how both kaJamas would vote: Rush the camp today, right now, before the element of surprise is lost and the British realize they were out in the open without the wagon laager that had proven insurmountable to the Zulu forty years ago at Blood River.

Jojo's running form caught Mbeki's attention, and soon every Invincible watched their comrade sprint towards them as if a legion of tokoloshe dogged his heels. When he came to a halt at Ingonyama's feet, he leaned forward with his hands on his knees, sucking in gasps of air.

"Well, are we going?" Mbeki asked, trying to sound unconcerned about charging a regiment of breech-loading rifles, backed by cannons and rockets.

"They can't decide," Jojo coughed and wheezed. Ingonyama had told him to return as soon as he had news, and he had run the length of the valley at full tilt to bring his induna advanced warning.

If the impi was to attack, the Invincibles must be the first men ready; if they were to hold fast they must be ready to show their patience in front of the anxious youths around them. Ingonyama was at a loss what to do if the decision between the two simple choices could not be made. *What example can I set when all I want to do is run towards the white tents and not stop until there are no more redcoats standing?*

"We could be in their camp before noon. When are those grey heads planning on finding their balls?" Sompisi complained. He had stood watch during the wee hours of the morning and his temper was frayed. His hand was clenched around his assegai, as if he was worried he might lose it.

"They say the moon is wrong. The ancestors may not favour the attack." Jojo dropped down next to Ingonyama. He reached up to move Ingonyama's sun screen, but the King's Champion slapped his hand away.

"The moon? Shaka never decided his campaigns based on where the damned moon was," Sompisi spat. A few of the superstitious men made the sign to ward off evil, and even Mbeki made the gesture beneath his shield. This was not a day to insult the ancestors.

"How long do they think we can hide here? Even with our diversion they will have patrols out. How many valleys can hide the Great Impi?" Bambatha's point raised murmurs among the Invincibles.

A drawn out yawn stopped their debate, and heads turned to watch Ingonyama's jaw swing wide open in an unintentional parody of the great lion whose skin he wore. Whatever troubled him at home, Ingonyama in the field had not a care in the world. At last finished with his expression of indifference, Ingonyama grinned at them. "A hero dies in heroism, boys. We aren't going home again until we're living heroes or dead ones, so what does the when really matter?"

Young boys walked freely through the camp, bringing firewood, amasi, boiled millet, and mugs of beer to the men. Other boys drove cattle in the dongas around the valley, always careful not to silhouette themselves against the skyline. They were vital to the war effort for without them, large portions of good fighting men would have needed to attend to such trivial camp chores.

Still, these little boys could not be expected to have the discipline of warriors, nor a working knowledge of the overall strategy of the impi. When a British cavalry patrol discovered a few dozen boys picking corn out of an abandoned homestead's granary the thought of leading the mounted men away from the Ngwebeni Valley never occurred to them. Only the security of their brothers and cousins came to their frightened minds, and so they fled straight back to the impatient warriors, British cavalry in tow.

Mbeki watched the boys spill over the crest of the hill overlooking the ravine and felt his stomach flip as the first horse followed them. The rider was surprised too, for his horse reared up and kicked the air in frustration as the blue-jacketed Englishman hauled back on the reins. Below him, stretching as far to the right and left as the contours of the valley would allow him to see, crouched the Zulu impi. Twelve regiments stared up at him in surprise and sudden bloodlust.

"Shit!" Ingonyama muttered, giving up any pretence of ease. The Skirmishers ibutho was already off and running, and the Red Needles were snatching up their spears to follow them. "Stop! Back to your places! Wait for the order!" The junior regimental izinduna came out of their surprised stupor and began echoing Ingonyama's commands. Men began to drift back to the camp, but every eye was on the rider. Within moments another horse came over the ridge's spine, then another, then a dozen.

Mbeki watched as the British dismounted. One soldier would hold the reins for four horses while the other three riflemen took their places in a growing formation. When the entire troop was formed up in their ranks the officer gave an order and thirty rifles roared, bullets smacking into warriors as they returned to their breakfasts.

There was no holding them now, and the Red Needles roared a long drawn out, "uSuthu!" The whole valley repeated the war cry. Mbeki could only imagine the sight of a hundred old men, the senior izinduna, running from the council as fast as their individual ages and weights would allow, desperate to get among their men so that the attack would move forward with some semblance of order.

"We haven't doctored for war yet! There's been no general address, no magic medicine!" Bambatha protested.

"Do it on the run. The Invincibles will not be in the rearguard!" Ingonyama barked, jumping to his feet with his shield and assegai in either hand. Released by their master, the hundred men bolted from their places, Bambatha running behind each one to smack the back of his head with a tassel full of war magic. Thousands of warriors did not even receive this minor protection from the British bullets.

The Zulu impi shuddered and convulsed; the center became the left, the right became the center, and the left, the only group that Ntsingwayo could restrain from moving directly at the cavalry patrol, became the extreme right. With little coercion the impi formed the head and horns of the fighting bull buffalo; the main mass of men formed the head, while the outer regiments formed the encircling horns designed to whip around the enemy's flanks to cut off his retreat.

The Invincibles fell into the head of the buffalo alongside the Red Needle Ibutho. Now that the amabutho were on the move, the izinduna regained enough control over the warriors to straighten out their formations. The Zulu would not advance in human waves, easily shot down at great distances. Instead, the warriors worked themselves into long skirmishing lines; no man was within five paces of his comrade to the left or right, and each of these ranks was twenty or thirty paces from the line ahead and behind them. They advanced at the relentless jog trot, and the ground flew beneath their feet without effort or notice.

The warriors moved from cover to cover, disappearing and reappearing so that their numbers were impossible to count. All the while they drummed on their shields and hummed in the back of their throats, making the whole plain between their valley and the British camp at the foot of the Isandhlwana kopje tremble with the noise of thunder and angry bees. To Mbeki the army seemed to be dancing: Five steps forward, squat down, two steps over to the right, up and running again. He crawled through the grass and ran along dongas, always working forward, forward, forward.

The grassy plain between the valley and the British camp was corrugated with crisscrossing dongas and depressions, all leading to the rocky summit of the Isandhlwana kopje that sat like a sphinx in profile with hundreds of white tents clustered around its base. Mbeki could hear the clarion sound of bugles calling men to arms and the white specks of British helmets flew together into rectangular blocks of men, each company forming in two ranks, ready to face the advancing impi's chest.

Confident of the stopping power of the Martini-Henry, the British regiment advanced well out from their camp until only a thin red line covered the entire front with no reserves in the camp and very little protection on the flanks. Mbeki smiled; it would be hard on the chest, but the horns could not have asked for a better deployment.

Mbeki was down in a donga when the first cannon fired, but he saw the effect; a white cotton ball appeared in the sky to his right as a shell burst in the air, and he heard the whistle of fragments and the shriek of the wounded warriors below. From twelve hundred paces the British cannons could kill his comrades. The thought was chilling.

When he climbed out of the donga he saw the camp before him, and he watched as the crew of the other seven pounder stood clear. Someone else saw it too, and he heard a deep voice call out, "Air!" The Zulu ranks thinned in reply. When the deadly cotton ball appeared again only two men fell to the ground this time, never to rise again.

Now Mbeki found himself on a flat patch of grass with very little cover for the next hundred paces. The Zulu lines began to bunch as the faster men in the rear ranks ran to get back into cover, passing the slower warriors in the front ranks. It was a mistake; the British officer had saved the first volley of massed rifle fire for just such a concentration of men; fifty rifles barked, and before the dead warriors had finished falling the next rank of fifty fired too.

The heavy bullets sent running men cartwheeling backwards. All around Mbeki men were twisting and flipping in impossible feats of gymnastics, their crumpled landings lost in the waving grass. None of the acrobats rose to run with their friends again.

Mbeki dove headfirst into the next donga, glad to be out of the line of fire. He looked to his left and right and the Invincibles looked back at him, their chests heaving. They had just experienced the first rifle salvo of their lives. "That wasn't so bad," Jojo lied.

"We aren't doing any good here. Over the top!" Ingonyama threw his arm over his head, and the group rose as one. The British officer commanding the company facing them had expected the sudden rush but ordered the first volley too early; the first three men up into the air were thrown back into the creek bed, but the next twenty warriors made it over and into cover before the second volley knocked another ten off their feet, dropping their corpses back down into the ditch.

So it went, every yard costing the Zulu without their blooding a single spear in retribution. Holes appeared in the lines, first small, then gaping. The warriors stopped smiling, stopped singing. Now their war cries were angry, and they heaped curses upon the cowardly redcoats who fired from such a distance that they could not even see the individuals they were shooting at. The British regulars volleyed into a mass of black humanity, and every salvo took its toll, leaving broken bodies bleeding out on the plain.

The rifles barked, the cannons roared, the rockets hissed, but always the Zulu moved forward, leaving scores of dead and wounded in their wake. Many of the Zulu carried old muskets and a few had newer guns, but though they fired them as often as they bothered to reload, no one saw a single redcoat fall. The poor Zulu marksmanship was made worse by the misconception that the further the rifles' sights were set, the faster the bullet would go. This resulted in the men who owned decent rifles firing at a target four hundred paces away with the sights set for eight hundred, so the bullet flew harmlessly over the redcoats' heads.

Within two hundred paces of the British line the Zulu centre could go no further. Every man threw himself behind cover, be it an ant bear hole, a bush, or even the body of another warrior. Anyone who rose up to move forward was shot down. The British company commander ahead of them had ordered his front rank to fire at will, keeping his rear rank ready for a massed volley if the Zulu tried a sudden rush. Ingonyama snorted his frustration, "We can't lie here forever! It's only a little further."

"There's no cover between there and here," Mbeki said. The ground ahead of them was flat as water on a calm day: The British oxen had cropped the grass too short to hide in. They were pinned down and were being picked off one by one until only the men whose cover kept them completely out of sight were left alive.

"I'm going!" Ingonyama shoved himself up from his belly but Jojo and Sompisi each jumped onto his back. A third man rose up onto his knees to help force Ingonyama down but he took a bullet in the throat and fell back, hissing and gurgling for the short while he had left.

Somewhere down the line a man wept and another cursed. The firing above their heads picked up whenever a man rolled over or shifted. The British were watching for the slightest movement, the smallest target. Jojo and Sompisi were both stacked on top of Ingonyama, so he finally grunted his submission, allowing them to slither off him and deeper into their shallow sheltering depression.

They lay like that for a long time with bullets cracking over their heads. Mbeki watched in horror as the sun, already shrouded by the overcast, grew dimmer and gloomier. Something stood between the bright spot in the sky and the miserable hole in which he lay. With a start Mbeki realized the moon was blocking some of the sun, and he felt a tremor run through him at the thought that the moon really was against them.

Some of the warriors cracked, jumping up onto their feet and falling down dead. Others took to firing at the Whites with their guns, but even at this range they could not hit one. To the right and left they heard the horns of the Bull close in on the British flanks and the firing got closer and closer as the horns drove the British back towards their camp. The head was pinned down, and until that changed the battle would not be won.

The horns continued to whip around the flanks of the British regiment so that the ends of the British front began to bend backwards to keep their rifles perpendicular to the Zulu advance. At last a bugle sounded ordering the British center, including the company opposite the Invincibles, to fall back into a tighter defensive formation around the camp.

"Now!" Ingonyama ordered. A hundred men jumped to their feet. There was a thunderclap of rifle fire and a hundred men fell back into shelter, only half of them still alive. Mbeki spat the dirt out of his mouth from his hard landing, but he saw Jojo and Sompisi struggling to hold Ingonyama down, so he rolled over onto the back of his brother's thighs.

"They'll shoot you!" Mbeki hissed.

"I'm as good as dead lying here!" He roared.

"What is this?" A voice called from behind them. Careful not to reveal themselves to the retreating British, every man craned back to see a thin man zigzagging crazily from cover to cover. He had the brass armbands of a royal favourite, and his willow wood necklace was so long it was looped three times around his throat. This induna ran among the prone men, gesturing them forward as one would shoo reluctant children. "Why are you lying down?" He cried. "Cetshwayo did not order this!" Ingonyama knew the man; he was from Ntsingwayo's staff. Still buried under three friends he ordered his men to charge.

Indecisive, a few men raised up onto their knees, but a bullet smashed through the back of the skinny induna's head and the few rallying men dropped back onto their bellies before the thin man's lifeless corpse hit the ground.

Ingonyama could be restrained no longer, and he threw off all three of the men pinning him to stand proud and tall, alone in the killing field. All eyes watched as he playfully moved his head from side to side as if dodging the bullets whizzing around him. His lopsided grin warmed their hearts, and suddenly they felt ashamed at their safety.

"You can only die once in kwaZulu," He boomed in his command voice. "And if today is your day, you will be remembered." He let that sink in. A passing bullet blew a piece of lion's mane off of his cloak, but Ingonyama did not flinch. "If you survive, will you be remembered as a coward or a hero?"

"Ingonyama!" Jojo called, and the Invincibles leapt to their feet. The hundred men were joined by a thousand, and then ten thousand. Ingonyama cried, "uSuthu!" And the call was taken up by every regiment in the head of the buffalo. The Zulu center was up and running, uncaring of the horrific losses of those last frantic yards.

Mbeki watched as the redcoats fired in volleys, blowing the front runners back into the grass like dead leaves in a strong wind. Warriors tumbled end over end through the air to land in heaps of arms and legs and blood. Here a man took a bullet high in the chest. There one had his leg shot out from under him. The Zulus had given up moving from cover to cover; those last two hundred paces swept them up into a human wave, and within a few terrible moments the bulk of the Great Impi crashed into the strongest part of the British line.

The British company had fixed bayonets, and the extended reach that gave them should have been enough to let them retire in good order, but the Zulu were too long frustrated in their bloodlust to be held at bay; they ran onto the bayonets and grabbed the hot barrels so that their friends behind them could kill the now disarmed redcoats. Others used their throwing spears to break up the disciplined British lines. Still others leapt over the wall of bayonets to come crashing down on the white helmets. Their fury and fear overcame their reason, and all they wanted to do was finish their foes.

The company of redcoats in front of Mbeki dissolved from a fighting force to a hundred desperate men, and the thousand Zulus they had pinned down avenged themselves over and over until they were dripping in the blood of their tormentors. The battle madness had descended, and the Zulu could only see through a red haze. They were no longer bound by what they thought was good and right. They would kill until the killing was done, and only then would they feel shocked at their brutality.

Ingonyama disappeared into the mass of British regulars and Mbeki ran into the hole he had made. Everywhere men ran and cried out. Frantic knots of friends ran together, stabbing with spear and bayonet, shooting with rifle and musket. A white face appeared in Mbeki's path, and he smashed his shield into its high thin nose. He continued running, leaving it to the warriors behind him to stab the fallen enemy. He had to get into the camp. After all that time spent laying in the grass with the camp an unreachable dream, he had to get there.

Some Zulu from the Weepers ibutho beat him into the tents, but Mbeki was not far behind. A cook with a white apron appeared from a tent, shakily holding a rifle. Mbeki was in front of him before the man had fixed a bayonet, and he watched as the cook pulled the trigger on an empty chamber: He had not thought to load the thing. Mbeki stabbed him high in the chest, drenching the apron in blood, then he and ran on, terrified at how easy it was to kill a man.

Mbeki rounded a tent and ran headlong into a blue-coated officer. "Bloody hell!" The man said, fumbling for his revolver.

"I'll kill you!" Mbeki yelled in English. Surprised, the officer took off his helmet and cracked Mbeki across the face with it, causing Mbeki to drop his spear at the unexpected blow. Enraged, Mbeki punched the man hard, spinning him around.

The man looked at Mbeki in confusion, still fumbling at the flap of his holster. Mbeki reached down to pick up his assegai. The officer gave up on the pistol and pulled a small knife from a sheath at his waist, slashing at the Zulu's head. Mbeki jumped back and the two stared at each other as the world came crashing down all around them. "You know, you should leave that holster unbuckled. You've tried a helmet and a knife, but the gun would have stopped me," Mbeki said. The man's eyes went wide again. Mbeki buried his assegai in the man's belly.

"Bloody hell," The man whispered. The officer died with his eyes wide open. Mbeki let the corpse drop to the ground and felt his bloodlust begin to drain out of him. He felt cold and clammy, feeling the spirits all around him, and he knew the white man had joined the ancestors. Mbeki was covered now in the magic pollution of the dead man's shade. Until he was purified he should carry something of the man's with him to placate his ghost.

Mbeki tried to unbuckle the man's holster, knowing if he was going to keep a memento it might as well be a weapon, but the clasp proved as difficult for his trembling fingers as it had for the white man's, and he gave up in disgust. Instead he took the man's fallen knife, slipping the sheath off the man's belt and running it through his loincloth. He did not know why the superstition was suddenly important to him, or why he was doing this with a battle still raging all around him, but he did it anyway and when he was done he ripped open the man's belly with his assegai to let his spirit escape.

Mbeki was swept up in the madness as the rest of the impi joined him among the white tents. Running warriors and redcoats mixed together, and only one or the other remained wherever they met. Chaos reigned as the dust, the smoke, the blood-sodden grass, and the partial eclipse of the sun all combined to lift the battlefield off the face of the Earth and dropped it in a confusing mass into a corner of Hell. There was no shelter from the storm, no resisting the orgy of destruction. The participants acted outside of themselves, and the notion of decent behaviour fell from their hearts.

When redcoats became scarce but the battle madness still clung to them the Zulu stabbed tents and sacks of flour because they were clothed; others smashed bottles of preserves because they would bleed jam. Maddened by thirst, the warriors drank anything they could find among the tents, and those who drank turpentine fell down and tripled up, their faces twisted with the rictus of pain until they threw up on the feet of their oblivious comrades. Their bile was runny with melting flesh.

Horses were clubbed to death. Cows and oxen were slaughtered without thought for their value. Each and every company dog was chased down, and the dying redcoats watched in disbelief as their beloved mascots were torn limb from limb. A party of Red Needles took turns taking axes to the dieselboom of a wagon for no better reason than because they had to smash something. They were compelled to.

Everywhere the air was torn with gunshots and cries of fear and pain and hatred. Chants of 'uSuthu!' and 'Ngadla' turned the British knees to jelly, and the thunder of bare feet slapping on the stony earth drove them back in dread. An ammunition wagon was set on fire, and the explosion killed whites and blacks alike as thousands of rounds cooked off, filling the air with flying death.

Groups of British regulars stood back to back in island-like circles as the black sea poured around and over them. They fired their rifles until their bullets ran out, and then kept the Zulus back with bayonets. Their faces were blackened with powder and streaked with sweat; many had lost their helmets. The Zulus were unable to break the walls of bayonets, so they threw spears into the packed ranks and waited for the enemy's numbers to become too small to hold formation.

The day dragged on. Zulus ran this way and that, their sight clouded by a red veil of fury. The dead called out to the living in whispers of insanity, demanding vengeance and blood. Men boiled from one end of the field to the other, joining their comrades in chasing down survivors. One by one the red islands of resistance were washed away until only a pile of stripped and disemboweled bodies lay partially concealed in the long grass. Sanity would return only slowly, and there would be many less left alive to enjoy it.

Mbeki felt it first as a weight in his stomach, but quickly it solidified into a shiver of dread up his spine; it was the old premonition coming back to him. Something was wrong. His hands traced the contours of his chest and legs but he was not hurt. He jumped up onto a wagon and strained his eyes, looking for some explanation to the cold pall that had fallen over him. The battle was over; the bloodlust was fading from the tens of thousands of exhausted warriors scattered across the field.

He watched as one man, who only moments before had been dancing wildly around a burning tent with his comrades, realized his arm had been cut to ribbons by a bullet some time ago. The warrior had not noticed at the time, and the loss of blood had only increased his light-headedness. Now he clutched the destroyed limb, shrieking with fear and the sudden overwhelming pain. He collapsed into a huddle in the grass but his friends, still in the grips of euphoria, stepped on and over him as they did all the other bodies in their path.

Mbeki had to find Ingonyama. What if he was down on the ground somewhere as Inyati had been all those years ago? What if he needed help? Mbeki looked for his brother, but there was no more fighting that might have drawn Ingonyama's attention. He would just be one of the thousands of warriors coming down from their bloodlust; Mbeki could think of no better means of finding him than to run across the plain shouting his brother's name.

Chapter 53

Ingonyama stood swaying with exhaustion over a mound of dead redcoats. Throughout the mayhem of the final melee he had worked his way through the camp, organizing warriors to break up the rallying white men. Now they were all dead, and his last duty was to make sure these British never harmed the Zulu people as spirits.

With shaking hands he fumbled to remove the first dead man's tunic. When the buttons refused to give he cut them off with his assegai, then he did the same to the blood spattered shirt underneath. He stared at the white man's pale chest, ignoring the red crater above his nipple where a Zulu had made a lucky hit with an old musket. He brought his broad-bladed assegai up against the man's navel and sliced open his abdomen.

This was not a desecration. Any fool can see that a corpse whose belly is not opened on the battlefield will soon swell and bloat in the sun as the spirit tries to force its way out. When the dead man's soul finally escaped its rotting body it would be furious at the delay and would stalk the warrior who had left it in its prison. Slicing open the abdomen allowed the spirit to leave at its convenience, a mark of respect and courtesy from victor to vanquished.

For Ingonyama it started off that way, but as the task of disemboweling the corpses became mechanical Ingonyama's mind began to wander. He thought of Nandhi and then of Inyati. Inyati should have died with that spear in his belly, he thought. That would have made everything easier. He stabbed the next man with more force, remembering the Matabele prince lying in the dust of oNdini, the spurting blood pouring out of his belly like water from a cleft spring.

Soon his spear was slashing the corpses as his memories drifted further and further. He remembered the day he had spared the son of the House of Kumalo; how he had wept with the effort it took to beat him. I spared the man who slept with my wife. I did it. He brought the flat of his spear against the side of a white man's head with such force that the corpse's neck broke, leaving the head to dangle at a ridiculous angle. The lifeless eyes looked at him, laughing at the Invincible, laughing at the cuckolded husband. I did it, he thought. I brought this on myself.

Ingonyama pictured his wife spread eagled on a sleeping kaross with

Inyati hovering over her, his naked form moving up and down through the air. She laughed and cried out, stroking the back of Inyati's head, shouting out his name, 'Inyati! Inyati! Inyati!'

Ingonyama roared like his namesake, tearing his throat with the volume of his emotion. He brought his assegai down like a club, staving in the skull of a redcoat. Unsatisfied, he skewered another through the throat and then hacked another's leg down to the bone. He could not get her voice out of his head; she kept saying it, crying it out as she had on their wedding night. 'Inyati!'

He roared again, but this time he said his torturer's name aloud. "Inyati!" He stabbed a corpse. "Inyati!" He stabbed another. Unsatisfied with this, he threw his spear aside and snatched up a discarded axe. "Inyati! Inyati! Inyati!" He brought the axe down on each corpse's belly, slicing them open in tribute to the lovable prince. "I hate you! Hate you! Hate you!" The dead men's blood splashed up onto his thighs and calves, painting him red and black with gore.

Ingonyama kicked one in the head, lost his footing, and fell back onto the heap. He hiccupped out a strangled laugh. "I look ridiculous," he said. "Absolutely ridiculous." He got back onto his feet, shaking his head with the return to sanity. He returned to opening the dead men's stomachs as ritual dictated; his only indulgence was to bring the axe down with unnecessary force, breaking into each man's belly as if he were chopping wood.

He became hypnotized with this exercise, needing only one blow to open a man's torso. He reveled in the movement of each muscle, grunted with every stroke, stomped down into the ground for a firmer footing as he moved on to a new corpse. Time passed, but he did not notice. There was nothing for him but the bodies and the axe.

So absorbed was he in his task that he did not see his brother come up behind him, nor did he hear his name said over and over again. "Ingonyama?" Mbeki repeated, watching his brother work. "Ingonyama!" Mbeki worried whose blood painting his brother from the waist down, and so he shook Ingonyama by the shoulders, snapping his head back and forth. The violent jarring finally broke Ingonyama from his daze; his eyes slowly rose from the mutilated flesh below him to Mbeki's worried face.

"What?" He asked, a sudden terrible thirst sucking all the moisture from his throat. He tried to spit, but could not muster enough saliva for the task.

"Something terrible has happened." Ingonyama looked at his brother and started to chuckle. His chuckle became a laugh, and soon he fell backward onto the corpses, roaring with the absurdity of it all. They were surrounded by thousands of dead men, with hundreds of warriors dealing with gunshot wounds beyond the ken of their medicine men, and his mind had thrown it all to one side with the assumption that Mbeki was about to tell him about Inyati and his wife. I have lost my mind, he decided. He did not care. The laughter would not stop.

Mbeki watched his brother uneasily; he could feel the madness on Ingonyama as real as the lion cloak on his back or the dried blood on his legs. Not knowing what to do, he gently shook his brother again until Ingonyama calmed himself. "What has happened?" His brother asked.

"I don't know. Something is wrong. I can feel it."

The idea that Mbeki's intuition could be wrong never occurred to him. "Is it Baba?" Ingonyama asked, his mind racing to the next worst possibility. "Or my men?"

Another measure of guilt settled on his uneasy mind for not thinking of them first. What kind of leader am I to butcher corpses when I don't even know where my men are? It occurred to him that he had not had a good thought since the first horse came over the ridge back at the Ngwebeni Valley. He shrugged off the idea; he was an Invincible again, and he tucked his doubts and worries under their familiar mountain.

"I don't know."

"Call them in. We'll do a head count, and then we'll go find Baba."

Ingonyama's tone of authority comforted Mbeki. He smiled with relief, cupped his hands to his mouth and shouted, "Invincibles, on me!" The call was taken up by every Invincible in earshot and soon the command was echoing off Isandhlwana's stony walls, racing across the Nyoni Heights, dropping into every donga between the Mzinyathi River and the Conical Kopje.

In ones and twos the Invincibles ran in, several with bloody compresses held to their injuries. Some were being carried in on their shields. Ingonyama did a head count and despaired. His men were the bravest in the Impi, and they had exposed themselves to enemy fire in order to inspire their comrades. A third of his men were lying out there on the battle field. Another ten were alive but would never fight again. Half of the rest were walking wounded.

"Brothers," He began, watching their eyes burn with fanaticism. He felt an inner shame knowing he did not deserve their adulation. "You stand on the victory of our people. You stand on your victory. You stand on the future of the Zulu!" A cheer went up, spoiled only by a wounded man spluttering on his own blood. "We have washed our spears. We have served our country well. We have seen red, and when our eyes cleared there were no more enemies to fight." They cheered again, but this time Ingonyama held up his hands for silence.

"Now I would ask one last thing from some of you before I release you to return to oNdini; Mbeki senses something is wrong, and far be it for me to doubt the word of the Wizard of kwaZulu." A few laughed, but most took his words seriously. "I want those of you who can still walk to stay with me just a little longer. I want to make sure my father is all right, and that there is nothing more the Invincibles need do here. In the meantime, Bambatha, tend to the wounded-- Where is Bambatha?" He looked at the men covered in blood and grime but could not see the face of his war doctor.

"Dead, Nkosi," Jojo said.

"Dead?" Ingonyama rocked back on his heels, stunned down to his core that Bambatha had died without his knowledge. "How?"

"Caught a bullet through his chin. It came out the back of his head." Jojo closed his eyes, and everyone knew he could still see his friend's skull blowing apart. A few reached out to touch his arm, but he jerked away. He would grieve in his own way, privately.

"Very well. Malanda," He named one of the walking wounded, "Get a healer here. If he argues, tell him it's on the orders of the King's Champion."

"Nkosi, we want to stay with you," One of the wounded men said. He lay upon his shield, shot through the liver. The black blood was welling up between the fingers of his left hand, but he managed to reach out with his right, beseeching his induna. "Let us go with you."

Ingonyama swallowed the lump in his throat, knowing the man before him would be dead before he was over the horizon. "Cha, you are ordered to get better. This battle destroyed one of the Enemy's five izimpi. I'll need you well to destroy the other four--" He choked back a sob: He wanted to tell them all what he had been doing to the corpses only a short while ago, but he could not. Commanders command; they do not confess. "Is it heard?"

"It is heard," The men shouted.

"uSuthu!" He raised his axe above his head.

"Ingonyama!" They roared back. Ingonyama adjusted his lion cloak, picked up his shield and trotted west without looking back. He was followed by only fifty of the hundred Invincibles he had led out of the valley that morning.

The wind whistled across the plain, ruffling the grass and chilling the corpses. Fifteen hundred men who had fought for the British Empire lay dead; a thousand Zulu lay with them. Another thousand Zulu would never live to return to their farms. Of the rest, hundreds of Zulu would never fight again, crippled for life by bullets and bombs. There were many battles ahead, and the Zulu would never again be able to afford a victory like this one.

Chapter 54

Even with his head buried in the dirt and the hellfire of the British centre pouring over his head, Ingonyama had seen the white shields of the Hunters ibutho swinging wide to form the extreme right horn of the fighting bull buffalo. He knew Jama and his Uncle Khandla would have been among the warriors who struck the camp from behind, forcing the British centre to fall back towards to tents. With all the fury and confusion of the final melee his father could have gone anywhere, but it made sense to begin his search on the west side of Isandhlwana and expand his search towards the Mzinyathi River in case Jama was pursuing any British survivors.

By a stroke of luck the two kaJama boys found the Hunters regiment reorganizing and forming up. The battle was over; the wounded were being collected, and the izinduna were taking head counts of their remaining warriors. Ingonyama trotted up to one of the commanders moving from man to man in his company, making sure they had collected their spears and shields. "I see you, Hunter. Have you seen Jama kaZuya or his company? He commands sixty Hunters from the Ntuli clan's holdings."

The man looked at Ingonyama's lion skin cape and brass armbands vacantly before murmuring, "Not here. Check further to the west." So Ingonyama went, towing Mbeki and the rest of the blood-spattered Invincibles behind him. Each induna they came across said to check further west, further west. Finally one remembered seeing Jama.

"His brother-in-law is in the Chieftains, yebho?"

"Yebho, that's my Uncle Punga," Mbeki replied.

"He broke off his company to follow the Chieftains and the Adult Mambas. They were in the reserves." The effort of speaking seemed to drain the last of his energy, so that the induna trembled down to the soles of his tough callused feet. His assegai was red half way up the handle, and he had powder burns on one shoulder where a British regular had fired over his shoulder at point-blank range.

"Which way did they go?" Ingonyama asked. The induna pointed west with his unburned arm. The Invincibles walked, unwilling to jog all the way to the Mzinyathi River. Every step of the way they passed the stripped corpses of white men who had run for the safety of the river only to be cut down by the pursuing Zulu. That was what the horns of the buffalo formation were for, to make retreat impossible.

Below them the Mzinyathi River flowed by waist deep, cold and furious, and spanning the turgid green waters was a human chain of warriors stretching from one bank to the other, slowly carrying a regiment of warriors across into Natal.

Mbeki pointed numbly at a man sitting on a rock, watching the spectacle. Ingonyama clamped down on his jaw to suppress his rage. "Nkosi Dabulamanzi, what are you doing?" He asked as he got closer.

"Ah, Ingonyama! It's nice to see you standing when so many young men are lying down!" The prince raised his glass of gin above his head in a silent toast and threw it back, tears brimming in the corner of his eyes as it burned down his throat in one hard gulp.

"What are you doing?" Ingonyama repeated, gesturing to the ibutho below him.

"I am crossing into Natal to burn a few farms and teach the Whites a lesson," The prince said simply, combing his mustache and pointed beard with his fingers to remove any stray drops of liquor.

"Your brother ordered us not to enter Natal," Ingonyama said, standing menacingly before the prince; he was still covered from the waist down in blood and from the waist up in a lion skin, but Dabulamanzi did not blink at the intimidating figure.

"Cetshwayo is not here. My men know their duty," He replied.

"Those men know their duty!" Ingonyama pointed further downstream to where another regiment turned back from the river despite the pleas of Prince Ndabuko.

"Those are the Weepers; they were the first men into the tents at Isandhlwana, and they chased the fleeing enemy all the way down here. They've had enough for today," Dabulamanzi said, standing up and pouring himself another glass of gin from a bottle carried by a herd boy. "Those men down there," He pointed to the human chain, "Are the Young Mambas. They were in the reserves with the Chieftains, the Adult Mambas and the Red Leopards. Their spears are spotless."

"So?" Ingonyama said rudely. He ached from head to toe, and the last of his great stamina was being used. All he wanted to do was sleep.

"So, the Humbler of Kings' girls refused to marry Chieftains; the Humbler of Kings started a regimental scale stick fight in the middle of an umKhosi Festival, and you would have the Chieftains spend the rest of their lives listening to those young men brag of their great deeds, while older men are spat upon for having clean spears after our greatest victory? Cha! These men will kill today, so that they won't live the rest of their life in their sons and nephews' shadows. I want to wash the spears of my men!" The prince's retainers voiced their support. They were all middle-aged men.

Ingonyama was exasperated. "You're not in command! The Young Mambas are Prince Zibhebhu's ibutho. Where is he?"

"Shot in the hand. He'll be fine, but he's had enough for today. Hamu's not here to lead the Chieftains, and the other two regiments' izinduna are nobodies. I'm the King's brother: I'm in charge, and I say we go into Natal."

Ingonyama knew he could not force Dabulamanzi to call back four thousand men, so he decided to settle for just one. "Where's my father? Do you have a company of the Hunters here?"

"They've already crossed the river." Dabulamanzi shrugged, taking a sip of his gin and turning his head back to enjoy the view.

Ingonyama led his men down to the water, but on the rocky shore he turned to the walking wounded and said, "No further. You men go back. The Invincibles will not fight again today, and I won't have you cross that river." The men were careful to hide their relief; the healthy Young Mambas coming out of the river on the opposite bank were shivering from head to toe. For men suffering from blood loss the cold could kill.

The rest of the Invincibles tried to wade across, but the current was so strong, and they were so tired, that they too used the human chain of shivering warriors, careful to give each a word of encouragement or gratitude as they passed. On the opposite bank, now in British territory, the Invincibles finally broke into a jog trot for both warmth and speed; Ingonyama hoped to collect his father and leave the rest of these men to their folly before anything happened.

The company of the Hunters sat in the grass taking snuff. Hundreds of men with the otter skin headbands of the Young Mambas were doing the same. "Baba!" Ingonyama shouted. Jama looked up at his son, saw the bloody spear, and smiled his lopsided grin. "You did the family proud today, I see."

"Yebho, Baba," Ingonyama said breathlessly, surprised at how much his father's praise touched him.

"Come here boys, and sit by me. Punga? Come over here and sit with your nephews." Ingonyama waived permission for his Invincibles to rest, and they gratefully sank into the grass. Mbeki and Ingonyama sat next to their father, taking a pinch of snuff from his container. Punga walked over from his company of Chieftains to join them.

"Baba, come back with us. Cetshwayo ordered us not to go into Natal," Ingonyama said.

"What about your Uncle Punga?" Jama asked.

Punga nodded. "Am I supposed to go back to the Valley and tell the families that I did nothing on this day? What a story for a storyteller. Jama fought. Mbeki fought. Ingonyama fought. Hlubi, Khandla, Bikwayo, Langa, all fought. Look at my spear: I might as well have slept the day away for all the work it has done."

"Baba..." Mbeki trailed off.

"Cha. There's more work to be done, and I will be here to help your uncle do it," Jama said firmly. "Now, let's talk of happier things." He put his arm around his youngest son. "When are you going to move back home with the family?"

Ingonyama rolled his eyes. "Baba, Mbeki is an Invincible."

"Exactly, he now has the right to wed. He could marry one of Ntsingwayo's daughters, leave the Invincibles, and come out to smith and drive cattle with his old man." Jama smiled, taking another pinch of snuff. His dreams were clear: One son to serve his king, one son for smithing, and one daughter to dote on. In a way he was glad he had only sired three children; his heart was only so big.

"Baba..." Mbeki shrugged. "The king--"

"Cetshwayo has Ingonyama, and that's more than he needs," Jama interrupted. Now Ingonyama was smiling at the compliment, and Mbeki was smiling from all the attention his father was giving him. For a moment their disagreements drifted away, and they were happy together.

The four of them sat in the grass like a pride of lions; they relaxed, comfortable in each other's company and drowsy from previous exertions, but an observer would have had only one impression: These men were dangerous. They drove off the flies with twitches of their heads. Their whispered conversations were deep rumbles from within their chests. Their best points were greeted with a flash of strong white teeth.

Their hands never let go of their assegais.

The Zulu did not stop, did not yield, and they took their foes eye to eye. Their bodies were trained from infancy to run all day, hide behind the smallest bush, and drive the underarm stabbing stroke of their broad assegais through bone, muscle, and blood.

They were Zulu, and the People of Heaven had the pride of lions, too. They were lords of all they surveyed, arrogant, dominant, imperious. This was their place, and they meant to keep it. Like lions on the plains they could be shot dead, but that did not remove their sovereignty. Some would live on, and the regal airs passed from father to son and mother to daughter in an unbroken chain. They belonged there like the kopjes and the sweetveld. It was their home, and they knew it down to their marrow.

The conversation drifted and flowed as if they were talking over a pot of beer at the homestead, rather than a snuff break after a battle to change the world. "Bhibhi is old enough to marry. Who would you choose?" Jama asked. He was teasing them. It was clear he had a surprise.

"Maybe one of the kaMajeke brothers, then she'd be close enough for you to visit," Mbeki said, sure that his father had a better idea than that.

"What about Inyati?" Jama asked.

Ingonyama had been drinking from a water gourd offered to him by a passing camp follower and now he sputtered, swallowing the wrong way. He managed to choke out, "Cha!"

"Why not?" Jama asked, surprised to hear his eldest refuse the idea. "He knows the family; he's our friend, and he has royal blood. Besides, if Mbeki sets up a homestead in the valley so will Inyati; that way I can visit Bhibhi every day, and, in time, his boys can help herd my cattle.

"I expect our family will be well rewarded after this war. Natal never suffered the lung sickness epidemic; Cetshwayo's canny enough to get fifty-thousand head when the British sue for peace. A lot of that will go to the Invincibles, and most of the rest will be divided among izinduna and royal favourites. All of us will be wealthy men." Jama did not mention that Bhibhi had been making his wives lean on him to arrange the marriage for years; he did not want Punga or his boys to know how many of the family's decisions were made by his women.

"You think the British will sue for peace?" Ingonyama sounded doubtful.

"Where were you during that battle?" Mbeki laughed. "I've seen how their governor works. The British officials had no orders to start this war. They hoped to conquer us before word got back to England. Instead they've lost an entire regiment of breech-loading riflemen to a Zulu impi, and that won't look good to their people over the ocean."

"Won't that just make them angry?" Ingonyama asked.

"Yebho, but Cetshwayo has whites speaking out for him. There's a bishop, a Christian wizard, who will tell the whole world that this war was unprovoked. Unless the British have a victory to hold on to, they'll make peace."

Ingonyama looked around before leaning into his brother's ear and whispering, "Do the British lose wars?"

Mbeki looked at his brother in surprise; he had never imagined Ingonyama had doubted the very possibility of a Zulu victory. "Yebho, they can be beaten; Holland Keech told me his country used to be part of Britain, and it fought for its independence."

Ingonyama imagined if Zibhebhu or Hamu ever tried for independence. *I'd kill every man, woman, and child in the North before I let that happen*, he decided.

Mbeki continued, "There have also been a number of wars where they fight just long enough to make their point, then they sign a peace. As long as Cetshwayo concedes something, like the free movement of Tsonga and Swazi labourers through kwaZulu to British farms and mines, then the British will give up. That was their main complaint anyway."

"Who is this riding on a pony?" Punga asked, pointing across the meadow. Prince Dabulamanzi was atop a white horse, the latest affectation of Zulu royals who had close ties with the British. In one hand he carried a stabbing assegai and in the other a throwing spear. He rode to the top of a prominent hillock, assured himself that he had every warrior's eye, and announced, "My brothers, we have come here to teach the English the error of their ways. We have come here to remind them that we make much better friends than foes. We have come here to prove to ourselves, and to our children, that our generation will stand and fight for our king and do so with courage."

He held aloft his throwing spear. "This is the weapon of a coward! Shaka said so. What brave man earns praise by killing his foe with a stick from the sky? He who kills knows not who is dead, and he who dies knows not who kills him!" He waited for the murmurs to die down. "Today I saw our sons use these spears when they lacked the courage to take cold steel to the redcoats. I tell you we need no such crutch!" He opened his hand and let the throwing spear clatter to the stones below. Now he raised the war assegai, pointing it to the heavens so that all could see the magnificent workmanship; it was one of Jama's spears.

"This is the weapon of a hero. If that hero dies in heroism his praise is still sung! When we go home and ours sons say, 'Where were you, Baba, when I was killing the enemies of my king?' We can say, 'I was killing my king's enemies with the stabbing spear of Shaka, not the toy spear I would use to hunt kudu!'" The men around the Invincibles smiled, imagining how sweet it would be to turn the young men's disrespect back against them.

"It is true they won at Isandhlwana, but I say we too can win glory. There is a place not far from here that we call kwaJim, and the English call Rorke's Drift. There are over a hundred redcoats there. If twenty-five thousand Zulu could cut down a regiment of British regulars with throwing spears this morning, surely four thousand can kill a hundred with the stabbing spear this afternoon, and ours will be the more glorious victory because we earned it as men! Eye to eye with the assegai! Throw aside your weapons of cowardice and onwards to kwaJim!"

Prince Dabulamanzi lowered his spear to point to the horizon and kicked his horse into a trot. All around him the regiments cheered their general and cast aside their throwing spears. With the discipline of veterans they formed up into the head, chest, and horns of the fighting bull buffalo and marched to Rorke's Drift.

Chapter 55

Jim Rorke built a mission station at a fordable section of the river several decades ago, and it later proved to be one of only three places on the border between Natal and kwaZulu where a modern wagon-supplied army could cross with ease. Rorke's Drift, or Jim's Place as the Zulu called it, had been turned into a hospital for the British Centre Column's sick. It was garrisoned by a company of the Twenty-Fourth, and there was also work being done to bridge the ford for easier resupply of the column from Natal.

Mbeki had seen it once, years ago, when Uncle Khandla had come here and bought sweaters, pots, beads, and sugar in exchange for some animal hides and the agreement to take a bible back with him into kwaZulu. As Mbeki crested the ridge and looked down onto the mission station his memory did not square with reality.

The hospital, the church, the storehouse, and the cattle kraal had all been linked by walls made up of mealie bags, biscuit boxes, and overturned wagons. The entire perimeter was lined with white-helmeted, red-coated British soldiers, their heavy rifles already pointing out with bayonets fixed. Even the windows and walls of the buildings bristled with muzzles protruding from loopholes. The place had become a fortress. "I don't like this," Mbeki said.

"I agree," Ingonyama answered. His soldier's eye told him things Mbeki had missed. While there was good cover up to within a hundred paces of the walls, the rest was a killing field, carefully cleared so that the riflemen could put up solid walls of volley fire, knocking warriors back as fast as they could rise up.

Once a charge reached the wall they would have to climb over shoulder-high fortifications. The redcoats could then fall back to an inner line of defenses and the Zulu warriors would be trapped between the wall they had just climbed over and the new one they would have to rush. There would be no cover to gather their numbers, and no way to fall back without being mowed down as they vaulted over the battlements.

This was going to be a difficult nut to crack, and he was not sure Dabulamanzi's men had the teeth for it. "Let's go talk some sense into the prince."

Dabulamanzi had dismounted from his horse and now sat in council with his izinduna, another glass of gin in his hand. He scowled at the arrival of the King's Champion. "I do not want to hear anything from you, Invincible, unless you plan to have your men support me."

Ingonyama set his jaw. "My men have been fighting and dying all day long. They will not fight and die here to save you from embarrassment." Dabulamanzi nodded. He had expected as much. He moved his hand in dismissal, but Mbeki refused to remain silent.

"You all know me," He spoke to the izinduna. "I am Mbeki kaJama. The King calls me the Wizard of kwaZulu. I am one of his favourites, a royal messenger, and an Invincible. I am entitled to speak at this war council as an equal." Dabulamanzi looked around at the izinduna who made no protest. The prince nodded for Mbeki to continue.

"Our King ordered us not to enter Natal, yet here we are on the wrong side of the Mzinyathi River. Our King ordered us not to attack a fortified position, but that mission station is a fortress. Our King ordered us not to tire the men, but you have driven the reserves of Isandhlwana all the way here, climbing a mountain, descending a ravine, crossing a river, and then marching across a plain. You defy the King three times, and all you will have to show for it is death. If you must disobey Cetshwayo, burn farms, kill livestock, slaughter any man, woman or child you find. Do not waste our most experienced warriors against those walls. You will lose hundreds, and even victory will not save from Cetshwayo's wrath."

Dabulamanzi caught the eye of each induna, and only when he was sure he had all their consent did he reply. "Those are words spoken by a man who is high in the King's favour, and whose deeds today will put him even higher. The young should never lose respect for their elders. If you will not fight with us, then leave us to our victory."

Mbeki and Ingonyama turned from the commanders, already discussing different directions for frontal assaults, and returned to their Invincibles. "Lie down, boys. We are always on the king's business, but that is not what is happening here. This fight is about the pride of old men. If that is the way things are to be, young men need take no part in it." The Invincibles nodded and sank down into the grass. Punga snorted, took Jama by the elbow, and trotted off to join his fellow Chieftains.

Resting on the heights surrounding the mission, the Invincibles could not have found better seats to watch the tragedy unfold. Concealed from the British but obvious to the Invincibles above, the four amabutho split up and went to ground, circling round to all quarters of the mission. Those Zulu with firearms were dismissed from their companies and ordered to the heights to lay down suppression fire, which they did with dismal accuracy.

Meanwhile, all Dabulamanzi's generals could think to do was to have a human wave of men rise up from the grass and charge the mealie bag ramparts, tumbling and dying under the ceaseless volleys of high-caliber rifle fire. The Invincibles watched as that solid wall of warriors became a floor, and still new walls rose up to climb over their dead to try again. Everywhere the gun smoke lay like a fog, and the war cries of 'uSuthu' were drowned out by the roar of the guns. The flower of their fathers' generation was being cut down like millet under the scythe.

Mbeki found a piece of wood and took out his captured knife, his smith's eye noticing the fineness of the steel and the strength of the edge. He began whittling to take his attention off the battle, but found he could not tear his eyes away from the charges below.

The day dragged on from the middle of the long summer afternoon and into the early evening. Finally, when the sun was dipping over the mountains and the heaps of dead Zulu were throwing long shadows on the ground Ingonyama muttered, "I can't watch this anymore." It was a rumble of discontent and heartbreak from deep within his chest.

"Those izinduna don't have any nerve. They've reached the outer wall five times, but they're always giving the order to fall back, and then they have to charge their way to the wall all over again!" Ingonyama rose to his feet, towering over the seated Invincibles. "Who isn't hurt?" Every man rose to his feet, even those who clearly were in no shape to fight. He gently ordered each of those by name to be seated. "This way!" He said to the rest.

They descended the heights with all the woodcraft their upbringing had taught them. They moved in the channels cut by erosion down the face of slope and then crawled through the long grass with such stealth that the heavy seed pods atop each blade of grass never swayed to betray their passage. Finally they reached the last good cover before the killing field, and the hundreds of men lying on their backs with their faces to the sky greeted them with silent, beseeching looks. The British fire overhead was murderous.

It was no coincidence that the company the Invincibles arrived at was

Jama's Hunters, now at half strength and mixed in with Punga's company of Chieftains. Ingonyama had watched them from the cliffs, and he knew that of all the companies theirs' had been the one that had reached the wall the most often. "I see you, Baba. Could you use an extra thirty men?"

Jama's face, stained with the soot of the floating powder clouds, pulled itself into a smile, not lopsided but beaming. "Yebho, thirty more would be excellent!"

The Invincibles slithered like snakes down into the last free space in the depression. "Where is Uncle Khandla, Baba?" Ingonyama asked, seeing Punga's dirty, sweating face among the Chieftains, but no sign of Khandla's among the Hunters.

"Out there, with three holes in him," Jama said it with such calm that Ingonyama thought there must be some other meaning to the words. "They shot him twice standing, and once more before he could hit the ground."

Ingonyama inched his head back, and then rolled over to get out of the line of fire. "We have to get over that wall, Baba." There was so little room in the depression that Ingonyama was laying on top of his father, so he spoke in only a whisper.

"How do you propose we do that?" Jama whispered back.

Ingonyama's honesty was brutal. "We stand up, run towards the wall, lose half our men getting there, another quarter getting over, and then hope the rest of the Chieftains follow us." Long moments passed as the two considered the slaughter that would entail.

"How is that any different from what we've been doing since we've gotten here?" Jama finally asked.

"My men will not fall back until I tell them to, and I am not going to order a retreat until the last redcoat is dead." Father and son lay there, their eyes less than a handsbreadth apart. Each took the measure of the other's courage. They could do it.

"He is a Lion!" Ingonyama called.

"He is a Lion!" Cried out Mbeki, Jojo, and Jama.

"He is even better than that: He is a Hippopotamus!
Master of his world, killer of the careless,
whose gut is huge, and penis pendulous!"

A hundred sang the song.

"uSuthu!" Ingonyama was on his feet in the full face of the gunfire.

"uSuthu!" Two hundred men replied. They were up and running, fast as springbok.

The words were in a language they did not know, but every Zulu knew what they meant: "Volley fire, present! Fire!" The thunder of the guns was answered a fraction of a moment later with the meaty thwack of bullets into flesh, and the little gasps of surprise and pain as air was forced out of the bodies of destroyed men. The Zulu kept running. "Present! Fire!" Another group of warriors fell, scattered across the entire front of the charge. It was like a smile in which one by one the teeth were falling out. "Present! Fire!"

Ingonyama felt his hand on the mealie bags and vaulted it with all his strength. He was inside. He swung his axe into the back of the redcoat standing next to him, not bothering to watch the man fall. All around him the Zulu were climbing over the barricade. He turned his back to the retreating redcoats and called over the battlements, "uSuthu! uSuthu!" But none of the Chieftains still under cover were rising to join him.

He swung back and watched his force whither like a spider engulfed in flames. The redcoats across a thirty-pace wide section of the wall had fallen back and been reinforced by men pulled from the opposite fortifications. Now they stood in two ranks, the one in front kneeling to reload, the one in the back firing. When the rear rank fired they walked forward and knelt to reload and the reloaded rank stood and fired. It was horrible and beautiful and deadly.

His men forward as fast as they could, but there was no cover to hide behind, no place to rally for a charge. He watched as five men tumbled back, only a pace from the kneeling front rank. Another six died moments later, five paces further back. Another four fell even further back. His men could not close as fast as the British regulars could reload their hateful guns, and even if they succeeded in getting into them, the redcoats all had bayonets, giving them a longer reach than the Zulu assegai.

Ingonyama stood there rooted to the ground, his mouth gummy with shock. We can't win, He admitted to himself. We've lost too many getting here; we're losing too many standing here, and no one is coming to help us. He opened his mouth to sound the retreat, but his father's voice stopped him.

"Come on, you bastards! We need you!" His father stood behind him atop the battlements with his back to the ranks of the enemy, calling out to the Chieftains still under cover. "We need you!" He called again. He was standing above everyone, Zulu and British alike, the most obvious target in the entire mission station. "We need you!" He called again. Ingonyama grabbed him by his ankle, trying to pull his father down. "uSuthu!" Jama called, and at that moment the bullet took his father in the back, lifted him high into the air surrounded by a cloud of pink mist and dropped him face down outside the wall.

"Baba!" Ingonyama shouted, his face sticky with his father's blood. He dove over the battlements to where Jama had landed on the hard ground. "Baba!" He looked at his father's back and the small hole the size of the end of his thumb. That doesn't look so bad, He lied to himself. He cradled his father in his arms, rolling him over to face the sky and saw the truth at once. The entry wound in the back was small, but the exit wound just below Jama's right nipple was big enough to put his fist into. "Baba!" Ingonyama cried again, tears streaming fast and hot down his bloody cheeks.

All around him the survivors of the attack were throwing themselves over the wall. Sompisi cleared it like a hurdle. Ignoring his bleeding shoulder and paralyzed arm, he kept on running until he was back and safe in the depression that had been their starting point. Jojo and Mbeki threw themselves over the battlements into a pile landing beside Ingonyama, who did not notice in his grief. Punga put one foot up on the mealie bags to jump over, but a bullet took him between the shoulder blades. He tumbled backwards onto the drift of dying Zulu. A handful more made it clear but that was all, all that was left of the hundred who had followed Jama and Ingonyama.

"Baba..." Ingonyama shook his father. Mbeki reached out and closed his father's open, vacant eyes. "Baba..."

It was Jojo who brought them back to reality. "We can't stay here."

The silence in both kaJamas' heads cleared, as if they had had stoppers in their ears that had just been removed. Suddenly they could hear the gunfire again, and the screams. The two ranks of redcoats were bayoneting the wounded on the far side of the wall. Within moments they would have taken their posts on the firing line again, and the muzzles of their rifles would hang over the grieving sons' heads. "He's not dead,"

Ingonyama lied. "He's not dead!" He used his command voice, as if he could order his father back to life. The corpse said nothing.

"Now, Ingonyama!" Jojo called, unwilling to leave his friend. It was Mbeki who heard what Jojo was saying.

"Ingonyama, we have to go!" The eldest son still cradled his father's body. Mbeki bunched his fist and punched his brother hard in the side of the head. "Now!" Ingonyama felt his teeth rattle at the blow, and finally he stood up. His head and shoulders were now above the battlements, in clear line of fire of the British who were killing the Zulu wounded, but they were so surprised to see him that none had reloaded their rifles. They fumbled to do so, but Ingonyama had other ideas.

He took off his lion cloak and draped it over his father's body like a shroud. "Ngwenyama," He said the past tense of his own name. "He was a lion." The cloak was the only burial the son could give his father. The single statement was the only eulogy. The three left Jama there below the British battlements and returned to the injured Invincibles upon the hillside.

Chapter 56

Throughout the evening and the long night the kaJama brothers were unceasing in their demands that Dabulamanzi call off his attacks. The bodies of the Zulu lay in drifts upon the field, and even the night attacks, so foreign to the Zulu's nature, availed them nothing. In the early twilight one side or the other had fired the thatch roof of the hospital, and the whole area was lit up; the slightest movement brought down a hailstorm of gunfire upon the Zulu.

"How many would you say we've lost?" Dabulamanzi finally asked; two empty gin bottles lay at his feet, and he had not shared a drop.

"Five hundred certainly, eight hundred probably, a thousand possibly," was Mbeki's blunt reply. "And if they've lost thirty men I would be surprised." Another human wave of black forms rose up; their long shadows thrown by the firelight pointed up at Dabulamanzi accusingly. Three salvos of rifle fire drove them to earth. The impi's frustration was palpable. Men began to cry out at their wounds, where before they had suffered them in silence. It was all for nothing, and the Impi knew it.

Dabulamanzi took out his fob watch, a gift from a white trader. "Two more hours until dawn," He said. Ingonyama stared at him blankly and Mbeki, who at least understood the concept of hours, still did not care. "Don't you two know what that means?" The prince tried to sound confident, but the edge of desperation had crept into his voice. "A dawn attack! The Zulu have always swept the field with a dawn attack!" Ingonyama could feel the panic in the prince's voice. The king's wrath would be terrible; the prince had lost somewhere between a fifth and a quarter of his force for nothing.

"You, Ingonyama, you shall lead it! One last assault will sweep them from behind their damned walls, eh?" The prince brought his gin glass to his mouth and threw it back, but it was already empty and had been since midnight.

"I won't," Ingonyama spoke softly, but his jaw was set. "Who would you have me lose this time? My best friend? My brother? All for your damned pride. This is not a battlefield; it is a place of slaughter."

"The dawn attack will--"

Mbeki interrupted the rising panic of the prince. "Haven't you learned anything from your family's history? A dawn attack did these men's fathers no good at Blood River. Forty years ago twelve thousand Zulu attacked a hundred Boers inside their laagered wagons and did not kill a single white man. Those Boers had muskets. These redcoats have breech-loading rifles. There were three times as many Zulu at Blood River, and they still did not win. Nothing you can do by dawn will change anything. This war is still winnable; this battle is not. Men you are killing for no good purpose today might carry a battle in the future. Don't be a fool!"

A scout ran up to them, his arm in a sling. "British cavalry are approaching from the southwest, Nkosi. What are your orders?"

Dabulamanzi sagged, admitting the situation to himself at last. "All I wanted to do..." His voice trailed off under the cold stares of the kaJama brothers. He wished his council of izinduna were here, but half of them were dead and the rest were down around the mission station, extorting the exhausted warriors for one last charge and then one more last charge. "Order the retreat."

The command went down the line, and the four broken regiments melted away under cover of darkness. A small rearguard would cover the withdrawal, outnumbered four times over by the dead. The rest formed a ragged column and marched after the white pony of Dabulamanzi, tears streaming down his face at the realization of how many he left behind.

The sun was up by the time they reached the Mzinyathi River, and every heart sank to see a column of British infantry marching towards them. Many thought they were the ghosts of the dead from Isandhlwana, but Mbeki knew better; these were the men who had left the camp yesterday morning to pursue the Zulu's decoy force. They had returned to spend a terrible night sleeping on the battlefield. When they awoke, they found that the entire camp had been looted and their friends disemboweled as demanded by Zulu custom. The faces of the redcoats were as exhausted and drawn as the Zulu opposite them.

It was ridiculous, impossible, unbelievable, but neither side wanted to fight. The two armies, companies of redcoats and regiments of Zulu, passed within a hundred paces of each other, eyeing their enemy with the detached loathing one used for reptiles in a menagerie. "This is not right," Sompisi muttered under his breath. The bayonet wound in his shoulder throbbed.

"Be quiet, Sompisi," Ingonyama ordered, the hollow voice surprising him as much as his followers. His father was dead, and the empty place in his heart would never be filled.

"There they are, right there! Closer than we were to the walls of kwa-Jim!" He pointed with one finger, raising his voice loud enough to carry across to the British.

"Shut up, Sompisi!" Ingonyama put steel into his voice. "There are hundreds of them, all with rifles, with bayonets. We've both had enough death." He tried to stare down his friend; he set his jaw, locked his eyes, and stood still as the rest of the Zulu marched past him. He could sense Sompisi's mind, and knew he was losing. He put a pleading look into his gaze, but still his junior would not give in.

"Coward," Sompisi spat; the accusation was like a slap across the King's Champion's face. "All of you! Cowards!" He shouted, waiving his good arm to attract their attention. Both columns froze, watching the drama play out. "There is your enemy! A hero dies in heroism! You rushed the guns at Isandhlwana! You rushed the guns at kwaJim! You are closer to those men than you ever were before, so what is different here from there? How can we meekly walk past these men?" Something in his brain had snapped, and he looked up and down the column of Zulu, seeking a single man who supported him.

"He is a lion..." He let the cheer trail off, knowing no one would pick it up. In despair he called out, "uSuthu!" and ran towards the foe.

"Sompisi!" Mbeki cried, taking a step after him. Ingonyama's broad arm held him back, tears running down his face. Sompisi ran across the open space, his body awkward as he could not swing one arm. He pointed with his assegai at the redcoats, his actions begging his brothers to join him. No one moved on either side.

The air was still, and every man could hear Sompisi's laboured breathing, his heartbreaking sobs. Clouds of dew exploded out of the grass as he ran, and soon his body was wet and sleek from the water. He was fifty paces out, twenty-five, ten. Everyone was frozen except for Sompisi, and Mbeki wondered if the redcoats would really allow the Invincible to reach them with his spear, as he was so intent on doing.

Finally a single private brought up his heavy Martini-Henry and shot Sompisi through the forehead when he was only a few paces away. Both sides stood there, still, waiting for the other to break the unspoken truce. "Wo..." Mbeki trailed off. Ingonyama released his hold on him.

The air hung heavy with the echo of that single blast. Each warrior remembering the barrages he had withstood and the men flying to pieces all around him. Each redcoat remembering their naked friends, sliced open and left to the jackals. For an eternity they stood there, then the Zulu began moving east again, and the British began moving west.

Only Sompisi did not move. He would never move again.

Chapter 57

Inyati dumped his basket of earth and wiped his sweating brow with the back of his dusty forearm. The sun beat down upon him, but he was exhilarated that at last he could work all day without the nagging cramps and spasms in his abdomen forcing him to stop.

"You, there! No slacking you, lazy kaffir!" The supervisor bellowed.

Inyati looked at the white man long enough to imply he did not comprehend the English words but understood their meaning. He picked up his basket and walked back down the slowly growing earthworks of Fort Pearson.

As he passed the other dusty labourers he amused himself with their careful expressions. Everyone knew he was a Zulu spy, but no one would say a word to the British, half because they were loyal to Cetshwayo and half because they feared the assegai in the night.

"Another basket," Inyati ordered, dropping the wicker container down and kneading the muscles in the small of his back with callused hands.

"Yebho, Nkosi," The men with the shovels murmured, digging deep into the hard ground.

"Enough Whites know what that means. Call me Inyati."

"Yebho, Inyati," They murmured again.

"How many riders did I miss?" The men digging at the base of the glacis could see the road while they worked, so they counted the traffic in and out of the fort for him.

"Four with blue coats, ten in hats with red headbands," One of the diggers said.

"Any wagons?"

"Not since your last trip, Nko--Inyati."

"Good work. I'll see you all get an extra beef ration." The diggers smiled among themselves; of all the bribes Inyati had invented since he had because spy master of the Zulu surveillance at Fort Pearson, recruiting the Zulu labourers' cook had proved the most popular.

Inyati scooped up his refilled load and began trotting back up the slope, joining in the workers' song and using its steady beat to pace his ascent. He would do nothing to make himself stand out.

He did another load, and another, slowing building up the useless fortifications of this useless fort. Fort Pearson would never come under artillery fire, so Inyati could see no purpose to the earthworks, and if the Zulu ever did cross into Natal they would bypass Fort Pearson and ravage their way through the countryside. Still, the Whites liked everything to be done just so, and so they built their fort to the same plans they would have used in Europe, and every British unit or officer attached to the Right Column of the invasion force had to check in at Fort Pearson before crossing the Thekula, making the fort the perfect observation point for a Zulu spy network.

Inyati returned to the diggers with his basket empty again. "Anyone new?" He asked.

"It's very strange, Inyati. Look." One of the diggers gestured with his chin to the main gate of the fort. Inyati glanced over to see a platoon of redcoats blocking the open gate as an officer on a horse addressed an armed party of Zulu warriors.

Inyati was careful not to mutter under his breath as he recognized their leader; dressed in a leopard skin cape and with a weather beaten revolver sticking out of his belt, the crushed nose of Jobe made him unmistakable.

"Okay, someone have an accident right now, and I'll double his beef ration for a month," Inyati whispered. The diggers did not ask him to repeat it. One promptly stabbed down with his spade, catching the top of his foot instead of the ground. He gave a little moan, and the others started shouting for the white foreman. Inyati dropped down into the hole, flashing them all a quick and easy grin as he put the injured man's arm over his shoulder to balance him while he took the weight off his bleeding foot.

"I'm going to take him to the doctor, Nkosi." Inyati said to the foreman when he sauntered over, and, though the white man spoke no Zulu, Inyati's meaning was clear.

"Well, be quick about it!" The man snapped, tossing the injured man's spade to one of the men waiting to have his basket filled.

Inyati supported the man as he hobbled towards the gate of the fort. Ahead of him the British officer allowed Jobe and his company to go inside, still armed. I wouldn't let an armed redcoat in to see the Cetshwayo, Inyati thought. He was waived through by the day sentry and promptly dropped the injured digger off at the base infirmary, where his flesh wound would be bandaged before he was sent back to light duties, painting a fence or tending a fire somewhere.

Inyati walked across the fort's parade square, easily spotting Jobe's escort waiting outside the base commander's office. Inyati picked up an empty pot and balanced it on his head to appear to be on an errand and walked around to the back of the building.

A window was open to allow air to circulate, and Inyati heard the fort's translator speaking. Inyati heard the word 'defection' in English before a hand clamped down on his shoulder.

"You there! The water was for B Barracks; you're heading to Officer Country!" The corporal spun Inyati around and sent him off down a side street; Inyati went without protest.

So Hamu is planning to switch sides? Inyati wondered, walking far enough that he was sure the corporal was no longer watching him before ducking down a row between two barracks and dropping the empty water jug for an armful of firewood. When would he do that? Will it be a civil war, or will he just run for the border with his followers? Will he head south or west or north? Inyati did not know enough to send a report, but he would send one anyway. Hamu's defection would be a huge blow for Cetshwayo.

The Matabele prince dropped the firewood off at the gatehouse and returned to his work on the glacis, hauling baskets of earth. He would have to be careful to be out of sight when Jobe left, and he would have to think who he could send to oNdini as a runner. There was a lot to do, running a spy network, and Inyati pretended to be so busy he did not have time to think about Nandhi or Ingonyama, or be grateful to be so far away from the whole sticky mess.

Chapter 58

The Great Place of oNdini was cold and empty. Most of the huts were vacant; all of the warriors had dispersed to their homes for the purification rights. The familiar smoke of cooking fires was absent. The cattle had been driven out to pasture by the few boys left in the ikhanda, depriving the palisades of the boys' echoing laughter, replacing it with the coughing and hacking of the few old men who were still garrisoning the capital to free younger men for war. Even the birds had deserted oNdini to eat the unharvested millet and mealie across the kingdom.

Three men were down on one knee, head bowed before their King. Cetshwayo stood over them and thundered, "You crossed in Natal; you attacked a fortified outpost, and you lost a thousand of my most experienced men, all for nothing?" The three did not move.

He reached out with a trembling hand to grab the back of Dabulamanzi's head, but stopped for a moment until the shaking subsided. How much I would like to see you dead for this, he thought. But that would be a waste, and this war will require everything I have. At last he laid his open palm on the back of his brother's head, who looked up with tears brimming in his eyes. "I forgive you, Dabulamanzi."

His councilors behind him shifted uneasily. It was their brothers and cousins who had died for this prince's ambition. "Cousin, kill him," Hamu begged.

"Hamu, shut up," Cetshwayo said rudely, looking down into his brother's eyes. "He has learned not to attack a fortified position, and he is twice the battlefield commander you are. I have a use for him."

"What possible use--"

"I said shut up," Cetshwayo repeated. Hamu nodded, taking a glass of gin from one of his pages, downing it, and returning it without his King seeing. Cetshwayo kept his eyes on Dabulamanzi and spoke slowly, as one would to a disobedient son. "Dabulamanzi, the British's Centre Column was destroyed at Isandhlwana, their Left Column is engaged with Mbilini out in the West. Their Right Column is the problem." The King looked into his brother's eyes, making sure the defeat at kwaJim had stamped itself upon his brother's soul.

"Godide's forces attacked them at Nyezane, but the battle was a draw.

We stopped the column, but did not destroy it. They've built a fort at the mission station of Eshowe, and they're staying there." Oh, how my brother flinches at the mention of a fort. He is the right man for the job. "The problem is that my Great Impi, between Isandhlwana and kwa-Jim, lost almost four thousand good fighting men killed and injured, and it takes an Impi the size of the one I brought against Isandhlwana to smash a column. Is it heard?"

Dabulamanzi nodded, his eyes still brimming with tears at the pain he heard in his brother's voice. "I am going to take four thousand men from the East to reinforce the Great Impi when it reforms after the purification rites and the harvest. That leaves only four thousand warriors to keep fifteen hundred redcoats, two thousand conscripted native levees, and two hundred cavalry in place."

"Cousin, four thousand men could never storm--"

"Shut up, Hamu, or I'll have your tongue!" Cetshwayo wheeled around to face the northern baron, who quailed before the royal rage. Cetshwayo's patience had stretched thin: The greatest victory in Zulu history had been completely negated by kwaJim. Every newspaper in the English-speaking world had carried the Battle of Rorke's Drift on the front page, a heroic victory to follow the defeat at Isandhlwana. Negotiations would never end the war now. Britain was determined to clean the stain upon her honour with total victory, now that it had proof the Zulu could be beaten.

Hamu gulped once, and took a step back to hide himself behind a screen of other Great Men. Cetshwayo wheeled back on Dabulamanzi, returning to his calm slow voice. "You have learned your lesson about fortresses, haven't you?" Dabulamanzi nodded again. "Four thousand men will hold the British in Eshowe. The British will need grazing for their oxen and horses, food for their men. When they sally out to get them you will harass and harry them. Keep them in their fort but never attack the walls. Keep them up at night with the sounds of men preparing to attack. Bother them. Worry them. Hold them in place."

"Yebho, my King."

"Do not fail me again, brother."

"Cha, my King."

"You have your orders. You and Godide will share command of the remaining four thousand. If either of you break my orders you will not live to regret it. Is it heard?" The threat was barely a movement of air.

Dabulamanzi nodded again. "Then get out of my sight." The Prince rose and departed, his face showing his horror at how close he had come to death.

The two kaJama boys still knelt with their heads lowered, but Cetshwayo did not have the same difficulty ordering them to rise. "Who is dead because of my brother's stupidity?" He asked.

"Jama..." Ingonyama paused for a moment after that name. "Punga, Sompisi, Khandla, Noziwana, Sobadli, Mdlaka, Madicane, Zikala, Ngini..." The list went on, and for each one Cetshwayo's face twitched in anguish. This was not just a list of the promising young Invincibles, each a royal favourite; Ingonyama was listing, in the detached and deadened tone he had adopted of late, some of Cetshwayo's oldest and dearest favourites, men who had been prominent in the days of his father. Almost all of the names on Ingonyama's list had worn brass armbands and willow wood necklaces. Ingonyama's list was the best men of two generations, and every one of them was dead. Hidden behind his comrades, Hamu polished off his bottle of gin before Ingonyama finished his list.

"Is that all?" Cetshwayo asked, dazed.

"Nkosi Nkulu, those are only the ones I personally saw fall. When men go to ground it takes an induna to get them up again, and when he stands up first too often he is the first one shot."

"How many Invincibles do you have left?" Cetshwayo asked.

"Twenty-five, Nkosi Nkulu." Ingonyama saw his king's face twitch again. Seventy-five of the finest warriors in the Kingdom were dead in just two battles against a single column.

"I absolve you of any responsibility for kwaJim. You both did what you could. Undergo the purification rituals and return here in half a moon. We will bring the Invincibles up to strength with the new heroes who have emerged from this war." Cetshwayo dismissed the Court, asking only Hamu to stay, who discreetly passed the empty gin bottle to the departing Zokufa.

"Cousin, there is a dog on the roof of my hut," Cetshwayo said, claiming an ancient sign of misfortune. "You are that dog." Hamu stood very still. "Well?"

"What would you have me say, Cousin?" Hamu replied.

"I would have you call me Nkosi Nkulu, for a start." Cetshwayo's voice was filled with steel.

"What would you have me say, Nkosi Nkulu?" Hamu said again, putting a touch of venom on the title of Great Chief.

"Where were you at Isandhlwana?" The King asked.

"I was here," Hamu replied.

"Yet your regiment, the Chieftains, was there, and when they won no glory they followed Dabulamanzi to kwaJim and died in their hundreds."

"Ah! I see. I am responsible for your brother's failures," Hamu spat.

"You are responsible for my headaches and my heartaches, Hamu," Cetshwayo spat back, letting all his anger pour out in the blackest tones Hamu had ever heard from his kind-hearted cousin. "May tokoloshe take you, and witches use your balls for their soup!" Hamu took an inadvertent step back, the gin had weakened his will.

"I am tired of your muttering, tired of your scheming, tired of your ambitions. I am tired of you, Hamu. There are a thousand men in your province who are not in any of my armies, maybe two or three thousand, and they are staying out of this war because you have ordered them to do so. Brave men died for the benefit of this entire kingdom, but you and your tribe will reap the rewards of this war without making a contribution."

"What rewards?" Hamu snarled, just as the gin had weakened his will, so it had given new life to his tongue, tearing down the last restraints between his thoughts and his words. "If you lose, my tribe will fall into civil war along with everyone else. If you win they are still your subjects. Why should I give you my Ngenetsheni to die for you, when if I leave them at home in a few years' time they can die for me?" His eyes flew open, realizing he had finally said the unspeakable.

"I see," Cetshwayo said, sinking down onto his throne stool. He snapped a finger, and Ingonyama and Jojo appeared from the royal quarters behind him, not yet departed for the purification rituals. "I have had enough of you, dear cousin." Hamu's liver hurt, and not just from the liquor. He could almost feel the tip of Ingonyama's eager assegai, so close now. "Today you will send a message to your followers in the north to present themselves here within ten days. Disobey me at your peril. Leave this ikhanda at your peril. I will have my kingdom fight for the common good, and that is not your good. Is it heard?"

Hamu concealed the smile of contempt from his face. Poor predictable Cetshwayo, never willing to dispose of someone if they are still of use to him. "It is heard, Cousin," Hamu said with all the oily charm he could muster.

"Get out of my sight." Hamu walked away without making any bows or genuflections; he had too much on his mind. The time had come; the preparations had already been made against this day. Arriving in his hut, Zokufa and Jobe waited for him, each with a bottle of gin for their chief. Hamu took the one from Jobe and drank straight from the neck, feeling the raw alcohol burn down his throat and form a warm pool in his stomach.

"Boy, run to my homestead. Tell my steward to launch Baobab Tree. Is it heard? Baobab Tree." Jobe's eyes went wide, recognizing the code name of that contingency plan. He had just returned from Fort Pearson faster even than Hamu's fleetest messengers, but he knew he could not plead exhaustion. He gave a quick 'Yebho, Baba' and departed before his father could cuff him for his tardiness.

"Nkosi, do you think this is wise?" Zokufa asked, handing over the other gin bottle as Hamu dropped Jobe's empty one to the floor.

"If I ever want to be king, I have no choice. Cetshwayo has forced me to it." The northern prince crammed the new bottle into his mouth and suckled from it as baby drinks from his mother's teat. He needed it more and more nowadays; it was his best advisor and his best friend. "I will be king of kwaZulu, even if my kingdom is one of ashes and corpses."

Chapter 59

The hundred Invincibles had no difficulty following the spoor of Hamu's escape. The man who would be king had not fled alone: He was running to the British with four thousand of his clansmen, complete with wagons and herds of cattle, all defecting to the British in exchange for favourable treatment after the war.

"We are gaining on them," Mbeki said, the jog trot left him more than enough wind to carry on a conversation.

"This country is no good for wagons," Ingonyama replied, his voice still missing some of its former confidence.

They were running through the west where Mbilini's followers fought from the mountains and caves against British cavalry, the only force capable of moving at speed through the foothills of the Drakensberg Mountains. All around them were kopjes and kloofs, thickets of thorn brush snarling up and over dongas.

"Remember, we're not supposed to kill him," Mbeki said.

"Yebho, but if one of our spears should slip, or if there should be some confusion during his surrender..." Ingonyama let the implications trail off. Mbeki was not shocked at the idea that in this one thing Ingonyama would disobey his king. They both knew what Cetshwayo really wanted was the fighting men and the cattle Hamu was taking with him. Hamu's death, especially his unordered death, would be a great relief to the Nkosi Nkulu.

Hamu's contingency plan had been carried out flawlessly by his northern followers. The Hamu ibutho had mustered, been blessed by the war doctors, and rounded up the tribe's cattle, women and children. Meanwhile Hamu had been snuck out of oNdini by his guards. Even with Inyati's warning of the coming defection, Hamu's entire force had been on the march for fifteen days before Ingonyama realized the occupant of Hamu's quarters was a double, eating the presented food and complaining just loud enough for the sentries to assure themselves the hut was occupied.

The hundred Invincibles, seventy-five of them only just elevated to the august position, moved easily across the rough ground. They knew that Hamu's warriors outnumbered them at least ten to one, so their eyes were always searching for ambushes. Even so, they almost missed Hamu's son Jobe, barring their path with a single double-barreled shotgun.

"Is this a joke?" Ingonyama asked, ordering his men to fan out to left and right to make sure Jobe did not have hidden support.

"No joke, kaJama. I have been asked to have a word with you," Jobe called out, dropping his shotgun to the ground, standing with arms above his head, palms forward to show he carried no other weapons.

"Kill him and let's go," Mbeki said. The two kaJama brothers were now only paces away from the kaHamu, who was standing between two wagon ruts.

"Oh have a heart, Mbeki. This is not a delaying tactic. You've got us. The empty gin bottle at my feet here is still wet from my father's spit." He gestured at the shattered bottle, discarded from the back of a wagon that must be only just out of sight.

"So what do you want, Jobe?" Ingonyama asked.

"I want you to let us go," Jobe said. Ingonyama and Mbeki laughed in his face. "Just be silent for a moment. My father has given me up to convey this one message." Mbeki made a point of putting his assegai into position for the stabbing stroke.

"Ingonyama, do you remember what my father said to you on the night you first met Nandhi?" Jobe asked, searching the Invincible's eyes for some flicker of remembrance. Hamu had planted the seed along time ago against such a day as this. "You remember, before he told you about Zungu the Great?" There it was, the spark. "He would ask you to remember what he told you then, and to think about what is happening here. If the Zulu win, then Cetshwayo is king and Hamu..." Jobe trailed off, knowing Ingonyama had to put it together for himself, and that the less specific he was, the less he gave Mbeki to argue against. "If the Zulu lose, kwaZulu will need someone with the British's ear to make sure..."

Silence hung between them. Mbeki looked at his brother incredulously. "What is all this about? Kill him, and let's get his father!"

"Cha, Mbeki," Ingonyama said. Jobe smiled.

"What did you say?" Mbeki was stunned.

"We're going to let them go. Both of them." Not waiting for Ingonyama to change his mind, Jobe picked up his shotgun and left at the jog trot. He would be with his father shortly, congratulating him and asking for an explanation as to how the prince had managed to manipulate the King's Champion so successfully.

"You heard him, Ingonyama. The shit they take now won't have flies on it by the time we find it. They can't be much further than that next kopje..." Still nothing from his brother. "What's the matter with you?"

"Just think about it, Mbeki," Ingonyama said, waving his men back in from their picket posts. "If we win, Hamu can never come back. He's as good as dead, turning traitor and defecting to the British. He's just banished himself with a few thousand Ngenetsheni forever. What have we lost? A few hundred warriors who would have deserted the impi anyway, and some cows that have been run out of condition."

Mbeki opened his mouth to argue, but Ingonyama was not done. "Now let's say we lose. I'm only speaking as a possibility, you understand." He held up his hand. "If we lose this war, Cetshwayo will not be allowed to remain King. Who will replace him? Ntsingwayo? The man who led us at Isandhlwana? Cha. Zibhebhu doesn't have enough support in the South to rule. None of Cetshwayo's brothers has anywhere near the influence to take the throne, and the British certainly aren't going to govern us themselves. As long as we provide cheap labour and don't have an army, they'll leave us to kill each other."

Mbeki closed his mouth, realizing Ingonyama's reasoning might have some logic. "Hamu has the bloodline to be king, and the whole Kingdom knows it. If he defects to the English with that many followers, they might make him Nkosi Nkulu after the war. Even a bad king is better than a civil war, Mbeki." Ingonyama put down his hands, ready now for his brother's barrage.

Mbeki surprised Ingonyama by not arguing against letting Hamu go. Instead he said, "And what about us, Ingonyama? With Hamu king, we're both dead."

Ingonyama turned his head to look his brother in the eye and smile his lopsided grin. "If Hamu is king, it is because we lost the war, and you and I will both be dead before that happens." Mbeki was chilled down to the bone despite the heat of the late summer day.

"Alright," He said and the two stood there, surrounded by their Invincibles as Hamu's followers got away. They made camp right there, their bonfires built up much higher and brighter than was necessary. When Mbeki asked his brother what he thought he was doing, revealing their position so blatantly, Ingonyama ordered his brother to add more wood. The dazzling fire was visible from every height all the way out to the horizon. Curiosity would make it irresistible to an observer.

Ingonyama was up all night, his insomnia more acute than usual. Always he ordered more wood, more wood, so that at one point ten men went into a patch of trees and hacked up two fallen trunks into manageable logs. The fire grew so hot that the sleeping men awoke and moved their karosses further from the flames. The light was thrown so far that it flickered and danced off the bare rock faces of the surrounding kopjes, graceful and graceless, solid and ethereal.

Towards dawn Ingonyama started smiling, and Mbeki, who was taking the last watch of the night, thought his brother might have lost grip with reality again. Nothing could have been further from the truth: Ingonyama's smile was one of pleasure, for his ears, straining for a specific sound all night, were finally rewarded.

At dawn everyone except Ingonyama was surprised to find the entire camp encircled by hundreds of glaring abaQulusi, stripped for fighting. Their axes and spears glinted in the early light like the last evening stars come down to earth. The Invincibles' night sentries who had been sent well out from the fire stood among the abaQulusi sheepishly. They had been captured and disarmed in the night with such stealth that not even the sleeping birds in the trees had stirred. Only the sound of hundreds of men slithering on their bellies through the grass had alerted Ingonyama, and he had only heard it because he had been straining to do so since sunset.

"Mbeki! Whose stupid idea was it to have all that light?" Mbilini called from the front rank of his warriors. He recognized the young man who had escorted the white hunter through these lands and arranged such a profitable night for him.

"Mine." Ingonyama stood, smiling his lopsided grin. A few of the abaQulusi muttered and took a step back, for the giant had looked nowhere near as imposing when he had been sitting in the grass, smiling like an idiot.

"Then you're a fool. The British cavalry is all through these hills; it could just as easily been a horse patrol as an abaQulusi one that found you."

"I have been listening. Give me enough credit to tell the different between a shoed horse on stony ground and the sound of a Swazi induna setting up an ambush. My men would have been long gone before a horseman reached us. Besides, this was the fastest way to find you." The lopsided grin remained unchanged.

"I take it from your unimpressive collection of young boys that you're the King's Champion, He is a Lion?" Mbilini said, walking from his circle towards Ingonyama.

"I take it from your crooked teeth that you're Mbilini waMswati, the Hyena of the Phongolo?" Ingonyama replied, stepping forward until the two stood toe to toe. Mbilini stared up into Ingonyama's eyes, undeterred that the King's Champion was more than a head taller than him. The two continued their smiles, then finally laughed heartily and took each other into a bear hug, shouting out, "You look good!" and "I haven't seen you since the last umKhosi Festival!"

At last the two broke apart, Mbilini wiping a tear of laughter from the corner of his eyes at the delicious joke they had played on the surrounding warriors. "What can I do for you, Ingonyama?"

"I have a hundred good fighters here. Do you have some action for them?" The two smiled again, eager as hunting dogs with the smell of bushbuck in their noses.

Mbilini laid his finger to the side of his nose, the crooked smile never leaving his face. "I just might."

"Where?" Ingonyama asked, looking around as if it might be within sight.

"Just to the north, on the Ntombe River." Mbilini smiled.

"Sounds like fun," Ingonyama replied. Mbilini waived his men to march and Ingonyama did the same. A thousand of the best warriors in kwaZulu were about to cause havoc among the invaders.

Chapter 60

"This is stupid," Mbeki said, balancing a stack of firewood on his head with both hands.

"I like it," Ingonyama replied. He carried a pot full of watery beer out in front of him, and his repeated attempts to contrive a pot belly joke had already irritated the others to anything he might have to say.

"It will work, and once we're inside you'll be glad for it." Mbilini also carried firewood, but his were kindling sized pieces put into a wicker basket that he carried on his back with the aid of a tumpline.

The three of them were walking across the wide plain of the Ntombe river valley in clear view of a company of British regulars. The hairs were standing up on the back of Mbeki's neck, but he was careful to appear relaxed. There were almost as many men in front of him as there had been at Rorke's Drift, but this time he did not have an impi at his back or even a spear in his hand. He was armed only with the bundle of firewood and the knife he still wore on his belt.

"Whoever's in charge is an idiot," Ingonyama muttered. "Just as I promised," Mbilini murmured.

The camp was a disgrace: It had begun as a supply convoy shifting ammunition and food from Natal to the British garrison at Luneberg, but it had reached the river in full spate, and the British had only managed to get two wagons across to the south bank before giving up.

The redcoats had formed their remaining wagons into a V-shaped laager on the north bank, but the fortification would not hold off a frontal assault: The wagons had wide gaps between them, and as the flood waters had receded an open space between the top of the V and the river had appeared. To further demonstrate his stupidity, the officer had sent a third of his force across the river to guard the two wagons on the south bank, and had pitched his own tent outside his laager.

The three warriors said nothing more once they were inside the perimeter. They were not challenged by any sentry, burdened as they were with items obviously destined for the camp cook. Finding that worthy lighting the first of supper's cooking fires, they dropped off their loads and were given a few mealie cakes for their trouble.

The three of them sat down on the dieselboom of a wagon and ate the food, coolly taking in their surroundings. There were seventy or eighty regulars on the north bank, and another thirty or forty on the south. Discipline was slack: The British who were not on picket duty walked about with their tunics undone and their helmets off. More than one was seen to take a discreet nip from a bottle when no superior was in sight. Mbeki looked at his brother with a merry twinkle in his eyes. They both looked at Mbilini, who finished his mealie cake with obvious enjoyment.

The three rose to their feet and began to filter out of the camp. As they were leaving the laager a voice called out to them in a cockney accent, "Right you mob... 'Ere! You lot! Mind your bloody betters!" Mbeki turned, sure they had been caught. The cook stood there scowling at them. "Don't you be goin' anywhere without these!" He threw a couple of woodcutter axes at them. "I want you to get some bigger logs, right? Bigger!" He made a gesture with his hands to show the diameter of wood he was looking for. Mbeki nodded dumbly, handed one of the axes to Ingonyama, and they walked out of the camp without further trouble.

The sun had set by the time they were back at Mbilini's camp atop the nearest kopje from the British convoy. The three laughed about the incident over mugs of beer, inordinately pleased they had been able to steal two of the fine British axes.

"They're soft," Ingonyama finally said, speaking of the British.

"Cha, they're tired. They've been getting those wagons out of the mud for days and days. Besides, they wouldn't dream of us attacking them," Mbilini said, quaffing another mug of beer.

"Why's that?" Mbeki asked, slipping his brass armbands back on.

"Because the rest of their regiment is just over the horizon." The two kaJama brothers stared at Mbilini in surprise. "Relax! All that means is that we hit them hard and run away. That's how we fight out here."

"What if that regiment comes after us?"

"If everything goes perfectly they'll never know we were there until every redcoat down at the river is dead."

"So we just have to be perfect?" Ingonyama said.

"Is that so much to ask?" Mbilini laughed.

Chapter 61

A thousand men moved from their mountain base in the deadest part of the moonlit night, making so little sound the sleeping meerkats at the base of the kopje were not disturbed. The moved at the jog trot with perfect discipline, forming a great semi-circle opening towards the British camp. Five hundred paces from the wagons, without a word spoken, the impi stopped. Two hundred men broke off and swung wide of the camp, swimming across the river so as to attack the British on both sides of the Ntombe at once.

The moon played eerie games with the night mists rolling off the river. The eight hundred squatted in the grass, growing more and more anxious for the two hundred's signal. A single shot, certain to alert the night sentries but so indiscrete that it would not be taken as a sign of impending attack, shattered the silence. As one, on both sides of the river, the warriors rose up and moved towards the wagons.

Standing almost shoulder to shoulder the thousand formed a ring around both camps, divided only by the river. Fifty paces away from the tents the warriors stopped again. Mbilini gave a great cry of, "Now!" And a thousand muskets were pulled out from behind the warriors' shields, leveled in the general direction of the laager, and discharged.

A thousand guns, each clumsily overcharged with gunpowder and loaded with pebbles, pieces of scrap iron and broken glass, tore the calm night apart. The blast of the volley raced to every rock and hill in sight, echoing back like the growl of feeding lions. The whiz and hiss of the uneven projectiles was mixed with the screams of the wounded.

"How do you like it?" a thousand throats roared, glad that finally the enemy had been at the receiving end. Every warrior dropped his gun into the grass, took up his assegai, and charged.

The camp was a confused tangle of running white men. Some snatched up rifles and climbed up onto the wagons; others hurried to their sergeants and officers; most just ran from the wall of advancing black men. Ingonyama was at his best, running from man to man, stabbing them in some vital area and moving on to let the warriors behind him finish them off.

The British commander had scampered up onto a wagon, shooting down at the swirling mass of Zulu all around him. Mbeki reached up and stabbed him through the belly. The officer cried out, "Fire away, boys! Death or glory! I'm done!" He tumbled down and was cut to pieces by the abaQulusi below.

By the time the sun came up the slaughter was over. A few British had tried to swim for it, but the Zulu had dived in after them and finished them in the water. Only one sergeant had the presence of mind to bring his squad together, and he led a fighting retreat back towards Luneberg and the rest of his regiment. Mbilini ordered his men to let them go.

Ingonyama supervised the slitting open of the redcoats' bellies to allow their souls to escape, careful not to repeat his unrepeatable episode of madness. In keeping with another tradition, that of taking a memento of the dead, Ingonyama stripped one of the corpses of his red tunic but found the sleeves to thin to take his arms, and his shoulders and chest were too broad to do up the buttons. Smiling, Ingonyama took his assegai and removed the sleeves and wore the tunic open at the front like a vest, receiving playful whistles and catcalls from the surrounding warriors at his fashion sense.

The looting was as organized as the attack: Two hundred and fifty cattle were driven off; the Martini-Henry breech-loading rifles of more than a hundred dead men were gathered up; food enough to feed the abaQulusi's dependants for months was divided among the men. The greatest booty was discovered by Mbeki. His whoop of triumph stilled the Zulu, and all heads turned to see him emerge from one of the covered wagons. He whooped again, raising his hands above his head and pumping his fists into the air.

"What is it?" Ingonyama asked.

Mbeki could not form words through his smile. Instead, he reached in and pulled out an ammunition crate.

"So?" Mbilini said.

"There are a thousand cartridges in here." Mbeki said, recognizing the one and three zeroes on the top of the box.

"So?" Mbilini and Ingonyama chorused again. A thousand rounds of ammunition was a good prize, but it was hardly exceptional.

"There are thirty of these boxes in this wagon, thirty more in that wagon, and thirty more in that wagon over there!" Mbeki pointed. The whole impi erupted in cheers and spontaneous giyas. Ninety thousand bullets for rifles worked out to three bullets for every fighting man in kwaZulu. This was the most successful raid the abaQulusi had ever achieved.

"Alright! Two companies in front of me, now!" Mbilini barked. His izinduna snapped to attention, calling their men together. Quickly the wagons were unloaded with every crate of ammunition being carried by two warriors, who then heaped their own personal loot onto the box's flat top. "Let's go!" The impi cheered again and set off into the hills, singing their war songs and praises.

Chapter 62

They marched into the broken wilderness, leaving sentries on every ridge and throwing scouts out to either flank, all armed with horns and whistles to signal a pursuit. Mbilini led them unerringly through a warren of rocky kopjes and yawning kloofs, twisting dongas and engulfing thickets, until the impi finally stopped in a great bowl-shaped depression. Unsatisfied with his precautions thus far, Mbilini threw out three concentric rings of pickets, each man within shouting distance of a man to his left, right, and in the ring behind him. The impi was too heavily laden with booty to make a quick retreat, so nothing must be allowed to catch the warriors by surprise.

As the sun began to set Mbilini ordered a great celebration, for every man had seen the favours the ancestors had bestowed upon them: Where Rorke's Drift had seen four times as many warriors fail, this morning they had prevailed. Where every battle had seen the Zulu lose hundreds of men, today the British dead outnumbered the fallen warriors two to one. The Invincibles had lost only five men. Only the ancestors could have given them such a victory, and proper appreciation for their assistance would be demonstrated.

Teams of fifty men were sent into the tangled and twisted forests; each team found a tree, dead long enough to have dried all the way through, and tethered it in a dozen places with strong riem ropes. While five men hacked at its base with axes, the rest heaved and hauled until the tree came down and the whole thing was dragged out of the forest. The branches were used for kindling and the trunk was cut into huge sections so that the bonfires were four times taller than a man and burned so high and bright that they lit up every rock and hill in the valley with cheery light.

Seven of the captured oxen were wounded by gunfire, so they were spit whole and rotated from the late afternoon and through the night, the cooking fires only being allowed to die down when the skin was crackling and the meat inside was falling off the bone. Long accustomed to retreating into the hinterland to escape Boer raiding parties, the abaQulusi had stored supplies in a nearby cave; soon beer pots and bottles of captured European liquor were circulating, increasing the revelry wherever they went.

Mbilini was too crafty to join the party before he was absolutely secure, but when a third inspection of the pickets satisfied him that every man was vigilant and no one would risk execution by deserting his post for the festivities, he took a mug of beer for himself. Mbeki and Ingonyama again found themselves surprised by the little man, but for once not by his strengths: Though he was tough as the mountains around him, Mbilini could not hold his liquor. By the second mug Mbilini was tipsy, and the fourth had him hanging from Ingonyama's neck like a dead weight. By his sixth mug he was crying.

"What's wrong?" Ingonyama had long since lowered Mbilini to a log waiting for its turn on the flames. The two kaJama brothers were sitting on the ground, each eating from a platter of beef, washing their food down with great gulps of frothy beer.

"We're going to lose," Mbilini said miserably. He swayed and decided it was better to get off the log and sit on the ground than to fall backwards and land on his head, so he leaned forward enough to topple in an untidy heap. All the while he had kept his cup steady, proving he had not completely lost control of his faculties.

"What?" Mbeki had cut a generous portion of beef off one of the rotating cows with his knife, but he threw the meat down onto his platter to point at Mbilini with a hand dripping with juice. "Three British columns have not been able to beat us in three months. We can hold them!"

Mbilini shook his head, and the sensation seemed to fascinate his drink-addled senses for he kept doing it as he spoke. "So we won at Isandhlwana. So what? So we have them besieged at Eshowe. So what? We won at Isandhlwana because they underestimated us, and we are holding them at Eshowe because they are too cautious. What about me? What about the man my people are facing?"

"What about him?" Ingonyama asked. He downed another mug of beer and decided he would wait a while before having another.

Mbilini looked up, and Ingonyama shivered at what he saw in the man's eyes. The Hyena of the Phongolo was afraid. "The abaQulusi have to deal with Lukuni, and he is neither overconfident nor timid. He just attacks and attacks and attacks, and every time I hear his name I am told which of my izinduna is dead; how many abaQulusi are refusing to respond to the musters; how many cows he has driven off."

Mbeki knew the British commander's name was Wood, but the Zulu had difficulty saying a name which did not end in a vowel, so they had dubbed the man Lukuni: Lukuni was the type of wood used to made war clubs. It was hard as iron, like Wood.

Wood commanded a column dominated not by infantry, as in the other two columns, but by colonial volunteer cavalry, perfect for raiding in the mountainous country defended by the abaQulusi. Knowing a drive on oNdini would see him cut down in the passes, Wood chose instead to destroy Mbilini's ability to resist him. He had burned the ikhanda of the abaQulusi ibutho, torched homesteads, driven off cattle, and promised that only those chiefs who came over to the British cause would be spared. He had a dug in at Khambula and set out his irregular horse patrols, reducing each of Mbilini's mountain fortresses until only the great bastion of Hlobane remained.

Wood's tactics were working; where before Mbilini had been able to summon three thousand crack abaQulusi warriors, now he could gather only a thousand. The rest were hiding: Wood had convinced them that they could not win.

"This battle will bring them back to you," Mbeki said gently. "Here we have proof for your men that we haven't lost."

"Cha!" Mbilini spat, straightening up. It seemed anger raised his tolerance for liquor, because Mbeki could not detect any trace of fogginess in his gaze or slur in his voice. "That wasn't Lukuni: We beat a lazy simpleton who could not be bothered to build a decent laager for his men. Lukuni has hundreds of soldiers at Khambula. He outnumbers me, though he doesn't know it. I'm holding him in place with a giant bluff, and only one thing is keeping him there."

"Hlobane," Ingonyama said, quaffing another mug; his resolution was forgotten.

"Hlobane." Mbilini nodded, and then continued nodding, as he was calming down the liquor took its hold again.

"But Hlobane is invincible, surely?" Mbeki said. The mountain was famous: A giant kopje with a flat top big enough to graze several thousand head of cattle, Hlobane was surrounded on all sides by sheer cliffs, and its two approaches could be held by a small force of warriors on the high ground.

"It's only a matter of time before he tries, and he might be able to take it. When my scouts say, 'Lukuni is coming' a fifth of my force flees before I can issue orders." The Swazi prince sat with his back against the log and took another pull from his mug. "Do you know what will happen when he gets on top of that kopje?" He did not wait for them to answer. "He'll take the last of my cattle. My last loyal men will run to their families. I'm too important for him to ignore and have been against him too long for him to spare me and mine. I have three wives on Hlobane."

"Wives! What are they good for?" Mbilini and Mbeki both looked at Ingonyama in surprise. "Don't look at me like that! What are they good for? Misery, that's what. The only time I'm happy with my wife is when I'm busy or she's far away." Ingonyama jumped up from the ground and began to pace, running his hands through his hair.

"And why is that, Ingonyama?" Mbilini asked with the blunt innocence of one who has no stake in the reply and is drunk enough not to care what the answer might be.

"Because she sleeps around!" Ingonyama roared, kicking his beer mug, sending it flying. All around the three of them the laughter stopped; all eyes turned to the King's Champion, shocked. Ingonyama was too angry to be embarrassed; it was out, and finally he could rage. "She sleeps around! She has cuckolded me! My wife—-"

Mbeki launched himself from his seat, hurtling up towards his brother with arms spread wide. He caught Ingonyama in a flying tackle, knocking the wind out of him and throwing him to the ground. Mbeki was straddling Ingonyama's chest and pinned both of his arms down with his knees. Eye to eye with his prostrated brother he said, "She isn't, and she hasn't."

"She has!" Ingonyama wheezed, trying to get his breath back.

"She hasn't. I promise you on our father, she has never slept with Inyati--" Now it was Mbeki's turn to be interrupted, for the mention of the Matabele's name from his brother's lips in connection with his wife was too much for Ingonyama. His arms broke out from under Mbeki's knees as if they had been free the whole time. With another roar Ingonyama pushed Mbeki in the chest, but Mbeki held on to his brother with his legs, and when he had recovered from that first shove he punched Ingonyama in the face. "She hasn't slept with--"

"Inyati!" Ingonyama snarled, and his hands clenched into fists, smashing into Mbeki's chest again and again. Mbeki relaxed his legs' grip on Ingonyama, and the next punch sent him flying back to land at his brother's feet. The two scrambled up, each taking up a boxer's stance, fists out in front, eyes looking for the weaknesses.

"Nandhi never--" Mbeki put up his guard as Ingonyama sent two hammer blows for his head, each time grunting, 'Inyati!' "Would you shut up and listen to me?" Ingonyama's eyes were glazed over with hatred, so Mbeki planted a fist between them. The Invincibles around the two of them stood frozen in surprise at this unlikely brawl. The abaQulusi began to shift forward as if to intervene, but Mbilini held them back with a small move of his hand.

Ingonyama swished his head from side to side, shaking away the blow like a bull freeing himself of a stinging fly. Then he bellowed, dropped his head, and charged. Mbeki jumped to one side and Ingonyama tripped over the log Mbilini had been leaning against, landing headfirst in the dust on the other side. Mbeki was over the log and on his brother before Ingonyama could get up, and every time his brother struggled or snarled, Mbeki punched him in the head. Finally, Ingonyama sagged into submission.

"Nandhi and Inyati never did anything. Do you hear me?" Mbeki picked up his brother's lolling head by its short hair and dropped it back into the dust. "They've been waiting for me to tell you that for months, but I was afraid you would go crazy, embarrass yourself in front of your men, and then try to beat me to a pulp." Mbeki waited for Ingonyama's eyes to come into focus. "But as that has already happened I guess I should put your mind at ease. They are not now, nor have they ever, cuckolding you. They are making a point never to be within a hundred paces of each other. Is it heard?"

Ingonyama looked up at him sullenly. When Mbeki clenched his fist Ingonyama finally said, "Do you know what she said on our wedding night?"

"I do," Mbeki said, deciding if he was going to lance this boil on his brother's soul he would have to probe long and deep to get out even the oldest of the bad blood. "I also know why she said it. When Inyati was stabbed in the belly, he flirted with her before you two were engaged." Mbeki stressed the word before and waited for Ingonyama's eyes to flicker his impatience. "What else would you expect with her nursing him every day? That's why he was involved in her prank. He had a thing for her. Then you went away for months, off to kwaTsonga, and she was left with him for company. He knew she was engaged, so he did nothing untoward, but in all that time she grew very fond of him. There was an attraction. That was all. That was as far as it ever went."

Mbeki decided not to mention the poison. "When I found out I beat him with the sticks, and it was months before he explained to me that there was nothing to it. I checked with Nandhi and she confirmed everything. They both think too much of you to disgrace you that way. Though I don't know why they'd care." He got off his brother, careful to keep an eye on both of those powerful fists.

Ingonyama lay there, ignoring the complete silence as every man waited to see what he would do. Gradually he felt a weight come off his chest, far heavier than when his brother had been sitting on him. It made sense, it all made sense. "Is my wife..?" He licked his lips. "Does Nandhi still..?" Mbeki nodded and Ingonyama felt tears of relief come to his eyes. "Then go and tell her that you've told me. Tell her... Tell her that I'll make it right with her."

Mbilini cleared his throat, and the kaJama brothers looked at him, mildly angry at the intrusion. "What?" Mbeki asked rudely.

"If you're going back to oNdini, shouldn't it be for the war effort and not to deal with your brother's estranged wife?"

"Of course," Ingonyama said before Mbeki could snap at the Hyena of the Phongolo. "What do you have in mind?"

"Tell Cetshwayo that I can't hold here. Have him call up the Great Impi, and if he has already done that make sure it heads for Hlobane." Mbilini stood in the firelight, and his men saw the rare snaggletoothed smile slowly spread across his face. It was the snarl of a predator that smelled blood in the air. The abaQulusi knew that look, and someone behind the front rank of onlookers began chuckling. Soon others were smiling, and laughing, and the liquor and beef began to circulate again. Someone started up the chant, 'uSuthu! abaQulusi! Mbilini!' and the kopje walls echoed with their cheers.

Mbilini waited until his men were beyond noticing what he did, then he helped up Ingonyama and pulled the two brothers' heads close to his mouth and said in a whisper, "Lukuni could attack today or tomorrow or the day after that. I need that impi here now. The moment Hlobane falls, Cetshwayo has lost western kwaZulu. Is it heard?"

"It is heard," Mbeki replied.

Ingonyama felt refreshed by the truth as a thirsty man is relieved by a cold mountain stream. He even felt his sense of humour return. "Mbeki, you have ten days to get back to oNdini, rally the impi, and bring it Hlobane. That's a lot of time," Mbeki frowned. It was not a lot of time at all. "And to make it even longer I want you to get to oNdini within two days." Ingonyama smiled.

Mbeki licked his lips, sensing his brother's challenge. "How about three days?"

"Two days." It was a game they had played as boys, Ingonyama asking Mbeki to do something that was just physically possible if everything went well. The more extreme the request, the more bragging Mbeki was allowed to do. Ingonyama's challenge was a compliment as long as Mbeki met it.

"What will you give me?" Mbeki smiled, suddenly a little boy again.

"Respect."

"I have that now," Mbeki said smugly.

Ingonyama smiled at his brother, his first smile that was from a carefree heart in a long time. "And you want to keep it. Any royal messenger I ever met could make it from here to there in five days. I expect better from my brother." Mbeki and Ingonyama looked into each other's eyes and an understanding passed between them; there was a war on and the country was being torn apart around them, but from this day forward the healing would begin in their family. Their father and uncles would be honoured and remembered and the suspicion and fear of Nandhi and Inyati would be set aside and forgotten. From this day forward the kaJama brothers would be happy again.

"Two days?" Mbeki murmured, feeling his heart beat faster with the knowledge of how difficult the challenge would be.

"Two days. I'm going to check with Nandhi the next time I see her." Ingonyama chuckled. He could think of a few other things he would do when he saw his wife again.

"See you soon." Mbeki wiped the beef juice and dirt from his hands onto his loincloth, gave Mbilini a little wave, and took off at the jog trot right then and there.

"Go well, Mbeki," Ingonyama said. "And tell my wife to stay well!" He shouted to his brother's receding form.

Chapter 63

If Mbeki had been a bird he would simply have flown into the rising sun, turning slightly to the south once he had his bearings on the plains beyond the last mountain and forest. On foot that route would have taken twice his allotted time, and Mbeki had no intention of losing the bet. It would take all his experience as a messenger to reach oNdini twice as fast as normal. His feet turned south.

He ran well, feeling as if he had lost weight, realizing only now the heaviness of the burden Nandhi and Inyati had placed upon him. Not far from Mbilini's temporary camp lay the first tiny mountain stream, which joined others to form the first burbling brook, running into other brooks to form a stream, eventually coalescing with other streams to form the headwaters of the great White Mfolozi.

The river followed a roundabout way to flow down into the plains, turning far to the south before cutting west and slowly flowing northward again, but Mbeki knew along its course the river had chosen the low ground, avoiding the rocky kopjes to form a smooth route that Mbeki would be able to run at full tilt, even at night, even when the lack of sleep and the constant exertion would weary his brain too much to be exactly sure of his navigation without the aid of always keeping the river on his right.

If this had been the only benefit, Mbeki would have cut west, across the foothills of the Mountains of the Up Thrust Spears. There was another benefit to the banks of the Mfolozi: The river valleys were heavily inhabited, whereas the rocky wilderness was not, and its inhabitants were sometimes rich enough to own the object of his desire.

Mbeki ran south from Mbilini's camp through the night so that when the sun came up it was on his left. The warm and welcome light allowed his eyes to assist his ears in the search for a horse; over the broken wilderness a Zulu impi could move as fast as a cavalry patrol, but on the flat of a river valley the horse's canter would outdistance even the most forced jog trot. Mbeki pinned his hopes on making his way to oNdini on four legs instead of two.

It was rare for a Zulu to own a horse, but not unheard of. Most of the horses in kwaZulu were owned by rich chiefs with trading connections to the whites, and most of them had a horse merely as a status symbol.

Prince Zibhebhu and Dabulamanzi could ride, and Mbeki imagined Mbilini probably knew how as well, though to his knowledge the Swazi renegade did not own a horse.

Mbeki had never ridden, but careful observation of Holland Keech on his brown mare had shown him most of the nuances. He was sure the hard part would be finding a horse to ride, and it was with relief, then, that when the stream he had been following finally grew wide enough to be called the White Mfolozi there sat a large homestead with two dun colored horses being put out to pasture with the herds.

When the herd boys saw a lone warrior running towards them faster than the normal jog trot, bearing the brass armbands of a royal favourite and the white shield of the Invincibles, they quickly sent an even faster runner, aided by youth and his ability to sprint without pacing himself, back to their chief's kraal. By the time Mbeki reached the gates of the homestead, decorated with bull skulls set high up on posts, the chief and several of his wives were there to greet him.

"I see you, Invincible," The chief said gravely, worried that there was only one returning when his kinsmen had told him a hundred had skirted his lands in pursuit of Hamu's ponderous procession.

"I see you, Nkosi," Mbeki panted. One of the chief's wives had a gourd of water, and he drank deeply before speaking again. "I bring urgent dispatches from Mbilini to Cetshwayo, including news of a great victory against the whites on the bank of the Ntombe."

"Wo!" The chief said, pleased and abashed at the same time; he was one of the abaQulusi leaders who had forsaken Mbilini, believing the war unwinnable. Perhaps I should take my company back to Hlobane? He thought.

"Yebho, Nkosi. I also carry several other messages that need to reach oNdini quickly," Mbeki said. "I need your help to get there as fast as possible."

The man's eyes narrowed. He knew whatever was asked of him he would have to provide, so he decided to preemptively turn down the Invincible. "I will give you what you need, but I'm afraid I don't have any men faster than you, and if Mbilini's communications could be trusted to the far caller network you would not be running at all."

"Cha, Nkosi. I don't need an extra runner or a relief. I want to borrow one of your horses. Both if I can."

The chief was stricken; having never anticipated the warrior would be able to ride, he had not thought to make an excuse about them. He had received the pair, a stallion and a mare, as a gift from a Boer farmer to whom he had returned a herd of lost cattle. The chief had planned to breed the horses and did not want to be parted with them. "The horses were expensive..." He lied, preferring to guilt the young man than reveal his breeding plan. This Invincible would know royals, and if word got to Zibhebhu or Dabulamanzi they would be able to throw their wealth around and breed enough horses to drive down the price of the colts and foals the chief was sure he could produce.

"I will return your horses. My name is Mbeki kaJama of the Cube clan. I am a royal favourite and a royal messenger. You have my word your property will be returned to you." Mbeki quickly looked at the surrounding heights and the river's fork, memorizing the landmarks around the chief's kraal.

After the promise there was very little the chief could do but agree, and in his heart of hearts he was a little pleased to give Mbeki the horses. He recognized the name, not as the brother of the King's Champion, but as an up and coming smith of promising skill. The chief had two of Mbeki's assegais in his chief wife's hut; one of them had already been washed in blood. The blades were impeccable.

The two horses were brought to Mbeki. Patiently the chief explained the workings of the Boer riding tack, made unusual by long stirrups and a comfortable saddle. He gave Mbeki a long list of dos and don'ts about care, like a mother trusting a young daughter to mind a baby, but Mbeki's impatience eventually brought the litany to an end. "Yebho, Nkosi, I promise I will take the snaffle out when I stop to graze them. How else will they eat?" Mbeki said, knowing he would not be stopping to let the horses eat. He only had a day and a half left because of this man's prattling. *The horses will drink when I drink, and they'll eat when I get to oNdini, which is also when I'll eat.* His stomach rumbled; he had taken only a strip of biltong with him from the party, and it had long since been wolfed down.

"Very well then, up you go," The chief said, gesturing to the mare's saddle. Mbeki looked blank for a moment then remembered how Holland had used a stirrup and one foot to swing his other leg up and over the horse's back. Clumsily Mbeki did so, landing heavily on the saddle, crushing his privates under him.

The chief saw him wince and hid a smile, recognizing an amateur rider. He ordered one of his grooms to hand Mbeki the leader for the stallion. Mbeki double thumped the mare's flanks with his bare heels and only her gentle temperament prevented her from breaking into a full gallop from the start. Mbeki's head whipped back and forth as the horse began to canter, the stallion following only at the insistence of the leader tied to the mare's pommel. Behind him he heard the chief repeating the more choice pieces of advice, but he had no time to listen; all his concentration was on balance and guiding the horse.

"How did Holland make this look so easy?" Mbeki muttered, the bouncing raising his bottom up out of the saddle only to have it crash back down with a smack, painful on the inside of his bare thighs. Fortunately, after the first terrible experience he had moved his manhood out of way, but the ride was still painful.

Mbeki followed the river, carefully keeping to the flattest path both to avoid exhausting the horses and to provide the smoothest ride for himself. He was not sure how much of the steering was being done by the reins and his calves and how much was the mare picking her ground, but Mbeki was covering the distance faster than he would have on foot, so he was satisfied. By noon he had made up the time lost talking to the chief, and by mid-afternoon the worst of the rocky wilderness was behind his left shoulder. It was only then, in the terrible heat, that the mare began to slow.

At first Mbeki assumed he had given her some kind of signal to reduce her pace; he had no frame of reference as to how long a horse could canter and had assumed she could do it as long as he could jog trot. Mbeki thumped the sides of his mare with his heels again and she gamely broke into a full gallop with the stallion running beside. It was faster than he wanted to go, but at least she was moving quickly again.

All too soon she was back down to a walk, and this time his heels could not make her move faster. Without his doing anything to the reins she veered to the right, and when he tried to correct her she whinnied and pulled to the right again. "What's to the right?" He muttered irritably, his thighs killing him and the mare's truculence offered a relief from riding he feared might become seductive. He looked ahead and saw the river. "Oh! You want a drink?" He asked the horse, laughing. The mare reached the bank and stood there. "I guess you want me to get down." He laughed again. The horse seemed to be nodding.

Mbeki lifted one foot out of the stirrup and tried to swing his leg over, but the limb froze half way, his thigh spasmed, and he fell from the saddle to land on the sandy river bank. The shock of impact winded him, and when he tried to stand he groaned. He felt as if the place where the top of his thighs met his hips had been pulled apart and now they would not come together again. Painfully, Mbeki rolled onto his front and crawled to the water's edge, taking a few welcome mouthfuls and splashing some water onto his face. The water here was clear and swift flowing, so there was little fear of a lurking crocodile. He lay there for quite a while, letting the two horses drink deep and his legs ache, then finally he resolved to get up.

It took much effort and curses he barely remembered the saltiest of warriors using, but Mbeki made it to his feet, though he found he could not bring those feet together; he was stiff and aching and his upper thighs seemed to be set in sheaths of stone. Stunned at his body's refusal, he tried to get his foot up to the stirrup but found he could not lift his knee high enough anymore. "Come on," He muttered. "Think, Mbeki."

After letting his mind play upon the problem for a spell, during which he eased himself down to a sitting position, Mbeki decided he should ride the stallion, as it was almost certainly fresher for having come this far without his weight on its back. Next he decided if he could not raise his foot high enough to reach the stirrup, the stirrup would have to come down to him. He tried everything short of stabbing the horse with his knife but he could not get it to kneel down. Next he tried building a pile of stones to create a platform high enough for him to get his foot into the stirrup, but the sight of him pulling the river rocks out of the shallows and the clacking of them being stacked upon one another spooked the stallion and he would not come close while Mbeki stood upon the stones.

Exasperated, Mbeki tried to coax the stallion into the water so that he could stand behind him on the bank and climb on that way, but now he found that the horse, after satiating its thirst, would not get so much as a hoof wet. Finally Mbeki risked all and simply leaned against the animal, reaching over the horse's back with his arms. With a quick jerk he was lying with his belly on the saddle, his head hanging on the far side of the horse with his feet dangling just below stirrup level opposite his head. As he had feared the stallion began to walk, the mare following on the now reversed leader. He was being carried on the stallion's back like a set of panniers, and the movement of the saddle threatened to batter his belly just as his thighs were already bruised.

His discomfort was increased as the horse, unguided by his rider and spooked by the unusual means of mounting, was working his way back to the east instead of the west, and was choosing rocky ground, creating a lot of bumping. Mbeki tried to spin on his belly to turn head towards the stallion's neck and feet towards the trailing mare, but found the saddle's pommel prevented him from completing the maneuver. He laughed at the ridiculousness of his situation, his laughter making his stomach hurt even worse. "What would Ingonyama do?" He murmured. "Ingonyama would never have gotten on this damned horse."

In his mind he pictured Ingonyama in his place. He saw Ingonyama using his enviable strength to twist over, spin on his back, kick his stiff feet into the air over the stallion's head and then slide on his buttocks so that his feet pointed down and his head pointed up. Ingonyama would be able to do that because he had excellent balance and a strength Mbeki could never dream of. "And if I get it wrong I'm going to fall off and there's no sand to break my fall this time." Still, Mbeki did not see another option. The stallion seemed to be making his way back to the chief's kraal, and lying on the horse's back until then to arrive in this ridiculous position was unthinkable. Mbeki bided his time.

Eventually the stallion cleared the rocky path and began to cross a grassy meadow. Muttering, "I play to win," under his breath, Mbeki twisted. He had rehearsed each movement in his head, sure that his body would rebel and that he would fall to the grass below and then have to chase the horses on his bowed legs; instead, as his head moved through three dimensions and his vision showed first the horse's neck, then the mountains, then the sky, and then finally the back of the stallion's head as normal, his stiff legs actually worked in his favour, forming a perfect cantilever to balance him out and perform the acrobatic shift with something approaching grace.

"uSuthu! He is a lion!" He shouted in triumph. The horse, already skittish at the unprecedented movement on his back, broke into a gallop, and it was all Mbeki could do to tuck his feet into the Boer's deep stirrups and put his head down. When the stallion had finally calmed, Mbeki swung him back to the east and dug his heels in, gritting his teeth as it cantered, feeling each bruise on his belly and thighs scream their humiliation and pain.

He trotted and cantered through the night, stopping once more at dawn to water the horses again and switch to the rested mare. He was beyond the foothills now, and the horses had covered the extra distance necessitated by the Mfolozi route; his original plan had been to dismount here, leave the horses with a homestead, and jog trot the rest of the way, but the stiffness in his legs made that impossible. He continued to ride, treating himself to occasionally slowing the horses to a mere walk as it became clearer that he would arrive on time.

Finally, he crested the last shallow sloped ridge and saw oNdini, King Cetshwayo's Great Place, with Ingonyama's small homestead on a nearby hill totally dwarfed by its opulent neighbour. The King's ikhanda had grown and matured, with fifteen hundred huts forming five great concentric rings around the parade square. The huts in the royal quarters were gigantic, some of them five times as tall as a man could stand, and the entrances to the royal quarters were marked with elephant's skulls, still holding tusks, mounted on posts that had once been the trunks of full grown trees. Mbeki clicked his tongue, putting the horses back up to a trot.

The sight of a lone man with two horses coming out of the west had been reported to the king at dawn by the amakhanda izinduna between the capital and the lands of the abaQulusi. By noon their messengers had informed him the rider was his favourite, Mbeki, the wizard of kwaZulu, who refused to speak to anyone or impart his message. Cetshwayo's messengers shuddered, saying that the wizard's eyes were dead with exhaustion and were always focused east towards oNdini. They said that his face and chest were coated in the dust of hard riding, and that his belly, back, and legs were bruised and bleeding. The king's messengers had said that surely it was only the wizard's magic that kept him seated.

"We'll see," The king had said breezily. "We could use some magic." Cetshwayo was careful to keep a twinkle out of his eyes when he looked at the nearby izangoma. Cetshwayo had squatted over the inkatha, the magic charm of the nation, throughout much of the battle at Isandhlwana, but had gotten up once to relieve himself, and abandoned it again at dusk, sure that the battle would be over. His izangoma had blamed the heavy casualties at Isandhlwana and the subsequent embarrassment at kwaJim on these lapses. He, in turn, had asked them what had happened to the magic charms designed to render the white's bullets impotent. Their response was that the Whites must have magic of their own.

He had muttered something about it being called gunpowder. Now there was a carefully veiled rift between the king and his magicians.

At last Mbeki passed through the kraal's main gate and, still upon the horse's back, he stopped in front of his king and gave the royal salute, "Bayete."

"I see you, Mbeki," Cetshwayo answered. *Indeed I do. My messengers were not exaggerating.* Mbeki had an otherworldly expression upon his face, carved there by exhaustion and pain and concentration.

"I bring word from the West, Great Elephant."

Cetshwayo did not see the usual good humour in his messenger's eyes and dreaded news of Mbilini's defeat. *I have just sent five thousand new men to the East to stop the British attempt to relieve Eshowe. Was that a mistake?* "Go on."

"I bring word of victory, Nkosi Nkulu." The word *victory* raced across the ikhanda, whispered from eavesdropper to friend to neighbour.

"When and where?" Cetshwayo asked.

"Two days ago at Ntombe, my King. A company of redcoats lies dead, and ninety thousand bullets sit in Mbilini's armoury." Cetshwayo was more than impressed that Mbeki had gotten word to him within two days, but as good as this news was, Cetshwayo's heart still fell; he had hoped Lukuni's western column had been destroyed as had the one at Isandhlwana.

"And what of Hamu?"

"Hamu has escaped with his kin to the Whites." Cetshwayo nodded, accepting the news. He opened his mouth to dismiss Mbeki but the young man interrupted him. "I bring word from Mbilini, Nkosi Nkulu." There were mutters behind him that a favourite had interrupted his king, but Cetshwayo did not mind. Clearly, Mbeki's mind was elsewhere. He nodded for the mounted man to continue. "He says the Ntombe victory will strengthen his supporters' numbers, but nothing like enough to hold off Lukuni. He says the western column is cavalry heavy, and that they could reach oNdini in four days if Hlobane falls."

There was more muttering behind him. "Is that likely?"

"Mbilini says it is only a matter of time, if things stay as they are, before Lukuni takes Hlobane. After that happens the abaQulusi will be out of the war, and you will have lost all the easily defendable ground between here and Luneberg." Mbeki's eyes were empty. He was speaking as if from rote.

"And what does Mbilini suggest I do to prevent that. Should I attack Lukuni's position at Khambula?" Cetshwayo tried to keep his voice level, but part of his incredulity slipped through. He knew the area from his youth, and he would not want his impi to attack any of those mountains if there were rifles on the top.

Mbeki's eyes flickered; Mbilini had never suggested a strategy. "Cha, Nkosi Nkulu, Mbilini suggests you call up the Great Impi and send it well south of Khambula to attack the white settlements beyond the Ncombe and Mzinyathi rivers. That will force Lukuni to abandon his fortress and fall back on his own territory. We can either engage him in the open or fall back into abaQulusi lands after reoccupying Khambula." Mbeki saw heads nod, including Cetshwayo's. "Great Elephant, a request?"

"Ask it," Cetshwayo said.

"Excuse me from duty for two days to attend to a personal matter." Cetshwayo wondered if the personal matter would be to heal his legs, as he could see the extent of the damages hard riding had produced. "Also," Mbeki slid from the back of the mare, offering the reins to a startled grey-headed warrior who nervously led the horses away. "Please have these horses returned to their owner." He gave the chief's name and the location of his homestead. "Last," Finally a trace of Mbeki's smile cracked his features, "Tell Ingonyama when next you see him that I won our bet."

"All of your requests are granted. Go well, Mbeki."

"Bayete." Mbeki bowed awkwardly from the waist, turned, and walked painfully away. He was bow legged,and his stride was accomplished by leaning to one side to lift a foot and then swinging the whole leg, as if it was dead weight, forward, repeating on the other side only when he was sure of his balance. Behind him the Court began to snicker, but Cetshwayo silenced them with a glare.

Slowly Mbeki made his way to Ingonyama's homestead on the hill. His eyes felt like they had two yawning caves behind the balls, pulling his eyes back from their sockets and into his skull. He had not slept for over three days, had not eaten for a day and a half, and he was sore all over, yet his painful stride was carefree; he thought he could see Nandhi even from here.

Chapter 64

Two moons ago the Great Impi had marched to Isandhlwana; ever since, Nandhi's universe had unraveled a little more each day. First news of Jama's death had arrived, and her wail of lament had risen and fallen to join the mournful shrill of a hundred other bereaved within earshot. Within a day of this bad news Ingonyama had returned for the bare minimum of purification rituals, more distant than ever, and then had left to chase down her defecting father without even taking his leave of her or their son. Then Jama's homestead, his three wives, daughter, and, worst of all, Inyati, had arrived at her door, begging to be given a home.

"With Khandla and Punga dead, there are no adult men in the valley," Inyati had said apologetically. "I mean, well, obviously there's me," he stammered. It was the first time they had spoken since before he left with Mbeki and Holland Keech over three years ago. "But Jama's widows and daughter... They want to live here until it's all over."

"I thought you were in the South, spying for Zibhebhu?" Nandhi asked, more to delay answering his request than out of curiosity.

"I came north of the Thekula to receive instructions now that Eshowe is besieged, but security at Fort Pearson tightened in my absence, so Zibhebhu sent me back to the valley."

Nandhi had cast a veiled appraising eye over Inyati, seeing the vicious scar across his belly but no other physical defect. Nandhi took a longer look at Jama's womenfolk: *Three widows, each of whom will try to take over my homestead, and Bhibhi, who is probably well into her rebellious teenage phase.*

Still she could not turn away family. "Of course you can stay for a few moons..." With that, her mothers-in-law had moved in. Mbeki and Ingonyama's mother Manase, the senior widow of Jama, had deposed Nandhi from her hut, and with Inyati taking a hut to himself to avoid sleeping with any of Mbeki or Ingonyama's women, Nandhi and Galazi had been forced to share a hut with Bhibhi, who, uncharacteristically for a young woman, snored.

The days passed slowly with Nandhi and Inyati always careful to spend as little time together as possible. Inyati took to chopping firewood, but soon, unknown to him, Nandhi was having dreams about the Matabele prince's muscles rippling as he brought that axe down over and over again.

Then Inyati had taken to teaching Galazi a few manly pursuits: The boy was still hardly more than a baby in her eyes, but it was never too young to learn stick fighting, dancing, singing, swimming, running, wrestling, and all the other past times of Zulu youth that would one day hone body and mind into a warrior of note. Nandhi had watched her baby from a distance, knowing this was the sort of education Ingonyama should have been giving and annoyed that Inyati was doing so well.

Soon her son took to sitting on the man's side of the hut at dinner, so that instead of eating beside his mother he would sit beside his hero, Inyati. Despite that, Galazi could not be trusted to load his own platter, and it would be unseemly for Inyati, as a man, to serve the boy, so Nandhi found herself constantly leaning across the hut while Galazi ate. Occasionally she had to hide a hot flush of embarrassment as she noticed Inyati's carefully concealed examination of her still perfect breasts.

Then there had been the night only a few days ago when Galazi had awoken from a nightmare and called out not for his mother but for his father. "Your Baba's not here," Nandhi had said, stroking his small back.

"I want Baba. I want Inyati." He had trembled. She too had trembled, knowing the rage that would descend if Ingonyama had heard his son call her supposed paramour father. Reluctantly she had gotten up, setting her kaross over her son and slipping out of the hut. The evening had been warm with the heat of the late summer day lingering long into the night. When she had tugged at Inyati's door flap there had been no answer.

"Heavy sleeper," She muttered, remembering her time as his nursemaid; many was the time she had come in, even burdened with clattering pots, and he had been blissfully unaware, requiring a tap on the shoulder to bring him out of his stupor. She pulled aside the flap and ducked inside.

The hut was even warmer than outside, for he had set a fire to burn all night in an attempt to go through some of the overstocked woodpile before Ingonyama came back and made a caustic comment. She felt a bead of sweat form on her brow, but it did not have much to do with the heat; uncomfortable by the fire's warmth, Inyati had sloughed aside his kaross in his sleep and lay there, completely naked, without even the gourd to hide his penis from her view.

He lay on his back, stretched out like a cat, which had unintentionally pulled every muscle into perfect viewing position. His head was held off the floor with a wooden head rest, and the upturned corners of his dreaming smile melted her heart. She was struck by the memory of the night she had snuck into Ingonyama's hut with a rope, the other end of which was attached to a bull. But for the scar and the smile, they look almost identical, she thought. Finally, embarrassed to be standing over him, she said, "Inyati." He had not moved. "Inyati!"

He awoke at once and, realizing who had come to visit him, his hands flew to screen his genitals. "What are you doing here?" He said, being careful not to put a sting in his tone in case she had come for the reason she had come in his dream.

"Galazi wants you." She averted her eyes while he put on his penis cover, and he had followed her back to her hut only to find her son asleep again, safe and warm beneath his mother's kaross.

They had stepped back into the cattle pen, she murmuring some pleasantry about disturbing him for no reason, and he doing his best not to show how much he wanted to keep talking with her. Before he knew it his arms were around her, and before she knew it her lips were on his, and they stood there in the moonlight; she began to pull away, but he held her. With an effort she put her hands on his strong chest and pushed, breaking the moment.

"That was wrong," She said. "Ingonyama--"

"Already thinks we've done much worse."

"I've told Mbeki to straighten that out." She had seen a flicker of surprise in his eyes. "He's waiting for an opportunity to say something where he won't embarrass Ingonyama or get himself killed."

"I can't stand to be within ten paces of Ingonyama. He always had his spear with him, and the last King's Champion with half an excuse used his spear to good effect." He shivered, and her heart went out to him, knowing his pain and fear would never completely vanish.

"I don't think you can stay here anymore," She whispered.

"I don't think I can leave without everyone assuming a reason, and we don't want Ingonyama's mothers repeating any of those reasons to him." She had not thought of that; only the warmth of that kiss and how much she wanted another, and how much she feared another.

"Then everything is as before." She turned to leave.

"Cha." His word had stopped her. "Things are different now. Before I was an invalid, and now I am a man. Before you were a girl, but now you are a married woman. Things will have to appear as before..." He had waited for her to say something, or turn to face him again, or leave, but when none of those things happened he continued. "But if anything should ever happen to change that, I want you to remember that I want you to be with me."

Still not facing him she had nodded and walked away. Nandhi went out of the homestead and onto the hill overlooking oNdini, wanting time to think and time for him to make his way back to his own hut. She had stood under the stars and thought of Ingonyama.

A hand had clamped over her mouth, smothering the scream. Someone had been stalking her, silent as a leopard through the waving grass. "Stay away from Inyati." A woman had whispered in her ear. "You have a husband, a good husband. My brother could have any woman in kwaZulu, and he chose you." Nandhi could not conceive the venom in that whisper, coming as it did from sweet and innocent Bhibhi. Illumination had come with the last hiss. "Inyati is not for you, but one day he will be for me." The hand left her mouth, but, though Nandhi turned around as soon as her feet had come unrooted from the ground, Bhibhi was gone.

The next day Bhibhi had been her bright and cheery self at the dinner meal, complimenting Nandhi on another recipe; the only change in her behaviour was that she moved in with her mother, leaving Nandhi and Galazi to the hut by themselves. Inyati, too, was his same old self, laughing and joking with the widows of his friends' father. Nandhi wondered if the night had really happened, if she alone had changed. Galazi said he did not even remember having a nightmare.

From that day to now she had been on eggshells around both Bhibhi and Inyati, but she had carefully noticed how Ingonyama's sister often looked at the Matabele prince when he was not paying attention. Inyati, for his part, cast more than the odd glance at Bhibhi too, but that was to be expected; she was the only available woman and he the only bachelor, and he saw her every day. Besides, at fifteen Bhibhi was young and nubile with a fine figure, good country manners, and a gentle temperament, when she was not threatening her sister-in-law in the dead of night. If Nandhi did not have a personal stake in Inyati, she would have suggested a match between the two.

Word of the lone rider had reached her ears almost as quickly as the king's, for a number of royal favourites came to visit her each day. It was no hardship for them to walk the short distance to Ingonyama's homestead, and, aside from paying respects to the wife of the King's Champion, favourites were treated to her cooking, her beauty, and her wit. She was kept well abreast of court gossip. "I have a new rumour for you today," Ntsingwayo said, sampling her amasi.

"Oh?" She arched an eyebrow, smiling at the old man.

"An Invincible riding a horse and leading another one is on his way to oNdini. My sources tell me it's Mbeki." Her heart had beat faster, worrying what news would put Mbeki on the back of a horse and whether something had happened to Ingonyama. She felt her stomach drop with the fear of that, and yet, at the same time, there was Inyati's voice whispering to her again.

At length the chief had left and she had watched from the gate of her homestead as the horses had entered oNdini, and the bowlegged figure of her brother-in-law had painfully limped up the hill towards her.

"He knows?" She had meant to make pleasantries first; he looked like death, and she knew some food and beer would have been appreciated. Instead she blurted out what she wanted to know with all the tact of a four year old.

"He knows," Mbeki said, swaying.

"And?"

"And he feels like a fool. He will spend the rest of his life making it up to you, and making sure you're happy. From this day forward, you have nothing to worry about." Behind her Bhibhi laughed, and Inyati joined her, but Nandhi was not relieved. Her worries were not over; they were living with her.

"Mbeki!" Bhibhi said, running up to her brother and hugging him. He nearly sagged at the effort it took to keep standing with her hanging from his neck.

"I see you, Bhibhi," He said instead, patting her on the back. "I see you, Inyati." He waved with his free hand.

"How do you feel?" Inyati said, noticing the bruises.

"Like sleeping for a day and then waking up to a feast." The four of them laughed and Mbeki was led to Inyati's hut. As he settled on the floor he sensed something tickling in the back of his mind. There was something he had seen, or not seen, something he had sensed between Inyati and Nandhi, something else between Nandhi and Bhibhi. He closed his eyes, banishing his mind's attempt to concentrate and slipping backwards into soothing slumber.

Chapter 65

A bead of sweat trickled down Ingonyama's face, but he did not wipe it away. He wanted to appear strong in front of Mbilini. The two of them sat in the mouth of a cave behind a waist-high stone barricade. Their gun barrels were balanced on the lip of the wall. Mbilini's rifle was one of the breechloaders captured from Ntombe, but Ingonyama's poor marksmanship did not warrant such a superb weapon, and so he was using a musket. To his left a third man, an abaQulusi, also had a musket.

"Not long now," Mbilini muttered. The cave was cold and clammy, a result of the night's violent thunderstorm. The predawn breeze did not move enough air to drive out the musty smell, so Mbilini tried to ignore his discomfort, focusing his mind on the plan.

There were only two approaches to the summit on opposite sides of the Hlobane mountain where portions of the rock face had fallen to leave a jumbled heap of caves and tunnels, perfect for a series of ambushes. The defense of Hlobane was just the sort of running fight the Swazi prince preferred. "We must hold them," He whispered.

From the highest point of the east end of the mountain Mbilini's men could see the distant glow of thousands of fires; the Great Impi would arrive at Hlobane tomorrow. With a little grit they could suck the British cavalry up onto the top of the mountain and then close down all the passes, making it impossible for them to escape. Lukuni's column was cavalry-heavy and his units were made up of colonial horsemen. Born in the saddle and natural shots, they had already shown their worth in the West. If Mbilini could strip his adversary of his most frightening force, the war would progress much more to the Swazi's liking.

His spies had whispered the horse soldiers' departure from Khambula at midnight, word moving from picket to picket through a series of daytime birdcalls cooed at night. His garrison --those who had been willing to stay after word that Lukuni's invincible horsemen were on their way-- had scrambled to deploy among the rock clefts and caves of the two approaches; their positions were set up with both cover, like Mbilini's wall, and an escape route that would not be in the enemy's line of fire from below.

The sun was not yet up, and the three men in the cave strained the rest of their senses, listening for the soft sound of muffled hooves, the clinking of metal equipment together, the whinny of an impatient horse restrained by the darkness and the necessity of stealth. The cool air did nothing to stop the three of them from sweating; their position was the furthest forward, and they would have to displace to another prepared firing position quickly or be overrun. "I would feel better with the sun up," The third man said.

Mbilini grunted. He was glad Ingonyama did not know that the witch doctors had told him as a boy that he would die in darkness but that as long as the sun shined he would be safe. The prophecy had never stopped him from launching his trademark night attacks, including this trap, but the third warrior in the cave knew that if Mbilini were to die the abaQulusi would flee. The Swazi prince did not need to be reminded that he was the only thing holding the western half of kwaZulu out of British hands.

"Me too," Ingonyama whispered, not understanding the undertones about Mbilini's fate or the defense of the realm. His aim was abysmal, always had been, and without some good shooting light all he would be able to do was fire his gun in the general direction of the enemy.

All three stiffened as they heard it. A clink, as if the rim of a metal canteen were hitting a holstered revolver. It was faint but straight ahead of them. The two muskets were already charged and now Mbilini dropped the first bullet into his breech, snicking it shut. The three men each brought the rifle butts up to their shoulders, staring over the iron sights into the darkness below.

A pebble skittered out from under a leather padded hoof less than a hundred paces ahead of them. "Now?" Ingonyama whispered. His musket would only be accurate to a third that distance, but as he could not see what he was shooting at and he could not have hit something at thirty paces even if he had been able to see, he saw no disadvantage in starting now. The sooner they began firing, the more shots they could put down range before having to relocate to their next firing position.

"Mbilini?" Mbilini suggested a war cry.

"abaQulusi," The third man said, not making it a suggestion.

"Ingonyama," Ingonyama said, just as firmly. The three smiled together, barely able to see each others' teeth; all of them had known which cry to use.

"uSuthu!" The roar of gunfire drowned out the long, drawn out ending of the cheer. The flash from their muzzles had just lit up their position in the darkness, but it had also illuminated a portion of the torturous path below them with hundreds of men and horses upon it.

"How can we miss them?" Ingonyama shouted, slightly deafened by the three gunshots' echo within the cave. He was frantically ramrodding his next shot. Mbilini, whose breechloader was ten times faster, was already shooting again. They heard a white man give orders in a barbarous language, and the next time the three fired in unison most of the targets had gone to ground, laying their horses down and taking up prone firing positions.

Bullets began coming back at them, much better aimed as they were directed by skilled marksmen into the area of the muzzle flashes. The wall in front of them began to scream and whine with the ricochet of bullets. Another shot went over their heads, hitting the roof and then the wall before burying itself in the floor behind them.

"Fall back?" The third man asked.

"Not yet," Mbilini and Ingonyama both said, feeling the man's rising panic and cursing themselves for picking a coward out of all the men who had volunteered to accompany them. They fired again, this time hearing a horse scream downhill.

"I think one of them is walking home," Mbilini joked, secretly furious that there was not enough light for him to pick off the men instead of wasting his precious bullets in any direction as if his rifle was no more accurate than the tower muskets in the other two men's hands. "Let's fire another together; we need the light." They shot again, and now they saw the dark forms of black men wearing the red calico cloth headbands of the Natal Native Contingent working their way through the boulders. In this darkness these warriors fighting for the Whites could advance into uncoordinated rifle fire with impunity.

"Look!" Ingonyama hissed. Behind the advancing blacks stood Hamu kaNzibe and Jobe kaHamu, urging the Hamu ibutho forward while keeping themselves out of the effective range of Mbilini's ambush. "I should have killed them when I had the chance." Hamu had not just defected into neutrality; he and his followers were actively serving the Whites in hopes of better treatment after the war. Ingonyama felt sick to his stomach, knowing he had been manipulated into letting the traitor go. "Can you get a shot off?"

Mbilini squinted over the sights, lining up on Hamu, when he saw a red headband appear from behind a boulder, only paces away from the front of their cave. He fired at the new man instead, taking him in the chest. "Time to go!" He ordered, Hamu forgotten for the moment.

The three raced back around a corner and out the back of their cave, shouting, "Cover! Cover!" Half of Mbilini's men were above them in other caves, and as one they all began firing down into the white cavalry and black infantry below. A bullet whistled by Mbilini's ear from his own men but he ignored it, knowing that one was no longer a threat, while bobbing and weaving might very well run him into the next stray shot.

The three dove over a stone parapet into the next redoubt, loading their guns again. "I didn't expect them to have Zulus," Ingonyama huffed, his side bruised from his landing.

"The whistle system is an alarm, not a code. There was no way for my pickets to tell me what the raiding party consisted of. It just means we will have to fall back faster." The first pre-dawn light was warming the eastern horizon, and the three pairs of eyes now easily saw a black man with a red headband appear from their exit passage; their old position had already been overrun.

Mbilini fired his rifle and the man spun around like a top. "There. That should slow the monkeys down." As the light came up he was proven right, and by the time the lowest part of the sun had risen above the edge of the Earth they had only had to fall back twice more, finding themselves now half way up the side of the hill.

The light worked against the abaQulusi too, though; the Whites below were much better shots, and they were picking off Mbilini's snipers now that they could see.

Ingonyama's face and chest were covered in the grimy blackness of burned gunpowder, and his nose burned with its sulphurous contents. His eyes watered at its sting, and his pride hurt at his poor marksmanship. Still, he fired and fired again, glad that the noise, if nothing else, was keeping his enemies' heads down. He longed to run among them with his assegai, but he knew the difference between bravery and suicide. He wiped one sweaty hand on his red vest and returned to loading.

A bullet tore through the third man's throat, and he stood with both hands around his neck, burbling his surprise. His eyes were open wide and his mouth was trying to form a word but no more air passed through his lips. He fell backwards into a growing pool of his own dark blood. Ingonyama and Mbilini looked at each other. "Time to fall back," they said in unison. They rose into a half crouch to shuffle to the back of the cave when a bullet struck the rocks in front of them, a sliver of stone smacking into Mbilini's forehead, lifting him off his feet before dropping him down onto the floor.

Mbilini gnashed his teeth together to hold back the scream that boiled up out of his lungs. Blood ran down his face and chest. It was the worst kind of flesh wound: The heavy bleeding combining with the blow to his head making him dizzy and weak.

"I'm fine," He woofed when he was sure he could open his mouth without expressing his pain. Ingonyama had crouched back down out of the line of fire, analyzing the situation. "You'll have to carry me and my rifle."

Ingonyama's eyes were on the wound. "All the fight is going to go out of your men if they see me carrying you. Can you walk?"

Mbilini cursed himself for not having thought of that, knowing that his injury was clouding his instincts. "Yebho, Help me up." The two men crouched even lower and escaped through the back of the cave, four more bullets ricocheting off the roof adding urgency to their actions. When they emerged from their latest position there was enough light for the abaQulusi further uphill to see the blood pouring down from Mbilini's head. The fire slackened.

"Shit," Mbilini spat, moving his schedule forward again. Before the native contingent had arrived he had expected to keep the Whites off the mountain until the afternoon. Before his wounding he had expected to keep them off until midmorning. Now they would reach his cattle before the sun was two handspans over the horizon. "Ingonyama, take me all the way to the top. I'm going to have to coordinate the fall back." The Invincible nodded, supporting the Swazi's weight with a shoulder now that the men had lost the will to fight.

From the top they watched as the British made their way uphill, moving from cover to cover while maintaining a suppression fire on their enemies. When the Whites were three quarters of the way to the top Mbilini sighed, "Order the fall back." He had hoped for half a day more, but that was now impossible. He shifted to look east, wincing at the pain, eyes straining for a sign of the Great Impi. Now he had to hope that the Zulu reinforcements would arrive in time to save the day from ending in catastrophe.

Ingonyama left Mbilini with his abaQulusi advisors and gathered his Invincibles. With the fall back ordered, most of the abaQulusi would melt away into the rocky rim of mountain, allowing the Whites to gather up the waiting cattle. When the Whites began to descend the mountains, laden with booty, the abaQulusi would choke the routes and hold the Whites as long as possible to give the Great Impi time to reach Hlobane and finish off Lukuni's greatest tactical asset.

Ingonyama's Invincibles task was to recover Mbilini's cattle. "Not a lot of glory in it, but three thousand cows is more than our Swazi host can give up, even for a victory." Ingonyama commiserated. There were some mutters from his warriors, but most just took a pinch of snuff and pretended that they did not want to be in the thick of it.

As if the Whites had agreed to Mbilini's plans they rode up on to the top of the mountain, convinced that the Zulu retreat was a rout, and began rounding up the cattle. By midmorning they completed the round up and began to move back to the paths only to find them choked, this time not just with gunfire but with throwing spears and the broad-bladed stabbing assegai as well.

The firefight was fierce; the abaQulusi were of roughly the same strength in numbers as their British foes but without as many guns. The Whites were better armed and were all mounted, but they were unwilling to give up their captured cattle or commit to the casualties necessary to force their way through. It was a stand off, one the Whites were pleased to enter in to, knowing their rifles would eventually pick off enough of the abaQulusi to escape without many casualties on their own part. Unknown to the Whites, Mbilini and Ingonyama's men were just as happy to delay, because the longer the Whites waited the more time the Great Impi had to come to their aid.

At last the remaining British soldiers left their native contingent to guard the captured herd in an attempt to force the escape route. Seeing the new vulnerability Ingonyama ordered his men forward, and not one of the red headbanded natives in the British employ stood to face the coming Invincibles. Before Ingonyama had even wet his spear all but three hundred of the three thousand cows were back in his men's hands.

"Good work." Ingonyama laughed, ruffling the hair of one of his Invincibles.

"Ingonyama!" The cheered. "He is a lion! He is a lion! He is a lion!"

He smiled his lopsided smile.

"Ingonyama!" A man ran up. At first he thought the man was joining the cheer, but a tug on the hem of his vest told him otherwise.

"What is it?" He asked, not recognizing the man, which would make him an abaQulusi.

"There! There in the east!" The man gestured with an open hand, shaking with excitement. Ingonyama ran to an outcropping and scaled it; the view taking his breath away. Laid out below him was the Great Impi, looking like a black leopard skin thrown across the plain, every hair a running Zulu warrior. As if it knew it was being reviewed, the impi pulsed with sudden movement and the sound followed moments later, three booms of rolling thunder as twenty-five thousand shields were slammed with open, calloused hands.

"You see that boys?" He shouted to the Invincibles below him. "Now we'll make them pay!

Chapter 66

As darkness fell and the last of the harrying pursuit parties returned to Hlobane, Ntsingwayo detailed Mbeki to count the white dead. Mbeki did so with a length of twine and a bucket of pitch borrowed from what was left of Mbilini's damaged Hlobane homestead. He walked the field from one end to the other, circling the bottom of the mountain to count the bodies thrown from the cliffs and sweeping the top for the men cut down in their panicked flight. Upon each corpse or grave, for two of the British had been buried in the heat of battle by their comrades, he put a splash of tar so as not to count the same body twice, and then tied a knot in the rope. When he returned to Ntsingwayo's war council that evening to the west of Hlobane his numbers were encouraging.

"Fifteen dead officers, seventy-nine dead Whites of lower ranks, and at least a hundred of their native contingent; it's hard to tell about the last because some of them stripped off their calico headbands." There were grins around the fire, but Mbeki feared the smiles were too confident, especially his brother's.

"Fifteen dead officers? Almost two hundred dead altogether? That's the biggest victory since Isandhlwana!" Ingonyama burst, his enthusiasm infecting the younger commanders at the council, who began smiling and nodding.

"It was no victory." Mbilini winced, turning to face the King's Champion. The pressure bandage on his head was soaked through with blood. "We drove them back, and they retreated stupidly, taking more casualties than they had to, but the point of our ambush was to wipe out Lukuni's cavalry, and we haven't done that."

"They came here to destroy you, prove Hlobane was not impregnable, and drive off your cattle, and they did not do any of that. They were defeated," Ingonyama said. Mbeki could feel the council polarizing to his side of the argument.

"Neither side won," Mbilini said at last, offering the compromise. Ingonyama grunted his agreement.

"If I can bring us back to the point of this council," Ntsingwayo rumbled, "What should we do now?"

"Drive on to Khambula," Ingonyama said it before greyer heads could speak. Many of the young commanders murmured their agreement.

Mbeki sat there flabbergasted at his brother's words. "Have you forgotten Rorke's Drift already? That was a hundred men behind walls they built in a day on flat ground. We did not win there. What makes you think we can defeat over a thousand men in fortifications that have been in the building for over a moon up on top of a hill?" Mbeki watched his brother's face storm over.

"Today they ran. Our morale is high while theirs' is low. We have as big an impi as we had at Isandhlwana, bigger, because at Isandhlwana we did not use the reserves, which is why we went to kwaJim in the first place," Ingonyama spat, remembering the fist-sized hole in his father's chest. "Last, we have all night to brief the men to encircle the camp from outside the range of their guns. If we all charge forward together, they can't be strong everywhere! As soon as we breach their walls every last redcoat, and every last Zulu who supported them --including Hamu-- is dead!" He stood there in all his terrible glory, emphasizing each point of his plan with a thrust of his assegai.

"Sit down," Ntsingwayo muttered, knowing how difficult the Invincible had just made this council. Ingonyama looked at him, the bloodlust still in his eyes. "I said sit down!" There was the old cold steel in his voice now, and he saw the madness leave his protégé's eyes.

At length, stiffly, the Invincible sank into the grass, shifting closer to the fire, as if the reprimand had left him cold. "I have heard from the side that says to strike the camp. Does anyone hold the contrary opinion?" When the younger kaJama raised his hand, Ntsingwayo nodded. "The Wizard of kwaZulu will speak."

"Ingonyama and Mbilini would not know this because they were not at the grand muster at oNdini, but Cetshwayo has already laid out the strategy—-"

"Your strategy," The induna of the Humbler of Kings hissed. He wanted to hit Khambula, to be the first in among the tents as the Weepers had been at Isandhlwana. The shame of the lost stick fight still burned, and he longed for his regiment to billet in oNdini once more.

"Don't interrupt!" Ntsingwayo barked in his command voice, most of the council leaning back at the violence of it. "Continue, Mbeki," He said.

"Cetshwayo has already laid out the strategy we are to follow. We are to pass well south of Khambula, out of range of their artillery but within sight of their scouts. We are to cross into the Boer lands, and we are to destroy everything. Men, women, children, cattle, farms, villages, roads, everything will be put to the assegai or the torch until Lukuni comes down off Khambula to chase after us."

"Then what?" Ingonyama asked.

"Then we hit them in the open across an extended front with only an unlaagered camp to fall back on, as we did at Isandhlwana. Or we cut them down on the river fords, or in the mountain passes, or, if Lukuni is too clever to be caught, as I'm sure Mbilini was about to say he is, we leave the abaQulusi with a couple of the younger regiments in enemy territory to force Lukuni's column on the defensive while the rest of the Impi falls back to oNdini to deal with Eshowe or any relief column the British may be sending.

"With a minimum of lives and a no chance of failure we either destroy or immobilize another of the three white izimpi that came against us. If we charge uphill against a laagered camp tomorrow we will lose."

"I can't believe you just said that," Ingonyama said. "What ever happened to, 'A hero dies in heroism?'"

"What ever happened to, 'I play to win, and I always win'?" Mbeki replied, smiling now. "My plan will have us win in the West. We've already won in the South. All we have left to do is the East and the Whites will spend a year trying to regroup, during which our supporters among them will be screaming at their leaders for peace. My way will give us victory; yours will give us the death of heroes. Which are you more likely to enjoy in your old age, Ingonyama?" There were some chuckles now, including some from the young commanders. Ingonyama grunted his reluctant agreement.

"Then that's settled," Ntsingwayo said, hiding his unease. "Tomorrow we will pass well south of Khambula." The council rose to their feet and drifted off to their various regiments to sleep.

"Ingonyama," Mbeki called, catching up with his brother. "I did not mean to be so harsh."

"Of course you did," Ingonyama was smiling his lopsided grin, and Mbeki was glad to see his brother was not upset with him. "But that's all right. I was just as firm in my opinion, and I have found that anger is very persuasive among soldiers." The two laughed. "How's Nandhi?" He said at last.

"Relieved," Mbeki smiled. "She sends her best."

"Good," He continued smiling.

The two walked back to where the Invincibles had camped down for the night, laughing together over childhood memories and swapping the latest gossip. They relieved the night sentries, taking their place, watching over the sleeping Invincibles against any sudden threat.

"I'm sleeping better now," Ingonyama whispered.

"It shows," Mbeki replied; his brother had never spoken of his nightmares or his insomnia, but Mbeki was too canny an observer, and rumours had also come to him from Jojo. "The bags under your eyes aren't as drawn out and you smile more."

Ingonyama nodded. He felt like whistling, or singing, or shouting with happiness and jumping up and down. His life was his own again. That's why I really wanted to charge the walls at Khambula, he admitted to himself. I want this campaign over tomorrow, so that I can go home to my wife for the first time in my life as a happy husband.

Mbeki read some of Ingonyama's thoughts and smiled his own smile. The two sat there for a long while, the night breeze calming and cooling them so that it took all their discipline for their heads not to droop. Finally, Ingonyama decided it was time to broach the subject of family. "So when are you going to take advantage of your Invincible privileges?"

"What do you mean?" Mbeki asked.

"You haven't sewn on the head ring yet, but you're in the royal guards. When do you plan to marry?" He was pleased to see surprise in his brother's eyes. He's not the only one with shocking ideas, Ingonyama chuckled.

Mbeki's mind was awhirl; Jama had spoken of his marrying, but he had never considered the possibility. There were no eligible women of his age near the Valley of the Three Homesteads, and he moved about too much as a messenger to have formed a relationship with a girl at oNdini. "I hadn't really thought about it," He admitted, leaving himself open to anything Ingonyama wanted to say.

"Well start thinking. Who has a kindly disposition and a number of daughters?" Ingonyama's smile grew broader as his brother's mouth hung open, completely lost in thought. "What about Ntsingwayo?" He suggested.

"Is that something he's said to you?" Mbeki asked, remembering Jama, too, had suggested Ntsingwayo.

"Oh, give over! The man has twenty or thirty daughters, and he thinks well of both of us. You could be married next month and have a baby by the end of the year." Mbeki's mouth still hung open, but now it was in shock. "How can you not have considered what you're going to do?" Ingonyama teased but became serious within moments. "Baba and Punga and Khandla are dead, Mbeki. Most of our cousins are either dead or will die by the end of this war. What's going to happen to the family's herd and the family's valley? That's some of the best grazing land between the Thekula and the Mhlathuze. We have to reaffirm our claim to it before squatters move in."

"What about Invincibles having to live near oNdini?" Mbeki asked, trying to stall for time as his mind worked over this new thought.

"I'm thinking of giving it up," Ingonyama said.

"What?" Mbeki said loud enough to provoke a muttered 'shut up' from the sleeping forms behind them. "What?" He returned to his whisper.

Ingonyama chuckled again, pleased. "When this war is over, Cetshwayo will be cemented as king for life. Hamu will be in permanent exile. Zibhebhu's service has been so great, he will probably be granted the autonomy that Mbilini receives. His Mandlakazi are essentially in the same position as the abaQulusi anyways; a warlike clan on our borders who protect us from raiders."

Ingonyama leaned in, not wanting his men to overhear him. "I'm going to retire to the family holdings with Nandhi, and have a normal life with her and my son." He patted his brother on the back. "I want you and Inyati to set up homesteads there too. Inyati can marry Bhibhi, and the three of us can take care of our mothers and aunts and any cousins who aren't old enough to set out on their own."

"You'd give it all up?" Mbeki asked.

"This is my last war, Mbeki. I have a son who deserves a father and a wife who deserves a husband. Ever since I married, I've been going from battle to battle. I'm done with it. I'm ready to stop."

"So..." Mbeki trailed off, mind following the possibilities. "That could work."

"It could. You smith, Inyati and I herd. We serve our regiments if there's a full scale mobilization, but other than that we just get honours heaped on us every umKhosi Festival as royal favourites. Ten years down the road you'll be an induna in the Flycatcher Birds, and I'll be an induna in the Humbler of Kings. By the time we're grandfathers we'll be Great Men of the Nation." Ingonyama, the impulsive man who lived for the moment, had a long-term plan, and Mbeki was surprised with its scope.

"Yebho," Mbeki breathed. "Who will take over as King's Champion?" He asked.

"Jojo is good enough. There won't be any further threats to the throne with Hamu and Zibhebhu dealt with." "This all depends on our winning the war," Mbeki said, voicing the unspeakable.

"I told you before: I'll be dead before we lose." Ingonyama said it with his most confident laugh. Death was very far from his mind.

"Get some sleep. I'll set up the next sentries."

Ingonyama rubbed the back of his neck, grateful that his brother had suggested the break. "Yebho, Nkosi," He replied with mock difference.

Mbeki sat in the long grass for some time before getting replacement sentinels. He had the heavy feeling in his stomach, the premonition of bad tidings to come, and he sat very still for a long time convincing himself it was indigestion.

Chapter 67

The British camp of Khambula sat on the back of a ridge known as Ngaba kaHawana, Hawana's Stronghold, and whoever Hawana was, he had chosen a fine position to have named after him. The ridge rose up in the center of a valley, so that an attacking impi would run down the slope to the valley floor only to find their unconscious speed had tired them for the sprint up the side of the hill.

Even from a great distance to the southeast of the camp Mbeki could see the defenses at Khambula were fearsome. Aside from the laager of wagons at one end of the ridge whose encompassing area was filled with redcoats and white tents, on the opposite end of the ridge there was a redoubt, and a number of cannons filled the space between the two fortifications.

Downhill from the artillery stood a stone cattle kraal whose walls would serve as a chest-high barricade for defenders. There was a dead space beneath the nearest walls where an impi could gather, but there was no cover on the approaches. Mbeki was glad they would not have to attack.

That was, at least, until the impi halted and the five columns of warriors closed up with word flying from company to company that all izinduna were to report to Ntsingwayo immediately. "What is this?" Mbeki asked his brother as they jog-trotted to the council. "What are we talking about today that we did not settle yesterday?"

The council was even bigger than last night, as a number of the younger regiments had sent company commanders along with their izinduna to the meeting. The young men were tense and eager, eyes always turning to Khambula and the distant white helmets that were driving cattle inside the laager. "Alright, we are all here and we have no need to dither. You want to attack Khambula, and I want to obey my king. As I've already ordered the Humbler of Kings twice to stop from marching against the British, I thought I should call a meeting and settle this now." Ntsingwayo had the steel in his voice again.

Fool, Mbeki thought harshly. If you had just kept ordering them, they would have been forced to obey. Every moment we're halted within sight of that fort is another moment where our warriors are sure we're committing them to an attack.

"Nkosi," The induna of the Humbler of Kings began, "The British are right there." He pointed with a single finger. "It's only noon. There's plenty of time until nightfall. They are afraid. We killed many of them yesterday. This Lukuni is cunning. If we let him chase us into White territory, who knows what he might do to us? Today we know where he is, what he has with him, and that his people are scared." The man took a little pinch of snuff as if he did not care what Ntsingwayo decided. Mbeki noticed the induna's hands trembled with excitement.

"He's on ground that he's chosen, and that he's had time to prepare." Ntsingwayo's mind was on the kloof battle he had led against the Swazi eight years earlier. This is the same thing, he thought. Except we are the Swazi: We will run down one slope and then up another, and if we lose, we will have to retreat the same way. Of course, this time we'll be doing it under rifle and cannon fire, and when we run they will chase us with their cavalry. I must convince them!

"I want to fight him on my ground, where I have had a chance to prepare. Lukuni is not worried. He need only wait up there for us to come to him, and then he can shoot us down as fast as we can climb up." Ntsingwayo's heart ached at what he had seen at Isandhlwana. There, at least, one of my horns tied down their cavalry to fight as infantry. At Khambula there was even more cavalry, and they would be in the laager until the opportunity presented itself for a charge.

"Nkosi, look! He is scared! He's striking his tents!" All eyes turned to the distant fort, and they watched in silence as the white bell tents were coming down. Their ears heard the feint clarion call of the bugler playing something fast and strident.

"Could he be--" Ntsingwayo clamped his mouth shut. He was walking the thin line between leading his impi onto an offensive and dashing it to pieces at the base of that hill. Inside he was finishing his thought: Could Lukuni be pulling out? Could he be so weak? Have I misread the man that much?

"Nkosi! He's just as likely to strike his tents to clear the center of his laager to move troops from one side to the other, and to prevent us from firing them," Mbeki blurted, having to shout over the men saying he was wrong.

"Quiet!" Ntsingwayo barked. "You, talk!" The general pointed to the King's Champion.

Mbeki held his breath, knowing now that whatever side Ingonyama supported would win. "Nkosi, I do not know whether Lukuni is withdrawing or preparing to fight, and I agree that it would be better to move on than attack today." Mbeki breathed out in relief, too soon. "But that's not really up to us. No matter what we order, our boys are expecting us to rush that fort. It's all they're talking about; all they're thinking about. They will not be dragged away. Look at them."

The council looked to the impi, squatting in the grass in their thousands, every man focused on the tents coming down. There was a buzz of conversation, excited words flying between clusters of friends. It was not an army eager to move on.

"Our duty is to preserve the impi, and as they seem determined to attack, we must make sure they suffer as few casualties as possible." Mbeki stifled a curse. Around him the younger regiments' representatives were voicing their support. "We must use the horns of the buffalo and completely surround the camp outside the range of their guns. Send the Humbler of Kings around to the far side; as they're the fastest, they should be in position across the longer distance by the time the rest of us are ready.

"We rush them all at once: The left and right horns taking the laager from the north, south, and west; the chest and loins rolling up over the redoubt and the cattle kraal, and finally taking the laager in the east. We can have the last redcoat killed by sundown."

Mbeki was desperate now, seeing the danger of those seductive words. "And how many will we lose, Ingonyama?"

His brother set his jaw, knowing he would have to tell the truth to appear objective when in his heart all he heard was his wife's tinkling laughter. "Between the dead and the crippled we lost two thousand at Isandhlwana. We can expect to lose that many again."

Someone cursed under their breath, but Mbeki knew it was not enough. He had to convince them. "If we go through with Cetshwayo's plan," he used the king's name, trying to remind Ntsingwayo of his duty, "We won't lose two hundred. This impi will be needed against Eshowe." He heard the whine creep into his voice and knew he was going to lose.

"Enough! The king is not here. The average warrior cares nothing for strategy when all he can see is red." Ntsingwayo looked out over the impi; he could feel their battle madness. "I am the king's general. It is my decision, and I say we attack today. Word has already come from our spies that the Whites are sending a relief column against Eshowe. This impi cannot be tied down out here for a moon to do what can be done in an afternoon."

Mbeki sagged back, defeated. He listened with half an ear as battle plans were given and confirmed; his counsel was not requested again, so he kept his mouth shut. When the council broke up, he followed his brother back to the waiting Invincibles in silence.

"We are attacking Khambula!" Ingonyama boomed. A cheer went up from his men. "We will be with the Weepers ibutho in the left horn, and our objective is to cut the redoubt and the cattle kraal off from the laager by pushing the redcoats out of the ground in between. That will bring us behind their north-facing cannons, so try to take those before they can be pulled back into the laager."

"Ingonyama!" Jojo cheered. The whole company took it up, except Mbeki:

"He is a Lion! He is a Lion!

He is even better than that:

He is a Hippopotamus!

Master of his world, killer of the careless,

whose gut is huge, and penis pendulous!"

Ingonyama flashed them his lopsided grin and gestured them forward with his assegai, "uSuthu!"

"uSuthu!" They replied, up and running as fast as a flock of birds can lift off the roost and into formation.

When they began their assault Khambula was so small that Mbeki could block it from his view with a finger on his outstretched hand; it did not take long to grow bigger and bigger until he could make out the ant bear holes and termite mounds at its base and count the individual white helmets looking over the battlements of the laager; there were hundreds of them.

The Great Impi formed the fighting buffalo easily, with the younger regiments thrown out to the left and right to cover the extra distance to encircle the enemy, and with the older amabutho forming the powerful crushing head and the unstoppable loins, held in reserve to pound through the enemy when they began to waiver.

On top of Khambula, Prince Hamu kaNzibe watched the impi come with well-concealed anxiety. The army was as big as the one which had smashed into Isandhlwana; when the horns were deployed to their fullest extent the impi spread across a ten-mile front, moving through the grass as silent as ghosts.

"Lukuni!" He said, an interpreter getting Wood's attention; Hamu had already proven himself a valuable source of military intelligence.

"What is it, Nkosi?" The interpreter asked. Wood had not called Hamu a lord, but it was best to be polite.

"The right horn is made up of the Humbler of Kings regiment, and they have been ordered to circle to your north and meet up with the Red Needles ibutho to our west before attacking. If you let that happen you will be attacked on all sides at once."

The mustachioed colonel looked at Hamu, squinting for a moment before saying something sharp in his own harsh language. "You have a suggestion instead of an observation?" The translation came.

"Yebho, Lukuni. When the Humbler of Kings are north of you, sally out with your cavalry and force them to charge after you. If they attack without the rest of the impi you can double the men on the north walls and break them. Then they will never link up with the Red Needles. You won't need to protect the west wall of the laager in strength, giving you a fifth of your men to deploy to weak spots." Hamu's former appointment as head of the Chieftains ibutho had not been entirely political; in his youth he had been a passable general.

"Why would they ruin their plans to chase after a few horses they have no chance of catching?" Wood asked through his interpreter; he had already decided on this course of action, but his plan had hoped for such a reaction, not expected it.

"The Humbler of Kings have scores to settle: Their traditional rivals are the Red Needles ibutho, and so their izinduna will spur them to do better than the Red Needles. They also lost a stick fight to the King's favourite regiment, the Chieftains, so the Humbler of Kings will also want to show themselves to be braver than their older foes. Also, despite taking the worst losses at Isandhlwana, it was the Weepers ibutho which first made it into the tents; the Humbler of Kings have promised the entire Impi that next time that will be their honour."

"Very well, a spoiling attack shall be carried out." Wood nodded, not liking a man who would betray his own people, but appreciating the access to his enemy's reasoning. Hamu watched as the British officer moved through the laager, ordering a wagon to be moved out of position and a cavalry unit to form up in the breach.

Hamu moved to the wall, summoning Jobe and Zokufa with a practiced twitch of his hand. They were facing north, and the Humbler of Kings ibutho was streaming past on the lower slopes of the hill opposite them, just out of range of the heavy British rifles. The cannons began firing, sending sullen-looking cotton ball shaped clouds to appear over the regiment with the crash and boom of thunder, but he could see that the men went to ground as soon as the white gunners stood clear of their cannons so casualties would be minimal. "Jobe, you have your pistol? Zokufa, your gun?"

"Yebho, Nkosi," The two said in unison. Zokufa handed Hamu an extra rifle without being asked. All three stepped up to rest their guns on the wall. The rest of Hamu's men, those few who had escaped Hlobane, were only armed with assegais, so they were keeping the cows calm in the center of the laager. Only Hamu and his immediate retinue would contribute their firepower to Khambula's defense.

"There they go!" Jobe shouted, watching the cavalry commander lead his troop out at the trot, dismounting within a hundred yards of the Humbler of Kings and firing volley after volley into their dispersed ranks. "Come on..." Jobe muttered as the Humbler of Kings induna called out to them to maintain discipline, the warrior's voice carrying even this far.

"Look!" Zokufa hissed. The British were mounting up to fall back, and the ibutho was surging after them, heedless of their orders. The cavalry fell back only a hundred paces before dismounting to fire another volley.

"Come back Johnny! We want to speak to you!" A warrior taunted as the British fell back again.

"We're the boys from Isandhlwana!" Another called. The sound of flying hooves grew closer, and soon the horsemen were tearing through the hole in the laager wall. At the walls the redcoats waited for their officers to order them to shoot. The company commanders wanted the Zulu to get too close to fall back easily.

At last an officer called out, "Volley fire, present! Fire!" The warriors below fell in drifts, winnowed at random by gunfire aimed not at men but at a moving mass.

Zokufa, Hamu, and Jobe fired as fast as they could reload. The gunfire went on and on, sounding like gin bottles being smashed over deep drums. The cannons roared too, pointed straight downhill, firing case shot into the ranks of the Zulu, blowing them back down, end over end, as if they were bits of flotsam caught in the monsoon winds.

The warriors no longer rushed forward; they cowered behind any shelter they could find in the killing field. Any induna who stood to urge his warriors on was targeted by British sharpshooters; soon the ibutho began crawling backwards on their bellies. They never made it within a hundred paces of the northern wall.

Mbeki and Ingonyama were on the south side of Ngaba kaHawana, unable to see what was happening to the Humbler of Kings, but when the volleys stopped they knew the regiment had failed. "Idiots," Mbeki muttered under his breath. The encirclement plan was impossible now.

"Enough." Ingonyama spat. "Doctor the men." They were at the bottom of the steep slope leading up to the ground between the laager and the redoubt, a blind spot out of the redcoats' field of fire, and here Mbeki performed the last act of war doctoring --Bambatha's duty until he had been shot in the head. Mbeki produced a gourd filled with a white powder, a battle magic so potent it was applied only moments before courage was needed.

With a cow's tail fly whisk he took the powder and thumped it on the head and chest of the surrounding men, whispering incantations. Almost at once the men felt it, a trembling in the limbs, a red veil coming down over their eyes. They were ready to kill or be killed, ready for the charge. "Jojo, give me a throwing spear," Ingonyama barked. His men watched as he took off his red vest, once a British tunic, and attached it to the shaft of the spear. "I let go of this flag when it's buried in the center of Khambula. Not before." A cheer went up. "uSuthu!" He called.

"uSuthu!" The call was taken up, not just by the Invincibles but by the Weepers and Skirmishers regiments who shared the dead space. They surged up in their hundreds, rushing the surprised redcoats in the cattle kraal. Without a single casualty they were already closer to the stone walls than the Humbler of Kings had managed on the opposite side of the hill.

Mbeki ran up the hill at Ingonyama's left with Jojo on his right. The bloodlust was in their hearts, remembering Jama and Sompisi and Bambatha. The cattle kraal was held by less than a hundred redcoats, and Mbeki was vaulting over the fieldstone wall before he realized that he had made it. The British company had gotten off only three or four volleys. "uSuthu!" He shouted, charging forward with his assegai. The redcoated regulars were falling back in good order, walking backwards, bayonets towards the enemy. In fury Mbeki realized he could not get amongst them.

All around him Skirmishers were pouring into the kraal, and though the redcoats' resistance was stiffening it would only be a matter of time before the kraal belonged to the Zulu. Ingonyama stood on top of the wall, waving his flag back and forth and pointing the men forward. A shower of throwing spears flew in among the redcoats and a number of them spun out of their neatly retreating line. The Zulu around them were making a deep humming noise, drumming their shields, forcing them to go back or attack and be swallowed up. A number of Skirmishers with guns had already taken up firing positions against the main laager, and to their left the Weepers ibutho was now filling the space between them and the nearest part of the wagon wall.

"Victory!" Mbeki shouted, too soon. The red glaze dropped from his eyes and he could see clearly as the laager wall opened as two wagons were pulled aside. Another company of regulars marched out of the opening and wheeled perfectly, as he had seen them do on the parade square at Pietermaritzburg. With a sharp command the bayoneted rifles were off the redcoats' shoulders and pointed forward; with another command the white men screamed a war cry as good as anything a Zulu company could do and charged.

"What is this?" Jojo gawked. The bayonet charge hit the surprised Zulu like a wave crashing into the shore, except the shore gave way. The bayonets gave the redcoats a decisive reach over the warriors, and their rifles all had a round in the chamber if they had no time to take the cold steel to their foes. The hundred pushed back a thousand, roaring the whole time. The Invincibles had been well back from the front, rallying around Ingonyama and preparing for the charge on the laager itself. Now they found themselves pushed back by the men in front of them.

The cattle kraal was littered with bodies, wet with pools of blood, and was so crowded with the frightened living that the Invincibles could not move forward against the redcoats; instead they were swept back and back with the press of bodies. Just before Ingonyama lost his footing on the wall he threw his flag into the advancing British. The red tunic flag retarded its flight, so instead of smacking one of the men in the chest it hit his thigh. Ingonyama barely had a chance to smile his lopsided grin before he fell over backwards to be caught and carried by the men behind him.

As if the bayonet charge was not surprise enough, the cannons that had blasted the Humbler of Kings ibutho to the north were swung around to point into the Weepers and the Skirmishers; the range was so close that the Zulu could not take cover. Hundreds died in the ten salvoes it took for the amabutho to reach the dead zone at the base of the hill again.

Mbeki lay on his back in the mud, chest heaving from his headlong run down the hill. He stared up into the sky, hearing the bullets and the shells still firing, uselessly now, as most of the warriors had gone to ground. He gulped air, tasting the pasty gum of dried saliva in his mouth. The wet earth beneath him seemed so comforting, embracing him if only he would stay there and not subject himself to further danger. He wanted to lie there forever, but he knew the battle was not yet lost, and it would take every Invincible to win it.

At last he hauled himself up and looked around. The Invincibles were scattered across two regiments, every pair of eyes he looked into were wide with fright. "Ingonyama!" He called and the cheer was taken up. The Invincibles began coalescing towards him. "What do we do? There're two companies of redcoats and four cannons guarding this approach now," He asked them when enough of them had gathered to hold a war council.

"We can't just stay here. The Chest will be moving on the redoubt in a minute, and if we don't keep up the pressure they'll be able to move their cannons and companies again," Jojo bellowed. The roar of the cannons had his ears ringing, so that he could hardly hear anything.

"Where's Ingonyama?" Mbeki asked.

"Right here. Come with me." Ingonyama moved into their circle and out again, every Invincible following him without question. They skirted the base of the hill, wading through two streams, to fall in with the Red Needles ibutho at the extreme tip of the Left Horn. With the premature attack by the Humbler of Kings their orders to link up with the Right Horn were now useless, so thousands of men had gone to ground, their only useful contribution to the fight were from the few warriors in a nearby rubbish heap who were using captured Martini-Henrys to pin down the redcoats managing this stretch of the laager.

"Okay, this is the weak spot! The Humbler of Kings on the far side of Ngaba kaHawana should be working up for another charge. The Chest will be rolling over the redoubt soon. I bet the defenses above us have been thinned out. We can get in here and storm the laager."

The warriors looked at him, ready to follow where he led. The Red Needles were only a year or two older than Ingonyama. If any regiment could rush the laager wall it was the Red Needles, and they knew it. "uSuthu! uSuthu! uSuthu!" The war cry echoed over and over as they tensed themselves like hunting cheetahs, readying for the sprint that would see them kill.

"He is a lion!" The Invincibles yelled, and the charge began; it was like an avalanche in reverse, as the men flew up the side of the hill so fast it was as if gravity was in their favour. Above them the rifles roared, but there were no cannons here to stomp the charge flat.

The front ranks of warriors dropped, men shot through the head, the heart, the lungs. Here a heavy bullet ripped off a man's arm; there another one was shot through the ankle and somersaulted forward in surprise, snapping his neck as he landed on his head. It made no difference. The charge could not be stopped. Though their lungs burned and they no longer had the air left to cheer, the Zulu reached the wagon wall.

Mbeki had long since dropped his shield, and with his free hand he grabbed the still hot barrel of a redcoat's rifle and wrenched it from his grip, stabbing the man high in the chest. He felt the assegai bounce off the man's ribs, and he screamed his outrage as the wounded man fell backwards where he could not kill him. Another redcoat turned his muzzle to point at Mbeki's face, but Jojo brought his war club against the back of the man's head. "Ngadla!" He cried. The two began to climb over the laager wall but froze as the impossible happened again.

Like a choreographed dance, a wagon was wheeled out of place and a company marched out with perfect drill. "Charge Bayonets!" The order rang out, clear to Mbeki's ears, and in that moment the Zulu assault crumpled. Jojo and Mbeki sat there with one leg over the wall, in shock. Ingonyama and a few other Invincibles were still moving forward to join them, but the hundreds, the thousands that they would need to support them were flying backwards in fear of the British bayonets.

Jojo and Mbeki locked eyes, an understanding passing between them that they would have to drag Ingonyama off the hill if they wanted to see him alive tomorrow. The two moved together, dropping off the wall and running straight at him, taking him across the chest, one on either side, grabbing him by the arms. Their combined weight moving downhill at speed was too much for him to bear, and they pulled Ingonyama back kicking and screaming from the laager wall.

He was still cursing when they reached the dead zone again, the blind spot where they were safe from British fire. Only when the company of bayonet men had retired back into the laager did the two Invincibles let him go. "Why did you do that?" Ingonyama shouted, slapping Jojo across the face.

Jojo took the blow, answering as calmly as he could while shouting to be heard over the ringing in his head, "Because the charge is over."

"It's not over! Nothing is over!" Ingonyama turned from Invincible to Invincible, but no one would hold his gaze.

"Ingonyama, they're ready for us now. They have twice as many rifles up there as before, and that company of bayonet men isn't going anywhere. Two amabutho on top of the hill could not stand against a company of charging bayonet men in the kraal. What chance does one regiment have charging uphill against them?"

"Those men have the right idea!" He said stubbornly, pointing to Red Needles warriors trying to rush through the hole left by the moved wagon. The company of bayonet men halted just inside the laager, blocking the gap, and fired five volleys into the packed mass of warriors. Ten redcoats were detached to go out and bayonet the few wounded in the new mound of dead.

"Cha!" Ingonyama roared like a lion. "This will not stand! This battle is not over!" He set his jaw, daring one of his men to disagree.

Mbeki did for the good of them all. "We're dying here, Ingonyama. We should not have attacked Khambula. There were better ways, but you didn't see that, and now we're dying."

Ingonyama's whole body trembled. Here, today, the war could end and he could go home. The British would never stand the loss of two columns. Ingonyama saw the rest of his life fall into place exactly as he wanted it, starting tomorrow, but he knew tomorrow would never come unless the Grand Impi smashed Wood's Column here and now.

"He is a lion!" He roared, and without looking back to see who was following him he ran up the hill.

The Invincibles sat there for a shocked moment before their instincts kicked in and they followed their induna. The surviving Red Needles did not join them. They lay in the mud and in the grass, exhausted and demoralized.

Mbeki and Jojo tried to catch up with Ingonyama, tried to drag him back as they had done before, but they were exhausted. Ingonyama ran on, oblivious of the massed volleys whizzing past his head. Behind him Invincibles were dying as the heavy bullets made a mockery of flesh and bone. The slope was so steep that as they fell, many of them rolled backwards so that their friends had to vault the bodies as they climbed. The gunfire roared, and each blast thinned the ranks of the Invincibles until at last even their terrible courage was exhausted, and they dropped prone into the grass half way up the hill, unwilling to fall back without their leader.

Mbeki and Jojo dropped down into a furrow in the earth, still affording them a perfect view of Ingonyama running alone against the entire camp of Khambula. They called to him, begging him to stop, but he ran on, his white shield and broad killing assegai in either hand.

The first bullet caught Ingonyama in the right shoulder, spinning him around in a crazy tuneless dance. His shield flew from startled fingers, but he regained his bearings and continued to run, the only target on the hill.

The second bullet struck him a glancing blow in the thigh, the shot moving through the muscle and flying out the other side of his leg without hitting bone. Ingonyama stumbled, trying to get his legs under him.

The third bullet caught him just below the navel and blew out the small of his back. Mbeki saw a flake of white bone fly from of the exit wound, a piece of his brother's spine. Ingonyama dropped to the grass, paralyzed from the waist down. He began to crawl forward with his hands, his useless legs trailing behind him.

Mbeki sobbed, seeing the redcoats ignore his brother, knowing his slow advance were the last movements of a dying man. Ingonyama made it close enough to touch one of the redcoat's dust-stained boots; then a bayonet plunged down between Ingonyama's shoulder blades, bursting his great heart. Mbeki watched the redcoat twist his rifle to free the blade from his brother's back.

Mbeki and Jojo lay in their cover for a long time, opening and closing their mouths at the shock of it. No more Ingonyama: Never again the lopsided grin or the booming laugh. It was the end of an age, and none of his redcoated murderers knew it.

"He is a lion!" Mbeki choked at last, beginning to rise. Jojo's arm dragged him back down and held him there.

"Cha!"

"He is a lion!"

"Cha! Not Ingonyama! Ngwenyama!" He was a lion. Mbeki sagged. He turned his head into Jojo's shoulder and wept.

They lay there together, embracing one another, until they were left limp and spent and empty with their grief. At last Mbeki said, "I have had enough of this." He looked back up at where Ingonyama lay and saw Hamu and Jobe standing over his brother's body. He watched in numbed disbelief as Hamu took his son's revolver and emptied all six shots into the back of Ingonyama's head and chest.

Mbeki watched, powerless to stop it. There were no more tears in him, but he would not have wept if he could. His anger was too hot. He waited until he could speak without screaming, which was long after the two traitors had left the wall. Finally he said, "Let's go, Jojo." He had had enough.

The two snaked their way down the slope, gathering up the few surviving Invincibles, forced to leave the dead and the dying to lie there in the open. When they reached the dead zone they stood up at last. Even here the corpses lay thick where the mortally injured had crawled into safety to die. Metallic green flies had already appeared out of nowhere to crawl over the bodies. The sight of them made Mbeki sick. "I have had enough of this," He repeated.

He led his Invincibles south and east, heading to the high point where Ntsingwayo had set up his command post. The general was dictating orders to a waiting messenger; only when the man took off as if he had a tokoloshe on his heels did he turn to Mbeki. "What does Ingonyama say?"

"He says this is all that is left of the Invincibles," Mbeki said.

Ntsingwayo eyed the dozen men. "And Ingonyama?" He asked, knowing they would never have retreated without him.

"Ngwenyama," Jojo choked. Ntsingwayo felt the lump in his throat, and hated himself for it. An induna must not play favourites, not even with his favourites. A thousand men lay dead out on the field so far. To mourn one was criminal.

"Rest here. You have done enough today."

Mbeki sank down into the grass, the sound of the guns and rifles carrying to his ears, sending goosebumps up and down his arms. By the late afternoon wave upon wave of warriors had thrown themselves uselessly against the laager, the redoubt, and the cattle kraal. The whole area was a killing field. Ntsingwayo's messengers ran out to the regiments again and again, sending ever more desperate attacks against the British, hoping by some miracle to break in. Just one breakthrough into the redoubt or the laager would turn this disaster into a bloody victory.

The redcoats moved their artillery and riflemen right up to the edge of the hill and fired down into the previously dead zone, catching thousands of men who thought they were lying in safety. As the sun began to set over the ridge to the west of Ngaba kaHawana the cannons switched to canister shot and the redcoats launched bayonet charges into the last refuges of the exhausted warriors. The bugler sounded the cavalry to mount up, and soon every man with a horse was riding down on the shattered impi.

Ntsingwayo stirred at the sight of the horsemen. "Now's our chance! They're out of their walls! If we can reform them, catch them in the open--"

Zibhebhu interrupted Ntsingwayo. "All we can do is run away, Nkosi. Maybe one man in twenty would stand if you asked him to, but he'd die for his trouble. Let them go. At least the fast ones will get away." The two Great Men of the Nation locked eyes and Ntsingwayo slumped. He would not try to rally defeated men.

The rout began, and no one could stop it as the trickle became a stream, and soon that stream became a river in full spate. There was no cohesion left on the battlefield. Men ran in any direction they could. Ntsingwayo waved his staff to disperse, and the Invincibles staggered away, getting separated in the mass of moving men. The sound of horses and guns grew ever closer.

"No quarter boys! Remember yesterday!" A horseman called out.

"I wish we had sabers! It takes too long to reload!" Another laughed.

Mbeki watched as the horsemen fired revolvers and carbines down into the staggering masses Zulus. The warriors no longer had the will to run, and many just dropped in the grass, feigning death. This sealed the fate of many, as Hamu's men and the rest of the Whites' native contingent followed the horsemen, spearing all the Zulu left behind.

Mbeki realized he had lost his assegai, and though his mind blanked at what possible use it might serve he picked up a discarded throwing spear, using the butt as a walking stick. It was familiar and comfortable to hold the spear, and he walked in silence, his mind refusing to focus on any one thought for fear of seeing his brother's destroyed body again in his mind.

"There's one! I've got him!" He heard, and he knew the man was talking about him. Mbeki's mind refused to respond, but his body acted for its preservation without conscious thought, and so he turned to see the horse galloping down upon him. The rider was one of the colonial volunteers, and so instead of a military uniform he wore a broad brimmed hat with a red band and a blue shirt; the white man had snatched up a fallen assegai and held it awkwardly, point forward and down, ready to run Mbeki through and disengage as if he had a sword.

Still without thought Mbeki's body dropped to one knee, ground the butt of the long hunting spear into the hard earth, and took the brown horse high in the chest; the spearhead broke off as the horse reared back, mortally wounded, and the man fell from the saddle, his assegai flying. The knife Mbeki had taken at Isandhlwana came out of his loincloth and with a savage scream he jumped astraddle the dazed man.

Holland Keech looked up at him, terrified, and Mbeki looked down at him in horror. It was the last blow, the final affront. Mbeki's mind rebelled and his body swayed at the further loss of conscious control. Mbeki's legs were on either side of Holland's chest, but he could not feel the contact. He felt as if he was floating, for nothing else could surprise him on this day when his whole world had turned upside down. Ridiculously, his mind turned to the knife held high over his head, ready for the killing stroke. He felt himself worry that he might cut himself with it, and slowly put it back into its sheath.

"Oh Jesus, Mbeki," Holland said, realizing who was kneeling over him. The voice brought Mbeki back to a reality he wanted no part of, a universe where Hamu won, Ingonyama died, and his friend Holland fought with the British to kill Zulu and destroy Cetshwayo's kingdom. He got up without realizing he was standing and ran away with an energy he had not realized he had, driven not by fear of death but by a desire to leave it all behind him. Holland's voice called out of the dusk over his shoulder, begging him, "Mbeki, wait!" Mbeki ran as if he had no reason to be tired. He flew across the plain faster than a horse could follow. He ran into the night that swallowed him whole.

No one could say for certain how many Zulu died that day. Somewhere between one and two thousand were blown to pieces on and around Ngaba kaHawana. Another one or two thousand were cut down by Wood's irregular horse units, who worked back and forth across the impi's axis of retreat for hours, retiring to Khambula only when they had used up every bullet and had no light left to see their retreating foes. Another one or two thousand warriors were injured too severely to ever fight again, many of those dying of their wounds at home. Thousands more returned to their families and never left again. In the end numbers did not matter; the Great Impi was like an assegai blade, fearsome when whole but useless when broken. It would never be reforged to the same strength.

Mbeki knew all that in the corner of his mind that was not screaming. It was the end of an era, the era in which there was a possibility the Zulu might win the war. Tomorrow there would be no Ingonyama, no Great Impi, no check on Lukuni's advances. Holland being among the men who had fought and killed the Zulu was far from the worst thing that had happened to Mbeki that day, but Holland's beseeching, "Mbeki, wait!" came to sum up the cold shock in his heart. Mbeki could never have predicted losing his brother, and he could never have conceived Holland's betrayal.

He ran with his back to the sunset, knowing that it was not just the end of the day. The sun was setting on the Zulu Kingdom, on the land of his birth. He did not know what the sun would rise upon the next day. He ran on and on, Jojo's brief eulogy playing over in his mind. 'Not Ingonyama! Ngwenyama!'

A lion roared in the distance, signaling the pride that it was dark enough to begin the hunt. Mbeki pointed towards the sound with a single finger, as if it was the lion's fault. "My brother is dead!" He hissed. The lion roared again. "My brother is dead!" Mbeki wailed.

Chapter 68

It was as if a blanket of gloom had been thrown across the autumn kingdom; children no longer played in the pastures. Women sang only funeral dirges as they harvested the last of the crops. Dogs barked less. Cows lowed less. Even the hyenas cackling from the darkness seemed subdued in respect for the Zulus' grief. Rain poured out of the sky as if every one of the Nkulunkulu's thousand eyes was weeping a river of tears. The nation's heart was broken.

Khambula was cause enough, but there was another source of despair: At the same time as the Great Impi was smashing itself to pieces on the side of Ngaba kaHawana in the west, the British had crossed the Thekula near the coast in the east with the intention of ending the three-month siege at Eshowe. Within three days, Dabulamanzi attempted to stop the relief column near the burned out ruins of the Gingingdhlovu ikhanda, but eleven thousand men had been too few to sweep the British camp, and within half a day another thousand irreplaceable warriors were lost.

Word of the two defeats reached oNdini at almost the same time, and the wail of mourning had swept across the surrounding plain. Every woman knew her husband was dead or crippled or, at best, he had tested the ancestors' patience and charity to stay alive. Worst of all, each wife would have to wait until a relative, a friend, or a neighbour returned from the battlefield and said which of those possible fates had occurred. The waiting would be an agony.

The despair was palpable. The Great Impi and the Coastal Impi, almost forty thousand men between the two of them, had each been shattered. The survivors returned to their homes, and many would no longer answer the King's call to muster. The Kingdom's offensive power was dead, and its ability to defend itself was crippled. To make matters worse, British reinforcements from around the world had gathered in Natal to avenge the fallen of Isandhlwana, and soon a second invasion with even more powerful columns would come against them.

The King sighed, his small smile gone from his face. The tension in his body was a constant grinding ache. "How long before the Impi will reform?" He asked his advisors.

"Those who will come will be here in a month."

"Very well," The king sighed. "Order every homestead to defend itself against cavalry raids until then."

"Yebho, Great Elephant." The councilor backed away, glad he did not live in the age of Shaka or Dingaan, either of whom would have killed him for such a report.

"Mbeki?" The King turned to his favourite, squatting down at one end of a line of councilors. "Where is Ingonyama?" The King knew, of course, but he had no details.

"Ngwenyama." Mbeki could not bring himself to say his brother's name or that he had died.

"Did he die well?" Cetshwayo said woodenly.

"He threw his life away," Jojo murmured, sitting next to Mbeki. Of the twelve Invincibles who had squatted at Ntsingwayo's feet in the late afternoon of Khambula, only nine escaped Wood's cavalry pursuit. Without the impi coming to the Great Place for purification rituals there was no way to bring the Royal Guards back up to full strength, and so the nine just sat there in a row, spurning the fine dress of the other councilors: From now on they would always be stripped for fighting, until the end came when the fighting would stop.

"Did he die in the attack?" Cetshwayo trailed off, knowing he would never be able to finish saying, 'Or was he shot in the back running away like a thousand others?'

"He was a lion," Mbeki and Jojo repeated. Cetshwayo tried other questions, but he could get no solid details out of them. They would not tell him how his Champion died.

"Mbeki, I make you leader of the Invincibles," He said, glad that there was one piece of good news he could give the man.

"Cha, Great Elephant." There were murmurs and mutters from some of the other favourites; no one should refuse the King.

"Why not?" Cetshwayo asked, careful not to put steel in the question for fear someone might put steel into Mbeki for his refusal.

"Give it to Jojo, Nkosi Nkulu. After I tell Nandhi about--" His voice broke, still unable to say his brother's name. "About her husband I have nothing left to do before I die, which will happen before this war is over." He said it as if he was saying it would rain tomorrow, and a number of the men at Court made the sign to ward off evil; the wizard of kwaZulu had prophesized his own death.

"Then go and tell her. My Champion will stay here." Jojo did not show any pleasure at his promotion. He did not want it either.

Mbeki left without giving the royal salute, walking from the royal kraal in a daze to climb the same hill he had visited over half a moon ago. His message was like a physical weight making each footfall an effort of will. He was out of breath by the time he reached the gates of the homestead.

Nandhi stood inside her courtyard helping Galazi tie his loincloth without the tight leather riem cutting into his skin. She was smiling her most dazzling smile, a tinkling laughter spilling out of her mouth. There was no hunch to her shoulders or weariness about her eyes. Of all the worried women in the land, Nandhi was at peace with the knowledge that it could not happen to her.

Nandhi saw him and patted Galazi on the bottom to send him away. Mbeki ached to have as much life stretching out before him as he had enjoyed at Galazi's age. Mbeki was only twenty-three, but he felt old in his bones.

The smile slipped from her face to be replaced with concern at Mbeki's stagger. "Are you alright?" She asked, a guiding hand coming out to take her brother—in-law's elbow.

Mbeki said nothing, unwilling to blurt out the truth, incapable of small talk. Inside the kraal Galazi was screaming to the world that 'Uncle Mbeki is home! Uncle Mbeki is home!' People poured out of every hut: Jama's wives, Bhibhi, Inyati, all there to hug him and rock him back and forth, relieved to tears that Mbeki was alive and safe where so many others were not. He was guided to a stool, and when he was seated a mug of Nandhi's beer was pressed into his hand. They gathered around, knowing a natural storyteller was in their midst and wanting to hear the whole sad tale from someone with the gift of words.

The idea of telling it made him queasy, and long before he was ready to begin Nandhi asked, "How much further behind you is Ingonyama? I'd imagine he's quite busy rounding up the scattered warriors, but when is he expected back? I'll prepare a feast."

Mbeki's stomach dropped and he gagged, knowing now how she had deluded herself for so long. The circle around him backed off, and when he was done gasping and swallowing he sat back on his stool and looked Nandhi in the eyes, silently, waiting, unwilling to speak but knowing his gaze would tell her.

Nandhi looked into Mbeki's eyes for the first time and realized he was not exhausted: He was all used up. The spark of life had left him. His eyes were dead, glazed over like the eyes of a fish; there was no soul lurking in the murky deep. The linchpin upon which his life had revolved, the certainty he had never doubted, was gone. Like a bucket of cold water over the head the truth washed over her. She sank to her knees.

"Cha," She managed to choke. "Cha!" She made it an order, and beside her Galazi recoiled as if struck. "Cha!" The last was heavy with grief, and soon every woman in the homestead was ululating the high pitched wail of the bereaved.

Mbeki sat there, time passing him by unnoticed. Inyati put a hand on his friend's shoulder, but Mbeki did not acknowledge it. He sat there, listening to the mourning songs, sometimes incoherent and other times so poignant they would have summoned tears if he had not cried himself out on the long return from Khambula.

You have a decision to make, Mbeki. He thought. She knows, and she will be well taken care of, so how serious were you about this being the end? He was surprised at how cold he felt, how calm he was in contemplating his end.

It won't be suicide. I will die in the next battle. I will run when everyone else cowers, and they will shoot me down as they did to my brother. Afterwards I shall go to the Nkulunkulu and spit in each of his thousand eyes for making the white men ingenious enough to create their rifles when black men were already good enough at killing with spears to need no more death in the world.

He sat there until the sun went down, surrounded by the weeping but not touched by it. He sat rock still, so that the others began to worry about him through their grief, but he did not respond.

He stared into space, watching the stars as he had as a little boy, wondering what they really were, and how far away, and if he would get the answers when he died, and whether he should make that sooner or later. It's so easy to be brave when you decide not to survive, Mbeki thought. But what about Hamu and his son? They betrayed us, and laughed over brother's corpse. If I die, who will avenge him?

It was the argument he had denied himself until his decision was almost made, but he brought it into play now and felt its weight. The

Zulu Kingdom will fall, and Hamu will prosper. What can I do to prevent that?

The moon came up, and Inyati took Nandhi by the shoulder to lead her to her hut, mouthing platitudes and telling her she would feel better after sleeping. My brother's widow will not be single for long, Mbeki thought without rancour. He was not a good husband to her, and those two will only grieve as long as is appropriate before moving on. Who am I to stand in their way, when my opposition would do nothing and I may or may not be long for this world? Mbeki's eyes strayed to Bhibhi and he was shocked to see anger on her face.

He followed her stare to see Inyati helping Nandhi through the low door of her hut, and then setting off for his own. Ah, Mbeki thought, coming back to the now and leaving his thoughts of mortality for later. My sister is growing up, and she has set her sights on a Matabele prince. That will take care of itself in its own time. Without warning he rose from his stool, surprising those around him with his sudden movement. He walked to Inyati's hut and ducked through the door. "I'm sleeping here tonight," He said distantly.

"Of course," Inyati replied, taking a second headrest from the back of the hut.

"And so are you."

"Of course," Inyati said in the same light tone as before. We have the rest of our lives, his mind whispered, knowing he had the patience to wait six moons or a year for appearances sake. "How did Ingonyama--"

"Ngwenyama," Mbeki interrupted. He would never speak his brother's name again. Inyati nodded, understanding Mbeki's wishes. He gave Mbeki the headrest and offered him a kaross, which was refused. Neither man slept that night, preferring to lay in silence and listen to their secret hearts.

Chapter 69

The rain was heavy, forcing the war council into one of the biggest huts in the royal quarters. The top of the dome was so high, three men standing on the shoulders of the man below would only just have reached it. A fire was going in a scallop-ringed hearth to drive off the worst of the chill. Cetshwayo was flanked by Jojo and Mbeki, both carrying assegais dulled and scratched from battle use. The message was clear: No one would defy the King simply because the war was failing. No one else in the hut was armed.

"What do the British say?" Cetshwayo sighed.

"They will negotiate the surrender of any chief except you. A number of chiefs on the coast and in the West are taking them up on the offer, including several of our brothers," Prince Ndabuko murmured.

Some of the grey light coming through the door was blocked, and all eyes turned to see a royal messenger, drenched to the bone, waiting to be allowed to speak. "Come to the fire and tell us what you must say," Cetshwayo said kindly, knowing the news would not be good.

"Great Elephant," the messenger said, "Mbilini waMswati is dead." The room went colder.

"How?" One of the great men asked.

"He was leading a night raid and was shot in the back. The bullet came in through his shoulder blade and exited out through his front below the waist. It took him three days to die." Men cursed. Few in the hut claimed a close friendship with Mbilini, but all had respected him, especially as a warrior. With him gone the West was out of the war.

"Go well. There will be hot food and a place to rest two huts further over." Cetshwayo waited for the man to leave. "Mbeki, will Lukuni come straight at us or wait in the West?" Of all his councilors he was coming to rely on Mbeki the most; the young man neither honeyed his words nor spoke to put down his king; he spoke with logic and without emotion or personal agenda, and his assumptions usually played out even if Cetshwayo wished they were better for his future.

"My King, Lukuni will stay for at most half a moon, making sure all resistance has collapsed. He's not strong enough to march against us unopposed, now that your warriors have agreed to muster in such numbers." Cetshwayo was careful not to smile, lest one of his councilors realize what he had done. A rumour had flown across kwaZulu that the British were so impressed with the fighting ability of the Zulu warriors that after the war all Zulu maidens would be married off to redcoats to breed strong British warriors, and all the Zulu men would be castrated to prevent a new generation of Zulus from making war on the Whites.

Mbeki had suggested it to him half a moon ago, and he had ordered the King's spies to spread the rumour in the farthest corners of the Kingdom so that the rumour only came back to oNdini in the last few days and seemed to have come from over the borders. Cetshwayo was not proud of deceiving his people, but the story had doubled the number of warriors willing to muster into an impi after Khambula, though they had asked and been granted leave to bring in the last of their crops.

"So what will he do?"

"The British have gathered two new izimpi on our borders; one on the coast whose job seems to be to tie down the forces they defeated at Gingindhlovu, and a larger one half way between Lukuni's position at Khambula and where the column destroyed at Isandhlwana crossed the Mzinyathi. I would assume Lukuni's cavalry-heavy column would be greatly desired by that impi because they know exactly how to do the scouting and raiding necessary to keep the column safe on a march to oNdini."

"What do you suggest?"

"There is no way to stop the two from linking up and no way to prevent them from reaching oNdini, and when they get here there will be no way to beat them." The room muttered at such defeatist talk, especially from the wizard of kwaZulu, who was rapidly gaining the reputation for predicting the future. "The only thing I could suggest is to step up the border raids across all the frontiers. Do not target white settlements; they require too many men to strike and will be well defended. Attack the homes of their black servants. Half their armies are made up of Black contingents, so they might slow down or divert men to protect the border."

"What good is your strategy if we can't stop them from reaching us?" Godide spat. If border raids were stepped up there would be retaliatory raids, and his homestead would be destroyed as sure as the sun rose in the east and bulls mounted cows from the rear.

"I must explain the white command structure to you," Mbeki said, intentionally leaving off the Nkosi. His pact with Death made him blunt and bold, for there was no consequence to any action which could hurt him after his demise. "This war started without the permission of the Great White Queen or her Parliament." He used the English word, pronouncing it correctly, something most of the Great Men of the Nation could not do. "Her commissioner here, Sir Bartle Frere, wants our people and the tribes north of us to work on white sugar fields and gold mines, so he started this war without orders, hoping to break us quickly before he could be reprimanded."

Most of the Great Men knew this, but they waited patiently, glad to be out of the rain. "Frere's general, Chelmsford," again he used the proper name instead of the Zulu nickname, "Did not win the war fast enough. We destroyed an entire regiment of British regulars at Isandhlwana, something which has never been done before without a proper rifle-armed army." The Great Men nodded wisely, trying to imagine where this was going.

"We humiliated Frere and Chelmsford, and the war has continued now for four moons with victories on both sides. That is unacceptable to them. All the British reinforcements on our borders are there because they refuse to be beaten by a small black Kingdom. They are calling in troops from across their Empire to crush us."

Godide let his impatience slip. "So why delay them if we can't beat them?"

Mbeki continued as if he had not been interrupted. "Along with these reinforcements will be a new general to replace Chelmsford. Chelmsford must come to oNdini and crush us before he is relieved. He will take the King away in chains and destroy the kingdom in the most thorough way possible so that he can claim the hard won victory. The new general might be willing to negotiate, because he has been sent here to end the war and has no personal stake in smashing us. We can't beat them, but if we delay Chelmsford long enough for his replacement to arrive we might be able to surrender without the final battle that will destroy the kingdom and send Cetshwayo into exile."

It was the first time the word exile had been spoken in regards to the King. "Is that likely?" Cetshwayo finally asked.

"Great Elephant, if we do not make a peace between you and the Whites before you fall into their hands they will take you from kwaZulu, and you may never see it again." With a tired wave of his hand

Cetshwayo dismissed the council and the men left in silence; they would whisper about Mbeki's impertinence and the King's weakness only when they were back to their huts with their own guards stationed to intercept eavesdroppers.

When everyone had left except Jojo and Mbeki, Cetshwayo stood and faced them, eye to eye. "What are my chances, Mbeki?"

"Barring a miracle there will be no peace until after a last decisive battle. If that battle happens the peace will be in whatever terms they dictate, and if that happens one of the terms will be your removal from the throne." Cetshwayo shivered, looking into Mbeki's dead eyes. For days after the young Invincible's return he had assumed it was shock at his brother's loss and that with time the old Mbeki would return. No spark of life flashed in those eyes. They were bottomless pits.

"Do you have the ability to see into the future?" He whispered, a superstitious dread running down his spine to send butterflies aflutter in his belly.

The wizard of kwaZulu licked his lips absently, framing a reply. "Nkosi Nkulu, I do not see the future as I see you now. I simply know what has happened and what is happening, and from this I can say what will come to pass."

Cetshwayo nodded, making a decision. "From now on you are promoted to full councilor. You will sit at my right and you will give me what advice you have when you have it, not fearing to interrupt whatever self-serving fool is talking to me. Invaders are at my gates, and many of my followers stand ready to throw them wide open. I need you."

"I cannot save you," Mbeki said, the aura of omnipotence hanging around him. Cetshwayo felt a wave of panic wash over him, and then laughed boldly, trying to inspire them with confidence.

"I didn't ask you to save me. I asked for your advice." Cetshwayo tried to keep the note of desperation out of his voice.

"You will have my loyalty as long as I live, Nkosi Nkulu." Mbeki bowed low, but his eyes did not show gratitude or pleasure. Cetshwayo wondered if he had slapped the man across the face if there would have been anger. His eyes tell me nothing, Cetshwayo shuddered again, but they see all. With a flick of the wrist he dismissed the two of them and only when he was quite alone did he rub himself all over to remove the sudden goosebumps.

Chapter 70

Two moons passed. The Zulu raids along the border were more successful than their enemies', but Godide did indeed lose his kraal to the torch, and Mbeki's plan failed to delay the second great invasion. The new white impi, twice as big as any of the columns from the first invasion and linked up with Wood's cavalry column, crossed the Mzinyathi and began to move ponderously towards Cetshwayo's Great Place.

The new column was equipped with so many wagons and oxen that from the time it took to inspan the wagons, to form a defendable column, to outspan the wagons, and to graze the oxen and form a laager it could move only three thousand paces a day; with so little progress, it took the British an entire moon to cover the distance from the Mzinyathi to the heights overlooking oNdini. Once there they built an impenetrable fortress and waited for the Zulu to be foolish enough to attack.

Mbeki sat alone on a hill and watched the flawless dawn vault over the horizon and light the panorama below him. The British fort sprawled grim and foreboding to his right. The White Mfolozi lay below him, its surface cut and broken by the shallows of a ford. To his left lay the plain with a dozen royal amakhanda, including Cetshwayo's great place, scattered across the meadows like intricate cowry shell necklaces, each tiny shell really a hut big enough to comfortably sleep six men. The kraals were full now; the last impi had mustered.

A rock skittered below and behind him, and Mbeki hid his smile without difficulty, knowing that only one person would have come looking for him on this day. "I see you, Inyati," He said without turning.

"You can't have seen me! I've been stalking you since you got up here." Inyati pretended to pout, wishing Mbeki would fall into the easy joking they had enjoyed before Nandhi's wedding.

"That's right. If you were a stray herd boy you would not have been so careful to hide your movements," Mbeki answered in the mysterious airs he had lately assumed. He was not angry at the intrusion; he had been hoping to have a quiet talk with Inyati soon. "Come here and sit with me."

The Matabele prince rose from the cover he had been using and walked up to sit on the ground next to Mbeki, looking down onto the field below. "I'm surprised you're not down there," Inyati murmured, gesturing to the long grass that seemed undisturbed from up here, but was swarming with

Zulu warriors. "All you've been talking about is the last battle, the last battle. Isn't that the last battle?"

"Cha," Mbeki said, not looking at his friend. He focused instead on the cavalry columns now fording the river below him. "This is the Hlobane to Khambula. If this battle goes exactly as we plan it, Chelmsford will lose his horses as Wood should have lost his. If it fails, then our retreat after the last battle will be horrific." They sat in silence, watching the cavalry column come across a party of Zulu who had orders to retreat in feigned panic; following the plan, the Zulu ran from the river in carefully organized disarray, the cavalry in hot pursuit.

"You don't plan on surviving the last battle, do you?"

"No one can decide to live through a battle and believe that their decision will make the difference," Mbeki answered, eyes always on the horses.

"That's not what I said. I said you're planning on dying. That's something you can decide to do. Don't be in such a hurry to die, Mbeki."

"If I should die, you're the last of the kaJamas, Inyati," Mbeki said, as if he had not heard his friend. "You will have to take care of Nandhi and Bhibhi. Marry them both and have lots of children." Mbeki smiled, the first smile Inyati had seen on Mbeki's face since Khambula, but it was sickly, like the smile a drunk had when he threw up and his stomach was finally quieted.

"What?" Inyati knew there was something behind that smile.

"This is the third time the head of my family suggested you marry Bhibhi, and every time it happens the head of the family dies." Mbeki laughed. Inyati eyed him as he would the demented. "I guess my sister is a curse."

"That's not funny, Mbeki."

"I sometimes remember," Mbeki said, as if he had not heard anything, "When my brother came back from kwaTsonga. Do you remember?"

"I remember," Inyati murmured.

"He told me about Zungu's tokoloshe, and how it was supposed to follow our family and rob us of peace and happiness in our final days." Mbeki looked down at his feet, the distant smile still on his face. "I think I believe in that tokoloshe."

"Don't be stupid--"

"Oh, I don't mean I think an actual tokoloshe stalks us in the night." Mbeki said without pause, again as if he had not heard Inyati. "I mean the spirit of the tokoloshe, the nature of the curse. Since that day --before

Nandhi and my brother's marriage-- I don't think our family has ever been happy."

"Mbeki..." Inyati did not know what to say.

"I feel sorry for him."

"Who?"

"The tokoloshe," Mbeki said. Inyati looked at him as he would look at a dog that was snarling in its sleep, a look of wariness mixed with concern. "He can't rest until he completes his master's bidding. That's the fate of a tokoloshe, isn't it? It must be terrible to be undead. I think I will help him to rest." Inyati opened his mouth to say something, but Mbeki pointed with an open hand to the plain below. "Look."

Below them the cavalry had run the Zulu diversion to ground but were now distracted by some Zulu on horseback, led by Prince Zibhebhu himself. The British broke off their pursuit of the Zulu on foot, going after the more elusive Zulu horse contingent. They ran closer and closer to the river, and the British commander seemed to sense the ambush. He halted his troop just short of the kill zone. "Wo," Inyati muttered.

"Wo, indeed. It looks like there will be cavalry to chase us down after our last defeat," Mbeki said. Fifty paces ahead of the white horsemen the grass had been cunningly woven into tripwires, nooses, and snares to tangle the horses' legs. At that point four thousand warriors, predominantly from the Mongrels ibutho and Zibhebhu's Mandlakazi, would have risen up and slaughtered the whites piecemeal. Their trap ruined, the warriors rose up now in frustration and the cavalry fired several volleys before beating a hasty retreat, leaving only a few dead horsemen behind them to be stripped and disemboweled. "Well that's disappointing," Was Mbeki's final word on the subject.

"Mbeki, did you mean that, about Nandhi?" Inyati asked, wanting Mbeki's blessing more than anything.

"Absolutely, but Bhibhi too. She likes you, even if you're too stupid to notice. Settle in the Valley of the Three Homesteads."

"They burned it." Inyati gestured to the retreating cavalry. Wood's cavalry had blazed a trail of destruction one day's hard ride in all directions from Chelmsford's axis of advance: The Valley of the Three Homesteads had been put to the torch and the cattle stolen. Seven more of Mbeki's cousins, the youngest just six years old, had been killed trying to protect the herd.

"I know. Grass grows back, and after this war there will be enough empty farms that you will get a cow or two. Breed them. Build a herd." The two sat in silence, both imagining the future; Mbeki's ended tomorrow.

"What if you survive the last battle?" Inyati asked. "It would be a lot easier to build up a herd if you're smithing and doing some magic."

Mbeki was irritated to be pulled from his purpose but answered anyway. "If I live, then I will help you." The promise cost him nothing; he was not planning to survive.

The riders crossed the ford below them and returned through the gates of their fortifications. "Are you going to have to rush the fort?" Inyati asked, keeping his tone level, pleased with his small victory.

"Cha, there isn't a general left in kwaZulu who would charge that, and I doubt there are many warriors who would do it if ordered. Besides, Chelmsford doesn't want us to break on his walls. He will march out and defeat us in the open, as his subordinate tried to do at Isandhlwana. Only then will he wash the stain off his honour and the honour of his army."

"Can't you beat them in the open? Isn't that what every Zulu general has been wanting them to do since the beginning of the war?" Inyati opened and closed his hand, knowing the carnage of the coming battle and that all the kraals and amakhanda would be burned, including Nandhi's. *She won't leave without Mbeki, alive or dead*, he knew. *We will have to stay here and hope we are not cut down.*

Mbeki saw the old telltale of Inyati's hand and smiled again, this time in real pleasure. He reached over and put a comforting arm around Inyati's shoulder and for the first time the two looked into each other's eyes; Mbeki's were no longer dead. There was a twinkle, a small but noticeable twinkle. "We can't win," He said, "But a hero dies in heroism."

"I've always hated that motto." Inyati smiled, touching the scar on his stomach.

"I know. I chose it to irritate you." The two laughed, but it was the forced laugh of the doomed.

The next day five thousand Whites came out of their fort, formed a square, and marched on oNdini.

Chapter 71

It was early in the morning, and Mbeki had not slept. He had been up all night playing with an exhausted Galazi, hoping the boy would remember that evening and, by extension, remember him. It's possible, he thought. I remember things from when his age. If he can just picture my face, imagine my voice, than I am not really gone. He ran his thumb along the edge of his assegai, feeling no burrs or blunt spots. If I even get blood on this it will be more than I hope for, he thought grimly.

The British square was two hundred paces to a side with red-coated infantry standing in ranks four deep, shoulder to shoulder, fronting the entire perimeter. Inside the square, blocks of cavalry stood ready to charge out through the infantry when the Zulu were in retreat. Twelve field guns were divided evenly across the faces and corners of the square, and two of the new Gatling guns that Holland had told Mbeki about were also present. Mbeki decided it would be a last indulgence to his curiosity to get a good look at one before he died.

The hill behind him was dotted with women ready to watch the coming battle, and their calls were giving heart to the warriors around him. I hope Nandhi, Inyati and Bhibhi aren't up there, but they almost certainly will be. Would I miss this show in their place?

"Steady," He called to the warriors around him, smelling the peculiar odour of fear sweat on several. The battle had not yet begun, but a number of them were ready to give up now. "Move from cover to cover and don't bunch up. They have only beaten down the grass for a few paces in front of them. We should be able to get close," he lied.

The British infantry was in four ranks with the first two kneeling. They would put their bullets down range at every possible height, and all of the Zulus' efforts would not allow them to reach close combat. The men around him heard his words and eased, heartened at having the nine surviving Invincibles with them.

Jojo was not relaxed; he was incensed. "Pompous asses haven't even fixed bayonets," Jojo murmured, pointing with a single finger at the redcoats.

"Bayonets are for desperate situations. We have to earn the honour of them putting on bayonets," Mbeki soothed his commander.

"I've never fought a battle where they did not have bayonets."

"Maybe no bayonets will be your good luck charm." The two chuckled.

"Maybe we'll be cut down a hundred paces from their front rank."

"I bet ten cows we get to fifty."

"Done." They laughed again at betting on where they would die with cows stolen by their future killers. The warriors around them heard them laugh and marveled at the Invincibles' calm outlook, never suspecting the macabre nature of the quiet conversation.

"There," Mbeki pointed with an open hand. From the first battle of the war to now, the horns of the buffalo had never successfully encircled a white army. Even at Isandhlwana the horns had been two hundred paces shy of completely surrounding their enemy. That changed today; for the first time in the war, the British were cut off on all sides. Ten thousand Zulu warriors now ringed the Whites, with another ten thousand in reserve. Twenty thousand warriors were still willing to serve the king, of the forty thousand in his kingdom.

"Good." They stood in silence, waiting for part of the impi to charge. The waiting stretched. "How far do you think Cetshwayo has gone?" Jojo asked, trying to end the silence.

"Two, three times over the horizon. He'll go further once word comes back that we've lost."

"May the ancestors watch over him," Jojo murmured. Neither doubted they would lose the battle.

"Don't worry. We will." The two laughed again. Gunfire started up as a cavalry unit provoked a regiment to charge before the order was given. "Just like Khambula," Mbeki murmured.

"Ngwenyama!" Jojo shouted.

"uSuthu!" The regiment around him replied. With a dozen paces between each man and moving from cover to cover, the warriors began to advance.

Jojo and Mbeki stayed side by side, keeping a slow and comfortable pace. In front of them the British cannon began to belch flame. "Air!" A warrior called behind them. Mbeki had every intention of continuing to run, ignoring all enemy fire, so he was surprised to find himself face down in the grass; Jojo had tackled him.

"What do you think you're doing?" Mbeki spat a clod of dirt out of his mouth.

"You aren't going to die uselessly," The King's Champion huffed, having winded himself in the collision. "I promised Ingonyama if anything ever happened to him I'd take care of you." Jojo, who could count the number of lies he had told in his life, lied now. There had been no time for Ingonyama to ask that promise of him, but he made it anyways.

Mbeki felt tears sting his eyes at the mention of his brother's name, and he heard the sound of running feet passing him in the long grass. They were no longer in the first ranks. "Let me up."

"Just understand if you die today, so be it, but don't throw your life away. Ingonyama died out of despair, or maybe he was trying to inspire us. Either way he made it to the laager wall. If you let a cannon strike you down a thousand paces from the redcoats because you were too dumb to duck, where's the point in that?" It was the most Mbeki had ever heard Jojo speak.

"Alright," Mbeki nodded. The two were up and running again, but this time in the third rank of warriors, moving forward in admirable skirmishing order. The gatling gun began to chatter like the sound a boy makes when he runs a stick along the side of a palisade, but now each rat-tat-tat-tat was the sound of a heavy caliber bullet being thrown at them, and Mbeki watched in disbelief as the gun traversed from left to right, knocking down fifteen men from the front rank, one next to the other.

"Why did it stop firing?" Jojo asked, never more than a pace away from Mbeki, open order be damned.

"It can't be out of bullets. That's the first we've seen it fire. It must be jammed." The rifles began to volley, and the two watched as men in the ranks ahead of them either spun around at the impact of the bullets or dropped down into the grass seeking cover. Jojo tapped Mbeki on the shoulder, and he got down without being knocked off his feet this time.

"How long until they fix it?" Jojo asked, the two now slithering forward through the grass.

"I don't even know how it works." Above them the chattering started again, interspersed between the roars of rifle volleys. "That answers that question." The gun jammed again. "Let's go!"

They were up on their feet again, but now most of the warriors around them had gone to ground, preferring the slow crawl that would not expose them to enemy fire until the battle was over. "uSuthu!" They roared together, shoulder to shoulder against five thousand redcoats. A few warriors rose up out of the grass around them and ran on. The four ranks of riflemen knocked ten back, then fifteen, then seven more, each of the dead bearing the tremendous gouge of the heavy bullet's exit wound. "Down!" Jojo roared, pushing Mbeki in the back and following him into a weedy donga. Overhead the gatling gun began to fire and the grass hissed and whizzed with the movement of the heavy bullets. All too soon the gatling gun fell silent again.

There was groaning amid the grass now, and weeping, and Mbeki and Jojo felt shame that the warrior spirit of the nation had been so broken. "They won't hold much longer," Mbeki whispered. Jojo nodded. They were only half way from where they had started to the front ranks of the British infantry; it was up to them to set the example. "Let's go!"

Up again and running, this time only half as many responded to their rallying cry. With all their battlefield instincts the two moved from cover to cover, never exposing themselves or running in a straight line long enough for a good shot to bring them down. It would be a random barrage that killed them at this distance. With five hundred paces gone and another five hundred to go they weaved and ducked, up and down and left to right through the grass and brambles so that to the British they looked like ghosts and seemed to appear randomly out in the field.

Another hundred paces behind them, and another. The gatling gun began to issue out its death rattle, and Mbeki saw five more men tumble before the machine coughed its last. He was close enough now to see the operators waving their hands over their heads in frustration and set to it with a will. It looked like a small cannon except the barrel was a cylinder of smaller barrels bound together, all mounted on a wheeled carriage. Mbeki wished he could get close enough to see it fire without the muzzle blast blocking his view. "Down," Jojo insisted, and the two dropped behind a bush, their lungs sucking in great gulps of air. "No one is following us anymore," He stated the obvious.

"We haven't lost that many," Mbeki said, unsure. The casualties had not seemed as bad as at Isandhlwana, but then at Isandhlwana the war had looked winnable. "How do you think the rest of the battle is going?" Jojo shrugged, furrowed his brow for a moment, then knit his fingers together and squatted down. "Seriously?" Mbeki smiled in child-like anticipation of what that would look like to the men trying to kill him.

"Yebho," The King's Champion said, his hands still set up like a stirrup.

Mbeki put his foot into Jojo's hands and jumped up from his squatting position, the other Invincible lending his support by throwing him. Mbeki rose straight up from behind the bush, faster and higher than any man could have jumped, and he surveyed the battlefield at a glance, dropping back down before the British in front of him had time to do anything besides curse in surprise.

"We're attacking all four sides of the square at once."

"Then we will win," Jojo said. He was among those who thought the British could not possibly survive an all around attack without fortifications.

"Jojo, four ranks of infantry and machine guns are as good as any wall. No regiment is closer than we are."

"Do you think the other Invincibles are still alive?" Mbeki blinked at the question and shrugged. "Ngwenyama!" Jojo called. The answering call came to their left, right, and behind, and soon the seven other Invincibles had crawled to their location. "Once more, boys; if we go to ground again without the regiment behind us, this battle is over and we can call it quits." They nodded.

The nine rose, three to Jojo's left and four to Mbeki's right, only a pace between them, and they roared, "Ngwenyama! uSuthu!" The regiment behind them responded as it had not for the last five rushes; the charge was on.

The nine of them running would have made any enemy quail; nine warriors, with lean, muscled bodies wetted down with dew and sweat, broad killing assegais in one hand and snow white shields in the other, each running as fast as a cheetah with the scent of a gazelle in his nostrils. For a moment the British stood in awe that their enemy had this kind of fight left in them, and then the gatling gun team cleared the unejected casing from the breech and its operators swung the barrels towards the best target they had seen all day.

For the third and last time in Mbeki's life the world slowed and his mind accelerated. He could see each brass cartridge eject out the side of the gatling gun, see each muzzle flash momentarily light up the operators' faces. He saw as its barrel swung, and then he heard the gasp as the left-most man was struck down. There was no time to duck, no time to even turn his head. The gatling gun continued to chatter, but in Mbeki's mind it had slowed to a steady boom-click-boom-click, then there was another gasp as the next furthest man was also struck down.

We shall be cut down from left to right, Mbeki thought, the bitter saliva of terror gushing into his mouth. A scream was cut short by a low grunt as the man to Jojo's left dropped, and this time Mbeki just managed to look over as Jojo's bullet arrived.

The machine gun took Jojo in the left kidney, and the impact snapped his head over to look at Mbeki's with regret and sadness. Both knew it was a fatal wound. The gatling gun continued to traverse and the next bullet also struck Jojo, this time drifting slightly lower, smashing the top of his right femur.

Perhaps it was losing the top of his leg and the fact that he was falling to the right that inspired Jojo, or perhaps he had intended to do it all along. With a grunt of exertion that in Mbeki's mind stretched on forever, Jojo launched himself up and to his right, putting his ruined body between Mbeki and the hate-spewing gun.

Mbeki never saw where the three bullets meant for him were supposed to go; they burst through Jojo's back, spraying him from head to toe in Jojo's gore, and then he felt all three crash into his own body. The world sped up again and Mbeki was lying on his back, his eyes blinded by blood, with Jojo's shattered corpse sprawled across his chest and waist so that only his head could move. He knew he had been hit but he could not tell where, and he could not wipe the blood from his eyes for the weight of his friend's body pinning his arms.

Mbeki lay there, listening as the last battle reached its inevitable conclusion. Rifles roared, cannon boomed, gatling guns laughed, and then a mighty cheer went up from the British square and the very earth shook with the pounding of horses' hooves. Mbeki was only half aware of what was happening. His chest hurt, it was hard to breathe, and his mind wandered.

For a while he was a child again with his brother sitting on his ribs to settle some argument. Then he was an old man with the rattle in his chest that spoke of coming death. He was asleep and awake, but unable to open his eyes. The blood had dried into a glue. There was a coppery tang in his mouth, and when he was lucid enough to think clearly he wondered if he had been shot through the belly and that this was gut blood welling up his throat now. He explored his mouth with his tongue and found he had bit his cheek, probably in the fall. He slept again.

He awoke and felt the warmth of the sun on a different part of his face and the cool of shadows had moved to where previously he had been warm. It was the late afternoon now, and he was still alive, trapped under Jojo and blinded by his blood. What woke me? Mbeki wondered, then he heard it again; the unmistakable sound of an assegai being driven into flesh, and the sucking noise as it was pulled out again. The native contingent of the British army was killing the Zulu wounded.

"Here's one!" A man called out. There was the stabbing noise and a little mew of protest. "And another!" Mbeki felt footfalls, but was careful to stare straight ahead for fear the movement of his eyelids would betray him. "Look at these two! Those white devils must have shot this one into that one!" The footfalls receded, the sound of assegais still coming to his sensitive ears.

Is it so bad I'm not even worth spearing for safety? Mbeki wondered, trying to move something, anything. He succeeded finally with a toe. He could also move his foot, but not his leg. One of Jojo's arms was pinning him below the knees, and he lacked the strength to push it away. That's blood loss, he thought. I'm bleeding to death. It was a peaceful death to die; he felt no real pain. He slept again.

He awoke a third time with a gasp, and he tried to open his eyes and screamed silently at his inability. He had forgotten it all, and it took a moment for his heart to stop racing as he remembered his situation. He felt the cool of twilight, and knew he did not want to survive until the jackals and the vultures found him. He would call the red headbands to him, have them spear him or shoot him or strangle him. Anything to escape the tentative nibbles and then the tearing, rending gulping when the scavengers were sure he was helpless.

With difficulty he opened his mouth, hearing the crackle as Jojo's dried blood reluctantly parted over his lips. The taste of copper reinforced the last traces of the blood in Mbeki's mouth, and he spluttered for a moment. He lay there, trying to think of something to say. Do I call out help when I expect a mercy killing? Do I call out uSuthu, defiant to the last? He settled on Ngwenyama, but when he tried to speak his tongue was too swollen. He was suddenly consumed with a terrible thirst, and all he could do was moan.

Mbeki lay there, eyes unseeing, his entire purpose focused on his moan. He played with the sound, making it rise and fall, stretch out or speed up, warble and stutter and slide. Such a simple thing to do, mostly from the chest, but it consumed his attention for hours. He knew true darkness had fallen before he heard a sound besides his groans and the wind in the grass. "Do you hear that?" He gave his loudest moan, absently worried that he did not have enough control to call for help. "It came from over there."

He moaned again, hearing the grass part. "Wo," one of the voices said.

"Is it him?" Another asked. Mbeki did not understand the question, waiting for the release of death.

"Yebho," He felt Jojo's weight shift off of him and gasped as the dried blood that had fused them together broke loose. One of the voices muttered a curse, and Mbeki felt a warmth across his chest; one of his wounds, plugged and compressed by Jojo's body, had reopened. He was bleeding again.

Mbeki gurgled as someone pressed down on the bullet hole, feeling each finger across his breast. The ends had nails, long nails. Is that a woman's hand?

"Mbeki?" He could not decide who was speaking or how many there were. He licked his cracked and bloody lips, desperate to speak a word.

He coughed once, feeling three lightening bolts of pain as the movement tugged at his wounds, one high in the shoulder, one in the breast, and one at waist level but well to the right of the navel. "Eyes," He managed to mutter.

"Eh?" Mbeki lacked the strength to say it again.

Another one of the voices said, "Clean off his eyes." And with blessed relief he felt a cool, wet cloth touch each eyelid, gently massaging away the caked pools of dried gore. He slowly opened his eyes to see Inyati, Nandhi, Bhibhi, and Magema the Healer leaning over him with torches. Galazi was not present, but Mbeki knew he was someplace safe, out of sight of the battlefield. The stars hung overhead, a silent audience. He opened his mouth again and closed it. "Give him something to drink," Magema the Healer said. Nandhi held a water gourd to his lips and Mbeki drank deep, feeling strength returning to him.

"What about his wounds?" Inyati asked, taking over from Bhibhi in holding down the bleeding rupture on Mbeki's chest.

"He's not dead yet, which is a good sign for a man shot three times and left out all day without help. I'd say the bullets lost most of their power going through Jojo. They haven't blown out Mbeki's back, so they're still in there. Taking them out will be more dangerous than leaving them in." Mbeki felt tears trickle down his face.

"Yebho, but what are his chances?" Inyati persisted.

"He can hear us," Magema the Healer said.

"He's probably been expecting to die since morning. It's midnight. He's tired and he wants to know whether he'll see dawn as much as I do, now say it."

"One chance in five, now get a big shield. We'll carry him on it." They lifted Mbeki's shattered body up onto a shield. Mbeki watched as they dropped another shield over Jojo's body.

"Let's go home, Mbeki," Inyati said. Mbeki looked out at the plain as they began to carry him south, watching eight glowing rings of embers that had once been the most powerful amakhanda in kwaZulu. The inkatha is gone, he thought. Cetshwayo will soon be caught. The Impi will never reform. This is the death of the Zulu Kingdom. With that dreary prediction the wizard of kwaZulu closed his eyes again and fell asleep.

Chapter 72

Over three years had passed since the war ended with the capture and exile of Cetshwayo. The Valley of the Three Homesteads had become the Valley of the Wizard Smith, and Mbeki sat upon a stool dispensing the first of his services to a worried customer.

"You seek your cattle. Your herd has dwindled with the continued fighting, and now more cows are missing while your herd boys swear up and down they did not lose them." Mbeki hid his smile as the man's face went limp with surprise and the hope of impending relief. Mbeki had heard of the man's misfortunes yesterday: One of the advantages of having so many visitors.

"Yebho, Nkosi. They have been gone three days now."

"I know where you can find your cows, but, as you know, I have family to provide for. What compensation would you provide me in these troubled times?" In Mbeki's experience it was better to let the customer name a price and feel insulted than miss the opportunity to be overpaid.

"I've lost twelve cows, and with the number of bandits roaming kwaZulu, I'm not likely to see any of them back if I don't find them soon. If your advice restores them to me, you can have a heifer from among them."

Mbeki nodded his acceptance, inside gleeful that the man would pay so much for a simple divination. Mbeki threw off the kaross he had wrapped around him, revealing for the first time the three puckering bullet wounds that would forever remind him of Jojo's gift of life.

Mbeki attached the rattles to his wrists and ankles, already knowing what he would tell the man before the ceremony but knowing his customer was paying as much for the show as for the advice. Mbeki broke into a giya; the rattles filling the air around him with a frenzy of commotion. Inside his mind was weighing the evidence, working the problem, making sure he had not missed anything. A client with cows to spare was worth cultivating.

The man's valley was shallow, and the spring rains and winds would be a torment to his herds. The sweetveld was still brown, so they would be in search of good grazing in a sheltered spot. It would have to be somewhere the man had not immediately checked, which threw the net further out. Mbeki froze suddenly, the rattling around him dying. The man waited with baited breath, but Mbeki had not stopped to give his prophecy: He heard something in the distance.

Slowly now, keeping the rattling to a minimum to better hear the sound, Mbeki began to sway and twitch, enjoying the sickly fascination on his guest's face. Another of his clients had told of passing untended cows in the thornveld to the North of his homestead. The right distance, the right seclusion, the right shelter, the right grass. "Your cows are in the thickets to the North of Zikala's homestead. When you have them back, put blankets over them and erect a windbreak for them to shelter themselves in storms; they will not run again." The man bowed and scuttled off, frightened to be in the presence of such power.

Mbeki lifted the blanket back over him again, moving the knife he had taken at Isandhlwana into position. The approaching sound was closer now, a clucking that triggered distant carefree memories that were heavy with significance now. For dramatic effect he turned around on his stool so that his back was to the gate of his and Inyati's kraal.

They had founded their homestead on the ashes of Jama's, but they had built it much bigger. There were huts for each of Jama's widows, plus a hut for Nandhi and Bhibhi, both married to Inyati and the mothers of two children each by him. Galazi and Mbeki slept in a hut to the right of the gate, and Mbeki's smithing and wizard tools were in the hut opposite. It was a well structured kraal with a generous cattle pen for the herd Mbeki's two skills were rapidly accumulating; the civil wars that followed Cetshwayo's exile made both spear manufacturing and divination lucrative businesses, and the fear of a wizard's wrath kept the ubiquitous cattle thieves at bay.

The clucking stopped on the far side of the nearest ridge, and now Mbeki heard the lowing of cattle and the swish swish of legs moving through the grass growing close to his home. He was only sure of his hunch when he heard a foot hit a stone, not with the dull thump of flesh but with the bouncing thwack of leather.

"Hello, Judas." He had made a point of asking a missionary for the name of the man who had betrayed Jesus, and the gasp of surprise was his reward. "Or would you prefer I called you Holland again, old friend?" He said it in English; he did not want his family to understand.

"How did you do that?" The white man behind him asked.

"It doesn't matter how he did it. Do what you have come here to do!" Another man hissed. The wizard of kwaZulu recognized that voice too.

"Ah, I see you, Jobe kaHamu," He said this in Zulu. Mbeki's family was looking out from their huts now, but he ordered them to stay back with a hand gesture. When he was sure they would obey, he turned around on his stool to face his uninvited guests. Eight armed black men stood behind Holland and Jobe, their eyes everywhere for signs of danger. They were not Hamu's men: Mbeki recognized many of them as Holland's camp servants from their hunting trip over six years ago now. "What is it exactly you have come to do?"

Holland spoke before Jobe could. "What do you think about the government of kwaZulu, Mbeki?"

Mbeki snorted. "What government? You took away our king but did not replace him with any meaningful government. You gave fiefs to traitors like John Dunn and Hamu, and fiefs to men who were too important to ignore like Ntsingwayo and Zibhebhu, and then you left us to kill each other. As long as you get your workers, why bother to rule us?" Hundreds had died since the end of the war. The kingdom had fallen into lawless anarchy, with rape and pillage sweeping from valley to valley. The Zulu squabbled over the rotting carcass of their once great nation; their cattle pastures were bathed in the blood of innocents.

Holland adjusted the brim of his hat to better block the sun. He ran his other hand down the front of his lucky blue shirt. The revolver on his hip was conspicuous. "You know there's a myth going around kwaZulu, a story from happier times." He waited for Mbeki to comment, but continued as if he had not been met with silence. "It's a tale about a wizard, the only true wizard some say. He sat at Cetshwayo's right hand, and every word he said was the right way to do things. He was overruled at Rorke's Drift and Khambula and by then the war was lost, but if Cetshwayo's generals had listened to him, kwaZulu would still be united. You're the wizard they're talking about, Mbeki."

"Your point?" Mbeki asked, his eyes fixed on Holland's revolver.

"You're too important to leave lying around. If one of these warlords like Zibhebhu or Ntsingwayo were to scoop you up, warriors would join them just because they had you. It would alter the balance of power, and the civil war would move from cattle raiding and homestead burning to full out campaigning." Jobe stood next to Holland, but he only had an assegai. Mbeki kept his eyes on Holland's revolver.

"I have already offered my services to Ntsingwayo, but he's an old man now and his loyalty is with Cetshwayo, wherever he may be. I would not serve anyone else," Mbeki said.

"And if Cetshwayo were to come back?" Holland asked.

"My allegiance is to my king. I would serve him as best I could."

Jobe smiled in triumph; Holland sighed and brought his hand to rest on the butt of his revolver. "I'm sorry, Mbeki. That's the wrong answer. We can't have a united and militant Zulu kingdom on the borders of Natal again. I didn't want to do--"

"Uncle Mbeki! Uncle Mbeki!" Galazi ran out of his hut and hugged Mbeki from behind. Holland looked into the boy's terror-filled eyes, and his heart was in his throat at the duty assigned to him.

"Let's do this over the hill," Mbeki suggested. He waited for Holland to nod his agreement before calling out to his family. "Inyati! Nandhi! Bhibhi!" The three were out of their huts at once. "Take Galazi and make sure no one goes over that ridge until you can't hear Holland's damned chickens." The blond man arched an eyebrow. "That's how I knew it was you: Who else takes chickens with him to kill a friend?"

Mbeki rose, still wrapped in his kaross, and felt Galazi's hands being gently pulled from his back. He turned to the boy and smiled. "You are your father's son. Remember that, and be brave." Galazi smiled, recognizing his uncle's highest praise but not understanding why it was being given. Mbeki followed the ten men up and over the crest of the ridge and down the other side, never looking back to see the stricken looks on his family's faces.

"Here?" He asked at last.

"Here's good," Holland agreed, turning back to face the wizard. His hand went to his gun again.

"One question," Mbeki said, waiting for the hand to still before going on. "Why did you join the colonial cavalry under Wood? Why did you kill Zulus?"

Holland chewed his lower lip before answering. "My farm's not doing so well, Mbeki. I needed the money, and irregular cavalry got a portion of the captured cattle as a bounty." He thought about his next words before deciding it would do no harm to say it to a dead man. "Also, I couldn't believe your people won at Isandhlwana. I joined for the money, but I also fought to make sure we deserve to rule here. If we had lost this war, half of Africa would be back under black rulers by now."

"My question is answered," Mbeki said, steeling himself. Holland's hand closed around the gun. "But of all the people they could send, why you, and why him?"

The hand relaxed again. "It was Hamu who pointed out how much support you would lend to Cetshwayo's cause," Holland said. Mbeki nodded, knowing Hamu's real reason was their personal feud. "But you're outside his fief, and the British aren't willing to let him set the precedent of sending assassins outside his territory, so I'm here." It was Mbeki turn to arch a questioning eyebrow. "They chose me because I know you, and I need the money; more importantly, I'm not wearing a red coat. If they catch hell for it, they can say I'm a colonial working without their authority." Mbeki turned his eyes to Jobe. "He's here as Hamu's observer to confirm the kill."

Mbeki nodded again. "Then shoot me down, Holland. Just know if our roles were reversed my king would not be ordering me to kill you, and if he did I wouldn't do it."

He saw Holland flush. "That's not fair, damn it. The Zulu were no angels! At Isandhlwana you took the Twenty-Fourth Regiment's drummer boys, put them up on meat hooks, and cut off their balls. Because of you the British army will never take drummers into the field again."

"Well I'm glad my brother and father died to keep the redcoats from marching to musical accompaniment."

"Enough of this!" Jobe burst, stepping up to Mbeki, his assegai underhand for the killing stroke. "If you don't have the stones for it, I do."

With the same sleight of hand that had earned him his nickname, Mbeki made his knife appear and buried it to the hilt under Jobe's jaw, driving the blade up into his brain. "That's for my brother," He said into the man's dead eyes. The corpse sank to the ground, but Mbeki held on to the knife. He looked up to the sound of the revolver hammer clicking back to full cock. Holland had it drawn and leveled at him.

"Drop the knife."

Mbeki let it fall to the grass. He looked at the gun, knowing he wanted to live. His heart beat fast; his pulse boomed in his ears. "Go for the head shot," He whispered.

Holland's eyes burned with unshed tears as he raised the gun to eye level. Mbeki looked down the muzzle of the gun, watching right up to the end, his ever-curious mind taking it all in. Holland pulled the trigger, and the sound of the shot echoed off the ridges.

Chapter 73

In the homestead on the far side of the ridge the wailing went up, but Inyati forbade anyone to go over the hill to collect the body. Mbeki's assassins must be given time to get away: That was the unspoken agreement that had kept Mbeki's family safe. If there had been any doubt as to what the gunshot signified, a vulture, the first of many, arrived to investigate. The carrion bird's circling confirmed something lay dead on the far side of the ridge.

Mbeki's eyes closed and his shoulders slumped. Long moments passed as Holland holstered his revolver and called out muffled orders to his servants, who ran back to the wagon to obey him. Holland stood there watching Mbeki, knowing something more would have to be said, a justification made.

Mbeki opened his eyes, his ears ringing from the close discharge of the gun. In front of him Holland had his finger to his lips and Mbeki nodded that he would be silent. Behind Holland servants were running forward with a blanket and a chicken, and Mbeki watched in surprise as the bird's head was cut off at his feet, and the animal ran all about, trampling down the dead sweetveld with its thrashings and spewing blood all over the place. One of the servants scooped up its body when it at last lay still; the rest looked to Holland for permission to continue.

"You can't stay here Mbeki. I was sent to do away with you, and if you're still here when Cetshwayo arrives in a few months they will send someone else. That means you have to come with me. I'll have eliminated you from the situation, so I will get paid, and you will still be alive. It's the best possible arrangement. Don't you agree?"

"What will I do?" Mbeki shouted, overcompensating for the ringing. Holland shushed him again, eyes on the crest of the ridge above for an observer. "What will I do?" Mbeki's whisper was so quiet that he could not hear himself.

"You're in good enough shape to box, or you can go on a lecture circuit, or write a book, or learn to blacksmith the modern way. I don't care. My farm is folding, and I'm going to see some more of the world. You can come with me, or you can stay here as worm food." Mbeki nodded, and Holland gave the order: His servants wrapped Mbeki in the blanket and carried him away horizontally, as one would carry a corpse. Through the rolled end of the blanket Mbeki looked back to the bloody patch in the grass and knew this possibility had been in Holland's mind the whole time. Holland was still his friend.

The men carrying the blanket shifted their grip, and Mbeki saw Jobe's body lying beside the trampled patch of grass. He was glad Hamu's son would be left for the vultures. It was partial payment --the best he would ever be able to do-- for the wrongs Hamu had done against his family. In his heart Mbeki hoped the booze would be Hamu's downfall, but he had no way of making sure.

"Let me ask you something," Holland's voice came through the blanket. "When Cetshwayo comes back, what do you think will happen? Will he put kwaZulu back together again?"

Mbeki thought for long moments before replying. "Without me to temper the hotheads on his council, there will be a civil war of campaigns rather than raids, as you said."

"Hamu?"

"Hamu's not a real force in the land anymore. His clan is loyal, but no one else will forgive or forget his betrayal during the war. No, Zibhebhu's Mandlakazi will be the ones to oppose Cetshwayo. Zibhebhu's war record will attract the rest of Cetshwayo's opponents to his side."

"So what will happen to Cetshwayo?"

"Enough men consider their allegiance oaths voided that they can kill him. He'll be dead within three or four years, poisoned or stabbed or shot. The how does not matter. Dead is dead," Mbeki said.

He felt the hard bump as he was lifted up into the wagon and dropped down hard onto the boards. "Holland?" He called softly through the blanket.

"Yes?"

"Will I ever be able to come home again?"

"I don't know, Mbeki. Not for a long time."

Chapter 74

The sound of the wagon-mounted chicken coop faded into the distance only as the sun began to set, and even then Inyati refused to allow anyone else to come with him. He kissed Nandhi and Bhibhi once each, touched the heads of his children, and set off. It was only when he was half way up the ridge that he saw the telltale movement of the tops of the sourveld. He was being stalked.

"Galazi!" his tone was stern. The boy rose out of the grass, his father's lopsided grin on his face. "Go home!"

"Cha, Baba."

Ancestors help me, Inyati beseeched. I know that look. That's Mbeki trying to solve a problem. What is he going to say to convince me? "What is over that hill is not for little boys to see."

"Then it's a good thing I'm here with you instead of one of your children."

Inyati snorted, amused. Short of carrying Ingonyama's son home and tying him to a post, there was nothing to be done about it. He gave a wave of his hand, allowing Galazi to follow. They climbed the ridge in silence, reaching the crest and looking down below.

Two vultures had settled down on Jobe's body, going for the softest and easiest food first, the anus and the eyes. One of the birds pulled its head out from between Jobe's cheeks and gave a warning warble to the other. The two lifted off, their bodies not yet heavy enough with flesh to prevent flight. Inyati and Galazi descended the slope, watched the whole time by Jobe's empty orbits.

The trampled bloody grass was unmistakable, and the wagon ruts were deep and fresh. Why would they take his body and leave Jobe's? Inyati wondered.

Galazi's eyes were wide at the sight of his first corpse. He saw the perfect incision under the jaw and found the bloody knife nearby in the grass. "Wo," He muttered under his breath. Outnumbered ten to one and armed only with a knife, his uncle had managed to take one of his killers with him.

Inyati worked back and forth over the scene, his hunter's senses reading the spoor without true understanding until he found the dimple in the earth behind where Mbeki had stood. Digging at it with his finger he produced a revolver slug. He furrowed his brow for a moment and then realized what it meant. Tears of relief streamed down his face, but he knew he would never be able to tell a soul. A deal had been made on this ground, and his silence would have to be a part of it.

Galazi saw the only father he remembered weeping, and he reached up to put his hand on a grieving shoulder. The two stayed like that for a long time, and then Galazi whispered the only eulogy that would be said over Mbeki, "Ngwenyama."

He was a lion.

Historical Note

There is a wealth of information about the Zulu available to modern historians, and my original intention was to tell the story of that remarkable people as it really happened, day by day and deed by deed. As you might imagine, the result was an unintelligible muddle, a textbook without the grace to call itself fact. Men like Ian Knight and John Laband among others have written remarkable tomes collating primary documents and period interviews to bring a civilization's rise and fall into the light of day. That is the true history, but that is only the starting point for a work of historical fiction. I strayed from the hard and true early and often to tell the Zulu's story from their own perspective in a relatable, readable, and entertaining way. I encourage all of you who found my book interesting to delve deeper to learn the true story.

So how much of this novel really happened? Whenever something shaped the story of kwaZulu --the court politics, the clan power struggles, the cattle plague, the stick fight, the British ultimatum, the war-- what you've read is recorded fact. The rest is often fabrication to move my characters between the great events of their civilization to make them witnesses and participants in the improbable but true.

My first draft of this novel was impenetrable without the glossaries. For instance, all of the regiments originally appeared with their Zulu names, but it was easier for my proofreaders to understand Chieftains and Humbler of Kings and Red Needles than uThulwana, iNgobamakhosi, and Khandempemvu. I made that compromise, and I do not regret it. I also felt it necessary to streamline the number of Zulu nobles I would ask you to remember, so great men of the nation like Mavumengwana and Sigcwelegcwele who had little impact in the first three quarters of my story were taken out for the sake of clarity and brevity.

There are more outright inventions than I would care to repeat if I started over again from a blank sheet of paper. The British embassy of the first chapter is fiction, and their unrecorded historical counterparts would likely have been made up of colonial horse rather than redcoats. Forgive me: I imagine most of you chose to read this novel because of some familiarity with the Anglo-Zulu War that makes up the last quarter of the novel, and so I felt it important to put Chekov's Gun on the wall from the very beginning, a promise and a context and a ticking clock that would allow me to tell the story of Jama, Ingonyama, Mbeki, Nandhi, and Inyati in their own time without trying your patience.

My glossary of characters lists who is based upon historical figures. Those people really lived and did the things I had them do. Their personalities are an extrapolated sketch of what their peers said of them, but in many cases those sentiments were expressed by their enemies. I did my best to be fair and tell their tales as I understood them. Hamu and Mbilini and Zibhebhu and Dabulamanzi and Cetshwayo are remembered largely as you have read them, and though I invented dialogue I never made up their motivations or decisions. For good or ill, they are as true as I could make them.

My single greatest fabrication is probably the Invincibles. I do not doubt that Cetshwayo had a royal guard --Shaka famously had his uFasimba-- but I could not find the name of the unit as of th 1870s. I wanted Ingonyama and Mbeki to have a reason to be at all the important moments of the war, and so I created the Invincibles from a very hazy probably truth. Putting Ingonyama and Mbeki in their age-appropriate regiments would have denied them Rorke's Drift, Ntombe, the Royal Court, and left them as minor participants with an incomplete worldview of the catastrophe that swallowed their way of life and left their kingdom in ashes. It was a necessary invention, but I must confess you can scour as many primary documents as you like without finding a reference to Cetshwayo's guardsmen.

I was careful to describe the war in as straight-forward and honest a way as possible through the eyes of my fictional characters. In fact, there is even more that I just could not include without slowing things down to a crawl: The battles of Nyezane and Gingingdlovu and the siege of Eshowe are mentioned only in passing, and the death of Napoleon III's heir just couldn't be made to fit. Again, I would be delighted if my novel inspired you to read the full and true account in a work of non-fiction. There are dozens of sterling works of scholarship available for the interested to learn exactly what happened.

It is worth pondering why that is so. Why is there so much written about the Zulu as opposed to the Xhosa or the Ashanti or the Matabele, known today as the Ndebele? I think the answer lies in what the Zulu accomplished. The Battle of Isandhlwana was the single greatest defeat ever inflicted upon a modern army by native forces. With all due respect to American history, it made Custer's Last Stand look like a minor skirmish. The British Empire at the height of its power found itself humbled by barefooted herdsmen, and it took six long, grueling months for a quarter of the world to crush a small iron age kingdom whose name is honoured to this day by friend and foe alike.

I can't help but wonder what history would look like if Sir Henry Bartle Frere hadn't defied his orders and provoked his quick and easy war. Would kwaZulu have survived into the 20th Century as a South African equivalent of Ethiopia? What would Apartheid have looked like with a strong and independent Bantu nation on the border of South Africa?

The Anglo-Zulu War was a tragedy on any number of levels. It devastated a proud and industrious people on the cusp of a golden age, and it robbed the world of a nation-state the equal of any of the polities of medieval Europe. It was my honour and pleasure to tell their story from their own perspective. Thank you for reading it.

Glossary of Names

(Asterisks denote characters based on recorded historical figures.)

Relations of Jama kaZuya:

Jama kaZuya, a smith and royal favourite
Ingonyama kaJama, his eldest son
Mbeki kaJama, his youngest son
Bhibhi, his daughter
Galazi, his grandson
Manase, his senior wife, mother to his sons
Mpikasi, his second wife
Namgoqu, his junior wife, mother to his daughter
Punga, his brother-in-law
Hlubi, Punga's son, his nephew
Kandhla, another brother-in-law
Langa, one of Kandhla's sons, his nephew
Bikwayo, one of Kandhla's sons, his nephew
The kaMajeke Brothers, his neighbours

Members of the Ngenetsheni Clan:

Prince Hamu kaNzibe,* a rebellious northern baron, chief of the Negenetsheni
Jobe kaHamu, his eldest son and heir
Nandhi, one of his daughters
Mnkabayi, one of his wives
Zokufa, his head steward

Zulu Nobility:

Mpande kaSenzangakhona,* King of kwaZulu
Prince Cetshwayo kaMpande,* his son and heir

Prince Mbuyazi,* his favourite son, now dead
Prince Dabulamanzi,* another son
Prince Ndabuko,* another son, one of the youngest
Zibehbhu,* a northern baron, chief of the Mandlakazi
Ntsingwayo,* chief of the Khoza clan, a famous general
Prince Mbilini waMswati,* a Swazi renegade prince, chief of the abaQulusi, defender of the northwest borders
Sihayo,* chief of a southern tribe
Godide,* chief of an eastern tribe

Other Zulus:
Mbejane, induna of the King's Bodyguard, the Invincibles
Jojo, an Invincible
Sompisi, an Invincible
Bambatha, an Invincible and war doctor
Magema, the royal healer
Phalo, a Zulu who serves the British
Zungu Nkulu, a famous wizard
Mbambo, an abaQulusi warrior

Members of the Matabele Royal House of Kumalo:
Mzilikazi,* King of the Matabele, now dead
Matshobana,* his son and heir, now dead
Lobengula,* another son, now King of the Matabele
Inyati, another son, now a fugitive

White Men:
John Dunn,* an Englishman who has gone native and lives among the Zulu. They call him Jonani
Holland Keech, an American adventurer
Gentleman Jim, a boxer

Lord Carnarvon,* Britain's Colonial Secretary in South Africa

Sir Bartle Frere,* his successor

General Chelmsford,* commander of Britain's army in Natal

Colonel Evelyn Wood,* commander of Chelmsford's cavalry-heavy western-most column. Nicknamed Lukuni, a very hard wood.

Glossary of Terms and Places

abaQulusi A Zulu ibutho and a semi-autonomous tribe associated with the Zulu Kingdom.

Afrikaans The language of the Boers, a bastardized form of Dutch.

Amabutho (Sing. Ibutho) Regiments. Each regiment is made up of every able-bodied man who is between the age of seventeen and twenty upon the formation of the unit. As a result each ibutho is comprised of every man in the nation of a given age.

Amakhanda (Sing. Ikhanda) Royal homesteads of 60 to 1200 huts that serves as a center of government, a barracks for the military, a religious fairground, and a political nerve center. After Dingaan, many of the larger regional chiefs established their own, which should have been beyond their power.

Amasi Soured milk, a staple of the Zulu.

Baba Diminutive of Father: Dad or Papa.

Bayete A salute reserved exclusively for the king.

Biltong Jerky.

Boers 'Farmers,'. descendants of the Dutch colonists of South Africa

Cha Zulu negative.

Dingaan A king who murdered Shaka. He made war with the Boers, lost, and was ousted from the throne by his brother Mpande.

Donga A dried creek bed.

Giya The shadow fighting dance of a Zulu warrior.

Head ring A black rubber-like fungus woven around a man's head to mark him as a married head of a household.

Ibutho (Pl. Amabutho) Regiment. Each regiment is made up of every able-bodied man who is between the age of seventeen and twenty upon the formation of the unit. As a result each ibutho is comprised of every man in the nation of a given age.

Ikhanda (Pl. Amakhanda) A royal homestead of 60 to 1200 huts that serves as a center of government, a barracks for the military, a religious fairground, and a political nerve center. After Dingaan, many of the larger regional chiefs established their own, which should have been beyond their power.

Impi (Pl. izimpi) Army.

Induna (Pl. izinduna) Commander.

Ingonyama "He is a lion."

Inkatha A magical charm of grass and black magic ingredients, sheathed in snake skin.

Isangoma (Pl. izangoma) Wizard, witch doctor, witch hunter, magician.

Izangoma (Sing. isangoma) Wizards, witch doctors, witch hunters, magicians.

Izimpi (sing. impi) Armies.

Izinduna (Sing. induna) Commanders.

IziNkosi (Sing. Nkosi) Lords, Chiefs. The title given to anyone who is of higher station, including seniority in age or marital status.

Ka Son of.

Kaross A blanket.

Kleza Literally to drink milk from the teat of a cow: It is the process in which all the young men of a certain age muster to form a new ibutho.

Kloof A deep, steep-sided ravine.

Kopje A rocky outcropping or hill formed by wind erosion as top soil is blown off up-thrust bedrock.

Kraal A cattle pen of indeterminate size; because Zulu build their domiciles in rings around the cattle pens this can also be interchangeable with homestead or ikhanda.

Kudu A solitary forest antelope with impressive horns.

Kumalo Once one of the most royal of the Zulu clans; they went renegade and formed the Matabele nation.

Kwa Place of (the).

kwaBulawayo Shaka's capital, literally the Place of Killing.

kwaZulu Place of the Zulu, the Zulu's Place, the Zulu Kingdom, The Kingdom of Heaven.

Laager Wagons drawn into a circle to make a fortification.

Lukuni A very hard wood, the praise name of Sir Evelyn Wood.

Mamba A poisonous snake.

Mandlakazi A northern clan led by Prince Zibhebhu.

Matabele A wildly successful raider nation, 'the People of the Long Shields.'

Mealie Dried maize, a staple.

Mfolozi The white and black Mfolozi rivers bracket the heart of kwaZulu.

Mzinyathi The Buffalo River, part of the Zulu's southern and western border.

Ncombe Blood River, part of the Zulu's western border and site of a great battle between the Zulu and the Boers in the time of King Dingaan.

Ndondakusuka The site of the bloodiest battle in Zulu history between the rival factions of two crown princes of Mpande.

Ngadla "I have eaten," The Zulu war cry confirming a kill. It is taken from the Zulu term for making war; when warriors fight for their king, they are eating up the king's enemies, so Ngadla actually could be translated colloquially as, "I am doing what the King requires."

Ngenetsheni A northern clan led by Hamu kaNzibe.

Ngwenyama "He was a lion."

Nkhandla A great forest, home to the Cube clan and most of the kingdom's smiths.

Nkosi (Pl. iziNkosi) Lord, Chief. The title is given to anyone who is of higher station, including seniority in age.

Nkulunkulu The Great Great One, the one-thousand eyed creator of the world.

Ntombe A small river in the northwest of kwaZulu, a tributary of the Phongolo.

Phongolo A river that unofficially marks the Zulu's northern border.

oNdini Cetshwayo's Great Place, his capital. The British call it Ulundi.

Riem Cured leather cut and twisted into rope.

Shaka Literally translated as stomach beetle, he was the king who launched the Zulu tribe from obscurity into dominance over their many neighbours.

Sindebele The language of the Matabele, a bastardized form of Zulu.

Sourveld Grass that ripens late but can be grazed upon throughout the year.

Swazi A troublesome tribe to the North that the Zulu never conquered.

Sweetveld Grass that ripens early but suffers from the effects of frost and drought.

Tokoloshe A monster of Zulu legend: A zombie whose spirit is trapped inside a corpse and forced to do the bidding of the witch or wizard who reanimated it.

Thekula One of the rivers marking kwaZulu's southern border.

Tshitsilikazi A magical word said about lightning and other dangerous occurrences in the sky, something to the effect of 'The sky is dangerous.'

Tunga To sow on the head ring of full adulthood which entitles a man to marry, own property, and retire from constant service in the impi.

umKhosi The Festival of First Fruits in which the nation gathers to ensure good harvests, strong leadership, and prevent misfortune from the spirit world. It is held every year and reaffirms the king's authority.

uSuthu A breed of large black cattle. During the political and military battles to name Mpande's crown prince it came to represent the faction supporting Cetshwayo. It became the national war cry upon his ascension to the throne.

Veldt Grassland, prairie.

Wa Son of in the Swazi language.

Wo An exclamation of surprise, dread, fear or other intense emotion.

Yebho Zulu affirmative.

Zanzi A Matabele bloodline that can be traced all the way back to the original House of Kumalo with no intrusion from conquered people.

Zulu Literally translated the People of Heaven, preferred translation the People. In truth, it was a small tribe which rose to place itself in a hierarchy above many other tribes under the leadership of Shaka kaSenzangakhona.

About the Author

Geoff Micks has a BA Honours with High Distinction from the University of Toronto and a diploma in Journalism from Centennial College.

He has worked for the National Post, The Woolwich Observer, Toronto Community News, the Canadian Institute, Infonex Inc., and the World Trade Group.

His twitter account is @faceintheblue and his blog is faceintheblue.wordpress.com.

He lives in Toronto, Ontario, Canada.

Printed in Great Britain
by Amazon.co.uk, Ltd.,
Marston Gate.